ALIEN
EMERGENCIES

ALSO BY JAMES WHITE

The Secret Visitor (1957)
Second Ending (1962)
Deadly Litter (1964)
Escape Orbit (1965)
The Watch Below (1966)
All Judgement Fled (1968)
The Aliens Among Us (1969)
Tomorrow Is Too Far (1971)
Dark Inferno (1972)
The Dream Millennium (1974)
Monsters and Medics (1977)
Underkill (1979)
Future Past (1982)
Federation World (1988)
The Silent Stars Go By (1991)
The White Papers (1996)
Gene Roddenberry's Earth:
    Final Conflict—The First Protector (Tor, 2000)

THE SECTOR GENERAL SERIES

Hospital Station (1962)
Star Surgeon (1963)
Major Operation (1971)
Ambulance Ship (1979)
Sector General (1983)
Star Healer (1985)
Code Blue—Emergency (1987)
The Genocidal Healer (1992)
The Galactic Gourmet (Tor, 1996)
Final Diagnosis (Tor, 1997)
Mind Changer (Tor, 1998)
Double Contact (Tor, 1999)
Beginning Operations (Tor, 2001)

ALIEN EMERGENCIES
A SECTOR GENERAL OMNIBUS

JAMES WHITE

A TOM DOHERTY ASSOCIATES BOOK
NEW YORK

ALIEN EMERGENCIES: A Sector General Omnibus

Copyright © 2002 by the Estate of James White. This book is an omnibus edition composed of the novels *Ambulance Ship,* copyright © 1980 by James White; *Sector General,* copyright © 1983 by James White; *Star Healer,* copyright © 1984 by James White.

Introduction copyright © 2002 by David Langford

Edited by Teresa Nielsen Hayden

An Orb Edition
Published by Tom Doherty Associates, LLC
175 Fifth Avenue
New York, NY 10010

www.tor.com

Library of Congress Cataloging-in-Publication Data
White, James.
    Alien emergencies : a sector general omnibus / James White.—1st Orb pbk. ed.
        p.   cm.—(Sector General ; 2)
        ISBN 0-312-87770-6 (pbk. : alk. paper)
        1. Science fiction, English. 2. Human-alien encounters—Fiction.
3. Life on other planets—Fiction. 4. Space medicine—Fiction.
5. Hospitals—Fiction. I. Title.
PR6073.H494 A6 2002
823'.914—dc21

                                        2001056852

Printed in the United States of America

0 9 8 7 6 5 4 3 2

CONTENTS

INTRODUCTION

BY
DAVID
LANGFORD

Sector Twelve General Hospital is one of the most charming and intelligently wish-fulfilling conceptions in science fiction, and its Irish creator James White—tall, bespectacled, balding, soft-spoken and eternally self-deprecating—was himself something of a charmer. Not merely a nice man, he was the cause of niceness in others. No one in the SF community could ever dream of being horrid to James.

While others joined literary or fan factions and entangled themselves in heated feuding, James could be found at British conventions solemnly inducting qualified attendees—those who like himself were several inches over six feet—into the S.O.P.O.A.H. or Society Of Persons Of Average Height. A luckily short-sighted few had the further credentials required for admission to the inner circle, the S.O.P.O.A.H. (W.G.) (With Glasses). Naturally James continued to treat the inner circle, the outer circle and the great unwashed masses beyond with identical benevolence, which somehow lent all those other embattled in-groups the same aura of gentle silliness.

James was and is much loved as a science fiction writer. I fondly remember scouring British bookshops in the 1960s for instalments of his Sector General space-hospital saga, which in those days was appearing in maddeningly brief instalments in E. John Carnell's original anthology *New Writings in SF*, later edited by Kenneth Bulmer. The last to feature there was the first story in this volume, "Spacebird" from Bulmer's *New Writings in SF 22*, published in 1973. British fans of Sector General had a long wait for this xenobiological extravaganza's inclusion in the 1980 *Ambulance Ship*. Americans had to wait longer still—until now, in fact—since the 1979 US version of *Ambulance Ship* omitted "Spacebird."

As every SF reader should know, Sector Twelve General Hospital is a huge interstellar construction built in a spirit of glorious idealism by many co-operating galactic races, with its 384 levels equipped to simulate the home environment of any conceivable alien patient. Conceivable, that is, to the builders' imaginations. From the outset James gleefully harassed his Sector General medics with a steady stream of inconceivables and seeming-impossibles, ranging in size from an intelligent virus and spacefaring barnacles, via beasties without hearts who must keep rolling forever to prevent their circulation from halting, and a levitating brontosaur called Emily, to "macro" life-forms like the miles-long Midgard Serpent which is discovered scattered through space in dismantled form and must be painstakingly reassembled, or the continent-sized inhabitant of planet Meatball whose treatment in *Major Operation* requires not so much surgery as military action.

In short, Sector General is the definitive medical SF series. Its precursors include L. Ron Hubbard's moderately dire *Ole Doc Methuselah* stories and the competent hackwork of Murray Leinster's Med Service tales. It may perhaps have helped inspire Piers Anthony's amusing exploits of an interstellar dentist in *Prostho Plus*. Nothing else in the genre is at all comparable.

To call these stories' repeated pattern of medical mystery and elucidation a formula is far from being a put-down. As with detective fiction, the basic pattern offers scope for endless variations limited only by ingenuity and narrative sleight, with James's lifelong fascination with medical techniques clearly visible throughout. There's even room in Sector General for G. K. Chesterton's favourite mystery trope of the Happy Surprise, whereby suitable illumination causes sinister and misleading clues to reverse themselves or cancel out, revealing that despite all appearances there has been no crime (or serious threat to health) at all.

Several well-loved props run through the sequence. The most famous is the species classification system which sums up a creature's shape and physiology in four terse letters. Theoretically this coding can extend to many further "decimal places," but the first four suffice for practical and narrative purposes. Earth-humans are DBDG and "similar" warm-blooded oxygen-breathers have similar codes, with teddy-bear Nidians and Orligians also being DBDG while the furry, caterpillar-shaped Kelgians are DBLF. Weirder creatures include chlorine-breathing PVSJs and psi-talented V-codes. One buried joke concerns the unfortunate Gogleskan species of *Star Healer,* classification FOKT, who are almost unable to prevent themselves from forming mindlessly destructive mobs. This, by intention, greatly tickled the local SF fan group in the traditionally tough city of Glasgow, Scotland: the Friends of Kilgore Trout.

The classification scheme began as homage to E. E. "Doc" Smith's perhaps unworkably human-centred version from *Gray Lensman* and *Children of the Lens,* in which true *Homo sapiens* is classed AAAAAA while the most alien monstrosities imaginable—the horrid Ploorans in their cryogenic winter metamorphosis—register as "straight Z's to ten or twelve places." It is a happy coincidence that James's first-ever published words, in his and Walt Willis's fanzine *Slant* 4, were firmly inserted into a contribution that was being horrid to Doc Smith: "[These opinions of the great Smith are not those of the typesetter, J. White.]"

Nearly half a century later he was honoured with the 1998 Skylark Award, presented by the New England SF Society in memory of Doc Smith and his Lensmen, and so consisting of an absolutely enormous magnifying lens. James found this practical as well as decorative, since by then his sight was failing to the stage where he needed such a glass to read even large type on the computer screen.

Besides demoting humans from AAAAAA to the modest DBDG, James distanced himself in other little ways from the traditional SF anthropocentrism of an era when John W. Campbell still stalked the earth. (It should be remembered that the first Sector General story appeared in 1957.) Smart and sympathetic aliens are foregrounded from the very beginning. Virtually all the hospital's top medical consultants, the eccentric Diagnosticians, are nonhuman. When a roving ambulance ship is introduced, it's named *Rhabwar* after a great doctor from the history of its Tralthan FGLI builders. When *Rhabwar*'s first mission appears to be a simple rescue of boring old humans and someone remarks, "There will be no juicy extraterrestrial cases on *this* trip," he is crushingly answered by a Kelgian nurse:

"To us, Earth-human DBDG's *are* juicy extraterrestrials." In three later novels beginning with *Code Blue—Emergency* (1987), the viewpoint characters are aliens who are not only as likeable as the human medics but every bit as accident-prone. Real equality includes the equal right to make blazing mistakes.

Another notable and fruitful series prop is Sector General's system of Educator tapes, which help prepare doctors for other-species surgery by uploading the skills of an expert from the relevant world. The dark side of this piece of narrative convenience is that a complete and often cantankerous e-t personality is loose in your head, objecting to your vile choice of food (a regular Sector General canteen sight is a Senior Physician eating "visually noncontroversial" sandwiches of uncertain content, with his eyes tight shut) and possibly imposing strange glandular urges. In the short "Countercharm," series hero Senior Physician Conway uses a tape recorded from a randy Melfan ELNT, and finds himself distracted from vital operations by an uncontrollable case of the hots for his gorgeous Melfan pupil—who happens to be a giant crab.

The regular human cast includes wiscracking, problem-solving Conway (who for ages appeared to have no first name—very late in the series it's revealed to be Peter); his busty girlfriend and eventual wife Nurse (later Pathologist) Murchison, whose forename I have yet to detect; and the irascible Chief Psychologist O'Mara, wielder of deadly sarcasm and—at his worst—a feared politeness. Reasons for O'Mara's peculiarly blunt, abrasive nature and multispecies insight lie at the heart of the penultimate Sector General novel, the elegiac *Mind Changer*, which allows us inside this thorny character's head for only the second time in the entire sequence.

Meanwhile Conway's closest friend is the universally popular Dr. Prilicla, a fragile GLNO e-t who resembles a giant and beautiful dragonfly, carries diplomacy to the point of fibbing since its empathic talent makes it cringe from hostile emotion, and likes to weave its canteen spaghetti into an edible cable to be chomped while hovering in mid-air. Sector General's staff and wards contain countless further aliens, each with their own quirky charm—engaging stock characters in a comedy of humours shaped by exotic racial traits. It's a running joke that the hottest hospital gossip concerns sexual antics in the methane level whose ethereal, crystalline SNLU patients live at 120–140 degrees below zero.

Thus the sequence offers copious fun and a warm feeling of extended community in addition to its xenobiological cleverness. "Almost wilfully upbeat," wrote John Clute in *The Encyclopedia of Science Fiction*. What it also contains—showing clearly through transparent storytelling that puts on no literary airs—is the compassion and rare anger of a good man. From that first novella in 1957 to *Double Contact* forty-two years later, it is repeatedly stressed that xenophobia in all its forms is a loathsome disease requiring salutary treatment. The Monitor Corps, this loose interstellar Federation's tough but kindly police force, hates war and stamps it out ruthlessly with nonlethal weapons like intimidation and sleepy gas. At Sector General's bleakest hour in *Star Surgeon,* when the hospital is besieged by a space fleet and under missile attack, the defending Monitors grit their teeth and accept that "fanatically tolerant" medical staff will—must—give enemy casualities the same degree of care as their own wounded.

It's impossible not to see these gentle stories' deep horror of war as fuelled by the author's revulsion at events in his home town of Belfast. Generally he downplayed his feelings, but the shades of melancholy emerged in his 1975 fanzine contribution "The Exorcists of IF," which miraculously preserved a light touch while mourning the ghosts of an older IF (Irish Fandom) then partly sundered by the Troubles, and which has with some justice been called the finest piece of fan fiction ever written. It is collected in *The White Papers* (1996).

On a related note, I have a vivid memory of James at the 1992 British national SF convention "Illumination," held in a Blackpool seafront hotel and featuring a hugely noisy fireworks display on the adjacent beach. Thunderous detonations of mortar shells could be felt as visceral jolts; the vibrations set off car alarms all around the hotel. Amid these terrific bangs and flashes and siren-wailings, James's plaintive Irish voice murmured into my ear: "They're trying to make me feel at home."

A later Sector General volume makes a deadpan gesture to the death-or-glory school of military SF, with war and violence being presented as a sick, enfeebled species's last remaining means of sexual stimulation. The Marquis de Sade might recognize his own face in that mirror. One early story spoke wistfully of "the diagnosis and treatment of a diseased interstellar culture, entailing the surgical removal of deeply rooted prejudice and unsane moral values . . ." If only.

It's worth noting that in the James White universe, outright villains are extraordinarily few. Even that "diseased culture" which despicably attacks the hospital (via armed forces duped into believing it a prison and torture chamber) is rotten only at the top, and reforms itself in the light of sweet reason. The most murderous-seeming threats within Sector General all prove to be confused innocents: examples include a traumatized, out-of-control pet, a pre-sentient saurian, and frightened alien children with odd biological defences.

One of the few characters ever to have engaged in deliberate killing is Monitor Fleet Commander (later Sector Marshal) Dermod, who has spent his life expiating his role in the small but bloody conflict of "Occupation: Warrior" (1959), a story whose Sector General links were removed by an editor who thought it too grim for the series. Now Dermod's colossal Emperor-class battleship *Vespasian* is chiefly called on for shows of force or vast rescue manoeuvres—as in *Major Operation*, where it literally has to hold a giant tourniquet, and the present volume's "Combined Operation."

That underlying moral sense illuminates such later and slightly darker segments as *Star Healer*, where after all the fireworks of his brilliant diagnoses and miracle cures, Conway is kicked upstairs to try his hand at the full responsibilities of a Diagnostician and to tackle cases that can't be solved with a single dazzling intuition. Instead he must brace himself for tougher tussles: with the grim evolutionary dilemmas of the Gogleskans who daren't approach each other and the reflexively violent Protectors who cannot be approached, with terminal injuries and recognition of the need for triage after major accidents, with normally cheerful and ultra-tough Hudlar FROB space roustabouts who have been reduced to a pitiable state by post-transplant shock or crippling senility.

Before this chance of promotion, though, the lighter-hearted *Ambulance Ship* and *Sector General* take Conway far away from the massive presence of the hospital and its permanent staff, to investigate medical enigmas with no immediate resources but the tiny *Rhabwar* team. This makes for a pleasant series of shorter adventures revisiting favourite auctorial themes.

Without too overtly giving away surprises, it can be said that most of *Ambulance Ship* and *Sector General* see our man working his way thoughtfully around two pet concepts which crop up elsewhere in the sequence. One is best phrased as a question: is there any inherent biological or physical handicap to space travel which sufficient intelligence and ingenuity cannot overcome? Series readers will remember that a certain immodest alien in *Major Operation,* whose deeply weird physiology should have trapped him for life on the sea bed, is first encountered as an orbiting astronaut.

Stories building on this question in *Ambulance Ship* and *Sector General* confront the baffled but eventually insightful Conway with five even more extreme cases. How can the dream of space possibly apply to e-t species who are blind, or limbless, or utterly devoid of mechanical technology, or helpless prisoners within insensately violent host-bodies, or larger than the greatest monsters of Earth's deep seas? Aha.

The stories' other repeated issue is the cheeky challenging of a Sector General axiom: that cross-species infection is as a rule impossible and that Conway and friends therefore need never fear catching something awful from their patients. Three clever exceptions are presented, though not of the kind that disprove the rule. Gulfs of time, a common chemistry, and the established (through Prilicla) premise of psychic empathy all sneak around the apparent constraints. A fourth and particularly far-out possibility—already planted in the early *Star Surgeon*—becomes the heart of the medical mystery in the later novel *Final Diagnosis.*

Among this volume's shorts the odd man out is "Accident," set before the building of Sector General and linking it to James's moving war or antiwar story "Tableau," which can be found in his 1970 collection *The Aliens Among Us*. An all too credible accident in a multi-species spaceport facility, and the resulting nightmare struggle with intractable wreckage in an increasingly toxic atmosphere, crystallize the need for medical and paramedical expertise that extends over many different physiologies and biochemistries. This plants the seed of Sector General, and of the recurring notion—found also in James's non-series stories—that being able to give medical assistance to a distressed alien brings a priceless bonus of goodwill to the ever-tricky SF situation of First Contact.

As already indicated, James White was a highly popular SF author and convention guest whom everyone liked and whose kindliness extended even to such loathed creatures ("straight Z's to ten or twelve places") as parodists and critics. I happen to know this, because in my wickedness I wrote both a Sector General parody and a critical essay on the series, and each time James replied with a letter too embarrassingly generous for even such an egotist as David Langford to quote.

His death from a stroke in 1999 came too soon—he was seventy-one—but was mercifully quick. A lot of us miss him badly. Reading the Sector General books yet again brings back so many happy memories. It's hackneyed but entirely true to say that I envy readers who are meeting them for the first time.

THE SECRET HISTORY OF SECTOR GENERAL

[NOTE: THIS WAS ORIGINALLY WRITTEN AS AN INTRODUCTION TO *AMBULANCE SHIP*.—ED.]

For a series that began twenty years ago and has so far run to over a quarter of a million words, Sector General got off to a very shaky start. In fact, had the late and sadly missed Ted Carnell, who was at that time the editor of the British SF magazine, *New Worlds*, not been desperate to fill a 17,000-word hole which had opened up in his November 1957 issue, the first novelette in the series, "Sector General," would not have been accepted without literary surgery of a drastic nature.

The birth of the Sector General idea was a natural, if perhaps a premature, occurrence. I had been writing professionally for just over four years and the joins were still showing in my work. But even in those early apprenticeship days I had a strong preference for medics or extraterrestrials as the chief characters in my stories, and gradually both types began appearing in the same stories. For example, in the Ballantine collection *The Aliens Among Us* there was a story called "To Kill or Cure," which dealt with the fumbling attempts of a navy doctor from a rescue helicopter to give medical assistance to the survivor of a crashed extraterrestrial spaceship. So it was only natural that a story that dealt with the problems inherent in human beings treating large numbers of extraterrestrial patients in hospital conditions, and aliens treating humans, would evolve.

The novelette "Sector General," however, had flaws. Ted Carnell said that it lacked a coherent plot; that the principal character, Doctor Conway, simply drifted into and out of medical situations without solving his main problem—the ethical conflict in his mind between the militaristic Monitor Corps, which maintained the hospital, and its intensely pacifist medical staff; and that the whole thing was so episodic that it resembled an interstellar *Emergency Ward 10,* a very corny British TV hospital series of the time. Comparing that series to my story was surely the unkindest surgical incision of all! He also said that I had spelled *efficient* two different ways in the story, and both ways were wrong. There were other flaws that became apparent only with hindsight, but these were corrected in the later stories of the series.

But Ted did like the basic idea. He said that the background of the huge hospital in space was one that I should keep going, if only occasionally. He also said that Harry Harrison had called him at his office and was somewhat irritated with me for beating him to the punch with the interstellar hospital idea, because he had been planning a series of four or five short stories with just such a background, reckoning that it was a new idea. Harry still intended doing the stories, Ted said, but his enthusiasm had been blunted.

This last piece of news scared me half to death.

At that time I had not met Harry Harrison, but I knew quite a lot about him. I knew since reading *Rockdiver* as a very young fan that he had been one of my favorite authors; that he spoke rather loudly to people when he was roused; and that he was probably *Deathworld* on two feet. And there was I, a fan and a professional writer still wet behind the ears, having the effrontery to actually blunt *his* enthusiasm! But Harry must be a truly kind and forgiving soul because nothing catastrophic has happened to me. At least not yet.

All the same, there must be a probability world somewhere in which he got in first with the idea and blunted my enthusiasm, and the SF shelves in the bookshops carry a series of books by Harry Harrison about an interstellar hospital. If someone would invent a transverse time-travel machine, I should dearly like to borrow it for a few hours to buy those books.

The second story in the series was "Trouble with Emily" and Ted was much happier with this one. It featured Doctor Conway—carrying a pint-sized alien with psi powers on his shoulder instead of a large chip—and a party of Monitor Corpsmen, who were assisting him with the treatment of a brontosaurus-like patient called

Emily, because one of the Corps officers had a fondness for reading the Brontë sisters.

But the function of the Monitor Corps, the law enforcement and executive arm of the Galactic Federation whose sixty-odd intelligent species were represented on the staff of Sector General, was something that needed clarification, I thought. The result was a very long novelette of some 21,000 words.

Essentially the Monitor Corps was a police force on an interstellar scale, but I did not want them to be the usual ruthless, routine-indoctrinated, basically stupid organization that is so handy to have around when an idealistic principal character needs a bit of ethical conflict. Conway was one of the good guys and I wanted them to be good guys too, but with different ideas as to the kind of activity that produces the greater good.

Their duties included interstellar survey and first-contact work as well as maintaining the Federation's peace—a job that could, if they were unable to discourage the warmongers, give rise to a police action that was indistinguishable from an act of war. But the Corps much preferred to wage psychological warfare aimed at discouraging planetary and interplanetary violence and when, despite their efforts, a war broke out, then they very closely monitored the beings who were waging it.

These warlike entities belonged to a psychological rather than physiological classification, and regardless of species they were the classification responsible for most of the trouble within the Federation. The story told of the efforts of the Monitor Corps first to attempt to prevent the war and then damp down the war, and Conway and Sector General came into it only when things went catastrophically wrong and large numbers of human and e-t casualties had to be dealt with. The original title of the story was "Classification: Warrior."

Ted, however, insisted that it was much too serious a story to be tied into the *Sector General* series, and he had me delete all references to the Monitor Corps (rechristening them the Stellar Guard), the Federation, Sector General hospital and Conway. The story was retitled "Occupation: Warrior." It appeared in the collection *The Aliens Among Us*, which also contained a proper Sector General story called "Countercharm."

With the next story, "Visitor at Large," later published in the collection entitled *Hospital Station*, the series was firmly back on the rails. Appearing for the first time in the hospital was the insectile, incredibly fragile and emotion-sensitive Doctor Prilicla, who was later to become the most popular character in the series. The patient that Conway and Prilicla were treating was physically incapable of becoming sick, although it was, of course, subject to psychological disturbances. This particular patient was amoebic, highly adaptable and had the ability to extrude any limbs or sensory organs required for any given situation. It reproduced by fission and inherited at the time of its "birth" all of the experience and knowledge of its parent, and of its parent's parent, and on back to the beginning of its evolution. The creature's problem was that it had suffered a trauma that had caused it to withdraw from all outside contact and it was slowly dissolving into water; and water turned out to be the solution in both senses of the word.

The next story featured a jump backwards in time to the period when the hospital was under construction, and the central character was O'Mara, who was later to become its Chief Psychologist. This was followed by a story that featured a patient with a most distressing collection of symptoms, which Conway steadfastly, and against all the advice and direct orders of his superiors, refused to treat. The stories were called "Medic" and "Outpatient" respectively, and they also appeared in the *Hospital Station* collection, which contained all five of the Sector General stories written at that time.

Around this time the one-hundredth issue of *New Worlds* was coming up and Ted Carnell had been writing to his regular authors asking them to produce something special for it. I submitted a 14,000-worder called "The Apprentice"—it later appeared in my *Monsters and Medics* collection—which he straightaway stuck into issue 99 because, he said, he had only a 7,000-word hole left in number 100. Could I fill it with a Sector General short story, within three weeks?

I badly wanted to make it into that one-hundredth issue with its lineup of top authors, but I did not have a single alien ailment in my head. In desperation I tried to build a story around an Earth-human condition that might have an extraterrestrial equivalent, an ailment of which I had firsthand experience, diabetes.

Now there is no great problem in pushing a hypodermic needle through the tegument and subcutaneous tissue of an Earth-human and injecting a measured dose of insulin—except sometimes I go "Ouch." But suppose the diabetic patient was a crab-like life-form, whose limbs and body were covered by a hard shell? Obviously the same procedure would not be suitable, unless one used a sterile power drill and even this, in time, would lead to grave weakening of the body structure by leaving it in the condition of an exoskeletal sieve. Solving this problem, with the help of a magnificently pro-portioned nurse and later an e-t pathologist called Murchison, was the plot line for the story "Countercharm," which dropped nicely into Ted's 7,000-word hole as well as appearing later in *The Aliens Among Us* collection.

Probably the next idea for the series came about because of a second or third re-reading of Hal Clement's *Needle*. The situation was that a Very Important Extraterrestrial Person had had a dis-agreement with its personal medic and as a result had been admitted to the hospital. Only much later in the story did Conway discover that the medic in question was an intelligent, organized virus life-form who lived and worked inside its patient. The story was called, inevitably, "Resident Physician" and was an introductory novelette to the first, and so far the only, Sector General novel-length work, "Field Hospital." "Resident Physician" and "Field Hospital" were later published together as *Star Surgeon*.

Normally I do not like stories of violence or the senseless killing that is war. But if a story is to hold the interest of the reader there must be conflict, which means violence or struggle of some kind. However, in a medical SF story of the Sector General type the vi-olence is usually the direct or indirect result of a natural catastrophe, a disaster in space or an epidemic of some kind. And if there *is* a war situation of the kind that occurred in *Star Surgeon,* then the medics are fighting only to save lives, and the Monitor Corps, like the good little policemen they are, are fighting to stop the war rather than win it—which is the essential difference between maintaining the peace and waging a war.

There is not enough space to go into the plot details of *Star Surgeon,* but one should be mentioned. In "Occupation: Warrior," which should have been the fourth Sector General story, "Classifi-

cation: Warrior," the leading character was a tactician called Dermod; and the same character turned up again as the Monitor Corps
Fleet Commander who defended the hospital in *Star Surgeon* as well
as having an important part to play in *Major Operation*. I don't
know why I went to the trouble of establishing this tenuous connection between the series proper and the Sector General story that
had been deliberately de-Sector Generalized, but it seemed important to me at the time.

There was a four-year gap before the next stories in the series
were written. These were five novelettes that were planned, like the
Ambulance Ship trio, to build progressively into a novel. They were
"Invader," "Vertigo," "Blood Brother," "Meatball" and "Major Operation," and with linking material added they were published as
the book-length *Major Operation*.

"Invader" set the stage by introducing to the hospital a thought-
controlled tool that caused havoc until Conway realized how valuable such a device could be in the hands of a surgeon who fully
understood its uses. During further investigation of the planet on
which the tool originated, the Monitor Corps rescued a doughnut-
shaped alien who had to roll all the time to live because it did not
have a heart but depended on a gravity feed system for blood circulation. This story was called "Vertigo," and the alien was a present
of my friend Bob Shaw, who called it a Drambon.

Bob thought it might be fun if I used his e-t and called it a
Drambon because he had used the Drambon species in one of his
stories; then we could wait and see how long it would take one of
the science-fiction buffs to spot the fact that a certain extraterrestrial
had cropped up, or rather rolled up, in the work of two different
authors. But up until now the widely traveled Drambon life-form
seems to have gone unspotted.

The next story in the series derived from an original idea by a
well-known English fan of the time, Ken Cheslin. We were at a
convention party when he said, as nearly as I can remember, "James,
you know how doctors used to be called leeches? Why don't you
write a story where the doctor really *is* a leech?" The e-t that resulted
was a life-form whose method of treatment was to withdraw practically all of its patient's blood—a very disconcerting process for the
being concerned—and remove the offending toxic material or

micro-organisms before returning the blood to the patient good as new. The story was called "Blood Brother." Thanks, Ken.

Regarding "Meatball" and the climactic "Major Operation," there is very little to say except that the poisoned and polluted living planet that was the patient in those stories required treatment on such a vast scale that the operation was a military as well as a medical one.

The next story in the series, so far published only in Britain in *New Writings in SF 22*, was called "Spacebird." The idea for an organic, completely non-metallic spaceship had been in my notebook for a long time, but it could not be used until I could discover a means of boosting such a bird to escape velocity. Then at one of the conventions I mentioned my problem to Jack Cohen. Jack, who is a very helpful person and a stickler for xenobiological verisimilitude, is senior lecturer in animal reproduction at the University of Birmingham in England. He knows so much about strange and alien life-forms that, when asked if a certain hypothetical extraterrestrial is physiologically possible, he invariably cites examples of a couple of terrestrial life-forms that are even weirder. The answer to my problem, Jack said, was the bombardier beetle—a small, mid-European insect that, when threatened with danger, expels and ignites gas from its rear so violently that it lands many inches away.

When the story was written, the launching of the spacecraft was from a Mesklin-type planet with high centrifugal force and low gravity at its equator to aid the process; and it was with millions of outsize bombardier beetles forming the multistaging sequences, all blasting away and hoisting the bird into space. Surely this was an idea to arouse the sense of wonder, I thought. Think of the technological achievement it represented for a race completely without metals, and think of the timing and delicacy of control involved. Try not to think of the smell . . .

The latest stories to be written are the three linked which comprise the book you are about to read. It deals with a new aspect of the work at Sector General—the hospital's special ambulance service—and concerns the extraterrestrial medical, physiological, psychological and engineering problems that must be solved, quickly and on the site of the accident by the ambulance ship's crew if the casualties are to survive until they reach the hospital. When these problems arise, the ambulance ships are inevitably far removed from the virtually limitless facilities of Sector General, so the alien technologists and medical specialists of the crews concerned must fall back on their own ingenuity and strictly limited resources. If they make a wrong decision, the consequences can be far-reaching indeed.

To date the Sector General series has run to one short story, fifteen novelettes and one novel. I hope to go on writing about extraterrestrials, their exotic physiologies, their alien viewpoints and the problems of communication and understanding they represent. But my problem in recent years has been that, when I dream up a really alien alien, it promptly falls sick or gets itself damaged in an accident and ends up becoming a problem for Sector Twelve General Hospital.

AMBULANCE SHIP

TO JACK COHEN
WHO IS A STICKLER FOR XENOBIOLOGICAL VERISIMILITUDE,
IN APPRECIATION

PART 1

SPACEBIRD

The Monitor Corps scoutship *Torrance* was engaged on a mission which was both highly important and deadly dull. Like the other units of its flotilla it had been assigned a relatively tiny volume of space in Sector Nine—one of the many three-dimensional blanks which still appeared in the Federation's charts—to fill in the types and positions of the stars which it contained and the numbers of planets circling them.

Because a ten-man scoutship did not have the facilities for handling a first contact situation, they were forbidden to land or even make a close approach to these planets. They would identify the technologically advanced worlds, if any, by analyzing the radio frequency and other forms of radiation emanating from them. As Major Madden, the vessel's captain, had told them at the start of the mission, they were simply going to count lights in the sky and that was all.

Naturally, Fate could not resist a temptation like *that* . . .

"Radar, sir," said a voice from the controlroom speaker. "We have a blip on the close-approach screen. Distance six miles, closing slowly, non-collision course."

"Lock on the telescope," said the Captain, "and let's see it."

"Yes, sir. Repeater screen Two."

On Corps scoutships discipline was strict only when circumstances warranted it, and normally those circumstances did not arise during a mapping mission. As a result the noises coming from the speaker resembled a debate rather than a series of station reports.

"It looks like a ... a bird, sir, with its wings spread."

"A plucked bird."

"Has anyone calculated the chances against materializing this close to an object in interstellar space?"

"I think it's an asteroid, or molten material which congealed by accident into that shape."

"Two lights years from the nearest sun?"

"Quiet, please," said the Captain. "Lock on an analyzer and report."

There was a short pause, then: "Estimated size, roughly one-third that of this ship. It's non-reflective, non-metallic, non-mineral and—"

"You're doing a fine job of telling me what it isn't," said the Captain dryly.

"It is organic, sir, and ..."

"Yes?"

"And alive."

For a few seconds the controlroom speaker and the Captain held their breath, then Madden said firmly, "Power Room, maneuvering thrust in five minutes. Astrogation, match courses and close to five hundred yards. Ordanace, stand by. Surgeon-Lieutenant Brenner will prepare for EVA."

The debate was over.

During the ensuing four hours Lieutenant Brenner examined the creature, initially at a safe distance and later as closely as his suit would allow. He was sure that the analyzer had been a little too optimistic over what was most likely a not quite frigid corpse. Certainly the thing was no threat because it could not move even if it had wanted to. The covering of what looked like large, flat barnacles and the rock-hard cement which held them together saw to that.

Later, when he was ending his report to the Captain, he said, "To sum up, sir, it is suffering from a pretty weird skin condition which got out of control and caused it to be dumped—certainly it didn't fly out here. This implies a race with space-travel who are subject to a disease which scares them so badly that they dump the sufferers into space while they are still alive.

"As you know," he continued, "I don't have the qualifications to treat e-t diseases, and the being is too large to fit into our hold.

But we could enlarge our hyperspace envelope and tow it to Sector General.

"That would make a nice break in the mapping routine," he added hopefully, "and I've never been to that place. I'm told that not all the nurses there have six legs."

The Captain was silent for a moment, then he nodded.

"I have," he said. "Some of them have more."

*   *   *

Framed in the rescue tender's aft vision screen the tremendous structure that was Sector Twelve General Hospital hung in space like a gigantic cylindrical Christmas tree. Its thousands of viewports were constantly ablaze with light in the dazzling variety of color and intensity necessary for the visual equipment of its patients and staff, while inside its three hundred and eighty-four levels was reproduced the environments of all the intelligent life-forms known to the Galactic Federation—a biological spectrum ranging from the ultra-frigid methane-breathers through the more normal oxygen- and chlorine-breathing types up to the exotic beings who existed by the direct conversion of hard radiation.

In addition to the patients, whose numbers and physiological classifications were a constant variable, there was a medical and maintenance staff comprising sixty-odd differing life-forms with sixty different sets of mannerisms, body odors and ways of looking at life.

The staff of Sector General prided themselves that no case was too big, too small or too hopeless, and their reputation and facilities were second to none. They were an extremely able, dedicated, but not always serious bunch, and Senior Physician Conway could not rid himself of the idea that on this occasion someone was playing a complicated joke on him.

"Now that I see it," he said dryly, "I still can't believe it."

Pathologist Murchison, who occupied the position beside him, stared at the image of *Torrance* and its tow without comment. On the controlroom ceiling, where it clung with six fragile, sucker-tipped legs, Doctor Prilicla trembled slightly and said, "It could prove to be an interesting and exciting professional challenge, friend Conway."

The musical trills and clicks of the Cinrusskin's speech were received by Conway's translator pack, relayed to the translation computer at the center of the hospital and transmitted back to his earpiece as flat, emotionless English. As expected, the reply was pleasant, polite and extremely non-controversial.

Prilicla was insectile, exo-skeletal, six-legged and with a pair of iridescent and not quite atrophied wings and possessing a highly-developed empathic faculty. Only on Cinruss with its one-eighth gravity and dense atmosphere could a race of insects have grown to such dimensions and in time developed intelligence and an advanced civilization. But in Sector General Prilicla was in deadly danger for most of its working day. It had to wear gravity nullifiers everywhere outside its own quarters because the gravity pull which most of its colleagues considered normal would instantly have crushed it flat, and when Prilicla held a conversation with anyone it kept well out of reach of any thoughtless movement of an arm or tentacle which could easily cave in its fragile body or snap off a leg.

Not that anyone would have wanted to hurt Prilicla—it was too well-liked for that. The Cinrusskin's empathic faculty forced it to be kind and considerate to *everyone* in order to make the emotional radiation of the people around it as pleasant for itself as possible.

Except when its professional duty exposed it to pain and violent emotion in a patient, and that situation might arise within the next few minutes.

Turning suddenly to Prilicla, Conway said, "Wear your light-weight suit but stay well clear of the being until we tell you that there is no danger of movement, involuntary or otherwise, from it. We shall wear heavy duty suits, mostly because they have more hooks on which to hang our diagnostic equipment, and I shall ask *Torrance*'s medic to do the same."

Half an hour later Lieutenant Brenner, Murchison and Conway were hanging beside the form of the enormous bird while Prilicla, wearing a transparent plastic bubble through which projected its bony mandibles, drifted beside the lock of their tender.

"No detectable emotional radiation, friend Conway," reported the empath.

"I'm not surprised," said Murchison.

"It could be dead," said the Lieutenant defensively. "But when we found it the body temperature was measurably above the norm for an object warmed only by a two light-years distant sun."

"There was no criticism intended, Doctor," said Murchison soothingly. "I was simply agreeing with our empathic friend. But did you, before or during the trip here, carry out any examinations, observations or tests on this patient, or reach any tentative conclusions as a result of such tests? And don't be shy, Lieutenant—we may be the acknowledged experts in xenological medicine and physiology here, but we got that way by listening and looking, not by gratuitous displays of our expertise. You were curious, naturally, and . . . ?"

"Yes, ma'am," said Brenner, his voice registering surprise that there was an Earth-human female inside the bulky suit. "I assumed that, lacking information on its planet of origin, you might want to know if there were any safe atmospheric compositions in which it could be examined—I was assuming that, being a bird, it needed an atmosphere to fly in and that it had been dumped in space because of its diseased condition . . ."

Listening, Conway could not help admiring the smooth way in which Murchison was getting the Corps medic to tell them about the things he had done wrong. As an e-t pathologist she was used to non-specialists interfering and complicating her job, and it was necessary that she discover as much as possible about the being's original condition before the changes or additional damage caused by inexpert examination—no matter how well-intentioned—had been introduced. She was finding out all that she needed to know quietly and without giving offense, as if she was Prilicla in human form.

But as Brenner continued talking it became increasingly clear that he had made few, if any, mistakes, and a fair proportion of Conway's professional admiration was being diverted towards the Lieutenant.

". . . After I sent the preliminary report and we were on our way," Brenner was saying, "I discovered two small, rough areas on the black stuff covering the creature—a small, circular patch at the base of the neck, right here, and an oval patch, a little larger, which you can see on the underside. In both these areas the black stuff is cracked but with the cracks filled, or partly filled, by more of the stuff, and a few of the barnacles in these areas have been damaged as well. This is where I took my specimens."

"Marking the places you took them from, I see," said Murchison. "Go on, Doctor."

"Yes, ma'am," said the Lieutenant, and went on. "The black material seems to be a near-perfect insulator—it is highly resistant to heat, including that of a cutting torch at medium power. At very high temperatures the area under test formed a black ash which flaked away but showed no sign of softening or cracking. The chips of shell from the damaged barnacles were not quite so heat-resistant unless they happened to be covered by the black material.

"The black stuff was also resistant to chemical attack," Brenner continued, "but not the pieces of shell. When the chips were exposed to various basic atmospheric types, the results seemed to indicate that they had not originated on one of the exotic environments— methane- or ammonia- or even chlorine-based atmosphere envelopes. Composition of the fragments seems to be basic hydrocarbon material, and they did not react to short-term exposures to an oxygen-rich mixture—"

"Give me the details of the tests you made," said Murchison, suddenly becoming very businesslike and, although the Lieutenant did not know it, very complimentary. Conway signaled Prilicla to come closer, leaving the professional and amateur pathologists to get on with it.

"I don't think the patient is capable of movement," he told the Cinrusskin. "I don't even know if it's alive. Is it?"

Prilicla's limbs trembled as it steeled itself to make a negative reply and by so doing, become just the slightest bit disagreeable. It said, "That is a deceptively simple question, friend Conway. All that I can say is that it doesn't appear to be quite dead."

"But you can detect the emotional emanations from a sleeping or deeply unconscious mind," said Conway incredulously. "Is there no emotional radiation at all?"

"There are traces, friend Conway," said the Cinrusskin, still trembling, "but they are too faint to be identifiable. There is no self-awareness and the traces which are apparent do not, so far as I am able to tell, originate from the being's cranial area—they seem to emanate from the body as a whole. I have never encountered this effect before, so I lack sufficient information or experience even to speculate."

"But you will," said Conway, smiling.

"Of course," said Prilicla. "It is possible that if the being was both deeply unconscious and at the same time was having the nerve endings in its skin constantly stimulated by severe pain, this might explain the effect which I can detect on and for some distance below the skin."

"But that means that you are detecting the peripheral nerve network and not the brain," said Conway. "That is unusual."

"Highly unusual, friend Conway," said the little empath. "The brain in question would have to have had important nerve trunks severed or have suffered major structural damage."

In short, Conway thought grimly, we may have been handed someone's cast-off patient.

II

Murchison and Brenner, using the pathologist's sterile drills, were taking deep samples as well as collecting and labelling chippings of shell and the black material which covered the patient—more accurately, Murchison took the samples while the Lieutenant sealed the tiny openings she made. Conway returned to the tender with Prilicla to arrange accommodation for the patient based on their sketchy knowledge—an evacuated chamber large enough to hold the thing, with provision for restraining it and for surrounding it with an oxygen-based atmosphere—and was followed shortly afterwards by the others.

It was then that Brenner saw for the first time the contents of the pathologist's spacesuit, and Prilicla began a slow tremble.

Unless covered by a heavy duty suit fitted with an opaque sun filter, Murchison displayed a combination of physiological features which made it impossible for any male Earth-human member of the staff to regard her with anything approaching clinical detachment. The Lieutenant finally managed to drag his eyes away from her and to notice Prilicla.

"Is something wrong, Doctor?" he asked, looking concerned.

"To the contrary, friend Brenner," said the empath, still trembling slowly. "This type of involuntary physical activity is my species' reaction to the close proximity of an intense but pleasurable source of emotional radiation of the kind usually associated with the biological urge to mate . . ."

The Cinrusskin broke off and stopped trembling because the Surgeon-Lieutenant's suddenly red face was clashing discordantly against his green uniform, and Prilicla was feeling his embarrassment.

Murchison smiled sympathetically and said, "Perhaps I am the cause, Lieutenant Brenner—I have intense feelings of pleasure over the way in which your earlier tests and deductions have saved me nearly four hours work in a very irksome spacesuit. Isn't that so, Prilicla?"

"Most certainly," said the empath, to whom lying was second nature so long as it made someone, especially itself, happy. "Empathy is not nearly as accurate as telepathy, you know, and mistakes of this kind frequently occur."

Conway cleared his throat and said, "I've arranged to see O'Mara just as soon as we have the patient accommodated which, initially, will be in an evacuated dock and storage chamber on Level 103. We will use the tender's tractor beam to transfer the patient to the hospital, so if you are needed on board *Torrance*, Lieutenant . . . ?"

Brenner shook his head. "The Captain would like to spend some time here, if possible, and so would I if I wouldn't be in the way. It's my first time to visit this place. Are there, ah, many other Earth-humans on the medical staff?"

If you mean like Murchison, Conway thought smugly, *the answer is no.* Aloud, he said, "We would welcome your help, of course. But you do not know what you are letting yourself in for, Lieutenant, and you keep asking about the Earth-humans on the staff. Are you xenophobic, even slightly? Uncomfortable near extraterrestrials?"

"Certainly not," said Brenner firmly, then added, "Of course, I wouldn't want to marry one."

Prilicla began the slow shakes again. The musical trills and clicks of its Cinrusskin speech formed a pleasant background to its translated voice as it said, "From the sudden flood of pleasant emotional radiation, for which I can see no apparent reason in the current situation and recent dialogue, I assume that someone has made what Earth-humans call a joke."

At Level 103 Prilicla left to check on its wards while the others supervised the transfer of the great, stiff-winged bird into the storage chamber. Looking at the swept-back, partially folded wings and stiffly extended neck, Conway was reminded of one of the old-time space shuttles. His mind began to slip off on an interesting but ridiculous, tangent and he had to remind himself that birds did *not* fly, in space.

With the patient immobilized under one full G of artificial gravity it still took another three hours before Murchison had everything she wanted in the way of specimens and x-rays. In part the delay was caused by them having to work in pressure suits because, as Murchison put it, there would be little risk in observing the patient for a few more hours in airless conditions until they had worked out its atmosphere requirements with exactness—otherwise they might simply end by observing its processes of decomposition.

But their information on the patient was growing with every minute that passed, and the results of their tests—transmitted direct from Pathology by the portable communicator beside them—were both interesting and utterly baffling. Conway lost all track of time until the communicator chimed for attention and the face of Major O'Mara glowered out at them.

"Conway, you arranged to see me here seven and one half minutes ago," said the Chief Psychologist. "No doubt you were just leaving."

"I'm sorry, sir," said Conway, "the preliminary investigation is taking longer than I estimated, and I want to have something concrete to report before seeing you."

There was a faint rustling sound as O'Mara breathed heavily through his nose. The Chief Psychologist's face was about as readable as a piece of weathered basalt, which in some respects it resembled, but the eyes which studied Conway opened into a mind so keenly analytical that it gave the Major what amounted to a telepathic faculty.

As Chief Psychologist of a multi-environment hospital he was responsible for the mental well-being of a staff of several thousand entities belonging to more than sixty different species. Even though his Monitor Corps rank of Major did not place him high in the chain of command, there was no clear limit to his authority. To O'Mara the medical staff were patients, too, and part of his job was to assign the right kind of doctor—whether Earth-human or e-t— to a given patient.

Given even the highest qualities of tolerance and mutual respect, potentially dangerous situations could still arise through ignorance or misunderstanding, or a being could develop xenophobia to a degree which threatened to affect its professional competence, mental stability, or both. An Earth-human doctor, for instance, who had a subconscious fear of spiders would not be able to bring to bear on a Cinrusskin patient the proper degree of clinical detachment necessary for its treatment. And if someone like Prilicla were to treat such an Earth-human patient . . .

A large part of O'Mara's job was to detect and eradicate such trouble among the medical staff while other members of his department saw to it that the problem did not arise where the patients were concerned. According to O'Mara himself, however, the true reason for the high degree of mental stability among the variegated and often touchy medical staff was that they were all too frightened of him to risk going mad.

Caustically, he said, "Doctor Conway, I freely admit that this patient is unusual even by your standards, but you must have discovered a few simple facts about it and its condition. Is it alive? Is it diseased or injured? Does it possess intelligence? Are you wasting your time on an outsize, space-frozen turkey?"

Conway ignored the rhetoric and tried to answer the questions. He said. "The patient is alive, just barely, and the indications are that it is both diseased—the exact nature of the disease is not yet known—and suffering from gross physical injury, specifically a punctured wound made by a large, high-velocity projectile or a tightly focused heat beam which passed through the base of the neck and the upper chestal area. The wound entrance and exit is sealed by the black covering or growth—we still don't know which—encasing the body. Regarding the possibility of intelligence, the cranial capacity is large enough not to rule this out, but again, the head is too deeply unconscious to radiate detectable emotion. The manipulatory appendages, whose degree of specialization or otherwise can give a strong indication of the presence or absence of intelligence, have been removed.

"Not by us," Conway added.

O'Mara was silent for a moment, then he said, "I see. Another one of your deceptively simple cases. No doubt you will have deceptively simple special requirements. Accommodation? Physiology tapes? Information on planet of origin?"

Conway shook his head. "I don't believe that you have a physiology tape that will cover this patient's type—all the winged species we know are light-gravity beings, and this one has muscles for about four Gs. The present accommodation is fine, although we'll have to be careful in case of contamination of or from the chlorine level above us—the seals to storage compartments like this are not designed for constant traffic, unlike the ward airlocks—"

"I didn't know that, of course."

"Sorry, sir," said Conway. "I was thinking aloud, and partly for the benefit of Surgeon-Lieutenant Brenner, who is visiting this madhouse for the first time. Regarding information on its planet of origin, I would like you to approach Colonel Skempton to ask him if it would be possible for *Torrance* to return to that area to investigate the two nearer star systems, to look for beings with a similar physiological classification."

"In other words," said O'Mara dryly, "you have a difficult medical problem and think that the best solution is to find the patient's own doctor."

Conway smiled and said, "We don't need full cultural contact— just a quick look, atmosphere samples and specimens of local plant and animal life, if *Torrance* wouldn't mind soft-landing a probe—"

O'Mara broke the connection at that point with a sound which was untranslatable and Conway, now that they had gone as far as they could with the patient without the path reports, suddenly realized how hungry he was.

III

To reach the dining hall reserved for warm-bodied oxygen breathers they had to travel through two levels, none of which required protective suits, and a network of corridors crowded with entities which flapped, crawled, undulated and occasionally walked past them. They were met at the entrance by Prilicla who was carrying a folder of green path reports.

As they entered the last Earth-human table was being taken by a bunch of crab-like Melfans and a Tralthan—Melfans could adapt themselves to the low stools and the Tralthans did everything including sleep on their six elephantine feet. Prilicla spotted an empty table in the Kelgian area and flew across to claim it before the party of Corps maintenancemen could get there. Luckily it was beyond the range of their emotional radiation.

Conway began eagerly leafing through the reports once he saw that the Lieutenant was being shown by Murchison how to balance on the edge of a Kelgian chair within reach of the food he had ordered. But for once Brenner's attention was not on the shapely pathologist. He was staring at Prilicla, his eyebrows almost lost in his hairline.

"Cinrusskins prefer to eat while hovering—they say it aids the digestion," explained Murchison, and added, "The slipstream helps cool the soup, too."

Prilicla maintained a stable hover while they concentrated on refuelling, breaking off only to pass around the reports. Finally Conway, feeling pleasantly distended, turned to the Cinrusskin.

"I don't know how you managed it," he said warmly. "When *I* want a fast report from Thornnastor the most he will let me do is just two places in the queue."

Prilicla trembled at the compliment as it replied "I insisted, quite truthfully, that our patient was at the point of death."

"But not," said Murchison dryly, "that it has been in that condition for a very long time."

"You're sure of that?" asked Conway.

"I am now," she answered seriously, tapping one of the reports as she spoke. "The indications are that the large punctured wound was inflicted by a meteorite collision some time after the disease, that is the barnacles and coating material were in position. The coating which flowed into and across the wound, effectively sealed it.

"As well," she continued, "these tests show that a very complex chemical form of suspended animation—not just hypothermia—

was used and that it was applied organ by organ, almost cell by cell, by micro-injections of the required specifics. In a way you could think of it as if the creature had been embalmed before it was quite dead in an effort to prolong its life."

"What about the missing legs or claws?" said Conway, "*and* the evidence of charring under the coating in the areas behind the wings? And the pieces of what seems to be a different kind of barnacle in those areas?"

"It is possible," Murchison replied, "that the disease initially affected the being's legs or claws, perhaps during its equivalent of nesting. The removal of the limbs and the evidence of charring you mention might have been early and unsuccessful attempts at curing the patient's condition. Remember that virtually all of the creature's body wastes were eliminated before the coating was applied. That is standard procedure before hibernation, anesthesia or major surgery."

The silence which followed was broken by the Lieutenant, who said, "Excuse me, I'm getting lost. This disease or growth, what exactly do we know about it?"

They knew that the outward symptoms of the disease were the barnacle-like growths, Murchison told him, which covered the patient's tegument so completely that it could have been a suit of chain mail. It was still open to argument whether the barnacles were skin conditions which had sprouted rootlets or a subcutaneous condition with a barnacle-like eruption on the surface, but in either event they were held by a thick pencil of fine rootlets extending and subdividing to an unknown depth within the patient. They penetrated not only the subcutaneous tissue and underlying musculature, but practically all of the vital organs and central nervous systems. And the rootlets were hungry. There could be no doubt from the condition of the tissue underlying the barnacles that this was a severely wasting disease which was far advanced.

"It seems to me that you should have been called in earlier," said Brenner, "and that the patient was sealed up just before it was due to die."

Conway nodded and said, "But it isn't hopeless. Some of our e-ts practice micro-surgery techniques which would enable them to excise the rootlets, even the ones which are tangled up in the nerve bundles. It is a very slow procedure, however, and there is the danger that when we revive the patient the disease will also be revived and that it might progress faster than the micro-surgeon. I think the answer is to learn as much as we possibly can about the disease before we do anything else."

When they returned to the patient there was a message waiting from O'Mara to say that *Torrance* had left with the promise of preliminary reports on the two solar systems nearest to the find within three days. During those three days Conway expected to devise procedures which would remove the coating and barnacles from the patient, arrest the disease and initiate curative surgery so that the scoutship's reports would be needed only to prepare proper accommodation for the patient's convalescence.

During those three days, however, they got precisely nowhere.

The material which encased barnacles and patient alike could be drilled and chipped away with great difficulty and an enormous waste of time—the process resembled that of chipping out a fossil without inflicting damage, and this particular fossil was fifty feet long and over eighty from tip to tip of its partially folded wings. When Conway insisted that Pathology produce a faster method of stripping the patient he was told that the coating was a complex organic, that the specifics they had devised for dissolving it would produce large quantities of toxic gases—toxic to the patient as well as the attending physicians—and that the shell material of the barnacles would be instantly dissolved by this solvent and that it would not be good for the patient's skin and underlying tissue, either. They went back to drilling and chipping.

Murchison, who was continually withdrawing micro-specimens from the areas affected by the rootlets, was informative but unhelpful.

"I'm not suggesting that you should abandon this one," she said sympathetically, "but you should start thinking about it. In addition to the widespread tissue wastage, there is evidence of structural damage to the wing muscles—damage which may well have been self-inflicted—and I think the heart has ruptured. This will mean major surgical repairs as well as—"

"This muscle and heart damage," said Conway sharply. "Could

it have been caused by the patient trying to get out of its casing?"

"It is possible but not likely," she replied in a voice which reminded him that he was not talking to a junior intern and that past and present relationships could change with very little notice. "That coating is hard, but it is relatively very thin and the leverage of the patient's wings is considerable. I would say that the heart and muscle damage occurred before the patient was encased."

"I'm sorry if . . ." began Conway.

"There is also the fact," she went on coldly, "that the barnacles are clustered thickly about the patient's head and along the spine. Even with our tissue and nerve regeneration techniques, the patient may never be able to think or move itself even if we are successful in returning it to a technically living state."

"I hadn't realized," said Conway dully, "that it was as serious as that. But there must be something we can do . . ." He tried to pull his face muscles into a smile. ". . . if only to preserve Brenner's illusions about the miracle-workers of Sector General."

Brenner had been looking from one to the other, obviously wondering whether this was a spirited professional discussion or the beginning of some kind of family fight. But the Lieutenant was tactful as well as observant. He said, "I would have given up a long time ago."

Before either of them could reply the communicator chimed and Chief of Pathology Thornnastor was framed in the screen.

"My department," said the Tralthan, "has worked long and diligently to discover a method of removing the coating material by chemical means, but in vain. The material is, however, affected by intense heat. At high temperatures the surface crumbles, the ashy deposit can be scraped or blown away and heat again applied. The process can be continued safely until the coating is very thin, after which it could be removed in large sections without harm to the patient."

Conway obtained the temperature and thickness figures, thanked Thornnastor and then used the communicator to call the maintenance section for cutting torches and operators. He had not forgotten Murchison's doubts regarding the advisability of attempting a cure, but he had to go on trying. He did not *know* that the

great, diseased bird would end as a winged vegetable, and he would
not know until they knew everything possible about the disease
which was affecting it.

Because the heat treatment was untried they began near the tail,
where the vital organs were deeply buried and where the area had
already been disturbed, presumably by the efforts of their medical
predecessors.

After only half an hour's continuous burning they had their first
stroke of luck in three days. They discovered a barnacle which was
embedded upside down in the patient—its bundle of rootlets fanned
out to link up with the other barnacles, but a few of them curved
down and past the rim of its shell to enter the patient. The surface
rootlet network was clearly visible as the flame of the torch burned
the rootlet material into a fine, incandescent web. One of the briefly
incandescent rootlets pointed towards a barnacle which was larger
and differently shaped.

Patiently they painted both objects and their immediate surroundings with the cutting torches, brushing away the crumbling
layers of coating until it was wafer thin. They cracked it, carefully
peeled back the remains of the coating and lifted away two perfect
specimens.

"They are dead," asked Conway, "not just dormant?"

"They are dead," said Prilicla.

"And the patient?"

"Life is still present, friend Conway, but the radiation is extremely weak, and diffuse."

Conway studied the area bared by the removal of the two specimens. Beneath the first was a small, deep hollow which followed
the contours of the reversed shell. The underlying tissues showed a
high degree of compression, and the few rootlets in evidence were
much too weak and fine to have held the barnacle so tightly against
the patient. Something or somebody had pressed the barnacle into
position with considerable force.

The second, and different, specimen had been held only by the
coating, apparently—it did not possess rootlets. But it did possess
wings folded into long slits in its carapace and so, on closer inspection, did the first type.

Prilicla alighted beside them, trembling slightly and erratically in the fashion which denoted excitement. It said, "You will have noticed that these are two entirely different species, friend Conway. Both are large, winged insects of the type which require a low-gravity planet with a thick air envelope—not unlike Cinruss. It is possible that the first type is a predator parasite and that the second is a natural enemy, introduced by a third party in an attempt to cure the patient."

Conway nodded. "It would explain why type one turned on to its back when approached by type two . . ."

"I hope," said Murchison apologetically, "that your theory is flexible enough to accept another datum." She had been scraping persistently at a piece of coating which was still adhering to a smaller slit in the barnacle. "The coating material was not applied by a third party, it is a body secretion of type one.

"If you don't mind," she added, "I'll take both of these beasties to Pathology for a long, close look."

For several minutes after she left nobody spoke. Prilicla began to tremble again and, judging by the expression of Brenner's face, it was at something the officer was feeling. It was the Lieutenant who broke the silence.

"If the parasites are responsible for the coating," he said sickly, "then there was no earlier attempt to cure the patient. Our heavy-gravity patient was probably attacked on the light-gravity planet of the flying barnacles, they sank in their rootlets or tendrils, paralyzed its muscles and nervous system and encased it in a . . . a shell of slowly feeding maggots when it wasn't even dead—"

"A little more clinical detachment, Lieutenant," said Conway sharply. "You're bothering Prilicla. And while something like that may have happened, there are still a few awkward facts which don't fit. That depression under the inverted barnacle still bothers me."

"Maybe it sat on one of them," said Brenner angrily, his feeling of revulsion temporarily overcoming his manners. "And I can understand why its friends dumped the patient into space—there was nothing else they could do."

He hesitated, then said, "I'm sorry, Doctor. But is there anything else that you can do?"

"There is something," said Conway grimly, "that we can *try* . . ."

IV

According to Prilicla their patient was, just barely, alive, and now that the barnacles were known to be the attacking organisms and not just surface eruptions, they and their coating must be removed as quickly as possible. Removal of the tendrils would require more delicate and time-consuming work, but the surface condition would respond to heat and, with the barnacles removed, the patient just might recover enough to be able to help Conway to help it. Pathology had already suggested methods for restarting its paralyzed life processes.

He would need at least fifty cutting torches operating simultaneously with high-pressure air hoses to blow the ash away. They would begin burning on the head, neck, breast and wing-muscle areas, freeing the patient of barnacle control of the brain, lungs and heart. If the heart was in a terminal condition emergency surgery would be necessary to bypass it—Murchison had already mapped out the arterial and venous processes in the area. And in case the patient twitched or began flapping its wings, they would need the protection of heavy-duty suits.

But no—Prilicla, who would be monitoring the emotional radiation during the op, would need maximum protection. The others would have to dodge until it could be immobilized with pressors. If emergency surgery was necessary, heavy-duty suits were too cumbersome anyway. As well, the communicator would have to be moved to a side compartment in case it was damaged, because the adjoining levels would have to be alerted and various specialist staff would have to be standing by.

While he gave the necessary orders Conway moved briskly but unhurriedly and his tone was quiet and confident. But all the time he had a vague but persistent feeling that he was saying and doing and, most of all, thinking all the wrong things.

O'Mara did not approve of his proposed line of treatment but, apart from asking whether Conway intended curing or barbecuing the patient, he did not interfere. He added that there was still no report from *Torrance*.

Finally they were ready to go. The maintenance technicians with cutting torches and air lines hissing—but directed away from the patient—were positioned around the head, neck and leading edges of the wings. Behind them waited the specialist and medical technicians with stimulants, a general purpose heart-lung machine and the bright, sterile tools of their trade. The doors to the side compartments were dogged open in case the patient revived too suddenly and they had to take cover. There was no logical reason for waiting any longer.

Conway gave the signal to begin only seconds before his communicator chimed and Murchison, looking disheveled and very cross, filled the screen.

"There has been a slight accident, an explosion," she said. "Our type two flew across the lab, damaged some test equipment and scared hell out of—"

"But it was dead," protested Conway. "They were both dead—Prilicla said so."

"It still is," said Murchison, "and it didn't fly exactly—it shot away from us. I'm not yet sure of the mechanics of the process, but apparently the thing produces gases in its intestinal tract which react explosively together, propelling it forward. Used in conjunction with its wings this would help it to escape fast-moving natural enemies like the barnacle. The gases must still have been present when I began work.

"There is a similar species, much smaller," she went on, "which is native to Earth. We studied the more exotic types of Earth fauna in preparation for the e-t courses. It was called a bombardier beetle and it—"

"Doctor Conway!"

He swung away from the screen and ran into the main compartment. He did not need to be an empath to know that something was seriously wrong.

The team leader of the maintenancemen was waving frantically and Prilicla, encased in its protective globe and supported by gravity nullifiers, was drifting above the man's head and trembling.

"Increasing awareness, friend Conway," reported the empath. "Suggesting rapidly returning consciousness. Feelings of fear and confusion."

Some of the confusion, thought Conway, *belongs to me . . .*

The maintenanceman simply pointed.

Instead of the hard coating he had expected to see there was a black, oily, semi-liquid which flowed and rippled and dripped slowly on to the floor plating. As he watched the area where the flame was being applied, the stuff rolled away from one of the barnacles, which twitched and unfolded its wings. The wings flapped, slowly at first, and it began pulling free of the patient, drawing its long tendrils out of the bird until it was completely detached and it went blundering into the air.

"Kill the torches," said Conway urgently, "but cool it with the air hose. Try to harden that black stuff."

But the thick, black liquid would not harden. Once initiated by the heat the softening process was self-sustaining. The patient's neck, no longer supported by solid material, slumped heavily on to the deck followed a few seconds later by the massive wings. The black pool around the patient widened and more and more of the barnacles struggled free to blunder about the compartment on wide, membranous wings, trailing their tendrils behind them like long, fine plumes.

"Back everybody! Take cover, *quickly!*"

Their patient lay motionless and almost certainly dead, but there was nothing that Conway could do. Neither the maintenancemen nor the medical technicians were protected against those fine, harmless-looking tendrils of the barnacles—only Prilicla in its transparent globe was safe there, and now there seemed to be hundreds of the things filling the air. He knew that he should feel badly about the patient, but somehow he did not. Was it simply delayed reaction or was there another reason?

"Friend Conway," said Prilicla, bumping him gently with its globe, "I suggest that you take your own advice."

The thought of fine, barnacle tendrils probing through his clothing, skin and underlying tissues, paralyzing his muscles and scrambling his brain made him run for the side compartment, closely followed by Brenner and Prilicla. The Lieutenant closed the door as soon as the Cinrusskin was inside.

There was a barnacle already there.

For a split second Conway's mind was like a camera, registering everything as it was in the small room: the face of O'Mara on the communicator screen, as expressionless as a slab of rock with only the eyes showing his concern; Prilicla trembling within its protective globe; the barnacle hovering near the ceiling, its tendrils blowing in a self-generated breeze, and Brenner with one eye closed in a diabolical wink as he pointed his gun—a type which threw explosive pellets—at the hovering barnacle.

There was something wrong.

"Don't shoot," said Conway, quietly but firmly, then asked, "Are you afraid, Lieutenant?"

"I don't normally use this thing," said Brenner, looking puzzled, "but I can. No, I'm not afraid."

"And I'm not afraid because you have that gun," said Conway. "Prilicla is protected and has nothing to fear. So who . . ." He indicated the empath's trembling feelers. ". . . *is* afraid?"

"It is, friend Conway," said Prilicla, indicating the barnacle. "It is afraid and confused and intensely curious."

Conway nodded. He could see Prilicla beginning to react to his intense relief. He said, "Nudge it outside, Prilicla, when the Lieutenant opens the door—just in case of accidents. But gently."

As soon as it was outside, O'Mara's voice roared from the communicator.

"What the blazes have you done?"

Conway tried to find a simple answer to an apparently simple question. He said, "I suppose you could say that I have prematurely initiated a planetary re-entry sequence . . ."

✳   ✳   ✳

The report from *Torrance* arrived just before Conway reached O'Mara's office. It said that one of the two stars had a light-gravity planet which was inhabitable while showing no indications of advanced technology, and that the other possessed a large, fast-spinning world which was so flattened at the poles that it resembled two soup bowls joined at the rims. On the latter world the atmosphere was dense and far-reaching, gravity varied between three Gs at the poles to one-quarter G at the equator, and surface metals were nonexistent. Very recently, in astronomical terms, the world had spiraled too close to its sun and planet-wide volcanic activity and steam had rendered the atmosphere opaque. *Torrance* doubted that it was still habitable.

"That supports my theory," said Conway excitedly when O'Mara had relayed the report to him, "that the bird and the barnacles, and the other insect life-form, originate from the same planet. The barnacles are parasites, of course, with a small individual brain capacity, but intelligent when linked and operating as a gestalt. They must have known that their planet was heading for destruction for centuries, and decided to escape. But just think of what it must have taken to develop a space-travel capability completely without metal . . ."

Somehow they had learned how to trap the giant birds from the heavy-gravity polar regions and to control them with their tendrils— the barnacles were a physically weak species and their ability to control non-intelligent hosts was the only strength they had. The birds, Conway now knew, were a non-intelligent species as were the tendril-less beetles. They had taken control of the birds and had flown them high above the equator, commanding maximum physical effort to achieve the required height and velocity for the link-up with the final propulsion stage—the beetles. They also had been controlled by the barnacles, perhaps fifty to each parasite, and they had attached themselves to the areas behind the wings in a gigantic, narrow cone.

Meanwhile the bird had been shaped and paralyzed into the configuration of a supersonic glider, its claws removed to render it aerodynamically clean, and injected with the secretions which would arrest the processes of decomposition. The crew had then sealed it and themselves in position and gone into hibernation for the duration of the voyage using the bird's tissue for life-support.

Once in position the propulsion cone comprising millions of insects, hundreds of thousands of which were the intelligent controllers, had begun firing. They had done so very evenly and gently, so as not to shatter or crush the narrow apex of the cone where it was attached to the bird. The beetles could be made to deliver their tiny modicum of thrust whether they were alive or dead and, even with their ability to seal themselves inside a hard coating, the propulsion controllers had not lived for very long—they also were expendable. But in dying they had helped an organic starship carrying a few hundred of their fellows to achieve escape velocity from their doomed planet and its sun.

"... I don't know how they intended to position the bird for re-entry," Conway went on admiringly, "but atmospheric heating was intended to trigger the organic melting process when they had braked sufficiently, allowing the barnacles to pull free of the bird and fly to the surface under their own wing-power. In my hurry to get rid of the coating I applied heat over a wide area of the forward section, which simulated re-entry conditions and—"

"Yes, yes," said O'Mara testily. "A masterly exercise in medical deduction and sheer blasted luck! And now, I suppose, you will leave me to clean up after you by devising a method for communicating with these beasties and arranging for their transport to their intended destination. Or was there something else you wanted?"

Conway nodded. "Brenner tells me that his scoutship flotilla, using an extension of the search procedure for overdue ships, could cover the volume of space between the home and destination stars. There are probably other birds, perhaps hundreds of them—"

O'Mara opened his mouth and looked ready to emulate a bombardier beetle. Conway added hastily, "I don't want them brought here, sir. The Corps can take them where they are going, melt them on the surface to avoid re-entry casualties, and explain the situation to them.

"They're colonists, after all—not patients."

PART 2

CONTAGION

Senior Physician Conway wriggled into a slightly less uncomfortable position in a piece of furniture that had been designed for the comfort of a six-legged, exoskeletal Melfan, and said in an aggrieved tone, "After twelve years' medical and surgical experience in the Federation's biggest multienvironment hospital, one would expect the next logical step up the promotional ladder would be to something more prestigious than . . . than an ambulance driver!"

There was no immediate response from the other four beings who were waiting with him in the office of the Chief Psychologist. Doctor Prilicla clung silently to the ceiling, the position it favored when in the company of more massive and well-muscled beings than itself. Sharing an Illensan bench were the spectacularly beautiful Pathologist Murchison and a silver-furred, caterpillar-like Kelgian charge nurse called Naydrad, also in silence. It was Major Fletcher, who as a recent visitor to the hospital had been given the office's only physiologically suitable chair, who broke the silence.

Seriously, he said, "You will not be allowed to drive, Doctor."

It was plain that Major Fletcher was still very conscious of the bright new ship commander's insignia decorating the sleeve of his Monitor Corps tunic, and that he was already concerned about the welfare of the vessel so soon to be his. Conway remembered feeling the same way about his first pocket scanner.

"Not even an ambulance driver," said Murchison, laughing.

Naydrad joined the conversation with a series of moaning, whistling sounds, which translated as, "In an establishment like this one, Doctor, do you expect logic?"

Conway did not reply. He was thinking that the hospital grapevine, a normally dependable form of vegetable life, had been carrying the news for days that a senior physician, Conway himself, was to be permanently attached to an ambulance ship.

On the ceiling, Doctor Prilicla was beginning to quiver in response to his emotional radiation, so Conway tried to bring his feelings of confusion and disappointment and hurt pride under control.

"Please do not concern yourself unnecessarily over this matter, friend Conway," said the little empath, the musical trills and clicks of its Cinrusskin speech overlaying the emotionless translated words. "We have yet to be informed officially of the new assignment, and the probability is that you may be pleasantly surprised, Doctor."

Prilicla, Conway knew, was not averse to telling lies if by so doing it could improve the emotional atmosphere of a situation. But not if the improvement would last for only a few seconds or minutes and be followed by even more intense feelings of anger and disappointment.

"What makes you think so, Doctor?" Conway asked. "You used the word *probability* and not *possibility*. Have you inside information?"

"That is correct, friend Conway," the Cinrusskin replied. "I have detected a source of emotional radiation that entered the outer office several minutes ago. It is identifiable as belonging to the Chief Psychologist, and the emoting is purposeful, with the type of minor-key worrying associated with the carriage of authority and responsibility. I cannot detect the kind of feelings that should be present if the imparting of unpleasant news to someone was being planned. At present Major O'Mara is talking to an assistant, who is also unaware of any potential unpleasantness."

Conway smiled and said, "Thank you, Doctor. I feel much better now."

"I know," said Prilicla.

"And I feel," said Nurse Naydrad, "that such discussion of the being O'Mara's feelings verges on a breach of medical ethics. Emotional radiation is privileged information, surely, and should not be divulged in this fashion."

"Perhaps you have not considered the fact," Prilicla replied, using the form of words which was the closest it could ever come to telling another being it was wrong, "that the being whose emotional radiation was under discussion is not a patient, friend Naydrad, and that the being most closely resembling a patient in this situation is Doctor Conway, who is concerned about the future and requires reassurance in the form of information on the non-patient's emotional radiation . . ."

Naydrad's silvery fur was beginning to twitch and ripple, indicating that the Kelgian charge nurse was about to reply. But the entrance of the non-patient from the outer office put an end to what could have been an interesting ethical debate.

O'Mara nodded briefly to everyone in turn, and took the only other physiologically suitable seat in the room, his own. The Chief Psychologist's features were about as readable as a lump of weathered basalt, which in some respects they resembled, but the eyes which regarded them were backed by a mind so keenly analytical that it gave O'Mara what amounted to a telepathic faculty.

Caustically, he began: "Before I tell you why I have asked for you four in particular to accompany Major Fletcher, and give you the details of your next assignment, which no doubt you have already learned in outline, I have to give you some background information of a non-medical nature.

"The problem of briefing people like yourselves on this subject," he went on, "is that I cannot afford to make assumptions regarding your level of ignorance in matters outside your specialties. Should some of this information seem too elementary, you are at liberty to allow your attention to wander, so long as I don't catch you at it."

"You have our undivided attention, friend O'Mara," said Prilicla, who, of course, knew this to be a fact.

"For the time being," Naydrad added.

"Charge Nurse Naydrad!" Major Fletcher burst out, his reddening face clashing with the dark green of his uniform. "You are being something less than respectful to a senior officer. Such offensive behavior will not be tolerated on my ship, nor shall I—"

O'Mara held up his hand and said dryly, "I didn't take offense, Major, and neither should you. Up until now, your career has been free of close personal contact with e-ts, so your mistake is understandable. It is unlikely to be repeated when you learn to understand the thought processes and behavior of the beings who will be working with you on this project.

"Charge Nurse Naydrad," O'Mara went on, politely for him, "is a Kelgian, a caterpillar-like life-form whose most noticeable feature is an all-over coat of silver-gray fur. You will already have noticed that Naydrad's fur is constantly in motion, as if a strong wind was continually blowing it into tufts and ripples. These are completely involuntary movements triggered by its emotional reactions to outside stimuli. The evolutionary reasons for this mechanism are not clearly understood, not even by the Kelgians themselves, but it is generally believed that the emotionally expressive fur complements the Kelgian vocal equipment, which lacks emotional flexibility of tone. However, you must understand that the movements of the fur makes it absolutely clear to another Kelgian what it feels about the subject under discussion. As a result, they always say exactly what they mean because what they think is plainly obvious—at least to another Kelgian. They cannot do otherwise. Unlike Doctor Prilicla, who is always polite and sometimes edits the truth to remove the unpleasant bits, Charge Nurse Naydrad will invariably tell the truth regardless of your rank or your feelings. You will soon grow used to it, Major.

"But I did not intend to give a lecture on Kelgians," he continued. "I did intend to discuss briefly the formation of what is now called the Galactic Federation . . ."

On the briefing screen behind him there appeared suddenly a three-dimensional representation of the galactic double spiral with its major stellar features and the edge of a neighboring galaxy, shown at distances that were not to scale. As they watched and listened a short, bright line of yellow light appeared near the rim, then another and another—the links between Earth and the early Earth-seeded colonies, and the systems of Orligia and Nidia, which were the first extraterrestrial cultures to be contacted. Another cluster of yellow lines appeared, the worlds colonized or contacted by Traltha.

Several decades had passed before the worlds available to the

Orligians, Nidians, Tralthans and Earth-humans were made available
to each other. (Beings tended to be suspicious in those days, on one
occasion even to the point of war.) But time as well as distance was
being compressed on this representation.

The tracery of golden lines grew more rapidly as contact, then
commerce, was established with the highly advanced and stable cultures of Kelgia, Illensa, Hudlar, Melf and, if any, their associated
colonies. Visually it did not seem to be an orderly progression. The
lines darted inwards to the galactic center, doubled back to the rim,
seesawed between zenith and nadir, and even made a jump across
intergalactic space to link up with the Ian worlds—although in that
instance it had been the Ians who had done the initial traveling.
When the lines connected the worlds of the Galactic Federation, the
planets known to contain intelligent and, in their own sometimes
peculiar fashions, technically and philosophically advanced life, the
result was an untidy yellow scribble resembling a cross between a
DNA molecule and a bramble bush.

"... Only a tiny fraction of the Galaxy has been explored by us
or by any of the other races within the Federation," O'Mara continued, "and we are in the position of a man who has friends in far
countries but has no idea of who is living in the next street. The
reason for this is that travelers tend to meet more often than people
who stay at home, especially when the travelers exchange addresses
and visits regularly..."

Providing there were no major distorting influences en route
and the exact co-ordinates of the destination were known, it was
virtually as easy to travel through subspace to a neighboring solar
system as to one at the other end of the Galaxy. But one had first
to find an inhabited solar system before its coordinates could be
logged, and that was proving to be no easy task.

Very, very slowly, a few of the smaller blank areas in the star
charts were being mapped and surveyed, but with little success.
When the survey scoutships turned up a star with planets, it was a
rare find—even rarer when the planets included one harboring life.
And if one of the native life-forms was intelligent, jubilation, not
unmixed with concern over what might be a possible threat to the
Pax Galactica, swept the worlds of the Federation. Then the Cultural
Contact specialists of the Monitor Corps were sent to perform the

tricky, time-consuming and often dangerous job of establishing contact in depth.

The Cultural Contact people were the elite of the Monitor Corps, a small group of specialists in e-t communications, philosophy and psychology. Although small, the group was not, regrettably, overworked . . .

". . . During the past twenty years," O'Mara went on, "they have initiated First Contact procedure on three occasions, all of which resulted in the species concerned joining the Federation. I will not bore you with details of the number of survey operations mounted and the ships, personnel and materiel involved, or shock you with the cost of it all. I mention the Cultural Contact group's three successes simply to make the point that within the same time period this hospital became fully operational and also initiated First Contacts, which resulted in seven new species joining the Federation. This was accomplished not by a slow, patient buildup and widening of communications until the exchange of complex philosophical and sociological concepts became possible, but by giving medical assistance to a sick alien."

The Chief Psychologist stared at each of them in turn, and it was obvious that he did not need Prilicla to tell him that he had their undivided attention. "I'm oversimplifying, of course. You had the medical and/or surgical problem of treating a hitherto unknown life-form. You had the hospital's translation computer, the second largest in the Galaxy, and Monitor Corps communications specialists to assist where necessary. Indeed, the Corps was responsible for rescuing many of the extraterrestrial casualties. But the fact remains that all of us, by giving medical assistance, demonstrated the Federation's good will towards e-ts much more simply and directly than could have been done by any long-winded exchange of concepts. As a result, there has recently been a marked change of emphasis in First Contact policy . . ."

Just as there was only one known way of traveling in hyperspace, there was only one method of sending a distress signal if an accident or malfunction occurred and a vessel was stranded in normal space between the stars. Tight-beam subspace radio was not a dependable method of interstellar communication, subject as it was to interference and distortion caused by intervening stellar bodies, as well as requiring inordinate amounts of a vessel's power—power which a distressed ship was unlikely to have available. But a distress beacon did not have to carry intelligence. It was simply a nuclear-powered device which broadcast a location signal, a subspace scream for help, which ran up and down the usable frequencies until, in a matter of minutes or hours, it died.

Because all Federation ships were required to file course and passenger details before departure, the position of the distress signal was usually a good indication of the physiological type of species that had run into trouble, and an ambulance ship with a matching crew and life-support equipment was sent from Sector General or from the ship's home planet.

But there were instances, far more than were generally realized, when the disasters involved beings unknown to the Federation in urgent need of help, help which the would-be rescuers were powerless to give.

Only when the rescue ship concerned had the capability of extending its hyperdrive envelope to include the distressed vessel, or when the beings could be extricated safely and a suitable environment prepared for them within the Federation ship, were they transported to Sector General. The result was that many hitherto unknown life-forms, being of high intelligence and advanced technology, were lost except as interesting specimens for dissection and study. But an answer to this problem had been sought and, perhaps, found.

It had been decided to equip one very special ambulance ship that would answer only those distress signals whose positions did not agree with the flight plans filed by Federation vessels.

". . . Whenever possible," O'Mara continued, "we prefer to make contact with a star-traveling race. Species who are intelligent but are not space travelers pose problems. We are never sure whether we are helping or hindering their natural development, giving them a technological leg up or a crushing inferiority complex when we drop down from their sky—"

Naydrad broke in: "The starship in distress might not possess a beacon. What then?"

"If a species advanced enough to possess starships did not make this provision for the safety of its individuals," O'Mara replied, "then I would prefer not to know them."

"I understand," said the Kelgian.

The Chief Psychologist nodded, then went on briskly, "Now you know why four senior or specialist members of the hospital's medical and surgical services are being demoted to ambulance attendants." He tapped buttons on his desk, and the Federation star map was replaced by a large and detailed diagram of a ship. "Attendants on a very special ambulance, as you can see. Captain Fletcher, continue, please."

For the first time, O'Mara had used Fletcher's title of ship commander rather than his Monitor Corps rank of major, Conway noted. It was probably the Chief Psychologist's way of reminding everyone that Fletcher, whether they liked it or not, was the man in charge.

Conway was only half-listening to the Captain as Fletcher, in tones reminiscent of a doting parent extolling the virtues of a favorite offspring, began listing the dimensions and performance and search capabilities of his new command.

The image on the briefing screen was familiar to Conway. He had seen the ship, hanging like an enormous white dart, in the Corps docking area, with its outlines blurred by a small forest of extended sensors and open inspection hatches, and surrounded by a shoal of smaller ships in the drab service coloring of the Monitor Corps. It had the configuration and mass of a Federation light cruiser, which was the largest type of Corps vessel capable of aerodynamic maneuvering within a planetary atmosphere. He was visualizing its gleaming white hull and delta wings decorated with the red cross, occluded sun, yellow leaf and multitudinous other symbols that represented the concept of assistance freely given throughout the Federation.

". . . The crew will mostly be comprised of physiological classification DBDG," Captain Fletcher was saying, "which means that they, like the majority of Monitor Corps personnel, are Earth-human or natives of Earth-seeded planets.

"But this is a Tralthan-built ship, with all the design and structural advantages that implies," he went on enthusiastically, "and we have named it the *Rhabwar,* after one of the great figures of Tralthan medical history. The accommodation for extraterrestrial medical personnel is flexible in regard to gravity, pressure, and atmospheric composition, food, furniture and fittings, providing they are warm-blooded oxygen-breathers. Neither the Kelgian DBLF physiological classification"—he looked at Naydrad, then up towards Prilicla—"nor the Cinrusskin GLNO will pose any life-support problems

"The only physiologically non-specialized section of the ship is the Casualty Deck and associated ward compartment," Fletcher continued. "It is large enough to take an e-t casualty up to the mass of a fully grown Chalder. The ward compartment has gravity control in half-G settings from zero to five, provision for the supply of a variety of gaseous and liquid atmospheres, and both material and non-material forms of restraint—straps and pressor beams, that is—should the casualty be confused, aggressive or require immobilization for medical examination or surgery. This compartment will be the exclusive responsibility of the medical personnel, who will prepare a compatible environment for and initiate treatment of the casualties I shall bring them.

"I must stress this point," the Captain went on, his tone hardening. "The responsibility for general ship management, for finding the distressed alien vessel and for the rescue itself is mine. The rescue of an extraterrestrial from a completely strange and damaged ship is no easy matter. There is the possibility of activating, by accident, alien mechanisms with unknown potentialities for destruction or injury to the rescuers, toxic or explosive atmospheres, radiation, the often complex problems associated with merely entering the alien ship and the tricky job of finding and bringing out the extraterrestrial casualty without killing it or seriously compounding its injuries . . ."

Fletcher hesitated and looked around him. Prilicla was beginning to shake in the invisible wind of emotional radiation emanating from Naydrad, whose silvery fur was twisting itself into spikes. Murchison was trying to remain expressionless, without much success, and Conway did not think he was being particularly poker-faced, either.

O'Mara shook his head slowly. "Captain, not only have you been telling the medical team to mind their own business, you have been trying to tell them their business. Senior Physician Conway, in addition to his e-t surgical and medical experience, has been involved in a number of ship rescue incidents, as have Pathologist Murchison and Doctor Prilicla, and Charge Nurse Naydrad has specialized in heavy rescue for the past six years. This project calls for close cooperation. You will need the cooperation of your medics, and I strongly suspect that you will get it whether you ask for it or not."

He turned his attention to Conway. "Doctor, you have been chosen by me for this project because of your ability to work with and understand e-ts, both as colleagues and patients. You should encounter no insurmountable difficulties in learning to understand and work with a newly appointed ship commander who is understandably—"

The attention signal on his desk began flashing, and the voice of one of his assistants filled the room. "Diagnostician Thornnastor is here, sir."

"Three minutes," said O'Mara. With his eyes still on Conway he went on: "I'll be brief. Normally I would not give any of you the option of refusing an assignment, but this one is more in the nature of a shakedown cruise for the *Rhabwar* than a mission calling for your professional expertise. We have received distress signals from the scoutship *Tenelphi*, which is crewed exclusively by Earth-human DBDGs, so there won't even be a communications problem. It is a simple search-and-rescue mission, and any charge of incompetence which may be brought against the survivors later will be a Corps disciplinary matter and is not your concern. The *Rhabwar* will be ready to leave in less than an hour. The available information on the incident is on this tape. Study it when you are aboard.

"That is all," he concluded, "except that there is no need for Prilicla or Naydrad to go along just to treat a few DBDG fractures or decompressions. There will be no juicy extraterrestrial cases on *this* trip—"

He broke off because Prilicla was beginning to tremble and Naydrad's fur was becoming agitated. The empath spoke first: "I will, of course, remain in the hospital if requested to do so," Prilicla said timidly, "but if I were to be given a choice, then I would prefer to go with—"

"To us," said Naydrad loudly, "Earth-human DBDGs *are* juicy extraterrestrials."

O'Mara sighed. "A predictable reaction, I suppose. Very well, you may all go. Ask Thornnastor to come in as you leave."

When they were in the corridor, Conway stood for a moment, working out the fastest, but not necessarily the most comfortable, route for reaching the ambulance ship docking bay on Level 83, then moved off quickly. Prilicla kept pace along the ceiling, Naydrad undulated rapidly behind him and Murchison brought up the rear with the Captain, who was all too plainly afraid of losing his medical team and himself.

Conway's senior physician's armband cleared the way as far as nurses and subordinate grades of doctor were concerned, but there were continual encounters with the lordly and multiply absent-minded Diagnosticians—who ploughed their way through everybody and everything regardless—and with junior members of the staff who happened to belong to a more heavily muscled species. Tralthans of physiological classification FGLI—warm-blooded oxygen-breathers resembling low-slung, six-legged and tentacled elephants—bore down on them and swept past with the mass and momentum of organic ground vehicles; they were jostled by a pair of ELNTs from Melf, who chittered at them reproachfully despite being outranked by three grades; and Conway certainly did not feel like pulling rank on the TLTU intern who breathed superheated steam and whose protective suit was a great, clanking juggernaut that hissed continually as if it was about to spring a leak.

At the next transection lock they donned lightweight protective suits and let themselves into the foggy yellow world of the chlorine-breathing Illensans. Here the corridors were crowded with the spiny, membranous and unprotected Illensan PVSJs, and it was the oxygen-breathing Tralthans, Kelgians and Earth-humans who wore, or in some cases drove, life-suits. The next leg of the journey took them through the vast tanks where the thirty-foot-long, water-breathing entities of Chalderescol swam ponderously, like armor-plated and tentacled crocodiles, through their warm, green wards. The same protective suits served them here, and although the traffic was less dense, the necessity of having to swim instead of walk slowed them down somewhat. Despite all the obstacles, they finally arrived in the ambulance bay, their suits still streaming Chalder water, just thirty-five minutes after leaving O'Mara's office.

As they boarded the *Rhabwar* the personnel lock swung closed behind them. The Captain hurried to the ship's gravity-free central well and began pulling himself forward towards Control. In more leisurely fashion, the medical team headed for the Casualty Deck amidships. In the ward compartment they spent a few minutes converting the highly unspecialized accommodation and equipment—which were capable of serving the operative and after-care needs of casualties belonging to any of the sixty-odd intelligent life-forms known to the Galactic Federation—into the relatively simple bedding and life-support required for ordinary DBDG Earth-human fracture and/or decompression cases.

Even though the casualties' stay in the ambulance ship would be a matter of hours rather than days, the treatment available during the first few minutes could make all the difference between a casualty who survived and one who was dead on arrival. Even Sector General could do nothing about the latter category, Conway thought; he wondered if any other preparations could be made to receive casualties whose number and condition were as yet unknown.

He must have been wondering aloud, because Naydrad said suddenly, "There is provision for twelve casualties, Doctor, assuming that each member of the scoutship's ten-man crew is injured, and further assuming that two of our crew-members are injured during the rescue, which is a very low probability. Eight of the beds have been prepared for multiple-fracture cases, and the other four for cranial and mandible fractures with associated brain damage necessitating a cardiac or respiratory assist. Self-shaping splints, body restraints and medication suited to the DBDG classification are readily available. When may we learn the contents of O'Mara's tape?"

"Soon, I hope," Conway replied. "Though I lack the empathic faculty of Prilicla, I feel sure our Captain would not be pleased if we were to discover and discuss the details of our mission without him."

"Correct, friend Conway," said Prilicla. "However, the combination of observation, deduction and experience can in many cases give a non-empathic species the ability to detect or to accurately predict emotional output."

"Obviously," said Naydrad. "But unless someone has something important to say, I shall go to sleep."

"And I," said Murchison, "shall press my not-unattractive face against a viewport and watch. It must be three years since I had a chance to see outside the hospital."

While the Kelgian charge nurse curled itself into a furry question mark on one of the beds, Murchison, Prilicla and Conway moved to a viewport, which at that moment showed only a featureless expanse of metal plating and the foreshortened cylinder of one of the hydraulic docking booms. But as they watched they felt a series of tiny shocks, which were being transmitted through the fabric of the ship. The hospital's outer skin began moving away from them, and the docking boom became even more foreshortened as it came smoothly to full extension, simultaneously releasing the ship and pushing it away.

The distance increased, allowing more and more details to crawl into the port's field of vision—the personnel and stores loading tubes, which were already being withdrawn into their housing; the flashing or steadily burning approach and docking beacons; a line of ports ablaze with the greenish yellow lighting characteristic of the Illensan chlorine-breathers; and a big supply tender sidling up to its docking boom.

Suddenly the picture began to unroll from the top to the bottom of the viewport as the *Rhabwar* applied thrust. It was a gentle, cautious maneuver aimed at placing the ship on a spiral course that would take it through the local hospital traffic to a distance where full thrust could be applied without inconveniencing other ships in the area or elevating the temperature of the hospital's skin—something that would be much more than an inconvenience if behind such a temporary hot spot there was a ward filled with the fragile, crystalline, ultra-frigid methane life-forms. The picture continued to shrink until the whole vast hospital structure was framed in the port, turning slowly as the ship spiraled away; then thrust was applied, and it slipped out of sight astern.

With the disappearance of the brilliantly lit hospital, their night vision returned slowly, and they watched, in a silence broken only by the hissing noises made by the sleeping Kelgian, while stars began to develop in the blank blackness outside the port.

The casualty deck speaker clicked and hummed. *"This is Control. We are proceeding at one Earth-gravity thrust until Jump-distance is reached, which will be in forty-six minutes. During this period the artificial-gravity grids will be deactivated on all decks for the purposes of system checking and inspection. Any e-t requiring special gravity settings please check and activate its personal equipment."*

Conway wondered why the Captain was not covering the Jump-distance at maximum thrust instead of dawdling along at one-G. He certainly could not Jump too close to the hospital, because the creation of an artificial universe that would allow faster-than-light travel—even a tiny one capable of enclosing the mass of their ship—would be much more than an inconvenience to Sector General. It could disrupt every piece of communications and control equipment in the place, with dire results for patients and staff alike. But Fletcher did not seem to be reacting with urgency to what was, after all, a distress call. Was Fletcher being overly careful with his nice new ship, Conway wondered, or was he proceeding carefully because the distress call had come before the ship was quite ready for it?

Though Conway's worrying was causing the Cinrusskin to tremble slightly, Prilicla seemed calm. "I check my gravity nullifiers every hour, since my continued existence as a living and thinking entity requires it. But it is nice of the Captain to worry about my safety. He appears to be an efficient officer and an entity in whom we can place full trust where the workings of the ship are concerned."

"I was a little worried for a moment," Conway admitted, laughing at the empath's unsubtle attempt at reassurance. "But how did you know I was worried about the ship? Are you becoming a telepath too?"

"No, friend Conway," Prilicla replied. "I was aware of your feeling and had already noted our somewhat leisurely departure, and I wondered if it was the ship or the Captain who was proceeding cautiously."

"Great minds worry alike," said Murchison, turning away from the viewport. "I could eat a horse," she added with feeling.

"I, too, have an urgent requirement for food," said Prilicla.

"What is a horse, friend Murchison, and would it agree with my metabolism?"

"Food," said Naydrad, coming awake.

They did not have to mention the fact that if the *Tenelphi* casualties were serious they might not have many opportunities to eat and it was always a good idea to refuel whenever an opportunity offered itself. As well, Conway thought, eating stopped worrying, at least for a while.

"Food," Conway agreed, and he led the way to the central well, which connected the eight habitable levels of the ship.

As he began climbing the connecting ladder against the one-G thrust aft, Conway was remembering the diagram of the ship's deck layout, which had been projected on O'Mara's screen. Level One was Control, Two and Three held the crew and medics' quarters, which were neither large nor overly well supplied with recreational aids, since ambulance ship missions were expected to be of short duration. Level Four housed the dining and recreational areas, and Five contained the stores of non-medical consumables. Six and Seven were the Casualty Deck and its ward, respectively, and Eight was the Power Room. Aft of Eight was a solid plug of shielding, then the two levels that could not be entered without special protective armor: Nine, which housed the hyperdrive generator, and Ten, which contained the fuel tanks and nuclear-powered thrusters.

Those thrusters were making Conway climb very carefully and hold tightly onto the rungs. A fall down the normally gravity-free well could quickly change his status from doctor to patient—or even to cadaver. Murchison was also being careful, but Naydrad, who had no shortage of legs with which to grip the rungs, began ruffling its fur with impatience. Prilicla, using its personal gravity nullifiers, had flown ahead to check on the food dispensers.

"The selection seems to be rather restricted," it reported when they arrived, "but I think the quality is better than the hospital food."

"It couldn't be worse," said Naydrad.

Conway quickly began performing major surgery on a steak and everyone else was using its mouth for a purpose other than talking when two green-uniformed legs came into sight as they climbed down from the deck above. They were followed by a torso and the features of Captain Fletcher.

"Do you mind if I join you?" he asked stiffly. "I think we should listen to the *Tenelphi* material as soon as possible."

"Not at all," Conway replied in the same formal tone. "Please sit down, Captain."

Normally a Monitor Corps ship commander ate in the isolation of his cabin, Conway knew, that being one of the unwritten laws of the service. The *Rhabwar* was Fletcher's first command and this his first operational mission, and here he was breaking one of those rules by dining with crew-members who were not even fellow officers of the Corps. But it was obvious as the Captain drew his meal from the dispenser that he was trying very hard to be relaxed and friendly—he was trying so hard, in fact, that Prilicla's stable hover over its place at the table became somewhat unsteady.

Murchison smiled at the Captain. "Doctor Prilicla tells us that eating while in flight aids the Cinrusskin digestion as well as cools everyone else's soup."

"If my method of ingestion offends you, friend Fletcher," Prilicla offered timidly, "I am quite capable of eating while at rest."

"I . . . I'm not offended, Doctor." Fletcher smiled stiffly. "I think *fascinated* would better describe my feelings. But will listening to the tape adversely affect anyone's digestion? The playback can certainly wait until you've all finished."

"Talking shop," said Conway in his best clinical manner, "also aids the digestion." He slotted in the tape, and O'Mara's dry, precise voice filled the compartment . . .

The Monitor Corps scoutship *Tenelphi*, which was currently engaged on preliminary survey operations in Sector Nine, had failed to make three successive position reports. The coordinates of the star systems assigned to the *Tenelphi* for investigation were known, as was the sequence in which they would be visited; and since the ship had not released a distress beacon, there was no immediate cause for concern over the fate of the missing vessel. The trouble, as so often happened, might turn out to be a simple communications failure rather than anything dramatic.

Stellar activity in the region was well above the norm, with the result that subspace radio communication was extremely difficult. Signals considered to be important—and they had to be very important indeed, because of the power required to penetrate the highly peculiar medium that was hyperspace—were taped and transmitted repeatedly for as long as was thought necessary, and safe, to do so. The transmission process released harmful radiation, which could not be effectively shielded if the signal was prolonged, especially where lightly built scoutships were concerned. The result was that a terse, highly compressed signal riddled with stellar interference was sent to be pieced together, hopefully in its entirety, from fifty or more identical but individually unreadable messages. Position-report signals were brief and therefore safe, and the power drain was relatively light, even for a scoutship.

But the *Tenelphi* had not sent a position report. Instead, it had transmitted a repeated message to the effect that it had detected and later closed with a large derelict that was falling rapidly into the system's sun, with impact estimated in just under eight days. Since none of the system's planets was within the life-spectrum—unless the life concerned was one of the exotic varieties that might be capable of flourishing on semi-molten rock under a small, intensely hot and aging sun—the assumption had been made that the vessel's entry into the system was accidental rather than the result of a planned mission. There was evidence of residual power remaining in the derelict, and of several pockets of atmosphere of various densities, but no sign of life. The *Tenelphi*'s intention was to board it and investigate.

In spite of the poor signal quality, there could be no doubt of the pleasure felt by the *Tenelphi*'s communications officer at this lucky break in the otherwise deadly monotony of a routine mapping assignment.

". . . Possibly they became too excited to remember to include a position report," O'Mara's voice continued, "or they knew that the timing of the signal, by checking it against their flight plans, would tell us where they were in general terms. But that was the only coherent message received. Three days later there was another signal, not taped but repeated, each time in slightly different form, by the sender speaking into a microphone. It said that there had been a serious collision, the ship was losing pressure and the crew was incapacitated. There was also some sort of warning. In my professional opinion the voice was distorted by more than the intervening subspace radio interference, but you can decide that for yourselves. Then, two hours later, a distress beacon was released.

"I have included a copy of the second signal, which may help you." The Chief Psychologist's voice added dryly, "Or help confuse you . . ."

Unlike the first signal, the second was virtually unreadable. It was like listening to a mighty storm through which a voice, badly distorted to begin with, was trying to make itself heard in a whisper. They listened intently to the words while trying even harder to ignore the rattling explosions of interstellar static accompanying them, so much so that Naydrad's fur rippled tensely with the strain and Prilicla, who was reacting to everyone else's feelings as well as to the noise, gave up its attempt to hover and settled, trembling, on the table.

"... idea if this ... getting out or ... crew incap ... collision with derelict and ... can't do ... distress beac ... work it inside ... manually ... but can't assume ... stupidity of specialization when ... if signal is getting out ... warning in case ... in collision ... internal pressure dropping ... can't do anything about that, either ... how to operate beacon from inside ... release it manually from ... al warning in case ... lets too stiff to ... confused and not much time ... only chance is ... sin chest ... derelict is close ... extra suit tanks ... my specialty ... ship Tenelphi in collision with ... crew incapable of any ... pressure dropping ..."

The voice went on for several minutes, but the words were lost in a prolonged burst of static. Shortly afterwards the tape ended. There were a few minutes of beautiful silence, during which Naydrad's fur settled down and Prilicla flew up to the ceiling.

"It seems to me that the gist of this message," Conway said thoughtfully, "is that the sender was unsure that the signal was being transmitted, possibly because he was not the communications officer and knew nothing about the equipment he was using, or maybe because he thought the subspace radio antenna had been damaged in the collision, which had, apparently, knocked out the rest of the crew. He did not seem to be able to help them, pressure was dropping, and again due to structural damage, he was unable to release the distress beacon from inside the ship. He would have to have set its timer and pushed it away from the ship with his hands.

"His doubts about the signal going out and his remarks regarding the stupidity of specialization," he went on, "indicate that he was probably not the communications officer or even the Captain, who would have a working knowledge of the equipment in all departments of his ship. The 'lets too stiff' bit could be 'gauntlets too stiff' to operate certain controls or suit fastenings, and with the ship's internal pressure dropping he might have been afraid to change from his heavy-duty spacesuit to a lightweight type with its thinner gauntlets. What an 'al warning' or a 'sin chest' is, I just don't know, and in any case the distortion was so bad that those may only be approximations of the words he used."

Conway looked around the table. "Maybe you can find something I missed. Shall I play the tape again?"

They listened again, and again, before Naydrad, in its forthright fashion, told him he was wasting their time.

"We would know how much credence to place on the material in this signal," Conway said, "if we knew which officer sent it and why he, of all the crew, escaped serious injury during the collision. And another point: Once he says the crew are incapable, and later he describes them as being incapacitated. Not hurt or injured, but incapacitated. That choice of word makes me wonder if he is perhaps the ship's medical officer, except that he hasn't described the extent of their injuries or, as far as his signal is concerned, done much to help them."

Naydrad, who was the hospital's expert in ship rescue procedures, made noises like a modulated foghorn, which translated as, "Regardless of his function in the ship, there is not much that any officer could do with fracture and decompression casualties, especially if everyone was sealed in suits or if the officer himself was a minor casualty. Regarding the, to me, subtle difference in meaning between the words *incapacitated* and *injured,* I think we are wasting time discussing it. Unless there is a deficiency in this ship's translation computer that affects only the Kelgian programing..."

The Captain bridled visibly at the suggestion that there might be anything at all wrong with his ship or its equipment. "This is not Sector General, Charge Nurse, where the translation computer fills three whole levels and handles simultaneous translations for six thousand individuals. The *Rhabwar*'s computer is programmed only to cover the languages of the ship's personnel, plus the three most widely used languages in the Federation other than our own—Tralthan, Illensan and Melfan. It has been thoroughly tested, and it performs its function without ambiguity, so that any confusion—"

"Undoubtedly lies in the signal itself," Conway contributed hastily, "and not in the translation. But I would still like to know who sent the message. The crew-member who used the words *incapacitated* and *incapable* instead of *hurt* or *injured,* who could not do something because he was confused and short of time and was hampered by gauntlets . . . Dammit, he might at least have told us *something* about the physical condition of the casualties so we'd know what to expect!"

Fletcher relaxed again. "I wonder why he was wearing a suit in the first place. Even if the ship was maneuvering close to the derelict and a collision occurred for whatever reason, it would not have been expected. By that I mean the crew would not normally be wearing spacesuits during such a maneuver. But if they were wearing them, then they were expecting trouble."

"From the derelict?" Murchison asked quietly.

A long silence followed, broken finally by the Captain. "Very unlikely, if it was, in fact, a derelict, and there is no reason to doubt the *Tenelphi*'s original report on the situation. If they were not expecting trouble, then we are back with this officer, not necessarily the ship's medic, who was able to get into a spacesuit and perhaps help some of the others into theirs—"

"Without compounding their injuries?" asked Naydrad.

"I can assure you that Monitor Corpsmen are trained to react to situations like this one," said Fletcher sharply.

Reacting to the Captain's growing irritation at the implied criticism of one of his fellow officers, Prilicla joined in: "The broken-up message we received did not mention injuries, so it is possible that the most serious damage is to the scoutship's structure and systems rather than to its crew. *Incapacitated* is not a very strong word. We may find that we have nothing to do."

While approving the little empath's attempt to halt the bickering between Naydrad and the overly touchy ship commander, Conway thought that Prilicla was being far too optimistic. But before anyone could speak there was an interruption.

"Control to Captain. Jump in seven minutes, sir."

Fletcher regarded his half-finished meal for a moment, then stood up. "There is no real need for me to go up there, you know," he said awkwardly. "We took our time coming out to Jump-distance to ensure that the ship was fully operational. It is, in every respect." He gave a short, forced laugh. "But the trouble with good subordinates is that sometimes they make a superior officer feel redundant . . ."

The Captain, Conway thought as Fletcher's legs disappeared up the well, was trying very hard to be human.

Shortly afterwards the ship made the transition into hyperspace, and just under six hours later it re-emerged. Because the *Rhabwar* had left the hospital at the end of the medical team's duty period, they had all used the intervening time to catch up on their rest. Nonetheless, there were a few interruptions whenever the Captain relayed what he thought were significant pieces of conversation from Control over the ship's PA system. Obviously, he was simply trying to keep the medics fully informed at every stage of the proceedings. If he had realized the reaction of Conway and the others at being repeatedly awakened to be given information that was either too technically specialized or too elementary, he would have dropped the idea.

Then, suddenly, a relay from Control that signaled the end of any further hope of sleeping for a long time to come.

"We have contact, sir! Two traces, one large and one small. Distance one point six million miles. The small trace matches the mass and dimensions of the Tenelphi.*"*

"Astrogation?"

"Sir. At maximum thrust we can match course, velocity and position in two hours, seventeen minutes."

"Very well, we'll do that. Power Room?"

"Standing by, sir."

"Four-gravities thrust in thirty seconds, Mr. Chen. Dodds, give Haslam your course figures. Would Senior Physician Conway report to Control as soon as convenient."

*   *   *

Because the physiological classification of the casualties and the general nature of their injuries were already known, it had been decided that Captain Fletcher would remain in the *Rhabwar* while Conway and the other Corps officers boarded the *Tenelphi* to assess the situation. Murchison, Prilicla and Naydrad were standing by on the Casualty Deck, ready to treat the cases as they came through. Since both the casualties and medical team had the same atmosphere and life-support requirements, it was expected that the examination and preliminary treatment time would be short, and that the *Rhabwar* would be returning to Sector General within the hour.

Conway sat in the supernumerary's position in Control, sealed up except for his helmet visor, watching the image of the *Tenelphi* growing larger on the Captain's screen. Flanking the Captain were Haslam and Dodds in the communications and astrogation positions, respectively, also suited except for their gauntlets, which had been removed to facilitate operation of their control consoles. The three officers muttered to one another in the esoteric language of their profession and occasionally exchanged words with Chen, who was in the Power Room aft.

The image of the distressed ship grew until it overflowed the edges of the screen, whereupon magnification was stepped down and it was suddenly tiny again—a bright silver cigar shape tumbling slowly in the blackness, with the immense spherical shape of the derelict turning slowly, like a battered, metal moon, two miles beyond it.

Like Conway, the derelict was being ignored for the present. For no other reason than to register his presence, he said, "It doesn't appear to be too badly damaged, does it?"

"Obviously not a head-on collision," Fletcher responded. "There is serious damage forward, but most of it is to the antennae and sensors, sustained, I think, when she struck and then rolled against the other ship. I can't see the extent of the damage in detail because of the fog. She's still losing a lot of air."

"Which could mean that she still has a lot of air to lose, sir," said Dodds. "Forward tractors and pressors ready."

"Right, check her pitch and roll," ordered the Captain. "But gently. The hull will be weakened, and we don't want to pull it apart. They might not be wearing suits . . ."

He left the sentence hanging as Dodds leaned stiffly over his console. All of the astrogator's attention was concentrated in his fingertips as he focused the immaterial cone-shaped fields of the pressor and tractor beams on the hull of the damaged ship, bringing it slowly and gently to rest with respect to the *Rhabwar*. Seen at rest, the *Tenelphi*'s bow and stern were still obscured by a fog of escaping air, but amidships the vessel seemed to have retained its structural integrity.

"Sir," Haslam reported excitedly, "the midships lock is undamaged. I think we can dock and . . . and walk aboard!"

. . . *And evacuate the casualties in a fraction of the time needed for an EVA transfer*, Conway thought thankfully. Medical attention was only minutes away for those who had been able to survive thus far. He stood up, closed and sealed his helmet.

"I'll handle the docking," said Fletcher briskly. "You two go with the Doctor. Chen, stay put unless they send for you."

They felt the tiny shock of the *Rhabwar* making contact with the other ship while they were still inside their own midships lock with the inner seal closed behind them. Dodds activated the outer seal, which swung slowly inwards to reveal the outer surface of an identical seal a few inches away. They could see a large, irregular patch of what seemed to be paint or oil, mottled brown and black in color, in the middle of the *Tenelphi*'s seal. The stuff had a ridged, blistered appearance.

"What is that stuff?" Conway asked.

"I haven't a clue," Haslam began, reaching out to touch it. His fingers left yellowish smears and some of the material stuck to his gauntlets. "It's grease, Doctor. The dark color fooled me at first. I expect the heat of the beacon melted and burned off most of it and left the rest looking like that."

"Grease," said Conway. "How did grease get spread over the outer seal?"

Haslam sounded impatient as he replied: "Probably one of the dispenser canisters broke loose during the crash and spun against the seal. There is a pressure nozzle at one end of the canister, which, if depressed with sufficient force, discharges several ounces of grease automatically. If you're very interested, Doctor, I can show you one of them later. Stand back, please, I'm going to open up."

The seal swung open, and Haslam, Conway and Dodds stepped into the *Tenelphi*'s lock chamber. Haslam checked the telltales as Dodds closed the outer seal. The pressure inside the ship was dangerously low, but not lethally low for a person who was fit and healthy. What it would do to an unprotected casualty who might be in shock—with decompression effects accelerating the loss of blood from even superficial cuts and lacerations—was another matter. Suddenly the inner seal opened; their suits creaked and swelled with the pressure differential, and they moved quickly inside.

Haslam gasped. "I don't believe it!"

The lock antechamber was filled with spacesuited figures drifting loosely on the ends of pieces of rope or webbing that had been attached to equipment support brackets or any other convenient tethering point. The emergency lighting system was functioning and bright enough to show all the figures in detail, including the webbing that bound each man's legs together, his arms tightly to his sides and extra air tanks on his back. The spacesuits were all of the rigid, heavy-duty type, so the tight webbing did not compress the underlying limbs and torsos and whatever injuries they might have sustained. In each case the helmet visor was covered by its almost opaque sun filter.

Moving carefully between two of the drifting figures, Conway steadied one and slid back the sun filter. The inside of the visor was badly fogged, but he could make out a face that was much redder than normal and eyes that squeezed themselves shut as soon as the light hit them. He slid back the filter of another casualty, then another, with similar results.

"Untether them and move them to the Casualty Deck, quickly," Conway said. "Leave the arm and leg restraints in place for the present. It makes them easier to move, and the strapping will support the fractured limbs, if any. This is not the complete crew?"

It was not really a question. Obviously, someone had trussed up the casualties and moved them to the *Tenelphi*'s airlock to be ready for a fast evacuation.

"Nine here, Doctor," said Haslam after a quick count. "One crew-member is missing. Shall I look for him?"

"Not yet," said Conway, thinking that the missing officer had been a very busy man. He had sent a subspace radio message, released a distress beacon when the automatic release mechanism had malfunctioned or he had been unable to work it, and he had moved his companions from their duty positions in various parts of their ship to the airlock antechamber. It was not inconceivable that during these activities he had damaged his spacesuit and had been forced to find himself an airtight compartment somewhere to await rescue.

The man who had accomplished all that, Conway swore to himself, was damn well going to be rescued!

While he was helping Haslam and Dodds transfer the first few casualties through to the *Rhabwar*, Conway described the situation for the benefit of those on the Casualty Deck and for the Captain. Then he added, "Prilicla, can you be spared back there for a few minutes?"

"Easily, friend Conway," the little empath replied. "My musculature is not sufficiently robust to assist directly in the treatment of DBDG casualties. My support is moral rather than medical."

"Fine," said Conway. "Our problem is a missing crew-member who may or may not be injured, perhaps sheltered in an airtight compartment. Will you pinpoint his position for us so we won't waste time searching through wreckage? Are you wearing a pressure envelope?"

"Yes, friend Conway," Prilicla replied. "I'm leaving at once."

It took nearly fifteen minutes for the casualties to be moved out of the *Tenelphi* and into the ambulance ship. By that time Prilicla was drifting back and forth along the exterior of the wreck's hull in an effort to detect the emotional radiation of the missing crew-member. Conway stayed inside the wreck and tried to keep his feelings of impatience and concern under control so as not to distract the Cinrusskin.

If anything lived in the *Tenelphi*, even if it was deeply unconscious or dying, Prilicla's empathic faculty would detect it.

"Nothing, friend Conway," Prilicla reported after twenty interminable minutes. "The only source of emotional radiation inside the wreck is yourself."

Conway's initial reaction was one of angry disbelief.

"I'm sorry, friend Conway," Prilicla replied. "If the being is still in the ship it . . . it is dead."

But Conway had never been one to give up easily on a patient. "Captain, Conway here. Is it possible that he's adrift? Perhaps injured or with his suit radio damaged as a result of releasing the beacon?"

"Sorry, Doctor," Fletcher replied. "We made a radar sweep of the area when we arrived in case the man had accidentally released himself along with the beacon. There is some loose metallic wreckage but nothing large enough to be a man. Nonetheless, I'll make another sweep to be absolutely sure." He paused for a moment, then went on: "Haslam, Dodds. Providing you will not be interfering with the medical treatment down there, check the ID tags and uniform insignias of the casualties and bring me a list. Quickly.

"Chen, you won't be needed in the Power Room for a while," he continued. "Seal up and search the wreck as thoroughly as possible in the time left to us. The casualties are supposed to be moved as quickly as possible to the hospital, and to add to our troubles, this system's sun is coming too close for comfort. You will be looking for the missing officer's body, ship's papers, tapes or anything that might explain what happened here. You should find a crew duty roster attached to the Recreation Deck notice board. By comparing it with the list of casualties, we will be able to tell the identity of the missing man as well as his specialty—"

"I know his specialty," Conway broke in suddenly. He was thinking of the highly professional way in which the missing man had moved the casualties, immobilized them against the possibility of further and perhaps self-inflicted injuries as well as extended the duration of their air supply, and of the amateurish way he had done everything else. "I'm sure he was the ship's medic."

Fletcher did not reply, and Conway began moving slowly around the *Tenelphi*'s lock antechamber. He had the uncomfortable feeling that something should be done, and quickly, but he had no idea what that something was. There was nothing unusual to be seen except, possibly, a wall-mounted clip that was designed to hold three cylindrical canisters about two feet long and that now held only two. Closer inspection showed identification labels on the cylinders, indicating that they contained type GP10/5B grease suitable for use on major actuator mechanisms and control linkages periodically or permanently exposed to low temperature and/or vacuum conditions. Feeling confused and impatient with himself—his job was on the Casualty Deck and not wasting time here—Conway returned to the *Rhabwar*.

Lieutenant Chen was already waiting to enter the lock Conway had just vacated. He opened his visor to speak to the Doctor without tying up the suit frequency and asked Conway if he had been forward to the damaged area of the wreck. Without unsealing his visor Conway shook his head. As Conway moved towards the communication well, Haslam, a piece of folded paper between his teeth to leave both hands free for climbing, came briefly into sight as he pulled himself in the direction of Control. Conway waited until the man had passed, then he stepped into the gravity-free well and began pulling himself aft towards the Casualty Deck.

Of the nine casualties, two of them had already had their spacesuits cut away in small pieces so as not to compound any underlying injuries. Murchison and Dodds were stripping a third without cutting the suit away, and Naydrad was removing the suit of a fourth casualty—also in normal fashion.

Without giving Conway time to ask the inevitable question, Murchison said, "According to Lieutenant Dodds here, all the indications are that these men were already encased in their spacesuits and strapped tightly to their couches *before* the collision occurred. I did not agree at first, but when we stripped the first two and found no injuries, not even bruising . . . ! And the suit fabric was marked by abrasive contact in areas corresponding to the positions of the safety strapping.

"The x-ray scanner lacks definition when used through a spacesuit," she went on, holding the casualty under the arms to steady him while Dodds tugged carefully at the leg sections, "but it is clear enough to show fractures or serious internal injuries. There are none, so I decided that cutting away the suits would be an unnecessary waste of time."

"And of valuable service property," Dodds added with feeling. To a spacegoing Monitor Corps officer, a spacesuit was much more than a piece of equipment, it was analogous to a warm, close-fitting, protective womb. Seeing them being deliberately torn apart would be something of a traumatic experience for him.

"But if they aren't injured," Conway asked, "what the blazes is wrong with them?"

Murchison was working on the man's neck seal and did not look up. "I don't know," she answered defensively.

"Not even a preliminary diag—"

"No," she said sharply, then went on: "When Doctor Prilicla's empathic faculty established the fact that they were in no immediate danger of dying, we decided that diagnosis and treatment could wait until they were all out of their suits, so our examination thus far has been cursory, to say the least. All I know is that the subspace radio message was correct—they are incapacitated, not injured."

Prilicla, who had been hovering silently over the two stripped patients, joined the conversation timidly. "That is correct, friend Conway. I, too, am puzzled by the condition of these beings. I was expecting gross physical injuries, and instead I find something which resembles an infectious disease. Perhaps you, friend Conway, as a member of the same species, will recognize the symptoms."

"I'm sorry, I did not mean to sound critical," Conway said awkwardly. "I'll help you with that one, Naydrad."

As soon as he took off the man's helmet he could see that his face was red and streaming with perspiration. The temperature was elevated and there was pronounced photophobia, which explained why the glare shields were in place over the visor. The hair was wet and plastered against the man's forehead and skull as if he had just been in for a swim. The drying elements in the suit had been unable to cope with the excessive moisture, so that the interior of the faceplate was opaque with condensation. For that reason Conway did not notice the medication dispenser attached to the collar piece until the helmet had been removed. The medication was in the usual form of an edible transparent plastic tube nipped off at intervals to enclose a single color-coded capsule in each division.

"Did any of the other helmets contain this anti-nausea medication?" asked Conway.

"All of them so far, Doctor," Naydrad replied, its four manipulators working independently on the suit fastenings while its eyes curled up to regard Conway. "The first casualty to be undressed displayed symptoms of nausea when I inadvertently applied pressure to the abdominal region. The being was not fully conscious at the time, so its words were not sufficiently coherent for translation."

Prilicla quickly joined in. "The emotional radiation is characteristic of a being in delirium, friend Conway, probably caused by the elevated temperature. I have also observed erratic, uncoordinated movements of the limbs and head, which are also symptomatic of delirium."

"I agree," said Conway. But what was causing it? He did not utter the question aloud because he was supposed to know the answer, but he had an uneasy premonition that even a really thorough examination might not reveal the cause. He began helping the charge nurse to remove the patient's sweat-soaked clothing.

There was evidence of heat prostration and dehydration, which, considering the patient's high temperature and associated loss of body fluid, was to be expected. Gentle palpation in the abdominal area caused involuntary retching movements, although there was no foreign material in the stomach so far as Conway could determine. The man had not eaten for more than twenty-four hours.

The pulse was a little fast but steady, respiration irregular and with a tendency towards intermittent coughing. When Conway checked the throat he found it seriously inflamed, and his scanner indicated that the inflammation extended along the bronchi and into the pleural cavity. He checked the tongue and lips for signs of damage by toxic or corrosive material, and noticed that the man's face was not, as he had first thought, wet only with perspiration—the tear ducts were leaking steadily, and there was a mucous discharge from the nose as well. Finally, he checked for evidence of radiation exposure or the inhalation of radioactive material, with negative results.

"Captain. Conway," he called suddenly. "Would you ask Lieutenant Chen, while he is searching the *Tenelphi* for the missing officer, to bring back samples of the ship's air and food and liquid consumables? Would he also look for evidence of a leakage of toxic material, solid or gaseous, into the life-support system, and bring them, tightly sealed, to Pathologist Murchison for analysis as quickly as possible?"

"Will do," Fletcher responded. "Chen, you overheard?"

"Yes, sir," said the engineer officer. "I still can't find the missing casualty, Doctor. Now I'm beginning to look in all the unlikely places."

Because Conway's helmet was still sealed, Murchison had been listening to the conversation on the Casualty Deck's speaker as well as hearing his side of it through his suit's external sound system. "Two questions, Doctor," she said irritably. "Do you know what's wrong with them, and has it anything to do with your using that overly loud suit speaker instead of opening your visor and talking normally?"

"I'm not sure," said Conway.

"Perhaps," she said angrily to Dodds, "he doesn't like my perfume."

Conway disregarded the sarcasm and looked around the ward. While he had been examining the casualty with Naydrad, Murchison and Dodds had stripped the others and were obviously waiting for instructions. Prilicla was already carrying out the instructions that Conway had yet to utter on the first two casualties, but then, Prilicla invariably said and did the right thing because it was an exceptionally fine doctor as well as an empath.

"If it wasn't for the very high temperature and general severity of their symptoms," Conway said finally, "I'd say we are dealing with a respiratory infection with associated nausea caused, perhaps, by swallowing infected mucus. But the sudden and incapacitating onset of the symptoms makes me doubtful of that diagnosis.

"But that is not the reason I stayed sealed," he went on. "There was no reason for doing so at first. Now, however, I think it would be a good idea if Lieutenant Dodds and you sealed up. It may be an unnecessary precaution."

"Or it may already be too late," said Murchison, unclipping one of the lightweight helmets, which, with its connecting hose, air tank and body webbing, converted the coveralls she was wearing into a protective suit, proof against anything but the most corrosive atmospheres. Dodds had already sealed his visor with remarkable haste.

"Until we can get them to the hospital," Conway said, "treatment must be supportive rather than curative. Replace the lost fluids intravenously, control the nausea and try to keep the temperature down. We may have to use body restraints to keep them from dislodging their monitor leads. Isolate them in pressure tents and raise the oxygen level. I think their condition is going to worsen, and we may eventually need to assist their breathing with a ventilator."

He paused for a moment, and when he looked at Murchison he knew that the concern on his face was concealed by the blurring effect of his visor and by the suit's external speaker, which distorted his voice.

"The isolation may be unnecessary," he said. "These symptoms could just as easily be due to inhaling and swallowing an as yet unidentified toxin. We can't be sure, and we haven't the proper facilities to find the answer in the limited time available. As soon as we find out what happened to the missing crew-man, we'll whisk them all back to Sector General and submit ourselves to a thorough—"

"While we are waiting," Murchison broke in, her voice and features now also distorted by a helmet, "I would like to try to discover what it was that hit them, and what it is that may hit everyone else but yourself."

"There may not be time for that," Conway began, but the voice of the engineer officer reporting to the Captain made him break off.

"Captain, Chen here. I've found the duty roster, sir, and I've checked it against the IDs of the casualties. The missing man turns out to be Surgeon-Lieutenant Sutherland, so the Doctor's guess was right. But his body is not here. I've searched thoroughly and he's not inside the wreck. There are things missing as well—the ship's portable sound and vision recorders, the crew's personal recorders, cameras, baggage containers, all missing. Clothing and personal effects are drifting about inside the crew's quarters as if they'd been scattered during a hurried unpacking.

"Practically all the spare air tanks have gone, and the equipment register shows that the crew's spacesuits were all logged out for a period of between two and three days, except for the Surgeon-Lieutenant's suit, which wasn't logged out and is missing. The ship's portable airlock is missing also.

"The Control area is badly damaged, so I can't be absolutely sure, but it looks as if they were trying to set up for an automatic Jump,

and the instrument settings in the Power Room, which wasn't dam-
aged, supports this. I'd say they were trying to move away from the
derelict because of the distortion such a large mass of metal would
introduce into the Jump calculations, but they collided with it instead."

"I have the samples for Pathologist Murchison. Shall I come back
now, sir?"

"Right away," the Captain ordered.

While Lieutenant Chen and the Captain had been talking, Conway had been trying to make sense out of the strange behavior of
the *Tenelphi*'s medical officer. Surgeon-Lieutenant Sutherland had
displayed professional competence of a very high order in his treatment of the casualties. Through no fault of his own, he had not
been able to communicate properly via the subspace radio although
he had made a good try, but he had managed to perform the tricky
job of manually releasing and activating the distress beacon. It
seemed to Conway that Sutherland was a sensible and resourceful
officer of the kind who did not panic easily. Neither was he the kind
who would get himself killed accidentally or go without leaving
some sort of message.

"If he isn't adrift and he isn't on the *Tenelphi*," said Conway
suddenly, "there is only one other place he can be. Can you land
me on the derelict, Captain?"

Knowing Fletcher's concern for his ship, Conway expected anything from a flat negative to a verbal explosion at the very suggestion. Instead, he received the kind of response an instructor gives
to a pupil of mediocre intelligence—a lecture couched in such elementary language that if the Captain had not been five levels forward in Control, Conway would have risked unsealing his visor to
spit in Fletcher's eye.

"I can conceive of no reason, Doctor, why the missing officer
should leave the *Tenelphi* when the obvious course would be to stay
with the other casualties and await rescue," the Captain began. Then
he went on to remind Conway that they did not have a lot of time
to waste. Not only should the casualties be hospitalized quickly, but
the derelict, the *Tenelphi* and their own vessel were closing with the
system's sun at an accelerating rate, which would make it uncomfortably warm for all concerned in two days and would cause their

hull to melt in four. There was also the fact that the closer they approached the sun, the more difficult it would be for them to make a Jump.

An added complication was that the *Tenelphi* and the *Rhabwar* were now docked and coupled fore and aft so that the ambulance ship could expand its hyperspace envelope to enclose the wreck, which would have to be taken back with them as evidence in the forthcoming investigation into the collision. With the two ships locked together and only one capable of exerting controlled thrust, delicate maneuvering of the order needed to land him on the derelict would be impossible. If Fletcher attempted it, the *Rhabwar* might well end up in the same condition as the *Tenelphi*. And then there was the sheer size of the derelict . . .

"The vessel is, or was originally, spherical," the Captain went on, and the image from the *Rhabwar*'s telescope appeared on the Casualty Deck's repeater screen. "It is four hundred meters in diameter, with residual power and pressure in a few compartments deep inside the ship. But the *Tenelphi* has already reported the absence of life on board—"

"Sutherland may be on board now, Captain."

Fletcher's sigh made rustling noises on the intercom; then he went on in his patient, lecturing and infuriating voice. "The other ship's findings are more dependable than ours, Doctor. A life indication is the result of a large number of sensor readings comprising the type and distribution of power sources, vibration associated with the mechanical aspects of life-support systems, pressure and temperature variations within the hull, detection of communication or lighting systems, and many more subtle indications. We both realize that many e-ts require ultra-low temperatures or do not see on our visual frequencies, but if anything, they are easier to detect as far as their life-support requirements are concerned.

"But right now," the Captain continued, "I could not say with certainty whether or not anyone or anything was alive inside that thing. The close approach to the sun has heated up the outer hull to such an extent that it is no longer possible to detect subtle differences of temperature inside, and the other sensor readings are badly distorted because of the effect of the heat expansion on the structure as a whole. Besides, that ship is big. Its hull is so torn and punctured by meteorite collisions that Sutherland could have found a way in anywhere. Where would you start looking for him, Doctor?"

"If he's there," said Conway, "he'll let us know where to look."

The Captain remained silent for a moment, and Conway, despite his irritation with Fletcher's manner towards him, could sympathize with the other's dilemma. No more than Conway did the Captain want to leave the area without finding or otherwise establishing the fate of the missing Surgeon-Lieutenant. But there was the welfare of the other casualties to consider, which properly was Conway's responsibility, and the safety of the ambulance ship, which was very definitely Fletcher's.

With all three vessels sliding down the gravity well of the system's sun with an acceleration that did not bear thinking about, the time allocated for a search for the missing officer would be strictly limited, and the Captain would not want to be placed in the position of having to abandon Senior Physician Conway of Sector General as well as the Monitor Corps medic on the derelict. Neither could he risk sending one of his officers with Conway because if he, too, was lost the Captain would have a very serious problem. The *Rhabwar*'s crew was small and there was no overlapping of specialties. Fletcher would probably be able to Jump back to Sector General eventually, but serious risks and delays would be involved that could adversely affect the casualties.

The wall speaker rustled with another sigh, and Fletcher said, "Very well, Doctor, you may search for the Surgeon-Lieutenant. Dodds, take the scope. You are searching for evidence of a recent entry into the derelict. Lieutenant Chen, forget the pathologist's samples for the time being and return to the Power Room. I want maneuvering thrust in five minutes. Doctor, I shall circle the derelict longitudinally at a distance of half a mile. Since it is rotating once every fifty-two minutes, this will enable us to scan its hull surface in four orbits. Haslam, do what you can with the sensors, and give the doctor some idea of the geography of the interior."

"Thank you," said Conway.

Dodds had been helping Murchison move one of the casualties into a pressure tent. As soon as he was finished he excused himself and headed for Control. Conway looked at the repeater screen and the image of the derelict, half of which was a featureless blackness and half a confusion of brilliantly reflective hull plating that was crisscrossed by black fissures and craters. He glanced at it from time to time while he was helping attach bio-sensors to the casualties, seeing it grow larger and begin to unroll from top to bottom of the screen. Suddenly the image flicked off, to be replaced by a diagrammatic representation of the derelict.

It showed the cross section of the spherical vessel, with its deck levels making concentric circles to its core. Near the center several compartments of different sizes were marked in various shades of green, and close to the inner wall of the hull at one point there was a large, rectangular compartment marked in red. Fine red lines joined this area with the green compartments at the center.

"Doctor, Haslam here. I'm projecting a sensor diagram of the derelict's interior. It is not detailed, I'm afraid, and a lot of it is guesswork . . ."

The derelict had been a generation transport, Haslam went on to explain, of the spherical configuration favored at a time when maximum living and cultivating space was a necessity. Direction of travel was along the vertical axis, with the control area forward and the reactor and drive units, which were marked in red, astern. The vessel could rotate fairly rapidly around the vertical axis so as to furnish the outer deck levels amidships with artificial gravity even when the ship was using thrust.

Haslam did not know whether it was one catastrophe or a number of them that had overtaken the ship, but whatever it was it had devastated the control area along with the rest of the outer hull and deck levels and in the process had checked the spin to a fraction of what it should have been. Heavy shielding around the reactors had protected them from serious damage.

The ship had virtually been depopulated, but a number of compartments deep inside the vessel had retained pressure and power, and a number of survivors must have been able to live in them for a time. These were the sections marked in green. The atmosphere inside some of these compartments was little more than a soft vacuum, Haslam added, but in others it was probably still breathable by the present-day members of the species who had built the ship, whoever and whatever they were.

"Is there any possibility . . . ?"

"No survivors, Doctor," Haslam stated firmly. "The *Tenelphi* reported the ship lifeless, derelict. The catastrophe probably happened centuries ago, and the survivors survived for only a short time."

"Yes, of course," said Conway. Then why would Sutherland go there?

"Captain. Dodds. I think I've found something, sir. Just coming into sunlight now. There it is on full magnification."

The repeater screen showed a small area of the derelict's ravaged outer hull. There was a black, jagged-edged opening leading into the depths of the ship, and beside it a section of buckled plating on which there was a large, brownish yellow smear.

"It looks like grease, sir," said Dodds.

"I agree," said the Captain, then impatiently: "But why would he use grease instead of fluorescent green marker paint?"

"Perhaps the stuff was handy, sir."

Fletcher ignored Dodds' reply—it had been a rhetorical question anyway. "Chen, we shall be closing with the derelict to one hundred meters. Haslam, stand by the pressors in case I miscalculate and blunder into that thing. Doctor, under the circumstances I'm afraid I cannot spare an officer to go with you, but a hundred meter flight should pose no serious problems. Just don't spend too much time in there."

"I understand," said Conway.

"Very well, Doctor. Be ready to go in fifteen minutes. Take extra air tanks, water and whatever medical supplies you consider necessary. I hope you find him. Good luck."

"Thank you," said Conway. He wondered what type of medication would be needed for a doctor who seemed to be physically fit but mentally deranged enough to go exploring in the derelict. Regarding his own requirements, he was less hesitant—he would simply increase the duration of his suit to forty-eight hours, at the end of which time the *Rhabwar* would depart, whether he found Sutherland or not.

While Conway was checking the extra tanks, Prilicla flew over and landed on the wall beside him. As they clung to the white plastic surface, the little empath's legs trembled as if it was being subjected to intense emotional radiation. When it spoke Conway was surprised to discover that the emotion was self-generated. It was frightened.

"If I might offer a suggestion, friend Conway," said Prilicla, "the job of finding the being Sutherland would be accomplished much more simply and quickly if I were to accompany you."

Conway thought of the tangle of metal plating and structural members that lay beneath the hull of the derelict, of the danger of rupturing their spacesuits practically every foot of the way, and of the other dangers they could not even guess at. He wondered what had become of the celebrated Cinrusskin cowardice, which in that incredibly fragile species was its most important survival characteristic.

"You would come with me?" Conway asked incredulously. "You are *offering* to come with me?"

Prilicla responded timidly. "Your emotional radiation is somewhat confused, friend Conway, but on the whole flattering to myself. Yes, I shall go with you and use my empathic faculty to help find Sutherland, if he is still alive. However, you already know that I am not a brave person, and I reserve the right to withdraw from the search should the element of risk pass beyond what I consider acceptable limits."

"I'm relieved," said Conway. "For a moment there I was worried about your sanity."

"I know," said Prilicla, beginning to add items to its own spacesuit.

They exited by the small personnel lock forward, the main one being connected to the *Tenelphi,* and had to listen to Captain Fletcher worrying out loud about the situation for several interminable minutes. Then they were outside, and the hull of the derelict was spread out ahead and all around them like a gigantic wall, so pitted and torn and ruptured by centuries of meteorite collisions that at close range the spherical shape of the enormous vessel was not apparent. As they guided themselves towards it, there was a sudden dizzying change of perspective. The derelict was no longer a vertical wall but a vast, metallic landscape on which they were about to touch down, and the two coupled ships were hanging in the sky above it.

Conway found it much easier to guide himself down to the marked area than to control his emotions at the thought of landing on one of the legendary generation ships. But it was likely that his emotional radiation would not inconvenience Prilicla too much because the empath's feelings would be very similar—even though it was physiologically impossible for a Cinrusskin to experience goose bumps or to have the non-existent hair at the back of its neck prickle with sheer wonder.

This was one of the generation ships which, before the discovery of hyperdrive, had carried colonists from their home worlds to the planets of other stars. All of the technologically advanced species of what was now the Galactic Federation had gone through their generation-ship phase. Melf, Illensa, Traltha, Kelgia and Earth had been among the scores of cultures which—between the time of their developing chemical- or nuclear-powered interplanetary travel and virtually instantaneous interstellar flight via the hyperdimension— had flung these planetary seed pods into space.

When a few decades or centuries later the cultures concerned had perfected hyperdrive or received it from one of the species of the emerging Galactic Federation, they had gone looking for these lumbering sub-light-speed behemoths and had rescued the majority of them a few decades or centuries after they had been launched.

This could be accomplished because the courses of the generation ships were known with accuracy, and their positions at any time during their centuries-long voyages could be computed with ease. Provided no physical or psychological catastrophe had occurred in the meantime—and some of the non-physical things that had gone wrong in the generation ships had given the would-be rescuers nightmares for the rest of their lives—the colonists were transferred to their target worlds within a matter of days rather than centuries.

Conway knew that the last of the generation ships to be contacted had been cleared, their metal and reactors salvaged. A few of them had been converted for use as accommodation for personnel engaged on space construction projects more than six hundred years ago. But this particular generation ship was one of the few which had not been contacted when hyperdrive was perfected. Either by accident or because of faulty design, it had gone off course to become a seedling destined never to reach fallow ground.

In silence they landed on the derelict's hull. Because of the vessel's slow spin, Conway had to use his feet and wrist magnets to keep from being tossed gently away again, while Prilicla used its gravity nullifiers in combination with magnetic pads on the ends of its six pipe-stem legs. Carefully they climbed through the gap in the plating and out of the direct sunlight. Conway waited until his eyes adjusted to the darkness, then he switched on his suit spotlight.

There was an irregular natural tunnel in the wreckage, leading down for perhaps thirty meters. At the bottom was a projecting piece of metal, which had been daubed with luminescent green marker paint and a smear of grease.

"*If the* Tenelphi's *officers marked a route for you,*" Fletcher said when Conway reported the find, "*it should speed the search for Sutherland. Always provided he hasn't been diverted from the marked path. But there is another problem, Doctor. The farther you go into the derelict, the more difficult it will be to work your radio signals. We have more power here than you have in your suit power pack, so you will be able to listen to us long after we will cease hearing you. I'm referring to spoken messages, you understand. If you switch on your radio deep inside the ship, we will still be able to hear it, as a hiss or a burst of static, and vice versa. So even if we can no longer talk to each other, switch on your radio every fifteen minutes to let us know you're still alive, and we'll acknowledge.*

"*It is possible to send messages by short and long bursts of static. It is a very old method of signaling still used in certain emergency situations. Do you know Morse?*"

"No," said Conway. "At least, only enough to send SOS."

"*I hope you don't have to, Doctor.*"

Following the marked path through the wreckage was slow, dangerous work. The residual spin on the derelict made them feel as if they were climbing up towards the center of the ship, while Conway's eyes and all of his instincts insisted that he was moving downwards. When they reached the first daub of paint and grease, another mark became visible deeper inside the ship, but the path inclined sharply to avoid a solid mass of wreckage and the next leg of the journey angled in a new direction for the same reason. They were progressing towards the center of the ship, but in a series of flat zigzags.

Prilicla had taken the lead to avoid the risk of Conway falling onto it. With its six legs projecting through its spherical pressure envelope—Prilicla's bony extremities were not affected by vacuum conditions—it looked like a fat metallic spider picking its way gracefully through a vast, alien web. Only once did its magnetic pads slip, when it began to fall towards him. Instinctively, Conway reached out a hand to check the creature's slow tumble as it was going past, then pulled his hand back again. If he had gripped one of those fragile legs, it would probably have snapped off.

But Prilicla checked its own fall with the suit thrusters, and they resumed the long, slow climb.

Just before communications with the ambulance ship became unworkable, Fletcher reported that they had been gone four hours, and asked if Conway was sure that he was following the missing Sutherland and not just the path marked by the party of the *Tenelphi* crew-members. Conway looked at the patch of luminous paint just ahead of them, and at the smear of grease beside it, and said he was sure.

I'm missing something, he told himself angrily, *something that is right in front of my stupid face . . . !*

As they moved deeper into the ship the wreckage became less densely packed, but the apparent gravity pull exerted by the spin had diminished so much that quite large masses of plating, loose equipment and demolished furnishings moved or slipped or settled ponderously whenever they tried to grip them. The suit spotlights showed other things, too—crushed, torn and unidentifiable masses of desiccated organic material, which were the remains of the crew or domestic animals caught in the centuries-old catastrophe. But separating the organic from the metallic wreckage would have been both highly dangerous and a waste of time. Finding Sutherland had to take priority over satisfying their curiosity regarding the physiological classification of the species that had built the ship.

They had been traveling for just under seven hours and had begun to move through levels that, although their structure was ruptured and contorted, were no longer choked with wreckage. This was fortunate because Prilicla kept blundering gently into walls and bulkheads through sheer fatigue, and every second or third breath that Conway took seemed to turn into a yawn.

He called a halt and asked the empath if it could detect any emotional radiation apart from Conway's own. Prilicla said no and was too tired even to sound apologetic. When Conway next heard the periodic hiss in his suit phones, he acknowledged by flipping his transmit switch on and off rapidly three times, pausing, then repeating the signal at short intervals for several minutes.

The Captain would realize, he hoped, that the repeated S signal meant that Prilicla and Conway were going to sleep.

They made much better time on the next stage of the journey, which involved simply walking along virtually undamaged decks and climbing broad ramps or narrower stairs towards the center of the ship. Only once did they have to slow to negotiate a plug of wreckage, which had been caused, apparently, by a large and slow-moving meteorite that had punched its way deep inside the ship. A few minutes later they found their first internal airlock.

Obviously the lock had been built by the survivors after the catastrophe, because it was little more than a large metal cube welded to the surround of an airtight door and containing a very crude outer seal mechanism. Both seals were open and had been that way for a very long time, because the compartment beyond was filled with desiccated vegetation, that practically exploded into dust when they brushed against it.

Conway shivered suddenly as he thought of the vast ship, grievously but not mortally wounded by multiple meteorite collisions, blinded but not powerless, and with groups of survivors living in little islands of light and heat and isolated by steadily dropping pressure. But the survivors had been resourceful. They had built airlocks, which had enabled them to travel between their islands and cooperate in the matter of life-support, and they had been able to go on living for a time.

"Friend Conway," said Prilicla, "your emotional radiation is difficult to analyze."

Conway laughed nervously. "I keep telling myself that I don't believe in ghosts, but I still won't believe me."

They went around the hydroponics room because the markers said that they should, and an hour or so later they entered a corridor that was intact except for two large ragged-edged holes in the ceiling and deck. There was a strange dilution of the absolute darkness of the corridor, and they switched off their spotlights.

A faint glow was coming from one of the holes, and when they moved to the edge it was as if they were looking down a deep well with a tiny circle of sunlight at the bottom. Within a few seconds the sunlight had disappeared, and for a few more seconds the wreckage at the other end of the tunnel was illuminated. Then the darkness was complete again.

"Now," Conway said with relief, "at least we know a shortcut back to the outer hull. But if we hadn't happened to be here at precisely the right time when the sun was shining in—"

He broke off, thinking that they had been very lucky and that there might be more luck to come, because at the end of the corridor containing the newly discovered exit they could see another airlock. It was marked with luminous paint and a very large smear of grease, and the outer seal was closed, a clear indication that there was pressure in the compartment beyond.

Prilicla was trembling with its own excitement as well as with Conway's as Conway began to operate the simple actuator mechanism. He had to stop for a moment because the suit radio was hissing at him and he had to acknowledge. But when he had done so it kept on hissing at him.

"The Captain is not a very patient man," said Conway irritably. "We've been gone just over thirty-eight hours and he said he would give me two days . . ." He paused for a moment and held his breath, listening to the faint, erratic hissing, which was quieter than the sound of his own breathing, so deep inside the derelict had they penetrated. It was difficult to tell when a hiss stopped or started, but gradually he detected a pattern in the signals. Three short bursts. Pause. Three long bursts. Pause. Three short bursts, followed by a longer pause, after which the sequence was repeated again and again. A distress signal. An SOS . . .

"There can't be anything wrong with the ship," he said. "That would be ridiculous. So it has to be a problem with the patients. Anyway, they want us back there and I would say the matter is urgent."

Prilicla, clinging to the wall beside the airlock, did not reply for several seconds. Finally it said, "Pardon the seeming unpoliteness, friend Conway, but my attention was elsewhere. It is at the limit of my range, but I have detected an intelligent life-form."

"Sutherland!" said Conway.

"I should think so, friend Conway," Prilicla said. It began to tremble in sympathy with Conway's dilemma.

Somewhere within a few hundred feet was the missing *Tenelphi* medic, physical condition unknown, but very definitely alive. It might take an hour or more to find him, even with Prilicla's help. Conway desperately wanted to find and rescue the man, not just for the usual reasons but because he felt sure that he possessed the answer to what had happened to the other *Tenelphi* officers. But he and Prilicla were wanted back on the *Rhabwar*, urgently. Fletcher would not send an SOS signal without good reason.

Obviously the ship was not in distress, so it had to be a problem involving the patients. A sudden worsening of their condition, perhaps, which was serious enough for Murchison and Naydrad—two beings who did not panic without reason—to agree to this method of recalling the two doctors. But, thought Conway suddenly, one doctor could satisfy them temporarily until they got two more a little later, one of whom, Sutherland, had a greater knowledge of the malady concerned than the ambulance ship medics.

Prilicla ceased trembling as soon as Conway made his decision. He turned to his companion. "Doctor, we'll have to split up. They need us urgently on the ship, or maybe they just want to talk to us urgently. Would you mind taking the shortcut to the outer hull? Find out what the problem is and give what advice you can. But don't move away from the outer end of that tunnel for at least an hour after you get there. If you do that you will be in line of sight with the *Rhabwar* and, via the tunnel, with me down here, and can relay messages in either direction.

"You should be able to get to the other end of the tunnel, with no zigzagging necessary and with the centrifugal force of the spin helping you along, in roughly two hours," Conway went on. "This should give me enough time to find Sutherland and start bringing him out. It has to be my job because it will need DBDG muscles rather than Cinrusskin sympathy to help him through that tunnel."

"I agree, friend Conway," said Prilicla, already moving along the corridor towards the opening. "I have rarely agreed to a request with more enthusiasm . . ."

The first surprise when he went through the airlock was that there was light. He found himself in a large, open compartment, which, judging from the remains of equipment attached to the deck, walls and ceiling, had been the ship's assembly and recreation area. The equipment, which had originally been used for weightless exercising and probably for competitive sports as well, had been drastically modified to provide supports for the sandwich hammocks, which were necessary for sleeping in the weightless condition. Apart from a few sections sheeted in with transparent plastic and containing vegetation, some of which was still green, the interior surfaces of the enormous compartment were covered with bedding and furniture modified for gravity-free conditions. It looked as if up to two hundred survivors of the original meteorite collisions, including their young, had once been packed into this compartment. The visual evidence indicated that they had lived there for a long time. The second surprise was that there were no traces of them other than the furniture and fittings they had used. Where were the bodies of the long-dead survivors?

Conway felt his scalp prickle. He turned up the volume of his external suit speaker to full and yelled "*Sutherland!*"

No response.

Conway launched himself across the compartment towards the opposite wall, where there were two doors. One of them was partly open and light was shining through. When he landed beside it he knew it was the ship's library.

It was not just the neat racks of books and tape-spools that covered the walls and ceiling of the empty room, or the reading and scanning equipment attached to the deck, or even the present-day tapes and portable recorders that had belonged to the *Tenelphi* officers but that had been abandoned to drift weightlessly about the room. He knew it was the library because he had been able to read the sign on the door, just as he was able to read the name below the ship's crest mounted at eye-level on the opposite wall. As he stared at that famous crest everything suddenly became clear.

He knew why the *Tenelphi* had run into trouble, why the officers had left their ship for the derelict, leaving only their medic as watch-keeping officer. He knew why they had returned so hastily, why they were sick and why there was so little he, or anyone else for that matter, could do for them. He also knew why Surgeon-Lieutenant Sutherland used grease instead of marker paint, and he had a fair idea of the situation confronting the doctor that had driven him back to the derelict. He knew because that ship's name and crest appeared in the history books of Earth and of every Earth-seeded planet.

Conway swallowed, blinked away the fog that was temporarily impairing his vision, and backed slowly out of the room.

The sign on the other door had read *Sports Equipment Stowage,* but it had been relettered *Sick Bay.* When he slid it open he found that it, too, was lighted, but dimly.

Along the walls on both sides of the door, equipment storage shelves had been modified to serve as tiers of bunks, and two of them were occupied. The bodies occupying them were emaciated to the point of deformity, partly because of malnutrition and partly because of being born and living out their lives in the weightless condition. Unlike the desiccated sections of bodies Prilicla and he had encountered on the outer decks, these two had been exposed to atmosphere, and decomposition had taken place. The process was not sufficiently advanced, however, to conceal the fact that the bodies were of classification DBDG, an old male and a girl-child, both Earth-human, and that their deaths had occurred within the past few months.

Conway thought of the voyage that had lasted nearly seven centuries and of the last two survivors who had almost made it, and he had to blink again. Angrily, he moved deeper into the room, pulling himself along the edge of a treatment table and instrument cabinet. In a far corner his spotlight illuminated a spacesuited figure holding a squarish object in one hand and supporting itself against an open cabinet door with the other.

"S . . . Sutherland?"

The figure jerked and in a weak voice replied, "Not so bloody loud."

Conway turned down the volume of his speaker and said quickly, "I'm glad to see you, Doctor. I'm Conway, Sector General.

We have to get you back to the ambulance ship quickly. They're
having problems there and . . ."

He broke off because Sutherland was refusing to let go of the
cabinet. Reassuringly, Conway went on: "I know why you used yellow grease instead of paint, and I haven't unsealed my helmet. We
know there is pressure in other parts of the ship. Are there any
survivors? And did you find what you were looking for, Doctor?"

Not until they were outside the sick bay with the door closed
behind them did Sutherland speak. He opened his visor, rubbed at
the moisture beading the inside of it. "Thank God somebody re-
members his history," he said weakly. "No, Doctor, there are no
survivors. I searched the other air-filled compartments. One of them
is a sort of cemetery of inedible remains. I think cannibalism was
forced on them at the end, and they had to put their dead somewhere where they would be, well, available. And no again, I didn't
find what I was looking for, just a means of identifying but not
curing the condition. All the indicated medication spoiled hundreds
of years ago . . ." He gestured with the book he was holding. "I had
to read some fine print in there, so I increased the air pressure inside
my suit so that when I opened my visor for a closer look it would
blow away any airborne infection. In theory it should have worked."

Obviously it had not worked. In spite of the higher pressure
inside his suit blowing air outwards through his visor opening, the
Surgeon-Lieutenant had caught what his fellow officers had. He was
sweating profusely, squinting against the light and his eyes were
streaming, but he was not delirious or unconscious, as the other
officers from the *Tenelphi* had been. Not yet.

"We found a quick way out," Conway said. "Well, relatively. Do
you think you can climb with my assistance, or should I tie your
arms and legs and lower you ahead of me?"

Sutherland was in poor shape, but he most emphatically did not
want to be tied and lowered, no matter how carefully, down a tunnel
whose walls were of twisted and jagged-edged metal. They compro-
mised by strapping themselves together back to back, with Conway
doing the climbing and the other medic fending them off the obstructions Conway could not see. They made very good time, so
much so that they had begun to catch up to Prilicla before the

Cinrusskin was more than halfway along the tunnel. Every time the sun shone into the other end, the dark circle that was the empath's spacesuited body seemed larger.

The continuous hissing of the SOS signal grew louder by the minute, then suddenly it stopped.

A few minutes later the tiny black circle that was Prilicla became a shining disk as the empath cleared the mouth of the tunnel and moved into sunlight. It reported that the *Rhabwar* and the *Tenelphi* were in sight, and that there should be no problem making normal radio contact. They heard it calling the *Rhabwar,* and what seemed like ten years later came the hissing and crackling sound of the ambulance ship's reply. Conway was able to make out some of the words through the background mush, so he was not completely surprised by Prilicla's relayed message.

"Friend Conway," said the empath, and he could imagine it trying desperately to find some way of softening the effect of its bad news. "That was Naydrad. All the DBDG Earth-humans on the ship, including Pathologist Murchison, are displaying symptoms similar to those of the *Tenelphi* officers, with varying degrees of incapacity. The Captain and Lieutenant Chen are the least badly affected so far, but both are in a condition that warrants their being confined to bed. Naydrad requires our assistance urgently, and the Captain says he'll leave without us if we don't hurry up. Lieutenant Chen is doubtful about our leaving at all, even if they weren't having to modify the hyperdrive envelope to accommodate the *Tenelphi.* It seems there are additional problems caused by the proximity of the system's sun that require a trained astrogator to—"

"That's enough," Conway broke in sharply. "Tell them to dump the *Tenelphi*! Decouple and undock and jettison any samples Chen took aboard for analysis. Neither Sector General nor the Monitor Corps will thank us for bringing back anything that has been in contact with the derelict. They might not be too happy to see us—"

He broke off as he heard Naydrad's voice relaying his instructions to the Captain and the beginning of Fletcher's reply. He went on quickly: "Prilicla, I'm receiving the ship direct, so I don't need you as a relay anymore. Return to the ship as quickly as possible and help Naydrad with the patients. We should be clear of this tunnel in fifteen minutes. Captain Fletcher, can you hear me?"

A voice which Conway did not recognize as the Captain's said, "I can hear you."

"Right," said Conway, and very briefly he explained what had happened to the *Tenelphi* and themselves . . .

Finding a derelict in the system they were surveying had been a welcome break in the monotony for the scoutship and for the off-duty officers who went on board to investigate and, if possible, identify the vessel. Like all scoutships on survey duty, the *Tenelphi* had a complement consisting of a Captain and his astrogation, communications, engineering and medical officers, while the remaining five were the survey specialists, whose work went on around the clock.

According to Sutherland, the first officers to board the derelict had identified the ship very quickly, because of a lucky find of a store requisition form, dated and headed with the ship's crest. The result had been that everyone, including the Captain, had hastily transshipped to the derelict. The sole exception was the ship's medic, whose specialty was considered the least useful on what had suddenly become a mass information-gathering exercise.

For the derelict was none other than the *Einstein*, the first starship to leave Earth and the only one of those early generation ships from that planet not to be rescued by the later hyperdrive vessels. Many attempts at rescuing it had been made over the centuries, but the *Einstein* had not followed its intended course. It had been assumed that the ship had suffered a catastrophic malfunction within a relatively short time of leaving the solar system.

And now here it was, the first and undoubtedly the bravest attempt by mankind to reach the stars the hard way, because at that time its technology had been untried, because nobody knew with absolute certainty that its target system contained habitable planets, and because its crew, the very best people that Earth could produce, wanted to go anyway. As well, the *Einstein* was a piece of technological and psychosociological history, the embodiment of one of the greatest legends of star travel. Now this great ship with its priceless log and records was falling into the sun and would be destroyed within the week. Small wonder, therefore, that the *Tenelphi* was left with only its medical officer on board. But even he did not realize that there was any danger in the situation until the crew, sick and sweating and near delirium, began to return. From the onset Sutherland had discarded Conway's first assumptions, that their condition was due to radiation poisoning, inhaling toxic material or eating infected food, because the returning officers told him about the conditions on board the derelict and how long some of the descendants of its crew had been able to survive.

Not only did the ship carry priceless records of man's first attempt at interstellar flight, it also contained an unknown quantity and variety of bacteria—preserved by the heat and atmosphere and recently living human organisms—of a type which had existed seven hundred years ago and for which the human race no longer had immunity.

Noting the rapidly worsening condition of his fellow officers and knowing there was little he could do for them, Sutherland insisted that they all wear spacesuits continually to avoid the possibility of cross-infection—he could not be absolutely sure they were all suffering from the same disease—and as protection in case of accidents while they were moving clear of the derelict. Their intention was to Jump to Sector General, where some high-powered medical assistance would be available.

When the collision—the inevitable collision, according to Sutherland, considering the semi-conscious and delirious condition of the crew—occurred, he moved the men to the lock antechamber in preparation for a quick evacuation, tried to send a subspace radio signal, and not knowing if he was doing the job properly, tried to eject the distress beacon. But the collision had damaged the release mechanism, and he had to push it out of the airlock. His patients' condition was worsening, and he wondered again if there was anything at all that he could do for them.

It was then that he decided to go aboard the derelict himself, to look for a cure in the very place the disease had originated. The solution might be in the derelict's medicine chest, the "sin chest" of the garbled radio signal. With pressure dropping steadily aboard the badly damaged *Tenelphi* and all the recorders abandoned on the derelict, he could not leave a proper warning for any would-be rescuers. But he had done his best.

He had smeared the *Tenelphi*'s airlock outer seal with yellow grease, not knowing that the heat from the distress beacon would turn it brown, and he had marked his path through the derelict in similar fashion. Few people these days realized, and even Conway had been slow to remember, that in pre-space-travel times a ship with disease on board flew a yellow flag . . .

"Sutherland discovered that the medication in the *Einstein*'s sick bay had long since spoiled," Conway went on, "but he did find a medical textbook which mentioned a number of diseases with symptoms similar to those shown by our people. It is one of the old influenza variants, he thinks, although in our case the loss of natural immunity over the centuries means that these symptoms are being experienced with much greater severity, and any prognosis would be uncertain. That is why I would like you to record this information for proper subspace transmission to Sector General, so that they will know exactly what to expect. And I suggest you make preparations for an automatic Jump, in case you aren't feeling well enough to—"

"Doctor," the Captain replied weakly, "I'm trying to do just that. How quickly can you get back here?"

Conway remained silent for a moment while he and Sutherland cleared the edge of the tunnel. "I have you in sight. Ten minutes."

Fifteen minutes later Conway was removing Sutherland's spacesuit and uniform on the Casualty Deck, which was rapidly becoming overcrowded. Doctor Prilicla was hovering over the patients in turn, keeping an eye and an empathic faculty on their condition, while Naydrad brought in Lieutenant Haslam, who had collapsed at his position in Control a few minutes earlier.

Neither of the extraterrestrials had anything to fear from terrestrial pathogens, even seven-hundred-year-old pathogens. The *Tenelphi* and *Rhabwar* crew-members and Murchison could only lie and hope, if they weren't already delirious or unconscious, that their bodies' defenses would find some way of fighting this enemy from the past. Only Conway had remained free from infection, because a smear of grease or something in a garbled radio signal had worried his subconscious to the extent that he had not unsealed his visor after the scoutship's officers had been brought aboard.

"Four-G thrust in five seconds," came Chen's voice from the speaker. "Artificial gravity compensators ready."

The next time Conway looked at the repeater screen it showed the *Einstein* and the *Tenelphi* shrunk to the size of a tiny double star. He finished making Sutherland as comfortable as possible, checked his IVs and moved on to Haslam and Dodds. He was leaving Murchison to the last, because he wanted to spend more time with her.

She was perspiring profusely despite the reduced temperature inside the pressure litter, muttering to herself and turning her head from side to side, eyes half-open but not really conscious of his presence. He was shocked to see Murchison like this. He realized that she was a very seriously ill patient instead of the colleague he had loved and respected since the days when she was a nurse in the FGLI maternity section, when he was convinced that all the ills of the Galaxy could be cured by his pocket x-ray scanner and his dedication to his profession.

But in Sector General, where the lowliest member of the medical staff would be considered a leading authority in a single-species planetary hospital, all things were possible. An able nurse with wide e-t experience could move up and across the lines of promotion to become one of the hospital's best pathologists, and a junior doctor with unconventional ideas bubbling about in a head that was much too large could learn sense. Conway sighed, wanting to touch and reassure her. But Naydrad had already done all that it was possible to do for her, and there was nothing he could do except watch and wait while her condition deteriorated towards that of the *Tenelphi* officers.

With any luck they would soon be transferred to the hospital, where more high-powered help and resources were available. Fletcher and Chen had been lucky in that the Captain had been in Control and the engineer officer in the Power Room while the infected *Tenelphi* officers were being brought aboard, so they had been the last two to be affected. Fortunately, they were still fit enough to work the ship.

Or were they . . . ?

The repeater screen was still showing an expanse of blackness in which the *Einstein* and the *Tenelphi* were indistinguishable among the background stars. But by now the screen should be showing the non-color of the hyperdimension. It would be much better for all concerned, Conway thought suddenly, if he stopped doing nothing for Murchison and tried to do something for Chen and the Captain.

"Friend Conway," said Prilicla, indicating with one of its feelers, "would you look at this patient, please, and at the one over there? I feel they are conscious and need reassurance by a member of their own species."

Ten minutes later Conway was in the well, pulling himself towards Control. As he entered he could hear the voices of the Captain and engineer officer calling numbers to each other, with frequent stops for repeats and rechecks. Fletcher's face was red and dripping with perspiration, his eyes were streaming and his delirium seemed to have taken the form of a rigid professional monomania as he blinked and squinted at the displays on his panel and read off the numbers. Meanwhile, Chen, who did not look much better, replied from the strange position of the astrogator's panel. Conway regarded them clinically and did not like what he saw.

"You need help," he said firmly.

Fletcher looked up at him through red-rimmed, streaming eyes. "Yes, Doctor, but not yours. You saw what happened to the *Tenelphi* when the medical officer tried to pilot it. Just tend to your patients and leave us alone."

Chen rubbed sweat from his face. "What the Captain is trying to say, Doctor, is that he can't teach you in a few minutes what it took him five years of intensive training to learn, and that the delay in making the Jump is caused by our having to get it right first time in case we aren't fit enough for a second try and we materialize in the wrong galactic sector, and that he is sorry for his bad manners but he is feeling terrible."

Conway laughed. "I accept his apology. But I have just come from speaking to one of the *Tenelphi* victims of what we now feel sure is one of the old influenza variants. He was one of the first to fall sick along with the other member of the original boarding party. Now his temperature is returning to normal and that of the other one is also falling rapidly. I would say that this outbreak of seven-hundred-year-old flu can be treated successfully with supportive medication, although the hospital will probably insist on a period of quarantine for all of us when we get back.

"However," he went on briskly, "the officer I speak of is the *Tenelphi*'s astrogator, and frankly, he is in much better shape than either of you two. You *do* need help?"

They were looking at him as if he had just produced a miracle, as if in some peculiar fashion Conway was solely responsible for all the complex mechanisms evolved by the DBDG Earth-human life-form to protect itself against disease—which was, of course, ridiculous. He nodded to them and returned to the Casualty Deck to send up the *Tenelphi* astrogator. He was thinking that within two weeks at most, everyone apart from the immune Prilicla and Naydrad would be fully recovered and convalescent, and he would no longer have to treat Pathologist Murchison as a patient.

PART 3

QUARANTINE

Immediately on its return to Sector General, the *Rhabwar* and the Earth-human personnel on board were placed in strict quarantine and refused admission to the hospital. Conway, who had had no direct physical contact with either the *Tenelphi*'s or his ambulance ship's crews since the infection had come aboard, was doubly quarantined in that he inhabited the man-shaped bubble of virus-free air that was his long-duration spacesuit and a cabin hastily modified to provide life-support independent of the ship's infected system.

There was no real problem in providing supportive treatment to both crews—who were either responding well or were in varying stages of convalescence—because he had Prilicla and Naydrad assisting him. As extraterrestrials they were, of course, impervious to Earth-human pathogens, and they were being very smug about this. Neither was there any difficulty in accommodating the two crews—the officers of the *Tenelphi* occupied the Casualty Deck, and the ambulance ship personnel had their own cabins. But there were periods, often as long as twenty-three hours in the day, when the *Rhabwar* was dreadfully overcrowded.

The real problem was that while the hospital refused them admittance, practically every Earth-human and e-t in Sector General was trying to find an excuse to visit the ambulance ship.

During the first week, combined medical and engineering teams worked around the clock flushing out the ship's air system and sterilizing everything with which the infected air had come in contact. There were also constant checks on the progress of the patients and constant supervision of the regimen, which would ensure that after their cure was effected they would not retain the ability of passing on the infection to any other member of the Earth-human DBDG classification. Lastly, there were those who came simply to talk to the patients and complain about Conway's handling of the *Einstein* incident.

These included Thornnastor, the elephantine Tralthan Diagnostician in charge of the Pathology Department, who came chiefly to raise the morale of its department-member Murchison by providing her with the latest hospital gossip, which in some of the e-t wards was colorful; and a variegated bunch of highly professional medics and bitterly disappointed amateur historians who wanted to talk to the *Tenelphi* crew about their experiences aboard the derelict, and to castigate Conway for not bringing back more in the way of specimens than a seven-hundred-year-old medical textbook, which had fallen apart as soon as it was exposed to present-day sterilization techniques.

Inside his suit-shaped bubble of sterile air, Conway tried, not always successfully, to remain emotionally cool and aloof. Captain Fletcher, whose convalescence had advanced to the stage where he was convinced that medical red tape was all that was keeping him from resuming active duty, could not remain cool at all. Especially when the *Rhabwar* personnel gathered together at mealtimes.

"You are a senior physician, after all, and you are still the ranking medical officer on this ship," the Captain observed in an aggrieved tone while he attacked the rather bland meal the hospital dietitians had prescribed for them. "Unlike us, Doctor, you never were a patient, so your rank was not taken away when you were issued a hospital gown. I mean, Thornnastor is all right as a person, but it's an FGLI, after all, and its movements are about as graceful as those of a six-legged baby elephant. Did you see what it did to the ladder on the Casualty Deck, and to the door of your cabin, ma'am?"

He broke off to smile admiringly at Murchison. Lieutenant Haslam muttered something about often feeling like breaking down the pathologist's door himself, and the Captain silenced him with a frown. Lieutenants Dodds and Chen, like the good junior officers they were, maintained a respectful silence, and in common with the other male Earth-human DBDGs present, exuded minor-key emotional radiation of a pleasurable nature, which Prilicla would have described as being associated with the urge to reproduce. Charge Nurse Naydrad, who rarely allowed anything to interfere with bodily refueling, kept on moving large portions of the green and yellow vegetable fiber it was pleased to call food, and ignored them.

The emotion-sensitive Doctor Prilicla, who could ignore nobody, hovered silently above the edge of the table, showing no signs of emotional distress. Obviously the Captain was not as irritated as he sounded.

". . . Seriously, Doctor," Fletcher went on, "it isn't just Thornnastor blundering into areas of the ship that were not meant for FGLIs. Some of the other e-ts take up a lot of space as well, and there are times when each crew-member of the *Tenelphi* has about half a dozen e-ts or Earth-humans sitting at his feet while he chatters on and on about the things he saw on that derelict, and they treat us as if we'd caught a mutated form of leprosy instead of the same influenza virus as the scoutship crew."

Conway laughed. "I can understand their feelings, Captain. They lost material of priceless historic value, which was already considered irretrievably lost for many centuries. That means they have lost it twice and feel twice as angry with me for not bringing back an ambulance shipful of records and artifacts from the *Einstein*. At the time I was tempted. But who knows what else I might have brought back with those records in the way of seven-hundred-year-old bacterial and viral infections from which we have little or no immunity? I couldn't take the risk, and they, when they stop being bitterly disappointed amateur historians and go back to being the hospital's top seniors and Diagnosticians, will know that, given the same circumstances, they would have done exactly what I did."

"I agree, Doctor," said Fletcher, "and I sympathize with your problem and theirs. I also know that they have to undergo a very thorough and, well, physically inconvenient decontamination procedure on leaving the ship, regardless of their physiological classifications, and this weeds out all but the most enthusiastic or masochistic amateur historians. All I want to know is whether there is a polite way, or any way, of telling them to stay off my ship."

"Some of them," said Conway helplessly, "are Diagnosticians."

"You say that as if it was some kind of answer, Doctor," said the Captain, looking perplexed. "What is so special about a Diagnostician?"

Everyone stopped eating to look at Conway, who alone among them could not eat anywhere outside his sterile cabin. Prilicla's hover became somewhat unstable, and Naydrad gave a short foghorn blast that was untranslatable but was probably the Kelgian equivalent of a snort of incredulity.

It was Murchison who finally spoke. "The Diagnosticians are very special, Captain," she said. "And peculiar. You already know that they are the top-ranking medical personnel in the hospital, and as such, cannot be readily ordered around. Another reason is that when you speak to one of them you can never be sure who or what you are talking to . . ."

Sector General was equipped to treat every known form of intelligent life, Murchison explained, but no single person could hold in his or its brain even a fraction of the physiological data necessary for this purpose. Surgical dexterity and a certain amount of e-t diagnostic ability came with training and experience, but the complete physiological knowledge of any patient requiring complex treatment was furnished by means of an Educator tape. This was simply the brain recording of some great medical authority belonging to the same species as or a species similar to that of the patient undergoing treatment.

If an Earth-human doctor had to treat a Kelgian patient, he took a DBLF physiology tape until treatment was completed, after which the recording was erased from his mind. The sole exceptions to this rule were senior physicians with teaching duties, which required the retention of one or two tapes, and the Diagnosticians.

A Diagnostician was one of the hospital elite, a being whose mind was considered stable enough to retain six, seven, and in a few cases, ten physiology tapes simultaneously. To these data-crammed minds were given projects such as original research in xenological medicine and the treatment of new diseases in hitherto unknown life-forms.

But the tapes did not impart only physiological data. Rather, the complete memory and personality of the entity who had possessed that knowledge was transferred as well. In effect, a

Diagnosticianan subjected himself or itself voluntarily to the most drastic form of schizophrenia. The entities apparently sharing a Diagnostician's mind could well be aggressive, unpleasant individuals—geniuses, whether medical or otherwise, were rarely pleasant people—with all sorts of peeves and phobias.

The original personality was never submerged completely, but depending on the case or research project currently being worked on and the depth of concentration required for it, one could never be sure of a Diagnostician's reaction to any request that was not of a medical nature. Even then it was considered good manners to find out who or what kind of personality was in partial mental control of the entity concerned before saying anything at all. As a class they were not people one gave orders to, and even the hospital's Chief Psychologist O'Mara had to treat them with a certain degree of circumspection.

". . . So I'm afraid you can't just tell them to go away, Captain," Murchison went on, "and the seniors accompanying those Diagnosticians will have sound medical reasons, as well as non-medical ones, for being here. You should also remember that for the past two weeks they have been checking us practically cell by cell, and they might become even more thorough if we were to suggest that they stop wasting time talking history to the scoutship crew and—"

"Not that," said the Captain hurriedly, and sighed. "But Thornnastor seems a friendly enough being, if a bit big and awkward, and it is our most frequent visitor. Could you suggest to it, ma'am, that if it came less often and without its medical retinue . . . ?"

Murchison shook her head firmly. "Thornnastor is Diagnostician-in-Charge in Pathology and as such is the hospital's senior Diagnostician. It is also a source of news, a friend, and my head of department. Anyway, I enjoy Thorny's visits. You may think it odd that a Tralthan FGLI, an oversized, elephantine, six-legged, warmblooded oxygen-breather with four manipulatory appendages and more eyes than seems decent should relish discussing a juicy piece of gossip from the SNLU section of the methane wards. You may even wonder how anything of a scandalous nature could occur between two intelligent crystalline entities living at minus one hundred and fifty degrees centigrade, or why their off-duty activities are of such interest to a warm-blooded oxygen-breather. But you must understand that Thorny's feeling for other e-ts, and even for us Earth-humans, is unique. It is, you see, one of our most stable and well-integrated multi-personalities..."

Fletcher held up both hands in a gesture of surrender. "As well as possessing the ability to instill a degree of personal loyalty in its staff, which is unusual, to say the least. All right, ma'am, you've convinced me. I am no longer ignorant about Diagnosticians, and I can do nothing about their overrunning my ship."

"I'm afraid not, Captain," Murchison agreed sympathetically. "Only O'Mara could do something about that. But he is very fond of his Diagnosticians and of saying that any being sane enough to be a Diagnostician is mad..."

While Murchison and Fletcher had been speaking, the illumination in the dining compartment had undergone a subtle change, caused by the vision screen lighting up to show the craggy features of the Chief Psychologist.

"Why is it that every time I break in on a conversation I find people talking about me," O'Mara asked sourly. "But don't apologize or explain; you would strain my credulity. Conway, Fletcher, I have news for you. Doctor, you can discard that spacesuit, reconnect your cabin to the ship's air system, and resume eating and direct physical contact with your colleagues." He smiled faintly, but did not look at Murchison as he went on. "The ship has been cleared as free from infection, but frankly, this business has uncovered a serious weakness in patient reception procedures.

"Up until now," he continued, "we have assumed, and rightly, that new patients or casualties pose no threat because e-t pathogens cannot affect entities of another species. And because any being traveling in space, even on an interplanetary hop, has to undergo strict health checks, we tended to be a bit lax regarding same-species infections. That is why we are being very cautious and are allowing only the *Tenelphi* crew off the ship while the rest of you must stay aboard the *Rhabwar* for another five days. They caught the disease first, then the ambulance ship crew did; if you don't come down with symptoms during the next five days, then your ship and everyone on it is clear. However, to keep you and everyone else from feeling bored with inaction we have a job for you. Captain Fletcher, you and your officers are returned to active duty. How soon can you be ready to leave?"

Fletcher tried hard not to show his eagerness as he replied: "We have been unofficially on active duty for the past week and the ship is ready, Major. Provided we can have immediate action in the matter of topping up stores and medical consumables and there are no oversized e-ts getting underfoot—"

"That I can promise," said O'Mara.

"—we can take off within two hours," Fletcher ended.

"Very well," replied the Chief Psychologist briskly. "You will be answering a distress beacon detected in Sector Five, well out on the rim. The radiation signature of the beacon indicates that it is not one of ours. There is no Federation traffic out there anyway, and the star destiny is so low that we didn't waste time trying to chart the area ourselves. But if there *is* a star-traveling race out there, they might let us copy their charts when we show them ours. Especially if you bail some of their friends out of trouble. Or perhaps I should not remind highly altruistic medical types like yourselves of the mutual profit aspect of this situation. Communications Center will let you have the coordinates of the beacon presently. The probability of this distress signal originating from a ship of a hitherto undiscovered species is close to being a certainty.

"And Conway," O'Mara ended dryly, "this time try to bring back a few ordinary, or even extraordinary, casualties, and not a potential epidemic . . ."

*   *   *

They wasted no time moving out to Jump distance because Fletcher was now fully confident of the capabilities of his ship. He did complain a little, although it seemed to Conway to be more in the nature of an apology, about the tuition during the first mission and this one. Theoretically, his officers and the medical team were supposed to become less specialized in their functions.

According to the ambulance-ship project directive, Conway was supposed to teach his officers the rudiments of e-t physiology, their physical structures, musculatures, circulatory systems and so on— enough of the subject, at least, for them not to kill some hapless casualty through good intentions. Meanwhile, Fletcher was supposed to reciprocate by lecturing the medical team on his particular specialty, e-t ship design and comparative technology, so that they would not make elementary errors regarding the vessel surrounding their patient.

Fletcher agreed with Conway that there would be no time to set up the lecture program on this mission, but that they would keep it in mind for the future. The result was that Conway spent most of the time in hyperspace with Naydrad, Prilicla and Murchison on the Casualty Deck, wondering whether they were properly prepared to receive an unknown number of casualties of an unknown physiological type. But he was in Control, at Fletcher's invitation, just before they were due to emerge.

A few seconds after the *Rhabwar* emerged into normal space, Lieutenant Dodds announced, "Wreckage ahead, sir."

"I don't believe . . . !" Fletcher began incredulously. "The accuracy of your astrogation is much too good, Dodds, to be due to anything but sheer luck."

"Oh, I don't know, sir," Dodds replied, grinning. "Distance is twelve miles. I'm locking on the scope now. You know, sir, this could be the fastest rescue ever recorded."

The Captain did not reply. He was looking pleased and excited and a little bit wary of so much good luck. On the screen the wreckage showed as a flickering gray blur spinning rapidly in the blackness. Out here on the Rim the stellar density was low, and most of the available light came from the long, faintly shining fog bank, which was the parent galaxy. Suddenly the image became brighter but even more blurred as Dodds switched to the infrared receptors and they saw the wreckage by its own heat radiation.

"Sensors?" the Captain asked.

"Non-organic material only, sir," Haslam reported. "No atmosphere present. Relative to the ambient temperature, it is very warm, suggesting that whatever happened occurred recently and probably as a result of an explosion."

Before the Captain could reply, Dodds said, "More wreckage, sir. A larger piece. Distance fifty-two miles. Spinning rapidly."

"Give me the numbers for closing with the larger piece,"

Fletcher ordered. "Power Room. I want maximum thrust available in five minutes."

"Three more pieces," said Dodds. "Large, distance one hundred plus miles, widely divergent bearings, sir,"

"Show me a distribution diagram," said the Captain, responding quickly. "Compute courses and velocities of all the pieces of wreckage, with a view to tracing the original point of the explosion. Haslam, can you tell me anything?"

"Same temperatures and material as the other pieces, sir," Haslam reported. "But they are at the limit of sensor range, and I could not say with certainty that it is composed entirely of metal. None of the pieces encloses an atmosphere, even residual."

"So if organic material is present," said Fletcher grimly, "it is no longer alive."

"More wreckage, sir," said Dodds.

This is not going to be a fast rescue, thought Conway. *It might not even be a rescue at all.*

Fletcher must have been reading Conway's mind, because he pointed at the big repeater screen. "Don't give up hope, Doctor. The first indications are that a ship has suffered a catastrophic explosion, and the distress beacon was released automatically as a result of the malfunction and not by one of the survivors, if any. But look at that display . . ."

The picture on the screen did not mean very much to Conway. He knew that the winking blue spot was the *Rhabwar* and that the white traces that were appearing every few seconds were wreckage detected by the ship's expanding radar and sensory spheres. The fine yellow lines that converged at the center of the screen were the computed paths taken by the wreckage from the point of the explosion, and what should have been a simple picture was confused by groups of symbols and numbers that flickered, changed or burned steadily beside every trace.

". . . The distribution of the wreckage seems a bit lopsided for an explosion," Fletcher went on, "and although the scale is too small for it to be apparent on the screen, it appears to have originated from a short, flat arc rather than a point. Then, there is the virtually uniform rate of spin on the pieces of wreckage, and their relatively small number and large size. When a ship is torn apart by an explosion, usually caused by a power-reactor malfunction, debris size is small and the rate of spin negligible. Also, the temperature of this wreckage is too low for it to have originated in a reactor explosion, which we now know would have to have occurred less than seven hours ago.

"The probability is," the Captain ended, "that it was a hyperdrive generator malfunction, Doctor, and not an explosion."

Conway tried to control his irritation at the other's lecturing and faintly condescending tone, realizing that the Captain could not help his academic background. Conway knew that if one of a matched set of hyperdrive generators was to fail, the other was supposed to cut out automatically; the vessel concerned would emerge suddenly into normal space somewhere between the stars, and sit there, unable to make it home on impulse drive, until either it repaired the sick generator or help arrived. But there had been instances when the safety cutoff on the good generator had failed or had been a split second late in functioning, which meant that a part of the ship had been proceeding at hyperspeed while the rest had been slowed instantaneously to sublight velocity. The effect on the vessel concerned was, at best, only slightly less catastrophic than a reactor explosion—but at least there would be no heat fusion, radiation and the other complications of a reactor blowup to worry about. The chance of finding survivors was very slightly increased.

"I understand," said Conway. He flipped the intercom switch on his console and said, "Casualty Deck, Conway here. You may stand down. Nothing will be happening for at least two hours."

"That is a pretty accurate estimate," Fletcher said dryly. "Since when have you become an astrogator, Doctor? Never mind. Dodds, compute a course linking the three largest pieces of wreckage, and put the figures on the Power Room repeater. Chen, we will apply maximum thrust in ten minutes. To save time I plan to make a close pass of the likeliest prospects and decelerate only if Haslam's sensors or Doctor Prilicla's empathy say it is worth doing so. Haslam, stay on the sensors and pick out a few more possibilities for us to look at once we've checked the first three. And continue searching the radio frequencies in case a survivor is trying to attract

AMBULANCE SHIP · 111

our attention in that fashion, and keep an eye on your scope in case it is trying to flash a light at us."

As Conway was leaving the Control Deck to rejoin his medical team aft, Haslam said in a quiet, respectful voice, "I've only got two eyes, sir, and they don't swivel independently..."

One hour and fifty-two minutes later they passed heart-stoppingly close to the first piece of wreckage. The sensors had already reported negatively on it—no organic material present other than structural plastic trimming panels and furniture, no pockets of atmosphere that might have contained a living entity. When they tried to put a tractor beam on it to check its spin, the whole mass began to fly apart and they had to take violent evasive action.

They caught up with the next piece in less than an hour. They had to decelerate and return to it, because the sensors reported small pockets of atmosphere inside the wreckage and organic material of a non-structural but not necessarily still-living kind. This time they did not risk trying to check its spin in case the loose mass of wreckage fell apart and the potentially life-giving pockets of air were lost to space. Instead, they set the sensor and vision recorders going during their slow, careful and extremely close approach. The close approach was for Prilicla's benefit, but the empath reported apologetically that none of the organic material was alive.

They had three hours to study the recordings before reaching the third piece of wreckage, which was the largest and most promising to be detected. In the process they learned quite a lot about the design philosophy of the alien ship-builders from the way the structural members and bulkheads had been twisted apart by the accident. The dimensions of the corridors and compartments gave an indication of the size of the life-forms that had crewed the ship. They had glimpses of things that looked like thick pieces of many-colored fur trapped and partially hidden in the wreckage. It might have been floor covering or bedding, except that a few of the pieces were restrained by webbing and many of them showed patches of reddish brown, which looked very much like dried blood.

"Judging by the color of those stains," Murchison observed as they studied one of the stills on the Casualty Deck repeater, "the chances are pretty good that they are warm-blooded oxygen-breathers. But do you think anyone could survive a disaster like that?"

Conway shook his head but tried to sound optimistic. "The staining on the fur does not appear to be associated with lacerations or punctured wounds of the kind suffered through violent deceleration or collision when the restraining body harness becomes deeply embedded in the body it was meant to protect. From these pictures it is impossible to tell which end of the body is which, but the staining seems to be located in the same areas of all the bodies. This suggests explosive decompression and the exiting of body fluid through natural openings, rather than massive external injury due to a sudden deceleration or collision. None of these people was wearing spacesuits, but if any of them was fast enough or lucky enough to be wearing suits, they should have been able to survive."

Before Murchison could reply the picture changed abruptly to show another mass of wreckage, and the excited voice of the Captain sounded from the wall speaker. "This looks like the best bet so far, Doctor. No spin to speak of, so we can board easily, if necessary. The fog you see is not all escaped air; some of it is boil-off from the vessel's water and hydraulic systems. If air is escaping, then there must be quite a lot of it still left on board. There is also what seems to be an emergency power circuit in use, weak and probably used for standby lighting. We may want to board this one. Is everyone ready?"

"Ready, friend Fletcher," said the empath.

"Of course," said Naydrad.

"We'll be at the Casualty lock in ten minutes," said Conway.

"Lieutenant Dodds and myself will accompany you," said the Captain, "in case structural or engineering problems are encountered. Ten minutes, Doctor."

There was not a lot of room to spare in the Casualty airlock with the Captain, Dodds, Naydrad and its already inflated pressure litter, Prilicla and Conway all clinging to its deck and walls with foot and wrist magnets while they watched the approach of the wreckage. It looked like a great rectangular metal thicket shrouded in fog and surrounded by smaller clumps of metal, some of which were spinning rapidly and some of which drifted motionless. When

Conway asked why this should be, the Captain turned silent in the manner of a person who has asked himself the same question and was unable to answer. They waited while the ambulance ship edged closer, passing between two of the wreckage's madly spinning satellites, and their suit spotlights as well as those of the ship reflected off the twisted metal plating and projecting structural members. They went on waiting until the little Cinrusskin began trembling inside its spacesuit.

"Someone," Prilicla finally managed to utter, "is alive in there."

Of necessity, it was a hurried but very careful search, because the emotional radiation of the survivor was weak and characteristic of a mind that was becoming more deeply unconscious by the minute. With Prilicla indicating if not leading the way, the Captain and Dodds cleared a path through obstructions with their cutters or pushed away free-floating debris and tangled cable looms with their insulated gauntlets—there was, after all, a live power circuit in use. Conway followed closely behind, pulling himself along in a kind of weightless crawl through corridors and compartments whose ceilings were only four feet high.

Twice his spotlight picked out the bodies of crew-members, which he freed and pushed gently back the way they had come so that the waiting Naydrad could load them into the unpressurized section of the litter. Should the survivor need urgent surgical attention, Conway would feel much better if Murchison had a few cadavers to take apart so that she could tell him how the living one should be put together again.

He still had no clear idea of what they looked like, because the bodies had been encased in spacesuits. But the suits and underlying tissue had been ruptured by violent contact with metallic debris, and if the resulting wounds had not killed the beings, the decompression had. Judging by the shape of the spacesuits, the beings were flattened cylinders about six feet long with four sets of manipulatory appendages behind a conical section that was probably the head, and another four locomotor appendages. There was a marked thickening at what was presumably the rear section of the suit. Apart from the smaller size and number of appendages, the beings physically resembled the Kelgian race, to which Naydrad belonged.

Conway could hear the Captain muttering to himself about the spacesuited aliens as they stopped at the entrance to a compartment that retained pressure. Prilicla felt carefully with its empathic faculty for the presence of life, in vain. The survivor was located somewhere beyond the compartment, the empath said. Before the Captain and Dodds burned away the door, Conway drilled through to obtain an atmosphere sample for Murchison so that she could prepare suitable life-support for the survivor.

Inside the compartment there was light—a warm, orange light, which would give important information about the planet of origin and the visual equipment of this species. But right then it illuminated only a shambles of drifting furniture, twisted wall plating, tangles of plumbing, and aliens, some of whom were spacesuited and all of whom were dead.

The thickened section at the rear of their spacesuits, Conway saw suddenly, was there to accommodate a large, furry tail.

"This is *collision* damage, dammit!" Fletcher burst out. "Losing a hypergenerator wouldn't have done all *this*!"

Conway cleared his throat. "Captain, Lieutenant Dodds, I know we haven't time to gather material for a major research project, but if you see anything in the way of photographs, paintings, illustrations, anything that would give me information about the alien's physiology and environment, take it along, please." He picked out another alien cadaver that was not too badly damaged, noting the pointed, fox-like head and the thick, broad-striped coat that made it look like a furry, short-legged zebra with an enormous tail. "Naydrad," he called, "here's another one for you."

"Yes, that must be it," the Captain said, half to himself. To Conway he added, "Doctor, these people were doubly unlucky, and the survivor doubly lucky . . ."

According to Fletcher, the hypergenerator failure had pulled the ship apart and sent the pieces spinning away. But in this particular place a number of the crew had survived and had managed to climb into their suits. They might even have had some warning of the approach of the second disaster—the overtaking of their section by another and equally massive piece of wreckage. When the collision occurred, the forward end of the first piece must have been swinging down while the afterpart of the second was swinging upwards. The kinetic energy of both sections had been cancelled out, bringing them both to rest and practically fusing them together. That, in the Captain's opinion, was the only explanation for the type of injuries and damage that had occurred here, and for the fact that this was the only section of the alien ship that was not spinning.

"I think you're right, Captain," said Conway, fishing out of the drifting mass of debris a flat piece of plastic with what looked like a landscape on one side of it. "But surely all this is academic now."

"Of course it is," Fletcher replied. "But I dislike unanswered questions. Doctor Prilicla, where now?"

The little empath pointed diagonally upwards at the compartment's ceiling. "Fifteen to twenty meters in that direction, friend Fletcher, but I must admit to some feelings of confusion. The survivor seems to be moving slowly since we entered this compartment."

Fletcher sighed noisily. "A spacesuited and still mobile survivor," he said in relieved tones. "That will make the rescue very much easier." He looked at Dodds, and together they began cutting through the roof plating.

"Not necessarily," said Conway. "We could have a rescue and a first-contact situation both at the same time. I much prefer new and injured e-ts to be unconscious so that first contact can be made following curative treatment and we can exercise more control over the—"

"Doctor," the Captain broke in, "surely a star-traveling species, with the technical and philosophical background which that capability implies, would be expecting to meet what it would consider extraterrestrials. Even if they did not have the expectation, they surely would realize that there was a strong possibility of it happening."

"Granted," said Conway, "but an e-t who is injured and only partly conscious might react instinctively, illogically, to the sight of an alien being who might physically resemble a natural enemy or a predator on its home planet. And the treatment of a conscious extraterrestrial, a stranger who has no prior knowledge of the beings carrying out the treatment, might be mistaken for something else—torture, perhaps, or medical experimentation. All too often a doctor has to be cruel to be kind."

At that moment a large, circular section of the ceiling came free, its edges still bright red with the heat of the cutting torches, and was pushed away by Dodds and the Captain. As it followed them through the gap, Prilicla said, "I'm sorry if I confused you, friends. The survivor is moving slowly, but it is too deeply unconscious to move itself."

Their spotlights played over a compartment that was open to space in several places, filled with drifting masses of debris, containers of various sizes, a shoal of bright objects that were probably sealed food packages, shelving and the bodies of three unsuited aliens, which were torn and swollen by the twin effects of massive external injuries and explosive decompression. The lights of the *Rhabwar* shone brightly through an open tangle of metal, illuminating the areas where their spotlights did not reach.

"It's here?" asked Fletcher in disbelief.

"It *is* here," said Prilicla.

The empath was indicating a large metal cabinet, drifting slowly past on the outer fringes of the wreckage. The container was deeply scratched and furrowed by violent contact with other metal, and there was one dent in particular that was at least six inches deep. There was a slight haze around the object, indicating that the air trapped inside was escaping slowly.

"Naydrad!" Conway called urgently. "Forget your pressure litter. The survivor has provided one of its own, but it is depressurizing. We'll push it outside where you can see it, then you can pull it on board with a tractor. As fast as you can, Naydrad."

"Doctor," the Captain asked as they were maneuvering the cabinet through a gap in the wreckage, "do we spend time here looking for information on this species, or do we go on looking for other survivors?"

"We go looking, Captain," responded Conway without hesitation. "With luck, the survivor will tell us all we want to know about its species during convalescence . . ."

When the cabinet had been transferred to the Casualty Deck, the Captain examined its door actuator. He said that the operating mechanism was straightforward and that the strength of the door and its surrounding structure had kept that particular face of the cabinet from being deformed during the collision.

"He means the door will open," Dodds translated dryly.

Fletcher glared at the Lieutenant. "The question is, Should we open it without taking precautions—more precautions than you are taking now, Doctor?"

Conway finished drilling, and he withdrew an air sample from the cabinet interior before replying. As he handed the sample to Murchison for analysis, he said, "Captain, the box does *not* contain an Earth-human DBDG with influenza. We *will* find an e-t of a hitherto unknown species in urgent need of medical attention, and as I have already explained, we are in no danger from extraterrestrial pathogens."

"I keep worrying about the exception that might prove the rule, Doctor," the Captain replied doggedly. But he unsealed his visor to show everyone that he was not too badly worried.

"Doctor Prilicla, please," came Haslam's voice from Control. "Minus ten minutes."

The little empath hovered briefly over the cabinet, assured them that there was no marked change in the survivor's emotional radiation—it was still deeply unconscious, but far from being terminal—and hurried to the airlock so that when the astrogator made a close approach to the next mass of wreckage Prilicla would be able to ascertain whether or not anything had survived in it. As the Cinrusskin left, Murchison straightened up from the analyzer display.

"If we assume that the first sample was taken from a compartment at normal atmospheric composition and pressure," she said, "then, apart from a few innocuous trace elements that our ship atmosphere does not contain, we would be quite happy breathing the same air as they do. But the sample from the cabinet is at half normal pressure and is high in carbon dioxide and water vapor. In short, the air inside that cabinet is dangerously thin and stale, and the sooner we get that beastie out of there the better."

"Right," said Conway. He removed the sampling drill without sealing the hole it had made, and as the Casualty Deck's air whistled into the cabinet, he said, "Open her up, Captain."

The cabinet was lying on its back with the door fastening, a rectangular metal plate with three conical indentations on it, facing upwards. Fletcher pulled off one of his gauntlets, pressed three fingers hard into the impressions and slid the plate aside. They heard a loud click, then he lifted the door open. Inside was a confused, bloody mess.

It took Conway several minutes to realize what had happened and to withdraw the bloodstained clothing or bedding from around the survivor. The cabinet had once contained upwards of twenty shelves, which had been pulled out hastily and the metal shelf supports padded with bedding or clothing to protect the occupant. But the collision had been a violent one, and there had been no time to attach the padding properly to the supports. As a result, both the padding and the survivor had been tumbled about the interior of the cabinet. The hapless e-t was jammed tightly into one end of the box, still bleeding sluggishly from a great many lacerations made by the shelf supports, and the colored bands of fur could barely be seen through tufted and matted patches of dried blood.

Very gently Murchison and Naydrad helped Conway lift out the survivor and lay it on the examination table. One of the gashes in its side began to bleed more freely, but as yet they did not know enough about the being to risk using one of their coagulants. Conway began going over its body with his scanner. "There must not have been any spacesuits in that compartment. But they must have had a few minutes' warning, enough for this one to clear and pad the cabinet and get inside, leaving the other three we saw to—"

"No, Doctor," said the Captain. He indicated the airtight cabinet. "It cannot be closed or opened from inside. The four of them must have decided which one was to survive, and they did their best for it, very quickly and, I should say, with minimum argument. As a species they seem to be very . . . civilized."

"I see," said Conway without looking up.

He did not know if there was any minor displacement of the survivor's internal organs, but his scanner indicated that none of the major ones were damaged or radically out of position. The spine also appeared to be undamaged, as did the elongated rib cage. On the back just above the root of the thick, furry tail was a bright pink area, which Conway thought at first was a patch where the fur was missing. But closer examination showed that it was a natural feature, and there were large flakes of what appeared to be some kind of pigment adhering to it. The being's head, which was tucked against its underside and partially covered by the tail, was conical, rodent-like and thickly furred. The skull itself appeared intact, but there was evidence of subcutaneous bleeding in several areas, which in a being without facial fur would have shown as massive bruising. There was some bleeding from the mouth, but Conway could not be sure whether it was due to an external blow or was the effect of lung damage caused by decompression.

"Help me straighten the poor thing out," he said to Naydrad. "It looks as if it tried to roll itself into a ball. Probably an instinctive defense posture it adopts when threatened by natural enemies."

"That is one of the things that puzzles me about this patient," said Murchison, looking up from her examination of one of the cadavers. "These creatures do not possess natural weapons of offense or defense as far as I can tell, or any signs of having had any in the past. Considering the fact that it is a planet's dominant life-form that develops intelligence, I don't see how these creatures came to dominate. Even their limbs are not built for speed, so they could not run from danger. The set used for walking are too short and are padded, while the forward set are more slender, less well-muscled and end in four highly flexible digits that don't possess so much as a fingernail among them. There are the fur markings, of course, but it is rare that a life-form rises to the top of its evolutionary tree by camouflage alone, or by being nice and cuddly. This is strange."

"It sounds like it comes from a nice world," said Prilicla, who had returned briefly from its airlock duty, "for Cinrusskins."

Conway did not join in the conversation, because he was re-examining the patient's lungs. The slight oral bleeding had worried him, and now that the survivor was properly presented for examination there was unmistakable evidence of decompression damage in the lungs. But moving the patient into the supine position had caused some of the deeper lacerations to start bleeding again. He could do very little about the lung damage with the facilities available on the ambulance ship, but considering the weakened state of the patient, the bleeding would have to be stopped quickly.

"Do you know enough about the composition of this beastie's blood at present," Conway asked Murchison, "to suggest a safe co-agulant and anesthetic?"

"Coagulant, yes. Anesthetic, doubtful," Murchison replied. "I'd prefer to wait until we get back to the hospital for that. Thornnastor would be able to suggest, or synthesize, a completely safe one. Is it an emergency?"

Before Conway could reply, Prilicla chimed in: "An anesthetic is unnecessary, friend Conway. The patient is deeply unconscious and will remain so. It is in a slowly deteriorating condition, probably caused by impaired oxygen absorption in the damaged lungs, and the loss of blood would be a contributing factor. Those cabinet-shelf supports were like blunt knives."

"I agree," said Conway. "And if you're trying to suggest that the patient should be hospitalized as soon as possible, I agree with that too. But this one is in no immediate danger, and I would like to be sure that there are no other survivors before we leave. However, if you continue to monitor its emotional radiation and report any sudden change in—"

"More wreckage coming up," Haslam's voice broke in from the wall speaker. "Doctor Prilicla to the airlock, please."

"Yes, friend Conway," said the empath as it scuttled rapidly across the ceiling on its way to the lock.

Before he could begin treating the survivor's surface injuries, he had to quell a minor revolt by Naydrad, who, in common with all of its beautiful silver-furred race, had an intense aversion towards any surgical procedure that would damage or disfigure a being's most treasured possession, its fur. To a Kelgian the removal of a strip or patch of fur, which in their species represented a means of communication equal to the spoken word, was a personal tragedy that all too often resulted in permanent psychological damage. A Kelgian's fur did not grow again, and one whose pelt was damaged could rarely find a mate willing to accept a Kelgian who was unable to display fully its feelings. Murchison had to assure the charge nurse that the survivor's fur was not mobile and emotion-expressive and that it would undoubtedly grow again before Naydrad was content. It did not, of course, refuse to assist Conway during the minor surgery; it simply argued, both vocally and with its rippling and twitching fur, while it was shaving and cleaning the operative field.

Murchison broke in occasionally while they were suturing and applying coagulant to the wounds crisscrossing the patient's body, giving them odd items of information gleaned from her continuing examination and dissection of the cadavers.

The species had two sexes, male and female, and the reproductive system seemed relatively normal. Unlike the patient, however, whose fur appeared duller and to have less color variation, the cadavers of both sexes had applied a water-soluble dye that enhanced artificially the bands of color on their body fur, which otherwise would have been of the same intensity as those of the patient. Clearly the dyes were applied for cosmetic reasons. But why the patient, who was female, had not used dye on its fur was something unclear to Murchison.

One reason might be that the survivor was not yet fully mature and there was some cultural reason why a preadolescent of the species did not use or was forbidden to use cosmetics. Or it might be that the patient was mature and small, or of a race within the species that did not believe in painting its fur. An equally valid reason might be that the disaster had occurred before it had a chance to apply cosmetics. The only substance at all resembling cosmetic material had been the few pieces of flaking brownish pigment adhering to the patient's bare patch above its tail, and that material had been removed during pre-op procedure. The action of its friends, or possibly its family, in placing the survivor in an airtight cabinet just before the collision led Murchison to believe that it was a young and probably preadolescent female, rather than a small mature female.

The Federation had yet to encounter an intelligent species in which the adults would not sacrifice themselves to save their young.

While they were busying themselves with the one living and three dead aliens, Prilicla returned from the lock from time to time to report negatively on the search for other survivors—and similarly on the one they had rescued, whose condition, according to the empath's reading, was still deteriorating. Conway waited until Prilicla had been called to the airlock once again, not wanting to inconvenience the Cinrusskin with what could well be a flood of unpleasant emotional radiation; then he called Fletcher in Control.

"Captain, I have to make a decision and I need your advice," Conway said. "We have completed running repairs on our survivor, so far as the superficial injuries are concerned, but there is decompression damage to the lungs, which requires urgent hospitalization. As an interim measure, we have it on an enriched-oxygen-content air supply. Despite this, its condition is deteriorating, not rapidly but steadily. What, in your opinion, are the chances of picking up other survivors if we are to remain in this area for another four hours?"

"Virtually nil, Doctor," the Captain replied.

"I see." Conway had expected the answer to be much more complicated and hedged with probability computations and verbal qualifiers. He felt both relieved and worried.

"You must understand, Doctor," Fletcher went on, "that the first three pieces of wreckage investigated offered the greatest possibilities of finding survivors, and since then, the likelihood of finding one has diminished sharply, as have the sizes of the collections of debris with every piece we look at. Unless you believe in miracles, Doctor, we are wasting our time here."

"I see," said Conway.

"If it will help you reach a decision, Doctor," the Captain went on, "I can tell you that subspace radio conditions are very good out here, and we have already made two-way contact with the survey and Cultural Contact cruiser *Descartes,* which I am required to do when evidence of a new intelligent species is discovered. As a matter of urgency the *Descartes* will investigate this wreckage with a view to obtaining all available data on the new species, and by analyzing the velocities and directions of those species, will roughly establish the alien ship's point of departure and its destination. There are relatively few stars out here, so they should locate the home planet and star system fairly easily, because they are specialists at that job. Quite possibly, communications will be established with the aliens within a few weeks, perhaps sooner. As well, the *Descartes* carries two planetary landers, which in space double as close-range search and rescue vessels. They won't have Prilicla on board, naturally, but those ships could cover the remaining wreckage much faster than we could, Doctor."

"When will the *Descartes* arrive?" Conway asked.

"Allowing for multiple Jump effects on the astrogation," said Fletcher, "four to five hours."

Conway made no attempt to hide his relief. "Right. If there are no survivors on the next piece of wreckage, let's head for home at once, Captain." He paused for a moment, looking at the survivor and the bodies of its friends who had not made it, then at Murchison. "If they find the home world and make contact quickly, will you ask the *Descartes* to request medical assistance for our friend here? Ask for a volunteer native medic to travel to Sector General to assist or, if necessary, to take charge of the treatment. In cases involving completely new life-forms we can't afford to be proud . . ."

He was also thinking that the native medic might, when it felt more at ease with the multiplicity of life-forms inhabiting the hospital, be agreeable to providing an Educator tape on its people so that the hospital staff would know exactly what they were doing if, on some future occasion, another member of its species became a patient.

*   *   *

"Identify yourself, please. Visitor, staff or patient, and species?" came a toneless translated voice from Reception a few minutes after they had emerged into normal space. The hospital was still little more than a large blurred star against a background of smaller, brighter ones. "If you are unsure of, or are unable to give, an accurate physiological classification because of physical injury, mental confusion or ignorance of the relevant data, please make vision contact."

Conway looked at Captain Fletcher, who drew down the corners of his mouth and raised one eyebrow in a piece of non-verbal communication which said that the person who understood the medical jargon was best fitted to answer the questions.

"Ambulance ship *Rhabwar,* Senior Physician Conway speaking," he responded briskly. "Staff and one patient, all warm-blooded oxygen-breathing. Crew classifications are Earth-human DBDG, Cinrusskin GLNO and Kelgian DBLF. The patient is a DBPK, origin unknown. It has sustained injuries which will require urgent—"

"You are expected, *Rhabwar,* and I have you flagged as priority traffic," the voice from Reception broke in. "Please use approach pattern Red Two and follow the red-yellow-red beacons to Lock Five—"

"But Lock Five is a—"

"—which is, as you know, Doctor, the principal entry port to the levels of the water-breathing AUGLs," Reception continued. "However, the accommodation being reserved for your casualty is close to Five; and Three, which you would normally use, is tied up with twenty-plus Hudlar casualties. There has been some kind of structural accident with radiation side effects during assembly of a Melfan orbiting factory, but I am aware only of the clinical details at present.

"Thornnastor did not know what, if anything, you were bringing in," Reception added, "but it thought it better not to subject the casualty even to residual radiation. Your ETA, Doctor?"

Conway looked at Fletcher, who said, "Two hours, sixteen minutes."

That would be ample time for their DBPK casualty to be transferred into a pressure litter capable of maintaining the integrity of the patient's life-support system against hard vacuum, water and a wide variety of lethal atmospheres, and for the *Rhabwar*'s medical team to don lightweight suits, which would enable them to accompany it. The intervening time could also be used to transmit and to consult with Diagnostician-in-Charge Thornnastor regarding their preliminary findings on the DBPK survivor and the results of Murchison's examination of the cadavers. Thornnastor would probably request the early transfer of those cadavers so as to make a thorough investigation that would give a complete picture of the DBPK life-form's metabolism. Conway relayed the Captain's estimate and asked who would be meeting the *Rhabwar* medics at Lock Five.

The voice from Reception made a number of short, untranslatable noises, possibly the e-t equivalent of a stammer, then went on, "I'm sorry, Doctor. My instructions are that *Rhabwar* personnel are still technically in quarantine and may not enter the hospital. But you may accompany the casualty, provided you do not unseal. The assistance of your team will not be required, Doctor, but the proceedings will be broadcast on the teaching channels so that you will be able to observe and, if necessary, advise."

"Thank you," said Conway. The sarcasm was lost, naturally, in the translation.

"You're welcome, Doctor," said Reception. "And now can I have your communications officer. Diagnostician Thornnastor has requested a direct link with Pathologist Murchison and yourself for purposes of consultation and preliminary diagnosis . . ."

A little more than two hours later, Thornnastor knew all that it was possible to know about the casualty at a distance, and the patient in its pressure litter was being transferred very gently from the *Rhabwar*'s boarding tube into the cavernous entry port that was Lock Five. Prilicla was also allowed to accompany the patient to monitor its emotional radiation. Reluctantly, the hospital authorities had agreed that the little Cinrusskin was unlikely to carry with it the virus that had affected the *Rhabwar*'s crew, and besides, it was the only medically qualified empath currently on the hospital's staff.

The reception and transfer team—Earth-humans in lightweight suits with the helmets, belts and boots painted bright fluorescent blue—quickly moved the pressure litter to Lock Five's inner seal. The outer seal closed ponderously and water poured in, bubbling and steaming coldly as it entered the recently airless chamber. By the time the turbulence had cleared and Conway was able to see, the team was already manhandling the litter into the tepid green depths of the ward devoted to the treatment of the water-breathing inhabitants of Chalderescol.

Conway was glad that their casualty was unconscious, because the Chalders, whose wide variety of ailments rarely left them immobile, swam ponderously around the litter, displaying the curiosity of all hospital patients towards anything that promised to break the monotony of ward routine.

The ward resembled a vast undersea cavern, tastefully decorated, to Chalder eyes, with a variety of artificial native plant life, some of which was obviously carnivorous. This was not the normal environment of the natives of Chalderescol, who were highly advanced both culturally and technically, but the type of surroundings sought by healthy young Chalders going on vacation. According to Chief Psychologist O'Mara, who was rarely wrong in these matters, the primitive environment was a significant aid to recovery. But even to an

Earth-human DBDG like Conway, who knew exactly what was going on, it was a spooky place.

A completely new life-form whose language had yet to be programed into the hospital's translation computer would not know what to think—especially if it was confronted suddenly with one of the AUGL patients.

An adult native of Chalderescol resembled a forty-foot-long crocodile, armor-plated from the rather overlarge mouth to the tail, and with a belt of ribbon tentacles encircling its middle. Even with Prilicla present to radiate reassurance, it was much better for the patient's peace of mind that it did not see the Chalder AUGLs, who swam to within a few meters of the litter to eye the newcomer and wish it well.

Prilicla drifted slightly ahead of the party, a vague insect shape inside the silvery bubble of its suit, twitching occasionally to the bursts of emotional radiation in the area. Conway knew from past experience that it was not the casualty or the curious AUGL patients who were responsible for this reaction, but the feelings of the transfer team maneuvering the litter past the sleeping frames, equipment and artificial flora of the ward and the stretch of water-filled corridor beyond it. The drying and cooling units in the team's issue lightweight suits did not operate at peak efficiency in the warm water of the AUGL level, and when strenuous physical effort was called for in that environment, the tempers shortened in direct proportion to the temperature rise.

The Observation Ward for the new patient had been part of the Casualty Department's initial treatment area for warm-blooded oxygen-breathers before that facility had been moved to Level 33 and extended. The intention had been to fit the original room as an additional AUGL operating theater as soon as the engineering section could get around to it, but at the present time it was still a large, square-sided bubble of air and light inside the watery vastness of the Chalder wards and service units. At the center of the room was an examination table, adjustable to the body configurations of a wide variety of physiological classifications and with provision for conversion to either an operating table or a bed. Ranged along opposing walls of the ward was the similarly non-specialized and complex equipment required for the life-support and intensive care of patients whose life processes were, at times, a partly open book.

Although large, the room was overcrowded—mostly with people who had no business being there and no reason other than professional curiosity. Conway could see one of the scaly, membranous Illensan PVSJs, its loose protective suit transparent except for the faint yellow fog of chlorine it contained, and there was even a TLTU encased in a pressure sphere mounted on caterpillar tracks, which was the only way a being who breathed superheated steam at high pressure could associate professionally with patients and colleagues with less exotic metabolisms. The remainder were warm-blooded oxygen-breathers—Melfans, Kelgians, Nidians and one Hudlar—with one thing in common besides their curiosity: the gold or gold-edged ID badges of Diagnosticians or senior physicians.

Rarely had Conway seen so much medical talent concentrated in such a small area.

They all stayed well clear of the transfer team as the patient was moved from the litter onto the examination table, supervised by Thornnastor itself. The litter was left unsealed and moved back to the ward entrance so as to be out of the way; then everyone began edging closer.

Murchison and Naydrad were watching on the *Rhabwar*'s screen, Conway knew, as Thornnastor began the preliminary examination, which was in all respects identical to the one carried out by Murchison and Conway on the ambulance ship—a careful check of the vital signs, even though at this stage nobody could be quite sure what was or was not a normal pulse, respiration or blood pressure reading for a DBPK—followed by deep and detailed scanning and gentle probing for physical injury or deformation. While it worked, Thornnastor described in detail everything it did, saw or deduced for the many medics who were observing on the teaching channels. Occasionally it paused to ask questions of Murchison on the ambulance ship or of Conway in the ward regarding the patient's condition immediately following its rescue, and for any comments that might be helpful.

Thornnastor had reached its unrivaled eminence in e-t pathology by asking questions and pondering the answers, not by listening to itself pontificate.

Finally, Thornnastor's examination was complete. It brought its massive body fully erect so that the osseous dome housing its brain was almost hidden by the curves of its massive triple shoulders. Its four extensible eyes regarded, simultaneously, the patient, the medics ranged around the examination table and the vision pickups through which the *Rhabwar* and the other non-present observers were viewing the proceedings. Then it spoke.

The most serious damage had been sustained by the patient's lungs, where decompression effects had ruptured tissue and caused widespread bleeding. Thornnastor proposed relieving this situation by withdrawing the unwanted fluid via a minor surgical intervention through the pleural cavity and into the trachea for the purpose of assisting the patient's breathing by positive pressure ventilation of the lungs with pure oxygen. There was a wide range of tissue-regenerative medication available for warm-blooded oxygen-breathers, but the tests that would be carried out on the DBPK cadavers to find one harmless to the DBPK species would be exhaustive and would require two days at least, by which time a safe anesthetic would also be available. Without immediate surgical intervention the patient would not live for more than a few hours. Neither of the proposed procedures was lengthy, the associated pain was minimal, and as Prilicla reported, the patient was too deeply unconscious to be aware of pain, so Thornnastor, assisted by a Melfan senior physician and a Kelgian theater nurse, would operate at once.

Considering the condition of the patient, Conway thought, it was the only sensible thing to do. He felt irked that it was not himself who was assisting Thornnastor, since he had had prior experience with the DBPK life-form. But then he realized, from listening to the respectful whispers coming from the other observers, that the Melfan senior assisting was Edanelt, one of the hospital's top e-t surgeons, the permanent possessor of four Educator tapes, and according to the grapevine, a being shortly to be elevated to Diagnostician status. If a surgeon of Edanelt's eminence could be big enough to assist, then Conway should be able to watch without radiating too much envy.

It had never ceased to amaze Conway, despite the hundreds of operations he had seen Tralthans perform, that such a monstrous and physically ungainly species could produce the Federation's finest surgeons. The DBPK patient did not know how fortunate it was, because it was said in the hospital that no life-form, no matter how hopeless its case might be, was ever lost if it came under Thornnastor's personal care. Such a thing was unthinkable, Thornnastor was reputed to have said, because it was not in its contract . . .

"Consciousness is returning," Prilicla announced suddenly, barely ten minutes after the operation was complete. "It is returning very rapidly."

Thornnastor made a loud, untranslatable sound, which probably signified satisfaction and pleasure. "Such a rapid response to treatment promises a favorable prognosis and, I should think, an early recovery. But let us withdraw for a short distance. Even though a member of a star-traveling race is accustomed to seeing other life-forms, in its weakened state our patient might be worried by the close proximity of a group of such large and diverse beings as ourselves. You agree, Doctor Prilicla?"

But the little empath did not have a chance to reply, because the patient had opened its eyes and was struggling so violently against the body restraints that its tracheal air hose threatened to become detached.

Instinctively, Thornnastor reached over the patient to steady the air hose, and the DBPK became even more agitated. The emotion-sensitive Prilicla began trembling so violently that it was in danger of coming unstuck from the ceiling. Suddenly the patient stiffened and remained absolutely still for several minutes, but then it began to relax again as the Cinrusskin radiated sympathy and reassurance.

"Thank you, Doctor Prilicla," said Thornnastor. "When communication has been established, I shall apologize to this patient for nearly frightening it to death. In the meantime, try to let it know that we wish it well."

"Of course, friend Thornnastor. It is feeling concern now, rather than terror, and it seems to be deeply worried about something which . . ." Prilicla broke off and began to tremble violently.

What happened next was utterly impossible.

Thornnastor began to sway alarmingly on its six stubby legs, legs which normally gave the Tralthan species such a stable base that they frequently went to sleep standing up; then it toppled onto its side with a crash that overloaded the sound pickup on Conway's suit. A few yards away from the treatment table the Melfan Edanelt, who had been assisting Thornnastor, collapsed slowly to the floor, its six multijointed legs becoming progressively more limp until the underside of its exoskeletal body hit the floor with a loud click. The Kelgian theater nurse had also slipped to the floor, the silvery fur on its long, cylindrical body undulating and puckering as if being affected by a tiny whirlwind. A member of the transfer team standing beside Conway dropped loosely to his hands and knees, crawled for a short distance along the floor and then rolled onto his side. Too many e-ts began speaking at once, and Earth-humans trying to outshout them, for Conway's translator to produce anything intelligible.

"This can't be happening . . ." he began incredulously.

Murchison's voice sounded in his helmet phones, speaking on the ship frequency. "Three extraterrestrial life-forms and one Earth-human DBDG, with four radically different metabolisms and inherent species-immunity . . . it's quadruply impossible! As far as I see, no indications of the other unprotected life-forms being affected."

Even when observing the impossible, Murchison remained clinical.

" . . . But it *is* happening," Conway went on. He turned up the volume of his suit external speaker. "This is Senior Physician Conway. Instructions. All transfer team-members, seal your helmets. Team leader, sound the alarm for Contamination One. Everyone else, move away from the patient . . ." They were doing so already, Conway could see, with a degree of haste that verged on panic. "Beings already wearing protective suits stand clear, unprotected oxygen-breathers go to the pressure litter and as many as possible seal yourselves inside. Everyone else should use the breathing masks and oxygen supplies for the ward ventilators. We seem to be affected by some kind of airborne infection—"

He broke off as the observation ward's main screen flicked on to show the features of the irate Chief Psychologist. As O'Mara spoke Conway could hear in the background the repeated long and two short blasts on the emergency siren, which gave added urgency to the words.

"Conway, why the blazes are you reporting lethal contamination down there? Dammit, there can't be a lethal contamination of air and water unless the place is flooded and you're all drowning, and I see no evidence of that!"

"Wait," said Conway. He was kneeling by the fallen transfer team-member, his hand inside the open visor, feeling for a pulse at the temporal artery. He found it, a fast, irregular beat that he did not like at all. Then he sealed the man's visor quickly and went on speaking to the ward: "Remember to close any breathing orifices not covered by your masks, nostrils, Melfan gills, the Kelgian speaking mouth. And you, the protected Illensan doctor, will you check Thornnastor and the Melfan Edanelt, quickly please. Prilicla, how is the original patient?"

The chlorine-breather waddled rapidly towards the fallen Thornnastor, its transparent suit rustling. "My name is Gilvesh, Conway. But all DBDGs look the same to me, so I suppose I should not feel insulted."

"Sorry, Gilvesh," said Conway. The chlorine-breathing Illensans were generally held to be the most visually repulsive species in the Federation as well as the most vain regarding their own physical appearance. "A snap diagnosis, please. There isn't time for anything else. What happened to it, and what are the immediate physiological effects?"

"Friend Conway," said Prilicla, still trembling violently, "the DBPK patient is feeling much better. It is radiating confusion and worry, but no fear and minimum physical discomfort. The condition of the other four concerns me deeply, but their emotional radiation is too faint to identify because of the high level of emotion pervading the ward."

"I understand," said Conway, who knew that the little empath could never bring itself to criticize, however mildly, another being's emotional shortcomings. "Attention, everyone. Apart from the four people already affected there is no immediate sign of the condition, infection, whatever it is, spreading. I would say that anyone protected by the pressure litter envelope or breathing through a mask is safe for the time being. And calm yourselves, please. We need Prilicla to help with a quick diagnosis on your colleagues, and it can't work if the rest of you are emoting all over the place."

While Conway was still speaking, Prilicla detached itself from the ceiling and fluttered across on its iridescent wings to the heap of silvery fur that was the Kelgian theater nurse. It withdrew its scanner and began a physical examination concurrent with its efforts to detect, isolate and identify the creature's emotional radiation. It was no longer trembling.

"No response to physical stimuli," Gilvesh reported from its examination of Thornnastor. "Temperature normal, breathing labored, cardiac action weak and irregular, eyes still react to light, but . . . This is strange, Conway. Obviously the lungs have been seriously affected, but the mechanism is unclear, and the curtailed supply of oxygen is affecting the heart and brain. I can find no signs of lung-tissue damage of the kind associated with the inhalation of corrosive or highly toxic material, nor anything to suggest that its immune system has been triggered off. There is no muscular tension or resistance; the voluntary muscles appear to be completely relaxed."

Using his scanner without unsealing the lightweight suit, Conway had examined the team-member's upper respiratory tract, trachea, lungs and heart with exactly similar results. But before he could say anything, Prilicla joined in: "My patient displays similar symptoms, friend Conway," it said. "Shallow and irregular respiration, cardiac condition close to fibrillation, deepening unconsciousness and all the physical and emotional signs of asphyxiation. Shall I check Edanelt?"

"I'll do that," said Gilvesh quickly. "Prilicla, move clear lest I walk on you. Conway, in my opinion they require intensive-care therapy as soon as possible, and a breathing assist at once."

"I agree, friend Gilvesh," the empath said as it fluttered up to the ceiling again. "The condition of all four beings is extremely grave."

"Right," Conway agreed briskly. "Team Leader! Move your man, the DBLF and the ELNT clear and as far from the patient as possible, but close to an oxygen supply outlet. Doctor Gilvesh will supervise fitting the proper breathing masks, but keep your team-member sealed up, with his suit air supply at fifty percent oxygen. Regarding Thornnastor, you'll need the rest of your team to move—"

"Or an anti-gravity sled," the Team Leader broke in. "There's one on the next level."

"—it even a few yards," Conway went on. "Considering its

worsening condition, it would be better to rig an extension to an oxygen line and assist Thornnastor's breathing where it is lying. And, Team Leader, do not leave the ward for a sled or anything else until we know exactly what it is that is loose in here. That goes for everyone . . . Excuse me."

O'Mara was refusing to remain silent any longer. "So there *is* something loose in there, Doctor?" said the Chief Psychologist harshly. "Something much worse, seemingly, than a simple case of atmospheric contamination from an adjacent ward? Have you finally discovered the exception that proves the rule, a bug that attacks across the species' lines?"

"I know Earth-human pathogens cannot affect e-ts, and vice versa," Conway said impatiently, turning to the ward screen to face O'Mara. "It is supposed to be impossible, but the impossible seems to be happening, and we need help to—"

"Friend Conway," Prilicla broke in, "Thornnastor's condition is deteriorating steadily. I detect feelings of constriction, strangulation."

"Doctor," the translated voice of Gilvesh joined in, "the Kelgian's oxygen mask isn't doing much good. The DBLF double mouth and lack of muscle control is posing problems. Positive pressure ventilation of the lungs with direct access through the trachea is indicated to avoid a complete respiratory failure."

"Can you perform a Kelgian tracheotomy, Doctor Gilvesh?" Conway asked, turning away from the screen. He could not think of anything to do to help Thornnastor.

"Not without a tape," Gilvesh replied.

"No tape," said O'Mara firmly, "or anything else."

Conway swung round to face the image of the Chief Psychologist to protest, but he already knew what O'Mara was going to say.

"When you raised the lethal contamination alarm, Doctor," the Chief Psychologist went on grimly, "you acted instinctively, I should think, but correctly. By so doing you have probably saved the lives of thousands of beings inside the hospital. But a Contamination One alarm means that your area is isolated until the cause of the contamination has been traced and neutralized. In this case it is much more serious. There seems to be a bug loose that could decimate the hospital's warm-blooded oxygen-breathers. For that reason your ward has been sealed off. Power, light, communication and translation facilities are available, but you are no longer connected to the main air supply system or to the automatic food distribution network, nor will you receive medical consumables of any kind. Neither will any person, mechanism or specimen for analysis be allowed out of your area. In short, Doctor Gilvesh will not be allowed to come to me for a DBLF physiology tape, nor will any Kelgian, Melfan or Tralthan doctor be allowed to volunteer to go to the aid of the affected beings. Do you understand, Doctor?"

Conway nodded slowly.

O'Mara's craggy features showed a deep and uncharacteristic concern as he stared at Conway for several seconds. It was said that O'Mara's normally abrasive and sarcastic manner was reserved only for his friends, with whom he liked to relax and be his bad-tempered self, and that he was quiet and sympathetic only when he was professionally concerned about someone.

He has an awful lot of friends, Conway thought, *and right now I'm in trouble . . .*

"No doubt you would like to have the life-duration figures based on the residual and tanked air remaining in the ward, and the number and species of the present occupants," the Major continued. "I'll have them for you in a few minutes. And, Conway, try to come up with an answer . . ."

For several seconds Conway stared at the blank screen and told himself that there was nothing effective he could do about Thornnastor or Edanelt or the Kelgian nurse or the team-member—all of whom had suddenly switched their roles from medics to critically ill patients—without Educator tapes.

In the normal course of events Doctor Gilvesh would have taken a DBLF tape and performed a tracheotomy on the Kelgian as a matter of course, and the Illensan senior would probably have insisted on O'Mara giving it the Tralthan tape for Thornnastor and the ELNT one for Edanelt, provided the Chief Psychologist considered Gilvesh's mind stable enough to take three tapes for short-term use. But Gilvesh was not allowed to leave the ward even if its chlorine-breathing life depended on it, which it would very shortly.

Conway tried not to think about the diminishing supply of air remaining in the pressure litter, where five or six e-ts were rapidly using up the tanked oxygen; or of the other beings ranged along opposing walls who were connected to breathing masks intended for patients; or of the four-hour supply carried by the transfer team-members and himself, or of the air in the ward, which was infected and unusable, or even of the strictly limited amount of breathable chlorine carried by Gilvesh, or of the superheated atmosphere re-quired by the TLTU. He had to think of the patients first, he told himself clinically, and try to keep them alive as long as possible. He would do this not because they were his friends and colleagues, but because they had been the first to be stricken and he had to chart the course of the infection as completely as possible so that the hospital medics of all grades and specialties would know exactly what they would have to fight.

But the fight would have to start here in the observation ward, and there were a few things Conway could do, or try to do.

"Gilvesh," he finally said, "go to the TLTU parked in the corner and the Hudlar on the mask beside it. I don't know if their trans-lators can receive me at this distance. Ask them if they will move Thornnastor to the clear area of wall beside the lock entrance. If they can do it, warn them that Tralthans must not be rolled onto their backs under normal gravity conditions, since this causes or-ganic displacement, which would increase its respiratory difficulties, and ask one of the transfer team to hold Thorny's mask in position while it is being moved.

"When it is at the wall," Conway went on, "position it with its legs pointing away from the wall and ask four team members to . . ."

While he talked Conway was thinking of all the Educator tapes he had had to digest during his career at Sector General and that, in a few cases, erasure had not been complete. None of the weird and wonderful personalities who had donated their brain recordings had remained, even in part, in his memory because that could have been psychologically dangerous. But there were odds and ends of data, pertaining chiefly to physiology and surgical procedures, which he had retained, because the Earth-human part of his mind had been particularly interested in them while the e-t personality had been in charge. The action he was considering taking with regard to the Kelgian theater nurse was dangerous—he had only the va-guest of memories regarding DBLF physiology in the respiratory tract area—and probably unprofessional. But first he had to do something for Thornnastor, even if it was little more than a first-aid measure.

The TLTU medic, whose race existed in an environment of edible minerals and superheated steam, had a protective suit that resembled a spherical pressure boiler bristling with remote handling devices and mounted on caterpillar treads. The vehicle had not been designated to move unconscious Tralthans, but it was quite capable of doing so.

The Hudlar doctor, classification FROB, was a blocky, pear-shaped being whose home planet pulled four Earth gravities and had a high-density atmosphere so rich in suspended animal and vegetable nutrients that it resembled thick soup. Although the FROB life-form was warm-blooded and technically an oxygen-breather, it could go for long periods without air if its food supply, which it absorbed directly through its thick but highly porous tegument, was adequate. The Hudlar's last meal had been sprayed on less than two hours earlier, Conway estimated, judging by the flaking condition of its covering of nutrient paint. It should be able to do without the oxygen mask long enough to help Thornnastor.

"... While they're moving Thornnastor," Conway went on, speaking to the transfer team leader, "have your men move the pressure litter as close as possible to the Kelgian nurse. There is another Kelgian, a Diagnostician, inside the litter. Ask it if it would direct me while I try to do the tracheotomy, and make sure it has a good view of the operation through the envelope of the litter. I'll be there in a few minutes, as soon as I check on Edanelt."

"Edanelt's condition is stable, friend Conway," reported Prilicla, who was keeping well clear of the Hudlar and the hissing metal juggernaut of the TLTU, who were moving Thornnastor. It made a feather-light landing on the Melfan's carapace for a closer feel of Edanelt's emotional radiation. "It is breathing with difficulty but is in no immediate danger."

Of the three e-ts affected, it had been the farthest away from the DBPK casualty—which should mean something. Conway shook his head angrily. Too much was happening at once. He was not being given a chance to *think* ...

"Friend Conway," called Prilicla, who had moved to the DBPK

casualty. "I detect feelings of increasing discomfort not associated with its injuries—feelings of constraint. It is also extremely worried, but not fearful, about something. The feeling is of intense guilt and concern. Perhaps, in addition to the injuries sustained in its ship, there is a history of psychological disturbance of the type common to certain preadolescents . . ."

The mental state of the DBPK survivor was low on Conway's order of priorities right then, and there was no way he could conceal his impatience from Prilicla.

"May I ease its physical restraints, friend Conway?" the empath ended quickly.

"Yes, just don't let it loose," Conway replied, then felt stupid as soon as he finished speaking.

The small, furry, utterly inoffensive being did not represent a physical threat—it was the pathogens it carried that provided the danger, and they were already loose. But when Prilicla's fragile pipe-stem manipulators touched the buttons that reduced the tightness of the restraining webbing holding the DBPK to the examination table, it did not try to escape. Instead it moved itself carefully until it lay like a sleeping Earth cat, curled up with its head pushed underneath its long and furry tail, looking like a mound of striped fur except for the bare patch at the root of its tail where the skin showed pinkish brown.

"It feels much more comfortable now, but is still worried, friend Conway," the Cinrusskin reported. Then it scuttled across the ceiling towards Thornnastor's position, trembling slightly because the unconscious Diagnostician was experiencing strong emotions.

The TLTU had taped Thornnastor's rear legs together, then withdrawn to enable the Hudlar and four team-members to do their work. With one man each grasping a middle or forward leg, they strained to pull them diagonally apart so as to expand the Tralthan's chest as much as possible. The Hudlar was saying, "Pull together. Harder. Hold it. Let go." When it said "let go" the legs resumed their natural position while simultaneously the Hudlar pressed on Thornnastor's massive rib-cage with its own not inconsiderable weight to ensure that the lungs were deflated before the process was repeated. Behind the visors of the men tugging on Thornnastor's legs were faces deep red and shining with perspiration, and some of the things they were saying were not suitable for translation.

Every medic, orderly and maintenance man in Sector General was taught the rudiments of first aid as it applied to members of the species that made up the Galactic Federation—those, that is, whose environmental requirements were not so exotic that only another member of their race could aid them without delay. The instructions for giving artificial respiration to a Tralthan FGLI was to tie the rear legs together and open and close the other four so as to suck air into the FGLI's lungs. Thornnastor's mask was in position, and it was being forced to breathe pure oxygen. Prilicla was available to report any change in its condition.

But a Kelgian tracheotomy was most decidedly not a first-aid measure. Except for a thin-walled, narrow casing that housed the brain, the DBLF species had no bone structure. The DBLF body was composed of an outer cylinder of musculature, which, in addition to being its primary means of locomotion, protected the vital organs within it. The Kelgian life-form was dangerously susceptible to lethal injury, because the complex and highly vulnerable circulatory system that fed those great bands of encircling muscle ran close under the skin and was protected only by its thick fur. An injury that most other species would consider superficial could cause a Kelgian to bleed to death in minutes. Conway's problem was that the Kelgian trachea was deeply buried under the neck muscles and passed within half an inch of the main artery and vein, which carried the blood supply to and from the brain.

With an Earth-human surgeon operating to the verbal instructions of another Kelgian, and hampered by the lack of a DBLF physiology tape and suit gauntlets, the procedure promised to be both difficult and dangerous.

"I would prefer," the Kelgian Diagnostician announced, its face pressed against the transparent wall of the pressure litter, "to perform this operation myself, Doctor."

Conway did not reply, because they both knew that if the Diagnostician left the litter it would be open to the air of the ward and whatever form of infection it contained, as would the other occupants of the litter. Instead, he began removing a narrow patch of fur from the Kelgian nurse's neck while Gilvesh sterilized the area.

"Try not to shave off too much fur, Doctor," said the Kelgian

Diagnostician, who had given its name as Towan. "It will not grow again on an adult and the condition of its fur is of great psychological importance to a Kelgian, particularly in premating approaches to the opposite sex."

"I *know* that," said Conway.

As he worked Conway found that some of the memories he retained from the Kelgian physiology tapes were trustworthy, while many others were not. He was very glad of the voice from the litter, which kept him from going disastrously wrong. During the fifteen minutes it took to perform the operation, Towan fumed and fretted and poured out a constant stream of instruction, advice and warnings, which at times were indistinguishable from personal insults—the fellow-feeling among Kelgians was very strong. Then, finally, the operation and the abuse ended, and Gilvesh began preparing to connect the nurse to a ventilator while Conway walked across the ward to have a closer look at Thornnastor.

Suddenly the ward screen lit again, this time to show the faces of O'Mara and the Monitor Corps officer in charge of hospital supply and maintenance, Colonel Skempton. It was the Colonel who finally spoke.

"We have been calculating the time left to you using the air supply currently available in your ward, Doctor," he said quietly. "The people on breathing masks, provided the bug doesn't get to them through one of their other body orifices or they don't fall asleep and dislodge the masks, have about three days' supply of air. The reason for this is that the six ventilator systems in that ward each carry a ten-hour supply of oxygen as well as other gases which are of no interest to you in the current situation—nitrogen, CO_2 and the like. The transfer team-members each have a four-hour supply in their lightweight suits, providing they conserve their oxygen by resting as much as possible—"

The Colonel broke off, and Conway knew that he was staring at the four team-members who were helping the Hudlar give artificial respiration to Thornnastor; then he cleared his throat and went on: "The Kelgian, Nidian and three Earth-humans sheltering inside the litter have less than an hour's supply remaining. However, it is possible for the team-members to recharge the litter and their own suits with air from the ventilator supply as this becomes necessary.

If this is done and everyone rests as much as possible, those of you who do not succumb to the bug should still be alive in, say, thirty hours, which gives us time to—"

"What about Gilvesh and the TLTU?" said Conway sharply.

"Recharging the TLTU's life-support system is a specialist's job," Colonel Skempton replied, "and any unqualified tinkering could result in a steam explosion down there to add to your other difficulties. As for Doctor Gilvesh, you will remember that that is an observation ward for warm-blooded oxygen-breathers. There is no chlorine available. I'm sorry."

Quietly but firmly, Conway said, "We need supplies of tanked oxygen and chlorine, a nutrient paint sprayer for the Hudlar, a recharging unit for the TLTU's vehicle, and low-residue rations complete with feeding tubes, which will enable the food to be taken without it being exposed to the air of the ward. With the exception of the TLTU's recharger—and I'm sure the team leader would be capable of handling that job if he had step-by-step instructions from one of the maintenance engineers—these items are not bulky. You could move them through the AUGL section and into our lock chamber with probably less trouble than it took getting the DBPK casualty here."

Skempton shook his head. Just as quietly and firmly he said, "We considered that method of supplying you, Doctor. But we noticed that your lock chamber was left open after the casualty was taken in, and as a result the chamber has been open to contamination for the same period as the rest of the ward. If the lock was cycled to enable us to load it with the needed supplies, water would be drawn in from the AUGL section. When your people pumped out the water to retrieve those supplies, that water, infected with whatever it is that is loose in there, would be returned to the AUGL section, with results we cannot even guess at. I have been told by a number of your colleagues, Doctor, that airborne bacteria can frequently survive and propagate in water.

"Your ward must remain in strict quarantine, Doctor," the Colonel added. "A pathogen that attacks the life-forms not only of its own planet but of four other off-planet species cannot be allowed to get loose. You must realize that as well as I do."

Conway nodded. "There is a possibility that we are overreacting, frightening ourselves unnecessarily because of—"

"A Tralthan FGLI, a Kelgian DBLF, a Melfan ELNT and an Earth-human DBDG became ill to the extent of requiring a mechanical assist with their breathing within a matter of minutes," the Colonel broke in. His expression as he looked at Conway was that of a doctor trying to tell a terminal patient that there was no hope.

Conway felt his face growing red. When he continued he tried to hold his voice steady so as not to appear to be pleading for the impossible. "The effects observed in the ward are totally unlike those experienced on board the *Rhabwar*. We handled and worked with the casualty and a number of DBPK cadavers without suffering any ill effects—"

"Perhaps some Earth-human DBDGs are naturally immune," Skempton broke in. "As far as the hospital is concerned, that is a small consolation."

"Doctor Prilicla and Nurse Naydrad also worked with the DBPKs," said Conway, "unprotected."

"I see," said the Colonel thoughtfully. "A Kelgian in the ward succumbs while another Kelgian on board the *Rhabwar* escapes. Perhaps there are naturally immune individuals in more than one species, and the *Rhabwar* personnel are fortunate. They, also, are forbidden contact with the hospital or other vessels in the area, although the problem of keeping them supplied is simple compared with yours. But we have thirty hours to work on that one if you conserve your air and—"

"By that time," said the TLTU in unemotional translated tones, "my air will have condensed into water and I shall have long since perished from hypothermia."

"I also," said Gilvesh, without taking its attention from the air hose it was connecting to the Kelgian nurse's neck, "and the bug you are all worried about would not even be interested in a chlorine-breather."

Conway shook his head angrily. "The point I'm trying to make is that we don't know anything at all about this bug."

"Don't you think, Doctor," said O'Mara, in a tone that had the incisive quality of the scalpel Conway had been wielding so recently, "it is high time you found out something about it?"

A long silence followed, while Conway felt his face growing hotter. Then the quiet was diluted by the Hudlar's voice as it directed the transfer team-members in their attempt to make Thornnastor breathe. Conway said sheepishly, "Things *were* a bit hectic for a while, and Thornnastor's analyzer is designed for Tralthan appendages, but I'll see what I can do with it."

"The sooner," said O'Mara caustically, "the better."

Conway disregarded the Chief Psychologist's tone, because O'Mara knew very well what had been happening in the ward and a display of hurt feelings would only waste time. Whatever ultimately happened to the people trapped in the ward, Conway thought, the rest of the warm-blooded oxygen-breathers in the hospital had to be given as much data as possible about the problem, including background information.

As he moved to Thornnastor's analyzer and started studying the Tralthan control console, Conway began to talk. He described for the people in the ward and the many others outside the search for survivors among the widely scattered wreckage of the DBPK vessel. No doubt Captain Fletcher could, and eventually would, give a more detailed description of the incident, but Conway was concerning himself solely with the medical and physiological aspects.

"The analyzer looks more fearsome than it really is," Murchison's voice explained at one point when he began looking, and feeling, baffled. "The labeled studs have been replaced by tactually coded pads, but the console is organized exactly the same as the one on the *Rhabwar*. I've helped Thorny use that thing on a few occasions. The displays are in Tralthan, of course, but the audio unit is linked to the translator. The air-sample flasks are kept behind the sliding blue panel."

"Thank you," said Conway with feeling, then went on talking about the rescue of the DBPK survivor and the examination and observations that followed. At the same time he cracked the valves of the sample flasks and resealed them after the ward's infection-laden atmosphere rushed in to fill their vacuums. He took samples from distances of a few inches from the patient out to the entry lock at the other end of the ward. Using a suction probe, he took samples from the patient's fur and underlying skin, and surface scrapings from the examination table, used instruments and the ward floor and walls. Then he had to break off to ask Murchison how to load the samples into the analyzer.

Gilvesh used the pause in the narrative to report that the Kelgian nurse's breathing was deep and steady, even though it was the mechanical ventilator that was actually doing the breathing. Prilicla said that Edanelt's condition remained stable as did Thornnastor's, but at a dangerously low level.

"Get on with it, Conway," O'Mara ordered harshly. "Practically every off-duty medic in the hospital is looking and listening in."

Conway resumed his account of the rescue and retrieval of the injured survivor and the transfer of the cadavers into the *Rhabwar*'s ward, stressing the fact that once inside the ship none of the crew or medical personnel wore masks while handling or examining the single living and several dead DBPKs. Because the survivor remained unconscious and its condition had been deteriorating steadily, the decision had been taken not to prolong the search for other possible survivors. The survey and Cultural Contact cruiser *Descartes* was asked to continue searching the area in case—

"You did *what*?" Colonel Skempton broke in. His face had turned to a sickly gray color.

"The *Descartes* was asked to continue the search of the area for other survivors," Conway replied, "and to gather and study the alien material, books, pictures, personal possessions and so on among the wreckage that might help them understand the new life-form prior to making formal contact. The *Descartes* is one of the few vessels possessing the equipment capable of analyzing the movements of widely dispersed wreckage and of deriving a rough approximation of the wrecked ship's original hyperspatial heading from them. You know the drill, Colonel. The policy in these cases is to backtrack and make contact with the survivor's world as quickly as possible and, if they have been able to find it, to request assistance of a doctor of its own species—"

He broke off because the Colonel was no longer listening to him.

"Priority hypersignal, maximum power," the Colonel was saying to someone off-screen. "Use hospital standby power to boost the service generator. Tell the *Descartes* not, repeat not, to take on board any alien artifacts, technical material or organic specimens from the wreckage. If any such material has already been taken on board they are to jettison it forthwith. On no account is the *Descartes* to seek out and make contact with the wreck's planet of origin, nor is the ship to make physical contact with any other vessel, base, satellite station or subplanetary or planetary body, inhabited or otherwise. They are to proceed at once to Sector General to await further instructions. Radio contact only is allowed. They are expressly forbidden to enter the hospital docking area, and their crew-members will stay on board and will allow no visitors of any species until further notice. Code the signal Federation Emergency. *Move!*"

The Colonel turned to look at Conway again, then continued. "This bug, bacterium, virus, whatever it is, affects warm-blooded oxygen-breathers and perhaps other life-forms as well. As you very well know, Doctor, three-quarters of the citizens of the Federation are warm-blooded oxygen-breathers, with the biggest proportion of those made up of the Kelgian, Tralthan, Melfan and Earth-human life-forms. We stand a good chance of containing the infection here, and of discovering something that might enable us to combat it. But if it hits the *Descartes* it could sweep through the ship so rapidly that they might not be given time to think about the problem, really think it through, before shooting out a distress beacon. Then the ship or ships that go to their aid will carry the infection home—or worse, to other ports of call. An epidemic on such a scale would certainly mean the end of the Federation, and almost certainly the end of civilization on a great many of its worlds.

"We can only hope that the *Descartes* gets the message in time," he added grimly. "With the hospital standby reactor boosting the output of the Corps transmitter, if they don't hear it they have to be deaf, dumb and blind."

"Or very sick," O'Mara observed quietly.

A long silence followed and was broken by the respectful voice of Captain Fletcher.

"If I might make a suggestion, Colonel," he said, "we know the position of the wreckage and of the *Descartes,* if it is still at the disaster site and, very approximately, of the sector that is likely to contain the wrecked ship's home planet. If a distress beacon is released in that area it is almost certain that it will come from the

Descartes. The *Rhabwar* could answer it, not to give assistance but to warn off any other would-be rescuers."

Obviously the Colonel had forgotten about the ambulance ship. "Are you still connected to the hospital by boarding tube, Captain?" he asked harshly.

"Not since the contamination alert," Fletcher replied. "But if you approve the suggestion we'll need power and consumables for an extended trip. Normally an ambulance ship is gone only for a couple of days at most."

"Approved, and thank you, Captain," said the Colonel. "Arrange for the material to be placed outside your airlock as soon as possible. Your men can load the stores on board later so as to avoid contact with hospital personnel."

Conway had been dividing his attention between the conversation and the analyzer, which looked as if it was about to make a pronouncement. He looked up at the screen and protested: "Colonel, Captain, you can't do that! If you take the *Rhabwar* away we lose Pathologist Murchison and the DBPK specimens, and remove any chance we have of quickly identifying and neutralizing this thing. She is the only pathologist here with first-hand experience of the life-form."

The Colonel looked thoughtful for a moment. "That is a valid objection, Doctor, but consider. There is no dearth of pathologists here at the hospital to help you study the live specimen, even second-hand, and the DBPK cadavers on the *Rhabwar* are staying there. We can contain and, in time, devise some method of treating this disease at the hospital. But the *Rhabwar* could be instrumental in keeping the *Descartes* from infecting the warm-blooded oxygen-breathers of dozens of planets. The original order stands. The *Rhabwar* will refuel and replenish and stand by to answer the expected distress signal from the *Descartes* . . ."

He had a lot more to say on the subject of probable future history, including the strong probability of having to place the DBPK patient's home planet and off-world colonies in strict quarantine and to refuse all contact with the new species. The Federation would have to enforce this quarantine in its own defense, and the result might well lead to interstellar war. Then, abruptly, the sound cut out, although it was obvious that Colonel Skempton was still talking to someone off-screen—someone, it was obvious, who was objecting to the *Rhabwar*'s imminent departure as strongly as Conway had.

But the objector, or objectors, was a medical staff-member concerned with solving what was essentially a unique medical problem in extraterrestrial physiology or pharmacology, while Colonel Skempton, like the dedicated Monitor Corps policeman that he was, wanted only to protect a frighteningly large number of innocent bystanders from he knew not what.

Conway looked over at the image of O'Mara. "Sir, I agree that there is the most fearful danger of letting loose a virulent infection that could bring about the collapse of the Federation and cause the technology of many of its individual worlds to slide back into their particular dark ages. But before we react we must first know something about the threat we are reacting against. We must stop and think. Right now we are overreacting and not thinking at all. Could you speak to the Colonel sensibly, sir, and point out to him that a panic reaction frequently does more harm than—"

"Your colleagues are already doing that," the Chief Psychologist replied dryly, "much more forcibly and persuasively than I could, so far without success. But if you feel that we are all guilty of a panic reaction, Doctor, perhaps you will demonstrate the kind of calm, logical reasoning that you think this problem demands?"

Why, you sarcastic . . . Conway raged silently. But before he could speak there was an interruption. Thornnastor's analyzer was displaying bright, incomprehensible symbols on its screen and vocalizing its findings through the translator link.

Analysis of samples one through fifty-three taken in Observation Ward One, AUGL Level, it began tonelessly. *General observations: All atmosphere samples contain oxygen, nitrogen and the usual trace elements in the normal proportions, also small quantities of carbon dioxide, water vapor and chlorine associated with the acceptable levels of leakage from the TLTU life-support system and the Illensan protective suit, and from the expired breaths of the DBDG, DBLF, ELNT, FGLI and FROB physiological types, as well as perspiration from the first, second and third of these types. Also present are the phenomes associated with the body odors of the species present who are not wearing overall body protection envelopes, including a hitherto unlisted set,* which, by elimination, belongs to the DBPK patient. There are very small quantities of dusts, flakings and fibers abraded from walls, working surfaces and instruments. Some of this material cannot be analyzed without a larger sampling, but it is biochemically inert and harmless. There are also present follicles of Earth-human hair, Kelgian and DBPK fur, flakes of discarded Hudlar nutrient paint, and scales from Tralthan and Melfan tegument.

Conclusion: None of the gases, dusts, colloidal suspensions, bacteria or viruses found in these samples are harmful to any oxygen-breathing life-form.

Without realizing it Conway had been holding his breath, and the inside of his visor misted over briefly as he released it in a short, heavy sigh of disappointment. Nothing. The analyzer could not find anything harmful in the ward.

"I'm waiting, Doctor," said O'Mara.

Conway looked slowly around the ward, at Thornnastor still undergoing artificial respiration, at the Kelgian theater nurse and the spread-eagled Melfan, at the silent Gilvesh and the TLTU hissing quietly in a corner, at the crowded pressure litter and at the beings of several different classifications attached to breathing masks—and found them all looking at him. He thought desperately: Something is loose in here. Something that did not show up in the samples or that the analyzer had classified as harmless anyway. Something that had been harmless, on board the Rhabwar . . .

Aloud, he said, "On the trip back to the hospital we examined and dissected several DBPK cadavers, and thoroughly examined and gave preliminary treatment to the survivor, without body protection and without suffering any ill effects. It is possible that the beings, Earth-human and otherwise, on the Rhabwar all had natural immunity, but that, to my mind, is stretching coincidence beyond its elastic limits. When the survivor was brought into the hospital, protection became necessary because four different physiological types practically dropped in their tracks. We have to ask ourselves, In what way were the circumstances aboard the ambulance ship and in the hospital different?

"We should also ask ourselves," Conway went on, "the question Pathologist Murchison asked after completing her first DBPK dissection, which was, How did a weak, timid and obviously nonaggressive life-form like this one climb to the top of its planet's evolutionary ladder and stay there long enough to develop a civilization capable of interstellar travel? The being is a herbivore. It does not even have the fingernails that are the evolutionary legacy of claws, and it appears to be completely defenseless."

"How about concealed natural weapons?" O'Mara asked. But before Conway could reply, Murchison answered for him.

"No evidence of any, sir," she said. "I paid particular attention to the furless, brownish area of skin at the base of the spine, since this was the only feature of the being's physiology that we did not understand. Both male and female cadavers possessed them. They are small mounds or swellings, four to five inches in diameter and composed of dry, porous tissue. They do not secrete anything and give the appearance of a gland or organ that is inactive or has atrophied. The patches were a uniform pale brown color on the adults. The survivor, who is a female adolescent or preadolescent, as far as we can judge, had a pale pink mound, which had been painted to match the coloration of the adult patches."

"Did you analyze the paint?" asked O'Mara.

"Yes, sir," said Murchison. "Some of it had already cracked and flaked off, probably at the time the survivor received its injuries, and we removed the rest of it while we were giving the patient a preoperative cleanup before moving it to the hospital. The paint was organically inert and chemically non-toxic. Giving regard to the patient's age, I assumed that it was a decorative paint applied for cosmetic purposes. Perhaps the young DBPK was trying to appear more adult than it actually was."

"Seems a reasonable assumption," said O'Mara. "So, we have a beastie with natural vanity and no natural weapons."

Paint, Conway thought suddenly. An idea was stirring at the back of his mind, but he could not make it take form. Something about paint, or the uses of paint, perhaps. Decoration, insulation, protection, warning . . . That must be it—the coating of inert, non-toxic, harmless paint!

He moved quickly to the instrument rack and withdrew one of the sprayers which a number of e-ts used to coat their manipulators instead of wearing surgical gloves. He tested it briefly, because its actuator had not been designed for DBDG fingers. When he was sure that he could direct the sprayer with accuracy, he moved across to the soft, furry and apparently defenseless DBPK patient.

"What the blazes are you doing, Conway?" asked O'Mara.

"In these circumstances the color of the paint should not worry the patient too much," Conway said, thinking aloud and ignoring the Chief Psychologist for the moment. He went on, "Prilicla, will you move closer to the patient, please. I feel sure there will be a marked change in its emotional radiation over the next few minutes."

"I am aware of your feelings, friend Conway," said Prilicla.

Conway laughed nervously. "In that case, friend Prilicla, I feel *fairly* sure that I have the answer. But what about the patient's feelings?"

"Unchanged, friend Conway," said the empath. "There is a general feeling of concern. It is the same feeling I detected shortly after it regained consciousness and recovered from its initial fear and confusion. There is deep concern, sadness, helplessness and . . . and guilt. Perhaps it is thinking about its friends who died."

"Its friends, yes," said Conway, switching on the sprayer and beginning to paint the bare area above the patient's tail with the bright red inert pigment. "It is worried about its friends who are alive."

The paint dried rapidly and set in a strong, flexible film. By the time Conway had finished spraying on a second layer the patient withdrew its head from underneath its furry tail to look at the re-painted patch of bare skin; then it turned its face to Conway and regarded him steadily with its two large, soft eyes. Conway restrained an impulse to stroke its head.

Prilicla made an excited trilling noise, which did not translate, then said, "The patient's emotional radiation shows a marked change, friend Conway. Instead of deep concern and sadness, the predominant emotion is one of intense relief."

That, thought Conway with great feeling, is *my own predominant feeling at the moment.* Aloud, he announced, "That's it, everyone. The contamination emergency is over."

They were all staring at him, and their feelings were so intense and mixed that Prilicla was clinging to the ceiling and shaking as if caught in an emotional gale. Colonel Skempton's face had disappeared from the screen, so it was the craggy features of O'Mara alone glaring out at him.

"Conway," said the Chief Psychologist harshly, "explain."

He began his explanation by requesting a playback of the sound and vision record of the DBPK's treatment from the point a few minutes before it fully regained consciousness. While they were watching Thornnastor, the Kelgian theater nurse and the Melfan Edanelt, who had moved back a short distance to check the patient's air line, Conway said, "The reason why nobody on board the *Rhabwar* was affected during the trip here was that at no time was the patient conscious. Now, the three attending physicians may or may not be handsome to other members of their respective species, but a being, an immature being at that, confronted with them for the first time might well find them visually quite horrendous. Under the circumstances the patient's fear and panic reaction are understandable, but pay particular attention to the physical response to what, for a few seconds, it regarded as a physical threat.

"The eyes opened wide," he continued as the scene unfolded on the main screen, "the body stiffened and the chest expanded. A fairly normal reaction, you'll agree. An initial moment of paralysis followed by hyperventilation so that as much oxygen as possible is available in the lungs either to scream for help or to drive the muscles for a quick getaway. But our attention was concentrated on what was happening to the three attending physicians and the affected team-member, so that we did not notice that the patient's chest remained expanded for several minutes, that it was, in fact, holding its breath."

On the screen Thornnastor toppled heavily to the floor, the Kelgian nurse collapsed into a limp heap of fur, Edanelt's bony undershell clicked loudly against the floor, the transfer team-member also collapsed and everyone else who was unprotected headed for the pressure litter or the breathing masks. "The effects of this so-called bug," Conway went on, "were sudden and dramatic. Respiratory failure or partial failure and collapse, and clear indications that the voluntary and involuntary muscle systems had been affected. But there was no rise in body temperature, which would be expected if the beings concerned were fighting an infection. If infection is ruled out, then the DBPK life-form was not as defenseless as it looked . . ."

To be the dominant life-form on its planet, the DBPKs had to have some means of defending themselves, Conway explained. Or more accurately, the beings who really needed it had a means of defense. Probably the adult DBPKs were mentally agile enough to avoid trouble and to protect their young when they were small and easily carried. But when the children grew too large for their parents to protect and were as yet too inexperienced to protect themselves, they had evolved a means of defense that was effective against everything that lived and breathed.

When threatened by natural enemies, the young DBPKs released a gas—which resembled in its effects the old Earth-snake venom curare, with the rapidity of action of some of the later nerve gases— so that the enemy's breathing stopped and it was no longer a threat. But it was a two-edged weapon in that it was capable of knocking out everything that breathed oxygen, including the DBPKs themselves. However, the event that triggered the release of the gas also caused the being concerned to hold its breath, which indicated that the toxic material had a complex and unstable molecular structure that broke down and became harmless within a few moments of release, although by that time the natural enemy was no longer a threat.

"With the rise of civilization and the coming of cities, leading to large numbers of the beings of all age groups living closely together, the defense mechanism of the DBPK children became a dangerous embarrassment. A suddenly frightened child, reacting instinctively, could inadvertently kill members of its own family, passers-by in the street or classmates in school. So the organ that released the gas was painted over and sealed until the child reached maturity and the organ became inactive." *There were probably psychological or sociological reasons,* Conway thought, *why the active organs were painted to resemble those of a 'safe' adult.*

"But the patient is a preadolescent of a race that has star travel, and it would expect to see alien life forms," Conway continued, turning away from the screen as the recording flicked off. "It reacted instinctively because of weakness and physical injury, and almost immediately realized what it had done. Judging by Prilicla's emotion readings, it felt guilty, was desperately sorry for what it had done to some of the friends who had rescued it, and was helpless because it could not warn us of the continuing danger. Now it has been rendered safe again and it is relieved, and judging by its emotional reaction to this situation, I would say that these are nice people—"

Conway broke off as the screen lit again to show the faces of both Colonel Skempton and Major O'Mara. The Colonel looked flustered and embarrassed and he kept his eyes on something he was holding off-screen as he spoke.

"We have received a signal from the *Descartes* within the past few minutes. It reads: *I am disregarding your recent signal. DBPK home planet located and first-contact procedure well advanced. Content of your signal suggests that survivor is a preadolescent DBPK and you are having problems. Warning, do not treat this being without using face masks or light protective suits, or move into the vicinity of the being without similar protection. If precautions have not been taken and hospital personnel are affected, they must be given immediate mechanical assistance with breathing for a period of two-plus hours, after which breathing will resume normally with no aftereffects. This is a natural weapon of defense possessed only by young DBPKs, and the mechanism will be explained to you when the two DBPK medics arrive. They should arrive within four hours in the scoutship* Torrance *to check on the survivor and bring it home. They are also very interested in the multienvironmental hospital idea and have asked permission to return to Sector General for a while to study and . . ."*

All at once it became impossible to hear the Colonel's voice or the *Descartes'* message because Doctor Gilvesh was shouting at Conway and pointing at the Kelgian nurse, whose fur was rippling in frustration because its tracheotomy tube was keeping it from vocalizing. A transfer team-member was also calling to him because Thornnastor was trying to climb to its six elephantine feet while complaining loudly at the indignity of it all. The affected Melfan was also up off the floor and loudly demanding to know what had happened; the Hudlar was shouting that it was hungry; and everyone who had been in the pressure litter began crawling out. The people who had been using masks had discarded them, and they were all trying to make themselves heard to Conway or each other.

Conway swung around to look at the DBPK, suddenly afraid of what the mounting bedlam might be doing to it. There was no longer any danger of their being knocked out by its panic reaction because of the painting exercise he had carried out a few minutes earlier, but the poor thing might be frightened out of its wits.

The DBPK was looking around the ward with its large, soft eyes, but it was impossible to read any expression on its furry, triangular face. Then Prilicla dropped from the ceiling to hover a few inches from Conway's ear.

"Do not feel concern, friend Conway," said the little empath. "Its predominant feeling is curiosity . . ."

Very faintly above the hubbub Conway could hear the series of long blasts on a siren signaling the Contamination All Clear.

PART 4

RECOVERY

The two Dwerlan DBPK medics arrived to collect their casualty, but after a brief consultation, decided that the patient was receiving optimum treatment and that they would be grateful if it was allowed to remain there until it could be discharged as fully recovered in two or three weeks' time. Meanwhile, the two visiting medics, whose language had been programed into the translation computer, wandered all over the engineering and medical miracle that was Sector Twelve General Hospital, carrying their tails erect in furry question marks of excitement and pleasure—except, of course, when those large and expressive members were squeezed inside protective suits for environmental reasons.

Several times they visited the ambulance ship, initially to thank the officers and medical team on the *Rhabwar* for saving the young Dwerlan, who had been the only survivor of the disaster to its ship, and later to talk about their impressions of the hospital or of their home world of Dwerla and its four thriving colonies. The visits were welcome breaks in the monotony of what, for the personnel of the *Rhabwar,* had become an extended period of self-education.

At least, that was how the Chief Psychologist described the series of lectures and drills and technical demonstrations that would occupy them for the next few months, unless a distress call was received before then.

"When the ship is in dock you will spend your on-duty time on board," O'Mara had told Conway during one brief but not particularly pleasant interview, "until you have satisfied yourselves, and me, that you are completely familiar with every aspect of your new duty—the ship, its systems and equipment, and something of the specialties of its officers. As much, at least, as they will be expected to learn about your specialty. Right now, and in spite of having to answer two distress calls in as many weeks, you are still ignorant.

"Your first mission resulted in considerable inconvenience to yourselves," he had gone on sourly, "and the second in a near panic for the hospital. But neither job could be called a challenge either to your extraterrestrial medical skill or Fletcher's e-t engineering expertise. The next mission may not be so easy, Conway. I suggest you prepare yourselves for it by learning to act together as a team, and not by fighting continually to score points like two opposing teams. And don't bang the door on your way out."

And so it was that the *Rhabwar* became a shipshaped classroom and laboratory in which the ship's officers lectured on their specialties in as much detail as they considered mere medical minds could take, and the medical team tried to teach them the rudiments of e-t physiology. Because so many of the lectures had to give a general, rather than a too narrowly specialized, treatment of their subjects, it was usually the Captain or Conway who delivered them. With the exception of the watch-keeping officer on duty in Control—and he could look and listen in and ask questions—all the ship's officers were present at the medical lectures.

On this occasion Conway was discussing e-t comparative physiology.

". . . Unless you are attached to a multienvironment hospital like this one," Conway was explaining to Lieutenants Haslam, Chen and Dodds, and with a brief glance at the vision pickup to include Captain Fletcher in Control, "you normally meet extraterrestrials one species at a time, and refer to them by their planet of origin. But here in the hospital and in the wrecked ships we will encounter, rapid and accurate identification of incoming patients and rescued survivors is vital, because all too often the casualties are in no fit condition to furnish physiological information about themselves. For this reason we have evolved a four-letter physiological classification system, which works like this:

"The first letter denotes the level of physical evolution," he continued. "The second letter indicates the type and distribution of limbs and sensory equipment, which in turn gives us information regarding the positioning of the brain and the other major organs. The remaining two letters refer to the combination of metabolism and gravity and/or atmospheric-pressure requirements of the being, and these are tied in with the physical mass and the protective tegument, skin, fur, scales, osseous plating and so on represented by the relevant letter.

"It is at this point during the hospital lectures," Conway said, smiling, "that we have to remind some of our e-t medical students that the initial letter of their classifications should not be allowed to give them feelings of inferiority, and that the level of physical evolution, which is, of course, an adaptation to their planetary environment, has no relation to the level of intelligence . . ."

Species with the prefix A, B or C, he went on to explain, were water-breathers. On most worlds, life had originated in the sea, and these beings had developed high intelligence without having to leave it. The letters D through F were warm-blooded oxygen-breathers, into which group fell most of the intelligent races in the Galaxy; and the G to K types were also warm-blooded but insectile. The L's and M's were light-gravity, winged beings.

Chlorine-breathing life-forms were contained in the O and P groups, and after that came the more exotic, the more highly evolved physically and the downright weird types. These included the ultra-high-temperature and frigid-blooded or crystalline beings, and entities capable of modifying their physical structures at will. Those possessing extrasensory powers sufficiently well developed to make ambulatory or manipulatory appendages unnecessary were given the prefix V, regardless of physical size or shape.

". . . There are anomalies in the system," Conway went on, "but these can be blamed on a lack of imagination by its originators. One of them was the AACP life-form, which has a vegetable metabolism. Normally, the prefix A denotes a water-breather, there being nothing lower in the system than the piscine life-forms. But then we discovered the AACPs, who were, without doubt, vegetable intelligences, and the plant came before the fish—"

"*Control here. Sorry for the interruption, Doctor.*"

"You have a question, Captain?" asked Conway.

"*No, Doctor. Instructions. Lieutenants Haslam and Dodds to Control and Lieutenant Chen to the Power Room, at once. Casualty Deck, we have a distress call, physiological classification unknown. Please ensure maximum readiness—*"

"We're always ready," said Naydrad, its fur bristling in irritation.

"*Pathologist Murchison and Doctor Conway, come to Control as soon as convenient.*"

As the three Monitor Corps officers disappeared rapidly up the ladder of the central well, Murchison said, "You realize, of course, that this means we will probably not be given the Captain's second lecture on control-system organization and identification in vessels of non-bifurcate extraterrestrials this afternoon." She laughed suddenly. "I am not an empath like Prilicla here, but I detect an overall feeling of relief."

Naydrad made an untranslatable noise, which was possibly a subdued cheer in Kelgian.

"I also feel," she went on, "that our Captain is merely being polite. He wants to see us up there as soon as possible."

"Everybody," said Prilicla as it began checking the e-t instrument packs, "wants to be an empath, friend Murchison."

They arrived in Control slightly breathless after their climb up the gravity-free well past the five intervening decks. Murchison had considerably more breath available than Conway, even though she had used a lot of it telling him that he was running to adipose and that his center of gravity was beginning to drop below his waistline—something that had not happened to the delightfully top-heavy pathologist over the years. As they straightened up, looking around the small, darkened compartment and at the intent faces lit only by indicator lights and displays, Captain Fletcher motioned them into the two supernumerary positions and waited for them to strap in before he spoke.

"We were unable to obtain an accurate fix on the distress beacon," he began without preamble, "because of distortion caused by stellar activity in the area, a small cluster whose stars are in an early and very active period of evolution. But I expect the signal has been received by other and much closer Corps installations, who will obtain a more accurate fix, which they will relay to the hospital before we make the first Jump. For this reason I intend proceeding at one instead of four-G thrust to Jump-distance, losing perhaps half an hour, in the hope of obtaining a closer fix, which would save time, a great deal of time, when we reach the disaster site. Do you understand?"

Conway nodded. On many occasions he had been awaiting a subspace radio message, usually in answer to a request for environmental information regarding a patient whose physiological type was new to the hospital, and the signal had been well-nigh unreadable because of interference from intervening stellar objects. The hospital's receptors were the equal of those used by the major Monitor Corps bases, and were hundreds of times more sensitive than any equipment mounted in a ship. If any sort of message carrying the coordinates of the distressed vessel's position was received by Sector General, it would be filtered and deloused and relayed to the ambulance ship within seconds.

Always provided, of course, that their ship had not already left normal space.

"Is anything known about the disaster area?" asked Conway, trying to hide his irritation at being treated as a complete ignoramus in all matters outside his medical specialty. "Nearby planetary systems, perhaps, whose inhabitants might have some knowledge regarding the physiology of the survivors, if any?"

"In this kind of operation," said the Captain, "I did not think there would be time to go looking for the survivors' friends."

Conway shook his head. "You'd be surprised, Captain," he said. "In the hospital's rescue experience, if the initial disaster does not kill everyone within the first few minutes, the ship's safety devices can keep the survivors alive for several hours or even days. Furthermore, unless faced with a surgical emergency, it is better and safer to institute palliative treatment on a completely strange lifeform and if it can be found, send for the being's own doctor, as we would have done with the Dwerlan casualty had its injuries been less serious. There may even be times when it is better to do nothing at all for the patient and allow its own healing processes to proceed without interruption."

Fletcher started to laugh, thought better of it when be realized that Conway was serious, then began tapping buttons on his console. In the big astrogation cube at the center of the control room there appeared a three-dimensional star chart with a fuzzy red spot at its center. There were about twenty stars in the volume of space represented by the projection, three of which were joined and enclosed by motionless swirls and tendrils of luminous material.

"That fuzzy spot," said the Captain apologetically, "should be a point of light signifying the position of the distressed ship. As it is, we know its whereabouts only to the nearest hundred million miles. The area has not been surveyed or even visited by Federation ships, because we would not expect to find inhabited systems in a star cluster that is at such an early stage in its formation. In any case, the present position of the distressed ship does not indicate that it is native to the area, unless it malfunctioned soon after Jumping. But a closer study of the probabilities—"

"What bothers me," said Murchison quickly as she sensed another highly specialized lecture coming on, "is why more of our distressed aliens are not rescued by their own people. That rarely happens."

"True, ma'am," Fletcher replied. "A few cases have been recorded where we found technologically interesting wrecks and a few odds and ends—the equivalent of e-t pin-ups, magazines, that sort of thing—but there were no dead e-ts. Their bodies and those of the survivors, if any, had been taken away. It is odd, but thus far we have found no civilized species that does not show respect for its dead. Also, do not forget that a space disaster is a fairly rare occurrence for a single star-traveling species, and any rescue mission they could mount would probably be too little and too late. But to the Galaxy-wide, multispecies Federation, space accidents are not rare. They are expected. Our reaction time to any disaster is very fast because ships like this one are constantly on standby; and so we tend to get there first.

"But we were discussing the difficulties of establishing the original course constants of a wrecked ship," the Captain went on, refusing to be sidetracked from his lecture. "First, there is the fact that a detour is frequently necessary to reach the destination system. This is because of pockets of unusual stellar density, black holes and similar normal-space obstructions that cause dangerous areas of distortion in the hyperspace medium, so very few ships are able to reach their destinations in fewer than five Jumps. Second, there are the factors associated with the size of the distressed ship and the number of its hypergenerators. A small vessel with one generator poses fewest problems. But if the ship is similar in mass to ourselves, and we carry a matched pair, or if it is a very large ship requiring four or six hypergenerators ... Well, it would then depend on whether the generators went out simultaneously or consecutively.

"Our ships and, presumably, theirs," Fletcher continued, warming to his subject, "are fitted with safety cutoffs to all generators, should one fail. But those safety devices are not always foolproof, because it takes only a split-second delay in shutting down a generator and the section of the ship structurally associated with it pops into normal space, tearing free of the rest of the vessel and in the process imparting an unbalanced braking motion, which sends the ship spinning off at a tangent to its original course. The shock to the vessel's structure would probably cause the other generator or generators to fail, and the process would be repeated, so that a series of such events occurring within a few seconds in hyperspace could very well leave the wreckage of the distressed ship strung out across a distance of several light-years. That is the reason why—"

He broke off as an attention signal flashed on his panel. "Astrogation, sir," Lieutenant Dodds announced briskly. "Five minutes to Jump."

"Sorry, ma'am," said the Captain. "We will have to continue this discussion at another time. Power Room, status report, please."

"Both hypergenerators at optimum, and output matched within the safety limits, sir," came Chen's reply.

"Life-support?"

"Systems also optimum," Chen said. "Artificial gravity on all deck levels at one-G Earth-normal setting. Zero-G in the central well, generator housings and in the Cinrusskin doctor's quarters."

"Communications?"

"Still nothing from the hospital, sir," Haslam replied.

"Very well," said the Captain. "Power Room, shut down the thrusters, and stand by to abort the Jump until minus one minute." In an aside to Murchison and Conway he explained: "During the final minute we're committed to the Jump, whether a signal comes from the hospital or not."

"Killing thrusters," said Chen. "Acceleration zero and standing by."

There was a barely detectable surge as the ship's acceleration ceased and the one-G was maintained by the deck's artificial-gravity grids. A display on the Captain's panel marked off the minutes and the seconds in a silence that was broken only by a quiet sigh from Fletcher as the figures marched into the final minute, then the final thirty seconds . . .

"Communications, sir!" said Haslam quickly. "Signal from Sector General, amended coordinates for the distress beacon. No other message."

"They certainly didn't leave themselves time for a tender farewell," said the Captain with a nervous laugh. Before he could continue, the Jump gong sounded and the ambulance ship and its occupants moved into a self-created universe where action and reaction were not equal and velocities were not limited to the speed of light.

Instinctively, Conway's eyes went to the direct-vision port and beyond it to the inner surface of the flickering gray globe that enclosed the ship. At first the surface appeared to be a featureless and absolutely smooth gray barrier, but gradually a sensation of depth, of far too much depth, became apparent and an ache grew behind his eyes as they tried to cope with the twisting, constantly changing gray perspectives.

A maintenance engineer at the hospital had once told him that in hyperspace, material things, whether their atomic or molecular building blocks were arranged into the shapes of people or hardware, had no physical existence; that it was still not clearly understood by the physicists why it was that at the conclusion of a Jump the ship, its equipment and its occupants did not materialize as a homogenous molecular stew. The fact that such a thing had never happened before, as far as the engineer knew, did not mean that it could not happen, and could the doctor suggest a really strong sedative that would keep the engineer non-existently asleep while he was Jumping home on his next leave?

Smiling to himself at the memory, Conway looked away from the twisting grayness. Inside Control the non-existent officers were concentrating all their attention on panels and displays that had no philosophical reality while they recited the esoteric litanies of their profession. Conway looked at Murchison, who nodded, and they both unstrapped and stood up.

The Captain stared at them as if he had forgotten they were there. "Naturally you will have things to do, ma'am, Doctor. The Jump will last just under two hours. If anything interesting happens I'll relay it to you on the Casualty Deck screen."

They pulled themselves aft along the ladder of the gravity-free well, and a few seconds later, staggered slightly as they stepped onto the Casualty Deck. Its one-G of artificial gravity reminded them that there was such a thing as up and down. The level was empty, but they could see the spacesuited figure of Naydrad through the airlock view panel as it stood on the wing where it joined the hull.

That particular section of wing was fitted with artificial-gravity grids to aid in the maneuvering of awkward loads into and out of the airlock, which was why the Kelgian charge nurse appeared to be standing horizontally on the, to them, vertical wall of the wing. It saw them and waved before resuming its testing of the airlock and wing exterior lighting system.

In addition to the artificial gravity holding it to the wing surface two safety lines were attached to Naydrad's suit. A person who became detached from its ship in hyperspace was lost, more utterly and completely lost than anyone could really imagine.

The Casualty Deck's equipment and medication had already been checked by Naydrad and Prilicla, but Conway was required to give everything a final checkout. Prilicla, who needed more rest than its much less fragile colleagues, was in its cabin, and Naydrad was busy outside. This meant that Conway could check their work without Prilicla pretending to ignore him and Naydrad rippling its fur in disapproval.

"I'll check the pressure litter first," said Conway.

"I'll help you," offered Murchison, "and with the ward medication stores downstairs. I'm not tired."

"As you very well know," said Conway as he opened the panel of the litter's stowage compartment, "the proper term is 'on the lower deck,' not 'downstairs.' Are you trying to give the Captain the idea that you are ignorant in everything but your own specialty?"

Murchison laughed quietly. "He seems already to have formed that idea, judging by the insufferably patronizing way he talks, or rather lectures, to me." She helped him roll out the litter, then added briskly: "Let's inflate the envelope with an inert at triple Earth-normal pressure, just in case we get a heavy-gravity casualty this time. Then we can brew up a few likely atmospheres."

Conway nodded and stepped back as the thin but immensely tough envelope ballooned outwards. Within a few seconds it had grown so taut that it resembled a thin, elongated glass dome enclosing the upper surface of the litter. The internal pressure indicator held steady.

"No leaks," Conway reported, switching on the pump that would extract and recompress the inert gas in the envelope. "We'll try the Illensan atmosphere next. Mask on, just in case."

The base of the litter had a storage compartment in which were racked the basic surgical instruments, the glove extensions that would enable treatment to be carried out on a casualty without the doctor having to enter the envelope, and general-purpose filter masks for several different physiological types. He handed a mask to Murchison and donned one himself. "I still think you should try harder to give the impression that you are intelligent as well as beautiful."

"Thank you, dear," Murchison replied, her voice muffled by the mask. She watched Conway use the mixing controls for a moment, checking that the corrosive yellow fog that was slowly filling the envelope was, in fact, identical to the atmosphere used by the chlorine-breathing natives of Illensa.

"Ten, even five years ago, that may have been true," she went on. "It was said that every time I put on a lightweight suit I upped the blood pressure, pulse and respiration rate of every non-geriatric male DBDG in the hospital. It was mostly you who said it, as I remember."

"You still have that effect on Earth-human DBDGs, believe me," said Conway, briefly offering his wrist so that she could check his pulse. "But you should concentrate on impressing the ship's officers with your intellect; otherwise, I shall have too much competition and the Captain will consider you prejudicial to discipline. Or maybe we are being a bit too unfair to the Captain. I heard one of the officers talking about him, and it seems that he was one of the Monitor Corps' top instructors and researchers in extraterrestrial engineering. When the special ambulance ship project was first proposed, the Cultural Contact people placed him first as their choice for ship commander.

"In some ways he reminds me of one of our Diagnosticians," Conway went on, "with his head stuffed so full of facts that he can only communicate in short lectures. So far, Corps discipline, the respect due his rank and professional ability have enabled him to operate effectively without interpersonal communication in depth. But now he has to learn to talk to ordinary people—people, that is, who are not subordinates or fellow officers—and sometimes he does not do a very good job of it. But he is trying, however, and we must—"

"I seem to remember," Murchison broke in, "a certain young and very new intern who was a lot like that. In fact, O'Mara still insists that this person prefers the company of his extraterrestrial colleagues to those of his own species."

"With one notable exception," Conway said smugly.

Murchison squeezed his arm affectionately and said that she could not react to that remark as she would have liked while wearing a mask and coveralls, and that it was becoming increasingly difficult to concentrate on Conway's checklist as time went on. But the high level of emotional radiation in the area was reduced suddenly by the Jump gong signaling the ship's return to normal space.

The Casualty Deck's screen remained blank, but Fletcher's voice came from the speaker a few seconds later. *"Control here. We have returned to normal space close to the position signaled by the beacon, but there is as yet no sign of a distressed ship or wreckage. However, since it is impossible to achieve pinpoint accuracy with a hyperspatial Jump, the distressed vessel could be many millions of miles away . . ."*

"He's lecturing again," Murchison sighed.

". . . but the impulses from our sensors travel at the velocity of light and are reflected back at the same speed. This means that if ten minutes elapsed before we registered a contact, the distance of the object would be half that time in seconds multiplied by the—"

"Contact, sir!"

"I stand corrected, not too many millions of miles. Very well. As-

trogation, give me the distance and course constants, please. Power Room, stand by for maximum thrust in ten minutes. Charge Nurse Naydrad, cancel your EVA immediately. Casualty Deck, you will be kept informed. Control out."

Conway returned his attention to the pressure litter, evacuating the chlorine atmosphere and replacing it with the high-pressure superheated steam breathed by the TLTU life-forms. He had begun to check the litter's thrusters and attitude controls when Naydrad slithered through the inner lock seal, its suit beaded with condensation and still radiating the cold of outside. The charge nurse watched them for a few moments, then said that if it was needed it would be in its cabin thinking beautiful thoughts.

They checked the compartment's restraints with great care. From experience Conway knew that extraterrestrial casualties were not always cooperative, and some of them could be downright aggressive when strange, to them, beings began probing them with equally strange devices of unknown purpose. For that reason the compartment was fitted with a variety of material and immaterial restraints in the forms of straps, webbing, and tractor- and pressorbeam projectors sufficient to immobilize anything up to the mass and muscle power of a Tralthan in the final stages of its premating dance. Conway devoutly hoped that the restraints would never be needed, but they were available and had to be checked.

Two hours passed before any news was forthcoming from the Captain. Then it was brief and to the point.

"Control here. We have established that the contact is not a naturally occurring interstellar body. We will close with it in seventy-three minutes."

"Time enough," said Conway, "to check the ward medication."

A section of the floor of the Casualty Deck opened downwards onto the deck below, which was divided into a ward and a combination laboratory-pharmacy. The ward was capable of accommodating ten casualties of reasonably normal mass—Earth-human size and below—and of producing a wide range of environmental life-support. In the laboratory section, which was separated from the ward by a double airlock, were stored the constituent gases and liquids used by every known life-form in the Galactic Federation and with the capability, it was hoped, of reproducing atmospheres of those yet unknown. The lab also contained sets of specialized surgical instruments capable of penetrating the tegument of and performing curative surgery on the majority of the Federation's physiological types.

The pharmacy section was stocked with the known specifics against the more common e-t diseases and abnormal conditions— in small quantities because of limitations of space—together with the basic analysis equipment common to any e-t pathology lab. All this meant that there was very little space for two people to work, but then Conway had never complained about working closely with Murchison and vice versa.

They had barely finished checking the e-t instruments when Fletcher's voice returned, and before the Captain had finished speaking they were joined by Prilicla and Naydrad.

"Control here. We have visual acquisition of the distressed vessel, and the telescope is locked on with full magnification. You can see what we can see. We are decelerating and will halt approximately fifty meters from the vessel in twelve minutes. During the last few minutes of our approach, I propose using my tractor beams at low intensity to check the spin of the distressed ship. Comments, Doctor?"

The shape on the screen appeared at first to be a pale, circular blur against the background luminosity associated with the nearby star cluster. Only after a few seconds of close examination of the image did it become apparent that the blurred circle was, in fact, a thick metallic-gray disk that was spinning like a tossed coin. Apart from three slight protuberances spaced equally around the circumference of the disk, there were no other obvious features. As Conway and the others stared the spinning ship grew larger, overflowing the edges of the screen until magnification was stepped down and they could once again see the vessel whole.

Clearing his throat, Conway said, "I should be careful while checking the spin, Captain. There is at least one species we know of which requires constant spin on their space and other vehicles to maintain life-support—"

"I'm familiar with the technology of the Rollers of Drambo, Doctor. They are a species which must roll, either naturally while traveling over the surface of their world or artificially if operating otherwise stationary machines, if their vital life-functions are to continue. They

do not possess a heart as such, but use a gravity-feed system to maintain circulation of the blood, so that to stop rolling for more than a few seconds means death to them.

"But this ship is not spinning around its vertical, lateral or longitudinal axis. In my opinion it is tumbling in a completely uncontrolled fashion, and its spin should be checked. Rather, it must be checked if we are to gain rapid entry to the ship and to its survivors, if any. But you're the doctor, Doctor."

For Prilicla's sake Conway tried hard to control his irritation. "Very well. Check the spin, Captain, but carefully. You wouldn't want to place an additional and unnecessary strain on the already damaged and weakened fabric of the ship, or cause wreckage to shift onto possible survivors, or to open a seam that might cause a lethal pressure drop in the vessel's atmosphere."

"Control out."

"You know, if you two stopped trying to impress each other with how much you know about the other person's job," Murchison said seriously, "Doctor Prilicla would not get the shakes so often."

On the screen the magnification was stepped down again as the ambulance ship closed with the distressed vessel, whose rate of spin was slowing under the tangential pull of the *Rhabwar*'s tractors. By the time both ships were motionless with respect to each other at a distance of fifty meters, the alien vessel had already presented its upper and lower surfaces for detailed inspection by eye and camera. One fact among many was glaringly obvious. But before Conway could comment on it, Control got there first.

"The distressed vessel appears to have retained its structural integrity, Doctor. There are no indications of external damage or malfunction, no signs of external substructures or antenna systems carried away or sheared off. Preliminary sensor analysis of the hull surface shows temperature variations with the highest readings in the areas of the bulges on the ship's rim. These three areas are also emitting residual radiation of the type associated with hyperdrive field generation. There is evidence of a major power concentration positioned around the central hub of the vessel, and several subconcentrations of power, all of which appear to be linked together by a system of power lines which are still active. The details are on the schematic . . ."

The picture of the alien ship was replaced by a plan view diagram showing the positions and intensities of the power concentrations in shades of red, with yellow dotted lines indicating the connecting power lines. The original image returned.

"*. . . There is no evidence of leakage of a gas or fluid which might constitute the atmosphere used by the crew, and neither, up to the present, can I detect a method of entry into the ship. There are no airlocks, either cargo or personnel, nor any of the markings associated with entry and exit points, inspection and maintenance panels, replenishment points for consumables. In fact, there are no markings or insignia or instructions or warning signs visible at all. The ship is finished in bare, polished metal, as far as we can see, and the only color variation is caused by different alloys being used in certain areas.*"

"No paint scheme or insignias," said Naydrad, edging closer to the screen. "Have we at last discovered a species completely devoid of vanity?"

"Perhaps the visual equipment of the species is in question," Prilicla added. "They may simply be color blind."

"*The reason is more likely to be aerodynamic than physiological.*"

"As far as we are concerned," Conway joined in, "the reason is much more likely to be medical when the crew of a seemingly undamaged ship releases a distress beacon. Whatever the reason, the condition of the occupants is likely to be grave. We must go over there at once, Captain."

"*I agree. Lieutenant Dodds will remain in Control. Haslam and Chen will accompany me to the ship. I suggest you wear heavy-duty suits because of their longer duration. Our primary objective is to find a way inside, and that could take some time. What are your intentions, Doctor?*"

"Pathologist Murchison will remain here," Conway replied. "Naydrad will suit up as you suggest and stand by with the litter outside the airlock, and Prilicla and I will accompany you to the ship. But I shall wear a lightweight suit with extra air tanks. Its gauntlets are thinner and I may have to treat survivors."

"*I understand. Meet at the lock in fifteen minutes.*"

The conversation of the party investigating the alien ship would be relayed to the Casualty Deck and recorded by Dodds in Control, and the three-view projection of the vessel would be updated as new data became available. But when they were in the *Rhabwar's* lock and about to launch themselves towards the other ship, Fletcher touched helmets with Conway—signifying that he wanted to talk without being overheard on the suit radio frequency.

"I am having second thoughts about the number of people making the initial investigation and entry," the Captain said, his voice muffled and distorted by its passage through the fabric of their helmets. "A certain amount of caution is indicated here. That ship appears to be undamaged and operational. It occurred to me that the crew rather than the ship are in a distressed condition and that their problem might be psychological rather than medical—they might be in a disturbed and non-rational state. So much so that they may react badly and possibly Jump if too many strange creatures started clambering all over their hull."

Now he has delusions of being a xenopsychologist! Conway thought. "You have a point, Captain. But Prilicla and I will not clamber, we will look carefully and touch nothing without first reporting what we have found."

They began by examining the underside of the disk-shaped vessel. It had to be the underside, Fletcher insisted, because there were four propulsion orifices grouped closely around its diametrical center. He was pretty sure the holes were the mouths of jet venturis because of the heat discoloration and pitting that surrounded them. From the position and direction of the thrusters it was clear that the ship's direction of travel was along its vertical axis, although the Captain thought that it would be able to skim edge on for aerodynamic maneuvering in an atmosphere.

In addition to the burned areas around the jet orifices there was a large, circular patch of roughened metal centered on the underside and extending out to approximately one quarter of the ship's radius. There were numerous other roughened areas, only a few inches across for the most part and of various shapes and sizes, scattered over the underside and around the rim. These rough areas puzzled Fletcher because they were really rough—rough enough to snag his gauntlets and pose a danger to anyone wearing a lightweight suit. But he was chiefly puzzled because the rest of the ship looked as if it had been put together by watchmakers.

There were three rough areas which corresponded with the swellings on the rim of the vessel and which were almost certainly the housings of its hypergenerators.

When they moved to the upper surface they found more tiny blemishes, raised very slightly above the surrounding surface, which seemed to be some kind of imperfection in the metal plating. Fletcher said they reminded him of corrosion incrustations except for the fact that there was no difference between their color and the color of the metal they had attacked.

Nowhere was there any evidence of transparent material being used in the ship's construction. None of its communications antennae or sensory receptors had been deployed, so, presumably, this equipment had been retracted before the distress beacon had been released, and was concealed below some of the ship's incredibly well fitting access panels and covers—a few of which had been distinguishable only because of slight color differences in the metal panels and the surrounding hull plating. After searching and straining their eyes for nearly two hours, they still found no sign of anything resembling an external actuator for any of these panels. The ship was locked up tight, and the Captain could give no estimate of the time needed to effect an entry.

"This is supposed to be a rescue attempt and not a leisurely scientific investigation." Conway sounded exasperated. "Can we force an entry?"

"Only as a last resort," the Captain replied. "We do not want to risk offending the inhabitants until we are sure their condition is desperate. We will concentrate our search for an entry port on the rim. The flat, disk-like configuration of the ship, which presents its upper surface to the direction of travel, suggests that its crew would enter via the rim. Its upper surface should, I feel sure, contain the control and living compartments and, hopefully, the survivors."

"Right," agreed Conway. "Prilicla, concentrate your empathic faculty topside while we search the rim. Again."

The minutes flew by without anyone reporting anything but negative results. Impatiently, Conway guided his suit along the edge of the rim until he was hanging just a few meters from Prilicla's position topside. On impulse, he energized his boot and wrist magnets, and when they had pulled him gently against the hull, he freed one foot and kicked hard against the metal plating three times.

Immediately, the suit frequency went into a howl of oscillation as everyone tried to report noise and vibration in their sensor pads at the same time. When silence had returned, Conway spoke.

"Sorry. I should have warned you I was going to do that," he said, knowing that if he had done so there would have been an interminable argument with the Captain, ending in refusal of permission. "We're using up too much time. This is a rescue mission, dammit, and we don't even know if there is anyone to rescue. Some kind of response is needed from inside the ship. Prilicla, did we get anything?"

"No, friend Conway," said the empath. "There is no response to your striking the hull, and no evidence of conscious mentating or emoting. But I cannot yet be sure that there are no survivors. I have the feeling that the total emotional radiation in the vicinity of the ship is not made up solely by the four Earth-humans present and myself."

"I see," said Conway. "In your usual polite and self-effacing fashion you are telling us that we are stirring up too much emotional mud and that we should clear the area so that you can work without interference. How much distance will you need, Doctor?"

"If everyone moves back to the hull of our ship," said Prilicla, "that would be more than adequate, friend Conway. It would also assist me if they engaged in cerebral rather than emotional thinking, and switched off their suit radios."

For what seemed to be a very long time they stood together on the wing of the *Rhabwar* with their backs to the alien ship and Prilicla. Conway had told them that if they were to watch the empath at work they would probably feel anxiety or impatience or disappointment if it did not find a survivor quickly, and any kind of strong feeling would cause emotional interference as far as Prilicla was concerned. Conway did not know what form of cerebral exercise the others were performing to clear their minds of troublesome emotional radiation, but he decided to look around him at the star clusters embedded in their billows and curtains of glowing star stuff. Then the thought came that he was exposing his eyes and his mind to too much sheer splendor, and the feeling of wonder might also be disturbing to an emotion-sensitive.

Suddenly the Captain, who had been sneaking an occasional look at Prilicla, began pointing towards the other ship. Conway switched on his radio in time to hear Fletcher say, "I think we can start emoting again."

Conway swung round to see the spacesuited figure of Prilicla hanging above the metal landscape of the ship like a tiny moon while it directed a spray of fluorescent marker paint at an area midway between the center and the rim. The painted area was already about three meters across and the empath was still extending it.

"Prilicla?" called Conway.

"Two sources, friend Conway," the Cinrusskin reported. "Both are so faint that I cannot pinpoint them with any degree of accuracy other than to say they are somewhere beneath the marked area of hull. The emotional radiation in both cases is characteristic of the unconscious and severely weakened subject. I would say they are in worse shape than the Dwerlan we rescued recently. They are very close to death."

Before Conway could reply, the Captain said harshly, "Right, that's it. Haslam, Chen, break out the portable airlock and cutting gear. This time we'll search the rim in pairs, except for Doctor Prilicla, with one man doing the looking with his light switched off while the other directs side lighting onto the plating so as to throw any joins into relief. Try to find anything that looks like a lock entrance, and cut a way in if we can't solve the combination. Search carefully but quickly. If we can't find a way through the rim inside half an hour, we'll cut through the upper hull in the center of the marked area and hope we don't hit any control linkages or power lines. Have you anything to add, Doctor?"

"Yes," said Conway. "Prilicla, is there anything else, anything at all, you can tell me about the condition of the survivors?"

He was already on the way back to the distressed ship with the Captain slightly ahead of him, and the little empath had attached itself magnetically to the marked area of hull.

"My data is largely negative, friend Conway," said Prilicla, "and comprises supposition rather than fact. Neither being is registering pain, but both share feelings suggesting starvation, asphyxiation and the need of something that is vital to the continuance of life. One of the beings is trying very hard to stay alive while the other appears merely to be angry. The emotional radiation is so tenuous that I cannot state with certainty that the beings are intelligent life-forms, but the indications are that the angry one is probably a nonintelligent lab animal or ship's pet. These are little more than guesses, friend Conway, and I could be completely wrong."

"I doubt that," said Conway. "But those feelings of starvation and strangulation puzzle me. The ship is undamaged, so food and air supplies should be available."

"Perhaps, friend Conway," Prilicla replied timidly, "they are in the terminal stages of a respiratory disease, rather than suffering from gross physical injury."

"In which case," said Murchison, joining the conversation from the *Rhabwar,* "I will be expected to brew up something efficacious against a dose of extraterrestrial pneumonia. Thank *you,* Doctor Prilicla!"

The portable airlock—a fat, lightweight metal cylinder swathed in the folds of transparent plastic that would form its antechamber—was positioned close to the alien ship. While Prilicla remained as physically close as possible to the survivors, Chen and Haslam joined the Captain and Conway in a final search for a fine line on the rim plating that might enclose an entry port.

He tried to be thorough without wasting time, because Prilicla did not think there was any time to waste as far as the two survivors were concerned. But the ship was close to eighty meters in diameter and they had an awful lot of rim to search in half an hour. Still, there had to be a way in, and their main problem was that, despite the many rough and incrusted patches, the ship's structure represented an incredibly fine piece of precision engineering.

"Is it possible," Conway asked suddenly, "that the reason for the ship's distress is these rough patches?" The side of his helmet was close to the hull as he directed his spotlight at an acute angle onto the area that Fletcher was scanning for joins. "Perhaps the troubles of the survivors are a secondary effect. Maybe the unnaturally tight fit of the plating and panels is meant as a protection against attack by some kind of galloping corrosion native to the survivors' home planet."

There was a lengthy silence, then Fletcher said, "That is a very disquieting idea, Doctor, especially since your galloping corrosion might infect our ship. But I don't think so. The incrusted patches appear to be made of the same material as the underlying metal and not a coating of corrosion. As well, they appear to avoid rather than attack the joins."

Conway did not reply. At the back of his mind an idea had begun to stir and take shape, but it dissolved abruptly as Chen's voice sounded excitedly in his phones.

"Sir, over here!"

Chen and Haslam had found what seemed to be a large, circular hatch or section of plating approximately a meter in diameter, and they were already spraying the circumference with marker paint when Fletcher, Prilicla and Conway arrived. There were no rough patches inside the circular line or outside it except for two tiny rough spots set side by side just beyond the lower edge of the circle. Closer examination showed a five-inch-diameter circle enclosing the two rough patches.

"That," said Chen, trying hard to control his excitement, "could be some kind of actuator control for the hatch."

"You're probably right," said the Captain. "Good work, both of you. Now, set up the portable lock around this hatch. Quickly." He placed his sensor plate against the metal. "There is a large empty space behind this hatch, so it is almost certainly an entry lock. If we can't open it manually we'll cut our way in."

"Prilicla?" called Conway.

"Nothing, friend Conway," said the empath. "The survivors' radiation is much too faint to be detectable above the other sources in the area."

"Casualty Deck," Conway said. When Murchison responded, he went on quickly: "Considering the condition of the survivors, would you mind coming over here with the portable analyzer? Atmosphere samples will be available shortly. It would save some time if we didn't have to send them to you for analysis, and shorten the time needed to prepare the litter for the casualties."

"I was expecting you to think of that," Murchison replied briskly. "Ten minutes."

Conway and the Captain ignored the loose folds of transparent fabric and the light-alloy seal that bumped weightlessly against their backs while Haslam and Chen drew the material into position around the entry lock and attached it to the hull with instant sealant. Fletcher concentrated on the lock-actuator mechanism—he insisted that the disk could be nothing but a lock—and described everything he thought and did for the benefit of Dodds, who was recording on the *Rhabwar*.

"The two rough areas inside the disk appear not to be corrosion," he said, "but in my opinion are patches of artificially roughened metal designed to give traction to the space-gauntleted mandibles or manipulatory appendages of the ship's crew—"

"I'm not so sure of that," said Conway. The idea he had had at the back of his mind was taking shape again.

"—to ease the operation of the actuator, this disk, that is," Fletcher continued, ignoring him. "Now, the disk may be turned clockwise or counterclockwise, screwed in or out on threads in either direction, pulled outwards, or pressed inwards and turned one way or the other into a locking position . . ."

The Captain performed the various twisting and pressing movements as he described them, but with no effect. He increased the power on his foot and wrist magnets so as to hold himself more firmly against the hull, placed his gauntleted thumb and forefinger on the two rough spots and twisted even harder. His hand slipped, so that momentarily all of the pressure was on his thumb and one rough area. That half of the disk tilted inwards while the other side moved out. The Captain's face became very red behind his visor.

". . . or, of course, it might turn out to be a simple rocker switch," he added.

Suddenly the large, circular hatch began to swing inwards, and the ship's atmosphere rushed out through the opening seal. The fabric of the portable lock they had attached to the hull bellied outwards and the metal cylinder of its double seal drew away from them, allowing them to stand up inside a large, inflated hemisphere of transparent plastic. As they were watching the hatch move inwards and upwards to the ceiling of the ship's lock chamber, a short loading ramp was slowly extruded. It curved downwards to stop at the position that would have corresponded to ground level had the ship been on the ground.

Murchison had arrived and had been watching them through the portable lock fabric. "The air that escaped was from the lock chamber, because the flow has already stopped. If I could measure the volume of that lock chamber and our own portable job, I could calculate the aliens' atmospheric pressure requirements as well as analyze the constituent gases . . . I'm coming in."

"Obviously a boarding hatch," said the Captain. "They should have a smaller, less complicated lock for space EVAs and—"

"No," said Conway, quietly but very firmly. "These people would not go in for extravehicular activity in space. They would be terrified of losing themselves."

Murchison looked at him without speaking, and the Captain said impatiently, "I don't understand you, Doctor. Prilicla, was there any emotional response from the survivors when we opened the lock?"

"No, friend Fletcher," the empath replied. "Friend Conway is emoting too strongly for the survivors to register with me."

The Captain stared at Conway for a moment, then he said awkwardly, "Doctor, my specialty has been the study of extraterrestrial mechanisms, control systems and communication devices, and my wide experience in this area led to my appointment to the ambulance ship project. The reason why I was able to operate this lock mechanism so quickly was partly because of my expertise and partly through sheer luck. So there is no reason why you, Doctor, whose expertise lies in a different area, should feel irritated just because—"

"My apologies for interrupting, friend Fletcher," said Prilicla timidly, "but he is not irritated. Friend Conway is feeling wonder, with great intensity."

Murchison and the Captain were both staring at him. Neither asked the obvious question, but he answered it anyway: "What would make a blind race reach for the stars?"

It took several minutes to make the Captain see that Conway's theory fitted all the facts as they knew them, but even then Fletcher was not completely convinced that the crew of the ship was blind. It was true that the rough areas on the vessel's underside, particularly those in the area of the thrusters, would give a being possessing only the sense of touch a strong tactual warning of danger, and that the smaller rough areas placed at regular intervals around the rim were probably the coverings of the less dangerous altitude jets. The smallest and most numerous patches of what at first they had thought was corrosion could well be opening or maintenance instructions on access panels, written in an extraterrestrial equivalent of Braille.

The total absence of transparent material, specifically direct vision ports, also gave support to Conway's theory, although it was not impossible that the ports were there but protected by movable metal panels. It was a very good theory, Fletcher admitted, but he preferred to believe that the ship's crew *saw* in a different part of the electromagnetic spectrum, rather than were completely blind.

"Why the Braille, then?" Conway asked. But Fletcher did not answer because it was becoming increasingly obvious on closer examination that the rough spots on the panels and actuators were not there simply to furnish traction—each one was as individual as a fingerprint.

Like the exterior of the ship, the lock interior was unpainted metal. The lock chamber itself was large enough for them to stand upright, but the two actuator disks visible below the inner and outer seals were only a few inches above deck level. There were also a number of short, bright scratches and a few shallow dents in evidence, as though something heavy with sharp edges had been loaded or unloaded fairly recently.

"Physiologically," said Murchison, "this life-form could be a weirdie. Is it a large being whose manipulatory appendages are at ground level? Or are they a small species whose ship was designed to be visited or used by a much more massive race? If the latter, then the rescue should not be complicated by xenophobic reactions on the part of the survivors, since they already know that there are other intelligent life-forms and that the possibility exists that an other-species group might rescue them."

"It is much more likely to be a cargo lock, ma'am," said the Captain apologetically, "and it is the cargo, rather than their extraterrestrial friends, if any, that was massive. Are we ready to go in?"

Without replying, Murchison switched her helmet spotlight to wide beam. The Captain and Conway did the same.

Fletcher had already checked that he could maintain two-way communication with Haslam and Chen outside the ship and with Dodds on the *Rhabwar* by touching the helmet antenna to the metal of the hull, in effect making the ship's structure an extension of his antenna. He knelt down and depressed the actuator, which was positioned just above deck level inside the outer seal. The hatch swung closed, and he repeated the operation on a similarly positioned actuator below the inner seal.

For a few seconds nothing happened. Then they heard the hiss of atmosphere entering the lock chamber, and they felt their suits becoming less inflated as air pressure built up around them. As the inner seal opened to reveal a stretch of dark, apparently empty corridor, Murchison was busy tapping buttons on her analyzer.

"What do they breathe?" Conway asked.

"Just a moment, I'm double-checking," Murchison replied. Suddenly she opened her visor and grinned. "Does that answer your question?"

When he opened his own helmet, Conway felt his ears pop at the slight difference in air pressure. "So, the survivors are warm-blooded oxygen-breathers with roughly Earth-normal atmospheric-pressure requirements. This simplifies the job of preparing ward accommodation."

Fletcher hesitated for a moment, then he, too, opened his visor. "Let's find them first."

They stepped into a metal-walled corridor, featureless except for a large number of dents and scratches on the ceiling and walls, which extended for about thirty meters toward the center of the ship. At the end of the corridor, lying on the deck, was an indistinct something that looked like a tangle of metal bars projecting from a darker mass. Murchison's foot magnets made loud scraping sounds as she hurried towards it.

"Careful, ma'am," said the Captain. "If the doctor's theory is correct, all controls, actuators, instruction or warning tags will have tactile indicators, and there is still power available within the ship; otherwise, the airlock mechanism would not have worked for us. If the crew live and work in complete darkness, you will have to think with your fingers and feet and not touch anything that looks like a patch of corrosion."

"I'll be careful, Captain," Murchison promised.

To Conway, Fletcher said: "The inner seal has an actuator just like the others under its lower rim." He directed his helmet light at the area in question, then indicated a smaller circle a few inches to the right of the actuator switch. "Before we go any farther I would like to know what this one does."

"Well," Conway said, "about the only thing we know for sure is that it isn't a light switch." He laughed as Fletcher depressed one side of the disk.

Murchison gave an unladylike grunt of surprise as bright yellow light flooded the corridor from an unseen source at the other end.

"No comment," said the Captain.

Conway felt his face burning with embarrassment as he muttered about the lights being for the convenience of non-blind visitors.

"If this was a visitor," said Murchison, who had reached the other end of the corridor, "then it was very severely inconvenienced. Look here."

The corridor made a right-angle turn at its inboard end, although access to the new section was blocked by a heavy barred grill, which had been twisted away from its anchor points on the deck and one wall. Behind the damaged grill, dozens of metal rods and bars projected at random angles into the corridor space from the walls and ceiling. But they did not pay much attention to the strange cage-like outgrowth of metal because they were staring at the three extraterrestrials who were lying in wide, dried-up patches of their body fluids.

There were two very different physiological types, Conway saw at once. The large one resembled a Tralthan, but less massive and with stubbier legs projecting from a hemispherical carapace, which flared out slightly around the lower edges. From openings higher on the carapace sprouted four long and not particularly thin tentacles, which terminated in flat, spear-like tips with serrated bony edges. Midway between two of the tentacle openings was a larger gap in the carapace, from which projected a head that was all mouth and teeth, with just a little space reserved for two eyes set at the bottom of deep, bony craters. Conway's first impression was that the entity was little more than an organic killing machine.

He had to remind himself that the Sector General staff included several beings whose species were highly intelligent and sensitive while retaining the physical equipment that had enabled them to fight their way to the top of their home planet's evolutionary tree.

The other two beings belonged to a much smaller species with much less in the way of organic weaponry. They were roughly circular, just over a meter in diameter, and in cross section, a slim oval flattened slightly on the underside. In shape they very much resembled their ship, except that *it* did not have a long, thin horn or sting projecting aft or a thin, wide slit on the opposite side, which was obviously a mouth. The upper lip of the mouth was wider and thicker than the lower, and on one of the dead beings it was curled over the lower lip, apparently sealing the mouth shut. Both of the beings were covered on their upper and lower surfaces and around the rims by some kind of organic stubble, which varied in thickness from pin size to the width of a small finger. The stubble on the underside was much coarser than that on the upper surface, and it was plain that parts of it were designed for ambulation.

"It is clear what happened here," said the Captain. "Two members of the species that crew this ship died when the large one broke free because of inadequate restraints, and presumably the survivors Prilicla detected were unable to cope with the situation and released a distress beacon."

One of the smaller beings, which had sustained multiple incised and punctured wounds, lay like a piece of torn and rumpled carpet under its killer's hind feet. Its companion, although just as dead, had suffered fewer wounds and had almost made its escape through a low opening in the wall at deck level before being immobilized and crushed by one of its attacker's forefeet. It had also, before it died, been able to inflict several deep puncture wounds on the larger alien's underside, and its broken-off horn or sting was still deeply embedded in one of them.

"I agree," said Conway. "But one thing puzzles me. The blind ones appear to have modified their ship to accommodate the larger life-form. Why would they go to so much trouble to capture such a dangerous specimen? They must need it very badly or consider it extremely valuable for some reason to risk confining it with a blind crew."

"Possibly they have weapons that reduce the risk," Fletcher said, "longer range, more effective weapons than that horn or sting, which these two omitted to carry for some reason and died because of the omission."

"What kind of long-range weapon," asked Conway, "could be developed by a being with only a sense of touch?"

Murchison tried to head off the argument that was impending. "We don't know for certain that they have only a sense of touch, although they are blind. As for the value of the large life-form to them, it could be a fast-breeding source of food, or its tissues or organs might contain important sources of valuable medication, or the reason maybe a completely alien one. Excuse me."

She switched on her suit radio. "Naydrad, we have three cadavers to transfer to the lab. Move them in the litter to avoid additional damage to the specimens by decompression." She turned to Conway and the Captain. "I don't think the other members of the crew would object to my opening up their friends, especially since the large one has already begun the process."

Conway nodded. They both knew that the more she was able to discover about the physiology and metabolism of the two dead specimens, the better would be their chances of helping the surviving blind ones.

With Fletcher's help they extricated the large cadaver from its cage and from the strange assortment of metal rods and bars that were pressing it against the deck. They had to widen the opening it had made in the grill. This required the combined efforts of the three of them and gave some indication of the strength of the being who had forced it apart. When they had the large alien free, its tentacles opened out and practically blocked the corridor as it floated weightless in the confined space.

While they were pushing it towards the airlock, Murchison said, "The deployment of the legs and tentacles is similar to the Hudlar FROB life-form, but that carapace is a thicker ELNT Melfan shell without markings, and it is plainly not herbivorous. Considering the fact that it is warm-blooded and oxygen-breathing and its appendages show no evidence of the ability to manipulate tools or materials, I would tentatively classify it as FSOJ, and probably non-intelligent."

"Certainly non-intelligent, considering the circumstances," said Fletcher as they returned to the caged section of corridor. "It was an escaped specimen, ma'am."

"We medical types," said Murchison, smiling, "never commit

ourselves, especially where a brand-new life-form is concerned. But right now I wouldn't even try to classify the blind ones."

Since she was the smallest person there, it was Murchison who wriggled carefully through the damaged grill and between the projecting rods and bars. If it had not been for the large alien warping a number of the bars out of true, she would not have been able to reach the blind one at all.

"This," she said breathlessly as she reached the cadaver, "is a very strange cage."

Although it was brightly lit, they could not see the other end of the caged section of corridor, because it followed the curvature of the ship, which at this distance from the center was sharp enough to keep them from seeing more than ten meters into it. The corridor walls and ceiling of the section they could see, however, were covered with projecting metal bars and rods. Some of them had sharp tips, others had spatulate ends and a few of them terminated in something that resembled a small metal ball covered in blunt spikes. The metal bars projected from slits in the walls, and the slots were long enough to allow their individual bars a wide angle of travel either up and down or from side to side. The rods protruded from circular holes and collar pieces in the ceiling and were designed only to move in and out.

"It is strange to me, too, ma'am," said the Captain. "None of the e-t technology I've studied gives me any ideas. For one thing, it is a large cage, or should I say a very long cage, if it is continued around the ship. Perhaps it was meant to house more than one specimen, or the one specimen required space in which to exercise. I'm guessing, but I would say that the bars and rods projecting into the corridor formed some kind of restraint whereby the specimen could be immobilized in any part of the caged section for feeding purposes or for physical examination."

"A pretty good guess, I'd say," said Conway. "And if there was a malfunction in the mobile restraints, then the metal grill formed a safety backup that couldn't, on this occasion, withstand the specimen's attack. But I'm wondering just how far this corridor follows the radius of the ship. Extending this arc to the other side of the vessel places it in the area where Prilicla detected the two survivors. One of those survivors, according to Prilicla, was emoting anger on a very basic, perhaps animal, level while the other being's emotional radiation was more complex.

"Let's suppose," Conway went on, "that there is another large alien at the other end of the corridor cage, maybe even outside the other end of the cage, with a badly injured blind one who wasn't as successful as its crew-mate here in killing the brute—"

He broke off as Naydrad's voice sounded in the suit phones, saying that it was outside with the pressure litter.

Murchison pushed the first blind one towards the lock. "Wait for a few minutes, Naydrad, and you can load all three specimens."

Fletcher had been staring at Conway while the doctor was talking, plainly not liking the thought of another large FSOJ being in the ship. He pointed anxiously at the second blind one's body. "This one nearly escaped after killing the FSOJ with its horn. If we knew where it was trying to escape to, we might know where to look for its crew-mate who did escape."

"I'll help you," said Conway.

Time for the survivors, whichever species they belonged to, was fast running out.

At deck level there was a low rectangular opening, which was wide and deep enough to allow entry to a blind one. Nearly one third of its flat, circular body was inside the opening, and when they tried to remove it they encountered resistance and had to give the creature a gentle tug to pull it free. They were pushing it towards Murchison, who was waiting to load it into the airlock with the other two specimens, when there was an interruption on the suit frequency.

"Sir! A panel is swinging open topside. It looks like . . . it is an antenna being deployed."

"Prilicla," Conway called quickly, "the survivors. Is one of them conscious?"

"No, friend Conway," the empath replied. "Both remain deeply unconscious."

Fletcher stared at Conway for a moment. "If the survivors did not extend that antenna, then we did, probably when we were pulling the blind one out from that opening." He bent suddenly and slid his foot magnets backwards until he was lying flat against the corridor floor. He moved his head close to the opening through which the blind one had tried to escape, and directed his helmet light inside. "Look at this, Doctor, I think we've found the control center."

They were looking into a wide, low tunnel whose internal dimensions were slightly larger than those of the bodies of the blind ones. Visibility was restricted because, like the corridor behind them, it followed the curvature of the ship. For a distance of about fifteen inches inside the opening the floor was bare, but the roof was covered with the tactually labeled actuators of the type they had found in the airlock. There were, naturally, no indicator lights or visual displays. Just beyond this area the tunnel had no roof, and they had a clear view of the first control position.

In shape it resembled a circular, elliptical sectioned sandwich open around the edges to facilitate entry by the blind ones of the crew. They could see hundreds of actuators covering the inside faces of the sandwich and, on the outer surfaces, the cable runs and linkages that connected the actuators with the mechanisms they controlled. The majority of the cable runs led towards the center of the ship while the rest curved towards the rim. There was no evidence of color-coding on the cables, but the sheathing carried various embossed and inset patterns that performed the same function for technicians who felt but could not see. A second control pod was visible beyond the first one.

"I can see only two control positions clearly," said Fletcher, "but we know that the crew numbered at least three. The survivor is probably out of sight around that curve, and if we could squeeze through the tunnel—"

"Physically impossible," said Conway.

"—without blundering against actuators every foot of the way," the Captain went on, "and switching on every system in the ship. I wonder why these people, who do not appear to be stupid, even if they are blind, placed a control position so close to the cage of a dangerous captive animal. That was taking a risk."

"If they couldn't keep an eye on it," said Conway dryly, "they had to keep closely in touch."

"Was that a joke?" the Captain asked disapprovingly while he detached one of his gauntlets and reached into the opening. A few seconds later he said, "I think I feel the actuator we must have snagged pulling the blind one out. I'm pressing it, now."

Chen's voice on the suit frequency broke in. "There is another antenna array deploying, close to the first one, sir."

"Sorry," said Fletcher. For a moment his face registered an expression of deep concentration as his fingers felt their way over the alien controls; then Chen reported that both antennae had retracted.

The Captain smiled. "Assuming that they group their controls together in sensible fashion, and the actuators for power, altitude control, life-support, communications and so on occupy their own specific areas on the control panels, I'd say that the blind one was touching its communications panel when it died. It managed to release a distress beacon, but that was probably the last thing it was able to do.

"Doctor," he added, "could you give me your hand, please?"

Conway gave his hand to the Captain to steady him and help him to his feet while Fletcher carefully withdrew his other hand from the opening. Suddenly one of Fletcher's foot magnets slipped along the deck. His arm jerked backwards instinctively to prevent him from falling, even though in the weightless condition he could not fall, sending the hand back inside the control area.

"I touched something." He sounded worried.

"You certainly did," said Conway, and pointed at the caged section of corridor.

"Sir!" said Haslam on the suit frequency. "We are detecting strong intermittent vibrations throughout the fabric of the ship. Also metallic sounds!"

Murchison came diving along the corridor from the airlock. She checked herself expertly against the wall. "What's *happening*?" Then she, too, looked into the caged corridor. "What *is* happening?"

For as far as they could see along the curvature of the corridor there was violent and noisy mechanical activity. The long metal bars projecting from their slots in the walls were whipping back and forth or up and down to the limits of their angles of travel, while the rods with their pointed or mace-like ends were jabbing up and down like pistons from the ceiling. Several of the bars and pistons were badly warped and were striking one another, which caused the awful din. As they watched, a small flap opened in the inboard wall of the corridor a few meters inside the grill, and a mass of something resembling thick porridge was extruded, to drift like a misshapen football into the path of the nearest wildly swinging bar.

The material splattered in all directions, and the smaller pieces were batted about by the other bars and pistons until they moved about the corridor like a sticky hailstorm. Murchison captured some of it in a specimen bag.

"Obviously a food dispenser of some kind," she observed. "An analysis of this stuff will tell us a lot about the large one's metabolism. But those bars and pistons are not, to my mind, a means of restraining the FSOJ. Not unless restraint includes clubbing it unconscious."

"With a physiological classification of FSOJ," said Conway thoughtfully, "that might be the only way to do it, short of using a heavy-duty pressor beam."

"All the same," Murchison went on, "I am feeling a slight attenuation of sympathy for the blind ones. That corridor looks more like a torture chamber than a cage."

Conway had been thinking the same thing and so, judging by his shocked and sickened expression, had the Captain. They had all been taught, and were themselves convinced, that there was no such thing as a completely evil and inimical intelligent race, and even the suggestion that they believed such a thing possible would have led to their dismissal from the Monitor Corps or from the Federation's largest multienvironment hospital. Extraterrestrials were different, sometimes wildly and weirdly different, and during the early stages of contact a great deal of caution was necessary until a full understanding of their physiological, psychological and cultural background was available. But there was no such thing as an evil race. Evil or antisocial individuals, perhaps, but not an evil species.

Any species that had evolved to the point of social and technological cooperation necessary for them to travel between the stars had to be civilized. This was the considered opinion of the Federation's most advanced minds, which were housed inside some sixty-odd different life-forms. Conway had never been the slightest bit xenophobic, but neither was he completely convinced that somewhere there wasn't an exception that would prove the rule.

"I'm going back with the specimens now," Murchison said. "I

may be able to find some answers. The trouble is finding the right questions to ask."

Fletcher was stretched out on the deck again with one hand inside the control area. "I'll have to shut off that . . . whatever it is. But I don't know where exactly my hand was when I switched it on, or if I switched on anything else at the same time." He tripped his suit radio toggle. "Haslam, Chen. Will you chart the extent of the noise and vibrations, please, and is there evidence of any other unusual activity within the ship?" He turned to Conway. "Doctor, while I'm trying to find the right button to push, would you do something for me? Use my cutting torch on the corridor wall midway between the L-bend here and the airlock—"

He broke off as they were suddenly plunged into absolute darkness, which seemed to augment the clanging and metallic screeching sounds to such an extent that Conway fumbled for his helmet light switch in near panic. But before he could reach it the ship's lighting came on again.

"That wasn't it," said the Captain, then he continued: "The reason I want you to do this, Doctor, is to find an easier path to the survivors than the one along the corridor. You probably noticed that the majority of the cable runs originating in the control pods go inboard towards the power generation area of the ship, with very few leading out to the periphery. From this I assume that the area of the vessel outboard of the corridor cage and control center is the storage or cargo sections, which should, if the blind ones follow basic design philosophy where their spaceships are concerned, be comprised of large compartments connected by simple doors rather than pressurized bulkheads and airlocks. If this is so, and the sensor readings seem to confirm it, we should have to move only some cargo or stores out of the way to be able to bypass the control pods and get to the survivors fairly quickly. We would not have to risk running through that corridor, or worry about accidentally depressurizing the ship by cutting in from topside . . ."

Before the Captain had finished speaking, Conway began cutting a narrow vertical rectangle in the wall plating, a shape that would enable both his eyes and the helmet light to be directed through the opening at the same time so that he could see into the adjoining compartment. But when he burned through the wall there was noth-

188 · JAMES WHITE

ing to see except a black, powdery substance, which spilled out of
the opening and hung in a weightless cloud until the movement of
his cutter flame sent it spinning into tiny three-dimensional whirl-
pools.

He worked his hand carefully into the hole, feeling the warmth
of the still-hot edges through his thin gauntlets, and withdrew a
small handful of the stuff to examine it more closely. Then he moved
to another section of the wall and tried again. And again.

Fletcher watched him but did not speak. All of the Captain's
attention was again concentrated in his fingertips. Conway began
working on the opposite wall of the corridor, reducing the size of
the test holes to speed up the process. When he had cut four widely
separated fist-sized holes without uncovering anything but the powdery material, he called Murchison.

"We are finding large quantities of a coarse black powder," he
told her, "which has a faint odor suggesting an organic or partly
organic composition. It could be a form of nutrient soil. Does that
fit the crew's physiology profile?"

"It fits," said Murchison promptly. "From my preliminary examination of the two small cadavers I would say that the atmosphere
in their ship is for the convenience of the larger FSOJ life-form. The
blind ones do not possess lungs as such. They are burrowers who
metabolize the organic constituents of their soil as well as any other
plant or animal tissue that happens to be available. They ingest the
soil via the large frontal mouth opening, but the larger upper lip is
capable of being folded over the lower one so that the mouth is
sealed shut when it needs to burrow without eating. We've noticed
atrophy of the limbs, or to be more accurate, the movable pads on
the underside that propel it, and of hypersensitivity in the upper-
surface tactual sensors. This probably means that their culture has
evolved to the stage where they inhabit artificially constructed tunnel systems with readily accessible food supplies, rather than having
to burrow for it. The material you describe could be a special loosely
packed nutrient soil that combines the ship's food supply with a
medium for physical exercise."

"I see," said Conway.

A blind, burrowing worm who somehow managed to reach the

stars! Then Murchison's next words reminded him that the blind ones were capable of seemingly petty and cruel activities as well as those that were great and glorious.

"Regarding the survivors," she went on, "if the FSOJ laboratory animal, or whatever it is, is too close to the surviving crew-member and we cannot rescue both without endangering ourselves or the blind one, a large reduction in atmospheric pressure, provided it is carried out gradually so as to avoid decompression damage to the blind one's tissues, would disable or more likely kill the FSOJ."

"That would be the last thing we would try," said Conway firmly. The rules were very strict in first-contact situations like this, where one could never be absolutely sure that an apparently sense-less and ferocious beast was, in fact, a non-sentient creature.

"I know, I know," Murchison replied. "And it will interest you to know that the FSOJ was in an advanced stage of pregnancy, a time during which most life-forms, regardless of their degree of intelligence, can feel overprotective, overemotional and over-aggressive if they think their unborn is being threatened. That might be the reason why the FSOJ broke out of its cage. As well, the blind one would not have been able to kill it with its horn if the FSOJ's underbody had not been locally weakened in preparation for the imminent birth."

Conway considered that for a moment. "The female FSOJ's con-dition and the beating and prodding it had to take in the—"

"I didn't say it was female," Murchison broke in, "though it may be. In many ways it is a far more interesting life-form than the blind one."

"Save your mental energy for the one we *know* is intelligent," Conway snapped at her. There was a moment's silence, broken only by the background hiss from the suit radio. Then he apologized: "Ignore me, please, I've got a bad headache."

"Me, too," Fletcher said. "I expect it is caused by the noise and subsonic effects of the vibration of all this moving machinery. If his headache is half as bad as mine you can forgive him, ma'am, and if you could have some helpful medication ready when we return to the ship—"

"Make that three," said Murchison. "My head has been aching

since I came back here, and I was exposed to the noise and vibration for only a few minutes. And I've bad news for you: The headache does not respond to medication."

She broke contact. "Doesn't it seem strange," Fletcher asked worriedly, "that three people who breathed the air in this ship are suffering from—"

"Back at the hospital," Conway broke in, "they have a saying that psychosomatic aches are contagious and incurable. Murchison's analyzer checked the ship's atmosphere for toxic material, and any alien bugs present are just not interested in us. This particular headache could be a product of anxiety, tension, or a combination of various psychological factors. But because it is affecting all three of us at once, and all three of us have spent some time inside the ship, it is probable that the headache is being caused by some outside agency, very likely the noise and vibration from that corridor, and you were right the first time. I'm sorry I mentioned it."

"If you hadn't," said Fletcher, "I certainly would have done so. It is quite unpleasant and is affecting my ability to concentrate on these—"

There was another interruption from the outer hull.

"Haslam, sir. Chen and I have finished charting the extent of the sounds and vibration. They occupy a narrow band, perhaps two meters wide, which coincides with what you have called the corridor cage. The corridor runs right around the ship in a constant-radius circle, which is completed by the arc containing the control pods. But that's not all, sir. The corridor intersects the area occupied by the two survivors."

Fletcher looked at Conway. "If I could only stop this mechanical torture chamber, or whatever it is, we might be able to squeeze through it to the survivors . . . But no, if it started up again when someone was inside, it would batter them to death. Very well," he said to Haslam, "is there anything else to report?"

"Well, sir," Haslam replied hesitantly. "This may not mean anything, but we have headaches too."

For a long time there was silence while the Captain and Conway thought about the two *Rhabwar* officers' headaches. The men had been outside the ship at all times, making contact with the hull plating infrequently and then only through their magnetic boots and gauntlets—both of which had padded and insulated interiors capable of damping out mechanical vibration. Besides, sounds did not travel through a vacuum. Conway could think of nothing that would explain the two men's headaches, but not so the Captain.

"Dodds," Fletcher said suddenly to the officer he had left in the *Rhabwar*. "Run a sensor recheck for radiation emanating from this ship. It may not have been present until I started pushing buttons. Also, check for possibly harmful radiation associated with the nearby star cluster."

Conway gave a nod of approval, which the Captain did not see. Even flat on his back with a thumping headache making it difficult to think and with one arm disappearing into an alien control pod in which an unguarded touch could cause anything from the lights going out to an unscheduled Jump into hyperspace, Fletcher was doing all right. But the sensor reading, according to Dodds, cleared the alien ship and the space around them of any trace of harmful radiation. They were still thinking about this when the timid voice of Prilicla broke the silence.

"Friend Conway," called the empath, "I have delayed making this report until I was sure of my feelings, but there can no longer be any doubt. The condition of both survivors is improving steadily."

"Thank you, Prilicla," said Conway. "That will give us more time to think of a way of rescuing them." To Fletcher, he added, "But why the sudden improvement?"

The Captain looked at the corridor cage and its outgrowth of furiously waving and jabbing metal and said "Could that have anything to do with it?"

"I don't know," said Conway, grinning in relief because the chances of a successful rescue had increased. "Certainly the noise alone is fit to wake the nearly dead."

The Captain looked disapprovingly at him, plainly unable to see anything funny in the remark or the situation. Very seriously, he said, "I have checked and rechecked all of the flat rocker switches within reach. That particular form of actuator is the only kind suited to the short feeler pads possessed by the blind ones, because as manipulators the pads lack strength and leverage. But I have found something that feels like a lever, several inches long and terminating in a narrow reverse-conical handle. The cone is hollow and is probably designed to accommodate the tip of the blind one's horn or sting. The lever is positioned at a forty-five-degree angle to its seating, which is the limit of its travel in the up direction. I intend moving it downwards.

"In case something calamitous happens as a result, we should seal our helmets," Fletcher added. He closed his helmet visor and replaced the gauntlet he had removed earlier. Then he reached inside the opening without hesitation, obviously knowing exactly where his hand was going.

In the corridor cage all mechanical activity ceased abruptly. The silence was so complete that when someone scraped a magnetic boot against the outer hull the noise made Conway start. The Captain was smiling as he got to his feet and opened his visor again.

"The survivors are at the other end of this corridor, Doctor," he said, then added, "if we can just get to them."

But they found it completely impossible to wriggle through the thicket of projecting metal rods and bars. Even when the Captain took off his spacesuit to try it, he was successful only in collecting a number of cuts and abrasions. Disappointed, Fletcher climbed into his suit again and began attacking the metal projections with his cutter. But the metal was tough and required several seconds at maximum power before each metal bar was burned through. There were so many of the things it was like weeding a metal garden a stalk at a time, the Captain observed crossly. He had cleared less than two meters of the corridor cage when they were forced back to the airlock because of the buildup of heat.

"It's no good," said the Captain. "We can cut a way through to them, but only in short stages with lengthy delays in between to allow the excess heat to dissipate by conduction through the fabric of the ship and to radiate into space. There is also the danger that the heat might melt the insulation on some of their power-control circuitry, with unknown results."

He tapped the wall beside him with his fist, so hard that it might almost have been a display of temper. "Emptying the storage spaces of nutrient soil would also be a long job, necessitating as it would the movement of the soil in installments from the storage spaces to the corridor to the lock and out, and we have no idea what structural problems could then arise inside those compartments. I'm beginning to think the only thing to do is cut a way in from outside. But there are problems there, too . . ."

Cutting down to the survivors through the double hull of the ship would generate a lot of heat, especially inside the portable lock they would have to use to guard against accidentally depressurizing the vessel. Once again, lengthy delays would be required to allow the heat to radiate away, although the process would be faster since they would already be on the outer hull. There was also the problem of cutting through the mechanical linkages to the bars and pistons projecting into the corridor, which would tend to generate a lot of heat inside the ship, heat which might have an adverse effect on the survivors. The only advantage was that they would not run the risk of being beaten to death by metal bars if as a result of their cutting operations the system switched itself on again.

". . . And by the way, Doctor," Fletcher added, changing from his lecturing tone, "my headache is fading."

Conway was telling him that his own headache was diminishing as well when Prilicla broke into the conversation. "Friend Fletcher, I have been monitoring emotional radiation of the survivors since you halted the corridor mechanisms. Their condition has deteriorated steadily since then, and they are now in the state similar to that detected on our arrival, or perhaps a little worse. Friend Fletcher, we could easily lose them."

"That . . . that doesn't make sense!" the Captain burst out. He looked appealingly at Conway.

Conway could imagine Prilicla trembling inside its spacesuit at the Captain's outburst and the emotional radiation accompanying it. But he could just barely imagine the effort it had taken for the little empath, who found it acutely painful to disagree with anyone, to speak as it had. "Perhaps not," he said quickly to Fletcher, "but there is one way of finding out."

Fletcher gave him an angry, puzzled look, but he moved to the control pod opening and a few seconds later the noise and mechanical activity in the corridor had returned. So had Conway's headache.

Prilicla said, "The condition of the survivors is improving again."

"How much did they improve last time?" asked Conway. "And would you be able to tell by their emotional radiation if one being was about to attack another?"

"Both survivors were fully conscious for a few minutes," Prilicla replied. "Their radiation was so strong that I was able to reduce the area of uncertainty of their position. They are within two meters of each other, and neither of them was or is contemplating an attack."

"Are you telling me," the Captain said in a baffled tone, "that a fully conscious FSOJ and a blind one are as close together as that without the animal wanting to attack it?"

"Maybe the blind one found a locker or something to hide in," said Conway, "and to the FSOJ it is a case of out of sight, out of mind."

"Excuse me," said Prilicla. "There is no way that I can tell with absolute certainty that the two beings are of different species. The quality of their emotional radiation strongly suggests this. One is emoting anger and pain and little else while the other's emotions possess the complexity of a rational mind. But would it help you if you considered the possibility that they are both blind ones, one of whom has suffered gross brain damage, which is causing the raw, mindless level of emoting which I have detected."

"A nice theory, Doctor Prilicla," said the Captain. He winced and instinctively put his hands to his head, only to have them stopped short by his helmet. "It explains their close proximity, but it does not explain why their condition is affected by the corridor mechanisms. Unless I damaged the controls in some fashion, and accidentally made a connection between the corridor control lever and some emergency life-support equipment, perhaps a medical therapy unit or . . . I feel completely and utterly confused!"

"Everyone is feeling confused, friend Fletcher," said the empath. "The general emotional radiation leaves no doubt of that."

"Let's go back to the ship," said Conway suddenly. "I need some peace and quiet to think."

They left the blind ones' ship with Chen on watch with instructions to keep his distance and on no account to make physical contact with the vessel's structure. Prilicla returned with them, saying that the emotional radiation from the two survivors was strong enough for it to be monitored at a distance, since the condition of both was continuing to improve while the corridor mechanisms were still operating.

Entering by the Casualty Deck lock, they headed straight for the lab, which was occupied by a bloodstained Murchison and numerous pieces of FSOJ and blind ones spread around the dissecting tables. Naydrad joined them as Conway asked the Captain to project a plan view diagram of the blind ones' ship, incorporating the latest data. Fletcher looked relieved at having something to occupy him, since it was obvious that he did not share the close professional interest of the others in the pieces of extraterrestrial raw meat scattered about the place.

When the diagram appeared on the lab's display screen, Conway asked the Captain to correct him if he went wrong anywhere, then he began reviewing their problem.

Like most major problems this one was composed of a number of smaller ones, some of which were susceptible to solution. There was the blind ones' ship, which preliminary technical investigation showed to be structurally sound and in a fully powered-up condition. The vessel's configuration was that of a disk that tapered in thickness towards the circumference. At the center was a circle of perhaps one third the radius of the ship, which enclosed the power generation and associated equipment. Outside this area and enclosing it was a circular corridor linked to the airlock by a straight section of corridor, giving the appearance in the plan view of a sickle with a circular blade whose tip almost reached its handle. The short arc that joined the tip to the top of the handle was occupied by the control pods of the blind ones.

Beyond the circular corridor was the life-support area for both the crew and their captives. Proportionately, the volume of the ship devoted to the FSOJ life-form meant that the vessel had been designed specifically for the purpose of transporting these creatures. The lighting, atmosphere, FSOJ food dispenser and exercise space left no doubt about that.

Conway paused for a moment to look at Fletcher and the others, but there were no arguments. Then he went on: "The arrangement of rapidly moving bars and pistons in the caged corridor, particularly the ones with pointed and club-like extremities, worries me because I cannot accept the idea that the FSOJs are being used solely

196 · JAMES WHITE

for the purpose of torture. I prefer the idea that they are being trained, perhaps domesticated, for a very special reason. One does not design an interstellar ship around a non-sentient life-form unless the creature is extremely valuable to the designers.

"We must therefore ask ourselves what the FSOJ has that the blind ones haven't," Conway went on. "What is it that they need most?"

They were all staring silently at the FSOJ cadaver. Murchison looked up at him suddenly, but it was the Captain who spoke first.

"Eyes?"

"Right," said Conway, then continued: "Naturally, I don't want to suggest that the FSOJs are the blind ones' equivalent of seeing-eye dogs. Rather, when their violent tendencies are curbed, a symbiotic or parasitic relationship is possible whereby the blind one attaches itself with its undersurface pads to tap into the FSOJ's central nervous system, in particular the vision network, so that it would receive—"

"Not possible," Murchison said firmly.

Prilicla began shaking to Conway's feelings of irritation and disappointment. His disappointment predominated because he knew that Murchison would not have spoken so bluntly had she not been certain of her facts.

"Perhaps with a surgical intervention as well as a training program . . ." Conway tried hopefully.

But Murchison shook her head. "I'm sorry," she said. "We now have enough information on both life-forms to know that a symbiotic or parasitic relationship is impossible. The blind ones, which I have tentatively classified as CPSD, are omnivorous and have two sexes. One of the cadavers is male, the other female. The sting is their only natural weapon, but the poison sac associated with it has long since atrophied. I found scratches on the osseous tip of both stings, which suggests that they are now used as a manipulatory appendage. They are highly intelligent and, as we already know, technologically advanced despite their physical and sensory handicaps.

"Their only sense seems to be that of touch," she continued, "but judging by the degree of specialization apparent in the sensor pads covering the upper surface of their bodies, their touch is extremely sensitive. It is possible that some of those sensors would 'feel' vibrations in a solid or gaseous medium, or 'feel' the taste of substances with which they came in contact. As well as feeling, hearing and tasting after a fashion, a refinement of the 'taste' pads might also enable them to smell by touch. But they cannot see and would probably have difficulty in grasping the concept of sight, so they would not know a visual nerve network if they touched one."

Murchison indicated the opened torso of the FSOJ, then went on. "But that is not the principal reason why they cannot have a symbiotic relationship. Normally, an intelligent parasite or symbiont has to position itself close to the brain or in an area where the main nerve bundles are easily accessible. In our own case that would be at the back of the neck or the top of the head. But this beastie's brain is not in its skull; it is deep inside the torso with the rest of the other vital organs and is positioned in a rather stupid place, just under the womb and surrounding the beginning of the birth canal. As a result, the brain is compressed as the embryo grows, and if it is a difficult birth its parent's brain is destroyed. Junior comes out fighting and with a convenient food supply available until it can kill something for itself.

"The FSOJ, which is bisexual, retains its young in the womb until it is well-grown and fully equipped to survive," she added. "Survival cannot be easy where it lives, and the blind ones must have found a much more suitable life-form for a symbiont, if that was what they were looking for."

Conway rubbed his aching head and thought that difficult cases usually did not have this effect on him. Occasionally he had lost sleep over patients, or felt anxious or even seriously worried and tense when the time came to make a crucial decision in their case, but up until now it had never given him headaches. Was he growing old? But no, that was much too simple an explanation, because at the blind ones' ship they had all had headaches.

"One way or another we will have to go after the survivors," Conway said decisively. "And soon. But it would be criminal and stupid to endanger the life of a sentient being by wasting time on an experimental animal, even one that the ship's crew consider as valuable as the FSOJ. Now, if we agree that the FSOJ is non-sentient—"

"We depressurize the ship, wait until Prilicla says the FSOJ is dead and cut our way in to the surviving blind one as quickly as possible," the Captain finished for him, then added, "Dammit, my headache's back."

"A suggestion, friend Fletcher," said Prilicla diffidently. "The blind one is small and could probably negotiate the corridor cage without being inconvenienced by the FSOJ training mechanisms. The emotional radiation from both beings is increasing to the point where I would say that they are almost fully recovered. One is radiating anger of the insensate, uncontrolled kind while the other is feeling increasing frustration and is straining hard to do something. And I, too, am having some cranial discomfort, friend Conway."

The contagious headache again! thought Conway. *This is too much of a coincidence . . .*

Suddenly his mind was back in time and space to his early years in the hospital, when he was insufferably proud to be on the staff of a multienvironment hospital even though at the time he was little more than a medical messenger boy. But then he had been given the assignment of liaison with one Doctor Arretapec, a VUXG who was teleportive, telekinetic and telepathic, and who had received Federation funding for his project of engendering intelligence in a race of non-sentient Saurians.

Arretapec had given Conway a headache in more ways than one.

He was only half-listening while the Captain was making the arrangements to depressurize the other ship. His plan was, first, to reposition the portable airlock above the survivors in case the blind one could not make its way along the corridor when the FSOJ was dead and they had begun the slow job of cutting a way in. But the sudden incredulity and anger in Fletcher's voice brought Conway's mind back to present time with a rush.

". . . And *why* can't you do it?" the Captain was demanding. "Start moving that lock at once. Haslam and I will be over to help you in a few minutes. What's the matter with you, Chen?"

"I don't feel well," said Lieutenant Chen from his position beside the blind ones' ship. "Can I be relieved, sir?"

Before the Captain could reply, Conway said, "Ask him if he has a headache of increasing severity, and is there a feeling of intense itching originating deep inside his ears. When he confirms this, tell him that the discomfort will diminish with distance from the blind ones' ship."

A few seconds later Chen was on his way back to the *Rhabwar*, having confirmed Conway's description of his symptoms. Fletcher asked helplessly, "What is happening, Doctor?"

"I should have been expecting it," Conway replied, "but it has been a long time since I had the experience. And I should have remembered that beings who, through physical damage or evolution, have been deprived of vital sensory equipment are compensated for the loss. I think—no, I know. We are experiencing telepathy."

The Captain shook his head firmly. "You're wrong, Doctor," he said. "There are a few telephathic races in the Federation, but they tend to be philosophically rather than technologically inclined, so we don't meet them very often. But even I know that their ability to communicate telepathically is confined to members of their own species. Their organic transmitter and receivers are tuned to that one frequency, and other species, even other telepathic species, cannot pick up the signals."

"Correct," said Conway. "Generally speaking, telepaths communicate only with other telepaths. But there have been a few rare exceptions recorded where non-telepaths have received their thoughts for a few seconds' or minutes' duration only, and more often than not the experimenters suffered great discomfort without making contact at all. The reason for their partial success is, according to the e-t neurologists, that many species have a latent telepathic faculty that became atrophied when they developed normal sensory equipment. But when my single, very brief experience took place I had been working closely with a very strong telepath on the same problem, seeing the same images, discussing the same symptoms and sharing the same feelings about our patient for days on end. We must have established a temporary bridge, and for a few minutes the telepath's thoughts and feelings were able to cross it."

Prilicla was shaking violently. "If the sentient survivor is trying to establish telepathic contact with us, friend Conway, it is trying very hard. It is feeling extreme desperation."

"I can understand that," said the Captain, "with a rapidly improving FSOJ nearby. Now what do we do, Doctor?"

Conway tried to make his aching head produce an answer before the surviving blind one suffered the same fate as its crew-mates. "If we could think hard about something we have in common with it. We could try thinking about the blind ones"—he waved his hand at the dissecting tables—"except that we might not have enough mental control to think of them whole and alive. If we thought about them as dissected specimens, however briefly, it would not be reassuring to the survivor. So look at and think about the FSOJ. As an experimental animal the blind one should not be bothered by seeing, feeling, experiencing or whatever, it in small pieces.

"I would like you all to concentrate on thinking about the FSOJ," he went on, looking at each of them in turn. "Concentrate hard, and at the same time try to project the feeling that you want to help. There may be some discomfort but no harmful after effects. Now think, think, *hard* . . . !"

They stared at the partially dismembered FSOJ in silence, and thought. Prilicla began trembling violently and Naydrad's fur was doing strange things indeed as it reflected the Kelgian's feelings. Murchison's face turned white and her lips were pressed together, and the Captain was sweating.

"Some discomfort, he said," Fletcher muttered.

"Discomfort to a medic," said Murchison, briefly unclenching her teeth, "can mean anything from the pain of a sprained ankle to being boiled in oil, Captain."

"Stop talking," Conway snapped. "Concentrate."

His head felt as if it could no longer contain his aching brain and there was a raging itch growing inside his skull, a sensation he had felt just once before in his life. Conway glanced quickly at Fletcher as the Captain gave an agonized grunt and started poking at his ear with a finger. And suddenly there was contact. It was a weak, unspoken message that came from nowhere, but it was there in their minds as silent words that formed both a statement and a question.

"You are thinking of my Protector . . ."

They all looked at each other, all obviously wondering if each had heard, felt, experienced the same words. The Captain let out his breath in an explosive sigh of relief, and said, "A . . . a Protector?"

"With those natural weapons," Murchison said, gesturing towards the FSOJ's horn-tipped tentacles and bony armor, "it certainly has the right equipment for the job."

"I don't understand why the blind ones need protectors," Naydrad said, "when they are technically advanced enough to build starships."

"They may have natural enemies on the home planet," began the Captain, "which they are incapable of controlling—"

"Later, later," Conway said sharply, breaking up what promised to become an interesting but time-wasting debate. "We can discuss this later when we have more data. Right now we must return to the ship. This must be extreme range for mind contact with non-telepaths like us, so we must get as close to it as possible. And this time we'll go for a rescue . . ."

With the exception of the Captain, the non-medical personnel remained with the ambulance ship. It was not thought that Haslam, Chen or Dodds could help very much unless or until they were required to burn a way into the other ship. Three extra minds that were not completely informed regarding the situation might, by their confused thinking, make it more difficult for the surviving telepath to communicate with the others, who, Conway thought dryly, were only slightly less confused than the crew-members.

Prilicla once again stationed itself near the hull to monitor emotional radiation in case the telepathy did not work. Fletcher carried a heavy-duty cutter intended, if necessary, to depressurize the ship rapidly and eliminate the Protector, and Naydrad had positioned itself with the pressure litter outside the airlock. In spite of their belief that the blind one could take decompression with much less danger than the FSOJ, Conway and Murchison would return with it inside the pressure litter should it require medical attention.

Their aching heads continued to feel as if someone were performing radical neurosurgery without benefit of an anesthetic. Since the few seconds of communication on the ambulance ship there had been nothing in their minds but their own thoughts and the maddening, itching headache, and there was no change as Murchison, Fletcher and Conway entered the lock chamber. As soon as they opened the inner seal, the noise of the corridor cage mechanisms thudding and screeching like an alien percussion section did nothing to improve their headaches.

"This time, try to think about the blind ones," said Conway as they moved inboard along the straight section of corridor. "Think about helping them. Try to ask who and what they are, because we need to know as much as possible about them if we are to help the survivor."

Even as he was speaking Conway felt that something was badly wrong, and he had an increasingly strong feeling that something terrible would happen if he did not stop and think carefully. But the raging, itching headache was making it difficult to think at all.

My Protector, the telepath on the ship had called the FSOJ. *You are thinking of my Protector.* He was missing something. But what?

"Friend Conway," Prilicla said suddenly. "Both survivors are moving along the corridor cage towards you. They are moving quickly."

They looked along the caged section with its screeching and clattering forest of waving metal bludgeons. The Captain unlimbered his cutter. "Prilicla, can you tell if the FSOJ is chasing the blind one?"

"I'm sorry, friend Fletcher," the empath replied. "They are close together. One being is radiating anger and pain, the other extreme anxiety, frustration and the emotional radiation associated with intense concentration."

"This is ridiculous!" Fletcher shouted above the suddenly increasing noise of the corridor mechanisms. "We have to kill the FSOJ if we're to rescue the blind one. I'm going to open the corridor to space—"

"No, wait!" said Conway urgently. "We haven't thought this through. We know nothing about the FSOJs, the Protectors. Think. Concentrate together. Ask, What are the Protectors? Who do they protect and why? What makes them so valuable to the blind ones? It answered once and it may answer again. Think hard!"

At that moment the FSOJ appeared round the curve of the corridor, moving rapidly in spite of the metal rods and clubs jabbing and battering at its body. The four horn-tipped tentacles whipped back and forth, pounding at the attacking metal bars and pistons and warping them out of shape, even tearing one of them out of its mounting. The noise was indescribable. The FSOJ was not quite running the course, Conway thought grimly as he saw the wounds overlaying the older scars on its body tegument and the distended underbelly, but it was moving fast, considering its condition. He felt a hand shaking his arm.

"Doctor, ma'am, are you both deaf?" Fletcher was shouting at them. "Get back to the airlock!"

"In a moment, Captain," said Murchison, shaking off Fletcher's hand and training her recorder on the advancing FSOJ. "I want to get this on tape. These aren't the surroundings I would choose in which to deliver my offspring, but then I suppose this one wasn't given any choice . . . Look out!"

The FSOJ had reached the section of corridor that had been partially cleared of the projecting metal by Fletcher's cutter. With nothing to stop it the being hurled itself through the damaged grill and was suddenly on them, floundering weightlessly now that the corridor mechanisms were no longer beating it against the floor, and spinning helplessly whenever a slashing tentacle struck the wall plating.

Conway flattened himself against the deck with his wrist and boot magnets and began crawling backwards in the direction of the airlock. Murchison was already doing the same, but the Captain was still on his feet. He was retreating slowly and waving his cutter, which he had turned up to maximum intensity, in front of him like a fiery sword. One of the FSOJ's tentacles was badly charred, but the being did not appear to be handicapped in any way. Suddenly Fletcher gave a loud grunt as one of the FSOJ's tentacles hit him on the leg, knocking him away from magnetic contact with the deck and sending him cartwheeling helplessly.

Instinctively Conway gripped an arm as it came whirling past him, steadied the Captain, then pushed him towards the lock where Murchison was waiting to help him inside. A few minutes later they were all in the lock chamber and as safe as it was possible to be within a few meters of a rampaging FSOJ.

But it was a weakening FSOJ . . .

As they watched it through the partly open inner seal, the Captain checked the actuator of his cutter and aimed it towards the outer seal. His voice was slurred with pain. "That damned thing broke my leg, I think. But now we can hold the inner seal open, cut a hole through the outer one, and depressurize the ship fast.

That'll fix the brute. But where's the other survivor? Where is the blind one?"

Slowly and deliberately, Conway covered the orifice of Fletcher's cutter with the palm of his hand. "There is no blind one. The ship's crew are dead."

Murchison and the Captain were staring at him as if he had suddenly become a mentally disturbed patient instead of the doctor. But there was no time for explanations. Slowly, and thinking hard about the words as he spoke them, he said, "We made contact with it once at long range. Now it is close to us and we must try again. There is so little time left to this being—"

The entity Conway is correct, came a soundless voice inside their heads. *I have very little time.*

"We mustn't waste it," said Conway urgently. He looked appealingly at Murchison and the Captain. "I think I know some of the answers, but we have to know more if we are to be able to help it. Think hard. What are the blind ones? Who and what are the Protectors? Why are they so valuable . . . ?"

Suddenly, they *knew*.

It was not the slow, steady trickle of data that comes through the medium of the spoken word, but a great, clear river of information that filled their minds with everything that was known about the species from its prehistory to the present time.

The Blind Ones . . .

They had begun as small, sightless, flat worms, burrowing in the primal ooze of their world, scavenging for the most part, but often paralyzing larger life-forms with their sting and ingesting them piecemeal. As they grew in size and number their food requirements increased. They became blind hunters whose sense of touch was specialized to the point where they did not need any other sensory channel.

Specialized touch sensors enabled them to feel the movements of their prey on the surface and to identify its characteristic vibrations so that they could lie in wait for it just below ground until it came within reach of their sting. Other sensors were able to feel out and identify tracks on the surface. This enabled them to follow their prey over long distances to its lair and either burrow underground and sting it from below, or attack it while the sound vibrations it was making told them it was asleep. They could not, of course, achieve much against a sighted and conscious opponent on the surface, and very often they became the prey rather than the hunters, so their hunting strategy was concentrated on variations of the ambush tactic.

On the surface they "built" tracks and other markings of small animals, and these attracted larger beasts of prey into their traps. But the surface animals were steadily becoming larger and much too strong to be seriously affected by a single Blind One's sting. They were forced to cooperate in setting up these ambushes, and cooperation in more ambitious food-gathering projects led in turn to contact on a widening scale, the formation of subsurface food stores and communities, towns, cities and interlinking systems of communication. They already "talked" to one another and educated their young by touch. Methods were even devised for augmenting and feeling vibrations over long distances.

The Blind Ones were capable of feeling vibrations in the ground and in the atmosphere, and eventually, with the use of amplifiers and transformers, they could "feel" light. They discovered fire and the wheel and the use of radio frequencies by transforming them into touch, and soon large areas of their planet were covered with radio beacons, which enabled them to undertake long journeys using mechanical transport. While they were aware of the advantages of powered flight, and a large number of Blind Ones had died experimenting with it, they preferred to stay in touch with the surface because they were, after all, completely unable to see.

This did not mean that they were unaware of their deficiency. Practically every non-sentient creature on their world had the strange ability to navigate accurately over short or long distances without the need of feeling the wind direction or the disturbances caused by vibrations bouncing off distant objects, but they had no real understanding of what the sense of sight could be. At the same time, the increasing sophistication of their long-range touching systems was making them aware that many and complex vibrations were reaching them from beyond their world, that there were sentient and probably more knowledgeable beings producing these faint touchings, and that these beings might be able to help them attain the sense that was possessed, seemingly, by all creatures except themselves.

Many, many more of the Blind Ones perished while feeling their way into space to their sister planets, but they learned eventually to travel between the stars they could not see. They sought with great difficulty and increasing hopelessness for intelligent life, feeling out world after world in vain, until finally they found the planet on which the Protectors of the Unborn lived.

The Protectors . . .

They had evolved on a world of shallow, steaming seas and swamps and jungles, where the line of demarcation between animal and vegetable life, so far as physical mobility and aggression were concerned, was unclear. To survive at all, a life-form had to move fast, and the dominant species on that world earned its place by fighting and moving and reproducing generations with a greater potential for survival than any of the others.

At a very early stage in their evolution the utter savagery of their environment had forced them into a physiological form that gave maximum protection to their vital organs—brain, heart, lungs, womb, all were deep inside the fantastically well muscled and armored body, and compressed into a relatively small volume. During gestation, the organic displacement was considerable because the embryo had to grow virtually to maturity before birth. It was rare that they were able to survive the reproduction of more than three of their kind; an aging parent was usually too weak to defend itself against attack by its last born.

But the principal reason why the Protectors rose to dominance on their world was because their young were well educated and already experienced in the techniques of survival before they were born. In the dawn of their evolution the process had begun simply as a transmission of a complex set of survival instincts at the genetic level, but the close juxtaposition of the brains of the parent and its developing embryo led to an effect analogous to induction of the electrochemical activity associated with thought. The embryos became short-range telepaths, receiving everything the parent saw or felt. And even before the growth of the embryo was complete, there was another embryo beginning to form within it that was also increasingly aware of the world outside its self-fertilizing grandparent. Then, gradually, the telepathic range increased, and communication became possible between embryos whose parents were close enough to see each other.

To minimize damage to the parent's internal organs, the growing embryo was paralyzed while in the womb, and the prebirth deparalyzing process also caused loss of sentience and the telepathic faculty. A newborn Protector would not last very long in its incredibly savage world if it was hampered by the ability to think.

With nothing to do but receive impressions from the outside world, exchange thoughts and try to widen their telepathic range by making contact with various forms of non-sentient life around them, the embryos developed minds of great power and intelligence. But they could not build anything, or engage in any form of technical research, or do anything at all that would influence the activities of their parents and protectors, who had to fight and kill and eat unceasingly to maintain their unsleeping bodies and the unborn within them.

This was the situation when the first ship of the Blind Ones landed on the planet of the Protectors and made joyful mental and savage physical contact.

Immediately it became obvious that the two life-forms needed each other—the Blind Ones, technically advanced despite their sensory deprivation, and the highly intelligent race with two-way telepathy who were trapped inside the mindless organic killing machines that were their parents. A species who had just one sensory channel open, hyperdeveloped though it was, and with the capability of traveling between the stars; and another that was capable of experiencing all sensory impressions and of relaying those experiences, who had been confined to within a few square miles of its planetary surface.

Following the initial euphoria and heavy casualties among the Blind Ones, the short- and long-term plans were made for assimilating the Protectors into their culture. To begin with, the Blind Ones did not possess many starships, but a construction program for hyperships capable of transporting Protectors to the world of the Blind Ones was begun. There, although the environment was not as savage as that of their home planet, the surface was still untamed, because the Blind Ones preferred to live underground. There they would be positioned above the Blind Ones' subsurface cities, hunting and killing the native animals while their telepathic embryos absorbed the knowledge of the citizens below them, showing the Blind Ones what it was like to *see*, for the first time, the animals and vegetation, the sky with its sun, stars and constantly changing meteorological effects.

Much later, if the Protectors bred true on the Blind Ones' planet, small numbers would be used on the hyperships to help extend the range of their exploration and search for other sentient beings. But to begin with, the Protectors were needed as the eyes of the Blind Ones on their home world, and they were brought there by specially designed transports two at a time.

It was an extremely hazardous proceeding and many ships had been lost, almost certainly because of the escape of the Protectors from confinement and the subsequent death of the Blind Ones of the crew. But the greatest loss was that of the Protectors concerned and their precious telepathic Unborn.

On the present occasion one of the Protectors had broken out of the corridor cage and had been slow to lose consciousness when the beating and pummeling of its environmental support system had been withdrawn. It had killed one of the crew whose fellow crewmember had also been killed while going to its mate's assistance, then it had died accidentally on the second Blind One's sting. But before the Blind One died, it had released the distress beacon and deactivated the corridor cage mechanisms so as to render the surviving Protector unconscious, thus avoiding danger to any would-be rescuers until the telepathic embryo could explain matters.

But the Blind One had made two mistakes, neither of which were its fault. It had assumed that all races would be capable of making telepathic contact with the embryo as easily as had the Blind Ones, and it had also assumed that the embryo would remain conscious after its Protector became unconscious . . .

The great flood of data pouring into their minds had slowed gradually. It became specific rather than general, a clear, narrow conversational stream.

. . . *The Protector life-form is under constant attack from the moment of its birth until it dies,* the silent voice in their minds went on, *and the continuous physical assault plays an important part in maintaining the physiological system at optimum. To withdraw this violent stimulation causes an effect analogous to strangulation, if I read the entity Conway's mind correctly, including greatly reduced blood pressure, diminished sensoria and loss of voluntary muscle activity. The entity Murchison is also thinking, correctly, that the embryo concerned is similarly affected.*

When the entity Fletcher accidentally reactivated the corridor mechanisms, the return to consciousness of my Protector and myself was begun, then checked again when they were switched off, only to be turned on again at the insistence of the entity whom you call Prilicla, whose mind I cannot contact although it is more sensitive to my feelings than my thoughts. Those feelings were of urgency and frustration because I had to explain the situation to you before I died.

While there is still time I would like to thank you with all the remaining strength of my mind for making contact, and for showing me in your minds the marvels which exist not only on my planet and the world of the Blind Ones, but throughout your Federation. And I apologize for the pain caused while establishing this contact, and for the injury to the entity Fletcher's limb. As you now know, I have no control over the actions of my Protector . . .

"Wait," said Conway suddenly. "There is no reason why you should die. The life-support systems, your corridor mechanisms and food dispensers are still operative and will remain so until we can move your ship to Sector General. We can take care of you. Our resources are much greater than those of the Blind Ones . . ."

Conway fell silent, feeling helpless despite his confident offer of help. The Protector's tentacles were lashing out weakly and in haphazard fashion as it drifted weightless and obviously dying in the center of the corridor, and each time one of them struck the wall or deck the reaction sent it spinning slowly. There was, therefore, a good if intermittent view of the whole birth process as first the head and then the four tentacles appeared. As yet, the Unborn's limbs were limp and unmoving because the secretions that would release the prebirth paralysis, and at the same time obliterate all cerebral activity not associated with survival, had not taken effect. Then, abruptly, the tentacles twitched, threshed about and began pulling the recently Unborn out of its parent's birth canal.

The soundless voice in their minds returned, but this time it was no longer sharp and clear. There was a feeling of pain and confusion and deep anxiety muddying up the clear stream of communication, but fortunately the message was simple:

To be born is to die, friends. My mind and my telephatic faculty are being destroyed, and I am becoming a Protector with my own Unborn to protect while it grows and thinks and makes contact with you. Please cherish it . . .

*   *   *

There had been some crepitation associated with the Captain's fractured tibia, and Conway had administered a strong painkiller to make him comfortable during the trip back to the ambulance ship. Fletcher remained fully conscious, and because of the relaxing of inhibitions that was a side effect of the medication, he talked continuously and anxiously about the Unborn telepaths and the Blind Ones.

"Don't worry about them, Captain," Murchison told him. They had moved Fletcher to the Casualty Deck, and she was helping Naydrad remove his spacesuit while Conway and Prilicla assembled the tools necessary for a piece of minor structural repair work. She went on: "The hospital will treat them with tender, loving care, never fear, although I can just imagine O'Mara's face when he learns that they have to be accommodated in what amounts to a torture chamber. And no doubt your Cultural Contact people will be there, too, hoping to obtain the services of a wide-range telepath . . ."

"But the Blind Ones need them most of all," Fletcher went on worriedly. "Just think of it. After millions of years in darkness they've found a way of seeing, even if their eyes can turn and quite literally kill them."

"Given a little time," Murchison said reassuringly, "the hospital will turn up the answer to that, too. Thornnastor just loves puzzles like this one. The continuous conception business, for instance, the embryo within an embryo. If we were able to isolate and inhibit the effects of the secretion that destroys the sentient portion of the Unborn's brain prior to birth, we would have telepathic Protectors as well as Unborn. And if the environmental beating they take all their lives was toned down gradually and eventually eliminated, they might get out of the habit of trying to kill and eat everything they see. The Blind Ones would have the telepathic eyes they need without danger to themselves, and they could roam all over the Galaxy if they wanted to."

She paused to help Naydrad cut away the trouser leg of the Captain's uniform, then addressed Conway. "He's ready for you now, Doctor."

Murchison and Naydrad were in position, and Prilicla was hovering above them, radiating feelings of reassurance. Conway said, "Relax, Captain. Forget about the Blind Ones and the Protectors. They will be all right. And so will you. After all, I'm a senior physician in the Federation's most advanced multienvironment hospital. But if you really feel the need to worry about something, think about my present problem." He smiled suddenly, and added, "It must be ten years since I last set a fractured DBDG tibia."

SECTOR
GENERAL

DEDICATED TO THE FRIENDS OF KILGORE TROUT,
WHO TREAT THE IMPOSSIBLE
WITH THE CONTEMPT IT DESERVES.

ACCIDENT

Retlin complex was Nidia's largest air terminal, its only spaceport, and, MacEwan thought cynically, its most popular zoo.
The main concourse was thronged with furry native airline passengers, sightseers, and ground personnel, but the thickest crowd was
outside the transparent walls of the off-planet departure lounge
where Nidians of all ages jostled each other in their eagerness to see
the waiting space travelers.

But the crowd parted quickly before the Corpsmen escorting
MacEwan and his companion—no native would risk giving offense
to an offworlder by making even accidental bodily contact. From the
departure lounge entrance, the two were directed to a small office
whose transparent walls darkened into opacity at their approach.

The man facing them was a full Colonel and the ranking Monitor Corps officer on Nidia, but until they had seated themselves he
remained standing, respectfully, as befitted one who was meeting for
the first time the great Earth-human MacEwan and the equally legendary Orligian Grawlya-Ki. He remained on his feet for a moment
longer while he looked with polite disapproval at their uniforms,
torn and stained relics of an almost forgotten war, then he glanced
toward the solidograph that occupied one corner of his desk and
sat down.

Quietly he began, "The planetary assembly has decided that you
are no longer welcome on Nidia, and you are requested to leave at
once. My organization, which is the closest thing we have to a neutral extraplanetary police force, has been asked to implement this

request. I would prefer that you leave without the use of physical coercion. I am sorry. This is not pleasant for me, either, but I have to say that I agree with the Nidians. Your peacemongering activities of late have become much too . . . warlike."

Grawlya-Ki's chest swelled suddenly, making its stiff, spikey fur rasp dryly against the old battle harness, but the Orligian did not speak. MacEwan said tiredly, "We were just trying to make them understand that—"

"I know what you were trying to do," the Colonel broke in, "but half wrecking a video studio during a rehearsal was not the way to do it. Besides, you know as well as I do that your supporters were much more interested in taking part in a riot than in promulgating your ideas. You simply gave them an excuse to—"

"The play glamorized war," MacEwan said.

The Monitor's eyes flickered toward the solidograph, then back to Grawlya-Ki and MacEwan again. His tone softened. "I'm sorry, believe me, but you will have to leave. I cannot force it, but ideally you should return to your home planets where you could relax and live out your remaining years in peace. Your wounds must have left mental scars and you may require psychiatric assistance; and, well, I think both of you deserve some of the peace that you want so desperately for everyone else."

When there was no response, the Colonel sighed and said, "Where do you want to go this time?"

"Traltha," MacEwan said.

The Monitor looked surprised. "That is a hot, high-gravity, heavily industrialized world, people by lumbering, six-legged elephants who are hardworking, peaceloving, and culturally stable. There hasn't been a war on Traltha for a thousand years. You would be wasting your time there, and feeling very uncomfortable while doing so, but it's your choice."

"On Traltha," MacEwan said, "commerical warfare never stops. One kind of war can lead to another."

The Colonel made no attempt to disguise his impatience. "You are frightening yourselves without reason and, in any case, maintaining the peace is our concern. We do it quietly, discreetly, by keeping potentially troublesome entities and situations under observation, and by making the minimum response early, before things can get out of control. We do a good job, if I do say so myself. But Traltha is not a danger, now or in the foreseeable future." He smiled. "Another war between Orligia and Earth would be more likely."

"That will not happen, Colonel," Grawlya-Ki said, its modulated growling forming a vaguely threatening accompaniment to the accentless speech coming from its translator pack. "Former enemies who have beaten hell out of each other make the best friends. But there has to be an easier way of making friends."

Before the officer could reply, MacEwan went on quickly, "I understand what the Monitor Corps is doing, Colonel, and I approve. Everybody does. It is rapidly becoming accepted as the Federation's executive and law-enforcement arm. But it can never become a truly multispecies service. Its officers, of necessity, will be almost entirely Earth-human. With so much power entrusted to one species—"

"We are aware of the danger," the Colonel broke in. Defensively he went on, "Our psychologists are working on the problems and our people are highly trained in e-t cultural contact procedures. And we have the authority to ensure that the members of every ship's crew making other-species contacts are similarly trained. Everyone is aware of the danger of uttering or committing an unthinking word or action which could be construed as hostile, and of what might ensue. We lean over backward in our efforts not to give offense. You know that."

The Colonel was first and foremost a policeman, MacEwan thought, and like a good policeman he resented any criticism of his service. What was more, his irritation with the two aging war veterans was rapidly reaching the point where the interview would be terminated. *Take it easy,* he warned himself, *this man is not an enemy.*

Aloud he said, "The point I'm trying to make is that leaning over backward is an inherently unstable position, and this hyperpoliteness where extraterrestrials are concerned is artificial, even dishonest. The tensions generated must ultimately lead to trouble, even between the handpicked and highly intelligent entities who are the only people allowed to make off-planet contacts. This type of contact is too narrow, too limited. The member species of the Federation are not really getting to know and trust each other, and they never will until contact becomes more relaxed and natural. As things

218 · JAMES WHITE

are it would be unthinkable to have even a friendly argument with an extraterrestrial.

"We must get to really know them, Colonel," MacEwan went on quickly. "Well enough not to have to be so damnably polite all the time. If a Tralthan jostles a Nidian or an Earth-human, we must know the being well enough to tell it to watch where it's going and to call it any names which seem appropriate to the occasion. We should expect the same treatment if the fault is ours. Ordinary people, not a carefully selected and trained star-traveling elite, must get to know offworlders well enough to be able to argue or even to quarrel nonviolently with them, without—"

"And that," the Monitor said coldly, rising to his feet, "is the reason you are leaving Nidia. For disturbing the peace."

Hopelessly, MacEwan tried again. "Colonel, we must find some common ground on which the ordinary citizens of the Federation can meet. Not just because of scientific and cultural exchanges or interstellar trade treaties. It must be something basic, something we all feel strongly about, an idea or a project that we can really get together on. In spite of our much-vaunted Federation and the vigilance of your Monitor Corps, perhaps because of that vigilance, we are *not* getting to know each other properly. Unless we do another war is inevitable. But nobody worries. You've all forgotten how terrible war is."

He broke off as the Colonel pointed slowly to the solidograph on his desk, then brought the hand back to his side again. "We have a constant reminder," he said.

After that the Colonel would say no more, but remained standing stiffly at attention until Grawlya-Ki and MacEwan left the office.

The departure lounge was more than half filled with tight, exclusive little groups of Tralthans, Melfans, Kelgians, and Illensans. There was also a pair of squat, tentacular, heavy-gravity beings who were apparently engaged in spraying each other with paint, and which were a new life-form to MacEwan. A teddybearlike Nidian wearing the blue sash of the nontechnical ground staff moved from behind them to escape the spray, but otherwise ignored the creatures.

There was some excuse for the chlorine-breathing Illensans to keep to themselves: the loose, transparent material of their protective envelopes looked fragile. He did not know anything about the paint-spraying duo, but the others were all warm-blooded, oxygen-breathing life-forms with similar pressure and gravity requirements and they should, at least, have been acknowledging each others' presence even if they did not openly display the curiosity they must be feeling toward each other. Angrily, MacEwan turned away to examine the traffic movements display.

There was an Illensan factory ship in orbit, a great, ungainly nonlander whose shuttle had touched down a few minutes earlier, and a Nidian ground transporter fitted with the chlorine breathers' life-support was on the way in to pick up passengers. Their Tralthan-built and crewed passenger ship was nearly ready to board and stood on its apron on the other side of the main aircraft runway. It was one of the new ships which boasted of providing comfortable accommodation for six different oxygen-breathing species, but degrees of comfort were relative and MacEwan, Grawlya-Ki, and the other non-Tralthans in the lounge would shortly be judging it for themselves.

Apart from the Illensan shuttle and the Tralthan vessel, the only traffic was the Nidian atmosphere craft which took off and landed every few minutes. They were not large aircraft, but they did not need to be to hold a thousand Nidians. As the aircraft differed only in their registration markings, it seemed that the same machine was endlessly taking off and landing.

Angry because there was nothing else in the room to engage his attention fully, and because it occupied such a prominent position in the center of the lounge that all eyes were naturally drawn to it, MacEwan turned finally to look once again at that frightful and familiar tableau.

Grawlya-Ki had already done so and was whining softly to itself.

It was a life-sized replica of the old Orligian war memorial, one of the countless thousands of copies which occupied public places of honor or appeared in miniature on the desks or in the homes of responsible and concerned beings on every world of the Federation. The original had stood within its protective shield in the central Plaza of Orligia's capital city for more than two centuries, during which a great many native and visiting entities of sensitivity and intelligence had tried vainly to describe its effect upon them.

For that war memorial was no aesthetic marble poem in which godlike figures gestured defiance or lay dying nobly with limbs arranged to the best advantage. Instead it consisted of an Orligian and an Earthman, surrounded by the shattered remnants of a Control Room belonging to a type of ship now long obsolete.

The Orligian was standing crouched forward, the fur of its chest and face matted with blood. A few yards away lay the Earth-human, very obviously dying. The front of his uniform was in shreds, revealing the ghastly injuries he had sustained. Abdominal organs normally concealed by skin, layers of subcutaneous tissue and muscle were clearly visible. Yet this man, who had no business being alive much less being capable of movement, was struggling toward the Orligian.

Two combatants amid the wreckage of a warship trying to continue their battle hand-to-hand?

The dozens of plaques spaced around the base of the tableau described the incident in all the written languages of the Federation.

They told of the epic, single-ship duel between the Orligian and the Earth-human commanders. So evenly matched had they been that, their respective crew members dead, their ships shot to pieces, armaments depleted and power gone, they had crash-landed close together on a world unknown to both of them. The Orligian, anxious to learn all it could regarding enemy ship systems, and driven by a more personal curiosity about its opponent, had boarded the wrecked Earth ship. They met.

For them the war was over, because the terribly wounded Earth-human did not know when he was going to die and the Orligian did not know when, if ever, its distress signal would bring rescuers. The distant, impersonal hatred they had felt toward each other was gone, dissipated by the six-hour period of maximum effort that had been their duel, and was replaced by feelings of mutual respect for the degree of professional competence displayed. So they tried to communicate, and succeeded.

It had been a slow, difficult, and extraordinarily painful process for both of them, but when they did talk they held nothing back. The Orligian knew that any verbal insubordination it might utter would die with this Earth-human, who in turn sensed the other's sympathy and was in too much pain to care about the things he said about his own superiors. And while they talked the Earth-human learned something of vital importance, an enemy's-eye view of the simple, stupid, and jointly misunderstood incident which had been responsible for starting the war in the first place.

It had been during the closing stages of this conversation that an Orligian ship which chanced to be in the area had landed and, after assessing the situation, used its Stopper on the Earth wreck.

Even now the operating principles of the Orligian primary space weapon were unclear to MacEwan. The weapon was capable of enclosing a small ship, or vital sections of a large one, within a field of stasis in which all motion stopped. Neither the ships nor their crew were harmed physically, but if someone so much as scratched the surface of one of those Stopped hulls or tried to slip a needle into the skin of one of the Stopped personnel, the result was an explosion of near-nuclear proportions.

But the Orligian stasis field projector had peaceful as well as military applications.

With great difficulty the section of Control Room and the two Stopped bodies it contained had been moved to Orligia, to occupy the central square of the planetary capital as the most gruesomely effective war memorial ever known, for two hundred and thirty-six years. During that time the shaky peace which the two frozen beings had brought about between Orligia and Earth ripened into friendship, and medical science progressed to the point where the terribly injured Earth-human could be saved. Although its injuries had not been fatal, Grawlya-Ki had insisted on being Stopped with its friend so that it could see MacEwan cured for itself.

And then the two greatest heroes of the war, heroes because they had ended it, were removed from stasis, rushed to a hospital, and cured. For the first time, it was said, the truly great of history would receive the reward they deserved from posterity—and that was the way it had happened, just over thirty years ago.

Since then the two heroes, the only two entities in the whole Federation with direct experience of war, had grown increasingly monomaniacal on the subject until the honor and respect accorded them had gradually changed to reactions of impatience and embarrassment.

"Sometimes, Ki," MacEwan said, turning away from the frozen

figures of their former selves, "I wonder if we should give up and try to find peace of mind like the Colonel said. Nobody listens to us anymore, yet all we are trying to tell them is to relax, to take off their heavy, bureaucratic gauntlets when extending the hand of friendship, and to speak and react honestly so that—"

"I am aware of the arguments," Grawlya-Ki broke in, "and the completely unnecessary restatement of them, especially to one who shares your feelings in this matter, is suggestive of approaching senility."

"Listen, you mangy, overgrown baboon!" MacEwan began furiously, but the Orligian ignored him.

"And senility is a condition which cannot be successfully treated by the Colonel's psychiatrists," it went on. "Neither, I submit, can they give psychiatric assistance to minds which are otherwise sane. As for my localized loss of fur, you are so lacking in male hormones that you can only grow it on your head and—"

"And your females grow more fur than you do," MacEwan snapped back, then stopped.

He had been conned again.

Since that first historic meeting in MacEwan's wrecked Control Room they had grown to know each other very well. Grawlya-Ki had assessed the present situation, decided that MacEwan was feeling far too depressed for his own good, and instituted curative treatment in the form of a therapeutic argument combined with subtle reassurance regarding their sanity. MacEwan smiled.

"This frank and honest exchange of views," he said quietly, "is distressing the other travelers. They probably think the Earth-Orligian war is about to restart, because they would never dream of saying such things to each other."

"But they do dream," Grawlya-Ki said, its mind going off at one of its peculiarly Orligian tangents. "All intelligent life-forms require periods of unconsciousness during which they dream. Or have nightmares."

"The trouble is," MacEwan said, "they don't share our particular nightmare."

Grawlya-Ki was silent. Through the transparent outer wall of the lounge it was watching the rapid approach of the ground transporter from the Illensan shuttle. The vehicle was a great, multi-wheeled silver bullet distinctively marked to show that it was filled with chlorine, and tipped with a transparent control module whose atmosphere was suited to its Nidian driver. MacEwan wondered why all of the smaller intelligent life-forms, regardless of species, had a compulsion to drive fast. Had he stumbled upon one of the great cosmic truths?

"Maybe we should try a different approach," the Orligian said, still watching the transporter. "Instead of trying to frighten them with nightmares, we should find them a pleasant and inspiring dream to—What is that idiot *doing*?"

The vehicle was still approaching at speed, making no attempt to slow or turn so as to present its transfer lock to the lounge's exit port for breathers of toxic atmospheres. All of the waiting travelers were watching it now, many of them making noises which did not translate.

The driver is showing off, MacEwan thought. Reflected sunlight from the canopy obscured the occupant. It was not until the transporter ran into the shadow of the terminal building that MacEwan saw the figure of the driver slumped face downward over its control console, but by then it was too late for anyone to do anything.

Built as it was from tough, laminated plastic nearly a foot thick, the transparent wall bulged inward but did not immediately shatter as the nose of the vehicle struck. The control module and its occupant were instantly flattened into a thin pancake of riven metal, tangled wiring, and bloody Nidian fur. Then the transporter broke through.

When the driver had collapsed and lost control, the automatic power cutoff and emergency braking systems must have been triggered. But in spite of its locked wheels the transporter skidded ponderously on, enlarging the original break in the transparent wall and losing sections of its own external plating in the process. It plowed through the neat rows of Tralthan, Melfan, Kelgian, and Illensan furniture. The heavy, complex structures were ripped from their floor mountings and hurled aside along with the beings unfortunate enough to still be occupying them. Finally the transporter ground to a halt against one of the building's roof support pillars, which bent alarmingly but did not break. The shock brought down most of the lounge's ceiling panels and with them a choking, blinding cloud of dust.

All around MacEwan extraterrestrials were coughing and floundering about and making untranslatable noises indicative of pain and distress, Grawlya-Ki included. He blinked dust out of his eyes and saw that the Orligian was crouched, apparently uninjured, beside the transporter. Both of its enormous, furry hands were covering its face and it looked as if it would shake itself apart with the violence of its coughing. MacEwan kicked loose debris out of the way and moved toward it. Then his eyes began to sting and, just in time, he covered his mouth and nose to keep from inhaling the contaminated air.

Chlorine!

With his free hand he grasped the Orligian's battle harness and began dragging it away from the damaged vehicle, wondering angrily why he was wasting his time. If the internal pressure hull had been ruptured, the whole lounge would be rendered uninhabitable to oxygen breathers within a few minutes—the Illensans' higher-pressure chlorine atmosphere would see to that. Then he stumbled against a low, sprawling, membranous body which was hissing and twitching amid the debris and realized that it was not only the damaged vehicle which was responsible for the contamination.

The Illensan must have been hit by the transporter and flung against a Kelgian relaxer frame, which had collapsed. One of the support struts had snagged the chlorine breather's pressure envelope, ripping it open along the entire length of the body. The oxygen-rich atmosphere was attacking the unprotected body, coating the skin with a powdery, sickly blue organic corrosion which was thickest around the two breathing orifices. All body movement ceased as MacEwan watched, but he could still hear a loud hissing sound.

Still keeping his mouth and nostrils sealed with one hand, he used the other to feel along the Illensan's body and pressure envelope. His eyes were stinging even though they were now tightly shut.

The creature's skin felt hot, slippery, and fibrous, with patterns of raised lines which made it seem that the whole body was covered by the leaves of some coarse-textured plant, and there were times when MacEwan did not know whether he was touching the skin or the ruptured pressure suit. The sound of the pulse in his head was incredible, like a constant, thudding explosion, and the constriction in his chest was fast reaching the stage where he was ready to inhale even chlorine to stop that fiery, choking pain in his lungs. But he fought desperately not to breathe, pressing his hand so tightly against his face that his nose began to bleed.

After what seemed like a couple of hours later, he felt the shape of a large cylinder with a hose connection and strange-feeling bumps and projections at one end—the Illensan's air tank. He pulled and twisted desperately at controls designed for the spatulate digits of an Illensan, and suddenly the hiss of escaping chlorine ceased.

He turned and staggered away, trying to get clear of the localized cloud of toxic gas so he could breathe again. But he had gone only a few yards when he tripped and fell into a piece of broken e-t furniture covered by a tangle of plastic drapery which had been used to decorate the lounge. His free arm kept him from injuring himself, but it was not enough to enable him to escape from the tangle of tubing and plastic which had somehow wrapped itself around his feet. He opened his eyes and shut them again hastily as the chlorine stung them. With such a high concentration of gas he could not risk opening his mouth to shout for help. The noise inside his head was unbelievable. He felt himself slipping into a roaring, pounding blackness, and there was a tight band gripping and squeezing his chest.

There *was* something gripping his chest. He felt it lifting him, shaking him free of the debris entangling his arm and legs, and holding him aloft while it carried him for an unknown distance across the lounge. Suddenly he felt his feet touch the floor and he opened his eyes and mouth.

The smell of chlorine was still strong but he could breathe and see. Grawlya-Ki was standing a few feet away, looking concerned and pointing at the blood bubbling from his nose, and one of the two paint-spraying extraterrestrials was detaching one of its thick, iron-hard tentacles from around his chest. He was too busy just breathing again to be able to say anything.

"I apologize most abjectly and sincerely," his rescuer boomed over the sounds being made by the injured all around them, "if I have in any fashion hurt you, or subjected you to mental trauma or embarrassment by making such a gross and perhaps intimate physical contact with your body. I would not have dared touch you at all had not your Orligian friend insisted that you were in grave danger and requested that I lift you clear. But if I have given offense—"

"You have not given offense," MacEwan broke in. "On the contrary, you have saved my life at great risk to your own. That chlorine is deadly stuff to all us oxygen breathers. Thank you."

It was becoming difficult to speak without coughing because the cloud of gas from the dead Illensan's suit was spreading, and Grawlya-Ki was already moving away. MacEwan was about to follow when the creature spoke again.

"I am in no immediate danger." Its eyes glittered at him from behind their hard, organic shields as it went on. "I am a Hudlar, Earthperson. My species does not breathe, but absorbs sustenance directly from our atmosphere, which, near the planetary surface, is analogous to a thick, high-pressure, semigaseous soup. Apart from requiring our body surface to be sprayed at frequent intervals with a nutrient paint, we are not inconvenienced by any but the most corrosive of atmospheres, and we can even work for lengthy periods in vacuum conditions on orbital construction projects.

"I am glad to have been of assistance, Earthperson," the Hudlar ended, "but I am not a hero."

"Nevertheless I am grateful," MacEwan shouted, then stopped moving away. He waved his hand, indicating the lounge which resembled a battlefield rather than a luxurious departure point for the stars, and started coughing. Finally he was able to say, "Pardon me, please, if I am being presumptuous, but is it possible for you to similarly assist the other beings who have been immobilized by their injuries and are in danger of asphyxiation?"

The second Hudlar had joined them, but neither spoke. Grawlya-Ki was waving at him and pointing toward the transparent wall of the Colonel's office where the Monitor Corps officer was also gesticulating urgently.

"Ki, will you find out what he wants?" MacEwan called to the Orligian. To the first Hudlar he went on, "You are understandably cautious in the matter of physically handling members of another species, lest you inadvertently give offense, and in normal circumstances this would be wholly admirable and the behavior of a being of sensitivity and intelligence. But this is not a normal situation, and it is my belief that any accidental physical intimacy committed on the injured would be forgiven when the intention is purely to give assistance. In these circumstances a great many beings could die who would otherwise—"

"Some of them will die of boredom or old age," the second Hudlar said suddenly, "if we continue to waste time with unnecessary politeness. Plainly we Hudlars have a physical advantage here. What is it you wish us to do?"

"I apologize most abjectly for my lifemate's ill-considered and hasty remarks, Earth-human," the first Hudlar said quickly. "And for any offense they may have given."

"No need. None taken," MacEwan said, laughing in sheer relief until the chlorine turned it into a cough. He considered prefacing his instructions with advance apologies for any offense he might inadvertently give to the Hudlars, then decided that that would be wasting more time. He took a deep, careful breath and spoke.

"The chlorine level is still rising around that transporter. Would one of you remove heavy debris from casualties in the area affected and move them to the entrance to the boarding tunnel, where they can be moved into the tunnel itself if the level continues to rise. The other should concentrate on rescuing Illensans by lifting them into their transporter. There is a lock antechamber just inside the entry port, and hopefully some of the less seriously injured chlorine breathers will be able to get them through the lock and give them first aid inside. The Orligian and myself will try to move the casualties not immediately in danger from the chlorine, and open the boarding tunnel entrance. Ki, what have you got there?"

The Orligian had returned with more than a dozen small cylinders, with breathing masks and straps attached, cradled in both arms. It said, "Fire-fighting equipment. The Colonel directed me to the emergency locker. But it's Nidian equipment. The masks won't fit very well, and with some of these beings they won't fit at all. Maybe we can hold them in position and—"

"This aspect of the problem does not concern us," the first Hudlar broke in. "Earthperson, what do we do with casualties whose injuries might be compounded by the assistance of well-meaning rescuers ignorant of the physiology of the being concerned?"

MacEwan was already tying a cylinder to his chest, passing the attachment over one shoulder and under the opposite armpit because the Nidian straps were too short to do otherwise. He said grimly, "We will have that problem, too."

"Then we will use our best judgment," the second Hudlar said, moving ponderously toward the transporter, followed closely by its lifemate.

"That isn't the only problem," Grawlya-Ki said as it, too, attached a cylinder to its harness. "The collision cut our communications and the Colonel can't tell the terminal authorities about the situation in here, nor does he know what the emergency services are doing about it. He also says that the boarding tunnel entrance won't open while there is atmospheric contamination in the lounge—it is part of the safety system designed to contain such contamination so that it won't spread along the boarding tunnel to the waiting ship or into the main concourse. The system can be overridden at this end, but only by a special key carried by the Nidian senior ground staff member on duty in the lounge. Have you seen this being?"

"Yes," MacEwan said grimly. "It was standing at the exit port just before the crash. I think it is somewhere underneath the transporter."

Grawlya-Ki whined quietly, then went on, "The Colonel is using his personal radio to contact a docked Monitor Corps vessel to try to patch into the port network that way, but so far without effect. The Nidian rescue teams are doing all the talking and are not listening to outsiders. But if he gets through he wants to know what to tell them. The number and condition of the casualties, the degree of contamination, and optimum entry points for the rescue teams. He wants to talk to you."

"I don't want to talk to him," MacEwan said. He did not know enough to be able to make a useful situation report, and until he did their time could be used to much better effect than worrying out loud to the Colonel. He pointed to an object which looked like a gray, bloodstained sack which twitched and made untranslatable sounds, and said, "That one first."

The injured Kelgian was difficult to move, MacEwan found, especially when there was just one Orligian arm and two human ones to take the weight. Grawlya-Ki's mask was such a bad fit that it had to hold it in position. The casualty was a caterpillar-like being with more than twenty legs and an overall covering of silvery fur now badly bloodstained. But the body, although no more massive than that of a human, was completely flaccid. There seemed to be no skeleton, no bony parts at all except possibly in the head section, but it felt as though there were wide, concentric bands of muscle running the length of the body just underneath the fur.

It rolled and flopped about so much that by the time he had raised it from the floor, supporting its head and midsection between his outstretched arms and chest—Grawlya-Ki had the tail gripped between its side and free arm—one of the wounds began bleeding. Because MacEwan was concentrating on holding the Kelgian's body immobile as they moved it toward the boarding tunnel entrance, his mind was not on his feet; they became tangled in a piece of decorative curtain, and he fell to his knees. Immediately the Kelgian's blood began to well out at an alarming rate.

"We should do something about that," the Orligian said, its voice muffled by the too-small mask. "Any ideas?"

The Service had taught MacEwan only the rudiments of first aid because casualties in a space war tended to be explosive decompressions and rarely if ever treatable, and what little he had learned applied to beings of his own species. Serious bleeding was controlled by cutting off the supply of blood to the wound with a tourniquet or local pressure. The Kelgian's circulatory system seemed to be very close to its skin, possibly because those great, circular bands of muscle required lots of blood. But the position of the veins were hidden by the being's thick fur. He thought that a pad and tight bandages were the only treatment possible. He did not have a pad and there was no time to go looking for one, but there was a bandage of sorts still wrapped loosely around his ankle.

He kicked the length of plastic curtain off his foot, then pulled about two meters free of the pile of debris which had fallen with it. The stuff was tough and he needed all his strength to make a transverse tear in it, but it was wide enough to cover the wound with several inches to spare. With the Orligian's help he held the plastic in position over the wound and passed the two ends around the cylindrical body, knotting them very tightly together.

Probably the makeshift bandage was too tight, and where it

passed around the Kelgian's underside it was pressing two sets of the being's legs against the underbelly in a direction they were not, perhaps, designed to bend, and he hated to think of what the dust and dirt adhering to the plastic might be doing to that open wound.

The same thought must have been going through the Orligian's head, because it said, "Maybe we'll find another Kelgian who isn't too badly hurt and knows what to do."

But it was a long time before they found another Kelgian—at least, it felt like an hour even though the big and, strangely, still-functioning lounge clock, whose face was divided into concentric rings marked off in the time units of the major Federation worlds, insisted that it was only ten minutes.

One of the Hudlars had lifted wreckage from two of the crablike Melfans, one of whom was coherent, seemingly uninjured but unable to see because of the chlorine or dust. Grawlya-Ki spoke reassuringly to it and led it away by grasping a thick, fleshy projection, purpose unknown, growing from its head. The other Melfan made loud, untranslatable noises. Its carapace was cracked in several places and of the three legs which should have supported it on one side, two were limp and useless and one was missing altogether.

MacEwan bent down quickly and slipped his hands and lower arms under the edge of the carapace between the two useless legs and lifted until the body was at its normal walking height. Immediately the legs on the other side began moving slowly. MacEwan sidled along at the same pace, supporting the injured side and guiding the Melfan around intervening wreckage until he was able to leave it beside its blinded colleague.

He could think of nothing more to do for it, so he rejoined the Hudlar excavating among the heavier falls of debris.

They uncovered three more Melfans, injured but ambulatory, who were directed to the boarding tunnel entrance, and a pair of the elephantine, six-legged Tralthans who appeared to be uninjured but were badly affected by the gas which was still leaking steadily from the transporter. MacEwan and Grawlya-Ki each held a Nidian breathing mask to one breathing orifice and yelled at them to close the other. Then they tried desperately not to be trampled underfoot as they guided the Tralthans to the casualty assembly point. Then they uncovered two more of the Kelgian caterpillars, one of whom had obviously bled to death from a deep tear in its flank. The other had five of its rearmost sets of legs damaged, rendering it immobile, but it was conscious and able to cooperate by holding its body rigid while they carried it back to the others.

When MacEwan asked the being if it could help the earlier Kelgian casualty he had tried to bandage, it said that it had no medical training and could think of nothing further to do.

There were more walking, wriggling, and crawling wounded released from the wreckage to join the growing crowd of casualties at the tunnel entrance. Some of them were talking but most were making loud, untranslatable noises which had to be of pain. The sounds made by the casualties still trapped by fallen wreckage were slight by comparison.

The Hudlars were working tirelessly and often invisibly in a cloud of self-created dust, but now they seemed to be uncovering only organic wreckage of which there was no hope of salvage. There was another Kelgian who had bled spectacularly to death; two, or it may have been three, Melfans with crushed and shattered carapaces and broken limbs, and a Tralthan who had been smashed flat by a collapsing roof beam and was still trying to move.

MacEwan was afraid to touch any of them in case they fell apart in his hands, but he could not be absolutely sure that they were beyond help. He had no idea of their ability to survive major injury, or whether specialized medical intervention could save them if taken in time. He felt angry and useless and the chlorine was beginning to penetrate his face mask.

"This being appears to be uninjured," the Hudlar beside them said. It had lifted a heavy table from a Tralthan who was lying on its side, its six massive legs twitching feebly and its domelike brain casing, multiple eye-trunk, and thick, leathery hide free of any visible signs of damage. "Could it be that it is troubled only by the toxic gas?"

"You're probably right," MacEwan said. He and Grawlya-Ki pressed Nidian masks over the Tralthan's breathing orifices. Several minutes passed with no sign of improvement in its condition. MacEwan's eyes were stinging even though he, like the Orligian, was using one hand to press the mask tightly against his face. Angrily, he said, "Have you any other ideas?"

The anger was directed at his own helplessness, and he felt like kicking himself for taking it out on the Hudlar. He could not tell the two beings apart, only that one tended to sound worried, long-winded, and overly polite, while its lifemate was more forthright. This one, luckily, was the former.

"It is possible that its injuries are to the flank lying against the floor and are presently invisible to us," the Hudlar said ponderously. "Or that the being, which is a squat, heavy-gravity creature with certain physical similarities to myself, is seriously inconvenienced by being laid on its side. While we Hudlars can work comfortably in weightless conditions, gravity if present must act downward or within a very short time serious and disabling organ displacement occurs. There is also the fact that all Tralthan ships use an artificial gravity system with multiple failsafe backup, which is just one of the reasons for the dependability and popularity of Tralthan-built ships. This suggests that a lateral gravity pull must be avoided by them at all costs, and that this particular being is—"

"Stop talking about it," the second Hudlar said, joining them, "and lift the thing."

The Hudlar extended its forward pair of tentacles and, bracing itself with the other four in front of the Tralthan's weakly moving feet, slid them over the creature's back and insinuated them between the floor and its other flank. MacEwan watched as the tentacles tightened, took the strain, and began to quiver. But the body did not move, and the other Hudlar positioned itself to assist.

MacEwan was surprised, and worried. He had seen those tentacles, which served both as ambulatory and manipulatory appendages, lifting beams, major structural members, and large masses of wreckage seemingly without effort. They were beautifully evolved limbs, immensely strong and with thick, hardened pads forming a knuckle on which the being walked while the remainder of the tentacle—the thinner, more flexible half tipped with a cluster of specialized digits—was carried curled inward against its underside. The Tralthan they were trying to move was roughly the mass of an Earthly baby elephant, and the combined efforts of both Hudlars were shifting it only slightly.

"Wait," MacEwan said urgently. "Both of you have lifted much heavier weights. I think the Tralthan is caught, perhaps impaled on a structural projection, and you cannot move it because—"

"We cannot move it," the polite Hudlar said, "because we have been expending large amounts of energy after insufficient sustenance. Absorption of our last meal, which was overdue in any case, was halted by the accident after the process was scarcely begun. We are as weak as infants, as are you and your Orligian friend. But if you would both go to the other side of the being and push, your strength, puny as it is, might make a difference."

Perhaps it wasn't the polite one, MacEwan thought as he and Grawlya-Ki did as suggested. He wanted to apologize to the Hudlars for assuming that they were simply organic pieces of heavy rescue machinery whose capabilities he had taken for granted. But he and Grawlya-Ki had their shoulders under the side of the Tralthan's cranial dome, their puny efforts *were* making a difference, and, unlike Hudlars, MacEwan needed breath with which to speak.

The Tralthan came upright, rocked unsteadily on its six, widely spaced feet, then was guided toward the other casualties by the Orligian. Sweat as well as chlorine was in MacEwan's eyes so he did not know which Hudlar spoke, but presumably it had been the one engaged in lifting injured Illensans into the damaged transporter.

"I am having difficulty with a chlorine breather, Earthperson," it said. "The being is abusive and will not allow me to touch it. The circumstances call for a very close decision, one I am unwilling to make. Will you speak to it?"

The area around the transporter had been cleared of casualties with the sole exception of this Illensan, who refused to be moved. The reason it gave MacEwan was that while its injuries were not serious, its pressure envelope had suffered two small ruptures. One of these it had sealed, after a fashion, by grasping the fabric of its envelope around the tear in both manipulators and holding it tightly closed, while the other one it had sealed by lying on it. These arrangements had forced it to increase the internal pressure of the envelope temporarily, so that it no longer had any clear idea of the duration of its chlorine tank and asphyxiation might be imminent. But it did not want to be moved to the relative safety of the transporter, which was also leaking, because that would allow the lethal atmosphere of the lounge to enter its envelope.

"I would prefer to die of chlorine starvation," it ended forcefully,

234 • JAMES WHITE

"than have my breathing passages and lungs instantly corroded by
your oxygen. Stay away from me."

MacEwan swore under his breath but did not approach the Illensan. Where were the emergency rescue teams? Surely they should
have been there by now. The clock showed that it had been just
over twenty-five Earth minutes since the accident. He could see that
the sightseers had been cleared from the lounge's inner wall, to be
replaced by a Nidian television crew and some uninformed ground
staff who did not appear to be doing anything at all. Outside there
were heavy vehicles drawn up and Nidians with backpacks and helmets scurrying around, but his constantly watering eyes and the
ever-present plastic hangings kept him from seeing details.

MacEwan pointed suddenly at the hangings and said to the
Hudlars, "Will you tear down a large piece of that plastic material,
please, and drape it over the Illensan. Pat it down flat around the
being's suit and smooth the folds out toward the edges so as to
exclude our air as much as possible. I'll be back in a minute."

He hurried around the transporter to the first Illensan casualty,
whose body had turned a livid, powdery blue and was beginning to
disintegrate, and tried to look only at the fastenings of the chlorine
tank. It took him several minutes to get the tank free of the body
harness, and several times his bare hands touched the dead Illensan's
flesh, which crumbled like rotting wood. He knew that oxygen was
vicious stuff where chlorine breathers were concerned, but now he
could really sympathize with the other Illensan's panic at the
thought of being moved in a leaking suit.

When he returned it was Grawlya-Ki who was smoothing out
the plastic around the Illensan while the two Hudlars were standing
clear. One of them said apologetically, "Our movements have become somewhat uncoordinated and the chlorine breather was worried lest we accidentally fall on it. If there is something else we can
do—"

"Nothing," MacEwan said firmly.

He turned on the tap of the chlorine tank and slipped it quickly
under the plastic sheet and pushed it close to the Illensan. The extra
seepage of the gas would make little difference, he thought, because
the whole area around the transporter was fast becoming uninhabitable for oxygen breathers. He pressed the tiny mask hard against

his face and took a long, careful breath through his nose, and used it to speak to the Hudlars.

"I have been thoughtless and seemingly ungrateful for the fine work you have been doing here," he said. "There is nothing more that you can do. Please go at once and spray yourselves with the necessary nutrient. You have acted most unselfishly, and I am, as are we all, most grateful to you."

The two Hudlars did not move. MacEwan began placing pieces of debris around the edges of the plastic and the Orligian, who was quick on the uptake, began doing the same. Soon the edges were held tightly against the floor, the gas escaping from the tank was beginning to inflate the plastic, and they had the Illensan in a crude chlorine tent. Still the Hudlars had not moved.

"The Colonel is waving at you again," Grawlya-Ki said. "I would say with impatience."

"We cannot use our sprayers here, Earthperson," one of the Hudlars said before MacEwan could reply. "The absorption mechanism in our tegument would ingest the toxic gas with our food, and in our species trace amounts of chlorine are lethal. The food sprayers can only be used in a beneficent atmosphere or in airless conditions."

"Bloody *hell*!" MacEwan said. When he thought of the way the Hudlars had worked to free the casualties, knowing that their time and available energy was severely limited and letting him assume that they had no problems, he should have had more to say—but that was all that came out. He looked helplessly at Ki, but the Orligian's face was covered by its furry hand holding the ridiculously small mask.

"With us," the other Hudlar added, "starvation is a rapid process, somewhat akin to asphyxiation in a gas breather. I estimate that we should lose consciousness and die in just under eight of our small time divisions."

MacEwan's eyes went to the concentric circles of the lounge clock. The Hudlar was talking about the equivalent of about twenty Earth minutes. Somehow they had to get that boarding tunnel open.

"Go to the tunnel entrance," he said, "and try to conserve your strength. Wait beside the others until—" He broke off awkwardly, then said to the Orligian, "Ki, you'd better get over there as well.

There's enough chlorine in the air here to bleach your fur. Keep passing the masks around and—"

"The Colonel," Grawlya-Ki reminded him as it turned to follow the Hudlars. MacEwan waved acknowledgment, but before he could leave the Illensan began speaking, its voice muffled by the fabric of the makeshift chlorine tent.

"That was an ingenious idea, Earthperson," it said slowly. "There is now a beneficent atmosphere surrounding my pressure envelope, which will enable me to repair the torn fabric and survive until Illensan assistance arrives. Thank you."

"You're welcome," MacEwan said, and began picking his way over the debris toward the gesticulating figure of the Colonel. He was still several meters from the wall when the officer pointed to his ear, then rapped with a knuckle on the interior surface. MacEwan obediently unfastened his mask on one side and pressed an ear against the transparent wall. The other's voice was low and indistinct, even though the color of the Colonel's face showed that he was shouting.

"Listen, MacEwan, and don't try to answer yet," the Colonel shouted.

"We'll have you out of there in fifteen, twenty minutes at most, and you'll have fresh air in ten. Medical help for all of the casualty species is on the way. Everybody on the planet knows about the accident because the TV channels were covering your deportation as a news item, and now this is big news indeed. Their contact mikes and translators are bringing us every word said in there, and the authorities are insisting that every effort be made to speed up the rescue. . . ."

Across the lounge Grawlya-Ki was waving a mask and air tank above his head. When the Orligian was sure that MacEwan had seen it; he threw it away. None of the other casualties were wearing masks so obviously they were useless, their air tanks empty. He wondered how long his own tank would last.

The equipment had been designed for the diminuitive Nidians, whose lungs were less than half the capacity of an Earthperson's. A lot of air had been wasted during the continual passing of masks between the casualties, and the furry face of the Orligian would have allowed air to leak past the edges of its mask, especially if Grawlya-Ki had increased the pressure to exclude the chlorine.

The Colonel had seen the Orligian's action and must have arrived at the same conclusion.

"Tell them to hang on for just a few more minutes," he went on. "We can't cut a way in from the main concourse because there are too many unprotected people out there. That plastic wall is tough and needs special, high-temperature equipment to cut it, and it won't be available soon enough. Anyway, it reacts with the plastic to produce large quantities of highly toxic fumes, bad enough to make your chlorine problem seem like a bad smell.

"So they're going in through the hole made by the transporter. There is only a few inches clearance around the vehicle's hull now, but they're going to pull the transporter out backward and you will be brought out through the hole it made and into the fresh air, where the medics will be standing by—"

MacEwan began banging with his fist and a foot against the plastic to attract the Colonel's attention, and breathing as deeply as he could through the mask. He had some shouting to do himself.

"*No!*" MacEwan said loudly, putting his mouth as close to the wall as the mask would allow. "All but one of the injured Illensans are inside the transporter. The structure was damaged in the collision and is leaking chlorine from every seam. If you drag it out like that it is likely to fall apart and the air will get to the casualties. I've seen what exposure to oxygen did to one of them."

"But if we don't go in there fast the oxygen breathers will die," the Colonel replied. His face was no longer red now, but a sickly white.

MacEwan could almost see the way the officer's mind was working. If the transporter with the chlorine-breathing casualties on board was hauled out and it broke up, the Illensan authorities would not be amused. But neither would the governments of Traltha, Kelgia, Melf, Orligia, and Earth if they did not act quickly to save those people.

This was how an interstellar war could start.

With the media covering every incident as it occurred, with their contact mikes picking up every translated word as it was spoken, and with fellow beings of the casualties' species on Nidia watching, judging, feeling, and reacting, there was no possibility of this incident being hushed up or diplomatically smoothed over. The decision to be taken was a simple one: Certain death for seven or eight chlorine-breathing Illensans to possibly save triple that number of Tralthans, Hudlars, Kelgians, Melfans, many of whom were dying anyway. Or death by chlorine poisoning for the oxygen breathers.

MacEwan could not make the decision and neither, he saw, could the pale, sweating, and silent Colonel trapped inside his office. He banged for attention again and shouted, "Open the boarding tunnel! Blast it open from the other side if you have to. Rig fans or pump in fresh air from the ship to raise the tunnel pressure and keep back this chlorine. Then send the emergency team to this end of the tunnel and open it from the inside. Surely the wiring of the safety system can be short-circuited and—"

While he was talking, MacEwan was thinking about the distance between the tunnel entrance and the take-off apron. It would take a long time to traverse the tunnel if the fast walkway was not operating. And explosives might not be quickly available in an air and space terminal. Maybe the Monitor Corps vessel in dock could provide some, given time, but the time they had was to be measured in minutes.

"The safety system is triggered from your end," the Colonel broke in. "The other end of the tunnel is too close to the ship for explosives to be used. The vessel would have to take off first and that would waste more time. The system can only be overridden at your end by a special key, carried by the Nidian on lounge duty, which unlocks the cover of the tunnel controls. The cover is transparent and unbreakable. You see, contamination can be a killer in a big complex like this one, especially when you consider that chlorine is mild compared with the stuff some of the offworlders breathe—"

MacEwan thumped the wall again and said, "The Nidian with the key is buried under the transporter, which can't be moved. And who says the cover is unbreakable? There is bar metal, furniture supports, among the wreckage. If I can't unlock the cover then I'll try levering or bashing it off. Find out what I'm supposed to do when it is off."

But the Colonel was ahead of him. He had already asked the Nidians that same question. In order to make accidental operation impossible for non-Nidian digits, the tunnel controls were in the form of six recessed buttons, which had to be depressed in a certain sequence. MacEwan would have to use a stylus or something similar to operate them because his Earthly fingers were too thick. He listened carefully, signaled that he understood, then returned to the casualties.

Grawlya-Ki had heard MacEwan's half of the shouted conversation and had found two lengths of metal. It was using one of them to attack the console when he arrived. The metal was a strong-enough alloy, but lacked the necessary weight and inertia. The metal bounced or skidded off the cover every time they swung at it, without leaving a mark.

Damn the Nidians and their superhard plastics! MacEwan raged. He tried to lever off the cover, but the join was almost invisible and the fastenings were flush with the console pedestal. He swore and tried again.

The Orligian did not speak because it was coughing all the time now, and the chlorine was affecting its eyes so badly that more often than not its blows missed the console altogether. MacEwan was beginning to feel an impairment in his own air supply, as if the tank were nearly empty and he was sucking at air which was not there, instead drawing in the contaminated air of the lounge through the edges of his mask.

Around them the casualties were still moving, but jerkily, as if they were struggling in the final stages of asphyxiation. The movements were not helping their injuries. Only the two Hudlars were motionless; their six tentacular limbs supported them just a few inches above the floor. MacEwan raised the metal bar high, stood on his toes, and brought it down as hard as he could.

He grunted in pain as the shock jarred his arms from wrist to shoulders and the bar slipped out of his hands. He swore again and looked around helplessly.

The Colonel was watching him through his glass-walled office. Through the inner wall of the lounge MacEwan could see the cameras of the Nidian TV networks watching him, listening and recording every word and cough and groan of those inside. Beyond the outer wall, now that the dust had settled and most of the intervening draperies had been pulled down, he could see the crews of the heavy Nidian towing vehicles watching him. He had only to signal to the Colonel and the emergency team would drag out the damaged transporter and medics would be attending the casualties within a few minutes.

But how would the Illensans as a species react to that? They were highly advanced technologically, occupying scores of colony worlds which they had had to adapt to their environmental needs, and, despite being the most widely traveled race in the Federation, they were a virtually unknown quantity because their worlds were so dangerous and unpleasant that few, indeed, were the visitors they received. Would they hold Nidia responsible for the accident and the deaths of their people? Or the worlds of the other warm-blooded, oxygen breathers whose people had survived at the expense of the Illensans?

And if everybody dithered and remained undecided until all but the Illensans had died, how would the world governments of Kelgia, Traltha, Melf, Orligia, and Earth react?

They would probably not gang up on Illensa, nor would the war start over this incident—not officially. But the seeds would have been planted no matter which races were saved or sacrificed, or even if all of them died. It would start, not because anyone wanted it, but because of a highly improbable accident with a number of contributing factors most of which could have been avoided.

Even the sudden collapse of the Nidian driver at the controls of the transporter could have been avoided by keeping closer medical checks on the ground staff. It had been sheer bad luck that the incident had happened when it did, and then the too rigidly designed safety system had done the rest. But most of the deaths would occur, MacEwan thought angrily, because of ignorance and fear—everyone was too frightened and over-polite to have asked the offworlders for a few basic lessons in first aid.

Beside him Grawlya-Ki was on its knees, coughing but still gripping its metal bar. At any moment the Colonel would make his decision because MacEwan, the Earth-being on the spot, was too much of a moral coward to make it. But whether the Colonel decided to save the Illensans or the others he would be wrong.

MacEwan moved closer to one of the motionless Hudlars and waved a hand in front of one of its large, widely spaced eyes.

For several interminable seconds there was no response. He was beginning to wonder if the being was already dead when it said, "What is it, Earthperson?"

MacEwan took a deep breath through his nose and found that his air had run out. For a moment he panicked and almost inhaled through his mouth, but stopped himself in time. Using the air remaining in his nearly empty lungs, he pointed to the console cover and said, "Are you able to break open the cover? Just the cover. I can . . . operate . . . controls . . ."

Desperately he fought the urge to suck the chlorine-laden air into his deflated lungs as the Hudlar slowly extended a tentacle and curled it around the cover. It slipped off the smooth, hemispheric surface. The Hudlar tried again without success, then it withdrew the tentacle slightly and jabbed at it with its sharp, steel-hard digits. A small scratch appeared on the cover but the material showed no sign of cracking. The tentacle withdrew, farther this time.

There was a roaring in MacEwan's head which was the loudest sound he had ever heard, and big, throbbing patches of darkness obscured the Hudlar as it made another attempt to break through the cover. MacEwan shrugged off his tunic, bunched it tightly in his fist and pressed it against his mouth as a makeshift filter. With his other hand he pressed the Nidian mask against his face to protect his eyes, at least, from the chlorine. He inhaled carefully and tried not to cough as the Hudlar swung its tentacle back for another try.

This time it struck like a battering ram and the cover, console, and even the floor supports exploded into their component parts.

"I am sorry for my clumsiness," the Hudlar said slowly. "Food deprivation impairs my judgment—"

It broke off as a loud, double chime sounded and the boarding tunnel doors slid open, bathing them suddenly in a wash of cool, pure air. A recorded voice was saying, "Will passengers please mount the moving way of the boarding tunnel and have their travel documents ready for inspection."

The two Hudlars found enough strength between them to lift the heavier casualties onto the moving way before they got on themselves, after which they began spraying each other with nutrient and making untranslatable noises. By then members of the Nidian emergency services, followed by a couple of Illensan and other offworlder medics, were hurrying in the opposite direction along the static borders of the moving way.

*　　*　　*

The incident had placed a six-hour hold on the Tralthan ship's departure, time for the less severe casualties to be treated and taken on board while the others were moved to the various offworlder accommodations in the city where they could be under the close supervision of medics of their own species. The transporter, empty of its Illensan casualties, had been withdrawn and a cold wind from the field blew through the gap in the transparent wall.

Grawlya-Ki, MacEwan, and the Colonel were standing beside the entrance to the boarding tunnel. The multichronometer above them indicated that take-off was less than half an Earth hour away.

The Colonel touched a piece of the demolished console with his boot and did not look at them when he spoke. "You were lucky. We were all lucky. I hate to think of the repercussions if you had failed to get all the casualties away. But you, both of you and the Hudlars, were instrumental in saving all but five of them, and they would have died in any case."

He gave an embarrassed laugh and looked up. "The offworld medics say some of your ideas on first aid are horrendous in their simplicity, but you didn't kill anybody and actually saved lives. You did it in full view of the media, with all of Nidia and its offworld visitors looking on, and you made your point about closer and more honest contact between species in a way that we are not going to forget. You are heroes again and I think—no, damn it, I'm sure—that you have only to ask and the Nidians will rescind their deportation order."

"We're going home," MacEwan said firmly. "To Orligia and Earth."

The Colonel looked even more embarrassed. He said, "I can understand your feelings about this sudden change in attitude. But now the authorities are grateful. Everybody, Nidians and offworlders alike, wants to interview you, and you can be sure that your ideas will be listened to. But if you require some form of public apology, I could arrange something."

MacEwan shook his head. "We are leaving because we have the answer to the problem. We have found the area of common interest to which all offworlders will subscribe, a project in which they will gladly cooperate. The answer was obvious all along but until today we were too stupid to see it.

"Implementing the solution," he went on, smiling, "is not a job for two tired old veterans who are beginning to bore people. It will take an organization like your Monitor Corps to coordinate the project, the technical resources of half a dozen planets, more money than I can conceive of, and a very, very long time. . . ."

As he continued, MacEwan was aware of excited movement among the members of the video team who had stayed behind hoping for an interview with Grawlya-Ki and himself. They would not get an interview but they were recording his final words to the Colonel. And when the Orligian and the Earthperson turned to leave they also got a not very interesting picture of the ranking Monitor Corps officer on Nidia standing very still, with one arm bent double so that the hand was held stiffly against the head. There was an odd brightness in the Earthperson's eyes and an expression on the pink, furless face which they were, naturally, unable to read.

✳　　✳　　✳

It took a very long time, much longer than the most generous estimates. The original and relatively modest plans had to be continually extended because scarcely a decade passed without several newly discovered intelligent species joining the Federation and these, too, had to be accommodated. So gigantic and complex was the structure required that in the end hundreds of worlds had each fabricated sections of it and transported them like pieces of a vast, three-dimensional jigsaw puzzle to the assembly area.

The tremendous structure which had finally taken shape in Galactic Sector Twelve was a hospital, a hospital to end all hospitals. In its 384 levels were reproduced the environments of all the different life-forms who comprised the Galactic Federation—a biological spectrum ranging from the frigid, methane life-forms through the more normal oxygen and chlorine-breathing types, up to the exotic beings who existed by the direct conversion of hard radiation.

Sector Twelve General Hospital represented a twofold miracle of engineering and psychology. Its supply, maintenance, and administration were handled by the Monitor Corps, but the traditional friction between the military and civilian members of the staff did not occur. Neither were there any serious disagreements among its ten thousand-odd medical personnel, who were composed of over sixty differing life-forms with the same number of mannerisms, body odors, and life views.

Perhaps their only common denominator, regardless of size, shape, and number of legs, was their need to cure the sick.

And in the vast dining hall used by the hospital's warm-blooded, oxygen-breathing life-forms there was a small dedication plaque just inside the main entrance. The Kelgian, Ian, Melfan, Nidian, Etlan, Orligian, Dwerlan, Tralthan, and Earth-human medical and maintenance staff rarely had time to look at the names inscribed on it, because they were all too busy talking shop, exchanging other-species gossip, and eating at tables with utensils all too often designed for the needs of an entirely different life-form—it was a very busy place, after all, and one grabbed a seat where one could. But then that was the way Grawlya-Ki and MacEwan had wanted it.

SURVIVOR

For more than an hour Senior Physician Conway had been dividing his attention between the interstellar emptiness outside the direct vision port and the long-range sensor display, which showed surrounding space to be anything but empty, and feeling more depressed with every minute that passed. Around him the officers on *Rhabwar*'s Control Deck were radiating impatience—but inaudibly, because they all knew that when their ship was at the scene of a disaster it was the senior medical officer on board who had the rank.

"Only one survivor," he said dully.

From the Captain's position, Fletcher said, "We've been fortunate on previous missions, Doctor. More often than not this is all an ambulance ship finds. Just think of what must have happened here."

Conway did not reply because he had been thinking of little else for the past hour.

An interstellar vessel of unknown origin and fully three times the mass of their ambulance ship had suffered a catastrophic malfunction which had reduced it to finely divided and widely scattered wreckage. Analysis of the temperature and relative motions showed the debris to be much too cool to have been at the center of a nuclear explosion less than seven hours earlier, when the distress beacon had been automatically released. It was obvious, therefore, that the ship had lost one of its hypergenerators and it had not been of a sufficiently advanced design for the occupants, with one exception, to have any chance of surviving the accident.

On Federation ships, Conway knew, if one of the matched set of hyperdrive generators failed suddenly, the others were designed to cut out simultaneously. The vessel concerned emerged safely into normal space somewhere between the stars, to sit there helplessly, unable to make it home on impulse drive, until it either repaired its sick generator or help arrived. But there were times when the safety cutoffs had failed or been late in functioning, which meant that while a part of the ship had continued for a split second at hyperspeed the remainder was braked instantaneously to sublight velocity. The effect on the early hyperships had been, to say the least, catastrophic.

"The survivor's species must be relatively new to hypertravel," Conway said, "or they would be using the modular design philosophy which we, from long experience, know to be the only structural form which enables a proportion of a ship's crew to survive when a sudden hypergenerator imbalance tears the vessel apart around them. I can't understand why the section containing the survivor wasn't fragmented like the rest."

The Captain was visibly controlling his impatience as he replied, "You were too busy getting the survivor out before the compartment lost any more air and decompression was added to its other problems, Doctor, to have time for structural observations. The compartment was a separate unit, purpose unknown, which was mounted outboard of the main hull and joined by a short access tube and airlock, and it simply broke away in one piece. That beastie was very lucky." He gestured toward the long-range sensor displays. "But now we know that the remaining pieces of wreckage are too small to contain survivors and frankly, Doctor, we are wasting time here."

"I agree," Conway said absently.

"Right," Fletcher said briskly. "Power Room, prepare to Jump in five—"

"Hold, Captain," Conway broke in quietly. "I hadn't finished. I want a scoutship out here, more than one if they can be spared, to search the wreckage for personal effects, photographs, solid and pictorial art, anything which will assist in reconstructing the survivor's environment and culture. And request Federation Archives for any information on an intelligent life-form of physiological classification EGCL. Since this is a new species to us, the cultural contact people will want this information as soon as possible, and if our survivor continues to survive, the hospital will need it the day before yesterday.

"Tag the signals with Sector General medical first-contact priority coding," he went on, "then head for home. I'll be on the Casualty Deck."

Rhabwar's communications officer, Haslam, was already preparing for the transmission when Conway stepped into the gravity-free central well and began pulling himself toward the Casualty Deck amidships. He broke his journey briefly to visit his cabin and get out of the heavy-duty spacesuit he had been wearing since the rescue. He felt as though every bone and muscle in his body was aching. The rescue and transfer of the survivor to *Rhabwar* had required intense muscular activity, followed by a three-hour emergency op, and another hour sitting still in Control. No wonder he felt stiff.

Try to think about something else, Conway told himself firmly. He exercised briefly to ease his cramped muscles but the dull, unlocalized aching persisted. Angrily he wondered if he was becoming a hypochondriac.

"Subspace radio transmission in five seconds," the muted voice of Lieutenant Haslam said from the cabin speaker. "Expect the usual fluctuations in the lighting and artificial gravity systems."

As the cabin lights flickered and the deck seemed to twitch under his feet, Conway was forced to think of something else—specifically, the problems encountered in transmitting intelligence over interstellar distances compared with the relative simplicity of sending a distress signal.

Just as there was only one known method of traveling faster than light, there was only one way of calling for help when an accident left a ship stranded between the stars. Tight-beam subspace radio could rarely be used in emergency conditions since it was subject to interference from intervening stellar material and required inordinate amounts of a vessel's power—power which a distressed ship was unlikely to have available. But a distress beacon did not have to carry intelligence. It was simply a nuclear-powered device which broadcast its location, a subspace scream for help which ran up and down the usable frequencies until it died, in a matter of a few hours. And on this occasion it had died amid a cloud of wreckage containing one survivor who was very lucky indeed to be alive.

But considering the extent of the being's injuries, Conway thought, it could not really be described as lucky. Mentally shaking himself loose of these uncharacteristically morbid feelings, he went down to the Casualty Deck to check on the patient's condition.

Typed as physiological classification EGCL, the survivor was a warm-blooded, oxygen-breathing life-form of approximately twice the body weight of an adult Earth-human. Visually it resembled an outsize snail with a high, conical shell which was pierced around the tip where its four extensible eyes were located. Equally spaced around the base of the shell were eight triangular slots from which projected the manipulatory appendages. The carapace rested on a thick, circular pad of muscle which was the locomotor system. Around the circumference of the pad were a number of fleshy projections, hollows and slits associated with its systems of ingestion, respiration, elimination, reproduction, and nonvisual sensors. Its gravity and atmospheric pressure requirements had been estimated but, because of its severely weakened condition, the artificial gravity setting had been reduced to assist the heart and the pressure increased so that decompression effects would not aggravate the bleeding.

As Conway stood looking down at the terribly injured EGCL, Pathologist Murchison and Charge Nurse Naydrad joined him at the pressure litter. It was the same litter which had been used to move the casualty from the wreck, and, because the patient should not be subjected to unnecessary movement, it would be used again to transfer the EGCL into the hospital. The only difference was that for the second trip the casualty had been tidied up.

In spite of his considerable experience with spacewreck casualties of all shapes, sizes, and physiological classifications, Conway winced at the memory of what they had found. The compartment containing the EGCL had been spinning rapidly when they discovered it, and the being had been rolling about inside and demolishing furniture and equipment with its massive body for many hours before it had lodged itself in a corner under some self-created debris.

In the process its carapace had sustained three fractures, one of which was so deeply depressed that the brain had been involved. One of the eyes was missing, and two of the thin, tentacular manipulators had been traumatically severed by sharp-edged obstructions—these limbs had been retrieved and preserved for possible rejoining—and there were numerous punctured and incised wounds to the base pad.

Apart from carrying out the emergency surgery to relieve some of the cranial pressure, controlling the major areas of bleeding with clamps and temporary sutures, and assisting the patient's breathing by applying positive pressure ventilation to the remaining undamaged lung, there had been very little that they could do. Certainly there was no way of treating the brain damage aboard *Rhabwar*, and their efforts at charting the extent of that damage had resulted in conflicting indications from the biosensors and Doctor Prilicla's empathic faculty. The sensor indications were that cerebral activity had virtually ceased, while the little empath insisted, insofar as the timid, shy, self-effacing Prilicla could insist, otherwise.

"No physical movement and no change in the clinical picture since you left," Murchison said quietly, anticipating his question. She added. "I'm not at all happy about this."

"And I am far from happy, Doctor," the Charge Nurse joined in, its fur twitching and rippling as if it was standing in a strong wind. "In my opinion the being is dead and we are simply insuring that Thornnastor receives a fresher than usual specimen to take apart.

"Doctor Prilicla," the Kelgian went on, "is often guilty of saying things which are not completely accurate just so long as they make the people around it happy, and the predominant emotional radiation it detected from the patient was of pain. The feeling was so intense, you will remember, that Prilicla asked to be excused as soon as the operation was completed. In my opinion, Doctor, this patient is no longer capable of cerebration but it is, judging by Prilicla's response, suffering intense pain. Surely your course is clear?"

"Naydrad!" Conway began angrily, then stopped. Murchison and the Charge Nurse had expressed exactly the same sentiments. The difference was that the Kelgian, in common with the rest of its species, was incapable of using tact.

Conway stared for a moment at the two-meters-long, caterpillar like life-form whose coat of silvery fur was in constant, rippling motion. This motion was completely involuntary among Kelgians, triggered by their reactions to external and internal stimuli, and the emotionally expressive fur complemented the vocal apparatus which lacked flexibility of tone. But the patterns of movement in the fur made it plain to any Kelgian what another felt about the subject under discussion, so that they always said exactly what they meant. The concepts of diplomacy, tact, and lying were therefore completely alien to them. Conway sighed.

He tried to conceal his own doubts about the case by saying firmly, "Thornnastor much prefers putting together a live specimen than taking apart a dead one. As well, on a number of occasions Prilicla's empathy has proved more trustworthy than medical instrumentation, so we cannot be absolutely sure that this case is hopeless. In any event, until we reach the hospital its treatment is my responsibility.

"Let's not become too emotionally involved with this patient," he added. "It is unprofessional and not like either of you."

Naydrad, its fur twitching angrily, made a sound which did not register on Conway's translator, and Murchison said, "You're right, of course. We've seen much worse cases and I don't know why I feel so badly about this one. Maybe I'm just growing old."

"The onset of senility could be one explanation for such uncharacteristic behavior," the Kelgian said, "although this is not so in my case."

Murchison's face reddened. "The Charge Nurse is allowed to say things like that but you, Doctor, had better not agree with it," she said crossly.

Conway laughed suddenly. "Relax. I wouldn't dream of agreeing with such a blatantly obvious misstatement," he said. "And now, if you have everything you think Thorny will need on our friend here, both of you get some rest. Emergence is in six hours. If you can't sleep, please try not to worry too much about the casualty or it will bother Prilicla."

Murchison nodded and followed Naydrad from the Casualty Deck. Conway, still feeling more like a not very well patient than a medic in charge, set the audible warning which would signal any change in the EGCL's condition, lay down on a nearby litter, and closed his eyes.

Neither the Earth-human DBDG or the Kelgian DBLF classifications were noted for their ability to exercise full control over their mentation, and it was soon obvious that Murchison and Naydrad had been worrying and, in the process, producing some unpleasant emotional radiation. With his eyes still closed he listened to the faint tapping and plopping sounds which moved along the ceiling toward him and came to a halt overhead. There was a burst of low, musical clicks and trills which came through his translator as "Excuse me, friend Conway, were you sleeping?"

"You know I wasn't," Conway said, opening his eyes to see Prilicla clinging to the ceiling above him, trembling uncontrollably as it was washed by his own and the patient's emotional radiation.

Doctor Prilicla was of physiological classification GLNO—an insectile, exoskeletal, six-legged life-form with two pairs of iridescent and not quite atrophied wings and possessing a highly developed empathic faculty. Only on Cinruss, with its dense atmosphere and one-eighth gravity, could a race of insects have grown to such dimensions and in time developed intelligence and an advanced civilization.

But in both the hospital and *Rhabwar,* Prilicla was in deadly danger for most of its working day. It had to wear gravity nullifiers everywhere outside its own special quarters because the gravity pull which the majority of its colleagues considered normal would instantly have crushed it flat. When Prilicla held a conversation with anyone it kept well out of reach of any thoughtless movement of an arm or tentacle which would easily have caved in its eggshell body or snapped off one of the incredibly fragile limbs.

Not that anyone would have wanted to hurt the little being— it was far too well liked. The Cinrusskin's empathic faculty forced it to be considerate to *everyone* in order to make the emotional radiation of the people around it as pleasant for itself as possible— except when its professional duties exposed it to pain and associated violent emotion in a patient or to the unintentionally unpleasant feelings of its colleagues.

"You should be sleeping, Prilicla," Conway said with concern, "or are Murchison and Naydrad emoting too loudly for you?"

"No, friend Conway," the empath replied timidly. "Their emotional radiation troubles me no more than that of the other people on the ship. I came for a consultation."

"Good!" Conway said. "You've had some useful thoughts on the treatment of our—"

"I wish to consult you about myself," Prilicla said, committing the—to it—gross impoliteness of breaking in on another's conversation without prior apology. For a moment its pipestem legs and body shook with the strength of Conway's reaction, then it added, "Please, my friend, control your feelings."

Conway tried to be clinical about the little Cinrusskin who had been his friend, colleague, and invaluable assistant on virtually every major case since his promotion to Senior Physician. His sudden concern and unadmitted fear of the possible loss of a close friend were not helping that friend and were, in fact, causing it even greater distress. He tried hard to think of Prilicla as a patient, only as a patient, and slowly the empath's trembling abated.

"What," Conway said in time-honored fashion, "seems to be the trouble?"

"I do not know," the Cinrusskin said. "I have no previous experience and there are no recorded instances of the condition among my species. I am confused, friend Conway, and frightened."

"Symptoms?" Conway asked.

"Empathic hypersensitivity," Prilicla replied. "The emotional radiation of yourself, the rest of the medical team, and the crew is particularly strong. I can clearly detect the feelings of Lieutenant Chen in the Power Room and those of the rest of the crew in Control with little or no attenuation with distance. The expected, low-key feelings of disappointment and sorrow caused by the unsuccessful rescue bid are reaching me with shocking intensity. We have encountered these tragedies before now, friend Conway, but this emotional reaction to the condition of a being who is a complete stranger is—is—"

"We do feel bad about this one," Conway broke in gently, "perhaps worse than we normally do, and the feelings are cumulative. And you, as an emotion-sensitive, could be expected to feel them much more strongly. This might explain your apparent hypersensitivity."

The empath trembled with the effort needed to express disagreement. It said, "No, friend Conway. The condition and emotional radiation of the EGCL, highly unpleasant though it is, is not the problem. It is the ordinary, everyday radiation of everyone else— the minor embarrassments, the bursts of irritation, the odd emotions associated with the feeling you Earth-humans call humor and the like, are registering so strongly with me that I find difficulty in thinking clearly."

"I see," Conway said automatically, although he could not see at all. "Apart from the hypersensitivity, are there any other symptoms?"

"Some unlocalized discomfort in the limbs and lower thorax," Prilicla replied. "I checked the areas with my scanner but could find no obstructions or abnormalities."

Conway had been reaching for his own pocket scanner but thought better of it. Without taking a Cinrusskin physiology tape he would have only a vague idea of what to look for, and besides, Prilicla was a first-class Diagnostician and surgeon and if it said that there were no abnormalities then that was good enough for Conway.

"Cinrusskins are susceptible to illness only during childhood," Prilicla went on. "The adults do occasionally suffer from nonphysical disturbances, and the onset of symptoms, as is expected with psychological disorders, takes many forms, some of which resemble my present—"

"Nonsense, you're not going insane!" Conway broke in. But he did not feel as sure as he sounded, and he was uncomfortably aware that Prilicla knew his feelings and was beginning to tremble again.

"The obvious course," Conway said, trying to regain his clinical calm, "is to desensitize you with a hefty sedative shot. You know that as well as I. But you are too good a doctor to self-administer the indicated medication which would, we both realize, simply be treating the symptoms, without first doing something about the disease, like reporting it to me. Isn't that so?"

"That is so, friend Conway."

"Right, then," Conway said briskly. "You also realize that we can't do anything about curing the condition until we have you back in the hospital. In the meantime we'll treat the symptoms with heavy sedation. I want you completely unconscious. You are relieved of all medical duties, naturally, until we have the answer to your little problem."

Conway could almost feel the little empath's objections while he was lifting it gently into a pressure litter fitted with gravity nullifiers and the incredibly soft restraints required by this ultrafragile species. Finally Prilicla spoke.

"Friend Conway," it said weakly, "you know that I am the only medically trained empath on the staff. Our patient will require extensive and delicate cerebral surgery. If my condition precludes me from taking a direct part in the operation, I wish to be treated in an adjacent ward where this abnormal hypersensitivity will better enable me to monitor the EGCL's unconscious emotional radiation.

"You know as well as I do," it went on, "that brain surgery in a hitherto unknown life-form is largely exploratory and very, very risky, and my empathic faculty enables me to sense when surgical intervention in any area is right or wrong. By becoming a patient I have lost none of my abilities as a diagnostic empath, and for this reason, friend Conway, I want your promise that I will be placed as close as possible to the patient and restored to full consciousness while the operation is in progress."

"Well—" Conway began.

"I am not a telepath, as you know," Prilicla said, so weakly that Conway had to increase the gain on his translator to hear it. "But your feelings, if you do not intend to keep this promise, will be clear to me."

Conway had never known the normally timid Prilicla to be so forthright in its manner. Then he thought of what the empath was asking him to do—to subject it, in its hypersensitive state, to the emotional trauma of a lengthy operation during which, because of the patient's strange physiological classification and metabolism, the effectiveness of the anesthetics could not be guaranteed. His hard-held clinical detachment slipped for a moment and he felt like any concerned friend or relative watching a patient whose prognosis was uncertain.

Prilicla began to shake in its harness, but the sedative was taking effect, and very soon it was unconscious and untroubled by Conway's feelings for it.

*   *   *

"This is Reception," a flat, translated voice said from the Control Deck's main speaker. "Identify yourself, please. State whether visitor, patient, or staff and give physiological classification. If unable to do so because of physical injury, mental confusion, or ignorance of the classification system, please make vision contact."

Conway cleared his throat and said briskly, "Ambulance ship *Rhabwar,* Senior Physician Conway. Staff and two patients, all warm-blooded oxygen-breathers. Staff classifications are Earth-human DBDG, Cinrusskin GLNO, and Kelgian DBLF. One patient is an EGCL, origin unknown, spacewreck casualty in condition nine. The second patient is also staff, a GLNO in condition three. We need—"

"Prilicla?"

"Yes, Prilicla," Conway said. "We need matching environment OR and postop intensive care facilities for the EGCL, treatment to begin on arrival, and adjacent accommodation for the GLNO whose empathic faculty may be required during the operation. Can do?"

There was silence for a few minutes, then Reception said, "Use Entry Lock Nine into Level One Six Three, *Rhabwar.* Your traffic coding is Priority Red One. ETA?"

Fletcher looked across at his astrogator, and Lieutenant Dodds said, "Two hours, seven minutes, sir."

"Wait," Reception said.

There was another silence, much longer this time, before the voice returned. "Diagnostician Thornnastor wishes to discuss the patient's condition and metabolic profile with Pathologist Murchison and yourself as soon as possible. Senior Physician Edanelt has been assigned to assist Thornnastor during the operation. Both require information on the type and extent of the EGCL's injuries and want you to transmit surface and deep-scan pictures at once. Until otherwise instructed you are assigned to the Cinrusskin patient. As soon as possible Chief Psychologist O'Mara wants to talk to you about Prilicla."

It promised to be a very busy two hours and seven minutes.

In *Rhabwar*'s forward viewscreen the hospital grew from a fuzzy smear of light against the stellar background until it seemed to fill all of space like a gigantic, cylindrical Christmas tree. Its thousands of viewports blazed with light in the dazzling variety of color and intensity necessary for the visual equipment of its patients and staff.

Within a few minutes of *Rhabwar* docking at Lock Nine, the EGCL and Prilicla had been moved into Operating Room Three and Ward Seven respectively on Level 163. Conway was not familiar with this particular level because it had still been in the process of conversion from the old FROB, FGLI, and ELNT medics' quarters when he had been detached for ambulance ship duty. Now the Tralthans, Hudlars, and Melfans had more spacious accommodations and their old abode had become the emergency admission and treatment level for warm-blooded oxygen breathers, with its own operating theaters, intensive care units, observation and recovery wards, and a diet kitchen which could reproduce the staples of every known warm-blooded, oxygen-breathing race.

While Naydrad and Conway were transferring the EGCL casualty from the litter's portable life-support and biosensor systems to those of the operating room, Thornnastor and Edanelt arrived.

Senior Physician Edanelt had been the natural if not the inevitable choice for this case. Not only was it one of the hospital's top surgeons, the permanent possessor of four physiology tapes and, according to the grapevine, a being shortly to be elevated to Diagnostician status, the crablike Melfan's physiological classification of ELNT was perhaps the closest of all the life-forms on the medical staff to that of the EGCL survivor—a vitally important factor when no physiology tape was available for the patient being treated. Where Thornnastor, the elephantine Diagnostician-in-Charge of Pathology, was concerned there were no physical similarities to the patient at all, other than that they breathed the same air.

In spite of being a Tralthan FGLI and as such one of the more massive intelligent species in the Federation, Thornnastor was no mean surgeon itself. But on this case its primary responsibility was the rapid investigation of the survivor's physiology and metabolism and, using its own vast experience in the field of e-t pathology together with the facilities available in its department, the synthesizing of the required medication which would include a safe anesthetic, coagulant, and tissue regenerative.

Edanelt and Conway had already discussed the case in detail on the way in, as had Murchison and her chief, Thornnastor. He knew that their initial efforts would be directed toward repairing the grosser structural damage, after which would come the extremely delicate, dangerous, and perhaps impossible operation to relieve the pressure on and repair the damage to the brain and adjacent organs caused by the extensive depressed fracturing of the carapace. At that stage the assistance of Prilicla and its wonderfully sensitive and precise empathic faculty would be required to monitor the operation if the EGCL was to continue to survive as something more than a vegetable.

Conway's presence was no longer needed, and he would be more usefully employed discussing Prilicla's condition with O'Mara.

As he excused himself and left, Edanelt waved a pincer which it was spraying with the fast-setting plastic film favored by the Melfan medics instead of surgical gloves, but Thornnastor's four eyes were on the patient, Murchison, and two separate pieces of its equipment so that it did not see him leave.

In the corridor Conway stopped for a moment to work out the fastest route to the Chief Psychologist's office. The three levels above this one, he knew, were the province of the chlorine-breathing Illensans, and if he had not known that then the anticontamination warnings above the interlevel airlocks would have told him. There was no danger of contamination from the levels below since they housed the MSVK and LSVO life-forms, each of which breathed oxygen, required a gravity pull of one-quarter Earth normal, and resembled thin, tripedal storks. Below them were the water-filled wards of the Chalders and then the first of the nonmedical treatment levels where O'Mara's department was situated.

On the way down a couple of the Nallajim MSVK medics chirped a greeting at him and a recuperating patient narrowly missed flying into his chest before he reached the lock into the AUGL section. For that leg of the journey he had to don a lightweight suit and swim through the vast tanks where the thirty-meters long, water-breathing inhabitants of the water world of Chalderscol drifted ponderously like armorplated crocodiles in their warm, green wards. With his suit still beaded with Chalder water, he was in O'Mara's office just twenty-three minutes later.

Major O'Mara indicated a piece of furniture designed for the comfort of a DBLF and said sourly, "No doubt you have been too busy in your professional capacity to contact me, Doctor, so don't waste time apologizing. Tell me about Prilicla."

Conway insinuated himself carefully into the Kelgian chair and began describing the Cinrusskin's condition, from the symptoms at onset to their intensification to the degree where complete sedation was indicated, and the relevant circumstance pertaining at the time. While he was speaking, the Chief Psychologist's craggy features were still and his eyes, which opened into a mind so keenly analytical that it gave O'Mara what amounted to a telepathic faculty, were likewise unreadable.

As Chief Psychologist of the Federation's largest multienvironment hospital, he was responsible for the mental well-being of a staff of several thousand entities belonging to more than sixty different species. Even though his Monitor Corps rank of Major did not place him high in the hospital's Service chain of command, and anyway had been given for purely administrative reasons, there was no clear limit to O'Mara's authority. To him the medical staff were patients, too, regardless of seniority, and an important part of his job was to ensure that the right doctor was assigned to each of the weird and often wonderful variety of patients who turned up at the hospital, and that there was no xenophobic complications on either side.

He was also responsible for the hospital's medical elite, the Diagnosticians. According to O'Mara himself, however, the real reason for the high level of mental stability among the diverse and often touchy medical staff was that they were all too frightened of him to risk his displeasure by going mad.

O'Mara watched him closely until Conway had finished, then he said, "A clear, concise, and apparently accurate report, Doctor, but you are a close friend of the patient. There is the possibility of clouded judgment, exaggeration. You are not a psychologist but an e-t physician and surgeon who has apparently already decided that the case is one which should be treated by my department. You appreciate my difficulty? Please describe for me your feelings during this mission from the rescue until now. But first, are *you* feeling all right?"

All that Conway could feel just then was his blood pressure rising.

"Be as objective as possible," O'Mara added.

Conway took a deep breath and let it out again slowly through his nose. "After our very fast response to the distress signal there was a general feeling of disappointment at the rescue of just one survivor, a survivor who was barely alive. But you're on the wrong track, Major. The feeling was shared by everyone on the ship, I believe, but it was not strong enough to explain the Cinrusskin's hypersensitivity. Prilicla was picking up emotional radiation of distressing intensity from crew members stationed at the other end of the ship, a distance at which emoting would normally be barely detectable. And I am given neither to maudlin sentimentality nor exaggeration of symptoms. Right at this moment I feel the way I usually do in this blasted office and that is—"

"Objectively, remember," O'Mara said dryly.

"I was not trying to do your diagnostic work for you," Conway went on, bringing his voice back to a conversational level, "but the indications are that there *is* a psychological problem. The result, perhaps, of an as yet unidentified disease, or organic malfunction or an imbalance in the endocrine system. But a purely psychological reason for the condition is also a possibility which—"

"Anything is *possible,* Doctor," O'Mara broke in impatiently. "Be specific. What are you going to do about your friend, and what exactly do you want me to do about it?"

"Two things," Conway said. "I want you to check on Prilicla's condition yourself—"

"Which you know I will do anyway," O'Mara said.

"—and give me the GLNO physiology tape," he went on, "so that I can confirm or eliminate the nonpsychological reasons for the trouble."

For a moment O'Mara was silent. His face remained as expressionless as a lump of basalt, but the eyes showed concern. "You've carried Educator tapes before now and know what to expect. But the GLNO tape is ... different. You will feel like a very unhappy Cinrusskin indeed. You are no Diagnostician, Conway—at least, not yet. Better think about it."

The physiology tapes, Conway knew from personal experience,

fell somewhere between the categories of mixed blessing and necessary evil. While skill in e-t surgery came with aptitude, training, and experience, no single being could hope to hold in its brain the vast quantity of physiological data needed for the treatment of the variety of patients encountered in a hospital like Sector General. The incredible mass of clinical and anatomical information needed to take care of them had therefore to be furnished, usually on a temporary basis, by means of the Educator tapes, which were the brain recordings of the great medical specialists belonging to the species concerned. If an Earth-human doctor had to treat a Kelgian patient, he took one of the Kelgian physiology tapes until treatment was completed, after which he had it erased. But for the medic concerned, whether the tape was being carried for as long as it took to perform an other-species operation or for a teaching project lasting several months, the experience was not a pleasant one.

The only good thing about it from the medic's point of view was that he was much better off than one of the Diagnosticians.

They were the hospital's elite. A Diagnostician was one of those rare entities whose mind had proved itself stable enough to retain up to ten physiology tapes simultaneously. To their data-crammed minds was given the work of original research in xenological medicine and the diagnosis and treatment of disease and injury in hitherto unknown life-forms. There was a saying current in the hospital, reputed to have originated with O'Mara himself, that anyone sane enough to be a Diagnostician was mad.

For it was not only physiological data which the tapes imparted; the complete memory and personality of the entity who had possessed that knowledge was impressed on the receiving mind as well. In effect, a Diagnostician subjected himself or itself voluntarily to a form of multiple schizophrenia, with the alien personalities sharing its mind so utterly *different* that in many cases they did not have even a system of logic in common. And all too frequently the foremost medical authorities of a planet, despite their eminence in the field of healing, were very bad-tempered, aggressive, and unpleasant people indeed.

Such would not be the case with the GLNO tape, Conway knew, because Cinrusskins were the most timid, friendly, and likable beings imaginable.

"I've thought about it," Conway said.

O'Mara nodded and spoke into his desk set. "Carrington? Senior Physician Conway is approved for the GLNO tape, with compulsory postimpression sedation of one hour. I'll be in Emergency Admissions on Level One Six Three—" he grinned suddenly at Conway "—trying not to tell the medics their business."

*   *   *

Conway woke to see a large, pink balloon of a face hanging over him. Instinctively he tried to scramble up the wall beside his couch in case the enormous, heavily muscled body supporting the face fell and crushed the life out of him. Then suddenly there was a mental shift in perspective as the features registered concern and withdrew and the slim, Earth-human body in Monitor Corps green straightened up.

Lieutenant Carrington, one of O'Mara's assistants, said, "Easy, Doctor. Sit up slowly, then stand. Concentrate on putting your two feet onto the floor and don't worry because they aren't a Cinrusskin's six."

He made good time back to 163 in spite of having to walk around a large number of beings who were much smaller than himself just because the Cinrusskin component of his mind insisted that they were big and dangerous. From Murchison he learned that O'Mara was in Prilicla's ward, having first called in to the OR to discuss the EGCL's basic physiology and probable environmental and evolutionary influence with Thornnastor and Edanelt, both of whom had been too busy to speak to him.

They would not speak to Conway, either, and he could see why. The operation on the EGCL had become an emergency with an unknown but probably extremely short time limit.

When the splinters of depressed carapace had been removed from the brain over an hour earlier, Murchison explained quietly between rumbled instructions from Thornnastor, there had been a sudden and surprising deterioration in the EGCL's condition. The change had been detected by Prilicla who, because of its condition, had been excluded from any part of the operation. But the Cinrusskin had continued to act like a doctor by making use of its abnormally heightened emotion-detection faculty. Prilicla had pulled rank to send Ward Seven's duty nurse to the operating theater with its empathic findings and a diffident suggestion that if they were to relay the operational proceedings to Seven's viewscreen, it would be able to assist them.

The cause of the deterioration was a number of large blood vessels in the cerebral area which had ruptured when the pressure from the depressed fracture had been removed. The two surgeons had been forced to accede to Prilicla's request because, without the empath's monitoring of the patient's level of consciousness, they had no way of knowing whether the delicate, dangerous, and perforce hurried repair work in the cerebral area was having a good or bad effect—if any.

"Prognosis?" Conway murmured. But before Murchison could reply, one of Thornnastor's eyes curled backward over its head to glare down at him.

"If this patient does not succumb to a massive cerebral hemorrhage within the next thirty minutes," the Diagnostician said crossly, "it is probable that it will perish, in time, from the degenerative diseases associated with extreme old age. Now stop distracting my assistant, Conway, and tend to your own patient."

On the way to Seven Conway wondered briefly how the empath's emotion sensitivity could detect the unconscious level of emoting of the EGCL without the signals beings swamped by the emotional radiation of dozens of fully conscious entities in the area. Maybe Prilicla's recent hypersensitivity was responsible, but there was a niggling doubt at the back of his mind which suggested that there was another reason.

O'Mara was still in the ward, steadying himself in the close to zero-gravity conditions with a hand on an equipment rack while he and Prilicla watched the scene in the operating theater.

"Conway, stop that!" O'Mara said sharply.

He had tried not to react when he had seen the empath's condition. But half his mind belonged to a Cinrusskin, a member of a species acknowledged to be the most sensitive and sympathetic intelligent life-form known to the Federation who was regarding a brother in extreme distress while the Earth-human half was feeling for a friend in the same condition, and it was difficult to be cool and clinical for both of them.

"I'm sorry," he said inadequately.

"I know you are, friend Conway," Prilicla said, turning toward him. "You should not have taken that tape."

"He was warned," O'Mara said gruffly, but his expression showed concern.

Conway was a member of an empathic race. All the memories and experience of his GLNO life were those of a normally healthy and happy empath, but now he was no longer an empath. He could see, hear, and touch Prilicla, but the faculty was missing which enabled him to share the other's emotions and which subtly colored every word, gesture, and expression so that for two Cinrusskins to be within visual range was unalloyed pleasure for both. He could remember experiencing empathic contact, remember having the ability all his life, but now he was little more than a deaf-mute. What he was feeling from Prilicla so strongly was a product of his imagination: It was sympathy, not empathy.

His human brain did not possess the empathic faculty, and it was not bestowed by filling his mind with memories of having had it. But there were other memories as well, covering a lifetime's experience of Cinrusskin clinical physiology, and these he could use.

"If you don't mind, Doctor Prilicla," Conway said with cool formality, "I would like to examine you."

"Of course, friend Conway." Prilicla's uncontrollable shaking had diminished to a steady, continuous trembling, an indication that Conway's emotional radiation was under control. "There are more symptoms, Doctor, which are causing severe discomfort."

"I can see that," Conway said as he gently moved aside one of the incredibly fragile wings to place his scanner against the empath's thorax. "Describe them, please."

In the two hours since Conway had last seen it, Prilicla had changed in ways which were individually subtle but cumulatively marked. There was a strange lack of animation and concentration in the large, triple-lidded eyes; the delicate structure which supported the wing membranes had softened and warped so that the translucent and iridescent membrane had fallen into unsightly folds and wrinkles; its four tiny, wonderfully precise manipulators, which should one day make it one of the finest surgeons in the hospital, were quivering in spite of being gripped tightly together, and the overall aspect was of a GLNO who was old and grievously ill.

While Conway continued the examination, the Cinrusskin part of his mind shared his bafflement at the findings and described symptoms. They were both sure, and in this their agreement was based on the GLNO tape donor's personal experience and Conway's knowledge acquired over many years in Sector General, that Prilicla was close to death.

The empath's trembling increased sharply, then diminished as Conway once again forced a feeling of clinical detachment on himself. He said calmly, "There is no evidence of deformation, obstruction, lesion, or infection which might cause the symptoms you describe. Neither can I see any cause for the respiratory difficulty you are experiencing. Some degree of empathic hypersensitivity occurs in adolescents of your species, my Cinrusskin alter ego tells me, but in nothing like the intensity you describe. It is possible, I suppose, that there is a nonpathogenic and nontoxic involvement with the central nervous system."

"You think it's psychosomatic?" O'Mara said harshly, jabbing a finger toward Prilicla. "This?"

"I would like to eliminate that possibility," Conway replied calmly. To Prilicla, he said, "If you don't mind I would like to discuss your case with Major O'Mara outside."

"Of course, friend Conway," the empath said. The constant trembling seemed as if it would shake the fragile body apart. "But please have that Cinrusskin tape erased as quickly as possible. Your heightened levels of concern and sympathy are helping neither of us. And consider, friend Conway, your tape was donated by a great Cinrusskin medical authority of the past. In all modesty, I can say that, before coming to Sector General and in preparation for my work here, I had reached a similar degree of eminence in the field.

"There is nothing in the clinical history of our species which even approximates this condition," it went on, "and absolutely no precedent for the symptomology. Regarding the possibility of a nonphysical basis for the condition, I cannot, of course, be completely objective about this. But I have always been a happy and well-adjusted person with no mental aberrations in childhood, adolescence, or adulthood. Friend O'Mara has my psych file and will confirm this. My hope is that these peculiar symptoms were so sudden in onset that their recession will be equally rapid."

"Perhaps Thornnastor could—" Conway began.

"The thought of that—that behemoth approaching me with investigative intent would cause me to terminate at once. And Thornnastor is busy—Friend Edanelt, be careful!"

Prilicla had switched its attention suddenly to the viewscreen. It went on, "Pressure, even temporary pressure in that area causes a marked decrease in the EGCL's unconscious emoting. I suggest you approach that nerve bundle anteriorly through the opening in the ..."

Conway missed the rest of it because O'Mara had gripped his arm and pulled him carefully out of the low-gravity compartment.

"That was very good advice," the Chief Psychologist said when they were some distance from Prilicla's ward. "Let's erase that tape, Doctor, and discuss our little friend's problem on the way to my office."

Conway shook his head firmly. "Not yet. Prilicla said all that could be said about its case back there. The hard facts are that the Cinrusskin species is not one of the Federation's most robust. They have no stamina, no reserves to resist over a long period the effects of any injury or disease, whatever the cause. We all know—myself, my alter ego and, I suspect, you yourself—that unless its condition is treated and relieved very quickly Prilicla will die within a few hours, perhaps ten hours at most."

The Major nodded.

"Unless you can come up with a bright idea," he went on grimly, "and I would certainly welcome it if you did, I intend to go on thinking with the Cinrusskin tape. It hasn't helped much up to now, but I want to think without constraint, without having to play mental games with myself to avoid emoting too strongly in the presence of my patient. There is something very odd about this case, something I'm missing.

"So I'm going for a walk," he ended suddenly. "I won't be far away. Just far enough, I hope, to be outside the range of Prilicla's empathy."

O'Mara nodded again and left without speaking.

Conway put on a lightweight suit and traveled upward for three levels into the section reserved for the spiney, membranous, chlorine-breathing Illensan PVSJs. The inhabitants of Illensa were not a sociable species by Earth-human standards, and Conway was hoping to walk their foggy yellow wards and corridors without interruption while he wrestled with his problem. But that was not to be.

Senior Physician Gilvesh, who had worked with Conway some months earlier on a Dwerlan DBPK operation, was feeling uncharacteristically sociable and wanted to talk shop with its fellow Senior. They met in a narrow corridor leading from the level's pharmacy and there was no way that Conway could avoid talking to it.

Gilvesh was having problems. It was one of those days, the Illensan medic said, when all the patients were demanding inordinate amounts of attention and unnecessary quantities of palliative medication, the administration of which required its personal supervision. The junior medics and nursing staff were under pressure, therefore, and there was evident an unusual degree of verbal overreaction and sheer bad temper. Gilvesh said that it was explaining and apologizing in advance for any seeming discourtesy encountered by such an important visiting Senior as Conway. There were several of Gilvesh's cases, it insisted, which he would find interesting.

In common with the other medics trained for service in a multienvironment hospital, Conway had a thorough grounding in the basics of extraterrestrial physiology, metabolism, and the more common diseases of the Federation's member species. But for a detailed consultation and diagnosis of the kind required here he needed an Illensan physiology tape, and Gilvesh knew that as well as he did. So the Illensan Senior, it seemed, was sufficiently worried by the current state of its patients to seek a quick, other-species opinion.

With the Cinrusskin tape and his intense concern for Prilicla confusing his clinical view, Conway could do little more than make encouraging noises while Gilvesh discussed a painful intestinal tract, a visually dramatic and undoubtedly uncomfortable fungoid infection involving all eight of the spatulate limbs, and sundry other conditions to which Illensans were heir.

While the patients were seriously ill, their conditions were not critical, and the increased dosages of painkilling medication which Gilvesh was administering against its better judgment seemed to be having the desired effect, albeit slowly. Conway excused himself from the frantically busy wards as soon as he could and headed towards the much quieter MSVK and LSVO levels.

He had to pass through Level 163 again on the way, and stopped to check on the condition of the EGCL. Murchison yawned in his face and said that the operation was going well and that Prilicla was satisfied with the patient's emotional radiation. He did not call on Prilicla.

But he found that the low-gravity levels were having one of those days, too, and he was immediately trapped into further consultations. He could not very well avoid them because he was Conway, the Earth-human Senior Physician, known throughout the hospital for his sometimes unorthodox but effective methods and ideas on diagnosis and treatment. Here, at least, he was able to give some useful if orthodox advice because his Cinrusskin mind-partner was closer temperamentally and physically to the Nallajim LSVOs and the MSVKs of Euril who were fragile, birdlike, and extremely timid where the larger life-forms were concerned. But he could find no solution, orthodox or otherwise, to the problem he most desperately wanted to solve.

Prilicla's.

He thought about going to his quarters where he would have peace and quiet in which to think, but they were more than an hour's journey away at the other end of the hospital and he wanted to be close by in case there was a sudden deterioration in Prilicla's already close to critical condition. So instead he continued listening to Nallajim patients describing their symptoms and feeling a strange sadness because the Cinrusskin part of his mind knew that they were suffering, feeling, and emoting on many levels but his Earth-human mental equipment was incapable of receiving their emotional radiation. It was as if a sheet of glass lay between them, through which only sight and sound could pass.

But something more was getting through, surely? He had felt some of the aches and pains of the Illensan patients as he was feeling, to a certain extent, those of the Eurils and Nallajims around him. Or was that simply the GLNO tape fooling him into believing that he was an empath?

A *sheet of glass,* he thought suddenly, and an idea began to stir at the back of his mind. He tried to bring it out into the light, to give it form. Glass. Something about glass, or the properties of glass?

"Excuse me, Kytili," he said to the Nallijim medic who was worrying aloud about an atypical case of what should have been an easily treated and nonpainful condition. "I have to see O'Mara urgently."

It was Carrington who erased the GLNO tape because the Chief Psychologist had been called to some trouble in the chlorine-breathing level lately vacated by Conway. As O'Mara's senior assistant, Carrington was a highly qualified psychologist. He studied Conway's expression for a moment and asked if he could be of assistance.

Conway shook his head and forced a smile. "I wanted to ask the Major something. He would probably have said no, anyway. May I use the communicator?"

A few seconds later the face of Captain Fletcher flicked onto the screen and he said briskly, "*Rhabwar*, Control Deck."

"Captain," Conway said, "I want to ask a favor. If you agree to do it then it must be clearly understood that you will not be held responsible for any repercussions since it will be a medical matter entirely and you will be acting under my orders.

"There is a way that I may be able to help Prilicla," he went on, and described what he wanted done. When he finished, Fletcher looked grave.

"I'm aware of Prilicla's condition, Doctor," the Captain said. "Naydrad has been in and out of the ship so often it is threatening to wear out the boarding tube, and each time it returns we get an update on the empath's progress, or rather lack of it. And there is no need to belabor the point about our respective responsibilities. Obviously you wish to use the ship for an unauthorized mission and you are concealing the details so that any blame attached to me as a result of a future inquiry will be minimal. You are cutting corners again, Doctor, but in this instance I sympathize and will accept any instructions you care to give."

Fletcher broke off, and for the first time in Conway's experience of the man the Captain's cold, impassive, almost disdainful expression softened and the voice lost its irritatingly pedantic quality. "But it is my guess that you will order me to take *Rhabwar* to Cinruss," he went on, "so that our little friend can die among its own kind."

Before Conway could reply, Fletcher had switched him to Naydrad on the Casualty Deck.

Half an hour later the Kelgian Charge Nurse and Conway were transferring Prilicla, who was barely conscious and trembling only slightly by then, from its supporting harness to a powered litter. In the corridor leading to Lock Nine none of the medical staff questioned their action, and when any of them looked as if they might, Conway tapped irritably at the casing of his translator pack and pretended that it was malfunctioning. But when they were passing the entrance to the EGCL's room, Murchison was just leaving it. She stepped quickly in front of the litter.

"Where are you taking Prilicla?" she demanded. She sounded desperately tired and uncharacteristically angry, so much so that the empath began to twitch weakly.

"To *Rhabwar*," Conway said as calmly as he could. "How is the EGCL?"

Murchison looked at the empath, then visibly tried to control her feelings as she replied, "Very well, all things considered. Its condition is stable. There is a senior nurse continually in attendance. Edanelt is resting next door, only seconds away if anything should go wrong, but we don't expect any problems. In fact, we are expecting it to recover consciousness fairly soon. And Thornnastor has returned to Pathology to study the results of the tests we did on Prilicla. That's why you shouldn't be moving Prilicla from—"

"Thornnastor can't cure Prilicla," Conway said firmly. He looked from her to the litter and went on, "I can use your help. Do you think you can stay on your feet for another couple of hours? Please, there isn't much time."

Within seconds of the litter's arrival on *Rhabwar*'s Casualty Deck, Conway was on the intercom to Fletcher. "Captain, take us out quickly, please. And ready the planetary lander."

"The planetary—" Fletcher began, then went on, "We haven't undocked yet, much less reached Jump distance, and you're worrying about landing on Cinruss! Are you sure you know what—"

"I'm not sure of anything, Captain," Conway said. "Take us out but be prepared to check velocity at short notice, and well within Jump distance."

Fletcher broke the connection without replying, and a few seconds later the direct vision port showed the vast metal flank of the hospital moving away. Their velocity increased to the maximum allowed in the vicinity of the establishment, until the nearest section of the gigantic structure was a kilometer, then two kilometers away. But nobody was interested in the view just then because all of Conway's attention was on Prilicla, and Murchison and Naydrad were watching him.

"Back there," the pathologist said suddenly, "you said that even Thornnastor could not cure Prilicla. Why did you say that?"

"Because there was nothing wrong with Prilicla," Conway said. He ignored Murchison's unladylike gape of surprise and Naydrad's wildly undulating fur and spoke to the empath. "Isn't that so, little friend?"

"I think so, friend Conway," Prilicla said, speaking for the first time since coming on board. "Certainly there is nothing wrong with me now. But I am confused."

"*You're* confused!" Murchison began, and stopped because Conway was again at the communicator.

"Captain," he said, "return at once to Lock Nine to take on another patient. Switch on all of your exterior lighting and ignore the traffic instructions. And please patch me through to Level One Six Three, the EGCL's recovery room. Quickly."

"Right," the Captain coldly said, "but I want an explanation."

"You'll get one—" Conway began. He broke off as the Captain's angry features were replaced by a view of the recovery room with the attending nurse, a Kelgian, curled like a furry question mark beside the EGCL. Its report on the patient's condition was brief, accurate, and, to Conway, terrifying.

He broke contact and returned to the Captain. Apologetically he said, "There isn't much time so I would like you to listen while I explain the situation, or what I think is the situation, to the others here. I had intended that the lander be fitted with remote-controlled medical servomechs and used as an isolation unit, but there isn't time for that now. The EGCL is waking up. All hell could break loose in the hospital at any minute."

Quickly he explained his theory about the EGCL and the reasoning which had led to it, ending with the proof which was Prilicla's otherwise inexplicable recovery.

"The part of this which bothers me," he concluded grimly, "is having to subject Prilicla to the same degree of emotional torture once again."

The empath's limbs trembled at the remembered pain, but it said, "I can accept it, friend Conway, now that I know the condition will be temporary."

But removing the EGCL was not as easy as had been the abduction of Prilicla. The Kelgian duty nurse was disposed to argue, and it took all of Naydrad's powers of persuasion and the combined ranks of Murchison and Conway to make it do as it was told. And while they were arguing, Conway could see the wildly rippling and twitching fur of the two nurses, the sudden, almost manic changes of facial expression in Murchison, and the emotional overreaction in all of them, in spite of his earlier warning of what would happen if they did not control their feelings. By the time the transfer of the patient to *Rhabwar*'s litter was underway, so much fuss had been created that someone was sure to report it. Conway did not want that.

The patient was coming to. There was no time to go through proper channels, no time for long and repeated explanations. Then suddenly he had to find time, because both Edanelt and O'Mara were in the room. It was the Chief Psychologist who spoke first.

"*Conway!* What do you think you're doing with that patient?"

"I'm kidnapping it!" Conway snapped back sarcastically. Quickly he went on, "I'm sorry, sir, we are all overreacting. We can't help it, but try hard to be calm. Edanelt, will you help me transfer the EGCL's support systems to the litter. There isn't much time left so I'll have to explain while we work."

The Melfan Senior dithered for a moment, the tapping of its six crablike legs against the floor reflecting its indecision, then it spoke. "Very well, Conway. But if I am not satisfied with your explanation the patient stays here."

"Fair enough," said Conway. He looked at O'Mara, whose face was showing the indications of a suddenly elevated blood pressure, and went on, "You had the right idea at the beginning, but everyone was too busy to talk to you. It should have occurred to me, too, if the GLNO tape and concern for Prilicla hadn't confused me by—"

"Omit the flattery and excuses, Conway," O'Mara broke in, "and get on with it."

Conway was helping Murchison and Naydrad lift the EGCL into the litter while Edanelt and the other nurse checked the siting of the biosensors. Without looking up he went on, "Whenever we encounter a new intelligent species the first thing we are supposed to ask ourselves is how it got that way. Only the dominant life-form on a planet has the opportunity, the security and leisure, to develop a civilization capable of interstellar travel."

At first Conway had not been able to see how the EGCL's people had risen to dominance on their world, how they had fought their way to the top of their evolutionary tree. They had no physical weapons of offense, and their snaillike apron of muscle which furnished locomotion was incapable of moving them fast enough to avoid natural enemies. Their carapace was a defense of sorts in that it protected vital organs, but that osseous shell was mounted high on the body, making it top-heavy and an easy prey for any predator who had only to topple it over to get at the soft underside. Its manipulatory appendages were flexible and dexterous, but too short and lightly muscled to be a deterrent. On their home world the EGCLs should have been one of nature's losers. They were not, however, and there had to be a reason.

It had come to him slowly, Conway went on, while he was moving through the chlorine and light-gravity sections. In every ward there had been cases of patients with known and properly diagnosed ailments displaying, or at least complaining about, atypical symptoms. The demand for painkilling medication had been unprecedented. Conditions which should have caused a minor degree of discomfort were, it seemed, inflicting severe pain. He had been aware of some of this pain himself, but had put that down to a combination of his imagination and the effect of the Cinrusskin tape.

He had already considered and discarded the idea that the trouble was psychosomatic because the condition was too widespread, but then he thought about it again.

During their return from the disaster site with the sole surviving EGCL, everyone had felt understandably low about the mission's lack of success and because Prilicla was giving cause for concern. But in retrospect there was something wrong, unprofessional, about their reactions. They were feeling things too strongly, overreacting, developing in their own fashions the same kind of hypersensitivity which had affected Prilicla and which had affected the patients and staff on the Illensan and the Nallajim levels. Conway had felt it himself; the vague stomach pains, the discomfort in hands and fingers, the overexcitability in circumstances which did not warrant it. But the effect had diminished with distance, because when he visited O'Mara's office for the GLNO tape and later for the erasure, he had felt normal and unworried except for the usual degree of concern over a current case, accentuated in this instance because the patient was Prilicla.

The EGCL was receiving the best possible attention from Thornnastor and Edanelt, so it was not on his mind to any large extent. Conway had been sure of that.

"But then I began to think about its injuries," Conway went on, "and the way I had felt on the ship and within three levels of the EGCL operation. In the hospital while I had the GLNO tape riding me, I was an empath without empathy. But I seemed to be feeling things—emotions, pains, conditions which did not belong to me. I thought that, because of fatigue and the stress of that time, I was generating sympathetic pains. Then it occurred to me that if the type of discomfort being suffered by the EGCL were subtracted from the symptoms of the medics and patients on those six levels and the intensity of the discomfort reduced, then the affected patients and staff would be acting and reacting normally. This seemed to point toward—"

"An empath!" O'Mara said. "Like Prilicla."

"*Not* like Prilicla," Conway said firmly. "Although it is possible that the empathic faculty possessed by the preintelligent ancestors of both species was similar."

But their prehistoric world was an infinitely more dangerous place than Cinruss had been, Conway continued, and in any case the EGCLs lacked the ability of the Cinrusskins quite literally to fly from danger. And in such a savage environment there was little advantage in having an empathic faculty other than as a highly unpleasant early warning system, and so the ability to receive emotions had been lost. It was probable that they no longer received even the emotional radiation of their own kind.

They had become organic transmitters, reflectors and focusers and magnifiers of their own feelings and those of the beings around them. The indications were that the faculty had evolved to the stage where they had no conscious control over the process.

"Think of the defensive weapon that makes," Conway explained. The EGCL's life support and sensors had been transferred to the litter and it was ready to leave. "If a predator tries to attack it, the anger and hunger it feels for its victim together with the fear and pain, if the victim was hurt or wounded, would be magnified, bounced back, and figuratively hit the attacker in the teeth. I can only guess at the order of emotional amplification used. But the effect on the predator, especially if there were others in the vicinity whose feelings were also being amplified, would be discouraging to say the least, also very confusing. It might have the effect of having them attack each other.

"We already know the effect of a deeply unconscious EGCL on the patients and staff three levels above and below this one," Conway went on grimly. "Now consciousness is returning and I don't know what will happen, or how far-reaching the effect will be. We have to get it away from here before the hospital's patients have their own as well as the EGCL's pain magnified to an unknown but major degree, and their medical attendants thrown into a steadily accelerating state of disorder and panic because they, too, will receive the reflected pain and—"

He broke off and tried to control his own growing panic, then he said harshly, "We have to get it away from the hospital now, without further delays or arguments."

O'Mara's face had lost its angry red coloration while Conway had been talking, until now it looked gray and bloodless. He said, "Don't waste time talking, Doctor. I shall accompany you. There will be no further delays or arguments."

When they reached *Rhabwar*'s Casualty Deck the EGCL was still not fully conscious and Prilicla was again being seriously affected by the ambient emotional radiation which was being amplified and bounced off their patient. The discomfort diminished sharply with increasing distance from the hospital, the empath told them, and the awakening EGCL was radiating only a relatively low intensity of discomfort from the sites of the recent surgery—but Prilicla did not have to tell them that because they could all feel it for themselves.

"I have been thinking about the problem of communicating with these people," O'Mara said thoughtfully. "If they are all high-powered transmitters and reflectors of emotional radiation, they may not be aware of what they are doing, only that they have an automatic, nonmaterial defense against everything and everyone wishing them harm. The job of establishing communications with them may not be easy and is likely to be a long-range affair, unless our basic premise is wrong and we—"

"My first idea," Conway broke in, "was to put it in the lander with remote-controlled medical servomechs. Then I thought there should be one medic, a volunteer, in attendance—"

"I won't ask who," O'Mara said dryly, and smiled as Conway's embarrassment bounced off the EGCL and hit them.

"—because if ever there was case demanding isolation," Conway ended, "this is it."

The Chief Psychologist nodded. "What I had been about to say was that we may have miscalculated. Certainly we could never treat EGCLs in hospital where the patients surrounding them were in pain, even slight pain. But the situation here in the ship isn't too bad. I can feel pains in the equivalent sites to where the EGCL is hurting, but nothing I can't handle. And the rest of you are emoting concern for the patient, and this is not unpleasant even when magnified. It seems that if you don't think badly toward the patient, it can't bounce anything too unpleasant back at you. It's surprising. I feel just the way I always do, except more so."

"But it is regaining consciousness," Conway protested. "There should be an intensification of—"

"There isn't," O'Mara cut in. "That is very obvious, Conway. Could the reason be *because* the patient is regaining consciousness? Think about it. Yes, Doctor, we can all feel you feeling 'Eureka!' "

"Of *course*!" Conway said, and paused because his pleasure and excitement at seeing the answer, magnified by the EGCL, was causing Prilicla's wings to go into the series of slow, rippling undulations which indicated intense pleasure in a Cinrusskin. It also counteracted the aches which he and everyone else were feeling from the patient. He thought, *What a weird experience the cultural contact specialists were going to have with this species.*

Aloud he said, "The process of reflecting and magnifying the feelings, hostile or otherwise, of the people around them is a defense mechanism which would, naturally, be at its most effective when the being is helpless, vulnerable, or unconscious. With a return to consciousness the effect seems to diminish but the empathic reflections are still strong. The result is that everyone around them will have an empathic faculty not unlike Prilicla's, and yet the EGCLs are deaf to each other's emotional radiation because they are transmitters only.

"Being like Prilicla," he went on, looking across at the empath, "is something of a mixed blessing. But the EGCL would be a nice person to have around if we were having a good time—"

"Control here," the voice of the Captain broke in. "I have some information on your patient's species. Federation Archives have signaled the hospital to the effect that this race—their name for themselves is the Duwetz—was contacted briefly by an exploring Hudlar ship before the formation of the Galactic Federation. Enough information was obtained for the basic Duwetz language to be programmed into the present-day translation computers, but contact was severed because of serious psychological problems among the crew. We are advised to proceed with caution."

"The patient," Prilicla said suddenly, "is awake."

Conway moved closer to the EGCL and tried to think positive, reassuring thoughts toward it. He noted with relief that the biosensors and associated monitors were indicating a weak but stable condition; that the damaged lung was again working satisfactorily and the bandages immobilizing the two rejoined appendages were firmly in position. The extensive suturing on the muscular apron and ambulatory pad at the base were well up to Thornnastor and Edanelt's high standards, as were the deftly inserted staples which gleamed in neat rows where the carapace fractures had been. Obviously the being was in considerable discomfort in spite of the painkilling medication Thornnastor had synthesized for its particular metabolism. But pain was not the predominant feeling it was transmitting, and fear and hostility were entirely absent.

Two of its three remaining eyes swiveled to regard them while the other one was directed toward the viewport where Sector Twelve General Hospital, now almost eight kilometers distant, blazed like some vast, surrealistic piece of jewelry against the interstellar darkness. The feelings which washed through them, so intensely that they trembled or caught their breaths or rippled their fur, were of curiosity and wonder.

"I'm not an organ mechanic like you people," O'Mara said gruffly, "but I would say that with this case the prognosis is favorable."

INVESTIGATION

The ambulance ship *Rhabwar* had made the trip from Sector General to the scene of the supposed disaster in record time and with a precision of astrogation, Conway thought, which would cause Lieutenant Dodds to exhibit symptoms of cranial swelling for many days to come. But as the information was displayed on the Casualty Deck's repeater screens, it became clear to the watching medical team that this was not going to be a fast rescue—that this might not, in fact, be a rescue mission at all.

The fully extended sensor net revealed no sign of a distressed ship, nor any wreckage or components of such a ship. Even the finely divided, expanding cloud of debris which would have indicated a catastrophic malfunction in the vessel's reactor was missing. All there was to be seen was the characteristic shape of a dead and partially fused distress beacon at a distance of a few hundred meters and, about three million kilometers beyond it, the bright crescent shape which was one of this system's planets.

Major Fletcher's voice came from the speaker. The Captain did not sound pleased. "Doctor," he said. "We cannot assume that this was a simple false alarm. Hyperspace radio distress beacons are highly expensive hunks of machinery for one thing, and I have yet to hear of an intelligent species who does not have an aversion to crying their equivalent of wolf. I think the crew must have panicked, then discovered that the condition of the ship was not as distressed as they at first thought. They may have resumed their journey or tried for a planetary landing to effect repairs. We'll have to eliminate the latter possibility before we leave. Dodds?"

"The system has been surveyed," the Astrogator's voice replied. "G-type sun, seven planets with one, the one we can see, habitable in the short term by warm-blooded oxygen-breathers. No indigenous intelligent life. Course for a close approach and search, sir?"

"Yes," Fletcher said. "Haslam, pull in your long-range sensors and set up for a planetary surface scan. Lieutenant Chen, I'll need impulse power, four Gs, on my signal. And Haslam, just in case the ship is down and trying to signal its presence, monitor the normal and hyperradio frequencies."

A few minutes later they felt the deck press momentarily against their feet as the artificial gravity system compensated for the four-G thrust. Conway, Pathologist Murchison, and Charge Nurse Naydrad moved closer to the repeater where Dodds had displayed the details of the target planet's gravity pull, atmospheric composition and pressure, and the environmental data which made it just barely habitable. The empathic Doctor Prilicla clung to the safety of the ceiling and observed the screen at slightly longer range.

It was the Charge Nurse, its silvery fur rippling in agitation, who spoke first. "This ship isn't supposed to land on unprepared surfaces," Naydrad said. "That ground is—is rough."

"Why couldn't they have stayed in space like good little distressed aliens," Murchison said to nobody in particular, "and waited to be rescued?"

Conway looked at her and said thoughtfully, "It is possible that their condition of distress was nonmechanical. Injury, sickness, or psychological disturbances among the crew, perhaps, problems which have since been resolved. If it was a physical problem then they should have stayed out here, since it is easier to effect repairs in weightless conditions."

"Not always, Doctor," Fletcher's voice cut in sharply from the Control Deck. "If the physical problem was a badly holed hull, a breathable atmosphere around them might seem more desirable than weightless and airless space. No doubt you have medical preparations to make."

Conway felt a surge of anger at the other's thinly veiled suggestion that he tend to his medical knitting and stop trying to tell the Captain his business. Beside him Murchison was breathing heavily and Naydrad's fur was tufting and rippling as if blown by a strong wind, while above them the emotion-sensitive Prilicla's six insectile legs and iridescent wings quivered in the emotional gale they were generating. Out of consideration for the empath, Conway tried to control his feelings, as did the others.

It was understandable that Fletcher, the ship's commander, liked to have the last word, but he knew and accepted the fact that on Sector General's special ambulance ship he had to relinquish command to the senior medic, Conway, during the course of a rescue. Fletcher was a good officer, able, resourceful, and one of the Federation's top men in the field of comparative extraterrestrial technology. But there were times during the short period while responsibility was being passed to Senior Physician Conway when his manner became a trifle cool, formal—even downright nasty.

Prilicla's trembling diminished and the little empath tried to say something which would further improve the quality of the emotional radiation around it. "If the lately distressed vessel has landed on this planet," it said timidly, "then we know that the crew belongs to one of the oxygen-breathing species and the preparations to receive casualties, if any, will be relatively simple."

"That's true," Conway said, laughing.

"Only thirty-eight different species fall into that category," Murchison said, and added dryly, "that we know of."

*   *   *

Rhabwar's sensors detected a small concentration of metal and associated low-level radiation, which on an uninhabited planet could only mean the presence of a grounded ship, while they were still two diameters out. As a result they were able to decelerate and enter atmosphere for a closer look after only two orbits.

The ambulance ship was a modified Monitor Corps cruiser and, as such, the largest of the Federation vessels capable of aerodynamic maneuvering in atmosphere. It sliced through the brown, sand-laden air like a great white dart, trailing a sonic shockwave loud enough to wake the dead or, at the very least, to signal its presence to any survivors capable of receiving audio stimulus.

Visibility was nil as they approached the grounded ship. The whole area was in the grip of one of the sandstorms which regularly swept this harsh, near-desert world, and the picture of the barren, mountainous surface was a sensor simulation rather than direct vision. It accurately reproduced the succession of wind-eroded hills and rocky outcroppings and the patches of thorny vegetation which clung to them. Then suddenly they were above and past the grounded ship.

Fletcher pulled *Rhabwar* into a steep climb which became a ponderous loop as they curved back for a slower pass over the landing site. This time, as they flew low over the other ship at close to stalling speed, there was a brief cessation in the storm and they were able to record the scene in near-perfect detail.

Rhabwar was climbing into space again when the Captain said, "I can't put this ship down anywhere near that area, Doctor. I'm afraid we'll have to check for survivors, if there are any, with the planetary lander. There aren't any obvious signs of life from the wreck."

Conway studied the still picture of the crash site on his screen for a moment before replying. It was arguable whether the ship had made a heavy landing or a barely controlled crash. Much less massive than *Rhabwar*, it had been designed to land on its tail, but one of the three stabilizer fins had collapsed on impact, tipping the vessel onto its side. In spite of this the hull was relatively undamaged except for a small section amidships which had been pierced by a low ridge of rock. There was no visible evidence of damage other than that caused by the crash.

All around the wreck at distances varying from twenty to forty meters there were a number of objects—Conway counted twenty-seven of them in all—which the sensor identified as organic material. The objects had not changed position between the first and second of *Rhabwar*'s thunderous fly-bys, so the probability was that they were either dead or deeply unconscious. Conway stepped up the magnification until the outlines became indistinct in the heat shimmer, and shook his head in bafflement.

The objects had been, or were, living creatures, and even though they had been partly covered by windblown sand, he could see a collection of protuberances, fissures, and angular projections which had to be sensory organs and limbs. There was a general similarity in shape but a marked difference in size of the beings, but he thought they were more likely to be representatives of different subspecies rather than adults and their young at different stages of development.

"Those life-forms are new to me," the pathologist said, standing back from the screen. She looked at Conway and the others in turn. There was no dissent.

Conway thumbed the communicator button. "Captain," he said briskly, "Murchison and Naydrad will go down with me. Prilicla will remain on board to receive casualties." Normally that would have been the Kelgian Charge Nurse's job, but nobody there had to be told that the fragile little empath would last for only a few minutes on the surface before being blown away and smashed against the rocky terrain. He went on, "I realize that four people on the lander will be a tight squeeze, but initially I'd like to take a couple of pressure litters and the usual portable equipment—"

"One large pressure litter, Doctor," Fletcher broke in. "There will be five people on board. I am going down as well in case there are technical problems getting into the wreck. You're forgetting that if the life-forms are new to the Federation, then their spaceship technology could be strange as well. Dodds will fetch anything else you need on the next trip down. Can you be ready at the lander bay in fifteen minutes?"

"We'll be there," Conway said, smiling at the eagerness in the other's voice. Fletcher wanted to look at the inside of that wrecked ship just as badly as Conway wanted to investigate the internal workings of its crew. And if there were survivors, *Rhabwar* would shortly be engaged in conducting another medical first contact with all the hidden problems, both clinical and cultural, which that implied.

Fletcher's eagerness was underlined by the fact that he rather than Dodds took the vehicle down and landed it in a ridiculously small area of flat sand within one hundred meters of the wreck. From the surface the wind-eroded rock outcroppings looked higher, sharper, and much more dangerous, but the sandstorm had died down to a stiff breeze which lifted the grains no more than a few feet above the ground. From the orbiting *Rhabwar,* Haslam reported occasional wind flurries passing through their area which might briefly inconvenience them.

One of the flurries struck while they were helping Naydrad unload the litter, a bulky vehicle whose pressure envelope was capable of reproducing the gravity, pressure, and atmosphere requirements of most of the known life-forms. Gravity nullifiers compensated for the litter's considerable weight, making it easily manageable by one person, but when the sudden wind caught it, Naydrad, Dodds, and Conway had to throw themselves across it to keep it from blowing away.

"Sorry about this," Lieutenant Dodds said, as if by studying the available information on the planet he was somehow responsible for its misdemeanors. "It is about two hours before local midday here, and the wind usually dies down by now. It remains calm until just before sunset, and again in the middle of the night when there is a severe drop in temperature. The sandstorms after sunset and before dawn are very bad and last for three to five hours, when outside work would be very dangerous. Work during the night lull is possible but inadvisable. The local animal life is small and omnivorous, but those thorn carpets on the slope over there have a degree of mobility and have to be watched, especially at night. I'd estimate five hours of daylight calm to complete the rescue. If it takes longer than that, it would be better to spend the night on *Rhabwar* and come back tomorrow."

As the Lieutenant was speaking, the wind died again so that they were able to see the wreck, the dark objects scattered around it, and the harsh, arid landscape shimmering in the heat. Five hours should be more than enough to ferry up the casualties to *Rhabwar* for preliminary treatment. Anything done for them down here would be done quickly, simple first aid.

"Did they bother to name this Godforsaken planet?" the Captain asked, stepping down from the lander's airlock.

Dodds hesitated, then said, "Trugdil, sir."

Fletcher's eyebrows rose, Murchison laughed, and they could see agitated movements of Naydrad's fur under its lightweight suit. It was the Kelgian who spoke first.

"The trugdil," it said, "is a species of Kelgian rodent with the particularly nasty habit of—"

284 · JAMES WHITE

"I know," the Astrogator said quickly. "But it was a Kelgian-crewed Monitor Corps scoutship which made the discovery. In the Corps it is customary for the Captain of the discovering ship to give his, her, or its name to the world which has been found. But in this instance the officer waived the right and offered it to his subordinates in turn, all of whom likewise refused to give their names to the planet. Judging by the name it ended with, they didn't think much of the place either. There was another case when—"

"Interesting," Conway said quietly, "but we're wasting time. Prilicla?"

Through his helmet phones, the empath's voice replied at once. "I hear you, friend Conway. Lieutenant Haslam is relaying an overall picture of the area to me through the telescope, and your helmet vision pickups enable me to see all that you see. Standing by."

"Very good," Conway said. To the others he went on, "Naydrad will accompany me with the litter. The rest of you split up and take a quick look at the other casualties. If any of them are moving, or there are indications of recent movement, call Pathologist Murchison or me at once."

As they moved off he added, "It is important that we don't waste time on cadavers at the expense of possible survivors. But be careful. This is a new life-form to us, and we are likewise strange to it. Physically we may resemble something it fears, and there is the added factor of the survivor being weak, in pain, and mentally confused. Guard against an instinctive, violent reaction from them which, in normal circumstances, would not occur." He stopped talking because the others were already fanning out and the first casualty, lying very still and partly covered by sand, was only a few meters away.

As Naydrad helped him scoop sand from around the body Conway saw that the being was six-limbed, with a stubby, cylindrical torso with a spherical head at one end and possibly a tail at the other extremity, although the severity of the injuries made it difficult to be sure. The two forelimbs terminated in long, flexible digits. There were two recognizable eyes, partially concealed by heavy lids, and various slits and orifices which were doubtless aural and olfactory sensors and the openings for respiration and ingestion. The tegument, which was pale brown shading to a deeper, reddish color on its top surface, showed many incised wounds and abrasions which had bled freely but had since congealed and become encrusted with sand—perhaps the sand had assisted in the process of coagulation. Even the large wound at the rear, which looked as if it might be the result of a traumatic amputation, was remarkably dry.

Conway bent closer and began going over the body with his scanner. There was no evidence of fracturing or of damaged or displaced organs, so far as he could see, so the being could be moved without risk of complicating its injuries. Naydrad was waiting with the litter to see whether it was a survivor for immediate loading or a cadaver for later dissection, when Conway's scanner's sensors detected cardiac activity, extremely feeble but undoubtedly present, and respiration so slow and shallow that he had almost missed it.

"Are you getting this, Prilicla?" he said.

"Yes, friend Conway," replied the empath. "A most interesting life-form."

"There is considerable tissue wastage," he went on, still using the scanner. "Possibly the result of dehydration. And there is a similarity in degree and type of the injuries which I find strange..." He trailed off into silence as Naydrad helped him lift the casualty into the litter.

"No doubt it has already occurred to you, friend Conway," Prilicla said, using the form of words which was the closest it ever came to suggesting that someone had missed the obvious, "that the dehydration and the deeper coloration on the upper areas of the epidermis may be connected with local environmental factors, and the redness is due to sunburn."

It had not occurred to Conway, but fortunately the emotional radiation associated with his embarrassment was well beyond the range of the empath. He indicated the litter and said, "Naydrad, don't forget to fit the sun filter."

In his phones he heard Murchison laughing quietly, then she said, "It hadn't occurred to me, either, so don't feel bad about it. But I have a couple of beasties over here I'd like you to look at. Both are alive, just barely, with a large number of incised wounds. There is a great disparity in mass between them, and the arrangement of the internal organs in the large one is, well, peculiar. For instance, the alimentary canal is—"

"Right now," Conway broke in, "we must concentrate on separating the living and the dead. Detailed examinations and discussions will have to wait until we're back on the ship, so spend as little time as possible on each one. But I know how you feel—my casualty has some peculiarities as well."

"Yes, Doctor," she replied coldly, in spite of his half apology. Pathologists, even beautiful ones like Murchison, he thought, were strange people.

"Captain? Lieutenant Dodds?" he said irritably. "Any other survivors?"

"I haven't been looking at them closely, Doctor," Fletcher replied. There was an odd harshness in his voice. Possibly the condition of the crash victims was distressing to a nonmedical man, Conway thought, and some of these casualties were in really bad shape. But before he could reply the Captain went on, "I've been moving around the area quickly, counting them and looking to see if any have been covered by sand or hidden between rocks. There are twenty-seven of them in all. But the positioning of the bodies is odd, Doctor. It's as if the ship was in imminent danger of blowing up or catching fire, and they used the last of their remaining strength to escape from it.

"The sensors show no such danger," he added.

Dodds waited for a few seconds to be sure that the Captain had finished speaking, then said, "Three alive and showing slight movement. One that looks dead, but you're the doctor, Doctor."

"Thank you," Conway said dryly. "We'll look at them as soon as possible. Meanwhile, Lieutenant, help Naydrad load the litter, please."

He joined Murchison then, and for the next hour they moved among the casualties, assessing the degree of injury and readying them for transfer to the lander. The litter was almost full and had space for two of the medium-sized casualties, which they had tentatively classified as belonging to physiological type DCMH, or one of the large DCOJs. The very small DCLGs, which were less than half the mass of the DCMH Conway had first examined, were left for the time being because they all showed flickerings of life. As yet neither Murchison nor Conway could make sense of them physiologically. She thought the small DCLGs might be nonintelligent lab animals or possibly ship's pets, while Conway was convinced that the large DCOJs were food animals, also nonintelligent. But with newly discovered extraterrestrial life-forms, one could never be sure of anything, and all of them would therefore have to be treated as patients.

Then they found one of the small aliens who was quite definitely dead. Murchison said briskly, "I'll work on it in the lander. Give me fifteen minutes and I'll have something to tell Prilicla about their basal metabolism before the casualties begin arriving."

A flurry of wind blew the sand disturbed by her feet ahead of her as she moved toward the lander, the small cadaver supported by her shoulder and one arm while the other hand, carrying her med kit, acted as a counterbalance. Conway was about to suggest that a proper examination on *Rhabwar,* where the full laboratory facilities were available, would be better. But Murchison would already have considered doing that and decided against it, for two obvious reasons: If she returned to the ambulance ship with Dodds and Naydrad, some of the casualties already loaded would have to be left behind, and she needed to tell Prilicla only enough for the empath to provide emergency surgery and supportive treatment until the survivors were taken to Sector General.

"Captain, you overheard?" Conway said. "I'd like Dodds and Naydrad to take off as soon as Pathologist Murchison is through. It looks as if three trips will be necessary to lift all of them, and another for ourselves. We're going to be pushed for time if this is to be wrapped up before the sunset storm hits the area."

There was no reply from Fletcher, which usually signified assent when Conway was in command. He went on, "Murchison will stay behind and assemble another batch of casualties for the next lift. We'll collect them where there is shelter from the sun and sand. The lee side of the wreck would do, or better still, inside it if there isn't too much debris."

"No, Doctor," the Captain said. "I'm worried about what we might find on that ship."

Conway did not reply, but the sigh he gave as he continued his examination of the casualty he was working on made his impatience clear. Fletcher was one of the Monitor Corps' acknowledged experts in the field of alien ship technology. This was the reason he had been given command of Sector General's most advanced ambulance ship—it had long been recognized that a rescue mission's greatest danger was to the rescuers, who would be looking for survivors in a distressed vessel whose technology and operating principles they did not understand. Fletcher was careful, conscientious, highly competent, and did not as a rule worry out loud about his work or ability to carry it out. Conway was still wondering about the Captain's uncharacteristic behavior when a shadow fell across the casualty he was examining.

Fletcher was standing over him and looking as worried as he had sounded. "I realize, Doctor," the Captain said awkwardly, "that during rescue operations you have the rank. I want you to know that I go along with this willingly. But on this occasion I believe the circumstances are such that complete authority should revert to me." He glanced back at the wreck and then down at the badly injured alien. "Doctor, do you have any experience in forensic medicine?"

Conway sat back on his haunches and simply gaped at him. Fletcher took a deep breath and went on. "The distribution and condition of the casualties around the wreck seemed wrong to me," he said seriously. "It indicated a rapid evacuation of a relatively undamaged ship, even though our sensors showed no radiation or fire hazard. As well, all of the casualties were severely injured to varying degrees and with the same type of wounding. It seemed to me that some of them would have been able to make a greater distance from their ship than others, yet all of them collapsed within a relatively small radius from the wreck. This made me wonder whether the injuries had been sustained inside the ship or close to where they were lying."

"A local predator," Conway said, "which attacked them as they came out already shocked and weakened as a result of the crash."

The Captain shook his head. "No life-form capable of inflicting such injuries inhabits this world. Most of the injuries I've seen are incised wounds or those caused by the removal of a limb. This suggests the use of a sharp instrument of some kind. The user of the instrument may or may not be still on board the ship. If it is on board, it may be that the beings who escaped were the lucky ones, in which case I hate to think of what we may find inside the wreck. But you can see now why I must resume overall responsibility, Doctor.

"The Monitor Corps is the Federation's law-enforcement arm," he concluded quietly. "It seems to me that a very serious crime has been committed, and I am a policeman first and an ambulance driver second."

Before Conway could reply, Murchison said, "The condition of this cadaver, and the other casualties I've examined, does not preclude such a possibility."

"Thank you, ma'am," the Captain said. "That is why I want the medical team back on *Rhabwar* while Dodds and I arrest this criminal. If things go wrong, Chen and Haslam can get you back to the hospital—"

"Haslam, sir," the Communications Officer's voice broke in. "Shall I request Corps assistance?"

The Captain did not reply at once, and Conway began thinking that the other's theory could very well explain why a previously undamaged ship had released a distress beacon and then left the scene to try for a planetary landing. Something had gotten loose among the crew, perhaps. Something which might have been confined had escaped, something very, very nasty. With an effort Conway brought his runaway imagination under control. "We can't be absolutely sure that a criminal was responsible for this. A nonintelligent experimental animal which broke loose, injured and perhaps maddened with pain, could have done—"

"Animals use teeth and claws, doctor," the Captain broke in. "Not knives."

"This is a completely new species," Conway replied. "We don't know anything about them, their culture or their codes of behavior. They may be ignorant of our particular laws."

"Ignorance of the law," Fletcher said impatiently, "has never been an acceptable excuse for committing a criminal act against another intelligent being. Just as ignorance of law by the innocent victim does not exclude the being concerned from its protection."

"I agree—" Conway began. "But I am not completely sure that a crime has been committed," he went on. "Until I am sure, you, Haslam, will not send for help. But keep a close watch on this area and if anything moves, apart from the survivors or ourselves, let me know at once. Very soon Dodds will be taking off with the lander and—"

"Naydrad and the casualties," Murchison ended for him. Quietly but firmly she went on, "Your theory scares hell out of me, Captain, but it is still only a theory. You've admitted as much yourself. The facts are that there are a large number of casualties all around us. They don't know it yet but they are entitled to the protection of Federation law. Whether their injuries are due to the crash or to being carved up by some psychopathic or temporarily deranged alien, they are also entitled, under that same law, to all necessary medical assistance."

The Captain looked toward the lander where the Pathologist was still working on the specimen, then back to the Doctor.

"I've nothing to add," Conway said.

Fletcher remained silent while Murchison completed her investigation and Dodds and Naydrad transferred two casualties into the lander. He did not speak while the vehicle was taking off or when Conway selected a spot under a large outcropping of rock which would give waiting casualties shelter from the sun and windblown sand. Neither did he offer to help them carry the injured e-ts to the assembly point even though, without the litter, it was hot, back-breaking work. Instead he moved among the e-ts with his vision pickup, recording them individually before and after the ground had been disturbed around them by Murchison and Conway, and always positioning himself between the two medics and the wreck.

Plainly the Captain was taking his strange, new role as a policeman and protector of the innocent bystanders very seriously indeed.

The cooling unit in his suit did not seem to be working very well and Conway would have loved to open his visor for a few minutes. But doing that, even in the shelter of the outcropping, would have meant letting in a lot of windblown sand.

"Let's rest for a while," he said as they placed another casualty beside its fellows. "Time we had a talk with Prilicla."

"That is a pleasure at any time, friends Murchison and Conway," the empath said promptly. "While I am, of course, beyond the range of the emotional radiation being generated down there, I sympathize and hope that your feelings of anxiety about the criminal are not too unpleasant."

"Our feelings of bewilderment are much stronger," Conway said dryly. "But maybe you can help relieve them by going over our information, incomplete as it is, before the first casualties reach you."

There was still a little doubt about the accuracy of the physiological classifications, Conway explained, but there were three separate but related types—DCLG, DCMH, and DCOJ. The wounds fell into two general categories, incised and abraded wounds which could have resulted when the ship's occupants were hurled against sharp-edged metal during the crash, and a traumatic amputation of major limbs which was so prevalent among the casualties that an explanation other than the crash was needed to explain them.

All of the survivors had body temperatures significantly greater than the norm for warm-blooded oxygen breathers, indicating a high metabolic rate and a hyperactive life-form. This was supported by the uniformly deep state of unconsciousness displayed by all of the casualties, and the evidence of dehydration and malnutrition. Beings who burned up energy rapidly rarely lingered in a semiconscious state. There were also signs that the beings had an unusual ability to control bleeding from severe wounds. Coagulation in the incised wounds, perhaps assisted by the presence of the sand, was rapid but not abnormally so, while the stumps at the amputation sites showed little evidence of bleeding.

"Supportive treatment to relieve the dehydration and malnutrition is all that can be done until we get them to the hospital," Conway went on. "Murchison has already specified the nutrients suited to their metabolism. You can also insert sutures as you see fit. If the load is too great for you, which in my opinion it is, retain Naydrad and send down only the pilot with the litter. Murchison can ride with the casualties on the next trip. She will stay with you while Naydrad comes down for the last batch."

There was a moment's silence, then the empath said, "I understand, friend Conway. But have you considered the fact that your suggestion will mean three members of the medical team being on *Rhabwar* for a lengthy period and only one, yourself, on the surface where medical assistance is most urgently needed? I am sure that, with the aid of the Casualty Deck's handling devices and the assistance of friends Haslam and Chen, I can cope with these patients."

It was possible that Prilicla could cope with the patients provided they remained unconscious. But if they came to suddenly and reacted instinctively to their strange and, to them, perhaps frightening surroundings, and to the giant but incredibly fragile insect medic hovering over them, Conway shuddered to think of what might happen to the empath's eggshell body and pipestem limbs. Before he could reply, Prilicla was speaking again.

"I am beyond the range of your emotional radiation, of course," the empath said, "but from long contact with the both of you I know of the strength of the emotional bond between friend Murchison and yourself. This, taking into account the strong possibility that there is a very dangerous life-form loose down there, is undoubtedly a factor in your decision to send her to the safety of the ship. But perhaps friend Murchison would suffer less emotional discomfort if she remained with you."

Murchison looked up from the casualty she was attending. "Is that what you were thinking?"

"No," Conway lied.

She laughed and said, "You heard that, Prilicla? He is a person utterly lacking in consideration and sensitivity. I should have married someone like you."

"I am highly complimented, friend Murchison," the empath said. "But you have too few legs."

There was the sound of Fletcher clearing his throat disapprovingly at this sudden and unseemly levity, but the Captain did not speak. He could no doubt appreciate as well as any of them the need to relieve fear tensions.

"Very well," Conway said. "Pathologist Murchison will remain with her feet, and too few legs, on Trugdil. Doctor Prilicla, you will keep Charge Nurse Naydrad with you, since it will obviously be of greater assistance in preparing and presenting the casualties for examination and treatment than would the Engineer and Communications Officer. Haslam or Dodds can return with the litter and medical supplies which we will specify later. Questions?"

"No questions, friend Conway," Prilicla said. "The lander is docking now."

Murchison and Conway returned their full attention to the casualties. The Captain was examining the hull of the wreck. They could hear him tapping at the outer skin and making the metallic scraping noises characteristic of magnetic sound sensors being moved across the surfaces. The wind kept changing direction so that the casualties in the shadow of the outcropping were sheltered only from the sun and not the wind-driven sand.

From *Rhabwar* Haslam reported that the area was being affected by a small, local sandstorm which should clear before the lander returned in half an hour. He added reassuringly that nothing was moving in the area except themselves and several patches of ambulating thorn bushes, which would lose a race against a debilitated tortoise.

All but three of the casualties had been moved to the outcropping, and while Conway was bringing them in the pathologist was protecting the others from the wind and sand by loosely wrapping them in transparent plastic sheets after first attaching a small oxygen cylinder to each survivor. The tanks released a metered quantity of gas calculated to satisfy the metabolic requirements of the entity concerned. They had decided that encasing the casualties in makeshift oxygen tents could do no harm since the pure oxygen would assist the weak respiration and aid in the healing of the wounds, but with a completely new life-form one could never be sure of anything. Certainly the treatment showed no sign of returning any of the casualties to consciousness.

"The uniformly deep level of unconsciousness bothers me," Murchison said as Conway returned carrying, with difficulty, one of the large aliens they had classified as DCOJ. "The level does not bear any relation to the number or severity of the wounds. Could they be in a state of hibernation?"

"The onset was sudden," Conway said doubtfully. "They were in the process of fleeing their ship, according to the Captain. Hibernation usually occurs in a place of safety, not when the being concerned is in immediate physical danger."

"I was thinking of an involuntary form of hibernation," Murchison said, "perhaps induced by their injuries, which enables them to survive until help arrives—What was *that*?"

That was a loud, metallic screeching noise which came from the wreck. It lasted for a few seconds, then there was a moment's silence before it was repeated. They could hear heavy breathing in their suit phones so it had to be coming from Fletcher.

"Captain," Murchison said, "are you all right?"

"No trouble, ma'am," Fletcher replied at once. "I've found a hatch in what appears to be a cargo hold. It is, or was, a simple hermetically sealed door rather than an airlock. When the ship tipped over the door couldn't open fully because the outer edge dug into the sand, which I've now cleared away. The hatch opens freely now but the hinges were warped in the crash, as you probably heard. Two of the occupants were trying to escape, but couldn't squeeze through the narrow opening. They are one of the large- and one of the medium-sized types, both with amputation wounds, neither of them moving. Shall I bring them to you?"

"I'd better look at them first," Conway said. "Give me a few minutes to finish with this one."

As they were placing the last casualty inside its makeshift oxygen tent, Murchison said, "Have you found any trace of the criminal, Captain?"

"Other than the wounding on these two, no ma'am," Fletcher replied. "My sensors pick up no trace of bodily movement inside the ship, nothing but a few quiet, intermittent sounds suggesting settling debris. I'm pretty sure it is outside the ship somewhere."

"In that case," she said, looking at Conway, "I'll go with you."

The wind died and the sand settled as they neared the wreck so that they could see clearly the black rectangular opening in the hull just at ground level, and the arm of the Captain waving at them from inside it. There were so many other openings caused by sprung plating and access hatches that without Fletcher's signal they would not have known which gap was the right one. From outside it looked as if the ship was ready to fall apart, but when they crawled through the opening and stood up their helmet lights showed little evidence of internal damage.

"How did the others get out?" Conway asked. He knelt and began running his scanner over the larger of the two casualties.

There was evidence of a traumatic amputation of a major limb but the other injuries were superficial.

"There is a large personnel hatch on the upper surface of the hull forward," Fletcher replied. "At least it was on the upper side after the ship toppled. Presumably they had to slide down the curve of the hull and jump to the ground, or move along the ship to the prow, which isn't very far from the ground, and jump from there. These two were unlucky."

"One of them was very unlucky," Murchison said. "The DCOJ is dead. Its injuries were not as severe as the other cases I've seen, but there is evidence of lung damage by a corrosive gas of some kind, according to my analyzer. What about your DCMH?"

"This one is alive," Conway said. "Similar general condition, including the lung damage. Probably it is simply a much tougher life-form than the other two."

"I wonder about this DCOJ life-form," Murchison said thoughtfully. "Is it intelligent at all? The small DCLG and the DCMH almost certainly are: The limb extremities terminate in specialized manipulators, and the former seems to have developed six hands and no feet. But the big DCOJ has four feet and two clawed forward appendages, and is otherwise made up of teeth and a large system of stomachs."

"Which is empty," Conway said. After a moment he added, "All of the cases I've examined so far had empty stomachs."

"Mine as well," Murchison said. They stared at each other for a moment, then Conway said, "Captain."

Fletcher had been working on what seemed to be the inboard entrance to the hold, reaching high above his head because he was standing on a wall with the floor and ceiling on each side of him. There was a loud click and a door swung downward and hung open. The Captain made a self-satisfied sound and joined them.

"Yes, Doctor."

Conway cleared his throat and said, "Captain, we have a theory about your criminal. We think that the condition of distress which caused this ship to release its beacon was hunger. All of the casualties we've examined so far have had empty stomachs. It is possible, therefore, that your criminal is a crew member who turned cannibal."

Before Fletcher could reply, the voice of Prilicla sounded in their phones.

"Friend Conway," the empath said timidly. "I have not yet examined all of the casualties you sent up, but those I have examined display symptoms of dehydration and tissue wastage indicative of hunger and thirst. But the condition is not far enough advanced for death to be imminent. Your hypothetical criminal must have attacked the other crew members before lack of food became a serious problem. The being was hungry but not starving to death. Are you sure that the creature is intelligent?"

"No," Conway said. "But if Murchison and I have missed it while examining the first of the casualties, and at that time we were more concerned with charting the injuries than in the contents, if any, of their stomachs, the beastie could be on *Rhabwar* now. So if you find a well-fed casualty, get Haslam and Chen to restrain it, quickly. The Captain has a professional interest in it."

"That I have," Fletcher said grimly. He was about to go on when Haslam, who had relieved Dodds as lander pilot, interrupted to say that he would be touching down in six minutes and would need help loading the litter.

By packing the litter and strapping casualties, sometimes two to a couch in the crew's positions, Haslam was able to lift just over half of the remaining survivors. There was no change in the condition of the remaining casualties. The shadow of the outcropping had lengthened, though the air was still warm; the sky remained clear and there was no wind. Murchison said that she could usefully spend the time until the lander returned investigating, so far as she was able with her portable equipment, the large DCOJ cadaver they had left in the wreck. The medium-sized DCMH survivor had gone up with Haslam.

It was obvious from the start that Fletcher found the dissection distasteful, and when Murchison told him that there was enough light for the work from the helmet spots of Conway and herself, he left quickly and began climbing among the containers fastened to the now-vertical deck beside them. After about fifteen minutes he reported that his scanner showed the contents to be identical and, judging by the amount of packing used, were almost certainly cargo rather than ship's stores. He added that he intended moving into the corridor outside the hold to explore, look for other casualties, and gather evidence.

"Do you have to do it now, Captain?" Murchison said worriedly, looking up. Conway turned to regard Fletcher, too, but somehow his eyes did not rise above the level of the other's waist and the weapon attached to it.

"Do you know, Captain," he said quietly, "you have been wearing a sidearm ever since *Rhabwar*'s first mission, and I've barely noticed it? It was just a part of your uniform, like the cap and insignia. Now it looks even more conspicuous than your backpack."

Fletcher looked uncomfortable as he said, "We're taught that the psychological effect of displaying a weapon is negligible among the law-abiding, but increases in direct proportion to the guilt or harmful intentions of the criminal or potential lawbreaker. However, the effect of my weapon was purely psychological until Lieutenant Haslam brought down the charges for it a few minutes ago." Defensively he added, "There was no need to wear a loaded weapon on an ambulance ship, and I'd no reason to believe that this would be a police operation."

Murchison laughed softly and returned to her work, and Conway joined her. As the Captain turned to go, he said, "We can't spend much time here, but I must make as full a report as possible of the incident and all relevant circumstances. This is a new species to the Federation, a different technology, and the purpose of this ship might have a bearing on the case. Was our criminal a responsible being, perhaps a captive, or an unintelligent animal? If it was intelligent was it deranged, and if so why? And was the distressed condition of the ship and crew a contributory factor? I know that it is difficult to conceive of extenuating circumstances for grievous wounding and cannibalism, but until all the facts are known—"

He broke off and placed his sensor against the deck beside him. A few seconds later he went on, "There is nothing other than ourselves moving inside the wreck. I've left the outside hatch open only a few inches. If anything tried to get in you will have plenty of warning, either from the beastie itself forcing it open against the sand or from the sensors on *Rhabwar*. I can get back to you in plenty of time in any case, so you have nothing to worry about."

While they resumed the dissection they could follow every step of the Captain's progress sternward, because he insisted on verbally describing and amplifying the pictures he was sending up to Dodds. The corridor was low and not very roomy by Earth-human standards, he reported. He had to crawl on hands and knees and it would be difficult to turn around to come back other than at an intersection. Cable looms and air or hydraulic pipelines ran along the sidewalls of the corridor, and coarse-mesh netting was attached to the floor and ceiling indicating that the ship did not possess an artificial gravity system.

Aft of the compartment occupied by the medics there was another cargo deck, and beyond that the unmistakable shapes of the hyperdrive generators. Further aft the reactor and thrusters were sealed from him and heavily shielded, but the sensor indications were that there had been a complete power shutdown—probably an automatic safety measure built into the design—when the ship had toppled. But he could detect a residue of power in some of the corridor lines which he thought might be associated with an emergency lighting circuit, and he thought he had identified a light switch.

It was a light switch, he confirmed a few seconds later. A large stretch of the corridor was illuminated. The lighting was uncomfortably bright but his eyes were adjusting to it. He was moving amidships.

They heard him pause outside their cargo hold, and suddenly the lights came on all over the ceiling beside them. Conway switched off his now-unnecessary helmet light.

"Thank you, Captain," he said, then continuing the discussion he had been having with Murchison, went on, "There is capacity for a large brain in the cranium, but we cannot assume that all of the available volume is used for cerebration. I don't see how a beastie with four feet and two manipulators which are little more than claws could be a tool user, much less a crew member of a starship. And those teeth bother me. They are certainly not those of a predator. In the distant past they might have been fearsome natural weapons, but now their condition shows that they have not much to do."

Murchison nodded. "The stomach system is overlarge in relation to the mass of the being," she said, "yet there is no evidence of adipose or excess edible tissue which would be present if it was an animal bred for food. And the stomach resembles that of an Earth-type ruminant. The digestive system is odd, too, but I'd have to work out the whole intake to elimination cycle to make any sense out of it, and I can't do that down here. I'd love to know what these things ate before their food ran out."

"I'm passing a storage deck of some kind," Fletcher said at that point. "It is divided into large racks with passages between them. The racks are filled with containers of different colors and sizes with funnellike dispensers at one end. There are wastebins holding empties, and some of the full and empty containers have spilled out into the corridor."

"May I have samples, please," Murchison said quickly, "of both."

"Yes, ma'am," the Captain replied. "Considering the starved condition of the survivors they are more likely to contain paint or lubricant than food. But I expect you have to eliminate all possibilities, like me. I am moving toward the next—Oh!"

Conway opened his mouth to ask what was happening but the Captain forestalled him.

"I switched on the lighting for this section and found two more casualties," he reported. "One is a DCMH, one of the medium-sized ones, which was crushed by a buckled structural member and certainly dead. The other is the small, DCLG life-form, with one amputation wound, not moving. I'm fairly sure that it's dead, too. This is the section of the ship which fell across the outcropping when she tipped over.

"The internal structure is badly deformed," he went on, "with sprung deck and wall plating all over the place. There are also two large, wall-mounted cylinders which seem to have been the reservoir for a hydraulic actuator system. Both have been ruptured and their connecting lines fractured, and there is a faint fog surrounding them as if some of the content remains and is evaporating.

"Ahead the corridor is partly blocked by wreckage," he continued. "I can move it but there will be a lot of noise, so don't—"

"Captain," Conway broke in. "Can you please bring us the DCLG and a sample of the hydraulic fluid with the other samples as soon as you can." To Murchison he added, "I'd like to know if the lung damage is associated with that leakage. It would eliminate another possibility."

Fletcher sounded irritated at having to break off his investigation of the ship. He said shortly, "They'll be outside your hold entrance in ten minutes, Doctor."

By the time Conway had retrieved the samples the Captain had already returned to the midships section, but once again his investigation was interrupted, this time by Lieutenant Dodds.

"The lander is ready to leave, sir," the Astrogator said. There was a certain hesitancy in his voice as he went on, "I'm afraid there will be time for only one round trip before sunset, so would the Doctor and you decide which casualties should be lifted and which left there for retrieval tomorrow? With you three and Haslam on board just over half of the remaining casualties can be lifted, less if you bring up all portable equipment."

"I'm not leaving unattended casualties down here," Conway said firmly. "The drop in temperature and the sandstorms would probably finish them!"

"Maybe not," Murchison said thoughtfully. "If we have to leave some of them, and it seems we've no choice, we could cover them with sand. They have a high body temperature, the sand is a good insulator, and they are already sealed up with a self-contained oxygen supply."

"I've heard of doctors burying their mistakes," Conway began dryly, but Dodds broke in again.

"Sorry, there is a problem there, ma'am," he said. "There are four large thorn patches moving toward the wreck. Slowly, of course, but we estimate their arrival just before midnight. According to my information the thorns are omnivorous and trap mobile prey by slowly encircling it, often at a distance, and allowing the animal to scratch itself on the thorns. These secrete a poison which is paralyzing or lethal, depending on the size of the prey and number of scratches. When the prey is immobilized the thorn clump inserts its roots and removes whatever nutrient material there is available.

"I don't think your buried casualties," he added grimly, "would survive till morning."

Murchison swore in very unladylike fashion, and Conway said,

"We could move them into the hold here and seal the hatch. We would need heaters and a medical monitor and—I'm still not happy about leaving them unattended."

"Obviously this is something which will have to be carefully considered, Doctor," the Captain said. "Your casualties will not only have to be attended, they may have to be defended as well. Dodds, how long can you delay the launch?"

"Half an hour, sir," the Astrogator said. "Then allowing another half hour for the trip and at least an hour on the surface to load up and make provision for the other casualties. If the lander does not leave in two and a half hours there will be serious problems with the wind and sand during take-off."

"Very well," Fletcher said. "We should reach a decision in half an hour. Hold the lander until then."

But there was very little discussion and the decision was made, in spite of anything Murchison and Conway could say to the contrary, by the Captain. Fletcher stated that the two medics on Trugdil had done everything possible for the casualties and could do nothing further without the facilities of *Rhabwar*, except keep them under observation. The Captain insisted that he was capable of doing that, and of defending them in case they were attacked again.

He was sure that the criminal responsible for their injuries was not currently on the ship, but it might return to the shelter of the wreck when the cold and the sandstorms returned, or even to escape the advancing thorn clumps. He added that the proper place for all of the medical team was on *Rhabwar* where the casualties there could be given proper attention.

"Captain," Conway said angrily, unable to refute his arguments, "in the medical area I have complete authority."

"Then why don't you exercise it responsibly, Doctor?" Fletcher replied.

"Captain," Murchison broke in quickly, trying to head off an argument which could sour relations on the ambulance ship for weeks to come. "The DCLG specimen you found was not badly injured, compared with some of the others, but it was defunct, I'm afraid. Severe inflammation of the breathing passages and massive lung damage similar to the one you found in the hold. Both sets of lungs contained traces of the sample you took from the hydraulic reservoir. That is lethal stuff, Captain, so don't open your visor anywhere near a leak."

"Thank you, ma'am, I won't," Fletcher said calmly, and went on, "Dodds, you can see that the stretch of corridor ahead has been crushed almost flat. There is enough space for crew members to squeeze through, but I will have to cut away a lot of this jagged metal—"

Conway switched off his radio and touched his helmet against Murchison's so that they could speak privately. He said furiously, "Whose side are you on?"

She grinned at him through her visor, but before she could reply Prilicla's voice rustled timidly from the phones. The empath, too, was trying to calm a potentially unpleasant source of emotional radiation.

"Friend Conway," it said, "while friend Fletcher's arguments are valid, and I would personally welcome the presence of friend Murchison and yourself back on board, friend Naydrad and myself are coping adequately with the patients, all of whom are in a stable condition with the exception of three of the small DCLGs who are showing a slight reduction in body temperature."

"Deepening shock, do you think?" Conway asked.

"No, friend Conway," Prilicla replied. "There seems to be a slight improvement in their general condition."

"Emotional radiation?"

"Nothing on the conscious level, friend Conway," the empath replied, "but there are unconscious feelings of deprivation, and need."

"They are all hungry," Conway said dryly, "except one."

"The thought of that one is abhorrent to me, too," Prilicla said. "But to return to the condition of the patients: The lung damage and inflammation of the breathing passages noted by friend Murchison is repeated, to a much lesser degree of severity, in the other survivors, and the cause is correctly attributed to the damaged reservoir. But it is possible that operating in Trugdil conditions with the less sensitive portable equipment—"

"Prilicla," Conway said impatiently, "what you mean is that we were too blind or stupid to spot an important medical datum, but you are too nice a person to hurt our feelings. But intense impatience and curiosity can be unpleasant emotions, too, so just tell us what you discovered, Doctor."

"I am sorry, friend Conway," said the empath. "It is that the food passage as well as the breathing passage is similarly inflamed. The condition is relatively mild, not obvious as are the other areas of inflammation, but is present in uniform intensity in all of the survivors regardless of physiological classification. I wondered if there was anything on their ship which would explain this.

"I am also puzzled by the amputation wounds," Prilicla went on. "I have been suturing incised wounds, none of which have penetrated to vital organs, and generally tidying up. But the stumps I have covered with sterile dressings only until the possibility of replacing the original limbs has been eliminated. Have you found anything down there which might be a missing limb or organ? Or have you given thought to the shape, size, and purpose of these missing parts?"

From amidships there were sounds of metal scraping against metal and of erratic, heavy breathing in their phones as the Captain cleared an obstruction. When it was quiet again, Murchison said, "Yes, Doctor, but I've formed no firm conclusions. There is a fairly complex nerve linkage to the stump in all three types and, in the case of the big DCOJ, a collapsed, tubular connection whose origin I have been unable to trace because of its close association with the very complex upper intestinal tract. But taking into account the positioning of these limbs or organs, which are at the base of the spine in the two smaller life-forms and on the medial underside of the large one, all I can say is that the missing parts must have been considered particularly edible by the attacker since it did not remove anything else. I have no clear idea of the size or shape of the missing parts, but my guess would be that they are probably tails, genitalia, or mammaries—"

"I'm sorry to interrupt a medical conference, ma'am," Fletcher broke in, in a tone which suggested that he was very glad to interrupt before it could go any farther. He went on quickly, "Doctor Conway, I've found another DCMH. It is tangled up in bedding, not moving, and seems to be uninjured. I thought you might like to examine it here rather than have it pulled through the wreckage in the corridor."

"I'm on my way," Conway said.

He climbed out of the hold and crawled along the corridor in the Captain's wake, listening as Fletcher resumed his commentary. Immediately forward of the cleared section of corridor the Captain had found the Dormitory Deck. It was characteristic of the early type of hyperships which did not have artificial gravity, and was filled with rows of sandwich-style double hammocks which retained the sleeper in weightless conditions. The hammocks were suspended on shock absorbers so as to double as acceleration couches for off-duty crew members.

There were three distinct sizes of hammock, so the ship had the DCLG, DCMH, and DCOJ life-forms in the crew—which proved that even the large and apparently unintelligent DCOJs were ship's personnel and not lab animals. Judging by the number and size of the hammocks, the two smaller life-forms outnumbered the large one by three to one.

He had made a quick count of the hammocks, the Captain said as Conway was passing the damaged hydraulic system reservoir, and the total number, thirty, agreed with the number of casualties found outside and inside the ship, which meant that the missing criminal was almost certainly not of any of the three species who served as the crew.

It was difficult to be precise regarding occurrences on the Dormitory Deck, Fletcher explained, because loose objects, ornaments, and personal effects had collected on the wall when the ship had fallen on its side. But one third of the hammocks were neatly stowed while the remaining two thirds looked as though they had been hastily vacated. No doubt the neat hammocks belonged to the crew members on duty, but the Captain thought it strange that if the ship operated a one-watch-on, two-off duty roster the rest of the crew were in their bunks instead of half of them being outside the dormitory on a recreation deck. But then he was forgetting the fact that the safest place during the landing maneuver would be inside the acceleration hammocks.

The Captain was backing out of the dormitory as Conway

reached it. Fletcher pointed and said, "It is close to the inner hull among the DCMH hammocks. Call me if you need help, Doctor."

He turned and began crawling toward the bows again. But he did not get very far because by the time Conway reached the casualty he could hear the hiss of the cutting torch and the Captain's heavy breathing.

It took only a few minutes to piece together what had happened. Two of the hammock's supports had broken due to the lateral shock when the ship had fallen—they had been designed to withstand vertical G forces, not horizontal ones—and the hammock had swung downward throwing its occupant against the suddenly horizontal wall. There was an area of subcutaneous bleeding where the DCMH's head had struck, but no sign of a fracture. The blow had not been fatal, but it had been enough to render the being unconscious or dazed until the highly lethal vapor from the damaged reservoir had invaded its lungs.

This one had been doubly unlucky, Conway thought as he carefully drew it the rest of the way from its hammock and extended his examination. There was one wound, the usual one, at the base of its spine. Conway's scalp prickled at the thought that the attacker had been inside the dormitory and had struck even at a victim in its hammock. What sort of creature was it? Small rather than large, he thought. Vicious. And fast. He looked quickly around the dormitory, then returned his attention to the cadaver.

"That's unusual," he said aloud. "This one has what seems to be a small quantity of partially digested food in its stomach."

"You think that's unusual," Murchison said in a baffled tone. "The sample containers from the storage deck contain food. Liquid, a powdery solid, and some fibrous material, but all high-grade nutrient suited to the metabolisms of all three life-forms. What was the excuse for cannibalism? And why the blazes was everybody starving? The whole deck is packed with food!"

"Are you sure—?" began Conway, when he was cut off by a voice in his phones which was so distorted that he could not tell who was speaking.

"What *is* that thing?"

"Captain?" he said doubtfully.

"Yes, Doctor." The voice was still distorted, but recognizable.

"You—you've found the criminal?"

"No, Doctor," Fletcher replied harshly. "Another victim. Definitely another victim—"

"It's moving, sir!" Dodds voice broke in.

"Doctor," the Captain went on, "can you come at once. You too, ma'am."

Fletcher was crouched inside the entrance of what had to be the ship's Control Deck, using the cutting torch on the tangle of wreckage which almost filled the space between the ceiling and floor. The place was a shambles, Conway saw by the light coming through the open hatch above them and the few strips of emergency lighting which were still operating. Practically all of the ceiling-mounted equipment had torn free in the fall; ruptured piping and twisted, jagged-edged supporting brackets projected into the space above the control couches on the deck opposite.

The control couches had been solidly mounted and had remained in position, but they were empty, their restraining webbing hanging loose—except for one. This was a very large, deep cupola around which the other couches were closely grouped, and it was occupied.

Conway began to climb toward it, but the foothold he had been using gave way suddenly and a stub of broken-off piping dug him painfully in the side without, fortunately, rupturing his suit.

"Careful, damn it!" Fletcher snapped. "We don't need another casualty."

"Don't bite my head off, Captain," Conway said, then laughed nervously at his unfortunate choice of words.

He cringed inwardly as he climbed toward the central cupola in the wake of the Captain, thinking that the crew on duty and those in the Dormitory Deck had had to find a way through this mess, and in great haste because of the toxic vapor flooding through the ship. They were much smaller than Earth-humans, of course, but even so they must have been badly cut by that tangle of metal. In fact, they *had* been badly cut, with the exceptions of the DCMH in the dormitory and the new life-form above them, neither of whom had attempted to escape.

"Careful, Doctor," the Captain said.

An idea which had been taking shape at the back of his mind dissolved. Irritably, Conway said, "What can it do except look at me and twitch its stumps?"

The casualty hung sideways in its webbing against the lower lip of the cupola, a great fleshy, elongated pear shape perhaps four times the mass of an adult human. The narrow end terminated in a large, bulbous head mounted on a walrus neck which was arched downward so that the two big, widely spaced eyes could regard the rescuers. Conway could count seven of the feebly twitching stumps projecting through gaps in the webbing, and there were probably others he could not see.

He braced himself against a control console which had remained in place and took out his scanner, but delayed beginning the examination until Murchison, who had just arrived, could climb up beside him. Then he said firmly, "We will have to remain with this casualty overnight, Captain. Please instruct Lieutenant Haslam to evacuate all the other casualties on the next trip, and to bring down the litter stripped of nonessential life-support equipment so that it will accommodate this new casualty. We also need extra air tanks for ourselves and oxygen for the casualty, heaters, lifting gear, and webbing, and anything else you think we need."

For a long moment the Captain was silent, then he said, "You heard the Doctor, Haslam."

Fletcher did not speak to them while they were examining the new casualty other than to warn them when a piece of loose wreckage was about to fall. The Captain did not have to be told that a wide path would have to be cleared between the big control cupola and the open hatch if the litter was to be guided in and out again carrying the large alien. It was likely to be a long, difficult job lasting most of the coming night, made more difficult by ensuring that none of the debris struck Murchison, Conway, or their patient. But the two medics were much too engrossed in their examination to worry about the falling debris.

"I won't attempt to classify this life-form," Conway said nearly an hour later when he was summing up their findings for Doctor Prilicla. "There are, or were, ten limbs distributed laterally, of varying thicknesses judging by the stumps. The sole exception is the one on the underside which is thicker than any of the others. The purpose of these missing limbs, the number and type of manipulatory and ambulatory appendages, is unknown.

"The brain is large and well developed," he want on, looking aside at Murchison for corroboration, "with a small, separate lobe with a high mineral content in the cell structure suggesting one of the V classifications—"

"A wide-range telepath?" Prilicla broke in excitedly.

"I'd say not," Conway replied. "Telepathy limited to its own species, perhaps, or possibly simple empathy. This is borne out by the fact that its ears are well developed and the mouth, although very small and toothless, has shown itself capable of modulating sounds. A being who talks and listens cannot be a wide-range telepath, since the telepathic faculty is supplemented by a spoken language. But the being did not display agitation on seeing us, which could mean that it is aware our intentions toward it are good.

"Regarding the airway and lungs," Conway continued, "you can see that there is the usual inflammation present but that the lung damage is minor. We are assuming that since the being was unable to move when the gas permeated the ship, it was able, with its large lung capacity, to hold its breath until most of the toxic vapor had dissipated. But the digestive system is baffling us. The food passage is extremely narrow and seems to have collapsed in several places, and with few teeth for chewing food it is difficult . . . to see how—"

Conway's voice slowed to a stop while his mind raced on. Beside him Murchison was making self-derogatory remarks because she, too, had not spotted it sooner, and Prilicla said, "Are you thinking what I am thinking, friends?"

There was no need to reply. Conway said, "Captain, where are you?"

Fletcher had cleared a narrow path for himself to the open hatch. While they had been talking they had heard his boots moving back and forth along the outer hull, but for the past few minutes there had been silence.

"On the ground outside, Doctor," Fletcher replied. "I've been trying to find the best way of moving out the big one. In my opinion we can't swing it down the sides of the wreck, too much sprung plating and debris, and the stern isn't much better. We'll have to lower it from the prow. But carefully. I jarred my ankles badly when I jumped from it to the sand, which is only about an inch deep over a gently sloping shelf of rock in that area. Obviously the big life-form needed a special elevator to board and debark, because the extending ladder arrangement below the hatch is usable only by the three smaller life-forms.

"I'm about to reenter the ship through the cargo hold hatch," he ended. "Is there a problem?"

"No, Captain," Conway said. "But on your way here would you bring the cadaver from the Dormitory Deck?"

Fletcher grunted assent and Murchison and Conway resumed their discussion with Prilicla, stopping frequently to verify with their scanners the various points raised. When the Captain arrived pushing the dead DCMH ahead of him, Conway had just finished attaching an oxygen tank and breathing tube to the patient and covering its head in a plastic envelope against the time when, during the night, the entry hatch would be closed and the fumes produced by the cutting torch against the metal and plastic debris might turn out to be even more toxic than those from the hydraulic reservoir.

They took the cadaver from Fletcher and, holding it above their heads, fitted it into one of the control couches designed for it. The big alien did not react and they tried it in a second, then a third couch. This time the patient's stub tentacles began to twitch and one of them made contact with the DCMH. It maintained the contact for several seconds then slowly withdrew and the big entity became still again.

Conway gave a long sigh, then said, "It fits, it all fits. Prilicla, keep your patients on oxygen and IV fluids. I don't think they will return to full consciousness until they have food as well, but the hospital can synthesize that when we get back." To Murchison he said, "All we need now is an analysis of the stomach contents of that cadaver. But don't do the dissection here, do it in the corridor. It would probably, well, upset the Captain."

"Not me," Fletcher said, who was already at work with his cutting torch. "I won't even look."

Murchison laughed and pointed to the patient hanging above

them. She said, "He was talking about the other Captain, Captain."

Before Fletcher could reply, Haslam announced that he would be landing in fifteen minutes.

"Better stay with the patient while I help the Captain load the lander," Conway told Murchison. "Radiate feelings of reassurance at it; that's all we can do right now. If we all left it might think it was being abandoned."

"You intend leaving her here alone?" Fletcher said harshly.

"Yes, but there is no danger—" Conway began, when the voice of Dodds interrupted him.

"There is nothing moving within a twenty-mile radius of the wreck, sir," he said reassuringly, "except thorn patches."

Fletcher said very little while they were helping Haslam move the casualties from the outcropping into the lander and while they were pushing the litter with its load of spare equipment to the wreck. It was unlike the Captain, who usually spoke his mind no matter who or what was bothering him, to behave this way. But Conway's mind was too busy with other things to have time to probe.

"I was thinking," Conway said when they reached the open cargo hatch, "that according to Dodds the thorn patches are attracted to food and warmth. We are going to create a lot of warmth inside the wreck, and there is a storage deck filled with food containers as well. Suppose we move as much food as we can from the wreck and scatter it in front of the thorn clumps—that might make them lose interest in the wreck for a while."

"I hope so," Fletcher said.

The lander took off in a small, self-created sandstorm as Conway was dragging the first containers of food toward the edge of the nearest thorn patch, which was about four hundred meters astern of the wreck. They had agreed that Fletcher would move the containers from the storage deck to the ground outside the hatch, and Conway would scatter them along the front of the advancing thorns. He had wanted to use the litter with its greater capacity and gravity neutralizers, but Naydrad had stated in its forthright fashion that the Doctor was unused to controlling the vehicle and if the gravity settings were wrong or a part of the load fell off, the litter would disappear skyward or blow weightlessly away.

Conway was forced to do it the hard way.

"Make this the last one, Doctor," the Captain said as he was coming in from his eighth round trip. "The wind is rising."

The shadow of the wreck had lengthened steadily as he worked and the sky had deepened in color. The suit's sensors showed a marked drop in the outside temperature, but Conway had been generating so much body heat himself that he had not noticed it. He threw the containers as far in front and to each side of him as he could, opening some of them to make sure that the thorns would know that the unopened containers also held food, although they could probably sense that for themselves. The thorn clumps covered the sand across a wide front like black, irregular crosshatching, seemingly motionless. But every time he looked away for a few minutes then back again, they were closer.

Suddenly the thorn patches and everything else disappeared behind a dark-brown curtain of sand and a gust of wind punched him in the back, knocking him to his knees. He tried to get to his feet but an eddy blew him onto his side. Half crawling and half running, he headed back toward the wreck, although by then he had no clear idea where it was. The storm-driven sand was hissing so loudly against his helmet that he could barely hear Dodds' voice.

"My sensors show you heading toward the thorns, Doctor," the Astrogator said urgently. "Turn right about one hundred ten degrees and the wreck is about three hundred meters distant."

Fletcher was outside the cargo hatch with his suit spotlight turned to maximum power to guide him in. The Captain pushed him through the hatch and closed it behind him. The crash had warped the hatch so that sand continued to blow in around the edges, except near the bottom where it came through in a steady trickle.

"Within a few minutes the outside of the hatch will be sealed by a sand drift," Fletcher said without looking at Conway. "It will be difficult for our cannibal to get in. Dodds will spot it on the sensors anyway and I'll have time to take the necessary steps."

Conway shook his head and said, "We've nothing to worry about except the wind, sand, and thorn patches." Silently he added, *If that wasn't enough.*

The Captain grunted and began climbing through the hatch

leading to the corridor, and Conway crawled after him. But it was not until Fletcher slowed to pass the leaking hydraulic reservoir, which was steaming very faintly now, that Conway spoke.

"Is there anything else bothering you, Captain?"

Fletcher stopped and for the first time in over an hour looked directly at the Doctor. He said, "Yes, there is. That creature in the Control Deck bothers me. Even in the hospital, what can you do for it, a multiple amputee? It will be completely helpless, little more than a live specimen for study. I'm wondering if it would not be better just to let the cold take it and—"

"We can do a great deal for it, Captain," Conway broke in, "if we can get it safely through the night. Weren't you listening to Murchison, Prilicla, and me discussing the case?"

"Yes and no, Doctor," Fletcher said, moving forward again. "Some of it was quite technical, and you might as well have been talking untranslated Kelgian so far as I was concerned."

Conway laughed quietly and said, "Then I had better translate."

The alien vessel had released its distress beacon, he explained, not because of a technical malfunction but because of serious illness on board which had affected the entire crew. Presumably the least affected crew members were on duty on the Control Deck while the rest were confined to their hammocks. It was still not clear why the ship had to put down on a planet. Possibly there were physiological reasons why a planetary gravity or atmosphere was needed, or maybe the weightless conditions on board aggravated the condition and they could not provide artificial gravity by using their thrusters because the crew were fast losing consciousness. Whatever the reason they had made an emergency landing on Trugdil. There were much better landing sites on the planet, but their degree of urgency must have been extreme and they had landed here.

Conway broke off as they entered the Control Deck because Murchison was high above them closing the personnel hatch. She said, "Don't let me interrupt you, but now that we will be using the cutting torches in a confined space, I'm going to take the patient off pure oxygen. It seems to be breathing easily now. Would one part oxygen to four inert be suitable, Doctor?"

"Fine," Conway said. "I'll help you."

The hissing of sand against the outer hull rose suddenly and the whole ship seemed to lurch sideways. There was a screeching and banging sound from amidships, which halted suddenly as a section of hull plating tore free and blew away.

"A piece of the wreck has blown away," Dodds reported unnecessarily, then went on, "The thorn patches have halted over the food containers, and those nearby are converging on the area. But there are other large clumps off to the side which are still heading directly for the wreck. They are moving quite fast. The wind is behind them and they are letting it carry them forward using only enough of their root system to maintain a loose hold on the ground. At this rate they could be at the ship in half an hour."

It was as if an enormous, soft pillow struck the side of the ship. The deck tilted under their feet, then righted itself. This time it sounded as if maniacs with sledgehammers were attacking three different sections of the hull until, a few seconds later, the banging ceased. But to the sound of the sand beating against the hull plating was added the discordant moaning and whistling of the wind as it forced its way into the wreck.

"Our defenses," the Captain said worriedly, "have become decidedly porous. But go on, Doctor."

"The ship made an emergency landing here," Conway resumed, "because they had no time to look for a better spot. It was a good landing, all things considered, and it was sheer bad luck that they toppled and as a result ruptured that hydraulic reservoir. If they hadn't done so it is possible that their illness, whatever the cause, would have run its course and in time they would have taken off again. Or maybe the first sandstorm would have knocked them over anyway. But instead they crash-landed and found themselves suddenly in a wreck which was rapidly filling with toxic fumes. Weakened by their condition as they were, they had to get out fast and, because the escape routes aft led past the source of the contaminant and were partly blocked by wreckage from the fall, they had to evacuate through the Control Deck here and along the upper surface of the hull, then slide to the ground.

"They injured themselves very seriously in doing so," Conway added.

He paused for a moment to help Murchison change over the patient's air supply. From the stern there was a clanking sound which reverberated steadily and monotonously throughout the ship. One of the pieces of wreckage was refusing to become detached. Conway raised his voice.

"The reason they did not move far from their ship was probably two-fold," he continued. "As a result of the debilitating effects of their illness, they did not have the strength to move farther, and I suspect there were strong psychological reasons for remaining close to their ship. Their physical condition, the high temperatures, and the indications of malnutrition observed, which we mistakenly assumed to be due to enforced starvation, were symptoms of the disease. The state of deep unconsciousness may also have been a symptom, or possibly some kind of hibernation mode which they adopt when injured or otherwise distressed and assistance is likely to be delayed, and which slows the metabolic rate and reduces bleeding."

Fletcher was readying his cutting torch and looking baffled. He said, "Disease and injuries caused by escaping from the wreck I can believe. But what about the missing limbs and—"

"Dodds, sir," *Rhabwar*'s Astrogator broke in. "I'm afraid the midnight drop in wind strength will not affect your area. There are local weather disturbances. Three large thorn patches have reached the stern and sections of the peripheral growth are entering the food storage deck. A lot of hull plating is missing there. Once they open that concentrated store of food they'll probably lose interest in anything else." His optimism sounded forced.

Murchison said, "We're not completely sure that it was a disease that caused the trouble, Captain. From the analysis of the stomach contents of the cadaver from the dormitory deck, the indications are that it was a severe gastrointestinal infection caused by a bug native to their home planet, and the symptom which led us to suspect malnutrition was total regurgitation of stomach contents in all of the other cases. The casualty from the dormitory had been knocked unconscious before the process was complete and was asphyxiated shortly afterward so that involuntary regurgitation did not take place. But it is also possible that the ship's own food supply was contaminated and that caused the trouble."

Conway wondered if it was possible for a mobile omnivorous vegetable to get food poisoning, and if it would take effect in time to save them from the thorns. He rather doubted it.

"Thank you, ma'am," Fletcher said, and went on, "About the missing limbs?"

"There are no missing limbs, Captain," she replied. "Or perhaps the crew are all missing the same organ, their head. The large number of the other injuries concealed the truth at first, but there are no missing limbs, and there is no criminal."

Fletcher looked at Conway, too polite to express his disbelief to the pathologist in words, and the Doctor took over the explanation. But he had to work as he talked because he and Murchison were faced with the long, difficult job of transferring the big alien from its cupola to the litter.

It was hard to imagine the set of environmental circumstances which had caused such an essentially helpless life-form to evolve, become dominant, and in time achieve a culture capable of star travel, Conway said, but these gross, limbless, and all too obviously immobile creatures had done just that. It was a host-symbiote, they now knew, who had developed multiple symbiotes specialized so as to act as short- and long-range manipulators and sensors. Its stumps and the areas which on the casualties had been mistaken for amputation sites were the interfaces which joined the host creature to its symbiotes when physical activity became necessary or the host required sustenance.

It was likely that a strong mental as well as physical bond existed between the host Captain and its crew, but continuous contact was not needed because in and around the wreck there had been three times the number of crew members as there were organic connectors on the host. It was also probable that the host entity did not sleep and provided continual, nonphysical support to its symbiotes. This was borne out by the type of emotional radiation being picked up on *Rhabwar* by Prilicla—confusion and feelings of loss. The host Captain's telepathic or empathic faculty did not reach as far as the ambulance ship's orbit.

"The smallest, DCLG life-form is independently intelligent and performs the finer, more intricate manipulative operations," Murchison joined in, clarifying the situation in her own mind as well as for the Captain, who had disappeared briefly into the corridor to check on the position of the thorns. "As is the slightly larger DCMH.

But the function of the big DCOJ is purely that of eating and supplying predigested food to the host. There is evidence, however, that all three of these life-forms have their own ingestion, digestion, and reproductive systems, but one of them must figure in the transfer of sperm or ova between immobile host creatures—"

She broke off as the Captain returned, his cutter in one hand and what looked like a short, tangled piece of barbed wire in the other. He said, "The thorns have grown out of the food storage deck and are halfway along the corridor. I brought you a sample, ma'am."

She took it from him carefully and Conway joined her for a closer look. It was like a dark-brown, three-dimensional zigzag with fine green thorns growing out of every angle, except one which sprouted a long, tapering hollow tube like the vegetable equivalent of a hypodermic needle, and which was probably a root. She snipped off the thorns with surgical scissors and let them drop into her analyzer.

"Why did we have to wear lightweight suits?" she said a few minutes later. "A scratch from a thorn won't kill you, but three or four would. What are you doing, Captain?"

Fletcher was unclipping the signal flare from his backpack. He said, "You can see from the charring on the stem that they burn. I removed that sample with the cutting torch. But the flame isn't self-sustaining. Maybe this will stunt its growth for a while. Stay clear of the corridor entrance, both of you. These things were not meant to be used in a confined space."

He set the timer on the flare and threw it as hard as he could into the corridor. The beam of light which poured out of the entrance was so intense that it looked almost solid, and the hissing of the flare was louder even than the sand lashing against the outer hull. The beam maintained its intensity but began to flicker as smoke poured from the entrance. *The thorns were burning*, Conway thought excitedly, and hoped that the pyrotechnics were not worrying their patient too much. It seemed to be unusually agitated—

There was a sudden, crashing detonation. Pieces of the flare, burning thorn branches, and parts of the dissected DCMH erupted from the corridor entrance, and the cupola edge Conway was gripping seemed to jerk in his hands. He hung on desperately as the vertical deck swung toward him, accompanied by the screech of tearing metal. There was a softer shock and the metallic noises ceased. The emergency lighting had died but there was enough illumination from the sputtering pieces of flare and their helmet lights to show that the patient had fallen out of its cupola and was hanging directly above him, suspended only by its webbing, sections of which were beginning to tear.

"The litter!" Conway shouted. "Help me!"

There was so much smoke from the flare that all he could see clearly were Murchison's and the Captain's helmet lights. He let go his hold with one hand and felt around for the litter, which had been left drifting weightlessly with repulsors set to one negative G so as to make the vehicle easier to maneuver in the confined space. He found it and a few seconds later felt other hands steadying it. Above him the alien hung like a great organic tree trunk with its stumps projecting between the webbing, ready to fall and crush him and probably kill itself on the charred but still poisonous thorns below them.

Suddenly it sagged closer. Conway flinched, but the rest of the webbing was holding it. He felt for the control panel of the litter. · "Get it under the things!" he shouted. "Right under its center of gravity, that's it."

Gradually he increased the repulsion until the litter was pressing firmly against the underside of the patient, and again until the being's entire weight was being supported and the webbing was simply holding it against any lateral movement. He became aware of the voice of Dodds in his phones, asking over and over again what had happened and were they all right.

"We're all right," Fletcher said angrily. "And you tell us what happened, Lieutenant. What are your sensors for?"

"An explosion at the site of the damaged hydraulic reservoir, sir," Dodds said, sounding relieved. "The stuff is highly inflammable as well as toxic, it seems, and the flare set it off. The explosion broke the back of the ship where it lies across that rock outcropping, and now the prow is lying on the sand, too. Amidships and stern sections have been stripped of plating by the explosion and the wind. The ship looks very open, sir."

The smoke had cleared but fine clouds of sand were blowing through the Control Deck from somewhere. Fletcher said dryly, "I believe you, Dodds. It is also very cold. How long until pickup?"

"Just under three hours, sir," Dodds replied. "Sunrise is in two hours and the wind should have abated an hour later."

The two portable heaters and spare cutting torch had been shaken loose by the explosion and had fallen into the thorns. One of the heaters was still functioning but its effect was severely reduced by the icy, sand-laden wind sweeping out of the corridor. Conway shivered and clenched his teeth, both to stop them chattering and in reaction to the indescribable noise of the wind screaming through the bare bones of the stern section and the irregular, thunderous din of the remaining plating shaking itself loose. He resited the portable lights, which had survived the explosion, so that they were within a few feet of the litter. They gave a little warmth.

More than an hour was spent completing the transfer of the alien from its cupola to the litter and securing it in the vehicle. The being, too, was suffering from the cold—its organic connectors twitched continuously and patterns of wrinkles marched across its smooth, featureless body. Conway tried to find something to wrap around it, but all that was available was the control cupola webbing from its own and the crew's positions. By the time he had finished, the being was virtually cocooned in the stuff and the few areas of skin visible were still twitching and wrinkling.

They moved it up to the sealed personnel hatch, hoping that the available heat would rise and it would be fractionally warmer up there. The difference, to Conway, was indetectable. He wondered if it would be possible to rescue the other heater, but when he looked down he saw that a fresh, uncharred tangle of thorns had grown in from the corridor and was climbing toward them.

"Doctor," said Fletcher quickly, indicating a large ceiling panel which was held in position by a single remaining support strut. "Hold onto that while I cut it free."

They dropped the panel onto the thorns and knotted loose pieces of webbing together into a rope so that the Captain could lower himself onto its center. The panel buckled slightly under his weight but the thorns beneath the plate were forced down by two meters or more. Fletcher kneeled carefully on his makeshift raft and unlimbered his cutting torch. With the flame focused down to a long, thin needle he attacked the thorns all around him.

After nearly six hours of constant use the power pack was exhausted. When the flame dimmed and died, Fletcher got carefully to his feet and began flexing and straightening his legs, bouncing the section of plating up and down. The thorns were forced lower. He paused for a rest and still the plate continued to sink. But now the needle-sharp thorns were growing in from the edges of the raft, slowly submerging it.

The rope of webbing was barely within reach. Fletcher steadied himself, jumped, and caught the end in a double grip as the plate teetered and disappeared sideways under the thorns. Conway climbed down as far as he could and pulled the rope close so that Fletcher could get his feet onto the edge of a projecting cabinet.

"Did you see the way that thing moved itself from under the plate and surrounded you, Captain?" Murchison said when they rejoined her. "It's very slow, but do you think we are hurting a potentially intelligent vegetable life-form?"

"Yes, ma'am," the Captain said with feeling, "but not nearly enough."

"Eighty minutes to go, sir," Dodds said.

They detached the few pieces of wreckage and equipment that could be dislodged by hand and dropped them onto the thorns, but with little effect. Fletcher and Conway took turns hacking at the growth with a metal support strut, but still it grew slowly toward them. Soon there was not enough space to move around freely or exercise to keep warm, or more accurately, less cold. They could only huddle close to the personnel hatch, teeth clenched together to keep from chattering, and watch the thorns creep closer.

The scene was being relayed to *Rhabwar* and was causing increasing concern. Lieutenant Haslam said suddenly, "I can launch now, sir, and—"

"No," the Captain said firmly. "If you touch down before it is safe to do so and the lander is blown over, nobody here will get out of this mess—"

He broke off because his voice had suddenly sounded very loud. The wind had died.

"Open up," Fletcher said. "Let's get out of here."

The dark-blue morning sky showed through the opening hatch and a negligible quantity of sand blew in. They maneuvered the litter and its trussed-up casualty through the opening and onto the upper surface of the hull.

"The lull may be temporary, sir," Dodds warned. "There are still a few squalls running through your area."

The rising sun was still hidden behind sand clouds, but there was more than enough light to see that the surface had been drastically altered overnight by the shifting of many sand drifts. From midships to stern the wreck was denuded of plating, but the skeleton had been filled out by a tightly packed tangle of thorns. The upper surface of the ship forward to the prow was intact, and the rocky shelf ahead was clear of thorns.

"One large squall will hit you in about twelve minutes," Dodds added.

They jammed the litter against the open hatch and attached its magnetic grapples to the hull. Then they secured their suit safety lines to the massive hinge and threw themselves across the litter, hooking their fingers into the webbing around the casualty. It was just one more physical indignity for the alien Captain, Conway thought, but by now the being was probably past caring about such things.

Abruptly the sky was dark again and the wind and sand tore at them, threatening to lift them bodily off the hull. Conway desperately gripped the webbing as he felt the magnetic grapples begin to slide and the litter slue around. He wondered briefly if the wind would blow him beyond the surrounding thorns were he to let go his grip and his safety line. But his fingers were locked in a cramp and he felt that his arms, like those of the alien Captain, were about to be separated from his torso. Then as suddenly as it had come the wind died and it was light again.

He saw that Murchison, Fletcher, and the patient were still safely attached to the litter. But he did not move. It grew brighter and he could feel the sun warming his side when the sand lashed at them again, accompanied by a high-pitched, screaming thunder.

"Extrovert!" Murchison yelled.

Conway looked up to see the lander hovering ahead of the ship and blasting sand in all directions with its thrusters. Haslam touched down on the shelf of rock which was clear of thorns, barely fifty meters from them.

There were no problems while moving the litter to the other ship, and no shortage of time to do it even though the thorns were already inching toward it. Before loading it on board, Conway removed the extra webbing and the makeshift eye protection from the patient and gave it a thorough examination. In spite of everything it had gone through it was alive and, in Conway's opinion, very well.

"How about the others, Prilicla?" he asked.

"The temperatures of all of them have come down, friend Conway," the empath replied. "They are radiating strong feelings of hunger, but not on the level of distress. Since the food supply on the wreck has been lost, and may have been contaminated anyway, they will have to wait until the hospital's synthesizers provide some. Otherwise they are emoting feelings of confusion and loss.

"But they will feel much better," Prilicla added, "when they rejoin their Captain."

COMBINED OPERATION

They emerged into normal space at a point whose coordinates placed them far out on the galactic rim and where the brightest object to be seen was a nearby sun burning coldly against a faint powdering of stars. But as Conway stared through Control's direct vision port, it became obvious that the emptiness was only apparent, because suddenly both the radar and long-range sensor displays were indicating two contacts, very close together and just under two thousand kilometers distant. For the next few minutes Conway expected to be ignored.

"Control, Power Room," Captain Fletcher said briskly. "I want maximum thrust in five minutes. Astrogator, give me the numbers to put us alongside that trace, and the ETA."

Lieutenants Chen and Dodds, seven decks below and a few feet away respectively, acknowledged. Then Lieutenant Haslam, from the Communications position, joined in.

"Sir," he said without taking his attention from his displays, "the sensor readings suggest that the larger trace has the mass, configuration, and antennae deployment of a scoutship engaged on survey duty. The other trace is currently unidentifiable, but their relative positions might indicate a recent collision."

"Very well," the Captain said. He touched his transmit stud and, speaking slowly and distinctly, he went on, "This is the ambulance ship *Rhabwar*, operating out of Sector Twelve General Hospital, responding to your distress beacon released six plus hours ago. We will close with you in—"

"Fifty-three minutes," Dodds supplied.

"—If you are able to communicate, please identify yourselves, specify the nature of your trouble, and list the type and number of casualties."

In the supernumerary's position Conway leaned forward intently, even though the difference of a few centimeters could not affect the clarity of any incoming message. But when the voice did come it sounded apologetic rather than distressed.

"The Monitor Corps scoutship *Tyrell* here, Major Nelson commanding," it said. "It was our distress beacon, but we released it on behalf of the wreck you see beside us. Our medical officer isn't sure, you understand, because its medical experience covers only three species, but it thinks that there may still be life on board."

"Doctor—" the Captain began, looking across at Conway. But before he could go on, Haslam was reporting again.

"Sir! Another, no, two more traces. Similar mass and configuration as the distressed vessel. Also smaller, widely scattered pieces of metallic wreckage."

"That's the other reason why we released our beacon," Nelson's voice sounded from *Tyrell*. "We don't have your long-range sensor equipment—our stuff is chiefly photooptical and computing gear associated with survey work—but this area seems to be littered with wreckage and, while I don't entirely agree with my medic that some of it must contain survivors, the possibility does exist that—"

"You were quite right to call for help, Captain Nelson," Conway said, breaking in. "We would much rather answer a dozen false alarms than risk missing one which might mean a rescue. Space accidents being what they are, most distress calls are answered too late in any case. However, Captain, as a matter of urgency we need the physiological classification of the wreck's survivors and the nature and extent of their injuries so that we can begin making preparations for accommodating and treating them.

"I am Senior Physician Conway," he ended. "May I speak to your medical officer?"

There was a long, hissing silence during which Haslam reported several more traces and added that, while the data were far from complete, the distribution of the wreckage was such that he was fairly certain that the accident had happened to a very large ship which had been blown apart into uniform pieces, and that the wreckage alongside *Tyrell* and the other similar pieces which were appearing all over his screens were lifeboats. Judging by the spread of the wreckage so far detected, the disaster had *not* been a recent occurrence.

Then the speaker came to life again with a flat, emotionless voice, robbed of all inflection by the process of translation. "I am Surgeon-Lieutenant Krach-Yul, Doctor Conway," it said. "My knowledge of other-species physiology is small, since I have had medical experience with only the Earth-human, Nidian, and my own Orligian life-forms, all of which, as you know, fall within the DBDG warm-blooded, oxygen-breathing classification."

The fact that the natives of Orligia and their planetary neighbor Nidia had a marked disparity in physical mass and one of them possessed an overall coat of tight, curly red fur was too small a difference to affect the four-letter classification coding, Conway thought as the other Doctor was talking. Just like the small difference which had, in the early days of their stellar exploration, caused Orligia and Earth to fight the first, brief, and so far only interstellar war.

For this reason the Orligians and Earth-humans were more than friendly—nowadays they went out of their way to help each other— and it was a great pity that Krach-Yul was too professionally inexperienced to be really helpful. All Conway could hope for was that the Orligian medic had had sense enough to restrain its professional curiosity and not poke its friendly, furry nose into a situation which was completely beyond its experience.

"We did not enter the wreck," the Orligian was saying, "because our crew members are not specialists in alien technology and there was the danger of them inadvertently contributing to the problem rather than its solution. I considered drilling through the hull and withdrawing a sample of the wreck's atmosphere, in the hope that the survivor was a warm-blooded oxygen breather like ourselves and we could pump in air. But I decided against this course in case their atmosphere was an exotic mixture which we could not supply and we would then have reduced their ship's internal pressure to no purpose.

"We are not certain that there is a survivor, Doctor," Krach-Yul went on. "Our sensors indicate pressure within the wreck, a small power source, and the presence of what appears to be one large mass of organic material which is incompletely visible through the viewports. We do not know if it is living."

Conway sighed. Where extraterrestrial physiology and medicine were concerned this Krach-Yul was uneducated, but it certainly was not unintelligent. He could imagine the Orligian qualifying on its home planet, moving to the neighboring world of Nidia, and later joining the Monitor Corps to further increase its e-t experience and, while treating the minor ills and injuries of an Earth-human scout-ship crew, hoping for something just like this to happen. The Or-ligian was probably one great, furry lump of curiosity regarding the organic contents of the wreck, but it knew its professional limitations. Conway was already developing a liking for the Orligian medic, sight unseen.

"Very good, Doctor," Conway said warmly. "But I have a request. Your vessel has a portable airlock. To save time would you mind—"

"It has already been deployed, Doctor," the Orligian broke in, "and attached to the wreck's hull over the largest entry port we could find. We are assuming it is an entry port, but it could be a large access panel because we did not try to open it. The wreck was spinning about its lateral axis and this motion was checked by *Ty-rell*'s tractor-beams, but otherwise the vessel is as we found it."

Conway thanked the other and unstrapped himself from his couch. He could see several new traces on the radar display, but it was the picture of *Tyrell* and the wreck growing visibly larger on the forward screen which was his immediate concern.

"What are your intentions, Doctor?" the Captain asked.

Indicating the image of the wreck, Conway said, "It doesn't seem to be too badly damaged and there isn't much sharp metal in sight so, in the interests of a fast recovery, my people will wear lightweight suits. I shall take Pathologist Murchison and Doctor Prilicla. Charge Nurse Naydrad will remain in the Casualty Deck lock with the litter, ready to pressurize it with the survivors' atmosphere as soon as Murchison analyzes it. You, sir, will come along to pick the alien airlock?"

Rhabwar was the first of its kind. Designed as a special ambulance ship, it had the configuration and mass of a Federation light cruiser, which was the largest type of Monitor Corps vessel capable of aerodynamic maneuver within a planetary atmosphere. As he pulled himself aft along the gravity-free central well, Conway was visualizing its gleaming white hull and delta wings decorated with the Occluded Sun, the Brown Leaf, the Red Cross, and the many other symbols which represented the concept of aid freely given throughout the worlds of the Federation.

It was a Traltha-built ship with all the design and structural advantages which that implied, and named *Rhabwar* after one of the great figures of Tralthan medical history. The ship had been designed for operation by an Earth-human crew, whose quarters were immediately below Control on Deck Two. The medical team occupied similar accommodation on Three except in the matter of furniture and bedding for the Kelgian Charge Nurse and reduced artificial gravity for the Cinrusskin empath.

Deck Four was a compromise, Conway thought as he pulled himself past it, a combination Mess Deck and recreation room where the people who worked together were expected, regardless of physiological classification, to play together—even though there was barely enough room to play a game of chess when everyone was present. The whole of Five was devoted to the ship's consumables, which comprised not only the food required by six Earth-humans, a Kelgian, and a Cinrusskin of classifications DBDG, DBLF, and GLNO respectively, but the storage tanks whose contents were capable of reproducing or synthesizing the atmosphere breathed by any species known to the Galactic Federation.

Six and Seven, where Conway was headed, were the Casualty Deck and underlying lab and treatment ward. Here the gravity, atmospheric pressure, and composition could be varied to suit the life-support requirements of any survivors who might be brought in. Deck Eight was the Power Room, the province of Lieutenant Chen, who controlled the ship's hyperdrive generators and normal space thrusters, the power supply for the artificial gravity grids, tractor and pressor beams, communications, sensors, and everything which made the energy-hungry ship live.

Conway was still thinking of the diminuitive Chen and the frightful powers available at the touch of one of his stubby fingers when he arrived on the Casualty Deck. He did not have to speak because his earlier conversation with the Captain had been relayed to Casualty, as were the more interesting and important displays on Control's screens. There was nothing for him to do except climb into his spacesuit—he had a very good medical team who kept their equipment and themselves at instant readiness, and who tried constantly to make their leader feel redundant.

Murchison was bending and stretching to check the seals of her lightweight spacesuit, and Naydrad was inside the casualty entrance lock testing a pressure litter, its beautiful silver fur rippling in slow waves along its caterpillarlike body as it worked. The incredibly fragile Prilicla, aided by its gravity nullifiers and a double set of iridescent wings, was hovering close to the ceiling where it would not be endangered by an accidental collision with one of its more massive colleagues. Its eight, pipestem legs were twitching slowly in unison, indicating that it was being exposed to emotional radiation of a pleasurable kind.

Murchison looked from Prilicla to Conway and said, "Stop that."

Conway knew that it was Murchison, albeit indirectly, and himself who were responsible for the Cinrusskin's twitchings. Prilicla, like the other members of its intelligent and sensitive race, possessed a highly developed empathic faculty which caused it to react to the most minute changes and levels of feeling in those surrounding it. Pathologist Murchison possessed that combination of physical attributes which made it extremely difficult for any Earth-human male DBDG to regard her with anything like clinical detachment—and while she was wearing a contour-hugging lightweight suit it was downright impossible.

"Sorry," Conway said, laughing, and began climbing into his own suit.

*　　*　　*

The wreck looked like a long section of metal tree trunk with a few short, twisted branches sprouting from it, Conway thought as they launched themselves from *Rhabwar*'s casualty lock toward the distressed alien ship, but apart from those pieces of projecting metal the vessel seemed to have retained its structural integrity. He could see two small viewports reflecting the ambulance ship's floodlights like two tiny suns. One of the ports was set about two meters back from the bows of the wreck and the other a similar distance from the stern, although it was impossible to say just then which was which, and he had learned that there were another two viewports in identical positions on the side hidden from him.

He could also see the loose, transparent folds of *Tyrell*'s portable airlock clinging to the hull like a wrinkled limpet and, beside it, the tiny figure of what could only be the scoutship's Orligian medic, Krach-Yul.

Fletcher, Murchison, and Conway landed beside the Orligian. They did not speak and they tried hard not to think so that Prilicla, who was slowly circling the distressed vessel, would be able to feel for survivors with the minimum of emotional interference. If anything lived inside that wreck, no matter how faintly the spark of life glowed, the little empath would detect it.

"This is very strange, friend Conway," said Prilicla after nearly fifteen minutes had passed and they were all radiating feelings of impatience in spite of themselves. "There is life on board, one source only, and the emotional radiation is so very faint that I cannot locate it with accuracy. And contrary to what I would expect in these circumstances, there are no indications that the survivor is in a distressed condition."

"Could the survivor be an infant?" Krach-Yul asked, "Left in a safe place by adults who perished, and too young to realize that there is danger?"

Prilicla, who never disagreed with anyone because to do so might give rise to unpleasant emotional radiation from the other party, said, "The possibility cannot be dismissed, friend Krach-Yul."

"An embryo, then," Murchison said, "who still lives within its dead parent?"

"That is not impossible, either, friend Murchison," Prilicla replied.

"Which means," the Pathologist said, laughing, "that you don't think much of that idea, either."

"But there *is* a survivor," the Captain said impatiently, "so let's go in and get it out."

Fletcher wriggled through the double seal of the portable airlock

and under the folds of tough, transparent plastic which, when inflated, would form a chamber large enough for them to work at
extricating the survivor and, if necessary, provide emergency treatment. Murchison and Conway, meanwhile, spent several minutes at
each of the tiny viewports, which were so deeply recessed that their
helmet lights showed only areas of featureless leathery tegument.

When they joined the Captain in the lock, Fletcher said, "There
are only so many ways of opening a door. It can hinge inward or
outward, unscrew in either direction, slide open, or dilate. The actuator for this one appears to be a simple recessed lever which—
Oh!"

The large metal hatch was swinging open. Conway tensed, waiting to feel the outward rush of the ship's air tugging at his suit and
inflating the portable lock, but nothing else happened. The Captain
grasped the edge with both hands, detached his foot magnets so that
his legs swung away from the hull, and drew his head deep inside
the opening. "This isn't an airlock but a simple access hatch to
mechanisms and systems situated between the inner and outer hulls.
I can see cable runs, plumbing, and what looks like a—"

"I need an air sample," Murchison said, "quickly."

"Sorry, ma'am," Fletcher said. He let go with one hand and
pointed carefully, then went on, "It seems obvious that only the
inner hull is airtight. It should be safe enough for you if you site
your drill in the angle between that support bracket and cable loom
just there. I don't know how efficient their insulation is, but that
cable is too thin to carry much power. The color coding suggests
that their visual range is similar to ours, wouldn't you say?"

"I would," Murchison agreed.

Conway said quickly, "If you use a Five drill it will be wide
enough to take an Eye."

"I intend doing that," she said dryly.

The drill whirred briefly, the sound conducted through the
metal of the hull and the fabric of Conway's suit, and a sample of
the ship's atmosphere hissed through the hollow drill-head and into
the analyzer.

"The pressure is a little low by our standards," she reported
quietly, "but that could be dangerously low or normal so far as the
survivor is concerned. Composition, the proportion of oxygen to

inert gases, makes it a warm-blooded, oxygen-breathing life-form. I shall now insert the Eye."

Conway saw her detach the analyzer from the hollow drill and, so expertly that she could not have lost more than a few cubic centimeters of ship's atmosphere in the process, replace it with the Eye. Very carefully she threaded in the transparent tube containing the lens, light source, and vision recorder through the hollow center of the drill, then attached the eyepiece and magnifier which would enable her to use the instrument while wearing a space helmet.

For what seemed like an hour but was probably only ten minutes she swiveled the lens and varied the light intensity, without speaking. Then she wriggled backward out of the opening to give Conway and the others a look.

"It's big," she said.

The interior of the wreck was a hollow cylinder completely free of compartment dividers or structural crossmembers and the floor— Conway was assuming it was the floor because it was flat and ran the length of the ship—had a double line of closely spaced holes three or four inches in diameter running down the middle. Seven or eight pairs of the survivor's feet disappeared into the holes so they were probably part of the vessel's system of safety restraints, as were the broad bands of torn webbing which floated loosely about its body.

The Eye was positioned close to floor level so that Conway could see the being's flank along the section whose feet were held in the deck holes. Farther along, where the feet had been pulled free by the force of the accident to its ship, he could see in detail the double line of stubby, centipedal legs and the pale-gray underside. In the opposite direction—he could not tell whether it was toward the being's head or tail—he could make out part of the upper surface of the creature and a single line of dorsal tentacular appendages. The long, cylindrical compartment did not give the being much room to maneuver and the twists and curves of the weightless, flaccid body seriously hampered viewing, but at the limit of his vision Conway could just make out three lengths of tubing, pencil thin, transparent, and apparently flexible, which sprouted from a container attached to the wall to disappear into the body of the survivor.

Despite the multiplicity of the being's arms and legs there seemed to be very little if anything for it to do. Apart from a large number of wall-mounted storage cabinets, the interior of the ship was bare of anything resembling control and indication systems or any obvious means by which the vessel could be guided by its occupant—unless, of course, there was a small control center forward in the area concealed by the survivor's body.

Conway must have been thinking aloud because the Captain, who had just returned from an external examination of the ship, said seriously, "There *is* nothing for it to do, Doctor. Except for a very unsophisticated power cell which, at present, is not being used to power anything, there is nothing. No propulsion unit, no attitude control jets, no recognizable external sensors or communications, no personnel lock. I'm beginning to wonder if this is a ship or some kind of survival pod. This would explain the odd configuration of the vessel, which is a cylinder of constant diameter with a perfectly flat face at each end. However, when I sighted along the hull in an effort to detect minor protrusions which could have housed sensor equipment, I observed that the cylinder was very slightly curved along its longitudinal axis. This opens up another possibility which—"

"What about power sources and comm equipment mounted outboard?" Conway broke in before the Captain's observations could develop into a lecture on ship design philosophy. "We have matched hyperdrive generators on our wingtips and perhaps these people had a similar idea."

"No, Doctor," Fletcher said in the cool, formal tone he used when he thought someone was trying to tell him his business. "I examined those external spars, which have been broken off too short to give any indication of the type of structure they supported, but the wiring still attached to them is much too thin to carry power to a hyperspace generator. In fact, I seriously doubt if these people had either hyperdrive or artificial gravity, and the general level of technology displayed is pretty elementary for a star-traveling race. Then there is the apparent absence of an entry port. An airlock for this beastie would have to be almost as long as the vessel itself."

"There are a few star-traveling species who do not use them,"

Conway said. "For purely physiological reasons they do not indulge in extravehicular activity, entering and leaving their ships only at time of departure and arrival."

"Suppose," Murchison said, "this vehicle is the being's space-suit."

"A nice idea, ma'am, but no," Fletcher said apologetically. "Apart from the four viewports, whose angles of vision are severely limited because of their small size and the space between the outer and inner hulls, there is no sensory input of any kind known to me and, more important, no external manipulators. But there must be some easy way of getting that beastie into and out of that thing, whether it is a ship, a survival pod, or something else."

There was a long silence, then Conway said, "I'm sorry, Captain. A few minutes ago you were about to mention a third possibility when I interrupted you."

"I was," Fletcher said in the tone of one graciously receiving an apology. "But you will understand, Doctor, that the theory is based on my initial visual observation only and not, as yet, supported by accurate measurements. Nevertheless, as I have already stated, this vessel is not a true cylinder but appears to be curved slightly along its longitudinal axis.

"Now, an explosion or collision sufficiently violent to warp the cylinder out of true," he went on, slipping into his lecturing manner, "would buckle and open up seams in the hull plating, and leave evidence of heat discoloration and indentations from flying debris. There are no such indications. So if the longitudinal axis of the vessel is, in fact, a very flat curve rather than a straight line, then the curvature was deliberate, built in. This would explain the lack of power and control linkages and an artificial gravity system be-cause they used—"

"Of course!" Conway broke in. "The hull beneath the flat deck was outward facing and free of structural projections, which means that they got their gravity the old-fashioned way by—"

"Will one of you," Murchison said crossly, "kindly tell me what you are talking about?"

"Certainly," Conway said. "The Captain has convinced me that this structure is not a ship or a lifeboat, but a section of a space station, an early Wheeltype of very large diameter, which suffered a collision."

"A space station away out here?" Murchison sounded incredulous. Then she began to realize the implications and added feelingly, "In that case we could have an awful lot of work ahead of us."

"Maybe not, ma'am," Fletcher said. "Admittedly there is a strong possibility of finding many more space station segments, but the survivors may be very few." His tone became suddenly forceful. "Transferring that creature to our Casualty Deck is out of the question. Instead I suggest we attach it to our hull, extend *Rhabwar*'s hyperspace envelope accordingly, and whisk it back to Sector General where their airlocks can easily handle a patient extraction problem of this size. I am not the e-t medical specialist, of course, but I think we should do this at once, leaving *Tyrell* to search for other survivors, and then return as soon as possible for the others."

"No," Conway said firmly.

"I don't understand you, Doctor." Behind his helmet visor Fletcher's face had gone red.

Conway ignored him for a moment while he addressed Murchison and Prilicla, who had drifted closer in spite of the strong emotional radiation being generated in the area. He said, "The survivor, so far as we are able to see, is linked to what appears to be some kind of life-support system by three separate sets of tubing. It is deeply unconscious but not physically distressed. There is also the fact that its vessel contains a reservoir of power which is not presently being used. Now, would either of you agree that the observed emotional radiation and apparent lack of physical injury could be the result of it being in a hibernation anesthesia condition?"

Before either of them could reply, Conway added, "Since there is no evidence of the presence of the power-hungry, complex refrigeration systems which we associate with suspended animation techniques, just three sets of tubing entering its body, would you also agree that the life-form is a natural hibernator?"

There was a short silence, then Murchison said, "We are familiar with the idea of long-term suspended animation being associated with star travel—that used to be the only way to do it, after all, and the cold-sleeping travelers would require neither air nor food during

their trips. In the case of a life-form with the ability to go periodically into a state of hibernation for planetary environmental reasons, a minimal supply of food and air would be required. It is quite
possible that the natural process of hibernation could be artificially
initiated, extended, and counteracted by specific medication and the
food supplied intravenously, as seems to be the case with our friend
here."

"Friend Conway," Prilicla said, "the survivor's emotional radiation pattern agrees in every particular with the hypothesis of hibernation anesthesia."

Captain Fletcher was not slow on the uptake. He said, "Very
well, Doctor. The survivor has been in this condition for a very long
time, so there is no great urgency about moving it or the other
survivors we might find to the hospital. But what are your immediate intentions?"

Conway was aware of a multiple, purely subjective silence as the
party on the alien's hull and the communications officers who were
listening in on *Rhabwar* and *Tyrell* held their collective breath. He
cleared his throat and said, "We will examine this section of space
station, if that is what it is, as closely as possible without entering
it, and simultaneously make as detailed a visual examination of the
survivor as we can using the Eye, and then we will all try to *think*."

He had the feeling, very strong and not at all pleasant to judge
by the trembling of Prilicla's spidery limbs, that this was not going
to be an easy rescue.

*　　*　　*

For a little over three hours, the duration remaining to their lightweight suits, they did nothing but think as they examined the exterior of the wreck and what little they could see of its occupant,
slowly adding data which might or might not be important. But
they thought as individuals, increasingly baffled individuals, so that
it was not until they met on *Rhabwar*'s Messdeck and recreation
level that they were able to think as an equally baffled group.

Tyrell was represented by its Captain, Major Nelson, and
Surgeon-Lieutenant Krach-Yul, while Major Fletcher and the astrogation officer, Lieutenant Dodds, furnished the required military
balance for *Rhabwar*. Murchison, Prilicla, Naydrad, and Conway—

who were, after all, mere civilians—filled the remainder of the deck space with the exception of the empath, who was clinging to the safety of the ceiling.

It was Prilicla, knowing that nobody else felt ready to contribute any useful ideas, who spoke first.

"I feel that we are all agreed," it said in the musical trills and clicks of the Cinrusskin tongue, which emanated from their translator packs as faultless if somewhat toneless speech in the languages of Kelgia, Orligia, and Earth, "that the being is in a state of suspended animation, that there is a high probability that it is not a patient but a survivor who should be returned to its home world as soon as convenient if this planet can be found, and that the need to move it is not an urgent one."

Lieutenant Dodds looked at Fletcher for permission to speak, then said, "It depends on what you mean by urgent, Doctor. I ran a vectors and velocities check on this and the other pieces of wreckage within detector range. These bits of alien vessel or space station occupied roughly the same volume of space approximately eighty-seven years ago, which is when the disaster must have occurred. If it was a ship I don't think it was heading for the nearby sun since there are no planets, but a lot of the dispersed wreckage will either fall into the sun or pass closely enough to make no difference to any other survivors in hibernation. This will begin to occur in just over eleven weeks."

They digested that for a moment, then *Tyrell's* Captain said, "I still say a space station way out here is impossible, especially one traveling at such a clip that its wreckage will reach the sun, there, in eleven weeks. It is far more likely that the survivor is in a lifeboat with suspended animation extending the duration of its consumables."

Fletcher glared at his fellow Captain, then he noticed Prilicla beginning to tremble. He visibly calmed himself as he said, "It is not impossible, Major Nelson, although it is unlikely. Let us suppose that the survivor's race, which is at the interplanetary flight level of technology, was beginning to experiment with hyperspace generation on its space station and inadvertently performed a random Jump and found themselves very far indeed from home, and subsequently went into hibernation for the reason you have stated.

Many such accidents have occurred during early experiments with hypertravel. In any case, I think we are drawing too many conclusions from what is, after all, only one small piece of a very large jigsaw."

Conway decided to join in before this spirited exchange of technical views could devolve into a quarrel. He said placatingly, "But what conclusions, however few and tentative, can we draw from the piece you have examined, Captain? And what, however vaguely, can you see of the complete picture?"

"Very well," said Fletcher. He quickly inserted his vision spool from the wreck into the Recreation Deck's display unit and began to describe everything he had observed and deduced during his examination of the distressed vessel, which he preferred to think of as a simple, pressurized container rather than a ship. It was a cylinder just over twenty meters in length and approximately three meters in diameter, with ends which were flat except for a set of eight couplings which would enable it to be connected at either end to other similar containers. The couplings had been designed to break open before any external shock or force applied to adjacent structures could damage or deform the container. If the dimensions of the other containers or space station sections were the same as the one examined, and if the longitudinal curvature was uniform in all of them, then approximately eighty of these sections would form a Wheel just under five hundred meters in diameter.

He paused, but Major Nelson still had his lips pressed tightly together, and the others, knowing that a reaction was expected of them, kept perversely silent.

The section had a double hull with only the inner one pressurized, Fletcher resumed, but it possessed no control, sensor, or power systems other than those associated with the suspended animation equipment. The level of technology displayed was advanced interplanetary rather than interstellar, so the station had no business being where it was in the first place. But the most puzzling feature of the container was the method used to enter and leave it.

They had already seen that there were no openings on the hull large enough to allow entry or exit by the survivor, which meant that it had to enter and leave via the flat, circular plate at each end of the cylinder. In Fletcher's opinion the creature went in one end and came out the other because physically it was too massive to turn itself around inside its container. But there was nothing resembling a door at either end of the cylinder, just the two large circular plates whose edges were set inside the thick rims which supported the couplings.

"So far as I can see there is no operating mechanism for these endplates," Fletcher went on with the hint of an apology creeping into his tone. "There are only so many ways for a door to open, and there has to be a door into and out of that thing, but I can't find one. I even considered explosive bolts, with the extraterrestrial sealed in until it arrived or was taken by its rescuers to an environmentally suitable position—either a planet or the hold of a rescue ship—whereupon it would blow the hatch fastenings and crawl out. But there are no hatch fastenings that I can see and the rim structure surrounding the hatches, if that is what they are, would not allow them to be blown open. Neither can they be opened inward because the diameter of the inner, pressurized hull is much smaller than that of the endplates."

Fletcher shook his head in bafflement and ended, "I'm sorry, Doctor. Right now I can see no way for you to get to your survivor without cutting its ship apart. What I need is another piece of this jigsaw puzzle to examine, a broken piece which will let me see how the other undamaged pieces were put together."

There was silence for a few seconds, during which Prilicla trembled in sympathy with the Captain's embarrassment, then Murchison spoke.

"I would like to examine a broken piece as well," she said quietly. "Specifically, a piece containing a nonsurvivor which would let me see how our survivor is put together."

Conway turned to Dodds. "Are there many pieces which look as if they had been broken up?"

"A few," replied the Astrogator. "Most of the traces give sensor readings similar to the first piece. That is, a vehicle of similar mass retaining internal pressure and containing a small power source. All of the pieces, including the few damaged ones, are at extreme sensor range. It is a long way to go on impulse drive, but if we jumped through hyperspace we would probably overshoot."

"How many pieces altogether?" asked Nelson.

338 · JAMES WHITE

"Twenty-three solid traces so far," said Dodds, "plus a few masses of what appears to be loose, structural debris. There is also one largish mass, unpressurized and radioactive, which I'd guess was part of a power center."

From its position on the ceiling, Prilicla said, "If I might make a suggestion, and if Major Nelson is willing to interrupt his survey mission . . . ?"

Nelson laughed suddenly and the other Corps officers present smiled. With great feeling he went on, "There isn't a scoutship crew on survey duty anywhere in the Galaxy who would not rather be doing something, *anything*, else! You only have to ask and give me half an excuse for accepting, Doctor."

"Thank you, friend Nelson," said the empath with a slow tremor of pleasure. "My suggestion is that *Rhabwar* and *Tyrell* act independently to seek out other survivors and return them to this area, using tractor beams if the distance is short enough for impulse drive or by extending the hyperspace envelopes to include them if a Jump is necessary. My empathic faculty enables me to identify sections containing living occupants and, because of the large mass of these beings, Doctor Krach-Yul and Nurse Naydrad should accompany me to assist with treatment, should this be possible. Pathologist Murchison and you, friend Conway, are well able to identify living casualties by more orthodox means if the ship's sensors are uncertain.

"This will halve the time needed to search for other survivors," Prilicla ended apologetically, "even though the period will still be a lengthy one."

Tyrell's medical officer spoke for the first time, its whining and barking speech translating as "I always assumed that a space rescue by ambulance ship would be a fast, dramatic, and decisive operation. This one appears to be disappointingly slow."

"I agree, Doctor," said Conway. "We need help if this job is not to take months instead of a few days. Not one scoutship but a flotilla, or better yet a squadron of them to search the entire—"

Captain Nelson began to laugh, then broke off when he saw that Conway was serious. He said, "Doctor, I'm just a major in the Monitor Corps and so is Captain Fletcher. We haven't got the rank to whistle up a flotilla of scoutships no matter how much you think we need them. All we can do is explain the situation and put in a very humble request."

Fletcher looked at his fellow Captain and opened his mouth to speak, then changed his mind.

Conway smiled and said, "I am a civilian, Captain, with no rank at all. Or considered in another way, I, as a specialist member of the public, have ultimate authority over people like yourselves who are public servants—"

Clearing his throat noisily, Fletcher said, "Please spare us the political philosophy, Doctor. Do you wish me to get off a subspace signal to Sector base requesting massive assistance because of a large number of widely scattered potential survivors of a hitherto un-known life-form?"

"That's it," said Conway. "And would you also take charge of assigning search areas to the scoutships if and when they arrive? In the meantime we'll do as Prilicla suggests, except that Murchison and I will go in *Tyrell,* if that is agreeable to you, Captain."

"A pleasure," said Nelson, looking at Murchison.

"Because your crew aren't used to our fragile friend scampering about on their ceilings and there might be an accident," he continued. "But right now we'll need help to transfer some of our portable equipment to your ship."

While their gear was being moved to the scoutship and Conway was trying hard to keep Murchison from transferring the Casualty Deck's diagnostic and treatment equipment in toto, *Tyrell's* portable airlock was detached from the alien vessel and restowed on board in case it would be needed on one of the other widely scattered sections. Several times as they worked, *Rhabwar's* lighting and grav-ity control fluctuated in momentary overload, indicating that Con-way's subspace signal was going out.

He knew that Fletcher was keeping the signal as brief as possible because the power required to punch a message through the highly theoretical medium of subspace from a vessel of *Rhabwar's* relatively small size would have Lieutenant Chen in the Power Room chewing his nails. Even so, that signal would be splattered with interstellar static and have audible holes blown through it by every intervening cloud of ionized gas, star, or quasistellar object, and for that reason the message had been speeded up many times and repeated so that the people at the receiving end would be able to piece together a normal-speed coherent message from the jumble reaching them.

But their response to the signal was an entirely different matter, Conway thought worriedly. Despite his seeming confidence before the others, he did not know what would happen because this was the first time he had made such a request.

* * *

Nelson had invited Murchison and Conway to Control so that they could observe *Tyrell*'s approach to the second section of alien space station to be investigated, and so that his crew could observe the pathologist. Since the subspace signal had gone out six hours earlier, the Captain had been regarding Conway with a mixture of anxiety and awe as if he did not know whether the Doctor was seriously self-deluded or a highly potent individual indeed.

The messages which erupted from his Control Room speaker shortly afterward, and which continued with only a few minutes' break between them for the best part of the next hour, resolved his doubts but left him feeling even more confused.

"Scoutship *Tedlin* to *Rhabwar*. Instructions please."

"Scoutship *Tenelphi* to *Rhabwar,* requesting reassignment instructions."

"Scoutship *Torrance,* acting flotilla leader. I have seven units and eighteen more to follow presently. You have work for us, *Rhabwar*?"

Finally Nelson muted the speaker and the sound of Captain Fletcher assigning search areas to the newly arrived scoutships, which were being ordered to search for sections of the alien space station and bring them to the vicinity of *Rhabwar*. With so much help available, Fletcher had decided that the ambulance ship would not itself join in the search but would instead remain by the first section to coordinate the operation and give medical assistance. Confident that the situation was under control, Conway relaxed and turned to face Captain Nelson, whose curiosity had become an almost palpable thing.

"You—you *are* just a doctor, Doctor?" he said.

"That's right, Captain," Murchison said before Conway could reply. She laughed and went on, "And stop looking at him like that, you'll give him an inflated sense of his own importance."

"My colleagues are constantly on guard against the possibility of that happening," Conway said dryly. "But Pathologist Murchison is right. I am not important, nor are any of the Monitor Corps officers or the medical team on *Rhabwar*. It is our job which is important enough to command the reassignment of a few flotillas of scoutships to assist."

"But it requires the rank of subfleet Commander or higher to order such a thing—" Nelson began, and broke off as Conway shook his head.

"To explain it I must first fill in some background, Captain," he said. "Some of this information is common knowledge. Much of it is not because the relevant decisions of the Federation Council and their effects on Monitor Corps operational priorities are too recent for it to have filtered down to you. And you'll excuse me, I hope, if some of it is elementary, especially to a scoutship Captain on a survey mission . . ."

Only a tiny fraction of the Galaxy had been explored by the Earth-humans or by any of the sixty-odd other races who made up the Galactic Federation, so that the member races were in the peculiar position of people who had friends in far countries but had no idea who was living in the next street. The reason for this was that travelers tended to meet each other more often than the people who stayed at home, especially when the travelers exchanged addresses and visited each other regularly.

Visiting was comparatively easy. Providing there were no major distorting influences on the way and the exact coordinates of the destination were known, it was almost as easy to travel through hyperspace to a neighboring solar system as to one at the other side of the galaxy. But first one had to find a system containing a planet with intelligent life before its coordinates could be logged, and finding new inhabited systems was proving to be no easy task.

Very, very slowly a few of the blank areas in the star maps were being surveyed and explored, but with little success. When a survey scoutship like *Tyrell* turned up a star with planets it was a rare find, even rarer if one of the planets harbored life. And if one of these life-forms was intelligent then jubilation, not unmixed with concern over what might possibly be a future threat to the Pax Galactica, swept the worlds of the Federation, and the cultural contact specialists of the Monitor Corps were assigned the tricky, time-consuming, and often dangerous job of establishing contact in depth.

The cultural contact people were the elite of the Monitor Corps, a small group of specialists in extraterrestrial communications, philosophy, and psychology. Although small, the group was not, regrettably, overworked.

"During the past twenty years," Conway went on, "they have initiated first-contact procedure on three occasions, all of which were successful and resulted in the species concerned joining the Federation. There is no need to bore you with such details as the fantastically large number of survey missions mounted, the ships, personnel, and material involved, or shock you with the cost of it all. I mention the cultural contact group's three successes simply to make the point that within the same period Sector Twelve General Hospital, our first multienvironment medical treatment center, became fully operational and initiated first contacts which resulted in seven new species joining the Federation.

"This was accomplished," he explained, "not by a slow, patient buildup and widening of communications until the exchange of complex philosophical and sociological concepts became possible, but by giving medical assistance to a sick alien."

This was something of an oversimplification, Conway admitted. There were the medical and surgical problems inherent in treating a hitherto unknown life-form. Sector General's translation computer, the second largest in the Federation, was available, as was the assistance of the Monitor Corps' hospital-based communications specialists, and the Corps had been responsible for rescuing and bringing in many of the extraterrestrial casualities in the first place. But the fact remained that the hospital, by giving medical assistance, demonstrated the Federation's goodwill toward e-ts much more simply and directly than could have been done by any time-consuming exchange of concepts.

Because all Federation ships were required to file course and passenger or crew details before departure, the position of a distress signal was usually a good indication of the ship and therefore the physiological classification of the beings who had run into trouble, and an ambulance ship with matching crew and life-support equipment was sent from Sector General or from the ship's home planet to assist it. But there had been instances, far more than was generally realized, when the disasters involved beings unknown to the Federation in urgent need of help, help which the would-be rescuers were powerless to give.

Only when the rescue ship concerned had the capability of extending its hyperspace envelope to include the distressed vessel, or the survivors could be extricated safely and a suitable environment provided for them within the Federation ship could they be transported to Sector General for treatment. The result was that many hitherto unknown life-forms, entities of high intelligence and advanced technology, were lost except as interesting specimens for dissection and study.

But an answer to this problem had been sought and, hopefully, found.

"It was decided to build and equip a very special ambulance ship," Conway continued, "which would give priority to answering distress signals whose positions did not agree with the flight plans filed by Federation vessels. The First Contact people consider *Rhabwar* to be the near-perfect answer in that we involve ourselves only with star-traveling species, beings who are *expecting* to encounter new and to them alien life-forms and who, should they get into trouble, would not be expected to display serious xenophobic reactions when we try to help them. Another reason why the Cultural Contact people prefer meeting star travelers to planetbound species is that they can never be sure whether they are helping or hindering the newly discovered culture's natural development, giving them a technological leg up or a crushing inferiority complex.

"Anyway," Conway said, smiling as he pointed at Nelson's main display where the newly arrived scoutships covered the screen, "now you know that it is *Rhabwar* which has the rank and not any member of its crew."

Nelson was looking only slightly less impressed, but before he could speak the voices of two scoutship commanders reporting to *Rhabwar* sounded in quick succession. Both vessels had emerged from hyperspace close to sections of alien space station and were already returning to the rendezvous point with them in tow on long-focus tractor beams. In both cases the sections gave sensor indications of life on board.

"The news isn't all good, however," Nelson said, pointing at his main display where an enlarged picture of the section toward which they were heading filled the screen. "That one has taken a beating and I don't see how the occupant could have survived."

Conway nodded, and as the wrecked section turned slowly to present an end view, Murchison added, "Obviously it didn't."

The alien cylinder had been dented and punctured by multiple collisions with some of the structural members which had furnished the supporting framework of the original space station and which was still drifting nearby. Amid the loose tangle of debris was one of the section's circular endplates, and from the open end of the compartment the body of its occupant protruded like an enormous, dessicated caterpillar.

"Can you relay this picture to *Rhabwar*?" Conway asked.

"If I can get a word in edgewise," Nelson replied, glancing at his speaker, which was carrying a continuous, muted conversation between Fletcher and the scoutships.

Murchison had been staring intently at the screen. She said suddenly, "It would be a waste of time examining that cadaver out here. Can you put a tractor on it, Captain, and take us back to *Rhabwar*?"

"We'll need to bring back the wreck for study as well," Conway said. "The life-support and suspended animation systems will give us important information on the being's physiology and—"

"Excuse me, Doctor," Nelson said. For several seconds the voices from *Rhabwar* and the scoutships had been silent and the Captain had seized the chance to send a message of his own. He went on, "*Tyrell* here. Will you accept a visual relay, *Rhabwar*? Doctor Conway thinks it's important."

"Go ahead, *Tyrell*," Fletcher's voice said. "All other traffic wait out."

There was a long silence while *Rhabwar*'s Captain studied the image of the slowly rotating wreck and the attached cadaver, long enough for it to make three complete revolutions, then Fletcher spoke. The tone and words were so uncharacteristic that they scarcely recognized his voice. "I'm a fool, a stupid damned fool for not seeing it!"

It was Murchison who asked the obvious question.

"For not seeing how that endplate opened," Fletcher replied. He made several more self-derogatory remarks in an undertone, then went on, "It *drops* out, or there is probably a spring-loaded actuator which pushes it out through the slot which you can see behind the coupling collar. No doubt there is an internal air pressure sensor linked to the actuator to keep the endplate from popping out accidentally when the section is in space or the adjoining section is airless. Do you intend returning with this section and not just the cadaver?"

The tone of the question suggested that if such was not the Doctor's intention, then forceful arguments would be forthcoming to make him change his mind.

"As quickly as possible," Conway said dryly. "Pathologist Murchison is just as keen to look inside that alien as you are to look inside its ship. Please ask Naydrad to stand by the Casualty Lock."

"Will do," Fletcher said. He paused for a moment, then went on seriously, "You realize, Doctor, that the manner in which these cylinders open means that their occupants were sealed into their suspended animation compartments while in atmosphere, almost certainly on their home planet, and the cylinders were not meant to be opened until their arrival on the target world. These people are members of a sublight colonization attempt."

"Yes," Conway said absently. He was thinking about the probable reaction of the hospital to receiving a bunch of outsize, hibernating e-ts who were not, strictly speaking, patients but the survivors of a failed colonization flight. Sector General was a hospital, not a refugee camp. It would insist, and rightly, that the colonists be transferred either to their planet of origin or destination. Since the surviving colonists were in no immediate danger there might be no need to involve the hospital at all—or the ambulance ship—except in an advisory capacity. He added, "We are going to need more help."

"Yes," Fletcher said with great feeling. It was obvious that his thinking had been parallelling Conway's. "*Rhabwar* out."

By the time *Tyrell* had returned to the assembly area, it was beginning to look congested. Twenty-eight hibernation compartments—all of which, according to Prilicla, contained living e-ts—hung in the darkness like a gigantic, three-dimensional picture showing the agglutinization of a strain of rod-shaped bacilli. Each section had been numbered for later identification and examination. There were no other scoutships in the area because they were busy retrieving more cylinders.

Even with the Casualty Deck's artificial gravity switched off and tractor beams aiding the transfer, it took Murchison, Naydrad, and Conway more than an hour to extricate the cadaver from its wrecked compartment and bring it into *Rhabwar*. Once inside it flowed over the examination table on each side and on to instrument trolleys, beds, and whatever else could be found around the room to support its massive, coiling body.

Fletcher paid them a visit some hours later to see the cadaver at close range, but he had chosen a moment when Murchison's investigation was moving from the visual examination to the dissection stage and his stay was brief. As he was leaving he said, "When you can be spared here, Doctor, would you mind coming up to Control?"

Conway nodded without looking up from his scanner examination of one of the alien's breathing orifices and its tracheal connection. The Captain had left when he straightened up a few minutes later and said, "I just can't make head or tail of this thing."

"That is understandable, Doctor," Naydrad said, who belonged to a very literal-minded species. "The being appears to have neither."

Murchison looked up from her microscopic examination of a length of nerve ganglia and rubbed her eyes. She said, "Naydrad is quite right. Both head and tail sections are absent and may have been surgically removed, although I cannot be certain of that even though there are indications of minor surgery having taken place at one extremity. All that we know for sure is that it is a warm-blooded oxygen breather and probably an adult. I say 'probably' despite the fact that the creature in the first cylinder was relatively more massive. Genetic factors generally make for size differences among the adults of most species, so I cannot assume that it is an adolescent or younger. Of one thing I am sure—Thornnastor is going to enjoy itself with this one."

"So are you," Conway said.

She smiled tiredly and went on, "I don't wish to give the impression that you are not helping, Doctor. You are. But I had the distinct feeling back there that the Captain was just being polite, and he wants to see you very urgently."

Prilicla, who had been resting on the ceiling between trips outside to monitor the emotional radiation of newly arrived survivors, made trilling and clicking noises which translated as "For a nonempath, friend Murchison, your feeling was remarkably accurate."

When Conway entered Control a few minutes later, both Captains were present and they looked relieved to see him. It was Nelson who spoke first.

"Doctor," he said quickly, "I think this rescue mission is getting out of hand. So far thirty-eight contacts have been made and the sensors report the presence of life on all but two of them, and more cylinders are being reported every few minutes. They are all uniform in size and the present indications are that there are many more sections out there than would be necessary to complete one Wheel."

"If, for technical or physiological reasons, the alien vessel had to have the configuration of a Wheel," Conway said thoughtfully, "then it could have been built, as were some of our early space stations, in a series of concentric circles, as wheels within wheels."

Nelson shook his head. "The longitudinal curvature on all sections is identical. Could there have been two Wheels, separate but identical vessels, which were in collision?"

"I disagree with the collision theory," Fletcher said, joining in for the first time. "At least between two or more Wheels. There are far too many survivors and undamaged sections for that. Their vessel seems to have fallen apart. I think there was a high-velocity collision with a natural body, the shock of which shook the hub and central support structure apart."

Conway was trying to visualize the finished shape of this alien jigsaw puzzle. He said, "But you still think there was more than one Wheel?"

"Not exactly," Fletcher replied. "Two of them mounted side by side, with a different alien or set of aliens in each. Right now we don't know whether we are retrieving single aliens who have been surgically modified for travel or pieces of much larger creatures, and we won't know how many we are dealing with until the scoutships begin bringing back heads and tails. I'm assuming that all of the occupants were in suspended animation and their ship ran itself, accelerating or decelerating along its vertical axis. If I'm right then the hub wreckage should contain the remains of just one propulsion unit and one section which contained the automatic navigation and sensor equipment."

Conway nodded. "A neat theory, Captain. Is it possible to prove it?"

Fletcher smiled and said, "All of the pieces are out there, even though some of them will be smashed into their component parts and difficult to identify, but given time and the necessary assistance we could fit them together."

"You mean *reconstruct* it?"

"Perhaps," Fletcher replied in an oddly neutral tone. "But is it really any of our business?"

Conway opened his mouth, intending to tell the other exactly what he thought of a damn fool question like that, then closed it again when he saw the expressions on both Captains' faces.

For the truth was that the situation which was developing here was no longer any of their business. *Rhabwar* was an ambulance ship, designed and provisioned for short-duration missions aimed at the rescue, emergency treatment, and transfer to the hospital of survivors of accident or disease in space. But these survivors did not require treatment or fast transport to the hospital. They had been in suspended animation for a long time and would be capable of remaining in that condition without harm for a long time to come. Reviving them and, more important, relocating them on a suitable planet would be a major project.

The sensible thing for Conway to do would be to bow out gracefully and dump the problem in the laps of the Cultural Contact specialists. *Rhabwar* could then return to its dock and the medical team could go back to treating the weird and wonderful variety of patients who turned up at Sector General while they waited for the next distress call for their special ambulance ship.

But the two men watching him so intently were a scoutship commander on survey duty, who would be lucky if he turned up one inhabited system in ten years of searching, and Major Fletcher, *Rhabwar*'s Captain and a recognized authority in the field of extra-terrestrial comparative technology—and the rescue of this e-t sub-light colonization transport could well be the biggest problem to face the Federation since the discovery and treatment of the continent-girdling strata creature of Drambo.

Conway looked from Nelson to Fletcher, then said quietly, "You're right, Captain, this isn't our responsibility. It is Cultural Contact's problem, and they would not think any the less of us, in fact they would expect us to hand it over to them. But I get the impression that you don't want me to do that."

Fletcher shook his head firmly and Nelson said, "Doctor, if you have any friends in authority, tell them I would willingly give an arm or a leg to be allowed to stay on this one."

A cool, logical portion of Conway's mind was urging him to do the sensible thing, to think about what he was letting himself in for and to remember who would be blamed if things went wrong, but it never had any hope of winning that argument.

"Good," Conway said, "that makes it unanimous."

They were both grinning at him in a manner totally unbefitting their rank and responsibilities, as if he had bestowed some great favor instead of condemning them to months of unremitting mental and physical hard labor. He went on, "As the ship responsible for making the original find, *Tyrell* would be justified in remaining, and as the medical team in attendance, the same applies to *Rhabwar*. But we are going to need a lot of help, and if we are to have any hope of getting it you will have to give me detailed information on every aspect of this problem, not just the medical side, and answers to the questions which are going to be asked.

"To begin with, I shall need to know a great deal more about the physiology of the survivors, and you will have to find me a couple of additional cadavers for Thornnastor, the hospital's Diagnostician-in-Charge of Pathology. It has six feet and weighs half a ton and if Murchison and I don't come up with some sensible conclusions about this life-form, and specimens for Thorny to investigate independently, it will walk all over me. And what O'Mara and Skempton will do—"

"They're public servants, Doctor," Nelson said, grinning. "You have the rank."

Conway got to his feet and said very seriously, "This is not simply a matter of whistling up another flotilla of scoutships, gentlemen, and something more than a hyperspace signal will be needed this time. To get the help we need I'll have to go back to the hospital and argue and plead, and probably thump the table a bit."

As he entered the gravity-free central well and began pulling himself toward the Casualty Deck he could hear Fletcher saying, "That wasn't much of an inducement, Nelson. Most of his highly placed friends have more arms and legs than they know what to do with."

*   *   *

Leaving *Rhabwar* and the rest of the medical team at the disaster site, Conway traveled to Sector General in *Tyrell*. He had requested an urgent meeting with the hospital's big three—Skempton, Thornnastor, and O'Mara—as soon as the scoutship had emerged into normal space. The request had been granted but Chief Psychologist O'Mara had told him curtly that there would be no point trying to start the meeting prematurely by worrying out loud over the communication channel, so Conway had to curb his impatience and try to marshal his arguments while Sector General slowly grew larger in the forward viewscreen.

When Conway arrived in the Chief Psychologist's office, Thornnastor, Skempton, and O'Mara were already waiting for him. Colonel Skempton, as the ranking Monitor Corps officer in the hospital, was occupying the only other chair, apart from O'Mara's own, which was suitable for the use of Earth-humans; Thornnastor, like the other members of the Tralthan species, did everything including sleeping on its six, elephantine feet.

The Chief Psychologist waved a hand at the selection of e-t furniture ranged in front of his desk and said, "Take a seat if you can do so without injuring yourself, Doctor, and make your report."

Conway arranged himself carefully in a Kelgian relaxer frame and began to describe briefly the events from the time *Rhabwar* had arrived in response to *Tyrell's* distress beacon. He told of the investigation of the first section of the fragmented alien vessel which was the product of a race in the early stage of spaceship technology, possessing sublight drive and gravity furnished by rotating their ship. Every undamaged section found had contained an e-t in suspended animation. For this reason additional scoutships had been requested to help find and retrieve the remaining survivors as a matter of urgency because the majority of these widely scattered suspended animation compartments would, in just under twelve weeks' time, fall into or pass so close to a nearby sun that the beings inside them would perish.

While Conway was speaking, O'Mara stared at him with eyes which opened into a mind so perceptive and analytical that it gave the Chief Psychologist what amounted to a telepathic faculty. Thornnastor's four eyes were focused equally on Conway and Colonel Skempton, who was staring down at his scratch pad where he was drawing a circle and going over it repeatedly without lifting his stylus. Conway found himself watching the pad as well, and abruptly he stopped talking.

Suddenly they were staring at him with all of their eyes, and Skempton said, "I'm sorry, Doctor, does my doodling distract you?"

"To the contrary, sir," Conway said, smiling, "you have helped a lot."

Ignoring the Colonel's baffled expression, Conway went on, "Our original theory was that a sublight vessel with the configuration of a rotating wheeltype space station suffered a catastrophic malfunction or collision which carried away its hub-mounted propulsion and navigation systems, and jarred the rim structure apart; the subsequent dispersal of the suspended animation containers was aided by the centrifugal force which furnished their ship with artificial gravity. But the number of sections found just before I left the area were more than enough to form three complete Wheels and, because I have been bothered by the fact that no head segments have been found so far, I have decided to discard the Wheel or multiple Wheel theory in favor of the more simple configuration suggested by the Colonel's sketch of a continuous—"

"Doctor," Thornnastor broke in firmly. As the Diagnostician-in-Charge of Pathology it had a tendency toward single-mindedness where its specialty was concerned. "Kindly describe in detail and give me the physiological classification of this life-form and, of course, your assessment of the number of casualties we will be required to treat. And are specimens of this life-form available for study?"

Conway felt his face reddening as he made an admission no Senior Physician on the staff of Sector General should ever have to make. He said, "We cannot classify this life-form with complete certainty, sir. But I have brought you two cadavers in the hope that you may be able to do so. As I have already said, the survivors are still inside their suspended animation compartments and the relatively few who did not survive are in a badly damaged condition—in several pieces, in fact."

Thornnastor made untranslatable noises which probably signified approval, then it said, "Had they not been in pieces, I would soon have rendered them so. But the fact that neither Murchison nor yourself are sure of their classification surprises and intrigues me, Doctor. Surely you are able to form a few tentative conclusions?"

Conway was suddenly glad that Prilicla was still on board *Rhabwar* because his embarrassment would have given the little empath a bad fit of the shakes. He said, "Yes, sir. The being we examined was a warm-blooded oxygen breather with the type of basic metabolism associated with that physiological grouping. The cadaver was massive, measuring approximately twenty meters in length and three meters in diameter, excluding projecting appendages. Physically it resembles the DBLF Kelgian life-form, but many times larger and possessing a leathery tegument rather than the silver fur of the Kelgians. Like the DBLFs it is multipedal, but the manipulatory appendages are positioned in a single row along the back.

"There were twenty-one of these dorsal limbs, all showing evidence of early evolutionary specialization. Six of them were long, heavy, and claw-tipped and were obviously evolved for defense since the being was a herbivore, and there were fifteen in five groups of three spaced between the six heavier tentacles. Each of the thinner limbs terminated in four digits, two of which were opposable, and were manipulatory appendages originally evolved for gathering and transferring food to the mouths, of which there are three on each flank opening into three stomachs. Two additional orifices on each side open into a very large and complex lung. The structure inside these breathing orifices suggests that expelled air could be interrupted and modulated to produce intelligence-bearing sounds. On the underside were three openings used for the elimination of wastes.

"The mechanism of reproduction was unclear," he continued, "and the specimen showed evidence of possessing both male and female genitalia on the forward and rear extremities respectively. The brain, if it was the brain, took the form of a cable of nerve ganglia with localized swellings in three places, running longitudinally through the cadaver like a central core. There was another and much thinner nerve cable running parallel to the thicker core, but below it and about twenty-five centimeters from the underside. Positioned close to each extremity were two sets of three eyes, two of which were mounted dorsally and two on the forward and rear flanks. They were recessed but capable of limited extension and together gave the being complete and continuous vision vertically and horizontally. The type and positioning of the visual equipment and appendages suggest that it evolved on a very unfriendly world.

"Our tentative classification of the being," Conway ended, "was an incomplete CRLT."

"Incomplete?" Thornnastor said.

"Yes, sir," Conway said. "The cadaver we examined had sustained minimum damage since it had died during a slow decompression while in suspended animation. We could be wrong, but there were signs of some kind of radical surgery having taken place, a double removal of what may have been the head and tail of the being. This was not a traumatic amputation caused by the disaster to their ship, but a deliberate procedure which may have been required to fit the being into its suspended animation container for the colonization attempt. The body tegument overall is thick and very tough, but at the extremities the only protection is a hard, transparent layer of organic material, and the underlying protrusions, fissures, orifices, and musculature look raw. This suggests—"

"Conway," O'Mara said sharply, with a glance toward the suddenly paling Colonel. "With respect to Thornnastor, you have moved too quickly from the general to the particular. Please confine yourself at this stage to a simple statement of the problem and your proposed solution."

Colonel Skempton was the man responsible for making Sector General function as an organization—but, as he was fond of telling his medical friends when they started to talk shop in grisly detail, he was a glorified bookkeeper, not a bloody surgeon! The trouble was that there was no way Conway could state his problem simply without offending the sensibilities of the overly squeamish Colonel.

"Simply," Conway said, "the problem is a gigantic, wormlike entity, perhaps five kilometers or more in length, which has been chopped into many hundreds of pieces. The indicated treatment is to join the pieces together again, in the correct order."

The Colonel's stylus stopped in mid-doodle, Thornnastor made a loud, untranslatable sound, and O'Mara, normally a phlegmatic individual, said with considerable vehemence, "Conway, you are not considering bringing that—that Midgard Serpent to the hospital?"

Conway shook his head. "The hospital is much too small to handle it."

"And so," Skempton said, looking up for the first time, "is your ambulance ship."

Before Conway could reply, Thornnastor said, "I find it difficult to believe that the entity you describe could survive such radical amputation. However, if Prilicla and yourself state that the separate sections so far recovered are alive, then I must accept it. But have you considered the possibility that it is a group entity, similar to the Telphi life-form which are stupid as individuals but highly intelligent as a gestalt? Physical fragmentation in those circumstances would be slightly more credible, Doctor."

"Yes, sir, and we have not yet discarded that possibility—" Conway began.

"Very well, Doctor," O'Mara broke in dryly. "You may restate the problem in less simple form."

The problem . . . thought Conway.

He began by asking them to visualize the vast, alien ship as it had been before the disaster—not the multiple Wheel shape first discussed but a great, continuous, open coil of constant diameter and similar in configuration to the shape on the Colonel's pad. The separate turns of the coil had been laced together by an open lat-ticework of metal beams which held the vessel together as a rigid unit and provided the structural support needed along the thrust axis during take-off, acceleration, and landing. Assembled in orbit, the ship had been approximately five hundred meters in diameter and close on a mile long, with its power and propulsion system at one end of an axial support structure and the automatic guidance system and sensors at the other.

The exact nature of the accident or malfunction was not yet known, but judging by the observed effects it had been caused by a collision with a large natural object which, striking the vessel head-on, had taken out the guidance system forward, the axial structure, and the stern thrusters. The shock of the collision had shaken the great, rotating coil into its component suspended animation com-partments, and centrifugal force had done the rest.

"This being—or beings—is so physiologically constituted," Conway went on, "that to assist it we must first rebuild its ship and land it successfully. Fitting the pieces together again can be done most easily in weightless conditions. The fact that the twenty-meter sections of the coil have flown apart but retained their positions with respect to each other will greatly assist the reassembly opera-tion—"

"Wait, wait," the Colonel said. "I cannot see this operation being possible, Doctor. For one thing, you will need a very potent com-puter indeed to work out the trajectories of those expanding sections accurately enough to return them to their original positions in this—this jigsaw puzzle—and the equipment needed to reassemble it would be—"

"Captain Fletcher says it is possible," Conway said firmly. "Piec-ing together the remains of an extraterrestrial ship has been done before, and much valuable knowledge was gained in the process. Admittedly, on previous occasions there were no living survivors to be pieced together as well and the work was on a much smaller scale."

"Much smaller," O'Mara said dryly. "Captain Fletcher is a the-oretician and *Rhabwar* is his first operational command. Is he happy ordering three scoutship flotillas around?"

The Chief Psychologist was considering the problem in the terms of his own specialty, Conway knew, and as usual O'Mara was a jump ahead of everyone else.

"He seems to enjoy worrying about it," Conway said carefully, "and there are no overt signs of megalomania."

O'Mara nodded and sat back in his chair.

But the Colonel could jump to correct conclusions as well, if not always as quickly as the Chief Psychologist. He said, "Surely, O'Mara, you are not suggesting that *Rhabwar* direct this operation? It's too damned big, and expensive. It has to be referred up to—"

"There isn't time for committee decisions," Conway began.

"—the Federation Council," the Colonel finished. "And anyway, did Fletcher tell you how he proposed fitting this puzzle together?"

Conway nodded. "Yes, sir. It is a matter of basic design philosophy . . ." Captain Fletcher was of the opinion—an opinion shared by the majority of the Federation's top designers—that any piece of machinery beyond a certain degree of complexity, be it a simple groundcar or a spaceship one kilometer long, required an enormous amount of prior design work, planning and tooling long before the first simple parts and subassemblies could become three-dimensional metal on someone's workbench. The number of detail and assembly drawings, wiring diagrams, and so on for even a small spaceship was mind-staggering, and the purpose of all this paper-work was simply to instruct beings *of average intelligence* how to manufacture and fit together the pieces of the jigsaw without knowing, or perhaps even caring, anything about the completed picture.

If normal Earth-human, Tralthan, Illensan, and Melfan practice was observed—and the engineers of those races and many others insisted that there was no easier way—then those drawings and the components they described must include instructions, identifying symbols, to guide the builders in the correct placing of these parts within the jigsaw.

Possibly there were extraterrestrial species which used more exotic methods of identifying components before assembly such as tagging each part with an olfactory or tactile coding system, but this, considering the tremendous size of the coil ship and the number of parts to be identified and joined, would represent a totally unnecessary complication unless there were physiological reasons for doing things the hard way.

The cadaver had possessed eyes which operated within the normal visible spectrum, and Captain Fletcher was sure that the alien shipbuilders would do things the easy way by marking the surface of the components with identifying symbols which could be read at a glance. Following a detailed examination of a damaged suspended animation cylinder and the remains of its supporting framework, Fletcher found that the system of identification used was groups of symbols vibro-etched into the metal, and that adjoining components bore the same type and sequence of symbols except for the final letter or number.

"Clearly they think, and put their spaceships together, much the same as we do," Conway concluded.

"I see," the Colonel said. He sat forward in his chair. "But decoding those symbols and fitting the parts together will take a lot of time."

"Or a lot of extra help," Conway said.

Skempton sat back, shaking his head. Thornnastor was silent also, but the slow, impatient thumping of its massive feet indicated that it was not likely to remain so for long. It was O'Mara who spoke first.

"What assistance will you need, Doctor?"

Conway looked gratefully at the Chief Psychologist for getting straight to the point as well as for the implied support. But he knew that O'Mara would withdraw that support without hesitation if he had the slightest doubt about Conway's ability to handle the problem. If Conway was to be confirmed in this assignment, he would have to convince O'Mara that he knew exactly what he was doing. He cleared his throat.

"First," he said, "we should initiate an immediate search for the vessel's home world so that we can learn as much as possible about this entity's culture, environment, and food requirements, as well as having somewhere to put it when the rescue is complete. It is almost certain that the disaster caused a large deviation in the coilship's course, and it is possible that the vessel suffered a guidance malfunction not associated with the accident which fragmented it, and it has already overshot the target world. This would complicate the search and increase the number of units conducting it."

Before the Colonel could react, Conway went on quickly, "I also need a search of the Federation Archives. For many centuries before the Federation came into being there were species who possessed the startravel capability and did a lot of independent exploration. There is a slight chance that one of them may have encountered or heard reports of an entity resembling an intelligent Midgard Serpent—"

He broke off, then for Thornnastor's benefit he explained that the Midgard Serpent was a creature of Earth-human mythology, an enormous snake which was supposed to have encircled the planet with its tail in its mouth. Thornnastor thanked him and expressed its relief that the being was mythological.

"Until now," the Colonel said sourly.

"Second," Conway went on, "comes the problem of rapid retrieval and placement of the scattered suspended animation cylinders. Many more scoutships will be required, supported by all of the available specialists in e-t languages and technical notation systems, and computer facilities capable of analyzing this material. A large, ship-borne translation computer should be able to handle the job—"

"That means *Descartes!*" Skempton protested.

"—In the time remaining to us," Conway resumed, "and I hear *Descartes* recently completed its first contact program on Dwerla and is free. But the third and most technically difficult part of the problem is the reassembly. For this we need fleet auxiliaries with the engineering facilities and space construction personnel capable of rapidly rebuilding those parts of the alien vessel's supporting framework which cannot be salvaged from the wreckage. Ideally the people concerned should be experienced Tralthan and Hudlar space construction teams.

"Four," he continued, allowing no time for objections, "we need a ship capable of coordinating the reassembly operation, and mounting a large number of tractor and pressor beam batteries with officers highly trained in their use. This will reduce the risk of collision in the assembly area between the retrieved sections and our own ships. The coordinating vessel will have its own computer capable of handling the logistic—"

"*Vespasian,* he wants," Skempton said dully.

"Yes, its tactical computer would be ideal," Conway replied. "It also has the necessary tractor and pressor batteries and, I believe, a very large cargo lock in case I have to withdraw some of the CRLTs from their suspended animation compartments. Remember, several segments of the entity were destroyed and surgery may be required in these areas to close the gaps. But until we know a great deal more about this entity's physiology and environment I have no clear idea of the type and quantity of medical assistance which will be needed."

"At last," Thornnastor growled through its translator, "you are about to discuss the needs of the patient."

"The delay was intentional, sir," Conway said, "since we must repair the ship before we can help the occupant. Regarding this entity, or entities, Pathologist Murchison and myself have examined one cadaver and we seek confirmation of our preliminary findings and as much additional physiological data as you can provide from the specimens brought back in *Tyrell,* and from the contents of the intravenous infusion equipment which is used, apparently, to induce, extend, and reverse the suspended animation process. Specifically, we require much more information on the nervous system, the linkages to the voluntary and involuntary musculature, the degree and rapidity of tissue regeneration we can expect if surgical intervention is necessary and additional data on the transparent material which covers and protects the raw areas at the forward and rear extremities. Naturally, sir, this information is required the day before yesterday."

"Naturally," Thornnastor growled. Its six elephantine feet, which had been silent while Conway was speaking, resumed their slow thumping. Clearly the Tralthan was eager to go to work on those specimens of the completely new life-form.

O'Mara waited for precisely three seconds, then he scowled up at Conway and said. "And that is all you require, Doctor?"

Conway nodded. "For the present."

Colonel Skempton leaned forward and said caustically, "*For the present* he needs the services of a Sector subfleet, including *Descartes* and *Vespasian*. Before we can recommend the deployment of so many Service units we should refer the matter to the Federation Council for—" He broke off because the thumping of Thornnastor's feet was making conversation difficult.

"Your pardon, Colonel," the Tralthan said, "but it seems to me that if we refer this matter to the Council they will ponder on it at great length and then decide to make it the responsibility of the beings best able to understand and solve the problem, who are the entities comprising the technical and medical crew of *Rhabwar*. The special ambulance ship program was designed to deal with the unexpected, and the fact that this problem is unexpectedly large is beside the point.

"This is an entity, or entities, of a hitherto unknown species," it went on, "and I recommend that Senior Physician Conway be given the assistance he requires to rescue and treat it. However, I have no objection to you recommending this course and referring the matter to the Council for discussion and ratification, and for amendment should they come up with a better idea. Well, Colonel?"

Skempton shook his head. He said doggedly, "It's wrong, I know it's wrong, for a newly appointed ship commander and a medic to be given so much authority. But the *Rhabwar* people are the only ones who know what they are doing at the moment. Reluctantly, I agree. O'Mara?"

All their eyes, the Colonel's and Conway's two and Thornnastor's four, were on the Chief Psychologist, who kept his steadily on Conway. Finally he spoke.

"If you have nothing else to say, Doctor," he said dryly, "I suggest you return to *Rhabwar* as quickly as possible before the area becomes so congested that you can't find your own ship."

*   *   *

The reaction time of the Monitor Corps to an emergency large or small was impressively fast. In *Tyrell*'s forward viewscreen the area resembled a small, untidy star cluster in which *Rhabwar*'s beacon flashed at its center like a short-term variable. Apart from acknowledging their arrival and giving them permission to lock on, Fletcher did not speak to them because, he explained, fifteen more scoutships had arrived unexpectedly and he was busy fitting them into his

retrieval program. For this reason Conway did not get an opportunity to tell him about the other unexpected things which were
about to happen until he was back on board the ambulance ship,
and by that time it was too late.

"*Rhabwar,*" a voice said from the wall speaker as Conway entered Control, "this is the survey and cultural contact vessel *Descartes,* Colonel Okaussie commanding. I'm told you have work for
us, Major Fletcher."

"Well, yes, sir," the Captain said. He looked appealingly at Conway, then went on, "If I might respectfully suggest, sir, that your
translation specialists—"

"I'd rather you didn't," Colonel Okaussie broke in. "Respectfully
suggest, I mean. When I know as much about this situation as you
do I'll accept suggestions, respectful or otherwise. But until then,
Major, stop wasting time and tell me what you want us to do."

"Yes, sir," Fletcher said. Speaking quickly, concisely, and, out of
habit, respectfully, he did just that. Then a few seconds after he
broke contact the radar screen showed a new trace which was even
larger than *Descartes.* It identified itself as the Hudlar-crewed depot
ship *Motann,* a star-going engineering complex normally used to
bring technical assistance to vessels whose hyperdrive generators had
failed noncatastrophically leaving them stranded in normal space
between the stars. Its captain, who was not a Monitor Corps officer,
was also happy to take his instructions from Fletcher. But then an
even larger blip appeared on the screen, indicating that a very large
ship indeed had just emerged from hyperspace. Automatically Lieutenant Haslam fed the bearing to the telescope and tapped for maximum magnification.

The tremendous, awe-inspiring sight of an Emperor-class bat-
tlecruiser filled the screen.

"*Rhabwar,* this is *Vespasian* . . ."

Fletcher paled visibly at the thought of giving instructions to
the godlike entity who would be in command of *that* ship, whose
communications officer was relaying the compliments of Fleet Commander Dermod and a request for full vision contact as soon as
convenient. Conway, who had not had time to tell the Captain what
to expect because it was already happening, got to his feet.

"I'll be in the Casualty Deck lab," he said. Grinning, he reached across to clap Fletcher reassuringly on the shoulder and added, "You're doing fine, Captain. Just remember that, a long, long time ago, the Fleet Commander was a major, too."

The conversation between Fletcher and the Fleet Commander, complete with visuals, was on the Casualty Deck's repeater when he arrived, but the sound was muted because Prilicla was on another frequency giving instructions to one of the scoutship medical officers regarding a cadaver the other had found and which Murchison wanted brought in for examination. Murchison and Naydrad were still working on the first specimen, which had been reduced to what seemed to be its component parts.

Murchison nodded toward the repeater screen and said, "You seem to have been given everything you needed. Was O'Mara in a good mood?"

"His usual sarcastic, helpful self," Conway said, moving to join her at the dissection table. "Do we know anything more about this outsize boa constrictor?"

"I don't know what *we* know," she said crossly, "but *I* know a little more and feel more than a little confused by the knowledge. For instance..."

The thick pencil of nerve ganglia with its localized bunchings and swellings which ran through the center of the cylindrical body was, almost certainly, the CRLT's equivalent of a brain, and the idea of a missing head or tail was beginning to seem unlikely—especially since the transparent material which covered the raw areas fore and aft was, despite its appearance, equally as tough as the being's leathery body tegument.

She had been successful in tracing the nerve connections between the core swellings and the eyes, mouths, and manipulatory appendages, and from both ends of the axial nerve bundle to the puzzling system of muscles which underlay the raw areas on the forward and rear faces of the creature.

The specimen appeared to be male—at least, the female genitalia at the other end were shrunken and seemed to be in a condition of early atrophy—and she had identified the male sperm generator and the method of transfer to a female.

"...There is evidence of unnatural organ displacement," she went on, "which can only be caused by weightlessness. Gravity, real or artificial, is a physiological necessity for this life-form. During hibernation the absence of weight would not be fatal, but weight-lessness while conscious would cause severe nausea, sensory im-pairment, and, I feel sure, intense mental and physical distress."

Which meant that the being would have to be in position on the rim of its rotating vessel or affected by natural gravity, that of its target world, when it was revived. *It isn't a doctor this patient needed,* Conway thought wryly, *it's a miracle worker!*

"With the Captain's help," Murchison continued, "we have es-tablished that the medication which produces and or extends the hibernation anesthesia occupies the larger volume of a dispenser mechanism which also contains a smaller quantity of the complex organic secretion which can only be the reviver. Fletcher also traced the input to the automatic sensor and actuator which switches the mechanism from the hibernation to the resuscitation mode and found that it reacted to the combined presence of gravity and ex-ternal pressure. The same actuator mechanism is also responsible for ejecting the endplates of its hibernation compartment which would enable the CRLT to disembark.

"Sooner or later we're going to have to revive one of these things," she ended worriedly, "and we'll have to be very sure that we know what we are doing."

Conway was already out of his spacesuit and climbing into his surgical coveralls. He said, "Anything in particular you'd like me to do?"

*   *   *

They worked on the cadaver while the hours flickered past on the time display to become days, then weeks. From time to time a terse, subspace message from Thornnastor would arrive confirming their findings or suggesting new avenues of investigation, but even so it seemed that their rate of progress was slow to nonexistent.

Occasionally they would look up at the Control Room repeater, but with decreasing frequency. Fletcher, a Hudlar space construction specialist, and variously qualified Monitor Corps officers were usu-ally showing each other pieces of twisted metal via their vision chan-nels, comparing identification symbols and talking endlessly about them. No doubt it was all vitally important stuff, but it made boring listening. Besides, they had their own organic jigsaw puzzle to worry about.

A pleasant break in the routine would occur when they had to go outside to look at one of the other cadavers which had been brought in and attached to the outer hull, there being room for only one CRLT at a time inside *Rhabwar*. On these occasions the investigations were conducted in airless conditions and only the organic material which was of special interest to them was excised for later study. As a result they found a bewildering variety of age and sex combinations which seemed to indicate that the older CRLTs were well-developed males whose raw areas at each extremity had a brownish coloration, while the younger beings were clearly female and the areas concerned were a livid pink under the transparent covering.

Once there was a break in the investigative routine which was not pleasant. For several hours they had been studying a flaccid, purplish lump of something which might have been the organic trigger for the being's hibernation phase, and making very little progress with it, when Prilicla broke into their angry, impatient silence.

"Friend Murchison," the empath said, "is feeling tired."

"I'm not," the pathologist said, with a yawn which threatened to dislocate her firm but beautifully formed lower mandible. "At least, I wasn't until you reminded me."

"As are you, friend Conway—" Prilicla began, when there was an interruption. The furry features of Surgeon-Lieutenant Krach-Yul replaced the pieces of alien hardware which had been filling the repeater screen.

"Doctor Conway," the Orligian medic said, "I have to report an accident. Two Earth-human DBDGs, simple fractures, no decompression damage—"

"Very well," said Conway, clenching his teeth on a yawn. "Now's your chance to get in some more other-species surgical experience."

"—And a Hudlar engineer, physiological classification FROB," Krach-Yul went on. "It has sustained a deep, incised, and lacerated wound which has been quickly but inadequately treated by the being itself. There has been a considerable loss of body fluid and associated internal pressure, diminished sensoria, and—"

"Coming," Conway said. To Murchison he muttered, "Don't wait up for me."

While *Tyrell* was taking him to the scene of the accident, an area where three of the coilship sections were being fitted together, Conway reviewed his necessarily scant surgical experience with the Hudlar life-form.

They were a species who rarely took sick, and then only during preadolescence, and they were fantastically resistant to physical injury, with eyes which were protected by a hard, transparent membrane, tegument like flexible armor, and no body orifices except for the temporary ones opened for mating and birth.

The FROBs were ideally suited to space construction projects. Their home planet, Hudlar, pulled four Earth gravities, and its atmospheric pressure—if that dense, soupy mixture of oxygen, inerts, and masses of microscopic animal and vegetable nutrient in suspension could be called an atmosphere—was seven times Earth-normal. At home they absorbed the food-laden air through their incredibly tough yet porous skin, while offplanet they sprayed themselves regularly and frequently with nutrient paint. Their six flexible and immensely strong limbs terminated in four-digited hands which, when the fingers were curled inward and the knuckles presented to the ground, served also as feet.

Environmentally, the Hudlars were a very adaptable species, because the physiological features which protected them against their own planet's crushing gravity and pressure also enabled them to work comfortably in any noncorrosive atmosphere of lesser pressure right down to and including the vacuum of space. The only item of equipment a Hudlar space construction engineer needed, apart from its tools, was a communicator which took the form of a small, air-filled blister enclosing its speaking membrane and a two-way radio.

Conway had not bothered to ask if there was an FROB medic on the Hudlar ship. Curative surgery had been a completely alien concept to that virtually indestructible species until they had joined the Federation and learned about places like Sector General, so that medically trained Hudlars were about as rare outside the hospital as physically injured ones inside it.

Captain Nelson placed *Tyrell* within fifty meters of the scene of the accident. Conway headed for the injured Hudlar. Krach-Yul had already reached the Earth-human casualties, one of whom was blaming himself loudly and unprintably for causing the accident and tying up the suit frequency in the process.

Conway gathered that the two Earth-humans had been saved from certain death by being crushed between two slowly closing ship sections by the Hudlar interposing its enormously strong body, which would have escaped without injury if the jagged-edged stump of an external bracing member had not snagged one of the FROB's limbs close to the point where it joined the body.

When Conway arrived, the Hudlar was gripping the injured limb with three of its hands, tourniquet fashion, while the two free hands remaining were trying to hold the edges of the wound together—unsuccessfully. Tiny, misshapen globules of blood were forming between its fingers to drift weightlessly away, steaming furiously. It could not talk because its air bag had been lost, leaving its speaking membranes to vibrate silently in the vacuum.

Conway withdrew a limb sleeve-piece, the largest size he carried, from his Hudlar medical kit and motioned for the casualty to bare the wound.

He could see that it was a deep wound by the way the dark red bubbles grew suddenly larger before they broke away, but he was able to snap the sleeve-piece in position before too much blood was lost. Even so there was a considerable leakage around both ends of the sleeve as the Hudlar's high internal pressure tried to empty it of body fluids. Conway quickly attached circlips at each end of the sleeve and began to tighten one while the Hudlar itself tightened the other. Gradually the fluid loss slowed and then ceased, the casualty's hands drifted away from the injured limb, and its speaking membrane ceased its silent vibrating. The Hudlar had lost consciousness.

Ten minutes later the Hudlar was inside *Tyrell*'s cargo lock and Conway was using his scanner to search for internal damage caused by the traumatic decompression. The longer he looked the less he liked what he saw, and as he was concluding the examination Krach-Yul joined him.

"The Earth-humans are simple fracture cases, Doctor," the Orligian reported. "Before setting the bones I wondered if you, as a member of their own species, would prefer to—"

"And rob you of the chance to increase your other-species experience?" Conway broke in. "No, Doctor, you treat them. They're on antipain, I take it, and there is no great degree of urgency?"

"Yes, Doctor," Krach-Yul said.

"Good," Conway said, "because I have another job for you— looking after this Hudlar until you can move it to Sector General. You will need a nutrient sprayer from the Hudlar ship, then arrange with Captain Nelson to increase the air pressure and artificial gravity in this cargo lock to levels as close to Hudlar-normal as he can manage. Treatment will consist of spraying the casualty with nutrient at hourly intervals and checking on the cardiac activity, and periodically easing the tightness of the sleeve-piece if your scanner indicates a serious reduction of circulation to the injured limb. While you are doing these things you will wear *two* gravity neutralizers. If you were wearing one and it failed under four-G conditions there would be another seriously injured casualty, you.

"Normally I would travel with this patient," he went on, stifling a yawn, "but I have to be available in case something urgent develops with the CRLT. Hudlar surgery can be tricky so I'll tape some notes on this one for the operating team, including the suggestion that you be allowed to observe if you wish to do so."

"Very much," Krach-Yul said, "and thank you, Doctor."

"And now I'll leave you with your patients and return to *Rhabwar*," Conway said. Silently he added, *to sleep.*

Tyrell was absent for eight days and was subsequently assigned to courier duty, taking specimens to Sector General and returning with information, advice, and detailed lists of questions regarding the progress of their work from Thornnastor. The great, spiral jigsaw puzzle which was the alien ship was beginning to take shape—or more accurately, to take a large number of semicircular and quarter-circular shapes—as the hibernation cylinders were identified, positioned, and coupled. Many of the cylinders were still missing because they had been so seriously damaged that their occupants had died or they had still to be found and retrieved by the scout-ships.

Conway was worried because the incomplete coilship and the

motley fleet of Monitor Corps vessels and auxiliaries were on a collision course with the nearby sun, which was growing perceptibly brighter every day. It was clearly evident that the growth rate of the alien vessel was much less perceptible. When he worried about it aloud to the Fleet Commander, Dermod told him politely to mind his own medical business.

Then a few days later *Tyrell* returned with information which made it very much his medical business.

Vespasian's communications officer, who was usually a master of the diplomatic delaying tactic, put him through to the Fleet Commander in a matter of seconds instead of forcing him to climb slowly up the ship's entire chain of command. This was not due to any sudden increase in Conway's standing with the senior Monitor Corps officer, but simply that while Conway was trying to reach Dermod, the Fleet Commander was trying to contact the Doctor.

It was Dermod who spoke first, with the slight artificiality of tone which told Conway that not only was the other in a hurry and under pressure but that there were other people present beyond the range of the vision pickup. He said, "Doctor, there is a serious problem regarding the final assembly phase and I need your help. You are already concerned over the limited time remaining to us and, frankly, I was unwilling to discuss the problem with you until I was able to present it, and the solution, in its entirety. This can now be done, in reverse order, preferably. My immediate requirement is for another capital ship. *Claudius* is available and—"

"Why—" Conway began, shaking his head in momentary confusion. He had been about to list his own problems and requirements and found himself suddenly on the receiving end.

"Very well, Doctor, I'll state the problem first," the Fleet Commander said, frowning as he nodded to someone out of sight. The screen blanked for a few seconds, then it displayed a black field on which there was a thick, vertical gray line. At the lower end of the line a fat red box appeared and on the opposite end a blue circle. Dermod went on briskly, "We now have a pretty accurate idea of the configuration of the alien ship, and I am showing you a very simple representation because I haven't time to do otherwise right now.

"The ship had a central stem, the gray line," Dermod explained, "with the power plant and thrusters represented by the red box aft and the forward-mounted sensors and navigation systems shown as a blue circle. Since the ship's occupant was unconscious, all of these systems were fully automatic. The stem also provided the anchoring points for the structure which supported the inhabited coil. You will see that the main supports are angled forward to compensate for stresses encountered while the vessel was under power and during the landing maneuver."

A forest of branches grew suddenly from the stem, making it look like a squat, cylindrical Christmas tree standing in its red tub and with a bright-blue fairy light at the top. Then the continuous spiral of linked hibernation compartments was attached to the ends of the branches, followed by the spacing members which separated each loop of the coil, and the picture lost all resemblance to a tree.

"The coil diameter remains constant throughout at just under five hundred meters," the Fleet Commander's voice continued. "Originally there were twelve turns of the coil and, with each hibernation cylinder measuring twenty meters in length, this means there were roughly eighty hibernating CRLTs in every loop of the coil and close on one thousand of the beings on the complete ship.

"Every loop of the coil was separated by a distance of seventy meters, so that the total height of the coilship was just over eight hundred meters. We were puzzled by this separation since it would have been structurally much simpler laying one on top of the other, but we now believe that the open coil configuration was designed both to reduce and localize meteorite collision damage and remove the majority of the hibernation compartments as far as possible from radiation leakage from the reactor at the stern. While encased in its rather unusual vessel we think the creature traveled tail-first so that its thinking end was at the stern to initiate disembarkation following the landing. Unfortunately, the stern section had to be heavier and more rigid than the forward structure since it had to support the weight of the vessel during deceleration and landing, and so it was the stern which sustained most of the damage when the collision occurred, and most of the CRLT casualties were from the sternmost loop of the coil."

According to *Vespasian*'s computer's reconstruction, the vessel had been in direct head-on collision with a large meteor, and the closing velocities involved had been such that the whole central stem had been obliterated, as if an old-time projectile hand weapon had been used to remove the core of an apple. Only a few scraps of debris from the power unit and guidance system remained—enough for identification purposes but not for reconstruction—and the shock of the collision had shaken the overall coil structure apart.

On the screen the widely scattered hibernation compartments came together again into a not quite complete coil: There were several sections missing, particularly near the stern. Then the stem, its power and guidance systems, and the entire support structure disappeared from the display leaving only the incomplete coil.

"The central core of that vessel is a mass of pulverized wreckage many light-years away," Dermod continued briskly, "and we have decided that trying to salvage and reconstruct it would be an unnecessary waste of time and materiel when there is a simpler solution available. This requires the presence of a second Emperor-class vessel to—"

"But why do you want—?" Conway began.

"I am in the process of explaining why, Doctor," the Fleet Commander said sharply. The image on the screen changed again and he went on, "The two capital ships and *Descartes* will take up positions in close line-astern formation and lock onto each other with matched tractor and pressor beams. In effect this will convert the three ships into a single, rigid structure which will replace the alien vessel's central stem, and the branching members which supported the coil will also be nonmaterial but equally rigid tractors and pressors.

"In the landing configuration *Vespasian* will be bottom of the heap," Dermod continued, with a tinge of pride creeping into his voice. "Our thrusters are capable of supporting the other two ships and the alien coilship during deceleration and landing, with *Claudius* and *Descartes* furnishing lateral stability and taking some of the load with surface-directed pressors. After touchdown, the power reserves of all three vessels will be sufficient to hold everything together for at least twelve hours, which should be long enough, I hope, for the alien to leave its ship. If we can find somewhere to put it, that is."

The image flicked off to be replaced by the face of the Fleet

Commander. "So you see, Doctor, I need *Claudius* to complete this—this partly nonmaterial structure and to test its practicability in weightless conditions before working out the stresses it will have to undergo during the landing maneuver. Of equal urgency are the calculations needed to extend the combined hyperspace envelope of the three ships to enclose the coil and Jump with it out of here before this damn sun gets too close."

Conway was silent for a moment, inwardly cringing at the thought of some of the things which could go catastrophically wrong when three linked ships performed a simultaneous Jump. But he could not voice his concern because ship maneuvers were most decidedly the Fleet Commander's and not the Doctor's business, and Dermod would tell him so with justification. Besides, Conway had his own problems and right now he needed help with them.

"Sir," he said awkwardly, "your proposed solution is ingenious, and thank you for the explanation. But my original question was not regarding the reason why you wanted *Claudius*, but why you needed my help in the matter."

For a moment the Fleet Commander stared at him blankly, then his expression softened as he said, "My apologies, Doctor, if I seemed a trifle impatient with you. The position is this. Under the new Federation Council directive covering extraterrestrial rescue operations by *Rhabwar*, I am required in a large-scale combined medical and military operation of this kind to obtain your approval for additional personnel and materiel, specifically another capital ship. I assume it is forthcoming?"

"Of course," Conway said.

Dermod nodded pleasantly despite his obvious embarrassment, but the lines of impatience were beginning to gather again around his mouth as he said, "It will be sufficient if you tape a few words as the physician-in-charge of the case to the effect that *Claudius* is urgently required to ensure the present safety and continued well-being of your patient. But you were calling me, Doctor. Can I help you?"

"Yes, sir," Conway said, and went on quickly, "You have been concentrating on joining the coilship sections in proper sequence. Now I have to begin putting the patient together, with special emphasis on the joining of segments which are not in sequence. That is, the ones which were separated by the hibernation compartments whose occupants died. We are now sure that the being is a group entity whose individual members are independently intelligent and may be capable of linking up naturally to their adjoining group members when the conditions are right. This is the theory, sir, but it requires experimental verification.

"The entities who are out of sequence could pose serious problems," Conway concluded. "They will have to be removed from their hibernation compartments and presented to each other so that I may determine the extent of the surgical work involved in reassembling the group entity."

"Sooner you than me, Doctor," Dermod said with a brief grimace of sympathy. "But what exactly do you need?"

He is like O'Mara, Conway thought, *impatient with confused thinking*. He said, "I need two small ships to bring in the CRLT segments I shall specify and to return them to their places in the coil. Also a large cargo hold which can accommodate two of the hibernation cylinders joined end to end and the two beings which will be withdrawn from them. The hold is to be fitted with artificial gravity grids and nonmaterial restraints in case the conscious CRLTs become confused and aggressive, and personnel to operate this equipment. I know this will mean using the cargo lock and hold in one of the largest ships, but I require only the hold; the vessel can go about its assigned duties."

"Thank you," the Fleet Commander said dryly, then paused while someone offscreen spoke quietly to him. He went on, "You may use the forward hold in *Descartes*, which will also provide the personnel and its two planetary landers for fetching and carrying your CRLTs. Is there anything else?"

Conway shook his head. "Only an item of news, sir. The Federation archivists think they have found the CRLTs home planet, although it is no longer habitable due to major orbital changes and associated large-scale seismic disturbances. The Department of Colonization has a new home for them in mind and will give us the coordinates as soon as they are absolutely sure that the environment and the CRLTs physiological classification are compatible. So we have somewhere to take Humpty-Dumpty when we've put it together again.

"However," Conway ended very seriously, "all the indications are that this was not simply a colony ship which ran into trouble, but a planetary lifeboat carrying the last surviving members of the race."

*　　*　　*

Conway stared anxiously around the enormous interior of *Descartes*'s forward hold and thought that if he had known there were going to be so many sightseers he would have asked for a much larger operating theater. Fortunately one of them was the ship's commanding officer, Colonel Okaussie, who kept the others from getting in the way and ensured that the area of deck containing the two joined hibernation cylinders was clear except for Murchison, Naydrad, Prilicla, Fletcher, and Okaussie himself. Conway was sure of one thing: Whether the initial CRLT link-up attempt was a success or a failure, there would be no chance at all of keeping the result a secret.

He wet his lips and said quietly, "Uncouple the cylinders and move the joined faces three meters apart. Bring the artificial gravity up to Earth-normal, slowly, and the atmosphere to normal pressure and composition for the life-form. You have the figures."

The fabric of his lightweight spacesuit began to settle against Conway's body and there was mounting pressure against the soles of his feet as he watched the facing ends of the two cylinders. Then abruptly the circular endplates jumped out of their slots to clank onto the deck and come to rest like enormous, spinning coins. The hibernation cylinders were now open at both ends, enabling the two CRLTs to move toward or away from each other, or from one compartment to the next.

"Neat!" Fletcher said. "When the coilship is spinning in its space-traveling mode, centrifugal force holds the being against the outboard surface of the cylinder, and when the spin ceases in the presence of real gravity and an atmosphere the airtight seals drop away, the individual compartments are opened to all of the others and the beastie, the complete group entity, that is, exits by working down the stern-facing wall until all of it reaches the surface. The gravity and pressure sensors are linked to the medication reservoirs,

Doctor, so you have just reproduced the conditions for resuscitation following a planetary landing."

Conway nodded. He said, "Prilicla, can you detect anything?"

"Not yet, friend Conway."

They moved closer so as to be able to look into the two opened cylinders, dividing their attention between the occupants who were lying flaccidly with their dorsal manipulators hanging limply along their sides. Then one of the enormous, tubular bodies began to quiver, and suddenly they were both moving ponderously toward each other.

"Move back," Conway said. "Prilicla?"

"Consciousness is returning, friend Conway," the empath replied, trembling with its own as well as everyone else's excitement. "But slowly; the movements are instinctive, involuntary."

As the forward extremity of one CRLT approached the rear of the other, the organic film which protected the raw areas on each creature softened, liquefied, and trickled away. At the center of the forward face a blunt, conical shape began to form surrounded by systems of muscles which twitched themselves into mounds and hollows and deep, irregular fissures. The rear face of the other CRLT had grown its own series of hollows and orifices which exactly corresponded with the protuberances of the other, as well as four large, triangular flaps which opened out like the fleshy petals of an alien flower. Then all at once there was just one double-length creature with a join which was virtually invisible.

And I was worried about joining them together, Conway thought incredulously. *The problem might be to keep them apart!*

"Are we observing a physical coupling for the purpose of reproduction?" Murchison said to nobody in particular.

"Friend Murchison," Prilicla said, "the emotional radiation of both creatures suggests that this is not a conscious or involuntary sex act. A closer analogy would be that of an infant seeking the physical reassurance of its parent. However, both beings are seeking physical and mental reassurance, and have feelings of confusion and loss, and these feelings are so closely matched that the only explanation is shared mentation."

"Tractor beamers," Conway said urgently. "Pull them apart, *gently!*"

He had been delighted to find that the beings who made up the vast group entity would link together naturally when the conditions were right, although that might not be the case if too many intervening segments had been destroyed in the accident, but he most certainly did not want a premature and permanent link-up between these two at this stage. They would have to be returned to a state of hibernation and resume their positions in the coil, otherwise they might find themselves permanently separated, orphaned, from the group entity.

Even though the tractor beamers were no longer being gentle, the two CRLTs stubbornly refused to separate. Instead they were becoming more physically agitated, they were trying to emerge completely from their hibernation cylinders, and their emotional radiation was seriously inconveniencing Prilicla.

"We must reverse the process—" Conway began.

"The sensors react to gravity and air pressure," Fletcher broke in quickly. "We can't evacuate the hold without killing them, but if we cut the artificial gravity only it might—"

"The endplate release mechanism was also linked to those sensors," Conway said, "and we can't replace them in their slots without chopping the two beasties apart, in the wrong place."

"It might stop the flow of resuscitation medication," Fletcher went on, "and restart the hibernation sequence. The needles are still sited in both creatures and the connecting tubing is flexible and still unbroken, although it won't be for long if we don't stop them from leaving their cylinders. If we put a clamp on the resuscitation line of each beastie, Doctor, I believe I could bypass the endplate actuator and restart the hibernation medication."

"But you will be working inside the cylinders," Murchison said, "beside two very massive and angry e-ts."

"No, ma'am," the Captain said. "I am neither foolhardy nor a xenophobe, and I shall work through an access panel in the outer skin. It should take about twenty minutes."

"Too long," Conway said. "They will have disconnected themselves from the tubing by then. We can calculate the dosage needed to put them back to sleep. Can you drill through the wall of the container, ignoring the sensors and actuators, and withdraw the required quantity of medication directly?"

For a moment there was silence while Fletcher's features fell into an angry, why-didn't-I-think-of-that? expression, then he said, "Of course, Doctor."

But even when injections of the CRLTs own hibernation medication were ready their troubles were far from over. The pressor beam operators who were responsible for immobilizing the creatures could not hold down the two joined e-ts without also flattening the medics who were trying to work on them. Their best compromise was to leave a two-meters clearance on each side of the operative field wherein the medical team would not be inconvenienced by the pressors. But this meant that there was no restraint placed on the movements of the creature along a four-meter length of its body, which wriggled and humped and lashed out with its dorsal appendages and generally made it plain that it did not want strange beings climbing all over it and sticking it with needles.

Several times Conway was knocked away from the patient and once, if it had not been for a warning from Fletcher, he would have lost his helmet and probably the head inside it. Murchison observed crossly that the big advantage in dealing with cadavers was that, regardless of their physiological classifications, they did not assault the pathologist and leave her normally peachlike skin pigmentation black and blue. But with Naydrad's long, caterpillarlike body wrapped around one appendage and both Fletcher and Colonel Okaussie hanging onto the other limb which threatened the operative field, and with Murchison steadying the scanner for him while he sat astride the creature like a bareback horserider, Conway was able to guide his hypo into the correct vein and discharge its contents before a particularly violent heave pulled the needle free.

Within a few seconds Prilicla, whose fragile body had no place in this violent muscular activity announced from its position on the ceiling that the being was going back to sleep. When they withdrew to turn their attention to its companion, its movements were already growing weaker.

By the time they had dealt similarly with the other CRLT, the two creatures had separated. The hollows and protuberances and flaps of muscle had collapsed and smoothed themselves out, and the raw interface areas began exuding the clear liquid which congealed into a thin, transparent film. Gently the tractor and pressor beam men lifted and pushed the two beings back into their respective hibernation cylinders. Conway signaled for the artificial gravity to be reduced to zero and, as expected, they were able to replace the cylinder endplates without trouble. The cargo hold's air pressure was reduced gradually so that they could check whether the premature opening of the hibernation compartments had caused a leak. It had not.

"So far so good," Conway said. "Return them to their positions in the coil and bring in the next two."

The first two had been the occupants of adjoining cylinders and their linking up had been automatic, a natural process in all respects. But the second two had been separated by a compartment which had been ruptured by a piece of flying debris and its occupant killed. The affinity between these two might not be so strong, Conway thought.

However, they merged as enthusiastically and naturally as had the first two. The resuscitation process was reversed before they were fully conscious so as to eliminate the multispecies wrestling match needed to put them into hibernation again. Prilicla reported a minor variation in the emotional radiation associated with the initial body contact—a feeling, very faint and temporary, of disappointment. But the two segments of the group entity were compatible and that particular break in continuity in the coil could be closed up.

Conway felt uneasy. Too much good luck worried him. Something was bothering Prilicla, too, because he had long since learned to recognize the difference between the little empath's reaction to its own feelings and those of the beings around it.

"Friend Conway," Prilicla said, while they were awaiting the arrival of the third set of CRLTs. "The first two beings were relatively immature and taken from the forward section of the coil, that is, from the tail segments of this multiple creature, and the second two came from a position considerably aft of amidships. Our own deductions, supported by the information on the creatures' probable planet of origin which arrived with *Tyrell*, suggest that the tail segments are immature beings, perhaps very young adults, and the head segments aft to be composed of the older, more experienced, and most highly intelligent of the beings since they are responsible for ship operations and disembarkation following a stern landing."

"Agreed," Conway said, wishing Prilicla would get to the point, no matter how unpleasant it was, instead of talking all around it.

"Aft of amidships, friend Conway," Prilicla went on, "the CRLTs should be older. The two who have just left us, judging by their emotional radiation, were even less mature than the first set."

Conway looked at Murchison, who said defensively, "I don't know why that should be, I'm sorry. Do the data on their home planet, if it *is* their home planet, suggest an answer?"

"I'm pretty sure it was their home planet," Conway replied thoughtfully, "because there couldn't possibly be another like it. But the data are old and sparse and predate the assembly and launching from orbit of the coilship, and we've been too busy since *Tyrell* brought back the information to discuss it properly."

"We have half an hour," Murchison observed, "before the next two CRLTs arrive."

＊　　＊　　＊

Many centuries before the formation of the Galactic Federation, the Eurils had ranged interstellar space, driven by a curiosity so intense and at the same time hampered by a caution so extreme that even the Cinrusskin race to which Prilicla belonged was considered brave, even foolhardy, by comparison. Physiologically they were classification MSVK—a low-gravity, tripedal, and vaguely storklike lifeform, whose wings had evolved into twin sets of multidigited manipulators. They had been and still were the galaxy's prime observers, and they were content to look and learn and record through their long-range probes and sensors without making their presence known to the large and dangerously overmuscled specimens, intelligent or otherwise, who were under study.

During their travels the Eurils had come upon a system whose single, life-bearing planet pursued a highly eccentric orbit about its primary which forced its flora and fauna to adapt to environmental conditions ranging from steaming polar jungles in summer to an apparently lifeless winter world of ice. Seeing it for the first time in its frigid, winter mode, the Eurils had been about to dismiss it as being uninhabitable until their probes showed evidence of a highly technical culture encased in the winter ice. Closer investigation revealed that the civilization was current and was awaiting the spring, like every other animal and vegetable life-form on the planet, to come out of hibernation.

It was not until the polar spring was far advanced that the members of this hibernating culture were identified as the large, loglike objects which had been lying in and around the cities under the ice.

"It is clear from this that the overall being is a group entity which, for reasons we do not yet understand, must separate into its individual parts before hibernation can take place," Conway went on. "Since hibernation is natural to them, the problem of artificially extending it and reversing the process for the purpose of interstellar migration was, medically speaking, relatively easy to solve.

"The following year a number of the beings were observed by the Eurils in a fully conscious state," he continued, "going about their business in small group gestalts inside heated domes under the winter ice, which indicates that they do not go into hibernation unless or until it is forced on them. It is unnecessary, therefore, to duplicate the extremes of temperature of their planet of origin on their new home since any world closely resembling their summer environment would suit them. Had this not been so, the near impossibility of finding another and identical planetary environment to the one they were trying to leave would have made the migration hopeless from the start. And the reasons for the CRLT life-form becoming a group entity, initially a small-group entity, are also becoming clear."

Even at the time of the Eurils' visit the CRLTs, despite their advanced technology, were not having things all their own way. They lived on an incredibly savage world which had no clear division between its animal and vegetable predators. In order to have any chance of survival at all, the young CRLTs had to be born physically well developed and remain under the protection of the parent for as long as possible. In the CRLT's case, parturition was delayed until the offspring was a young adult who had learned how to survive and how to aid the continued survival of its parent.

Separation took place every winter, when everything went to sleep and there was no physical threat, and the young one rejoined its parent in the spring to continue its lessons in survival. The young one, who at this stage was invariably female, reached physical maturity early and produced a child of its own. And so it went with the original adult, who had begun to change its sex to male, trailing a long tail of beings of diminishing degrees of masculinity and experience behind it as it moved up the chain of the group entity toward the head.

"The CRLT brain forms part of the central nerve core which during fusion is linked to the brains of the individuals ahead of and behind it via the interfaces at each end of the body," Conway went on, "so that an individual segment learns not only by its own experience but from those of its predecessors farther up the line. This means that the larger the number of individuals in the group, the smarter will be its male head and forward segments. Should the head segment, who is the elder of the group and probably its decision maker, die from natural or other causes, the male next in line takes over."

Murchison cleared her throat delicately and said, "If anyone wishes at this juncture to make a general observation regarding the superiority, physical or intellectual, of the male over the female, be advised that I shall spit in his, her, or its eye."

Conway smiled and shook his head. He said seriously, "The male head will, naturally, fertilize a number of young female tail segments of other group entities, but there is a problem. Surely there would be serious psychological difficulties, sex-based frustrations, with so many of the intervening segments neither fully male or female and unable to—"

"There is no problem," Murchison broke in, "if all mentation and, presumably, the pain and pleasure stimuli are shared by every individual in the group."

"Of course, I'd forgotten that aspect," Conway said. "But there is another. Think of the *length* of our survivor. If mentation and experience are shared, then this could be a very long-lived and highly intelligent group entity indeed—"

The discussion was cut short at that point by the lock cycling warning. The third pair of CRLTs had arrived.

These two had been taken from the sternmost loops of the coil-ship where the casualties among the most senior and intelligent CRLTs had been heaviest. According to *Vespasian*'s tactical computer and the findings of *Descartes*'s specialists in e-t written languages and numerical systems, fifty-three of the CRLT hibernation cylinders—and their occupants—had been destroyed as a result of the collision, and between these two segments there had been seventeen members of the group entity who had not made it.

The other breaks in the coil were much smaller—the largest missing five segments and the rest only three or four each. Conway hoped that if the largest gap could be closed successfully, then the smaller ones should pose fewer problems.

As with the previous two CRLTs, the combination of artificial gravity and atmospheric pressure triggered the actuators which opened the cylinders and reversed the hibernation process. Conway had already sited the IV needles which would put them back to sleep again should they become disorderly, and Prilicla reported that they were reviving and their emotional radiation indicated that they were beings who were fully mature, healthy, and highly intelligent. As consciousness returned they began moving out of their cylinders and toward each other.

They touched, and jerked apart.

"What?" Conway began. But Prilicla was already answering the question.

"There are feelings of intense discomfort, friend Conway," the empath said, trembling violently. "Also of confusion, disappointment, and rejection. There is background emotion, a combination of anxiety and curiosity, which is probably regarding their present surroundings."

Because he could think of nothing to say, Conway moved to a position directly between the forward and rear interfaces of the two CRLTs. He did not consider the position dangerous because, if Prilicla's emotional readings were correct, they were unlikely to come together. He began examining the two interfaces, both visually and with his x-ray scanner, and taking measurements. A few minutes later Murchison joined him, and Prilicla dropped to hover cautiously a few meters above the area.

"Even with unaided vision you can see that the two interfaces are not compatible," Conway said worriedly. "There are three areas which cannot be made to join without surgical intervention. But I am reluctant to start cutting without having a clearer idea of how to proceed. I wish I could obtain the consent and cooperation of the patients."

382 · JAMES WHITE

"That might be difficult," Colonel Okaussie said. "But I could have my men try to—"

"Lift them on tractor beams and force another contact," Conway finished for him. "I need one more attempted joining, at least, with vision recorders catching it in close-up from the anterior, posterior, and lateral aspects. I also need Prilicla to monitor their emotional radiation closely during the attempt so that we will know which particular areas give the most discomfort and are, therefore, most in need of surgical attention. During surgery, instead of using an anesthetic, we can return them into hibernation. Yes, Doctor?"

"Have you considered, friend Conway—" began Prilicla, but Conway cut it short.

"Little friend," he said, "I know of old your roundabout manner of expressing disagreement as well as your feelings regarding the causing of unnecessary discomfort to patients, and you know that I share those feelings. But much as I dislike causing pain, in this case it is necessary."

"Doctor Conway," Colonel Okaussie said, with an impatient edge to his tone, "a few moments ago I had been about to suggest that since the beings are fully conscious, intelligent, and their visual range is similar to our own, we should be able to obtain their co-operation by explaining the situation to them graphically. I think it is worth a try."

"It most certainly is," Conway said. He caught Fletcher's eye and muttered, "Now why didn't I think of that?"

Descartes's commanding officer smiled and said, "I'll have a projection screen set up as quickly as possible, Doctor." Conway began assembling the instruments he would need while Murchison and Naydrad took over the job of measuring the interfaces and Prilicla hovered above them radiating reassurance to the patients.

* * *

It was a large screen, set between the angle of the ceiling and the aft wall of the hold so that the dorsally mounted eyes of both CRLTs would be able to view it without distortion. *Descartes*'s officers were specialists in e-t communications and the presentation was short, simple, and very much to the point.

The opening sequence was familiar since it was part of the ma-

terial the Fleet Commander had used during his recent briefing to
Conway. It showed a diagrammatic reconstruction of the CRLTs
great, coillike interstellar transport complete with central stem, coil
supporting structure, thrusters, and guidance system moving slowly
against a starry backdrop. Suddenly a large meteor appeared at the
edge of the screen, heading directly for the coilship. It struck, moving along the inside of the coil and carrying away the thrusters,
guidance system, and all of the central supporting structure for the
continuous spiral of hibernation compartments. The impact shook
the coil apart, and the individual hibernation cylinders, because of
the vessel's rotation, went flying off in all directions like shrapnel
from a slow-motion explosion.

Because of the greater rigidity of the structure aft, the shock in
this area was much more severe and the casualties among the hibernating CRLTs were heavy; the cylinders whose occupants had not
survived were shown in red. Then there was a two-minute shot of
the scene as it actually was, with *Vespasian, Claudius* and *Descartes*
with a shoal of smaller vessels busy reassembling the coil followed
by a longer sequence, displayed graphically, which showed a modified coilship coming in to land on a fresh, green world with the
two capital ships and *Descartes* linked together so as to replace the
missing support structure and thrusters.

The presentation ended by showing the coilship with the missing segments indicated in throbbing red, then with the red sections
removed and the gaps closed up to make a slightly shorter coil, and
the final scene showed the successful link-up of the first two CRLTs.

As a piece of visual communication it left very little room for
misunderstanding, and Conway did not need Prilicla's empathic faculty to tell him that the message had been understood—the two
CRLTs were already moving cautiously toward each other.

"Recorders?" Conway said urgently.

"Running," Murchison said.

Conway held his breath as once again the two massive creatures
attempted fusion. The movements of their stubby, caterpillarlike legs
were barely perceptible and their dorsal appendages were tensely
still, making them resemble two enormous, alien logs being pushed
together by the current of an invisible river. When they were separated by about six inches, the forward face of the rearmost creature

had grown the pattern of bumps and fleshy projections which they had seen during the first two link-ups, and the rear interface of its companion had twitched itself into a pattern of fissures and a single deep recess. Around the periphery of the interface four wide, triangular flaps of muscle tipped with osseous material, features which had not appeared to be of any importance when examined on sleeping or dead CRLTs, had grown suddenly to nearly four times their size in the unconscious state and opened out like fleshy, horn-tipped petals. But with these two the interfaces did not correspond. They touched, held contact for perhaps three seconds, then jerked apart.

Before Conway could comment, they were coming together again. This time the forward creature remained still while the second twisted its forward interface into a slightly different position to try again, but with the same result.

It was obvious that the contacts were intensely uncomfortable, and the resultant pain had triggered off the involuntary movement which had jerked them apart. But the CRLTs were not giving up easily, although it appeared at first as if they had. They withdrew until their bodies were again inside their hibernation cylinders, then their stubby legs blurred into motion as they drove themselves at each other seeking, it seemed, by sheer brute force and bodily inertia to force a fusion. Conway winced as they came together with a sound like a loud, multiple slap.

But to no avail. They broke contact to lie a few feet from each other with their dorsal appendages twitching weakly and air hissing loudly as it rushed in and out of their breathing orifices. Then slowly they began to move together again.

"They are certainly *trying*," Murchison said softly.

"Friend Conway," Prilicla said, "the emotional radiation from both creatures has become more complex. There is deep anxiety but not, I would say, personal fear. Also a feeling of understanding and great determination, with the determination predominating. I would say that both entities fully understand the situation and are desperately anxious to cooperate. But these unsuccessful attempts at fusion are causing great pain, friend Conway."

It was characteristic of the little empath that it did not mention its own pain, which was only fractionally less severe than that of the emoting CRLTs. But the uncontrollable trembling of its pipestem legs and fragile eggshell of a body spoke more eloquently than words.

"Put them to sleep again," Conway said.

There was silence while the hibernation medication was taking effect, broken finally by Prilicla who said, "They are losing consciousness, but there is a marked change in the emotional radiation. They are feeling both anxiety and hope. I think they are expecting us to solve their problem, friend Conway."

They were all looking at him, but it was Naydrad, whose mobile, silvery fur was registering its bafflement and concern, who put the question everyone else was too polite to ask.

"How?"

Conway did not reply at once. He was thinking that two highly intelligent elder CRLTs from the coilship's stern, following their first abortive attempt at fusion, would have realized that a link-up was impossible for them. But they had made two further attempts—one when the rearmost creature had tried to twist itself and its interface into a new position, and again when it had tried to achieve fusion by sheer brute force. He was beginning to wonder whether the recent attempt at communicating with the aliens had been strictly one way. Until the *Descartes* linguists could be given the opportunity to learn the CRLTs language, an accurate exchange of ideas was impossible. But it had already been shown that pictures were very effective in putting across a message, and they were all forgetting that actions, like pictures, often spoke louder than words.

Recalling those three unsuccessful attempts at fusion, Conway wondered if the two CRLTs had in fact been trying to demonstrate that the link-up was impossible for them without assistance, but that by changing the positions and perhaps the dimensions of some of the surface features on the interfaces and forcing things a little, then a join might be achieved.

"Friend Conway," Prilicla announced, "is having feelings of optimism."

"Perhaps," Murchison said, "in his own good time, of course, he will explain to us nonempaths the reason for his optimism."

Ignoring the sarcasm, Conway briefly outlined his recent thinking, although he personally would have described his feeling as one of forlorn hope rather than optimism. He went on, "So I believe that the CRLTs were trying to tell us that surgical intervention is necessary for them to achieve fusion, not brute force. And it has just occurred to me that there is a precedent for this procedure. One of the cadavers examined on *Rhabwar* showed evidence of surgery on its forward interface and this could mean—"

"But that was a very youthful, although physically mature CRLT," Murchison broke in, "and the surgery was minor. We agreed that it had probably been performed for cosmetic reasons."

"I think we were wrong," Conway said. Excitedly he went on, "Consider the physical organization of this group entity. At the head is the most mature, male adult and at the tail the most recently born infant, although as we know the infant grows to physical maturity without separating from the parent. Between the head and the tail there is a gradual and steady progression from the most elderly and intelligent male entities down to the increasingly youthful and female segments which form the tail sections. But Prilicla has reported an anomaly in this progression. Young CRLTs positioned relatively close to the tail show evidence of greater physical age and brain development than entities in the midsections. Until now I could see no reason for this anomaly.

"But now let us suppose that this group entity," he continued quickly, "forming as it does a complete colonization project, has been artificially lengthened. The extraordinarily large number of individuals in this group entity has always bothered me, and now there is a simple explanation for it. Let us assume that there is one head or, more accurately, a fairly large number of linked elders forming the leading segments, and several tails connected one behind the other. These would be very youthful tails because it must be much easier to carry out the surgical modifications on young CRLTs which enable them to link up. So we have this colonist group entity with intelligence and experience at its head and linked to a number of young and inexperienced subgroups forming an artificially lengthened tail. The joins between these subgroups are surgically assisted and, I feel sure, temporary, because once established on the target planet they would be able to separate again, and in time the young heads would grow to full adulthood and the dangers from inbreeding would be avoided.

"Perhaps the head on this group entity has also been artificially

SECTOR GENERAL · 387

extended," Conway added, "so as to include elder CRLTs with specialist experience relating to the colonization project who would be available initially to protect the younger group entities, and subsequently to teach and train them and pass on the knowledge of their race's history and science."

Prilicla had flown closer while Conway had been speaking and was hovering a few inches above the Doctor's head. It said happily, "An ingenious theory, friend Conway. It fits both the facts as we know them and the type of emotional radiation received from the beings."

"I agree," Murchison said. "I, too, found difficulty in accepting the extreme length of this group entity, but the idea of a wise old head acting as guide and mentor to an as yet unknown number of young tails is much easier to believe. However, I can't help remembering that it was the head segments which suffered most of the casualties. Perhaps the head is no longer as wise as it should have been and an awful lot of vital knowledge has been lost to this multiple group entity."

Colonel Okaussie waited for a moment to see if anyone in the medical team would speak, then he cleared his throat and said, "Maybe not, ma'am. Most of the head segments who were killed in the collision were very close to the stern and to the ship's control and propulsion centres. One could reasonably expect that these segments were the beings charged with the responsibility for operating the ship and carrying out the landing maneuvers, functions which are now the responsibility of the Monitor Corps. It is likely that the scientist and teacher segments were positioned a little farther back in the chain and the majority of the casualties were suffered by the vessel's crew, whose specialist knowledge would no longer be of vital importance to the colonization project after the vessel had landed."

Before Murchison could reply Naydrad gave an impatient, modulated growl which translated as "Why don't we stop talking and get on with the job?"

*　　*　　*

The screen which had been used to communicate with the CRLTs was continuously displaying distant and close-up views of spacesuited figures of various physiological classifications busily at work

388 · JAMES WHITE

on the final stages of the coilship's reassembly. Conway could not decide whether *Descartes*'s commanding officer was screening the material to be helpful and informative or as a means of suggesting, very subtly, that the medical team display a similar degree of industry. The attempt was a failure in either event, Conway thought, because the *Rhabwar* medics were far too busy to look at Okaussie's pictures. They were concentrating instead on measuring and remeasuring the features on the CRLT interfaces and charting with their scanners the paths of underlying blood vessels and the distribution of the nerve ganglia. And with great care and accuracy they were marking the areas where surgical intervention was possible without causing either a major hemorrhage or sensory impairment.

It was slow, tedious work and visually not very dramatic. Colonel Okaussie could be forgiven for thinking that the ambulance ship personnel had gone to sleep on the job.

"Friend Conway," Prilicla said at one particularly awkward stage, "the physical differences between these two entities are so marked that I cannot help wondering if they belong to different subspecies."

All of Conway's attention at that moment was concentrated on what seemed to be the main sphincter muscle on the rear interface of the forward CRLT, so that by the time he was ready to reply Murchison had done it for him.

"In a sense you are right, Doctor Prilicla," she said. "It is a natural result of their method of reproduction. Think of this forward CRLT when it was the last and female link in its group entity chain. In due time it grew to maturity and, still attached to its parent, it was fertilized by the male head of another group entity. Its own infant grew and became mature and in turn produced another, and the process continued with different male heads adding their individual sets of genes at every stage.

"The physical connection between any given CRLT and its offspring is perfect," she continued, "and perfect fusion may even be possible between a parent and its grandchild or great-grandchild. But the effect of different males fertilizing each new endlink in the chain would be cumulative. So it is understandable when you think about it, Doctor, that the differences between the fusion interfaces of these two, which were separated by seventeen intervening segments, are considerable."

"Thank you, friend Murchison," Prilicla said. "My brain seems not to be functioning properly."

"Probably," Murchison replied in a sympathetic tone, "because your brain is more than half asleep, like mine."

"And mine," Naydrad joined in.

Conway, who had been trying not to think of how long it had been since he had last eaten or slept, decided that the best way to deal with an impending mutiny among his overworked medics was to ignore it. He indicated a small area on the rear interface of the first alien, midway between the central conical depression and the upper rim of the interface, then pointed to the corresponding area on the forward face of the second one. He said, "We can safely ignore these reproductive organs in both creatures, since this kind of link-up is temporary and physiologically independent of the parent-offspring fusion mechanism. As I see it the three areas we must concentrate on are the central conical projection and its corresponding recess, which are the connecting points for the central nerve core and our primary concern. Second is this narrow, semi-rigid tongue with the fleshy mushroom at its tip which locates with this slit in the other—"

"That connection is also of vital importance," Murchison broke in, "since it links up the nerve networks controlling the voluntary and involuntary muscles which move each CRLTs legs and enable the group entity to walk in unison. There would be small advantage to the group entity if it could share mentation but a number of its segments were unable to walk."

"Friend Murchison," Prilicla said timidly, "it seems to me that the original nerve impulse from the head segment, or whichever individual CRLT was responsible for initiating the movement, would not be sufficiently strong to trigger the ambulatory muscles throughout the enormous length of this group entity."

"That is true," the pathologist replied. "But there is an organic amplifier, consisting of a bunching of nerve ganglia situated just above the womb, or the position where the womb had been in the males, in an area where the surrounding tissue has a high mineral content and is particularly rich in copper salts. This biological booster ensures that the ambulatory muscles receive their signals with undiminished strength throughout the length of the chain."

"Third," Conway said, raising his voice slightly to discourage further interruptions, "there are these four flaps of muscle which terminate at their apexes in osseous hooks which locate in these four bone-reinforced orifices in the second creature. This is the primary mechanism by which the individual segments are held together nose to tail, and in this instance—"

"It is also the method by which the CRLT female at the end of the line held onto its developing offspring," Murchison broke in again. "At that stage the offspring had no choice in the matter. But as it matured, produced its own offspring, and moved farther up the line I feel sure that voluntary separation became possible. In fact, separation would be necessary during activities which did not require the entire group entity for their performance."

"That is most interesting, friend Murchison," Prilicla said. "I should think that the first time such a voluntary separation took place a certain amount of psychological trauma would be present. It would be analogous to a coming-of-age ceremony, perhaps, even though the separation might not be permanent—"

Before Conway could speak, Prilicla fell silent and began trembling in reaction to the Doctor's feelings of irritation and impatience. He said, "This is all very interesting, friends, but we do not have the time just now for a general discussion. In any case, following the type of temporary separation you mentioned, the young adult would rejoin its original parent segment and not a—I suppose you could describe it as an ancestor seventeen times removed, which is the problem currently facing us. And now, if you don't mind, we will concentrate on this problem and on the surgical procedures necessary to solve it.

"Feel free to interrupt at any time," he added dryly.

But the interruptions were few and pertinent, and very soon it became obvious even to the watching tractor beamers, *Descartes*'s commanding officer, and Fleet Commander Dermod, whose face appeared briefly but with increasing frequency on the overhead screen, that the medical team was also working hard.

Because Sector General was the Federation's foremost emergency hospital, the kind of surgery performed there, whether the patient was Earth-human or extraterrestrial, tended to be curative rather than cosmetic. It felt very strange to Conway, and he knew that his feelings were being shared by the other members of the team, to be operating on a perfectly healthy e-t with the purpose of simply modifying the size and contours of certain physiological features. But the operation itself was far from simple.

The greater proportion of the surgical work had to be performed on the second alien whose forward nerve coupling cone was too wide at its base to be retained by the sphincter muscle surrounding the corresponding orifice in the first CRLT. With the semiflexible tongue and groove connection which joined the two beings' locomotor nerve networks, the solution was much simpler. The deep recess in the first alien was surgically widened until measurement showed that it would accommodate the tongue comfortably, after which reinforcing sutures were inserted to prevent further accidental widening. But the four triangular flaps with their bony, hooklike extensions posed a completely different and more difficult problem.

Together the four members formed the principal organic coupling which held the considerable mass of the second e-t against the first, and they did not fit because the hooks did not quite reach the apertures meant to receive them.

Elongating the four triangular members was contraindicated since this would have entailed surgical interference and consequent serious weakening of the muscle systems concerned, and they could not foresee the effect on the network of blood vessels which became engorged and extended the members to quadruple their size when the being returned to consciousness. Instead they made molds of the four hooks and made artificial ones using a hard, biologically neutral plastic at the tips and a wide band of thinner, more flexible material around the bases. The result was a set of hollow, hook-tipped gloves which, when a little of the original hooks were filed away to make them fit, were slipped over the original members and secured in position with rivets and sutures.

Suddenly there was nothing left to do, but hope.

Above the two unconscious CRLTs the vision screen was displaying an overall picture of their coilship, complete now except for the segments whose occupants were awaiting surgical attention, and the dense but orderly mass of shipping moving in and around it. The thought came to Conway, no matter how hard he tried to avoid it, that the tremendous fleet of Monitor Corps and other units, from the great capital ships and auxiliaries down to the swarms of scout-ships and the army of specialists in engineering and communications they represented, were all wasting their time here if this particular operation was not a success.

For this responsibility he had argued long and eloquently with Thornnastor, O'Mara, and Skempton at Sector General. He must have been mad.

Harshly, he said, "Wake them up."

They watched anxiously as once again the two CRLTs came out of hibernation and began moving toward each other. They touched once, a brief, exploratory contact, then they fused. Where there had been two massive, twenty-meter caterpillarlike creatures there was now one of twice that length.

The join was visible, of course, but one had to look very carefully to see it. Conway forced himself to wait for ten interminable seconds, and still they had not pulled away from each other.

"Prilicla?"

"They are feeling pain, friend Conway," the empath replied, trembling slightly. "It is within bearable limits. There are also feelings of acceptance and gratitude."

Conway gave a relieved sigh which ended in an enormous, eye-watering yawn. He rubbed his eyes and said, "Thank you, everyone. Put them back to sleep, check the sutures, and reseal them in their hibernation cylinders. They will not have to link up again until after the landing, by which time the wounds should have healed to a large extent so that the fusion will be more comfortable for them. As for ourselves, I prescribe eight hours solid sleep before—"

He broke off abruptly as the features of Fleet Commander Dermod appeared on the screen.

"You appear to have successfully repaired a major break in our alien chain, Doctor," he said seriously, "but the time taken to do so was not short. There are many other breaks and we have three days during which a concerted Jump is possible, Doctor, after which the gravitational distortion effects caused by that rapidly approaching sun will make an accurate Jump out of the question even for single ships.

"Should we overrun the three-day deadline," he went on grimly, "single-ship Jumping within operational safety limits will be possible for an additional twenty hours. During this twenty-hour period, if the coilship is not to be abandoned to fall into the sun, it will have to be dismantled into sections small enough to be accommodated by the hyperspheres of the units available in the area. This, you will understand, would of necessity be a very hurried operation and our own accident casualties as well as those of CRLTs would be heavy.

"What I am saying, Doctor," he ended gravely, "is that if you cannot complete your organic link-ups within three days, tell me now so that we can begin dismantling the coilship in a safer and more orderly fashion."

Conway rubbed his eyes and said, "There were seventeen missing segments between the join which we have just effected, and this makes it the most difficult job of the lot. The remaining breaks are of two, three, or at most five segments, so that those linking operations will be correspondingly easier. We know the drill now and three days should be ample time, barring an unforeseen catastrophe."

"I cannot hold you responsible for one of those, Doctor," the Fleet Commander said dryly. "Very well. What are your immediate intentions?"

"Right now," Conway said firmly, "we intend to sleep."

Dermod looked vaguely surprised, as if the very concept of sleep was one that had become alien to him over the past few days, then he nodded grudgingly and broke contact.

*　　　*　　　*

Feeling rested, alert, and much more human—and, of course, more Kelgian and Cinrusskin—they returned to *Descartes*'s cargo hold to find another two CRLTs already waiting for them and the remaining segments to be joined clamped to the outer hull. The Fleet Commander, it was clear, was a man who believed in maintaining the pressure.

But achieving fusion with these two was remarkably easy. Only two intervening segments were missing so that the surgery required was minor indeed. The next pair were more difficult, nevertheless a satisfactory link-up was achieved within two hours and, with their growing confidence and expertise, this was to become the average time required for the job. So well did they progress that they became almost angry with themselves when they were forced to break for meals or sleep.

Then suddenly they were finished and there was nothing to do but watch the screen while the last gap in the coil was being closed and hundreds of spacesuited figures swarmed all over it to give a final check to the sensor actuators on each hibernation cylinder which would expel their endplates and initiate resuscitation on landing.

With the exception of *Rhabwar* and one of *Descartes*'s planetary landers, the great fleet of scoutships and auxiliaries withdrew to a distance of one and a half thousand kilometers, which was far enough to relieve the traffic congestion in the area but close enough for them to return quickly should anything go wrong.

"I do not foresee anything going seriously wrong at this end," the Fleet Commander said when the coilship was in one tremendous, spiral piece. "You have given us enough time, Doctor, to carry out all the necessary pre-Jump calculations and calibrations. This will be a time-consuming process since our three vessels, whose hyperspace envelopes will have to be extended to enclose the coilship, are Jumping in concert. Should a problem arise and we are unable to make this Jump, the units standing by will move in, dismantle the coilship as quickly as possible, and Jump away with the pieces and salvage what we can from this operation.

"There will be enough Monitor Corps medics on these ships to deal with the expected casualties," he went on, "and for this reason I would like *Rhabwar* to leave at once and position itself close to the CRLTs' new target planet. If trouble develops it is much more likely to be at that end."

"I understand," Conway said quietly.

The Fleet Commander nodded. "Thank you, Doctor. From now on this is purely a transport problem and my responsibility."

Sooner yours than mine, Conway thought grimly as Dermod broke contact.

He was thinking about the Fleet Commander's problem while they were wishing Colonel Okaussie and the *Descartes*'s tractor beam crew good-by and good luck, and it remained in his mind after the medical team boarded *Rhabwar* and the ambulance ship was heading out to Jump distance from the combined CRLT and Federation vessels.

Conway understood Dermod's problem all too well and the strong but unspoken reason why the Fleet Commander wanted the ambulance ship positioned in the target system. They both knew that the majority of single-ship accidents occurred because of a premature emergence into normal space when one of the unfortunate vessel's matched set of hyperdrive generators was out of synchronization. A single generator pod emerging into normal space while the rest of the vessel was in the hyperdimension could tear the ship apart and leave wreckage strewn across millions of kilometers. Timing, therefore, was critical even on a single ship where only two or perhaps four generators had to be matched. The Fleet Commander's problem was that *Vespasian, Claudius*, and *Descartes* together with the enormous coilship of the CRLTs were linked together by tractor and pressor beams into a single rigid structure.

The Emperor-class cruisers were the largest ships operated by the Monitor Corps, and each required six generators to move its tremendous mass into and out of hyperspace, while the survey and Cultural Contact vessel *Descartes* needed only four. This meant that sixteen generators in all would be required to perform a simultaneous Jump and subsequent emergence into normal space. And the problem was further complicated by the fact that all of the generators would be operating under controlled overload conditions because their combined hyperspace envelope had to be extended to enclose the coilship.

As *Rhabwar* made its Jump into hyperspace Conway was overcome by such an intense, gnawing anxiety that even Prilicla could not reassure him out of it. He had the awful feeling that they were about to witness the worst space disaster in Federation history.

*　　*　　*

The new home chosen for the CRLTs had been known to the Federation for nearly two centuries and was listed as a possible colony world for the Chalders. However, the denizens of Chalderescol Three—a water-breathing life-form resembling an outsize, tentacled crocodile which combined physical inaction with mental agility—were not very enthusiastic about it since they already possessed two colony worlds and their home planet was far from overcrowded. So when they learned of the plight of the CRLT colonists they willingly relinquished their claim to a planet which was of marginal interest to them anyway.

It was a warm, pleasant world with a continent, largely desert, encircling its equator like a wide, ragged belt and two relatively small bands of ocean separating the equatorial landmass from the two large continents centered at each pole; these were green, temperate, and free of icecaps.

Following exhaustive investigations of the cadavers available to them at Sector General both Murchison and Thornnastor were firmly of the opinion that this would be an ideal home for the CRLT life-form—moreover it was an environment which would not force them into periodic hibernation.

The landing area, a large clearing on the shore of a vast, inland sea, had already been marked with beacons. It awaited only the arrival of the CRLTs—as, with mounting anxiety, did the personnel on board *Rhabwar*. On the Casualty Deck Conway and the other members of the medical team each picked a direct visionport, hoping in some obscure fashion that by watching and worrying hard they might ensure the safe arrival of the coilship.

It was no surprise, considering the distances involved, that they learned of its emergence from the Control Room repeaters.

"Trace, sir!" Haslam's voice sounded excitedly. "The bearing is—"

"Are you sure it's them?"

"A single trace that size couldn't be anything else, sir. And yes, the sensors confirm."

"Very well," the Captain's voice replied, trying unsuccessfully to hide its relief. "Lock the scope on your radar bearing and give me full magnification. Dodds, contact astrogation on *Vespasian* and arrange a rendezvous. Power Room, stand by."

The rest of the crewmen's conversation was ignored as the medical team crowded around the Casualty Deck's repeater screen. One look was enough to tell them that their preparations to receive large numbers of casualties from the expected emergence accident had been wasted effort, but they did not care because it was immediately obvious that the concerted Jump had been completely successful.

Centered on the repeater screen was a small, sharp image of the coilship with its three Monitor Corps vessels spaced along its axis, looking like an exercise in alien three-dimensional geometry. *Vespasian*, the stern component, was already applying thrust, and the three linked ships were beginning to turn around their longitudinal axes in order to reproduce the original rate of rotation and centrifugal force conditions of the coilship before its accident. Gradually a voice from Control made itself heard above the sound of the medics' human and extraterrestrial jubilation.

". . . Rendezvous in four hours thirteen minutes," Haslam was saying. "No preliminary orbital maneuvering, sir. They intend going straight in."

*　　*　　*

Rhabwar, in its hypersonic glider configuration, circled the descending coilship at a distance of three kilometers using its thrusters only when necessary to maintain the same rate of descent. Rotating slowly and illuminated to near-incandescent brightness by the system's sun and noontime reflection from the planet's cloud blanket, it seemed to Conway as if it were boring its way into the lower reaches of the atmosphere like some gigantic, alien drill. Inside the enormous, dazzling coil the three Federation ships in their drab service liveries were virtually invisible except for the flare of *Vespasian*'s thrusters, which were supporting the weight not only of the coilship but the two vessels stacked above it. The great alien and Monitor Corps composite continued its descent until, three kilometers from the surface, tangential thrust was applied to begin killing its spin.

Vespasian's flare lengthened suddenly and brightened, slowing the descent until the ship was hovering a meter above the ground. Then simultaneously the coilship's rotation ceased, *Vespasian*'s stabilizers came to rest on the fused and blackened soil, and the sternmost segment of the coilship touched down.

For perhaps five seconds nothing happened, then, reacting to the cessation of spin and the presence of a suitable atmosphere, the sensor-actuators on every hibernation cylinder performed their function. The endplates which kept the individual CRLTs apart were ejected to fall like a shower of giant coins to the ground, and resuscitation of the group entity was initiated. Conway could imagine the individual CRLTs awakening, stretching, and linking up, the occupants of close on nine hundred hibernation compartments which had survived the eighty-seven years past collision. Then he began to worry in case some of them could not link up and there was an organic log-jam somewhere inside the coil trapping CRLTs above it . . .

But within a surprisingly short time the great group entity was leaving its ship, the leading head segments walking carefully around the fused earth under *Vespasian*'s stern and toward the vegetation on the edge of the clearing. And, like an endless, leathery caterpillar the younger segments emerged carrying equipment and stores and following the tracks of their elders.

When at last the tail was clear of the coilship, the power to the supporting tractor and pressor beams was gradually reduced so that the towering, open spiral collapsed slowly onto itself to lie like a great, loose coil of metal rope on the ground. A few minutes later *Vespasian*, *Claudius*, and *Descartes* took off and separated, the two capital ships to go into orbit and *Descartes* to land again a few kilometers along the shoreline to await formal contact with the CRLT group entity. Contact would occur, they knew, because the individual CRLTs who had undergone surgery knew that the beings inside the Federation ships wished them well and, since the CRLT life-form had shared mentation, the whole group would be aware of these good intentions.

By this time *Rhabwar*'s lander had also touched down and its medics were on the surface standing as close as they possibly could to the being who was marching endlessly past them. Ostensibly they were there to furnish any medical assistance which might be required. Actually they were simply satisfying their curiosity regarding a being which must surely have been the strangest life-form yet encountered.

Conway, as was his wont, was indulging in a bout of postoperative worrying. He waved, indicating the endless line of dorsal appendages which were either gathering pieces of edible vegetation or waving back at him, and said, "I realize that one or more of the head segments must have tried the local vegetation with no ill effects, and now the whole group entity knows what is safe to eat, but the procedure seems a bit slapdash to me. And I haven't been able to spot any of our surgical joins going past. There is bound to be a certain amount of muscular weakness in those areas, and perhaps an impairment in sensory communication and—What the blazes is *that*!"

That was a low, moaning and caterwauling sound which ran up and down the length of the kilometers-long entity, rising in volume suddenly until it became deafening. It sounded as if each and every CRLT was suffering intense physical or mental anguish. But strangely the outpouring of emotional radiation which must have accompanied it was not bothering Prilicla.

"Do not feel concern," the little empath said. "It is an expression of group pleasure, gratitude, and relief. They are cheering, friend Conway."

STAR
HEALER

CHAPTER 1

Something struck Conway as odd about the latest bunch of trainees as he stood aside to allow them to precede him into the observation gallery of the Hudlar Children's Ward. It was not that among the fourteen of them they comprised five widely different life-forms or that their treatment of him—he was, after all, a Senior Physician attached to the galaxy's largest multienvironment hospital—was condescending to the point of rudeness.

To be accepted for advanced training at Sector Twelve General Hospital a candidate—in addition to possessing a high degree of medical and surgical ability—had to be able to adapt to and accept people and circumstances which, back in their home-planet hospitals, they could barely have imagined. At home an off-planet patient would be a rarity indeed, while at Sector General they would be treating nothing else. Furthermore, many of them would find it difficult to make the transition from highly respected member of the local medical fraternity to mere trainee at Sector General, but they would soon settle in.

His mind was playing tricks on him, Conway decided—probably because he had so much on it at the present time. A rumor was going around about changes in his ambulance ship setup, and he was scheduled for an hour early that afternoon with the Chief Psychologist, always an unsettling prospect.

Conway was also irritated because he seemed to be coming in for more than his fair share of short-term projects and medical odd jobs—such as giving the trainees their initial orientation tour. His special ambulance-ship team had had very few calls in recent months.

"The patients in the ward below are infant Hudlars," Conway explained when the trainees had formed an untidy crescent around and behind him. "They belong to an immensely strong species and, as adults, are extremely resistant to physical injury and disease. So much so that the concept of curative medical treatment has been foreign to them. No medical profession exists on Hudlar, and the high infant mortality rate of the recent past was simply accepted. Their young fall prey to a large number of indigenous pathogens from the moment they are born, and those which do not quickly develop or inherit resistance to them perish. The hospital is trying to develop a wide-spectrum immunization procedure to be carried out during the prenatal stage, but so far with limited success."

He indicated a young Hudlar standing just below them, looking up. "You will already have deduced from this individual's general stance and musculature that the species evolved on a world with very heavy gravity and proportionately high atmospheric pressure, both of which have been reproduced in the ward. You will also observe no beds or rest furniture; patients who can move simply roam about at will. This is because their body tegument is so tough that padded rest areas are unnecessary. Because of the difficulty other species have in telling Hudlars apart, patient ID and case history are impressed magnetically on the metal band attached to the left forelimb. The Hudlars' six limbs can serve as either manipulatory or locomotor appendages.

"While gravity and atmospheric pressure have been duplicated here," Conway went on, "the exact constituents of their atmosphere have not been reproduced. Their home world's air is a thick, semi-liquid soup laden with tiny, airborne food particles which are absorbed and excreted by specialized areas of the skin. We find it more convenient to spray them periodically with a nutrient paint, as two of the armored medical attendants are doing now.

"With the facts now in your possession," he said, turning to regard them, "would anyone like to classify this life-form?"

For a moment there was no verbal response. The Orligian DBDGs moved restively, but the expressions on their humanoid features were concealed by facial hair. The silvery fur of the caterpillarlike Kelgian DBLFs was in constant motion, but the emotions which the movements expressed were readable only by a fellow member of the species or by a being carrying a Kelgian tape in its mind. As for the elephantine Tralthan FGLIs and the diminutive Dewatti EGCLs, their features were too decentralized to be visible in their entirety, while the hard, angular mandibles and deeply recessed eyes of the Melfan ELNTs were completely expressionless.

One of the four Melfan trainees first broke the silence. Its translator hummed briefly, "They belong to physiological classification FROB."

It was difficult to tell Melfans apart at the best of times, since all adult ELNTs possessed similar body mass and the only visible differences were the subtle variations in marking on the upper carapace. To make identification even more difficult, two of the four Melfan trainees seemed to be identical twins. One of these had spoken.

"Correct," Conway said approvingly. "Your name, Doctor?"

"Danalta, Senior Physician."

Polite, too, Conway thought. "Very well, Danalta. But you were slow in making the identification even though your colleagues were even slower. All of you must learn to quickly and accurately classify—"

"With respect, Senior Physician," the Melfan broke in, "I did not wish to offer gratuitous display of my medical knowledge, woefully limited as it is at present, until my colleagues had a chance to respond. I have studied all that was available to me regarding your physiological classification system. But I come from a backward world where the level of technology is low and intercultural communication has been limited, particularly where medical data on this hospital was concerned.

"Besides," it concluded, "the Hudlar life-form is distinctive, unique, and could only be FROB."

Conway would not have described Melf as a backward world and neither would any other member of the Galactic Federation, so this Danalta must have come from one of the colonies recently seeded by Melf. To qualify for Sector General with a background like that required determination as well as professional competence. It did not matter that the Melfan was turning out to be an odd combination of polite, self-effacing smart aleck—the operative word was "smart," and the best assistants an overworked Senior could have were those who strived to render their superiors redundant. He decided that he would keep a close watch on Danalta's progress, for purely selfish reasons.

"Since it is possible," Conway said dryly, "that a number of your colleagues are less well-informed on this subject than you, I shall outline very briefly the system of life-form identification which we use here. Your various specialist tutors will take you through it in more detail."

He looked for Danalta, but the trainees had changed their positions and Conway could no longer tell which of the two identical Melfans was which. He went on, "Unless you have already been attached to a multienvironment hospital, you will normally have encountered off-world patients one species at a time, probably on a short-term basis as the result of a ship accident or some emergency, and you would refer to them by their planets of origin. But here—where rapid and accurate identification of incoming patients is vital because all too often they are in no condition to furnish physiological data themselves—we have evolved a four-letter physiological classification system. It works like this.

"The first letter denotes the level of physical evolution reached by the species when it acquired intelligence," he continued. "The second indicates the type and distribution of limbs, sense organs, and body orifices, and the remaining two letters refer to the combination of metabolism and food and air requirements associated with the home planet's gravity and atmospheric pressure, which in turn gives an indication of the physical mass and protective tegument possessed by the being."

Conway smiled, although he knew that a long time would elapse before any of the trainees would be able to recognize that peculiarly Earth-human facial grimace for what it was. "Usually I have to remind some of our extraterrestrial candidates at this point that the initial letter of their classification should not be allowed to give them feelings of inferiority, because the degree of physical evolution is controlled by environmental factors and bears little relation to the level of intelligence . . ."

Species with the prefix A, B, or C, he went on to explain, were water-breathers. On most worlds life had originated in the sea, and these beings had developed intelligence without having to leave it. D through F were warm-blooded oxygen-breathers, into which group most of the intelligent races of the Federation fell, and the G and K types were also oxygen breathing, but insectile. The Ls and Ms were light-gravity, winged beings.

Chlorine-breathing life-forms were contained in the O and P groups, and after these came the more exotic, the more highly evolved physically and the downright weird types. Into these categories fell the radiation-eaters, the cold-blooded or crystalline beings, and entities capable of modifying their physical structures at will. However, those beings possessing extrasensory powers sufficiently well developed to make ambulatory or manipulatory appendages unnecessary were given the prefix V regardless of their size or shape.

"There are anomalies in the system," Conway went on, "and these must be blamed on a lack of imagination and foresight by the originators. The AACP life-form, for instance, has a vegetable metabolism. Normally the A prefix denotes a water-breather, there being nothing lower on the evolutionary scale than the piscatorial life-forms, but the AACPs are intelligent vegetables and plant-life came before the fish."

Conway pointed suddenly at a nurse who was spraying nutrient onto a young Hudlar at the other end of the ward, then turned toward Danalta. "Perhaps you would like to classify that life-form, Doctor."

"I am not Danalta," the Melfan Conway was addressing protested. Even though the process of translation tended to filter the emotional overtones from messages, the ELNT sounded displeased.

"My apologies," Conway said, looking around for its twin, in vain. He decided that Danalta, for reasons known only to itself, had hidden behind the group of Tralthan trainees. Before he could redirect the question, one of the Tralthans answered it.

"The being you indicate is encased in a heavy-duty protective suit," the big FGLI said, this deep modulated rumblings of its native speech reinforcing the ponderous and pedantic style of the translated words. "The only part of the being visible to me is the small area behind the visor, and this is indistinct because of reflections from the ward lighting. Since the protective suit is self-propelled, there is no evidence available as to the number and type of the locomotor appendages. But the overall size and shape of the suit together with the positioning of the four mechanical manipulators spaced around the base of the conical head section—assuming that for ergonomic reasons these mechanical extensions approximate the positions of the underlying natural limbs—leads me to state with a fair degree of certainty that the entity in question is a Kelgian of physiological classification DBLF. Glimpses of a gray, furry tegument and what appears to be one of the Kelgian visual sensors revealed, however unclearly, through the small area of the visor, supports this identification."

"Very *good*, Doctor!" But before Conway could ask the Tralthan its name, the entrance lock of the ward swung open and a large, spherical vehicle mounted on caterpillar treads rolled in. The sphere was encircled equatorially by a variety of remote handling and sensory devices, and prominently displayed on the forward upper surface was the insignia of a Diagnostician. Instead, Conway pointed to the vehicle and said, "Can you classify that one?"

This time one of the Kelgians spoke first.

"Only by inference and deduction, Senior Physician," it said as slow, regular waves rippled along its fur from nose to tail. "Plainly the vehicle is a self-powered pressure vessel which, judging by the external bracing evident on the sphere, is designed to protect the ward patients and medical staff as well as the occupant. The walking limbs, if there are any, are concealed by the pressure envelope, and I would say that the number of external handling and sensory devices is so large that it is probable the being has only a small number of natural manipulators and sensors, and operates the external devices as required. The walls of the pressure vessel are of unknown thickness, so that there is no accurate data available to me regarding the size and physical configuration of the occupant."

The Kelgian paused for a moment and sat back on its rearmost legs, looking like a fat, furry question mark. Silvery ripples continued to move slowly along its back and flanks, while the fur of its three fellow DBLFs twitched and tufted and flattened randomly as if there were a strong wind blowing in the observation gallery.

An air of restlessness, of low-key agitation, seemed to pervade the other members of the group. The Tralthans were each raising and lowering their stumpy, elephantine feet in turn. The continuous clicking and scraping sound was the Melfans tapping their crablike legs against the floor, while the teeth of the Origians showed whitely in their dark, furry faces. Conway hoped they were smiling.

"I am aware of two life-forms which use a pressure vessel of this kind," the Kelgian went on. "They are utterly dissimilar in environmental requirements and physiology, and both would be considered by the more common oxygen- and chlorine-breathing species to be among the exotic categories. One is a frigid-blooded methane-breather who is most comfortable in an environment at a few degrees above absolute zero, and who evolved on the perpetually dark worlds which have been detached from their original solar systems and drift through the interstellar spaces.

"Physically they are quite small," the Kelgian continued, "averaging one-third of the body mass of a being like myself. But during contact with other species, the highly refrigerated life-support and sensory translation systems which they are forced to wear are large and complex and require frequent power recharge . . ."

Three of them! Conway thought. He looked around for the Tralthan who had correctly tagged the suited DBLF, and Danalta, the Melfan trainee who had identified the FROB, to observe their reactions to the very knowledgeable Kelgian—but the group was milling about so much that he could not tell who was who. Certainly he had sensed something unusual about this bunch shortly after taking charge of them at the hospital's staff entry port.

". . . The other life-form," the Kelgian was saying, "inhabits a heavy-gravity, watery planet which circles very close to its parent sun. It breathes superheated steam and has a quite interesting metabolism about which I am incompletely informed. It, also, is a small life-form, and the large size of its pressure envelope is necessitated by its having to mount heaters to render the occupant comfortable, and surface insulation and refrigerators to keep the vicinity habitable by other life-forms.

"The environment of the Hudlar ward is warm with a high moisture content," the Kelgian continued, "and some measure of the low internal temperature required by a methane-breathing SNLU would be conducted, no matter how efficient the insulation, to the outer fabric of the vehicle, where condensation would be apparent. Since condensation is not present, the probability is high that the vehicle contains the high-temperature life-form, a member of which species is said to be a Diagnostician at the hospital.

"This identification is the result of deduction, guesswork, and a degree of prior knowledge, Senior Physician," the Kelgian ended, "but I would place the entity in physiological classification TLTU."

Conway looked closely at the slow, regular fur movements of the unusually unemotional and well-informed DBLF, and then at the agitated pelts of its Kelgian colleagues. Speaking slowly, because his mind was moving at top speed and little of it was free for speech, he said, "The answer is correct, no matter how you arrived at it."

He was thinking about the DBLF classification, and in particular about their expressive fur. Because of inadequacies in the speech organs, the Kelgian spoken language lacked emotional expression. Instead the beings' highly mobile fur acted, so far as another Kelgian was concerned, as a perfect but uncontrollable mirror to the speaker's emotional state. As a result the concept of lying was totally alien to them, and the idea of being tactful or diplomatic or even polite was utterly unthinkable. A DBLF invariably said exactly what it meant, and felt, because its fur revealed its feelings from moment to moment and to do otherwise would be sheer stupidity.

Conway was also thinking about the Melfan ELNTs and their mechanism of reproduction which made twinning an impossibility, and about the phrasing of the answers volunteered by Danalta and the other two, particularly that of the Kelgian who had implied that the TLTU life-form was not particularly exotic. From the moment they had arrived, he had felt that something was distinctly unusual about the group. He should have trusted his feelings.

He thought back to his first sight of the newcomers and of how they had looked and acted at different times since then, especially their nervousness and the general lack of questioning about the hospital. Was some kind of conspiracy afoot? Without being obtrusive about it, he looked at each of them.

Four Kelgian DBLFs, two Dewatti EGCLs, three Tralthan FGLIs, three Melfan ELNTs, and two Orligian DBDGs—fourteen in all. *But Kelgians are never polite or respectful or capable of much control over their fur,* Conway thought as he deliberately turned away from them and looked into the ward.

"Who's the joker?" he said.

No one replied, and Conway, still without looking at them, said, "I have no previous knowledge of the life-form concerned, and my identification is based, therefore, on inference, deduction, and behavioral observation . . ."

The sarcasm in his voice was probably lost in the translation, and the majority of extraterrestrials were literal-minded to a fault, anyway. He softened his tone as he went on. "I am addressing that entity among you whose species is amoebic in that it can extrude any limbs, sense organs, or protective tegument necessary to the environment or situation in which it finds itself. My guess is that it evolved on a planet with a highly eccentric orbit, and with climatic changes so severe that an incredible degree of physical adaptability was necessary for survival. It became dominant on its world, developed intelligence and a civilization, not by competing in the matter of natural weapons but by refining and perfecting the adaptive capability. When it was faced by natural enemies, the options would be flight, protective mimicry, or the assumption of a shape frightening to the attacker.

"The speed and accuracy of the mimicry displayed here," he continued, "particularly in the almost perfect reproduction of behavior patterns, suggests that the entity may be a receptive empath. With such effective means of self-protection available, I would say that the species is impervious to physical damage other than by physical annihilation or the application of ultrahigh temperatures, so that the concept of curative surgery would be a strange one indeed to members of that race. Virtual physical indestructibility would mean that they did not require mechanisms for self-protection, so they are likely to be advanced in the philosophical sciences but backward in developing their technology.

"I would identify you," Conway said, swinging around to face them, "as physiological classification TOBS."

He walked rapidly toward the three Orligians, for the good reason that there should have been only two of them. Quickly but gently he reached out to their shoulders and slipped a finger between the straps of their harnesses and the underlying fur. On the third attempt he could not do it because the harness and the fur would not separate.

Dryly, Conway said, "Do you have any future plans or ambitions, Doctor Danalta, other than playing practical jokes?"

For a moment the head and shoulders melted and slumped into what could have been the beginnings of a Melfan carapace—the sort of disquieting metamorphosis, Conway thought, which he would have to get used to—before it firmed back to the Orligian shape.

"I am most sincerely sorry, Senior Physician," Danalta said, "if my recent actions have caused you mental distress. The matter of physical shape is normally of complete indifference to me, but I thought that adopting the forms of the people within the hospital would be more convenient for purposes of communication and social intercourse, and I also wished to practice my mimicry as soon and as often as possible before a being who was most likely to spot any inconsistencies. On the ferrycraft I discussed it with the other members of the group, and they agreed to cooperate.

"My chief purpose in seeking a position at the hospital," Danalta went on quickly, "was to have the opportunity of working with so large and varied a group of life-forms. To a mimic of my capabilities—and at this point I should say that they are considered greater than average among my people—this establishment represents a tremendous challenge, even though I fully realize that there will be life-forms which I may not be able to reproduce. Regarding the word 'joker,' this does not seem to translate into my language. But if I have given offense in this matter, I apologize without reservation."

"Your apology is accepted," Conway said, thinking of some of the harebrained stunts his own group of trainees had been up to many years ago—activities which had only the most tenuous connection with the practice of medicine. He looked at his watch and added, "If you are interested in meeting a large number of different life-forms, Doctor, you will shortly have your wish. All of you, please follow me."

But the Orligian who was not an Orligian did not move. It said, "As you rightly deduced, Senior Physician, the practice of medicine is completely foreign to our species. My purpose in coming here is selfish, even pleasurable, rather than idealistic. I shall merely be using my abilities to reassure beings who are suffering from physical malfunctions by mimicking them if there are no members of their own race present to give such reassurance. Or to adapt quickly to environments which others would find lethal so that urgent treatment would not be delayed because of time wasted in the donning of protective envelopes. Or to extrude limbs of a specialized shape or function which might be capable of repairing otherwise inaccessible areas where an organic malfunction had occurred. But I am not, and should not be called, a Doctor."

Conway laughed suddenly. He said, "If that is the kind of work you plan to do here, Danalta, we won't call you anything else."

CHAPTER 2

Like a gigantic, cylindrical Christmas tree Sector Twelve General Hospital hung in the interstellar darkness between the rim of the parent Galaxy and the densely populated star systems of the Greater Magellanic Cloud. In its three hundred and eighty-four levels were reproduced the environments of all the intelligent life-forms known to the Galactic Federation, a biological spectrum ranging from the ultrafrigid methane life-forms through the more common oxygen-breathing types up to the weird and wonderful beings who did not breathe, or even eat, but existed by the direct absorption of hard radiation.

Sector General represented a two-fold miracle of engineering and psychology. Its supply and maintenance were handled by the Monitor Corps—the Federation's executive and law-enforcement arm—which also saw to its nonmedical administration. But the traditional friction between military and civilian members of the staff did not occur, and neither were there any serious problems among its ten thousand-odd medical personnel, who were composed of nearly seventy differing life-forms with as many different mannerisms, body odors, and ways of looking at life.

But space was always at a premium in Sector General, and whenever possible the beings who worked together were expected to eat together—though not, of course, of the same food.

The trainees were lucky enough to find two adjoining tables, unlucky in that the furniture and eating utensils were designed for the use of dwarflike Nidian DBDGs. The vast dining hall catered to the warm-blooded, oxygen-breathing members of the staff, and one look around made plain that different species dined or talked shop or simply gossiped together at the same table. Wrong-size furniture was a discomfort which the newcomers would get used to and, in this instance, things could have been much worse.

The Melfan's mandibles were at the right height above the table, and it was no inconvenience for the ELNTs to eat while standing. The Tralthans did everything including sleeping on their six blocky feet. The Kelgians could adapt their caterpillar shapes to any type of furniture, and the Orligians, like Conway himself, could sit without too much discomfort on the armrests of the chairs. The tiny Dewatti had no problems at all, and the polymorphic Danalta had taken the shape of a Dewatti.

"The food-ordering and delivery system is standard," Conway said, looking from one table to the other, "and the same as that used on the ships which brought you here. If you punch in your physiological classification, the menu will be displayed in your own written language. Except for Danalta. There are no special dietary requirements for the TOBS life-form, I suspect, but no doubt you have preferences? Danalta! . . ."

"Your pardon, Senior Physician," the TOBS said. While it watched the dining hall entrance, its body was twisted into a shape impossible for a Dewatti. "My attention was taken by the incredible assortment of beings who come and go here."

"What would you like to eat?" Conway asked patiently.

The TOBS spoke without turning its Dewatti head. "Virtually anything which is not radioactive or chemically corrosive, Senior Physician. Were nothing else available I could, in a short time, metabolize the material of this dining furniture. But I eat infrequently and will not need to do so again for several of your days."

"Fine." Conway tapped for a steak before going on. "And Danalta, while it is very pleasant, and rare in this establishment, to be addressed properly and with respect, it can be cumbersome. So it is customary to address interns, Junior and Senior Physicians, and even Diagnosticians as Doctor. Have you seen a physiological type which you cannot reproduce?"

Conway was beginning to feel irritated at the way Danalta kept looking at the entrance while he was speaking, and wondered if it

416 · JAMES WHITE

was a trait peculiar to the species and the impoliteness uninten-
tional. Then he nearly choked when he saw that the TOBS had
extruded a small eye from the back of its head to watch him.

"I have certain limitations, Doctor," it replied. "Shape changing
is relatively easy, but I cannot discard physical mass. This . . ."—it
indicated itself—"is a small but very heavy Dewatti. And the entity
who has just entered would be very difficult to reproduce."

Conway followed the direction of its other eyes, then stood up
suddenly and waved.

"Prilicla!"

The little being who had just entered the dining hall was a Cinrusskin GLNO—a six-legged, exoskeletal, multiwinged, incredibly
fragile insect. The gravity of its home world was one-twelfth Earth
normal, and only double sets of gravity nullifiers kept it from being
smashed flat against the floor, enabled it to fly or, when the unthinking movements of its more massive colleagues threatened life
and ultrafragile limb, to scamper safely along the walls or ceiling. It
was impossible for off-worlders to tell Cinrusskins apart; even Cinrusskins could only differentiate between members of the species by
the identification of individual emotional radiation. But there was
only one GLNO empath on the hospital staff; this one had to be
Senior Physician Prilicla.

The occupants of both tables were watching the little empath as
it flew slowly toward them on its wide, iridescent, almost transparent wings. As it came to a gentle halt above them, Conway noticed
a faint, erratic trembling in the six pipestem legs and its hover
showed definite signs of instability.

Something was distressing the little Cinrusskin, but Conway did
not say anything, because he knew that his own concern was already
obvious to the empath. He wondered suddenly if the sight of the
GLNO had triggered some deep-seated phobia in one of the new
arrivals and it was radiating fear or revulsion with sufficient intensity
to affect Prilicla's coordination.

He would have to put a stop to *that*.

"This is Senior Physician Prilicla," he said quickly, as if he was
making a simple introduction. "It is a native of Cinruss, a GLNO,
and possesses a highly developed empathic faculty which, among
other uses, is invaluable in detecting and monitoring the condition

of deeply unconscious patients. The faculty also makes it highly sensitive to the emotional radiation of colleagues such as ourselves who are conscious. In Prilicla's presence we must guard against sudden and violent mental reactions, even involuntary reactions such as instinctive fear or dislike at meeting a life-form which, on another species' home planet, is a predator or the object of a childhood phobia. These feelings and reactions must be controlled and negated to the best of your abilities because they will be experienced with greater intensity by the empath. When you become better acquainted with Prilicla, you will find that it is impossible to have unpleasant feelings toward it.

"And I apologize, Prilicla, for making you the subject of that impromptu lecture without first asking your permission."

"No need, friend Conway. I am aware of your feeling of concern, which was the reason for giving the lecture, and I thank you for it. But no unpleasant feelings exist among this group. Their emotional radiation is composed of surprise, incredulity, and intense curiosity, which I will be pleased to satisfy—"

"But you're still shaking ..." Conway began quietly. Uncharacteristically the Cinrusskin ignored him.

"... I am also aware of another empath," it went on, drifting along between the tables until it hovered above the psuedo-Dewatti with the extra eye. "You must be the newly arrived polymorph life-form from Fotawn. I look forward to working with you, friend Danalta. This is my first encounter with the extremely gifted TOBS classification."

"And I with a GLNO, Doctor Prilicla," Danalta replied as its Dewatti shape slumped and began to overflow the chair in what had to be a pleased reaction at such words from a Senior Physician. "But my empathic faculty is not nearly as sensitive and well developed as yours. It evolved with the shape-changing ability as an early warning of the intentions of nearby predators. Unlike the faculty possessed by your race, which is used as the primary system of nonverbal communication, mine is under voluntary control so that the level of emotional radiation reaching my receptors can be reduced or even cut off at will should it become too distressing."

Prilicla agreed that a shutoff was a useful option, and ignoring Conway, they turned to discussing their homeworld environments, the gentle, light-gravity world of Cinruss and Fotawn, the utterly frightful and inimicable planet of the TOBS. The others, to whom Cinruss and Fotawn were little more than names, listened with great interest, only occasionally breaking in with questions.

Conway, who could be as patient as anyone when all other options were closed to him, concentrated on finishing his meal before the downwash from Prilicla's wings cooled it into inedibility.

He was not surprised that the two empaths were getting on well together—that was a law of nature. An emotion-sensitive who by word, deed, or omission caused hostility in the people around it had those same feelings bounced back in its face, so it was in an empath's own interest to make the atmosphere as pleasant as possible for all concerned. Danalta, apparently, was somewhat different in that it could switch off incoming emotional radiation at will.

Neither was Conway surprised that the TOBS knew so much about Cinruss and its empathic natives—Danalta had already demonstrated its wide-ranging knowledge about everything and everybody. What did surprise him was that Prilicla seemed to know a lot about Fotawn that had not come up in the present conversation, and Conway had the impression that the knowledge was recently acquired. But from whom?

Certainly it was not common knowledge in the hospital, Conway thought as he kept his eyes on his dessert, with an occasional glance upward to where Prilicla was maintaining its unstable hover. From habit he did not look at the various unsavory, foul-smelling messes which the others were busy ingesting. Had news of Fotawn and its visiting TOBS leaked, the hospital grapevine would have been twitching with it in its every leaf and branch. So why had Prilicla alone been given the information?

"I'm curious," Conway stated during the next lull in the conversation.

"I know." The trembling in Prilicla's limbs increased momentarily. "I am an empath, friend Conway."

"And I," Conway replied, "after the number of years we have worked together, have developed a degree of empathy where you are concerned, little friend. There is a problem."

It was a statement rather than a question, and Prilicla's flying

became even more unstable, so that it had to alight on an unoccupied space at the table. When it spoke it seemed to be choosing
the words with great care, and Conway reminded himself that the
empath was not in the least averse to lying if in so doing it could
maintain a pleasant level of emotional radiation in the area.

"I have had a lengthy meeting with friend O'Mara," Prilicla said,
"during which I was given some disturbing news."

"Which was?" Conway felt that he should have obtained a degree in extraterrestrial dentistry; on this occasion getting information out of Prilicla was like pulling teeth.

"I am sure that I will adjust to it in time," the empath replied.
"Do not be concerned for me. I . . . I have been promoted to a
position of much greater responsibility and authority. Please understand, friend Conway, I accepted with reluctance."

"Congratulations!" Conway was delighted. "And there was no
need for the reluctance, or for you to feel badly about it. O'Mara
would not give you the job unless he was absolutely sure you could
do it. What exactly will you be doing?"

"I would rather not discuss it here and now, friend Conway."
Prilicla's tremor was increasing as it forced itself to say something
which verged on the disagreeable. "This is not the time or the place
to talk shop."

Conway choked on his coffee. In this place shop was normally
the only subject of conversation, and they both knew it. What was
more, the presence of the newcomers should have been no bar,
because they would have been interested in listening to a discussion
between senior members of staff of matters which they did not quite
understand, but which they soon would. He had never known Prilicla to behave like this before, and the intensity of his curiosity was
making the empath shake even harder.

"What did O'Mara say to you?" Conway asked firmly, and
added, "Exactly."

"He said," Prilicla replied quickly, "that I should assume more
responsibility, learn to give orders, and generally throw my weight
around. Friend Conway, my physical mass is inconsiderable, my
musculature virtually nonexistent, and I feel that the thought processes of the Chief Psychologist are, well, difficult to fathom. But

420 · JAMES WHITE

right now I must excuse myself. There are some routine matters to which I must attend on *Rhabwar,* and I had, in any case, planned on having lunch in the ambulance ship."

Conway did not have to be an empath to know that the empath was uncomfortable and did not want to answer any more questions.

A few minutes after Prilicla departed, he handed over the trainees to the instructors who had been waiting patiently for them to finish lunch, and he had a few more minutes in which to think before a trio of Kelgian nurses joined the next table and began moaning and twitching their fur at each other. He switched off his translator so that their conversation, a highly scandalous tale about another member of their species, would not distract him.

Prilicla would not display continuous emotional disturbance simply because it had received news of a promotion. It had borne heavy medical and surgical responsibilities on many previous occasions. Neither would it mind giving orders. True, it had no weight to throw about, but then it always gave its instructions in such a polite and inoffensive way that its subordinates would have died rather than make it feel unhappy by refusing to obey. And the newcomers had not been emoting unpleasantly and neither had Conway.

But suppose Conway *would* have felt badly if Prilicla had told him the details of its new job? That would explain the empath's uncharacteristic behavior, because the thought of hurting another being's feelings would be highly unpleasant for it—especially if the person concerned was a close friend like Conway. And for some reason Prilicla would not, or could not, speak about its new position in front of the newcomers, or perhaps before one of the newcomers.

Maybe it was not its new job which was worrying Prilicla but something it had learned during its meeting with O'Mara, something which concerned Conway himself and which the Cinrusskin was not at liberty to divulge. He checked the time and stood up quickly, excusing himself to the nurses.

The answers—and, he knew from long experience, very likely a whole new set of problems—would be found in the office of the Chief Psychologist.

CHAPTER 3

The inner office of the Chief Psychologist resembled in many respects a medieval torture chamber, and the resemblance was heightened not only by the wide variety of extraterrestrial couches and relaxers fitted with physical restraints, but by the graying, granite-featured Torquemada in Monitor Corps green who presided over it. Major O'Mara indicated a physiologically suitable chair.

"Sit down, Doctor," he said with a completely uncharacteristic smile. "Relax. You've been dashing about in that ambulance ship of yours so much recently that I've scarcely seen you. It is high time that we had a good, long talk."

Conway felt his mouth go dry. *This is going to be rough.* But what had he done or left undone to merit this sort of treatment?

The other's features were as unreadable as a lump of rock, but the eyes which were studying him, Conway knew from long experience, opened into a mind so keenly analytical that it gave the Major what amounted to a telepathic faculty. Conway did not speak and neither, for a long moment, did O'Mara.

As Chief Psychologist of the Federation's largest multienvironment hospital, he was responsible for the mental well-being of a huge medical staff belonging to more than sixty different species. Even though his Monitor Corps rank of major—which had been conferred on him for purely administrative reasons—did not place him high in the hospital's chain of command, there were no clear limits to his authority. To O'Mara the medical staff were potential patients, and a large part of the Psychology Department's work was

422 · JAMES WHITE

the assignment of the right kind of doctor to a given patient.

Even with the highest degrees of tolerance and mutual respect, dangerous situations could arise among the staff because of ignorance or misunderstanding, or a being could develop xenophobia—in spite of the strict psychological screening every Sector General candidate had to undergo before being accepted for training—to a degree which threatened to affect its professional competence, mental stability, or both. An Earth-human doctor, for example, who had a strong subconscious fear of spiders would not be able to bring to bear on a Cinrusskin patient the proper degree of clinical detachment necessary for its treatment. And if someone like Prilicla were to treat such an Earth-human patient . . .

A large part of O'Mara's responsibility was to detect and eradicate such trouble among the medical staff while the other members of his department saw to it that the problems did not arise again—to such an extent that Earth-humans knowledgeable in matters of planetary history referred to the process as the Second Inquisition. According to O'Mara himself, however, the true reason for the high level of mental stability among his charges was that they were all too frightened of him to risk publicly displaying even a minor neurosis.

O'Mara smiled suddenly and said, "I think you are overdoing the respectful silence, Doctor. I would like to talk to you and, contrary to my usual practice, you will be allowed to talk back. Are you happy with ambulance ship duty?"

Normally the Chief Psychologist's manner was caustic, sarcastic, and abrupt to the point of rudeness. He was fond of saying by way of explanation—O'Mara never apologized for anything—that with his colleagues he could relax and be his usual bad-tempered, obnoxious self while with potential patients he had to display sympathy and understanding. Knowing that, Conway did not feel at all reassured by his uncharacteristically pleasant Chief Psychologist.

"Quite happy," Conway said guardedly.

"You weren't happy in the beginning." O'Mara was watching him intently. "As I remember, Doctor, you thought it beneath the dignity of a Senior Physician to be given medical charge of an ambulance ship. Any problems with the ship's officers or the medical team? Any personnel changes you might care to suggest?"

"That was before I realized what a very special ambulance ship *Rhabwar* was," Conway said, answering the questions in order. "There are no problems. The ship runs smoothly, the Monitor Corps crew are efficient and cooperative, and the members of the medical team are . . . No, I cannot think of any possible change that should be made in the personnel."

"I can." For an instant there was a caustic edge to the Chief Psychologist's tone, as if the O'Mara that Conway knew and did not particularly love was trying to break through. Then he smiled and went on. "Surely you must have considered the disadvantages, the inconvenience and disruption caused by constantly remaining on ambulance ship standby, and you must have felt a degree of irritation that every operation you perform at Sector General requires that a surgical understudy be prepared in case you were to be suddenly called away. And the ambulance ship duty means that you cannot take part in some of the projects which your seniority would warrant. Research, teaching, making your experience available to others instead of dashing all over the Galaxy on rescue missions and—"

"So the change will be me," Conway broke in angrily. "But who will be my? . . ."

"Prilicla will head *Rhabwar*'s medical team," O'Mara replied, "but it accepted only on condition that in so doing it did not cause its friend Conway serious mental distress. It was quite adamant about that, for a Cinrusskin. Even though I told it not to say anything to you until you had been told officially, I expected it to go straight to you with the news."

"It did. But it only mentioned a promotion, nothing else. I was with a party of new trainees and Prilicla seemed more interested in an empathic polymorph called Danalta. But I could see that something was troubling our little friend."

"Several things were troubling Prilicla," O'Mara said. "It knew that when you moved from *Rhabwar*, it moved up to your job, and that Danalta had already been chosen to fill its vacancy. But the TOBS doesn't know about this yet, so Prilicla couldn't tell you the details of its new job, because if Danalta learned about its appointment at second hand it might decide that it was being insulted by being taken for granted. The TOBS are a very able species and justifiably proud of their abilities, and its psych profile indicates that it would certainly take umbrage in a situation like that. But the job it is being offered is physiologically challenging to a polymorph, and I expect Danalta to jump at it.

"Have you any serious objections to these changes, Doctor?" he added.

"No." Conway wondered why he did not feel angrier and more disappointed at losing a position which was the envy of his colleagues, and which he himself found exciting and professionally demanding. He added sourly, "If the changes are necessary in the first place."

"They are necessary," O'Mara said seriously, and went on. "I am not in the habit of paying compliments, as you know. My job here is to shrink heads, not swell them. Neither do I discuss my reasons for taking particular actions or decisions. But this is not a routine matter."

The psychologist's square, stubby hands were spread out on the desk before him, and his face was bent forward, looking at them as he spoke,

"First," he said, "you were the medical team leader on *Rhabwar*'s maiden flight. Since then there have been many successful rescue missions, the procedures for the recovery and treatment of survivors have been perfected, and you are leaving a most efficient ambulance ship in which nothing serious can go wrong because of a small change in operating personnel. Prilicla, Murchison, and Naydrad will still be there, remember. And Danalta . . . Well, with two empaths on the team, one of whom has muscles, can change shape at will, and get into normally inaccessible areas of a wrecked ship, there might even be an improvement in the rescue times.

"Second, there is Prilicla. You know as well as I do that it is one of our best Senior Physicians. But, for purely psychological and evolutionary reasons, it is incredibly timid, cowardly, and utterly lacking in self-assertion. Placing it in a position where it has overall responsibility and authority, at the site of a disaster, will accustom it to the idea of giving orders and making decisions without help from superiors. I realize that its orders may not sound like orders, and that they will be obeyed because nobody will want to hurt its feelings by objecting. But in time it should acquire the habit of command, and during the periods between rescue missions the habit will carry over to its work in the hospital. You agree?"

Conway tried to smile as he said, "I'm glad our little friend isn't here because my emotional radiation is anything but pleasant. But I agree."

"Good," the Major said. He went on briskly. "Third, there is Senior Physician Conway. We should be striving for objectivity in this matter, which is the reason why I am referring to you in the third person. He is a strange character in some ways, and has been since he joined us. A bit of a brat and very sure of himself in the early days, but he showed promise. In spite of this he remained a loner, didn't mix socially, and seemed to prefer the company of his extraterrestrial colleagues. Psychologically suspect behavior, that, but it conferred distinct advantages in a multispecies hospital where—"

"But Murchison isn't . . ." Conway began.

". . . An extraterrestrial," O'Mara finished for him. "I realize that. The processes of senile decay are not so advanced in me that I would fail to notice that she is an Earth-human DBDG female, and then some. But apart from Murchison, your close friends are people like the Kelgian charge nurse Naydrad, the Melfan Senior Edanelt, Prilicla, and, of course, that SNLU dietician with the un-pronounceable name from Level Three Oh Two, and even Diag-nostician Thornnastor. This is highly significant."

"What does it signify?" Conway asked, wishing desperately that the other would stop talking and give him time to think.

"You should be able to see that for yourself," O'Mara said sharply, then went on. "Add to this the fact that Conway has per-formed excellently over the years, has seen many important and unusual cases through to their successful conclusions, and has not been afraid to take personal responsibility for his professional de-cisions. And now there are indications that he may be losing his fine edge.

"It isn't serious as yet," the psychologist went on quickly before Conway could react. "In fact, neither his colleagues nor the man himself has noticed it, and there is no diminution of professional competence. But I have been studying his case very closely, and it has been apparent to me for some time that Conway is slipping into a rut, and must . . ."

"A *rut*! In this place?" Conway laughed in spite of himself.

"All things are relative," O'Mara said irritably. "Let us call it the increasingly routine response to the completely unexpected, if rut is too simple for you. But to resume, it is my considered opinion that this person requires a complete change of assignment and duties. This change should be preceded by the immediate removal from the ambulance ship responsibilities, some minor psychiatric assistance, and a period of mental reappraisal . . ."

"Agonizing reappraisal," Conway said, laughing again without knowing why. "Reappraisals are always supposed to be agonizing."

O'Mara studied him intently for a moment, then he exhaled slowly through his nose. Caustically, he said, "I don't approve of unnecessary suffering, Conway, but if you want to agonize while you're reappraising, feel free."

The Major's normally abrasive manner had returned, Conway noted. Apparently O'Mara no longer regarded him as a patient— which was pleasantly, or rather unpleasantly, reassuring. But his mind was fairly seething as it tried to assimilate and consider all the implications of this sudden and dramatic change in his situation, and he knew that he was temporarily incapable of responding coherently.

"I need time to think about this," he said.

"Naturally," O'Mara said.

"And I'd like to spend some time on *Rhabwar* to advise Prilicla on—"

"No!" O'Mara's open hand slapped the desk top. "Prilicla will have to learn to do the job in its own way, as you had to do, for the best results. You will stay away from the ambulance ship and not speak to the Cinrusskin except to wish it goodbye and good luck. In fact, I want you out of this hospital as quickly as possible. There is a Monitor Corps scoutship on courier duty leaving in thirty hours from now, so you won't have time for long goodbyes.

"I do not believe," he went on sardonically, "that there is any way that I can stop you saying a long goodbye to Murchison. Prilicla will already have broken the news of your imminent departure to her, and I can't think of anyone who could break it more gently, since it has been told what is going to happen to you over the next few months."

"I wish," Conway said sourly, "that somebody would tell *me*."

"Very well," the Chief Psychologist said, sitting back in his chair. "You are being assigned for an indefinite period to a planet which, in its most widely used language, is called Goglesk. They have a problem there. I don't know the details, but you will have plenty of time to brief yourself on it when you arrive, if it interests you. In this case you will not be expected to solve the problem; you will simply rest and—"

O'Mara's intercom buzzed, and a voice said, "Sorry, sir, but Doctor Fremvessith is here, early for its appointment. Shall I ask it to return later?"

"That's the PVGJ for the Kelgian tape erasure," O'Mara replied. "There are problems there. No, ask it to wait and administer sedation if necessary."

To Conway he went on. "As I was saying, while you are on Goglesk I want you to take things easy and think very carefully about your professional future, and take plenty of time to decide what you want to do or not do at Sector General. To assist the process, I'll provide some medication designed to enhance the memory and aid dream recall. There are no long-term side effects. If you are going to take a mental inventory, the least I can do is supply a light for the darker recesses."

"But *why*?" Conway said, and suddenly he was not at all sure that he wanted the answer.

O'Mara was watching him intently, his mouth a tight, expressionless line, but the look in his eyes was sympathetic. He said, "You are beginning to realize the purpose of this meeting at last, Conway. But to save wear and tear on your overworked brain, I'll make it simple for you.

"The hospital is giving you the chance," he ended very seriously, "to try for Diagnostician."

A Diagnostician! . . .

Many times Conway had had the disquieting experience of having his mind shared with an alien alter ego, as had the majority of the medics at Sector General. He had even, for one relatively short period, had his mind apparently taken over by several extra-terrestrials. But after that experience O'Mara had spent several days putting the mental pieces of the original Conway personality together again.

The problem was that although the hospital was equipped to treat every known form of intelligent life, no single person could hold in his or its mind even a fraction of the physiological data necessary for this purpose. Surgical dexterity was a product of experience and training, but the complete physiological information on a patient had to be furnished by means of an Educator tape, which was simply the brain record of some great medical genius belonging to the same or a similar species to that of the patient being treated.

If an Earth-human doctor had to treat a Kelgian patient, he took a DBLF physiology tape until treatment was completed, after which the tape was erased. The exceptions to this rule were the Senior Physicians of proven stability with teaching duties, and the Diagnosticians.

A Diagnostician was one of the medical *elite*, a being whose mind was considered stable enough to retain permanently six, seven, and in some cases ten physiology tapes simultaneously. To the data-crammed minds of the Diagnosticians were given the initiation and direction of original research in xenological medicine in addition to the practice and teaching of their considerable art.

But the tapes did not impart only the physiological data—the complete memory and personality of the entity who had possessed that knowledge was transferred as well. In effect a Diagnostician subjected himself or itself voluntarily to an extreme form of multiple schizophrenia. The entities apparently sharing one's mind could be aggressive, unpleasant individuals—geniuses were rarely charming people—with all sorts of peeves and phobias. Usually these did not become apparent during the course of an operation or treatment. Often the worst times were when the possessor of the tape was relaxing, or sleeping.

Alien nightmares, Conway had been told, were really nightmarish. And alien sexual fantasies or wish-fulfillment dreams were enough to make the person concerned wish, if he was capable of wishing coherently for anything, that he were dead. Conway swallowed.

"A response of some kind is called for," O'Mara said sarcastically, his manner indicating that he was back to being his usual, unlovable self and that the Conway interview was no longer a matter for concern. "Unless that gape is an attempt at nonverbal communication?"

"I . . . I need time to think about it," Conway said.

"You will have plenty of time to think about it," O'Mara said, standing up and looking pointedly at the desk chronometer, "on Goglesk."

CHAPTER 4

The officers of the Monitor Corps scoutship *Trennelgon* knew Conway, both by reputation and by the fact that on three separate occasions he had given instructions to their communications officer during the search and retrieval operation on the widely scattered life capsules of the gigantic coilship belonging to the CRLT group entity.

Virtually every scoutship in three Galactic Sectors had been called on to assist in that operation, and Conway had communicated with the majority of them at some stage, but this tenuous connection made *Trennelgon*'s crew act toward him as if he were a famous relative. So much so that there was no time to think, or feel morbid, or do anything but respond to their friendly curiosity regarding *Rhabwar* and its rescue missions until he began yawning uncontrollably in their faces.

He was told that the trip would require only two Jumps and that they were estimating arrival in the Goglesk system in just under ten hours, after which he was reluctantly allowed to retire.

But when he stretched out on the narrow Service bunk, it was inevitable that he would start thinking of Murchison, who was not stretched out beside him. And his recollections were sharp and clear as they always were of anything they had said or done together, so that O'Mara's memory-enhancing medication was superfluous.

She had begun by discussing the implications of Prilicla's new appointment and the effect of Danalta's shape-changing faculty on the established rescue procedures. Only gradually had she worked the conversation around to Conway's possible advancement to Diagnostician. It had been obvious that she was as reluctant to bring up the subject as Conway had been, but Murchison was less of a moral coward.

"Prilicla has no doubt about you making it," he heard her saying again, "and neither have I. But if you were unable to adjust, or could not for some reason accept the position, it is still a high professional compliment to have been considered."

Conway did not reply, and she turned toward him, raising herself on one elbow. "Don't worry about it. You'll be gone for a few weeks, maybe months, and you'll hardly even miss me."

They both knew that was untrue. He looked up at her faintly smiling but concerned features and said, "As a Diagnostician I might not be the same person anymore. That's what is worrying me. I might end up not feeling the same toward *you*."

"I'll make damned sure that you do!" she said fiercely. More quietly, she went on, "Thornnastor has been a Diagnostician for nearly thirty years. I've had to work very closely with it as my head of department, and apart from gossiping and purveying information on all and sundry on the sexual misdemeanors of every species on the hospital staff, no serious personality changes have been apparent to . . ."

". . . A non-Tralthan like you," Conway finished for her.

It was her turn to be silent. He went on. "A few years back I had a multiple carapacial fracture on a Melfan. It was a lengthy procedure, done in stages, so that I had the ELNT tape riding me for three days. The Melfans have a great appreciation of physical beauty, so long as the physique concerned is exoskeletal and has at least six legs.

"Assisting me was OR Nurse Hudson," he continued. "You know Hudson? By the time the op was completed, I was much impressed with Hudson, and I and my Melfan alter ego were regarding her as a very pleasant personality, professionally most competent, but physically as a shapeless and unlovely bag of dough. I'm worried that—"

"Some members of her own species," Murchison put in sweetly, "also regard Hudson as a shapeless and unlovely bag—"

"Now, now," Conway said.

"I know, I'm being catty. I'm worried about that, too, and sorry that I cannot fully appreciate the problems you will be facing, because the Educator tapes are not for the likes of me."

She drew her features into a mock scowl and tried to reproduce the deep, rasping voice of O'Mara at its most bitingly sarcastic as she went on. "Absolutely not, Pathologist Murchison! I am well aware that the Educator tapes would assist you in your work. But you and the other females or extraterrestrial female equivalents on the staff will have to continue using your brains, such as they are, unaided. It is regrettable, but you females have a deep, ineradicable and sex-based aversion, a form of hyperfastidiousness, which will not allow you to share your minds with an alien personality which is unaffected by your sexual . . ."

The effort of maintaining the bass voice became too much for her, and she broke into a fit of coughing.

Conway laughed in spite of himself, then said pleadingly, "But what should I, what should we, *do?*"

She placed her hand lightly on his chest and leaned closer. Reassuringly, she said, "It might not be as bad as we think. I cannot imagine anyone or anything changing you if you don't want to be changed. You're far too stubborn, so I suppose we have to give it a try. But right now we should forget it and get some sleep."

She smiled down at him and added, "Eventually."

＊　　＊　　＊

He had been given the supernumerary's position on the control deck—a courtesy not often offered to non-Service personnel—and was watching the main screen when *Trennelgon* emerged from hyperspace in the Goglesk system. The planet itself was a bluish, cloud-streaked globe similar in all respects, at this distance, to all the other worlds of the Federation which supported warm-blooded oxygen-breathing life. But Conway's primary interest was in the world's intelligent life-forms, and as diplomatically as possible he made that clear.

The Captain, an Orligian Monitor Corps Major called Sachan-Li, growled at him apologetically while its translator annunciated the words, "I'm sorry, Doctor. We know nothing of them, or of the planet itself beyond the perimeter of the landing area. We were pulled off survey duty to take the available Goglesk language data to the master translator in Sector General for processing, and to bring you and the translator program back here.

"Having you on board, Doctor," the Captain went on, "was a very welcome break in the monotony of a six-month mapping mission in Sector Ten, and I hope we didn't give you too hard a time with all our questions."

"Not at all, Captain," Conway said. "Is the perimeter guarded?"

"Only by wire netting," Sachan-Li replied. "To keep the non-intelligent grazers and scavengers from being cooked by our tail-blasts. The natives visit the base sometimes, I hear, but I've never seen one."

Conway nodded, then turned to watch the screen where the major natural features of the planet were becoming visible. He did not speak for several minutes, because Sachan-Li and the other officers—a diminutive, red-furred Nidian and two Earth-humans—were engaged in the pre-landing checks. He watched as the world overflowed the edges of the screen and its surface changed gradually from being a vertical wall ahead of them to the ground below.

Trennelgon, in its hypersonic glider configuration, shuddered its way through the upper atmosphere, slowing as it lost altitude. Oceans, mountains, and green and yellow grasslands swept past below them, still looking normal and familiar and Earth-like. Then the horizon dropped suddenly below the bottom edge of the screen. They climbed, lost velocity, and began dropping and decelerating tail-first for a landing.

"Doctor," Sachan-Li said after they had touched down, "would you mind delivering this language program to the base commander? We are supposed to drop you and take off at once."

"Not at all," Conway said, slipping the package into a tunic pocket.

"Your personal gear is inside the air lock, Doctor," the Captain said. "It was a pleasure meeting you."

They did not take off at once, but the heat from *Trennelgon's* tail-flare as it took off half a mile behind him warmed the back of Conway's neck. He continued walking toward the three closely grouped hemispheres which were the accommodation normally used for a non-permanent base with minimum personnel. He had not taken a gravity float for his gear, because his belongings fitted easily into a backpack and a large handgrip, but the late evening sun was warm, and he decided to put down his grip for a moment and rest—the degree of urgency on this job, after all, was zero.

It was then that the strangeness hit him.

He looked down at the earth which was not of the Earth; at the grass which was subtly different from that of his home world; and at the undergrowth, wildflowers, vegetation, and distant trees which, although looking superfically similar, were the products of a completely different evolutionary process. He shivered briefly despite the heat as the feeling of *intrusion* which he always felt on these occasions washed over him, and he thought of the less-subtle differences which would soon become manifest in this world's dominant lifeform. He lifted the handgrip and began walking again.

When he was still a few minutes away from the largest of the three bubble buildings, its main entrance slid open and a figure came hurrying out to meet him. The man was wearing the uniform and insignia of a lieutenant in the Monitor Corps's Cultural Contact section, and was capless—he was either a naturally sloppy person or one of the Corps's academics who had little time for worrying about their uniforms or any other clothing they might be wearing. He was well built, with fair, receding hair and highly mobile features, and he spoke when they were still more than three meters apart.

"I'm Wainright," he said quickly. "You must be the Sector General medic, Conway. Did you bring the language program?"

Conway nodded and reached into his tunic pocket with his left hand while proffering the right to the Lieutenant. Wainright drew back quickly.

"No, Doctor," he said apologetically but firmly. "You must get out of the habit of shaking hands here, or of making any other kind of physical contact. It isn't done on this planet, except in certain rare circumstances, and the natives find it, well, disquieting if they see us doing it. But that bag looks heavy. If you place it on the ground and move away, I'll be happy to carry it for you."

"I can manage, thanks," Conway said absently. There were several questions lining up in his mind, jostling each other for priority in vocalization. He began to walk toward the bubble with the Lieutenant at his side, but still separated from him by a distance of three meters.

"That tape will be very useful, Doctor," Wainright said. "Our translation computer should be able to handle the language now, with a lot fewer misunderstandings. But we weren't expecting someone from Sector General to be sent out so quickly. Thanks for coming, Doctor."

Conway waved away the thanks with his free hand and said, "Don't expect me to solve your problem, whatever it is, as easily as all that. I've been sent here to observe the situation, and think about it, and . . ." He thought of the principal reason O'Mara had sent him to Goglesk, to think about his future at the hospital, but he did not feel like telling the Lieutenant about that just yet, so he ended, ". . . And to rest."

Wainright looked at him sharply, his expression registering concern. But it was obvious that the Lieutenant was much too polite to ask Conway why a Senior Physician from the Federation's largest hospital, where every conceivable medical and psychological treatment was available, had come here to rest.

Instead, he said, "Speaking of rest, Doctor, where were you on ship time? Is it after breakfast, the middle of your day, or long past your bedtime? Would you like to rest now? It is late afternoon here, and we can easily talk in the morning."

Conway said, "I slept well and wakened less than two hours ago, and I want to talk now. In fact, if you don't stop me asking questions, Lieutenant, it is you who are going to miss a lot of sleep."

"I won't stop you, Doctor." Wainright laughed. "I don't want to suggest that my assistants are not always entertaining people, or that their digital dexterity is sometimes used to influence the laws of probability while playing cards, but it will be nice having someone new to talk to. Besides, the natives disappear at sunset, and there is nothing to do except talk about them, and that hasn't gotten us very far up until now."

He entered the building in front of Conway. There was a narrow corridor inside with a nearby door which had the Lieutenant's name on it. Wainright stopped in front of the door, looked quickly in both directions, and then asked Conway for the tape.

"Come in, Doctor," he said then, sliding open the door and walking across the large office to a desk which had a translator terminal on its top. Conway looked around the office, which was lit by the warm, orange light of the near-to-setting sun. Most of the floor space was empty of furniture, with the desk, filing and retrieval systems, projection equipment, and even the visitors' chairs crowded against the wall opposite to the window. Beside the window there was a large, dumpy cactuslike plant whose spikes and hair were richly colored in a pattern which seemed less random the more he looked at it.

He became aware of a faint odor coming from the planet, a smell which seemed to be a combination of musk and peppermint, and he moved across the office for a closer examination.

The cactus moved back.

"This is Khone." The Lieutenant switched on the translator. He indicated the Doctor and said, "This is Conway. He, too, is a healer."

While Wainright was talking, the translator had been producing a harsh, sighing sound which had to be the being's language. Conway thought for a moment, discarding in turn a number of polite, diplomatic phrases his own species used on occasions like this. It was better to be positive and unambiguous.

"I wish you well, Khone," he said.

"And I, you," the extraterrestrial said.

Wainright said quickly, "You should know, Doctor, that names are used only once during a conversation for the purposes of introduction, identification, or recognition. After the initial use, try to speak as impersonally as possible so as to avoid giving offense. Later, we can discuss this matter more fully. This Gogleskan person has waited until nearly sunset just to meet you, but now . . ."

". . . It must leave," the being ended.

The Lieutenant nodded and said, "A vehicle with a rear loading ramp has been provided, so that the passenger may board and travel while avoiding close physical proximity with the driver. The passenger will be home long before dark."

"Consideration has been shown," the Gogleskan said as it turned to go, "and gratitude is expressed."

During the conversation Conway had been studying the extraterrestrial. The mass of unruly hair and spikes covering its erect, ovoid body were less irregular in their size and placing than he had at first thought. The body hair had mobility, though not the high degree of flexibility and rapid mobility of the Kelgian fur, and the spikes, some of which were extremely flexible and grouped together to form a digital cluster, gave evidence of specialization. The other spikes were longer, stiffer, and some of them seemed to be partially atrophied, as if they had been evolved for natural defense, but the reason for their presence had long since gone. There were also a number of long, pale tendrils lying amid the multicolored hair covering the cranial area, but the purpose of these was unclear.

There was a thin band of dull metal encircling the domelike neckless head, and a few inches below the metal band were two widely spaced and recessed eyes. Its voice seemed to come from a number of small, vertical breathing orifices which encircled its waist. The being sat on a flat, muscular pad, and it was not until it turned to leave that Conway saw that it had legs as well.

These members were stubbly and concertinalike, and when the four of them were in use they increased the height of the being by several inches. He also saw that it had two additional eyes at the back of its head—obviously this species had had to be very watchful in prehistoric times—and he suddenly realized the purpose of the metal band. It was used to suspend a corrective lens over one of the Gogleskan's eyes.

Despite the physical configuration the being was a warm-blooded oxygen-breather and not an intelligent vegetable, and Conway classified it physiologically as FOKT. As it was leaving the room, it paused in the doorway, and a group of its digits twitched briefly.

"Be lonely," it said.

CHAPTER 5

Goglesk had been a borderline case so far as the Cultural Contact people were concerned. Full contact with such a technologically backward culture was dangerous, because when the Monitor Corps ships dropped out of their skies, they could not be sure whether they were giving the Gogleskans a future goal toward which to aim or a devastating inferiority complex. But the natives, in spite of their backwardness in the physical sciences and the obscure racial psychosis which forced them to remain so, were psychologically stable as individuals, and the planet had not known war for many thousands of years.

The easiest course would have been to withdraw and leave the Gogleskan culture to continue as it had been doing since the dawn of its history, and write their problem off as being insoluble. Instead, Cultural Contact had made one of its very rare compromises.

They had established a small base to accommodate a handful of observers, their supplies and equipment, which included a flyer and two general-purpose ground vehicles. The purpose of the base was to observe and gather data, nothing more. But Wainright and his team had developed a liking for those sorely tried natives and, contrary to their instructions, wanted to do more.

Problems had been encountered in obtaining accurate translations with their relatively simple equipment—the Gogleskan word-sounds were made by producing minor variations in the quantity of air expelled through four separate breathing orifices, and several potentially dangerous misunderstandings had occurred. They had decided to send their language data for checking and reprocessing to the big multitranslation computer at Sector General. So as not to disobey their instructions directly, they accompanied the material with a brief statement on the Gogleskan situation and a request to the hospital's Department of E-T Psychology for information on any similar life-form or condition which Sector General might have encountered in the past.

". . . But instead of sending information," the Lieutenant went on as he lifted the groundcar over a fallen tree which was blocking the path they were following through the forest, "they sent us Senior Physician Conway, who is—"

"Here simply to observe," Conway broke in, "and to rest."

Wainright laughed. "You didn't rest much during the past four days."

"That's because I was too busy observing," Conway said dryly. "But I wish Khone had come back to see me. You think I should visit it now?"

"That could be the correct behavior in these circumstances," the other replied. "They have some odd rules and, intensely individualistic as they are, they may consider two consecutive and uninvited visits to be an unwarranted intrusion. If a person's first visit is welcome, you may simply be expected to return it. We're entering the inhabited area now."

Gradually the forest floor had become clear of small trees and bushes, leaving only a thin carpet of grasslike vegetation between the massive trunks which served as the main structural supports for the Gogleskan dwellings. To Conway they looked like the log cabins of ancient history—but roofless because the overhanging branches provided all the necessary weather protection—and the wide variation in style and quality of workmanship made it clear that they had been built by their occupiers rather than by an organization specializing in home construction.

If a species' progress was based on group and tribal cooperation, it was easy to understand why there had been so little of it on Goglesk. But why, Conway wondered for the hundredth time since his arrival, did they refuse to cooperate with each other when they were so obviously intelligent, friendly, and nonaggressive?

"And highly accident-prone," the Lieutenant said, making Conway realize that he had been thinking aloud. "This looks like a good place to ask questions."

"Right," Conway said, opening the canopy. They had drawn level with three Gogleskans who were grouped, very loosely, around one of their spindly-legged draught animals and the contraption of unknown purpose to which it was harnessed. He went on. "Thanks for the ride, Lieutenant. I'll wander around and talk to a few people in addition to Khone, if I can find it, then walk back to base. If I get lost I'll call you."

Wainright shook his head and cut the vehicle's power, letting it settle to the ground. He said, "You aren't in your hospital now, where everybody is either a medic or a patient. The rule is that we go around in pairs. There is no danger of giving offense provided you don't move too close to them, or me. After you, Doctor."

Followed at a distance by the Lieutenant, Conway climbed down and walked toward the three natives, stopping several paces before he came to the nearest one. Not looking at anyone in particular, he said, "Is it possible to be given directions to the dwelling place of the entity Khone?"

One of the Gogleskans indicated the direction with two of its long spikes. "If the vehicle proceeds in that direction," it sighed at them, "a clearing will be encountered. More precise directions may be obtained there."

"Gratitude is expressed," Conway said, and returned to the groundcar.

The clearing turned out to be a wide crescent of grass and rocky outcroppings on the shore of a large inland lake, judging by the absence of sand and the small size of the waves. There were several jetties projecting into the deeper water, and most of the small craft tied alongside had thin smokestacks as well as sails. The buildings clustered near the water's edge were tall, three or four stories high, built of stone and wood, and with ascending ramps running up and around all four faces, so that from certain angles they looked like thin pyramids, an effect which was enhanced by their tall, conical roofs.

If it had not been for the all-pervading noise and smoke, the overall effect would have been one of picturesque, medieval charm.

STAR HEALER • 441

"It is the town's manufacturing and food-processing center," the Lieutenant said. "I've seen it several times from the flyer. The fish smell will hit you in a minute."

"It's hitting me already," Conway said. He was thinking that if this was what passed for an industrial area, then the healer, Khone, was probably the equivalent of a factory medic. He was looking forward to talking to the being again, and perhaps seeing it at work.

They were directed past a large building whose stonework and wooden beams were smoke-blackened and still smelling of a recent fire, to the edge of the lake where a large boat had sunk at its moorings. Opposite the wreck there was a low, partially roofed structure with a stream running under it. From their elevated position on the groundcar they could see into a mazelike system of corridors and tiny rooms which was Khone's dwelling and, presumably, an adjoining hospital.

A Gogleskan patient was having something done to its breathing orifices—a nonsurgical investigation, Conway saw, using long wooden probes and dilators, followed by the oral administration of medication also by a long-handled instrument. The patient occupied one cubicle during this procedure and the healer another. It was several minutes before Khone came outside and acknowledged their presence.

"Interest is felt," Conway said when the three of them were on the ground and standing at the points of an invisible equilateral triangle more than three meters on the side, "in the subject of healing on Goglesk. Comparisons of other-world knowledge and treatments might be made, of illnesses, injuries, and nonphysical disorders, and particularly of surgical procedures and anatomical studies."

Khone's center of attention was in the space between Wainright and Conway as it replied, "There is no curative surgery on Goglesk. Anatomical work is possible only on cadavers stripped of stings and residual poisons. Personal physical contact, except for the purposes of procreation or the care of nonadults, is dangerous for both the healer and patient. A certain minimum distance is essential for the performance of my work."

"But *why*?" Conway said, moving instinctively toward the healer.

Then he saw that Khone's fur was agitated and that the spikes all over its body were twitching. He turned toward the Lieutenant, ostensibly addressing Wainright when he spoke.

"An instrument in my possession enables a trained healer to observe the position and workings of internal organs and to chart the locations of bones and principal blood vessels," Conway said, and withdrew the scanner from its pouch at his side.

He began passing it slowly along his other arm, then moved it to his head, chest, and abdomen, describing in his most impersonal, lecturing voice the function of the organs, bone structure, and associated musculature revealed on the scanner's screen. Then he pulled the instrument's telescoping handle to full extension and moved it closer to Khone.

"The instrument provides this information without touching the patient's body," he added, "if that should be a requirement."

Khone had moved a little closer while he had been demonstrating the scanner, and the being had rotated its body so that the eye with the spectacle could be brought to bear on the instrument. Conway had angled the screen so that the Gogleskan could see its own internal structure while he could not. But he had also set the scanner to record so that he would be able to study the material later.

He watched the healer's spikes twitching and the long, multicolor hair rising up stiffly to lie flat again, several times in a minute. Some of the colored strands lay at right angles to the others, giving a plaid effect. The breathing orifices were making an urgent, hissing sound, but Khone was not moving away from the scanner, and gradually the being was growing calmer.

"Enough," it said. Surprisingly, it looked straight at Conway with its ridiculous, bespectacled eye. There was a long silence, during which it was obvious that the Gogleskan was coming to a decision.

"On this world," it said finally, "the art of the healer is a unique one, and the probability exists that this is true in other places. A healer may, while treating a patient, explore delicate areas and states of mind, and pry into material which is distressful or even shameful, but invariably personal. This normally forbidden and dangerous behavior is allowed because the speaker may not speak of anything learned, except to another healer who is being consulted in the interests of the patient . . ."

Hippocrates, Conway thought, *could not have said it better.*

". . . And it might be possible," Khone went on, "to discuss such matters with an off-world healer. But it must be understood that these matters are for the ears only of another healer."

"As a layman," the Lieutenant said, smiling, "I know when I'm not wanted. I'll wait in the groundcar."

Conway got down on one knee so that his eyes were on a level with those of the Gogleskan. If they were to speak together as equals, he thought, the process might be aided considerably if Conway did not tower over the other healer, whose hair and spikes were again twitching in agitation. They were less than two meters apart now. He decided to take the initiative.

He had to be careful not to overawe Khone with gratuitous accounts of medical superscience, so he began by describing the work of Sector General in very simple terms, but continually emphasizing the multispecies aspects and stressing the high degree of professional cooperation required for its performance. From there he worked gradually around to the subject of cooperation in general and its importance in fields other than medicine.

". . . Observations have been made," Conway went on, "which suggest that progress here has been retarded for reasons which, considering the high intelligence of individual Gogleskans, are not clear. Is an explanation possible?"

"Progress is impossible because cooperation is impossible," Khone replied, and suddenly it became less impersonal. "Healer Conway, we are constantly fighting ourselves and the behavior patterns imposed on us by survival instincts evolved, I suspect, at the time when we were the nonintelligent food source of every seadwelling predator on Goglesk. To successfully fight these instincts requires self-discipline in our thinking and actions if we are not to lose the very modest, nay, backward, level of culture that we now possess."

"If the exact nature of the problem could be explained in detail," Conway began, and then he, too, slipped into a more personal mode, "I would like to help you, Healer Khone. It might be that a completely strange healer, one who has a completely new and perhaps even an alien viewpoint, could suggest a solution which would not otherwise have occurred to the entities concerned . . ."

He broke off because an irregular, urgent drumming sound had started up from somewhere further inland. Khone drew away from him again. "Apologies are tendered for the immediate departure," it said loudly. "There is urgent work for a healer."

Wainright leaned out of the groundcar. "If Khone is in a hurry . . ." he began, then corrected himself. "If rapid transport is required, it is available."

The rear storage compartment was already open and the loading ramps extending groundward.

They reached the scene of the accident after ten minutes of the most hair-raising driving that Conway had ever experienced—the Gogleskan, probably because of its naturally slow method of ambulation, did not give directions for turning corners until they were abreast of the intersection concerned. By the time Wainright had grounded the vehicle beside the partly demolished three-story building indicated by Khone, Conway was wondering if for the first time in his adult life he would succumb to motion sickness.

But all subjective considerations were driven from his mind when he saw the casualties hobbling or tumbling down the cracked or slowly collapsing external ramps, or struggling out of the large, ground-level doorway which was partly blocked by fallen rubble. Their many-colored body hair was hidden beneath a layer of dust and wood splinters, and on a few of the bodies he could see the wet, red gleam of fresh wounds. But all of them were ambulatory, he saw as he jumped down from the vehicle, and they were all moving as fast as they could away from the damaged building to join the wide and surprisingly distant circle of onlookers.

Suddenly he caught sight of a Gogleskan shape protruding from the debris around the doorway, and heard the untranslatable sounds it was making.

"Why are they standing there?" he yelled at Khone, waving toward the onlookers. "Why don't they *help* it?"

"Only a healer may closely approach another Gogleskan when it is in distress," Khone said as its tiny manipulators drew thin wooden rods from a pouch strapped to its middle and began slotting them together. It added, "Or a person with sufficient mental self-control not to be affected by that distress."

Conway was following the healer as it moved toward the casualty. He said, "Perhaps a being of a completely different species could bring to bear on the case the required degree of clinical detachment."

"No," Khone said firmly. "Physical contact or even a close approach must be avoided."

The Gogleskan's rods had fitted together into a set of long-handled tongs to which, as the examination of the casualty proceeded, Khone added a series of interchangeable probes, spatulas, and lenses which were later substituted for fine brushes and swabs soaked in what must have been antiseptics for cleaning the wounds. This was followed by suturing of the larger incisions, using an ingenious device clipped to the end of the tongs. But the treatment was superficial and very, very slow.

Conway quickly extended the telescopic handle of his scanner until it was the same length as Khone's tongs, then went down onto his hands and knees and pushed the instrument toward the healer.

"Internal injuries may be present," he said. "This instrument will reveal them."

Thanks were not expressed—probably Khone was too busy to be polite—but the Gogleskan laid down its tongs at once and began using Conway's scanner. Its manipulators were awkward at first, but very soon they had adapted to the grips which had been designed for Earth-human fingers so that Khone began varying the focus and magnification in a manner that was almost expert.

"There is minor bleeding from the buried section of the body," the Gogleskan said a few minutes later. "But it will be observed that the greatest danger to the casualty is the interruption of the blood supply to the cranial area, just here, which is caused by pressure from a wooden beam lying across and compressing the main cranial artery. This has also caused unconsciousness, which explains the lack of recent sounds and body movements which will also have been observed."

"Rescue procedure?" Conway asked.

"Rescue is not possible in the time available," Khone replied. "There is no knowledge regarding the time units used by the offworld healer, but the conditions will be terminal in approximately one-fiftieth of the time period between our dawn and dusk. However, the attempt must be made . . ."

Conway looked at Wainright, who said quietly, "About fifteen minutes."

". . . To immobilize the beam with a wedge," the Gogleskan went on, "and remove the rubble from under the casualty so that the being will subside into a position where the constriction from the beam will be removed. There is also the risk of a further collapse of the structure, so the removal of beings other than the casualty and its healer is urgently requested in the interest of their safety."

It returned the scanner to Conway long handle first, and when he took it back the Gogleskan began fitting soil-moving claws to its tongs.

Conway had the nightmarish feeling of being faced with a simple problem requiring a minimal amount of manual activity, and having both hands tied behind his back. It was impossible for him to stand by and watch an injured being die when there were so many ways that he could try to save it. And yet he had been expressly forbidden to go near the creature, even though its fellow Gogleskan knew that he wanted only to help. It was stupid, of course, but there had to be something in this species' culture which made sense of the apparent stupidity.

He looked helplessly at Wainright, and at the stocky, heavily muscled body which made the Lieutenant's coveralls look tight, and tried again.

"If a casualty is unconscious," he said desperately, "it should not be adversely affected by the close presence or touch of other beings. It might be possible for the off-worlders to lift the beam sufficiently high for the casualty to be drawn free."

"Many others are watching," Khone said, and its indecision was shown by the way it raised and then lowered its tongs. Then it fitted a new set of tips to them, produced a coil of light rope from somewhere, and began using the tongs to loop it around the casualty's feet. It went on. "Very well. But there are risks. And the casualty and its healer must not be closely approached by off-worlders, or be seen by others to make such an approach, no matter how well-intentioned it is."

Conway did not ask how close "closely" was as he preceded the Lieutenant into the wide, low entrance, each putting a shoulder under the beam which was supporting one side of it. No doubt the physical proximity of Wainright and Conway was offensive to the onlookers, but the doorway was shadowed and perhaps the watching Gogleskans could not see them clearly. Right then Conway was too busy pushing to care what they thought.

Dust and fine rubble rained down on them as they lifted their end of the beam by three, four, and then nearly six inches. But at the other end where the casualty was trapped, it rose by barely two inches. Khone's tongs had successfully looped the rope around the casualty's legs, and it had wrapped the other end several times around its own middle. It took up the slack, braced its feet, and leaned against the rope like the anchorman in a tug-of-war team, but without effect. The Gogleskan FOKT life-form was too lightly built and physiologically unsuited to the application of the required traction.

"Can you hold it up yourself for a moment?" Wainright asked, crouching suddenly and disappearing further into the entrance. "I can see something that might help us."

It seemed much longer than a moment while the Lieutenant dug among the rubble inside the entrance and the beam dug into Conway's shoulder. His straining back and leg muscles were knotted in a continual, fiery cramp. He blinked the sweat out of his eyes and saw that Khone had changed its approach to the problem. Instead of pulling continuously, it had begun returning as close as was allowable to the casualty and then waddling as fast as it could away from it until the rope was pulled taut, trying to jerk the other Gogleskan free.

With every jerk the injured FOKT moved a little, but some of the sutures had opened and it was bleeding freely again.

Every single vertebra in his back was being compressed into a single osseous column, Conway thought angrily, which any second now would break.

"*Hurry*, dammit!"

"I *am* hurrying," Khone said, forgetting to be impersonal.

"Coming," the Lieutenant said.

Wainright arrived with a short, thick piece of timber which he quickly wedged between the beam and the ground. Conway collapsed thankfully onto his knees, easing his maltreated shoulder and back, but only for a moment. The Lieutenant's idea was for them to lift with a few seconds of maximum effort, and then use the prop to keep from losing the extra height gained, repeating the process until the casualty could be pulled free.

It was a very good idea, but the intermittent falls of dust and rubble were becoming a steadily increasing shower. The casualty was almost free when there was a low rumble and the sound of splintering timber from inside the building.

"Get clear!" Khone shouted as it got ready to give one last, desperate jerk on the rope. But as the healer came to the end of its waddling run, the loop slipped off the casualty's feet and Khone went tumbling and rolling away, entangled in its own rescue rope.

Later, Conway was to spend a long and agonizing time wondering whether he had done the right or the wrong thing just then, but there was simply no time to evaluate and compare extraterrestrial social behavior with that of Earth-humans—he did it because he could not do anything else. He checked his stumbling run away from the collapsing entrance, turned and grabbed the unconscious FOKT casualty by the feet.

With his greater weight and strength it came away easily, and crouched double and moving backward, he dragged it clear of the subsiding building. As the dust began to settle, he pulled it gently onto a patch of soft grass. Nearly all of Khone's sutures had pulled free, and the casualty had acquired a number of new wounds, all of which were bleeding.

The being opened its eyes suddenly, stiffened, then began making a loud, continuous, hissing sound which wavered up and down in pitch so that at times it was almost a whistle.

"*No!*" Khone said urgently. "There is no danger! It is a healer, a friend! . . ."

But the irregular hissing and whistling grew louder, and Conway was aware that the circle of onlookers, no longer distant, had joined in. He could scarcely hear himself think. Khone was stumbling around the casualty, sometimes approaching to within a few inches, then moving away again, as if it was performing an intricate ritual dance.

"Yes," Conway said reassuringly, "I'm not an enemy. I pulled you out."

"You stupid, stupid healer!" Khone said, sounding angry as well as personal. "You ignorant off-worlder! Go *away*! . . ."

What happened then was one of the strangest sights Conway had ever witnessed, and at Sector General he had seen many of those. The casualty rolled and jerked itself to its feet, still emitting the undulating whistling noises. Khone had begun to make the same sound, and the long, stiff body hair on both beings was standing out straight, so that the plaid effect caused by the different colors lying at right angles to each other was lost. Suddenly Khone and the casualty touched and were instantly welded or, more accurately, tightly woven together where they had made contact.

The stiff hairs covering their sides had insinuated into and through each other, like the warp and weft of an old-time woven rug, and it was plain that no outside agency would be able to separate them without removing the hair of both creatures and probably the underlying tegument as well.

"Let's get out of here, Doctor," Wainright said from the top of the groundcar, pointing at the Gogleskans who were closing in from all sides.

Conway hesitated, watching a third FOKT join itself in the same incredible fashion to Khone and the casualty. The long spikes whose purpose he had not known were projecting stiffly from the cranium of every Gogleskan, and there was a bright yellow secretion oozing from the tips. As he climbed into the vehicle, one of the spikes tore the fabric of his coveralls, but without penetrating the underlying clothing or skin.

While the Lieutenant moved the vehicle to higher ground for a better view of what was going on, Conway used his analyzer on the traces of yellow secretion which had been left along the edges of the tear in his suit. He was able to calculate that the contents of one of those stings introduced directly into the bloodstream would be instantly disabling, and that three or more of them would be fatal.

The Gogleskans were joining themselves into a group-entity which was growing larger by the minute. Individual FOKTs were hurrying from nearby buildings, moored ships, and even from the surrounding trees to add themselves to this great, mobile, spiky carpet which crawled around large buildings and over small ones as if it did not know or care what it was doing. In its wake it left a trail of smashed equipment, vehicles, dead animals, and even one capsized ship. The vessel had been tied up, and when the periphery of the group-entity has stumbled on board it had flipped onto its side, smashing the masts and superstructure against the jetty.

But the Gogleskans who had fallen into the water did not seem to be inconvenienced, Conway saw, and the movement of the land-based constituents of the group-entity pulled them out again within a few minutes.

"They're not blind," Conway said, aghast at the wholesale destruction. He stood on his bucket seat to get a better view and went on. "There are enough unobscured eyes around the periphery for them to see where they're going, but they seem to have great difficulty making up their mind. Oh, man, they're fairly wrecking that settlement. Can you put up the flyer and get me a detailed, high-level record of this?"

"Can do," the Lieutenant said. He spoke briefly into his communicator, then went on. "It isn't making straight for us, Doctor, but it's trying to get nearer. We'd better change position."

"No, wait," Conway said, gripping the edge of the open canopy and leaning out, the better to see the edge of the group-entity which had stumbled to within six meters' distance. Dozens of eyes regarded him coldly, and the long, yellow-tipped stings were like a thinly stubbled hayfield. "They are hostile, yet Khone itself was friendly. Why?"

His voice was almost drowned by the rushing, whistling sound made by the group, a sound which their translators did not register. But somewhere in that unintelligible mush there was a whisper of intelligence trying to fight its way out, the voice of the Gogleskan healer.

"Go away," it said. "Go away."

Conway had to drop quickly into his seat before Wainright closed the canopy on him and they moved away. Angrily, the Lieutenant said, "You can't *do* anything!"

CHAPTER 6

There was no need for the memory-enhancing medication which Conway had been taking since leaving Sector General to recall the incident—it was there in his mind, complete in every detail. And there was no arguing against the evidence, no escaping the damning conclusion that he alone was responsible for the whole sorry mess.

The vision tapes from the flyer had shown an immediate decrease in the destructive activity of the rampaging Gogleskans as soon as the groundcar carrying Wainright and Conway had left the scene. And within an hour the group-entity had fragmented into its individual members, who had stood immobile, widely separated from each other and giving the impression that they were suffering from extreme exhaustion.

He had gone over the visual material again and again, together with his scanner's playback of the self-examination by Khone and the later material on the FOKT whose rescue had precipitated the fusion of all the Gogleskans in the area. He tried to find a clue, a mere indication, the most tenuous of hints which would explain the reason for the FOKTs' incredible reaction to his touching one of their number, but without success.

At one stage the thought came that he was here to rest, to clear his mind so that he could make important decisions regarding his future. The Gogleskan situation was a nonurgent problem which, according to O'Mara, he could think about or ignore. But he could *not* ignore it, because, apart from making it fractionally worse, he had been presented with a puzzle so alien that even his long experience of extraterrestrial behavior and thought processes at the hospital was not of much help.

As an individual, Khone had been so *normal*.

Irritably he dropped into his bunk, still holding his scanner at eye level and trying to squeeze some meaning out of the FOKT recordings. In theory it was impossible to feel discomfort in a bunk with gravity controls set to a tiny fraction of one Earth-G, but Conway wriggled and tossed and managed to feel very uncomfortable indeed.

He was able to trace the shallow roots of the four FOKT stings, which at the time Khone had been examining itself had been lying flat against the upper cranium and partially concealed by the surrounding hair, and chart the positions of the fine ducts which connected the spikes to the poison sac which supplied them. There was also a nerve linkage between the base of the brain and the muscles for erecting the stings and for compressing the reservoir of venom, but he had no idea of the kind of stimulus which would trigger this activity. Neither had he any ideas regarding the function of the long, silvery strands which lay among the coarser cranial hair.

His first thought, that they were simply an indication of advancing age, had to be revised when closer study showed that the follicle structure was completely unlike that of the surrounding hair and that they, like the stings, had underlying muscle and nerve connections which gave them the capability of independent movement. Unlike the stings, they were much larger, finer, and more flexible.

Unfortunately he could not trace the subdermal nerve connections, if such were present, because his scanner had not been set for such fine work. His intention had been simply to impress the Gogleskan healer by showing it pictures of its own major organs operating, and no amount of magnification during playback could bring up details which were not already there.

Even so, had it not been for the utterly strange behavior of the FOKTs, Conway would have been highly satisfied with the physiological data he had obtained. But in this case he was not satisfied. He badly wanted to meet Khone again and examine it more closely—both clinically and verbally.

After today's debacle the chance of that happening was small indeed.

"Go away!" Khone had told him from somewhere within that rampaging mob of Gogleskans. And the Lieutenant, too, had been angry when he had shouted, "You can't *do* anything!"

Conway knew that he had slipped into sleep when he became aware that he was no longer on Goglesk. His surroundings had changed, but they were still familiar, and the problems occupying his mind had become much simpler. He did not dream very often— or, as O'Mara was fond of reminding him, he dreamed as frequently as any other so-called intelligent being, but was fortunate in that he recalled very few of his dreams. This particular dream was pleasant, uncomplicated, and bore no relation to his present situation.

At least, so it seemed at first.

The chairs were enormous and had to be climbed into instead of being sat upon, and the big dining table, which was also hand-built, required him to stand on tiptoe if he was to see onto the deeply grained and highly polished planking of its top. That, thought the mature, dreaming Conway, placed him at the age of about eight.

Whether the effect was due to O'Mara's medication or a psychological quirk which was all his own, Conway did not know, but he was viewing the dream as a mature and fully informed adult while his feelings about it were those of a not very happy eight-year-old.

His parents had been third-generation colonists on the mineral-rich, Earth-seeded world of Braemar which, at the time of their deaths, had been explored, tamed, and made safe—at least, so far as the areas occupied by the mining and agricultural towns and the single spaceport were concerned.

He had lived on the outskirts of that spaceport city, which was a great, sprawling complex of one-, two-, and three-story buildings, for all of his young life. He had not thought it strange that the log cabins greatly outnumbered the towering white blocks of the manufacturing complexes, the administration center, the spacefield buildings, and the hospital; or that the furniture, nonmetal household equipment, pottery, and ornaments were all home-produced.

With his mature hindsight he knew that wood was plentiful and cheap on Braemar while imported Earth furniture and gadgetry were very expensive and, in any case, the colonists took pride in their own handiwork and wanted it no other way.

But the log cabins were powered and lit by modern fusion generators, and the hand-built furniture supported sophisticated vision transceivers whose chief purposes were, so far as the young Conway was concerned, to educate during the day and entertain in the evening. Ground and air transportation was also modern, fast, and as safe as it was possible to make it, and only very occasionally did a flyer drop out of the sky with the loss of all on board.

It was not the loss of his parents which was making him unhappy. He had been too young to remember them as anything but vague, comforting presences, and when they had been called to the emergency at the mine he had been left in the charge of a young couple who were close neighbors. He had remained with them until after the burial, when his father's oldest brother had taken him to live with his family.

His aunt and uncle had been kindly, responsible, and very busy people who were no longer young. Their own children were young adults, so except for a period of initial curiosity, they had very little time for him. Not so the grandmother of the house, Conway's great-grandmother, who had decided that the newly orphaned infant would be her sole responsibility.

She was incredibly old—anyone who dared ask her age did not do it a second time—and as fragile as a Cinrusskin, but was still physically and mentally active. She had been the first child born to the Braemar colony, and when Conway began taking an interest in such things, she had an endless supply of stories about those early days of the colony which were far more exciting, if perhaps a little less factual, than the material in the history tapes.

Without understanding what they had been talking about at the time, Conway had heard his uncle tell a visitor that the kid and the old lady got on very well together because they were the same mental age. Except when she chastised him, which was not very often and not at all during the later years, she was always good fun. She covered for him when accidents occurred which were not entirely his fault, and she defended his pet-pen when it began to grow from a small, wired-in enclosure in the back garden to something resembling a miniature wildlife park, although she was most insistent that he not acquire pets which he could not care for properly.

He had a few Earth pets as well as a collection of the small and harmless native Braemar Herbivores—who sometimes took sick, frequently injured themselves, and multiplied practically all the time. She had called up the relevant veterinary tapes for him—such material was considered too advanced for a child—and with her advice and by his using practically all of his nonstudy time the inhabitants of his pet-pen prospered and, much to his aunt and uncle's surprise, showed a fair profit when the word got around that he was a prime source of healthy garden and household pets for the neighborhood children.

The young Conway was kept much too busy to realize that he was a very lonely boy—until his great-grandmother and only friend suddenly lost interest in talking about his pets, and seemed to lose interest in him. The doctor began visiting her regularly, and then his aunt and uncle took it in turn to stay in the room with her night and day, and they forbade him even to see his only friend.

That was why he felt unhappy. And the adult Conway, remembering as well as reexperiencing the whole incident, knew that there was more unhappiness to come. The dream was about to become a nightmare.

They had forgotten to lock the door one evening, and when he sneaked into the bedroom he found his aunt sitting on a chair by the bedside with her chin on her chest, dozing. His great-grandmother was lying with her face turned toward him, her eyes and mouth wide open, but she did not speak and she did not seem to see him. As he moved toward the bed, he heard her harsh, irregular breathing, and he became aware of the smell. Suddenly he felt frightened, but he reached forward to touch the thin, wasted arm which lay outside the bedclothes. He was thinking that she might look at him or say something, or maybe even smile at him the way she had done only a few weeks ago.

The arm was *cold*.

The mature and medically experienced Conway knew that circulation had already failed at the extremities and that the old lady had only minutes to live, and the very young Conway knew it, too, without knowing why. Unable to stop himself, he tried to call her, and his aunt woke up. She looked at his grand-grandmother, then grabbed him tightly by the arm and rushed him from the bedroom.

"Go away!" she had said, beginning to cry. "You can't *do* anything! . . ."

His adult eyes were damp when he awakened in his tiny room in the Monitor Corps base on Goglesk, and not for the first time he wondered to what extent the death of that incredibly old and fragile and warmhearted old lady had affected his subsequent life. The grief and sense of loss had faded, but not the memory of his utter helplessness, and he had not wanted to feel that way ever again. In later life, when he had encountered disease and injury and impending death, there had always been something, sometimes quite a lot, that he could do. And until his arrival on Goglesk he had never felt as helpless as that again.

"Go away," Khone had said when Conway's misguided attempt to help had resulted in the near-devastation of a town, and had probably caused untold psychological damage as well. And "You can't *do* anything," the Lieutenant had said.

But he was no longer a frightened, grieving young boy. He refused to believe that there was nothing he could do.

He thought about the situation as he bathed, dressed, and converted the room into its daytime mode, but ended by feeling angry with himself and even more helpless. He was a medic, he told himself, not a Cultural Contact specialist. The majority of his contacts were with extraterrestrials who were immobilized by disease or injury or examination-room restraints, and when close physical contact and investigative procedures were taken for granted. But not so on Goglesk.

Wainright had warned him about the phobic individualism of the FOKTs, and he had seen it for himself. Yet he had allowed his Earth-human instincts and feelings to take over when he should have controlled them—at least until he had understood a little more about the situation.

And now the only being who could have helped him understand the problem, Khone, would not want to meet him again except, perhaps, to offer physical violence.

Maybe he could try with another Gogleskan in a different area, presupposing that Wainright agreed to Conway's borrowing the base's only flyer for a lengthy period, and that the FOKTs had no means of long-distance communication. Certainly there had been nothing detected on the radio frequencies, and no evidence of visual or audible signaling systems or of messages carried by intelligent or nonintelligent runners or flyers.

But was it likely, he was thinking when his communicator beeped suddenly, that a species which so fanatically avoided close contact would be interested in keeping in touch over long distances?

"Your room sensors say that you're up and moving around," Wainright said, laughing. "Are you mentally awake as well, Doctor?"

Conway did not feel like laughing at anything, and he hoped the well-meaning Lieutenant was not intent on cheering him up. Irritably, he said, "Yes."

"Khone is outside," Wainright said, as if he was having trouble believing his own words. "It says that an obligation exists to return our visit of yesterday, and to apologize for any mental or physical distress the incident may have caused us. Doctor, it particularly wants to talk to you."

Extraterrestrials, thought Conway, not for the first time, *are full of surprises.* This one might have some answers, as well. As he left the room his pace could never have been described as the confident, unhurried tread of a Senior Physician. It was more like a dead run.

CHAPTER 7

In spite of the painfully slow and impersonal style of speech and the lengthy pauses between the sentences, it was obvious that Khone wanted to talk. What was more, it wanted to ask questions. But the questions were extraordinarily difficult for it to verbalize because they were of a kind which had never before been asked by a member of its species.

Conway knew of many member species of the Galactic Federation whose viewpoints and behavior patterns were utterly alien and even repugnant to an Earth-human, even to an Earth-human medic with wide extraterrestrial experience like himself. He could imagine the tremendous effort Khone was putting into trying to understand this frightful off-worlder who, among other peculiarities, thought nothing of actually *touching* another being for purposes other than mating and infant care. He had a lot of sympathy and patience for a being engaged in such a struggle.

During one of the seemingly endless pauses he had tried to move the conversation along by taking the blame for what had happened, but Khone dismissed the apology by saying that if the off-worlders had not precipitated the calamity then some Gogleskan combination of events would have done so. It gave details of the damage which had been done. This would be repaired and the ship rebuilt in time, but it would not be surprised if a similar disaster overtook them before the work was completed.

Every time a joining occurred they lost a little ground, were left with less of their technology—simple though it was by off-worlder standards—so that the minor advances they had been able to achieve were being slowly eroded away. It had always been thus, according to the stories which had been handed down from generation to generation and in the scraps of written history which had somehow survived their regular orgies of self-destruction.

"If any assistance can be given," Conway said in impersonal Gogleskan fashion, "whether it is in the form of information, advice, physical help, or mechanisms capable of furnishing such help, a simple request is all that is necessary for it to be made available."

"The wish," Khone said slowly, "is that this burden be lifted from our race. The initial request is for information."

If yesterday's events could be so graciously forgiven, surely Khone would not be too bothered by Conway omitting the cumbersome verbal niceties which were a part of the barrier between them. He said, "You may ask any question on any subject without fear of offending me."

Khone's hair twitched at being addressed directly, but the healer's reply was immediate. "Information is requested regarding other off-world species of your experience who have similar problems as those encountered on Goglesk. Particular interest is felt in those species who have solved them."

The healer, too, had become slightly less impersonal in its mode of speech. Conway marveled at the effort it must have cost the other to break, or at least bend a little, its lifelong conditioning. The trouble was that he did not have the information required.

To give himself time to think, Conway did not reply directly, but began by describing some of the more exotic life-forms who made up the Federation—but not as he had described them earlier. Now he drew on his hospital experience to describe them as patients undergoing surgical or nonsurgical treatments for an incredible variety of diseases. He was trying to give Khone hope, but he knew that he was doing little more than stalling by describing clinical pictures and procedures to a being, albeit a doctor of sorts, who could not even touch its patients. Conway had never believed in misinforming his patients, by word or deed or omission, and he did not want to do so to another medic.

". . . However," he went on, "to my own certain knowledge the problem afflicting your species is unique. If a similar case had been encountered, it would have been thoroughly investigated and discussed in the literature and be required reading for the staff of a multispecies hospital.

"I am sorry," he continued, "but the only helpful suggestion I can make is that the condition be studied as closely as possible by me, with the cooperation of an entity who is both a patient and a doctor, you."

As he waited for Khone's reaction, Conway heard Wainright moving behind him, but the Lieutenant did not speak.

"Cooperation is possible, and desirable," the Gogleskan said finally, "but not close cooperation."

Conway gave a relieved sigh. "The structure behind me contains a compartment designed for the confinement and study of local fauna under conditions of minimum physical restraint. For the protection of observers, the compartment is divided by an invisible but extremely hard wall. Would a close approach for purposes of physical examination be possible in those conditions?"

"Provided the strength of the invisible wall is demonstrated," the Gogleskan said cautiously, "a close approach is possible."

Wainright cleared his throat and said, "Sorry, Doctor. Until now there has been no need to use that room and I've been storing fuel cells in it. Give me twenty minutes to tidy up."

While Khone and Conway walked slowly around to the rear of the building, he explained that the compartment had, as the healer could see, an external opening which allowed confined life-forms to return to their own environment quickly after release. No restraints whatsoever would be placed on Khone, Conway reassured the other, and it could break off any discussion or examination at will.

His intention was to try to find some explanation for the Gogleskan behavior by a close study of the physiology of the species, with particular emphasis on the cranial area, which displayed features completely new to Conway and which, for this reason, might suggest a line of investigation. But it was not his intention to cause physical or mental distress.

"Some discomfort is expected," the FOKT said.

To further reassure Khone, Conway entered the compartment first, and while the Gogleskan watched from the external entrance, he demonstrated with his fists and feet the strength of the transparent wall. Indicating the ceiling, he briefly described the purpose of the two-way communicator and the projectors of the nonmaterial restraining and manipulation devices, which would be used only with Khone's express permission. Then he went through the small door, outlined in white for visibility in that totally invisible wall, and left the FOKT to get used to the place.

Wainright had already moved the fuel cells from the observer's half of the compartment, and had replaced them with a tri-di projector, recordings made the previous day as well as basic information tapes of the type used during other-species first contacts, and all of Conway's medical equipment.

"I'll monitor and record from the comm center next door," Wainright said, pausing for a moment in the internal entrance. "Khone has already seen the information tapes, but I thought you might want to rerun the five-minute sequence on Sector General. If you need anything else, Doctor, let me know."

They were left alone in the compartment, separated only by a thin, transparent wall and about three meters of distance, which was much too far.

Conway placed the palm of one hand against the transparent surface at waist level, and said, "Please approach as closely as possible and try to place a manipulatory appendage on the other side of the transparent wall occupied by mine. There is no urgency. The purpose is to accustom you to close proximity to me without actual physical contact . . ."

He went on talking reassuringly as Khone came closer and, after several attempts and withdrawals, placed its cluster of digits opposite Conway's hand. They were now separated by less than half an inch. Slowly he used his other hand to bring out his scanner and place that, too, against the wall on a level with the FOKT's cranium. Without being asked, the Gogleskan pressed the side of its head section against the invisible surface.

"Excellent!" Conway said, refocusing his scanner. He went on. "While there are elements of the Gogleskan physiology which are completely strange to me, as a whole the life-form is similar to many warm-blooded oxygen-breathing species. The differences are centered in the cranial area, and it is this which requires examination and an explanation which might not have a purely physical basis.

"In short," he went on, "we are examining a fairly normal life-form that occasionally behaves abnormally. Now, if we accept that behavior patterns are established by environmental and evolutionary factors, we should begin by examining your past."

He gave Khone a moment to think, then continued. "Lieutenant Wainright, who admits to being a fairly good amateur archeologist, tells me that your world has been remarkably stable since the time your presapient ancestors evolved. There have been no orbital changes, no major seismic disturbances, no ice ages or any marked alterations in the climatology. All of which indicates that your particular behavior pattern, the one which is presently hampering your progress as a culture, was evolved in response to a very early threat from natural enemies. What are, or were, these enemies?"

"We have no natural enemies," Khone replied promptly. "There is nothing on Goglesk which threatens us except ourselves."

Conway had trouble believing that. He moved his scanner to one of the areas where a sting lay partially hidden by cranial hair and then followed its connections to the poison sac while an enlarged picture of the process was projected onto the screen for Khone's benefit. He said, "That is a potent natural weapon whether it was used for attack or defense, and it would not have evolved without reason. Are there any memories, any written or spoken history, any fossil remains of a life-form so ferocious that it caused such a deadly defense to evolve?"

The answer was again no, but Conway had to ask the help of Wainright to explain fossils to the Gogleskan. It transpired that Khone had seen fossil remains from time to time but had not realized what they were or considered them of any importance. As a science archeology was unknown to its people. But now that Khone knew what the odd-shaped marks and objects in certain rocks signified, it seemed likely that the healer would father a new science.

"Have you experienced any dreams or nightmares about such a beast?" Conway asked, without looking up from his scanner.

"Only the phantasms of childhood," Khone said quickly, giving Conway the impression that it wanted to change the subject. "They rarely trouble adult minds."

"But when you do dream about them," Conway persisted, "is it possible to remember and describe this creature or creatures?"

Almost a full minute passed before the Gogleskan replied, and during that time Conway's scanner showed a perceptible bunching of the muscles surrounding the poison sac and at the base of the stings. Plainly he was moving into a very sensitive area. This answer, he thought, was going to be an important one.

But when it came the answer was disappointing, and seemed to invite only more questions.

"It is not a creature with a definite physical form," the FOKT said. "In the dreams there is a feeling of great danger, a formless threat from a fast-moving, ferocious entity which bites and tears and engulfs. It is a phantasm which frightens the young, and the thought of it distresses adults. The young may give way to their fears and join together for mutual comfort, because they lack the physical strength to inflict major damage to their surroundings. But adults must avoid such mental bad habits and remain mentally and physically apart."

Baffled, Conway said, "Are you telling me that young Gogleskans may link together at will, but not the adults?"

"It is difficult to stop them doing so," the FOKT replied. "But it is discouraged lest a habit develops which would be too difficult to break in adulthood. And while I realize that you are anxious to study the joining process without subjecting our artifacts to damage, to closely observe a joining between children without causing mental distress in the parents concerned, followed by an involuntary adult joining, would be impossible."

Conway sighed. Khone was way ahead of him, because that would have been his next request. Instead, he said, "Does my race in any way resemble this phantasm of your youth?"

"No," Khone replied. "But your close approach of yesterday, and in particular your physical contact with a Gogleskan, appeared to be a threat. The reaction and emission of the distress call was instinctive, not logical."

Helplessly, Conway said, "If we knew exactly what was responsible for what is clearly a species-wide panic reaction, we could try to negate it. But what *is* this bogeyman of yours?"

The lengthy silence which followed was broken by Wainright clearing his throat. Hesitantly, he said, "Considering the vague description, the speed and silence of its approach, and the fact that it rends and engulfs its prey, could it have been a large, airborne predator?"

Conway thought about that while he charted the nerve connections between the thin, shining tendrils lying in the coarser hair and the small, mineral-rich lobe at the center of the brain where they originated. He said, "Is there fossil evidence for such a creature? And isn't it possible, if this memory goes back to presapient times to the period when the FOKTs were sea-dwellers, that the predator was a swimmer rather than a flyer?"

The communicator was silent for a moment; then Wainright said, "I found no evidence of large avians on the few sites I examined, Doctor. But if we are going really far back to the time when all Gogleskan life was in the oceans, then some of it was very large indeed. There is an area of seabed which was thrown up fairly recently, in geological terms, about twenty miles south of here. I deep-probed a fossil-rich section which was once a deep subsea valley, meaning to work up a computer reconstruction whenever I had a few hours to spare. It made a very confusing picture, because a large number of the fossil remains are damaged or incomplete."

"Distortion due to seismic activity, do you think?" Conway asked.

"It's possible," the Lieutenant said doubtfully. "But my guess would be that it was inflicted by a contemporary agency. But the tape is in my room, Doctor. Shall I fetch it and see if the pictures, confusing as they are to me, jog our friend's racial memory?"

"Yes, please," Conway said. To Khone he went on. "If the recollection is not too distressing, can you tell me the number of times you have joined with other adults in response to a real or imagined threat? And can you describe the physical, mental, and emotional stages before, during, and subsequent to a joining? I do not wish to cause you pain, but it is important that this process be studied and understood if an answer to the problem is to be found."

It was obvious that the recollection was causing discomfort to Khone, and equally plain that the healer was going to cooperate to the best of its ability. Before yesterday, it told Conway, there had been three previous joinings. The sequence of events was, firstly, the accident or sudden surprise or physical threat which caused the being endangered to emit an audible distress signal which drew all of its fellows within hearing to it as well as placing them in the same emotional state. If one being was threatened then everyone within audible range was threatened and was under the same compulsion to react, to join and overcome the threat. Khone indicated the organ which produced the signal, a membrane which could be made to vibrate independent of the respiratory system.

The thought occurred to Conway that the membrane would have been even more effective under water, but he was too busy listening to interrupt.

Khone went on to describe the sense of increased safety as the body hair of the beings wove them together, and the pleasant, exciting feeling of increased intellect and awareness as the first few Gogleskans joined and shared minds. But that feeling died as more and more beings linked up and mentation became progressively more difficult and confused until it was submerged by the one, overwhelming need to protect the group by attacking anything and everything in the vicinity. Coherent thought at the individual level was impossible.

". . . When the threat has been neutralized," Khone went on, "or the incident which initiated the fusion is over and even to the dim understanding of the group-entity no longer poses a threat, the group slowly breaks up. For a time the individuals feel mentally confused, physically tired, and ashamed of themselves and of the destruction they have caused. To survive as an intelligent race, every Gogleskan must strive to be a lonely person."

Conway did not reply. His mind was still trying to adjust to the sudden realization that the Gogleskans had telepathy.

CHAPTER 8

T he telepathic faculty had limitations, because the distress signal which triggered the joining was an audible rather than a
mental one. It had to be telepathy by touch, then. He thought of
the fine tendrils concealed by the coarse cranial hair. There were
eight of them, which was more than enough to make contact with
those of the beings pressed tightly around during a linkup.

He must have been thinking aloud, because Khone announced
very firmly that such contact with another Gogleskan was acutely
painful, and that the tendrils lay alongside those of the other group
members but did not touch. Apparently the tendrils were organic
transmitting and receiving antennae which operated by simple induction.

But the problem with telepathic races—and there were several
of them in the Galactic Federation—was that the faculty worked
only between members of the same species; with other races whose
telepathic equipment operated on different frequencies or who did
not possess the faculty, it worked rarely if at all. Conway had had a
few experiences with projective telepaths—it was thought that
Earth-humans had a latent ability but had evolved away from it—
and the images he had received had been of short duration and
accompanied by prior mental discomfort. It was also thought that
races possessing a spoken and written language rather than a mental
one tended to progress further and faster in the physical sciences.

The Gogleskans possessed both, and for some reason had been
stopped dead in their cultural tracks.

"Is it agreed," Conway asked, very impersonally and carefully because he was about to suggest something unpleasant, "that it is the instinctive linkup, when there is no longer a major threat to make it necessary, which is the basis of your problem? Is it further agreed that the tendrils, which are almost certainly the mechanism which initiates and maintains the group as a single entity, require close and detailed study if the problem is to be solved? However, a visual examination is not sufficient, and tests requiring direct contact would be necessary. These would include nerve conductivity measurements, the withdrawal of minute tissue samples for analysis, the introduction of external stimuli to ascertain if . . . Khone! None of these tests are painful!"

In spite of his hasty reassurance the Gogleskan was displaying signs of growing panic.

"I know that the thought of any kind of physical contact is distressing," Conway went on quickly as he thought of a new approach, beautiful in its simplicity provided the personal dangers were ignored, "because there is an instinctive reaction to anyone or anything which might be a threat. But if it were demonstrated, on the instinctive as well as the cerebral level, that I am not a threat, then it might be possible for you to overcome this instinctive reaction.

"What I propose is this . . ."

Wainright returned while he was talking. The Lieutenant stood listening, the tape gripped tightly in his hand, until Conway had finished. Then he said in a frightened voice, "Doctor, you're mad."

It took a much longer time to obtain the Lieutenant's agreement than to get Khone's, but finally Conway had his way. Wainright drew a litter from stores and the Doctor was placed on it and securely restrained with straps around the feet, legs, arms and body—the restraints had a quick-release capability which could be remotely operated by the Lieutenant; Wainright had insisted on that—and he was moved into Khone's half of the observation compartment. The litter was set at a comfortable height for the Gogleskan healer to work, if it was able.

The idea was that if he could not physically examine Khone then the Gogleskan would examine Conway, while he was utterly helpless and incapable of any threatening behavior. It would accustom the healer to the idea of physical examination and investigation against the time when it would be Conway's turn. But that time, it soon became obvious, would be long delayed.

Khone approached him closely without too much distress and, under Conway's direction, used the scanner with a fair degree of skill. But it was the instrument which touched him, not Khone itself. Conway remained absolutely still on the litter, moving only his eyes to watch Khone's hesitant movements, or the Lieutenant, who was projecting his tape onto the big screen.

Suddenly he felt a touch, so light that it might have been a feather falling onto the back of his hand and then sliding off again. Then the touch was repeated, more firmly this time.

He tried not to move even his eyes lest Khone shy away, so he was aware from his peripheral vision of an expanse of stiff, Gogleskan hair and three of Khone's manipulators, two of which were holding the scanner, moving along the side of his head. He felt another light touch in the area of the temporal artery; then very gently, the tip of a manipulator began exploring the convolutions of his ear.

Abruptly Khone withdrew, its membrane vibrating softly in muted distress.

Conway thought of the strength of the conditioning Khone had been fighting just to touch him the first time, and he felt an admiration for the dumpy little creature so great, and concern for its species as a whole so intense, that he found it difficult to speak for a few minutes.

"Apologies for the mental distress," Conway said finally, "but it should lessen as the contacts are repeated. But audible distress signals are being generated even though you know that I have neither the wish nor the ability to endanger you. With your agreement the external door of this compartment should be closed lest members of your species within audible range think that you are being threatened and come to join with you."

"There is understanding," Khone said without hesitation, "and agreement."

On the big screen the Lieutenant was playing back the tape which showed the dense mass of fossilized remains revealed by his deep probes, rotating the viewpoint and overlaying a scale grid so that a true idea of the shapes and sizes could be shown. Khone paid little attention to the display because, Conway realized, a species with such a primitive level of technology would not immediately comprehend the solid reality represented by a few thin lines on a dark screen. It was much more interested in the three-dimensional reality of the Doctor and it was approaching him again.

Conway, however, was intensely interested in the images on the screen.

He kept his eyes on it while two of Khone's manipulators gently parted the hair on his scalp. To the Lieutenant, he said, "Those incomplete fossils look as if they have been torn apart, and I wouldn't mind betting that if you ask that computer to reconstruct one of them using the data available from the Khone physiological material, you will have a recognizable presapient FOKT. But what is that . . . that overgrown vegetable hanging in the middle of them?"

Wainright laughed. "I was hoping you would tell me, Doctor. It looks like a deformed, stemless rose, with spikes or teeth growing from the edges of some of the petals, and it's *big*."

"The shape doesn't make sense," Conway said quietly as the Gogleskan shifted its attention to one of his hands. "As a mobile sea-dweller it should have fins rather than limbs, but there is no sign of streamlining along its direction of motion, or even a basic symmetry about its center of . . ."

He broke off to answer a question from Khone regarding the hair on his wrist, and he took the opportunity of weakening the other's conditioning a little more by suggesting that it perform a simple surgical procedure on him. It would involve removing a small area of hair, and using a fine needle in conjunction with the scanner to withdraw a small quantity of blood from a minor vein at the back of Conway's hand. He assured Khone that the procedure would be painless and no harm would be done even if the needle were not positioned with complete accuracy.

He explained that it was the kind of test which was done count-less times every day at Sector General on a wide variety of patients, and later analysis of the sample taken revealed a great deal about the condition of these patients, and in many cases, the data obtained was instrumental in curing them.

There would be very little direct physical contact involved in taking the sample, because Khone would be using the scanner, swab, scissors, and a hypodermic, he added encouragingly. Just as there would be minimal body contact if or when Conway performed similar tests on the Gogleskan.

For a moment Conway thought that he had rushed things too much, because Khone had backed away until it was pressing against the inside of the closed external door. It remained there, its hair twitching while it fought another battle with its conditioning, then it slowly returned to the litter. While he waited for it to speak, Conway took a quick look at the amazingly lifelike picture which was taking form on Wainright's screen.

The Lieutenant had incorporated in the display all of the FOKT data as well as information he had gleaned earlier on the subsea vegetation of prehistoric times. The fossil remains, which the computer had reconstructed as slightly smaller versions of present-day Gogleskans, lay singly and in small, linked groups among the gently waving marine vegetation, lit by bright, greenish yellow sunlight which filtered down from the wave-wrinkled surface above. Only in the enormous, roselike object which lay in the center of the picture was there a lack of detail. An idea about it began to take shape at the back of Conway's mind, but Khone spoke suddenly before it could form.

The Gogleskan was still not taking any interest in the screen.

"If this test were to cause pain," Khone asked, "what would be the procedure then? And would it be preferable, in the present circumstances, for the blood sample to be taken by and from oneself?"

A helpful but cautious entity, this Khone, Conway thought, trying not to laugh. He said, "If a procedure is expected to cause discomfort, a quantity of the material contained in one of the phials colored in yellow and black diagonal bands is withdrawn and injected into the site. The quantity required is dependent on the period and degree of discomfort which one is expecting to cause.

"The material concerned is a painkiller for my species," he went on, "as well as a muscle relaxant. But it is not required in this instance . . ."

While he continued to give the directions for withdrawing the blood sample, he told Khone that it was much easier to perform such work on a subject other than oneself. He did not, at that time, make any mention of the fact that if he was to obtain a specimen of FOKT blood from Khone, the first thing he would have wanted to discover was if the yellow and black marked medication, or one of the other similar preparations in his supply, was suited to the Gogleskan metabolism. If one of them was suitable and there was an opportunity of injecting it, Khone would be left in such a pain-free, relaxed, and massively tranquilized state that subsequent and more revealing tests would have been no problem at all.

A muscle relaxed, he thought, his eyes going back to Wainright's display, *as opposed to a muscle in spasm!* . . .

The large object centering the screen lacked the symmetry and structural repetition of a vegetable—it looked like a sheet of paper which had been crushed and twisted into a loose ball. But if that idea was correct, the predator must have pulled itself into that shape. Conway shivered in spite of himself.

That Gogleskan venom was potent stuff.

To Wainright, he said quickly, "How does this sound? The FOKT fossils were those beings who did not survive the initial attack of the creature, and some of them are linked, indicating that they were part of a larger group. This FOKT group-entity attacked or defended itself against the predator with its stings, all of them. The quantity of venom injected must have sent the beastie into multiple muscular spasm, and it must have literally tied itself into a knot as it died. Can you get your computer to unravel that knot?"

Wainright nodded, and soon the twisted, convoluted shape at the center of the screen was surrounded by a fainter image of itself which was slowly unfolding. This had to be the answer for that weird shape, Conway thought, because nothing else made sense. Occasionally he asked for expanded views of the enormous fossil's skeletal structure, and each one supported his theory. But the Lieutenant was forced to reduce the size several times as the ghostly, unfolding image overran the edges of the screen.

"It's beginning to look like a bird," Wainright said. "Parts of the wing are very fragile. In fact, it seems to be *all* wing."

"That's because the fossil remains are of the skeleton and skin only," Conway replied. "There must have been almost total wastage of muscle and soft tissue which was attached to that bone structure. In the areas where you are indicating the wing . . . Now you've got me thinking of it as a bird ... The wing thickness should be increased by a factor of five or six. But with that bone structure the wing could not have been rigid. I'd say that it undulated rapidly rather than flapping, and propelled the beastie forward at great speed. And that lateral split in the wing inboard leading edges is interesting. It reminds me of the engine intakes of the old jet aircraft, except that these intakes have teeth ..."

He broke off because Khone was jabbing hesitantly at the back of his hand with the hypo. For the first time Conway understood what a patient had to go through at the hands of a trainee medical technician.

"The jointing at the base of the wings," he went on when the Gogleskan had found the proper vein, "suggests that the mouths on the wing leading edges opened and closed as it swam, eating everything that got in its way and passing the food through two alimentary canals to the stomach housed in that cylindrical bulge along the center line. The tegument was thicker along the leading edges, and probably sting-proof, and the stomach was probably capable of dealing with the FOKT venom even though it is lethal when injected through softer areas of tegument into the bloodstream.

"The only defense the FOKTs could offer was to link up and present themselves as a solid wall in its path," he continued excitedly. "Quite a few of them would die before the group entity folded around the predator and stung it to death. The incomplete fossil remains indicate that. But I hate to think of what it must have been like for the group-members as a whole while they were mentally linked to their dying friends ..."

He cringed inwardly as he thought of how they all must have suffered, and died, every time one of their group did so. And they would have done so many times if the predator's attacks were a regular occurrence. What was worse, prior to an attack they all knew what was ahead of them through the minds of previous survivors—all the fear and pain and multiple dying by proxy.

At last he understood the severity of the racial psychosis which gripped the whole Gogleskan species. As individuals they feared and hated a joining, or any close physical or mental contact or cooperation which might lead to the possibility of a linkup. Subconsciously to join was to suffer remembered pain, pain which could only be assuaged by a blind, berserker rage which in turn blotted out the capacity to think or to control their actions. Their fear of that particular species of predator must have been extreme, and even though their old enemy was extinct or was still a sea-dweller, they had not been able to forget it or develop a less self-defeating method of self-defense.

The main trouble was that the defense mechanism was so hypersensitive, even after the elapsed millennia since it was needed, that it could be triggered by an imagined or potential threat as well as an actual one.

Khone had finally completed withdrawing the blood sample. The back of Conway's hand felt like a pincushion, but he said highly complimentary things about the FOKT healer's first off-planet surgical procedure, and meant every word of them. While the other was carefully transferring the contents of the syringe into a sterile phial, he returned his attention to the screen.

The creature was completely unfolded now, and the Lieutenant had reduced the image again so that it would fit within the limits of the screen. Wainright had also added all the available data and theory on coloration, probable method of locomotion, and the wing-synchronized mouth and teeth movements. It moved slowly in the center of the big screen, a vast, dark gray, dreadful shape more than eighty meters across, undulating and flapping ponderously like an enormous, Earthly stingray, sucking in, tearing apart, and eating everything in its path.

This was the Gogleskan nightmare from their prehistoric past, and the figures of the reconstructed FOKT fossils were tiny blobs of color near the lower edge of the screen.

"Wainright!" Conway said urgently. "*Kill that picture! . . .*"

But he was too late. Khone, its work completed, had turned to look at the screen—and was confronted with the three-dimensional picture of a moving and seemingly living creature which up until then had inhabited only its subconscious. In the confined space of the compartment its distress call was deafening.

Conway cursed his own stupidity as the panic-stricken Gogleskan stumbled about the floor within a few feet of his litter. Khone had shown little interest in the display when it had been a collection of fine lines, since it lacked the experience to appreciate the three-dimensional reality which they represented. But the Lieutenant's final picture was much too realistic for any Gogleskan to view and remain wholly sane.

He saw the FOKTs dumpy body come toward him, then lurch past. Its multicolor hair was standing on end and twitching, its four stings were fully extended, droplets of venom oozing from the tips, but the sound coming from its membranes seemed fractionally less deafening. Conway lay rigid, not even swiveling his eyes as the being moved away and then came back again.

The reduction in the volume of its distress call made it obvious that Khone was fighting its conditioning and Conway had to help it in the only way possible, by remaining absolutely motionless. Out of the corner of his eye he saw the Gogleskan stop, one of its stings only inches away from the side of his face and the stiff, bristling hair touching his coveralls. He could feel its breath puffing gently across his forehead and smell the faint, peppermint smell which seemed to be its body odor. Khone was trembling, whether with fear at the Lieutenant's display or in indecision over whether or not to attack, Conway did not know.

If he stayed absolutely still, he told himself desperately, he should not represent a threat. If he moved, however, he knew with a dreadful certainty that the Gogleskan would sting him, instinctively, without thinking. But there was another aspect of the FOKT behavior pattern which he had forgotten.

They blindly attacked enemies, but any being who was not a threat and had managed to remain in such close physical proximity as Conway had done had to be a friend.

At times like this, friends linked up.

Conway was suddenly aware of the stiff bristles scratching against his clothing and trying to weave themselves into the fabric of his coveralls in the area of his neck and shoulder. The sting was still too close to the side of his face for comfort, but somehow it seemed to be less threatening. He held absolutely still, anyway. Then he saw, clearly because it was moving just two inches above his eyes, one of the long, fine tendrils. He felt it fall, feather-light, across his forehead.

A Gogleskan joining was mental as well as physical, Conway

knew, but he did not foresee any more success for the telepathic linkup than for the physical one.

He was wrong.

It began as a deep, unlocalized itch inside his skull, and if his hands and arms had not been immobilized he would have been poking desperately at his ears with his fingers. He was aware, too, of a maddening confusion of sounds, pictures, and feelings which were not his own. He had experienced the same sensation many times, after taking extraterrestrial physiology tapes at the hospital, but on those occasions the alien impressions had been coherent and orderly. He felt now as if he were watching a tri-di show with sensory augmentation when the channel selector control was malfunctioning. The bright but chaotic images and impressions became more intense, and he wanted to close his eyes in the hope that they would go away, but he dared not even blink.

Suddenly the picture held steady and the feelings were sharp and clear, and for a few seconds Conway knew what it was like to be the intensely lonely and intellectually frustrated entity that was an adult Gogleskan. The breadth of intelligence and sensitivity of Khone's mind awed him, and he was aware of the many ways in which the Gogleskan healer had used that mind, long before the Monitor Corps or Conway had arrived on Goglesk, to fight and circumvent the mind-destroying conditioning which their evolution had imposed on them.

He was sure, because he was in Khone's mind and the healer was sure, that its mind was nothing extraordinary so far as FOKT mental capacity was concerned. But their high intelligence could not be shared except by the slow, impersonal, and imprecise spoken language, and a true meeting of minds was possible only during the brief period between the initial linkup and the coarsening and confusion of intellect which immediately followed it. His admiration for this individual member of a race of intensely reluctant individualists was great indeed.

There is no coarsening or loss of definition in the thoughts we are exchanging.

The words which appeared in Conway's mind were overlaid by feelings of pleasure, gratitude, curiosity . . . and hope.

476 · JAMES WHITE

The process of establishing the mental linkup between your people must trigger an area of your endocrine system which desensitizes the entire cerebral process, probably to reduce the pain which was suffered in prehistoric times following a linkup and during the predator attack. But I am not a Gogleskan, so the desensitizing mechanism is absent. However, a precise study of the endocrinology involved should be undertaken without delay and the gland isolated, and if surgical intervention is indicated . . .

Too late he realized where that line of thought was taking him and the wide—and to Khone frightening—surgical associations it opened up. With a tremendous mental effort the Gogleskan had adapted to the close presence and physical contact with an offworlder, and Conway *knew* precisely how much of an effort that had been. But now the healer was sharing Conway's mind, sharing his thoughts and feelings and experience of entities who staffed or were being cured at Sector General and who made the seagoing nightmare from Goglesk's past seem like a domestic pet by comparison.

Khone could not take it, and its distress signal, which had grown quieter over the past few minutes, roared out again at full, frantic intensity. But the little being was maintaining contact in spite of the alien nightmare its thought tendril was receiving, and Conway was suffering with it.

He tried to think reassuring thoughts, tried to make the Gogleskan's mind as well as his own change the mental subject. He had blinked several times but had otherwise remained still, and he thought, or rather he hoped, that Khone would continue to treat him as an immobile and helpless nonthreat. But was it his imagination or had Khone's appearance changed suddenly?

The stiff, multicolor hair was more clearly defined and the nearest sting had developed new highlights. For a moment his fear became even greater than Khone's as he realized what was happening.

"No, don't! . . ." he began, as loudly as he could without moving his lips. But the Gogleskan membrane was vibrating too loudly for Wainright to hear him.

"I've opened the outer door, Doctor," the Lieutenant shouted, the communicator volume turned high so that he would be heard

over the noise Khone was making. "I'm cutting your restraints, *now.*
Get out of there!"

"I'm not in danger," Conway called, but his voice was drowned
out by that earsplitting distress signal and the overamplified Wainright. And he was lying anyway, because when the straps dropped
away he was in terrible danger.

He was potentially mobile again, no longer helpless, and had
therefore become a threat.

In the instant before the tendril was withdrawn Conway knew
that Khone did not want to sting him, but that made no difference
at all to what was a purely reflex action. As he rolled desperately
onto the floor, he felt the jab of the blunt point of the sting thudding
into his shoulder. One of his ankles was entangled in the foot restraints as he tried to crawl away, and another jab tore his coveralls
and scratched his thigh. Again he tried to crawl toward the outer
entrance, but first his arm and then his leg doubled up in muscular
spasm, and he toppled onto his side, unable to move and facing the
transparent partition. The two affected limbs seemed to be on fire.

The muscles in his neck and in the area of the scapula were
knotting in cramp, and the fire was spreading from the hip puncture
to the abdominal muscles. He wondered if the venom would affect
the involuntary muscle systems as well, specifically those operating
his heart and lungs. If it did then he had not long to live. The pain
was so intense that the thought did not frighten him as badly as it
should have. Desperately he tried to think of something he should
do before he passed out.

"Wainright . . ." he began weakly.

Khone's distress call had reduced in volume, and the healer had
not tried to sting him again—obviously he was no longer a threat.
The Gogleskan stood a few feet from him, its hair agitated by its
stings lying flat against its head, looking like a harmless multicolored
haystack. He tried again.

"Wainright," he said slowly and painfully. "The yellow and black
phial. Inject all of it . . ."

But the Lieutenant was not at the other side of the partition,
and the connecting door was still closed. Maybe Wainright intended
coming around to the external door to drag Conway out, but he

could not move himself around to see. It was becoming difficult to see anything.

Before he passed out, Conway was aware of regular fluctuations in the lighting which reminded him of something. A heavy power drain, he thought weakly, of the kind required to punch a signal through hyperspace . . .

CHAPTER 9

He seemed to be attached to every sensor and monitoring device in the unit, Conway thought as he looked up at the displays from the unfamiliar viewpoint of a patient, and luxuriated in the feeling of his limbs stretched to full extension and free of the excruciating cramp. He moved his eyes to see Prilicla regarding him from its position on the ceiling and the figures of Murchison and Naydrad at one side of his bed, also looking down at him. Between them was a large eye supported by a long tubular appendage which had been extruded by Danalta with the same purpose in mind. Conway moistened his lips.

"What happened?" he said.

"That," Murchison said, "is supposed to be the second question. The first is 'Where am I?'"

"I know where I am, dammit. On the casualty deck of *Rhabwar*. And why am I still wired up to that thing? Surely you can see that the biosensors are indicating optimum levels on all vital functions. What I want to know is how I got here."

The pathologist breathed gently through her nose. "Mentation and memory seem unimpaired, and you are your usual short-tempered self. But you must rest. The Gogleskan venom has been neutralized, and in spite of what the displays are showing, there is marked physical debility and the likelihood of delayed shock as a result of severe mental trauma. Massive rest is indicated, at least until we return to the hospital and you are given a thorough check-out.

"And don't think you can pull your Senior Physician's rank on me to get up," she said sweetly as Conway opened his mouth to do just that. "In this instance you are the patient and not the doctor, Doctor."

"This is a good time," Prilicla broke in at that moment, "for us to withdraw and so enable you to get the rest you require, friend Conway. We are all feeling pleased and relieved that you are recovering, and I think it would be less exhausting for you if we left and allowed friend Murchison to answer your questions."

Prilicla scuttled across the ceiling toward the entrance, Naydrad growled something which did not translate and followed the empath, and Danalta withdrew its eye support limb, stabilized as a dark green, lumpy ball, and rolled after them. Murchison began removing the unnecessary biosensors and switching off the monitors, silently and with more concentration than the work warranted.

"What *did* happen?" he asked quietly. When there was no response he went on. "That venom, I was trying to tie myself into knots. I wanted Wainright to inject the muscle relaxant, but he wasn't there. Then I seem to remember the lights dimming, and I knew he was using the hyperspace radio. But I didn't expect to wake up on *Rhabwar* . . ."

Or wake up ever again, he finished silently.

Still without looking at him she explained that the ambulance ship had been testing new equipment just beyond the Jump distance from Sector General, and with the full medical team on board. Because they knew the exact coordinates of Goglesk when the Lieutenant's hypersignal came in, they were able to emerge close to the planet, with their lander ready to launch, and they had been able to reach him in just under four hours.

They had found him still trying to tie himself in knots, but the muscular spasm had been reduced significantly by a massive dose of the relaxant DM82, so the knots were loose enough for him not to have broken any bones or torn any muscles or tendons. He had been very lucky.

Conway nodded and said seriously, "So the Lieutenant was able to get to me with the muscle relaxant in time. I'd say with seconds to spare."

Murchison shook her head. "It was the native Gogleskan,

Khone, who administered the DM82. After damn well nearly killing you, it saves your life! It kept asking if you would be all right when we were taking you away, shouting at us until the entry port was sealed. You make some peculiar friends, Doctor."

"It had to make a tremendous mental effort to give me that shot," Conway said, "a bigger effort, perhaps, than I could have made in similar circumstances. How close did it come while you were transferring me to the lander?"

Murchison thought for a moment, then said, "When Lieutenant Haslam, who was piloting, and I met Wainright at the lock, it came to within twenty meters. When Naydrad, Prilicla, and Danalta came out with the litter, it became nervous and moved back to about twice that distance. Wainright told us what had happened between it and you, but we did not act or say anything which could be construed as hostile even though, personally, I would have liked to give it a quick kick in whatever it uses as a *gluteus maximus* for what it did to you. Maybe it simply feared retribution."

"Knowing its feelings as I do," Conway said seriously, "I think it would have welcomed retribution."

Murchison breathed through her nose once again and sat down on the edge of the litter, twisting around so as to face him and placing her hands on the pillow beside his shoulders. Her face lost its cool, clinical expression and she said shakily, "Damn you, Doctor, you nearly got yourself killed."

Suddenly her arms were around him and her face was close to his. Conway moved his head away quickly, without thinking. She straightened up, looking surprised.

"I'm . . . I'm not feeling like myself today," he said. Again without thinking he had used the stock phrase which, at Sector General, was the acceptable excuse for strange or uncharacteristic behavior.

"You mean," she said furiously, "that you've an Educator tape riding you, and O'Mara sent you to Goglesk without erasing it? What are you carrying, a Tralthan, a Melfan? I know both of those species consider the Earth-human female body to be something less than desirable. Or did you *volunteer* to take an Educator tape on vacation? Some vacation!"

Conway shook his head. "It isn't a physiology tape, and O'Mara had nothing to do with it. There was a very close, and quite intense, telepathic contact with Khone. It was unexpected, an accident, but the Gogleskan FOKT classification has some remarkable behavior characteristics which include . . ."

Before Conway could stop himself he was describing the whole Gogleskan situation and his experience with the town-wrecking group entity and with Khone as an individual. As one of the hospital's leading pathologists, second only to the great Thornnastor itself, her professional interest should have been aroused, and it would be, in time. But right then it was obvious that she was not thinking about anything except the state in which she had found Conway a few hours earlier.

"The important thing," she said, trying to smile, "is that you don't want anyone to come close to you, unless it looks like a multicolor haystack. As an excuse it certainly beats having a headache."

Conway smiled back. "Not at all. Bodily contact can be made without initiating a Joining, at any time, provided the intention is associated with reproduction." He reached up with one hand, and with the palm pressed gently against the back of her neck he pulled her face down toward his. "Would you like to rerun that last bit again?"

"You are severely debilitated," she said, looking relieved and trying to duck from under his hand—but not working very hard at it. Conway spread his fingers through her hair and did not let go even when their faces were only a few inches apart. She went on softly. "You're making an awful mess of my hair."

Conway slipped his other hand around her waist and said, "Don't worry. It makes you look much more like a desirable haystack . . ."

He had no discomfort and he did not feel particularly debilitated, but suddenly he began to shake as the delayed shock from the Khone incident hit him, and with it the memory of those excruciating muscle spasms and the knowledge of just how close to death he had been. She held him tightly until the shaking had stopped, and for a long time afterward.

They both knew that the gentle and understanding Prilicla, from its quarters two decks above them, was aware of the emotional radiation of every being in the ship. The telepath would ensure that nobody interrupted them until curative therapy was concluded.

It was ten hours later—*Rhabwar* had not needed to break any records on the return trip—that they locked on to the Casualty Admission Port on Level 103. Charge Nurse Naydrad, who could be fanatical at times about the regulations, insisted on bringing him into the observation ward on the litter. Conway was equally insistent about sliding back the canopy and sitting up during the transfer, to reassure the Earth-human and extraterrestrial colleagues who were waiting inside the entry port to inquire worriedly about his condition. Murchison had left him to make her report to Thornnastor, and Prilicla had gone on ahead to escape the somewhat turbulent emotional radiation being generated in the vicinity of Conway's litter.

But it took less than an hour in the observation ward for the Physician-in-Charge and its staff to complete their examination and agree with Conway's self-diagnosis that he was in all respects physically fit.

An hour later he was in the office of Major O'Mara, who was not overly concerned with things physical.

"This is not the usual Educator tape impression," the Chief Psychologist said when Conway had described his experiences with Khone. "Normally a tape contains the complete mind record of the being who donated it, and in spite of the psychological tricks which the recipient plays on himself or itself, the taped-in personality of that of the being receiving the tape is completely distinct. The recording is not subject to alteration. For this reason an erasure can be performed without any ill-effects on the recipient's personality or mental state. But you, Doctor, had a full, two-way exchange with this Khone character, which means that you have assimilated a fairly large body of memories, feelings, and thought processes into the Conway mind matrix and, God help its future sanity, Khone has been impressed with quite a lot of your material, and the minds of both parties were aware of and were modified by the process. For this reason I cannot see any way that we can selectively remove the Gogleskan material without the risk of personality damage. In psychological terms there has been feedback from both minds.

"There is a possibility, a small one," O'Mara went on gruffly, "that if Khone could be persuaded to come here and donate its own Educator tape for study, something could be tried which—"

"It wouldn't come," Conway said.

"Judging by what you've told me, I'm inclined to agree," the Chief Psychologist said, a tinge of sympathy creeping into his tone. "This means that you are stuck with your Gogleskan alter ego, Conway. Is it . . . bad?"

Conway shook his head. "It is no more alien than a Melfan tape, except that there are times when I'm not sure whether it is Khone or myself reacting to a given situation. I think I can handle it without psychiatric assistance."

"Good," O'Mara said dryly, and added, "You're afraid the treatment might be worse than the condition, and you're probably right."

"It isn't good," Conway said firmly. "The Gogleskan business, I mean. Their whole species is being held back by what amounts to a racial conditioned reflex! We will have to do something about that berserker group-entity problem."

"*You* will have to do something about it," O'Mara said, "between a few other jobs we have lined up for you. After all, you are the Senior Physician with the most knowledge of the Gogleskan situation, so why should I assign anyone else? But first, I assume you found a little time between wrecking Gogleskan towns and being stung nearly to death by your FOKT colleague to decide whether or not you want to try for Diagnostician? And that you discussed some of the, er, ramifications with your personal pathologist?"

Conway nodded. "We've discussed it, and I'll give it a try. But these other jobs you mentioned, I'm not sure that I'm able to—"

The Chief Psychologist held up a hand. "Of course you are able. Both Senior Physician Prilicla and Pathologist Murchison have pronounced you in all respects psychologically and physically fit." He looked steadily at Conway's reddening face for a moment, then added, "She did not go into detail, just said that she was satisfied. You have another question?"

Warily, Conway asked, "How many other jobs?"

"Several," O'Mara replied. "They are detailed in the tape which you can pick up from the outer office. Oh, yes, Doctor, I expected you to decide as you have done. But now you will have to accept a greater measure of responsibility for your diagnoses, decisions, and treatment directives than you have been accustomed to as a Senior

Physician, and for patients which only your subordinates will see unless something goes badly amiss. Naturally, you will be allowed to seek the help and advice of colleagues at Diagnostician or any other level, but only if you can satisfy me, and yourself, that you can no longer proceed without such assistance.

"Knowing you, Doctor," he added sourly, "it would be difficult to say which of us would be harder to satisfy on that point."

Conway nodded. It was not the first time that O'Mara had criticized him for being too professionally proud, or pigheaded. But he had been able to avoid serious trouble by also being right on most of the occasions. He cleared his throat.

"I understand," he said quietly. "But it still seems to me that the Gogleskan situation requires early attention."

"So does the problem in the FROB geriatric unit," O'Mara said. "Not to mention the urgent need to design accommodation for a pregnant Protector and its offspring, as well as sundry teaching duties, lectures in theater, and any odd jobs which may come up and for which your peculiar qualities suit you. Some of these problems have been with us for a long time, although not, of course, for as many thousands of years as those of your Gogleskan friends. As a would-be Diagnostician you also have the responsibility for deciding which case or cases should be given priority. After due consideration, of course."

Conway nodded. His vocal chords seemed to have severed communications with his brain while it tried to absorb all the implications of a multiple assignment the individual sections of which were just this side of impossible. He knew of some of those problems and the Diagnosticians who had worked on them, and the hospital grapevine had carried some bloodcurdling accounts of some of the failures. And now, for the period of assessment as acting Diagnostician, the problems were his.

"Don't sit there gaping at me," O'Mara said. "I'm sure you can find something else to do."

CHAPTER 10

I t was an unusual meeting for Conway in that he was the only medic present—the others were exclusively Monitor Corps officers charged with the responsibilities for various aspects of hospital maintenance and supply, and Major Fletcher, the Captain of the *Rhabwar*. It was doubly unusual in that Conway, wearing his gold-edged acting Diagnostician's armband with a nonchalance he did not feel, was solely and completely himself.

There were no Educator tapes which could help him with this problem, only the experience of Major Fletcher and himself.

"The initial requirement," he began formally, "is for accommodation, food supply, and treatment facilities for a gravid FSOJ life-form better known to some of us as one of the Protectors of the Unborn. It is an extremely dangerous being, nonintelligent in the adult stage, which on its home planet is continuously under attack from the time it is born until it dies, usually at the tentacles and teeth of its last-born. Captain, if you please . . ."

Fletcher tapped buttons on his console, and the briefing screen lit with the picture of an adult Protector taken during one of *Rhabwar*'s rescue missions, followed by material on other FSOJs collected on their home world. But it was the way that the Protector's snapping teeth and flailing tentacles warped and dented the ambulance ship's internal plating which caused the watchers to grunt in disbelief.

"As you can see," Conway resumed, "the FSOJ is a large, immensely strong, oxygen-breathing life-form with a slitted carapace from which protrude those four heavy tentacles and a tail and head. The tentacles and tail have large, osseous terminations resembling organic spiked clubs, and the principal features of the head are the recessed and heavily protected eyes, and the jaws. You will also note that the four stubby legs which project from the underside of the carapace possess bony spurs which make these limbs additional weapons of offense. On their planet of origin all of these weapons are needed.

"Their young remain in the womb until physical development is sufficiently advanced for them to survive birth into their incredibly savage environment, and during the embryo stage they are telepathic. But this aspect of the problem is not in your area.

"Constant and savage conflict is such a vital part of their lives," Conway went on, "that they sicken and die without it. For that reason the preparation of accommodation for this life-form will be much more difficult than any you have been asked to provide hitherto. The compartment will have to be structurally robust. Captain Fletcher, here, will be able to give you information on the beastie's physical strength and degree of mobility, and if he sounds as if he is exaggerating, believe me, he is not. The cargo chamber on *Rhabwar* had to be completely rebuilt after the FSOJ had been confined in it during an eleven-hour trip to the hospital."

"My tibia needed repairing, too," Fletcher said dryly.

Before Conway could go on there was another interruption. Colonel Hardin, who was the hospital's Dietician-in-Chief, said, "I get the impression that your FSOJ fights and eats its food, Doctor. Now, you must be aware of the rule here that live food is never provided, only synthesized animal tissue or imported vegetation if the synthesizers can't handle it. Some of the food animals used in the Federation bear a close resemblance to other sentient Galactic citizens, many of whom find the eating of nonvegetable matter repugnant and—"

"No problem, Colonel," Conway broke in. "The FSOJ will eat anything. Your biggest headache will be the accommodation, which is going to resemble more closely a medieval torture chamber than a hospital ward."

"Are we to be given information regarding the purpose of this project?" asked an officer whom Conway had not seen before. He wore the yellow tabs of a maintenance specialist and the insignia of a major. He smiled as he went on. "It would help guide us in the initial design work, as well as satisfying our curiosity."

"The work is not secret," Conway replied, "and the only reason I would not like it to be discussed widely is that we may fall short of our expectations. This, considering the fact that I have been given charge of the project, could cause personal embarrassment, no more than that.

"Continuous conception takes place within every member of this species," he went on briskly, "and the intention is to closely study this process with the ultimate aim of inhibiting the effects of the mechanism which destroys the sentient and telepathic portion of the embryo's brain prior to its birth. If a newly born Protector retained its sentience and telepathic faculty, it could in time communicate with its own Unborn and, hopefully, establish a bond which would make it impossible for them to harm each other. We will also be trying to gradually reduce the violence of the environmental beating they take and stimulate, medically rather than physically, the release of the complex secretions which are triggered by this activity. That way they should gradually get out of the habit of trying to kill and eat everything they see. Also, the answers we find must enable the FSOJs to continue to survive on their frightful planet, and help them escape from the evolutionary trap which has rendered impossible any chance of the species' developing a civilized culture."

They have a lot in common with the Gogleskans, he thought. Smiling, he added, "But this is one of my problems. Another is making sure that you fully understand yours."

There followed a long and at times overheated discussion at the end of which they understood all of the problems—including the need for urgency. Their captive Protector could not be held indefinitely in the old Tralthan Observation Ward on Level 202 with a couple of FROB maintenance engineers taking turns at beating it with metal bars. The two Hudlars, despite their immense strength and fearsome aspect, were kindly souls, and the work—in spite of constant reassurances that the activity was necessary for the Protector's well-being—was causing them serious psychological discomfort.

Everybody had problems, Conway thought. But his own most immediate one, hunger, was easily solved.

He had timed his visit to the dining hall to coincide with the meal schedule of *Rhabwar*'s medical team, primarily to see Murchison, and he found Prilicla, Naydrad, and Danalta with her at a table designed for Melfan ELNTs. The pathologist did not speak until he had finished tapping out his food selection, an enormous steak with double the usual accessories.

"Obviously you are still yourself," she said, looking enviously at his plate, "or your alter egos are nonvegetarian. Synthetics are still fattening, you know. Why is it you don't grow an abdomen like a pregnant Crepellian?"

"It's my psychological approach to eating which is responsible," Conway said with a grin as he initiated major surgery on the steak. "Food is simply a fuel which has to be burned up. It must be obvious to you all that I am not enjoying this."

Naydrad made an untranslatable Kelgian noise and continued eating. Prilicla maintained its stable hover above the table without comment, and Danalta was in the process of growing a pair of Melfan manipulators while the rest of its body resembled a lumpy green pyramid with a single eye on top.

"I'm still myself," he said to Murchison, "with just a shade of Gogleskan FOKT. I've been given the Protector case, among others, and that is what I wanted to talk to you about. Temporarily I'm an acting Diagnostician, with full responsibility and authority regarding treatment, and may call on any assistance I require. I do need help, badly, but I don't know exactly what kind as yet. Neither do I want to pester other Diagnosticians, even politely, and certainly not the Diagnostician-in-Charge of Pathology. So I shall have to be devious and approach Thornnastor through you, its chief assistant, to get the sort of advice I need."

Murchison watched his refueling operation for a moment without speaking, then she said seriously, "You don't have to be circumspect with Thornnastor, you know. It badly wants to be involved in the Protector case, and would have been placed in charge if it hadn't been for the fact that you were the Senior with firsthand experience of the beastie, and you were already being considered for Diagnostician status. Thorny will be happy to assist you in every way possible.

"In fact, if you don't ask for its help," she ended, smiling, "our Chief of Pathology will walk all over you with its six outsize feet."

"I, too, would like to assist you, friend Conway," Prilicla joined in. "But considering the massive musculature of the patient, my cooperation will not be close."

"And I," Danalta said.

"And I," Naydrad said, looking up from the green mess which its Kelgian taste buds were finding so delectable, "will continue doing as I'm told."

Conway laughed. "Thank you, friends." To Murchison, he said, "I'll go back to Pathology with you and talk to Thornnastor. And I'm not proud. If I were to mention the Gogleskan problem, and the FROB geriatrics, and the other odds and ends which—"

"Thornnastor," Murchison said firmly, "likes to know, and stick its outsize olfactory sensor into everything."

He felt much better after the meeting with the Chief of Pathology which, because the Tralthan's waking and sleeping cycle was much longer than that of an Earth-human, took the remainder of his duty period. Thornnastor was the biggest gossip in the hospital; it just could not keep any of its mouths shut, but its information on virtually every aspect of extraterrestrial pathology, as well as in many areas not considered to be within its specialty, was completely dependable.

Thornnastor wanted to know everything, and it was certainly not reticent, about anything.

"As you are already aware, Conway," it said ponderously as he was about to leave, "we Diagnosticians are generally held in high regard among the members of our profession, and the respect shown us, insofar as it can be shown in a madhouse like this, is tempered by pity for the psychological discomfort we experience, and an almost lighthearted acceptance of the medical miracles we produce.

"We are Diagnosticians and, as such, medical miracles are expected of us," the Tralthan went on. "But the production of true medical miracles, or radical surgical procedures, or the successful culmination of a line of xenobiological research, can be personally unsatisfying to certain types of doctor. I refer to those practitioners who, although able and intelligent and highly dedicated to their art, require a fair apportionment of credit for the work they do."

Conway swallowed. He had never before heard the Diagnostician-in-Chief of Pathology talk to him like this, and the words would have been more suited to a lecture on his personal shortcomings from the Chief Psychologist. Was Thornnastor, knowing of his fondness for reaching solutions and initiating treatments with the minimum of consultation, suggesting that he was a grandstander and was therefore unsuitable material for a Diagnostician? But apparently not.

"As a Diagnostician one rarely obtains complete satisfaction from producing good work," the Tralthan went on, "because one can never be wholly sure that the work performed or the ideas originated are one's own. Admittedly the Educator tapes furnish other-species memory records only, but purely imaginary person-ality involvement with the tape donor leaves one feeling that any credit due for new work should be shared. If the doctor concerned is in possession of three, five, perhaps ten, Educator tapes, well, the credit is spread very thinly."

"But nobody in the hospital," Conway protested, "would dream of withholding the credit due a Diagnostician who had—"

"Of course not," Thornnastor broke in. "But it is the Diagnos-tician itself who withholds the credit, not its colleagues. Unneces-sarily, of course, but that is one of the personal problems of being a Diagnostician. There are others, for the circumvention of which you will have to devise your own methods."

All four of the Tralthan's eyes had turned to regard Conway, a rare occurrence and proof that Thornnastor's vast mind was con-centrating exclusively on his particular case. Conway laughed ner-vously.

"Then it is high time I visited O'Mara to take a few of those tapes," he said, "so that I will have a better idea of what my prob-lems will be. I think initially a Hudlar tape, then a Melf and a Kelgian. When I'm accustomed, if I ever become accustomed to them, I'll request some of the more exotic . . ."

"Some of the mental stratagems used by my colleagues," Thorn-nastor continued ponderously, ignoring the interruption, "are such that they might conceivably tell their life-mates about them, but certainly no person with a lesser relationship. In spite of my overwhelming curiosity regarding these matters, they have not confided in me, and the Chief Psychologist will not open its files."

Two of its eyes curved away to regard Murchison and it went on. "A few hours' or even days' delay in taking the tapes is not important. Pathologist Murchison is free to go, and I suggest that you take full advantage of each other while you are still able to do so without otherspecies psychological complications."

As they were leaving, Thornnastor added, "It is the Earth-human taped component of my mind which has suggested this . . ."

CHAPTER 11

"The theory is that if you are to accustom yourself to the confusion of alien thought patterns," O'Mara growled at him as Conway was still rubbing the sleep out of his eyes, "it is better in the long run to confuse you a lot rather than a little at a time. You have been given the tapes during four hours of light sedation, during which you snored like a demented Hudlar, and you are now a five-way rugged individualist.

"If you have problems," the Chief Psychologist went on, "I don't want to know about them until you're absolutely sure they're insoluble. Be careful how you go and don't trip over your own feet. In spite of what your alter egos tell you to the contrary, you only have two of them."

The corridor outside O'Mara's office was one of the busiest in the hospital, with medical and maintenance staff belonging to a large variety of physiological classifications walking, crawling, wriggling, or driving past in both directions. Seeing his Diagnostician's armband and realizing, rightly in his case, that a certain amount of mental confusion and physical uncoordination might be present, they gave him as wide a berth as possible. Even the TLTU inside a pressure sphere mounted on heavy caterpillar treads passed him with more than a meter to spare.

A few seconds later a Tralthan Senior he knew passed by, but the big FGLI was not known to Conway's other selves, so his reaction time was slowed. When he swiveled his head to return the Tralthan's greeting, he was overcome suddenly by vertigo, because the Hudlar and Melf components of his mind were of beings whose heads did not swivel. Instinctively he reached toward the corridor wall to steady himself. But instead of a hard, tapering Hudlar tentacle or a shiny black Melfan pincer, the member supporting him was a flaccid pink object with five lumpy digits. By the time he had steadied himself both physically and mentally, he had become aware of an Earth-human DBDG in Monitor green waiting patiently to be noticed.

"You were looking for me, Lieutenant?" Conway asked.

"For the past couple of hours, Doctor," the officer replied. "But you were with the Chief Psychologist on a taping session and could not be disturbed."

Conway nodded. "What's the trouble?"

"Problems with the Protector," the Lieutenant said, and went on quickly. "The Exercise Room—that's what we're calling it now even though it still looks like a torture chamber—is underpowered. Tapping into the main power line for the section would necessitate going through four levels, only one of which is inhabited by warm-blooded oxygen-breathers. The structural alterations in the other three areas would be very time-consuming because of our having to guard against atmosphere contamination, especially where the Illensan chlorine-breathers are concerned. The answer would be a small power source sited within the Exercise Room. But if the Protector broke free, the shielding around the power unit might not survive, and if the shielding went, the radiation hazard would necessitate five levels'—above and below the area—being evacuated, and a lot more time would be wasted cleaning the—"

"The room is close to the outer hull," Conway said, feeling that a lot of time was being wasted right now by asking a medical man's advice on purely technical questions, and fairly simple ones at that. "Surely you can set up a small reactor on the outer hull, safe from the Protector, and run a line into—"

"That was the answer I came up with, too," the Lieutenant broke in, "but it gave rise to other problems, administrative rather than technical. There are regulations regarding what structures can and cannot be placed on the outer hull, and a reactor there, where one had never been before, might necessitate alterations in the hospital's external traffic flow patterns. In short, there is a major tangle of red tape which I can unravel given time, and if I asked all of the people concerned nicely and in triplicate. But you, Doctor, considering the urgency of your project, could *tell* them what you need."

Conway was silent for a moment. He was remembering one of the Chief Psychologist's remarks prior to the taping session and just before the sedation had taken effect. O'Mara had smiled sourly and said, "You have the rank now, Conway, even though it may turn out to be temporary. Go out and use it, or even abuse it. Just let me see you doing something with it."

Striving to make his tone that of a Diagnostician to whom nobody in the hospital would say no, Conway said, "I understand, Lieutenant. I'm on my way to Hudlar Geriatric, but I'll deal with it at the first communicator I pass. You have another problem?"

"Of course I have problems," the Lieutenant replied. "Every time you bring a new patient to the hospital, the whole maintenance division grows ulcers! Levitating brontosaurs, Drambon rollers, and now a patient who hasn't even been born yet inside a . . . a berserker!"

Conway looked at the other in surprise. Usually the Monitor Corps officers were faultless in matters of discipline and respect toward their superiors, whether military or medical. Dryly, he said, "We can treat ulcers."

"My apologies, Doctor," the other said stiffly. "I've been in charge of a squad of Kelgians for the past two years, and I've forgotten how to be polite."

"I see." Conway laughed. Since he was carrying a Kelgian tape himself right then, the Lieutenant had his sympathy. "That problem I cannot help you with. Are there others?"

"Oh, yes," the other replied. "They are insoluble, but minor. The two Hudlars are still objecting to their continuous beating of the Protector. I asked O'Mara if he could find someone else for the job, someone who would suffer less mental distress while carrying it out. O'Mara told me that if such a person had escaped his screening and was currently working in the hospital, he would resign forthwith. So I'm stuck with the Hudlars, and their damn music, until the new accommodation is ready.

"They insist that it helps keep their minds off what they're do-ing, but have you ever had to listen to Hudlar music, continuously, day after day?"

Conway admitted that he had not had that experience, that a few minutes of it had been more than enough for him.

They had arrived at the interlevel lock, and he began climbing into one of the lightweight suits for the journey through the foggy yellow levels of the Illensan chlorine-breathers and the water-filled wards of the aquatic denizens of Chalderescol which lay between him and the Hudlar wards. He double-checked all the fastenings and reread the checklist, even though he had donned such pieces of hospital equipment thousands of times and could do it with his eyes shut. But he was not entirely himself just then, and the regu-lations stated that all medical personnel carrying Educator tapes, and as a consequence laboring under a degree of mental confusion, must use the checklist with their eyes wide open.

The Lieutenant was still standing patiently beside him. Conway said, "There's more?"

The officer nodded. "A fairly easy one, Doctor. Hardin, the Dietician-in-Chief, is asking about the consistency of the Protector's food. He says he can reproduce a synthetic mush tailored to fit its dietary requirements in all respects, but that there is a psychological aspect to the ingestion of food which may be important to the overall well-being of this particular patient. You had a brief tele-pathic contact with one of them and so have firsthand information on the subject. He would like advice."

"I'll talk to him later," Conway said, pausing before pulling the helmet over his head. "But in the meantime you can tell him that it rarely eats vegetation, and the food that it does eat is usually wrapped in a thick hide or exoskeleton and is fighting back. I suggest that he encases the food in long, hollow tubes with edible walls. The tubes can be incorporated into the exercise machinery and used to beat the patient in the interests of greater environmental realism. Its mandibles are capable of denting steel plating, and Hardin is right. It would not be happy eating the equivalent of thin, milky cereal."

He laughed again and added, "We wouldn't want to risk rotting its teeth."

The Hudlar Geriatric Ward was a comparatively new addition to Sector General's facilities, and it was the closest the hospital came to providing treatment for psychologically disturbed patients, and even then the treatment was available to only a statistically chosen few. This was because the solution to the problem, if one could be found, would have to be put into effect on a planet-wide scale on Hudlar itself.

The ward's artificial gravity had been set at the Hudlar normal of nearly four Earth-Gs, and the atmospheric pressure was a compromise which caused the minimum of inconvenience to both patients and nursing staff. There were three Kelgian nurses on duty, their fur twitching restlessly under their lightweight suits and gravity neutralizer harnesses as they sprayed nutrient paint onto three of the five patients. Conway buckled on a G-neutralizer suited to his Earth-human mass, signaled that he did not require a nurse to attend him, and moved toward the nearest unoccupied patient.

Immediately the Hudlarian component of his mind came surging up, almost obliterating the Melfan, Tralthan, Kelgian, and Gogleskan material and threatening to engulf Conway's own mind in a great wave of pity and helpless anger at the patient's condition.

"How are you today?" Conway asked ritually.

"Fine, thank you, Doctor," the patient replied, as he knew it would. Like the majority of other life-forms possessing immense strength, the Hudlarian FROBs were a gentle, inoffensive, and self-effacing race, none of whom would dream of suggesting that his medical ability was somehow lacking by saying that it was *not* well.

It was immediately obvious that the aging Hudlar was not at all well. Its six great tentacles, which normally supported its heavy trunk in an upright position for the whole of its waking and sleeping life, and which served as both manipulatory and ambulatory appendages, hung limply over the sides of its supporting cradle. The hard patches of callus, the knuckles on which it walked while its digits were curled inward to protect them against contact with the ground, were discolored and cracking. The digits themselves, usually so strong, rock-steady, and precise in their movements, were twitching continually into spasm.

The Hudlars lived in a heavy-gravity, high-pressure environment whose superdense air teemed with so much airborne vegetable and microanimal life-forms that it resembled a thick soup, which the inhabitants absorbed directly through the tegument of the back and flanks. But the absorption mechanism of the patient had begun to fail, so large areas of the skin were caked with discolored nutrient paint which would have to be washed off before the next meal could be sprayed on. But the condition was worsening, the patient's ability to absorb nourishment was diminishing, and that, in turn, was accelerating the deterioration in the skin condition.

Chemical changes caused by the incomplete absorption process caused the residual nutrient to smell. But even worse was the odor from the waste elimination area, no longer under voluntary control, whose discharge formed like milky perspiration on the patient's underside before dripping into the cradle's suction pan. Conway could not really smell anything at all, because his suit had its own air supply. But the FROB personality sharing his mind had experienced this situation many times in its life, and psychosomatic smells were, if anything, worse than the real kind.

The patient's mind was still clear, however, and there would be no physical deterioration in the brain structure until a few minutes after its double heart stopped beating, and therein lay the real tragedy. Rare indeed was the Hudlar mind that could remain stable inside a great body which was disintegrating painfully all around it, especially when the mind was fully and intensely aware of the process.

Hopelessly he searched for an answer, going through the material on gereology available at the time his tapes were donated as well as the painful data associated with his own childhood memories and subsequent medical experience. But there was no answer to be found anywhere in his multiple mind, and the consensus of all of them was that he should increase the dosage of painkilling medication so as to make the patient as comfortable as possible.

While he made the addition to the treatment chart, the Hudlar's speaking membrane vibrated stiffly, but that organ, too, was deteriorating, and this time the sounds it made were too distorted for his translator to make any sense of them. He murmured reassurances, which they both knew to be empty, and moved to the next cradle.

Its condition was fractionally better than the previous one, and its conversation with him was animated and covered every subject under the Hudlar sun except what ailed it. Conway was not fooled, much less his Hudlarian alter ego, and he knew that this particular FROB was enjoying—although that was scarcely the right word in these circumstances—its last few hours of sanity. The next two patients did not speak to him at all, and the last one was loudly articulate but no longer sane.

Its speaking membrane was vibrating continually inside the wide, cylindrical muffler which had been attached to reduce both the sound and the mental discomfort of those within earshot, but enough was escaping to make Conway feel very uncomfortable indeed. It was in poor physical shape as well. In addition to the breakdown of the absorption system over a large area of the body surface, the incontinence, and the marked deterioration evident in all of the limb extremities, two of the tentacles had lost mobility and resembled nothing so much as a couple of withered tree-trunks.

"Those limbs require urgent surgical attention, Doctor," the nurse engaged in spraying the patient with nutrient said, having first turned off its translator. In the forthright manner of all Kelgians it added, "Amputation is indicated to prolong the patient's life, if that is considered desirable."

In ordinary circumstances the prolongation of the patient's life was desirable and, in fact, was the prime consideration, and his mind was being flooded with information and suggestions for treating the equivalent condition in Melfans, Kelgians, Tralthans, and Earth-humans. But to the physiological classification FROB the very concept of curative medicine had been unknown until the discovery of Hudlar by the Federation, and to that species any major surgical intervention was hazardous in the extreme. On a heavy gravity, high-pressure world like Hudlar, the internal pressure and metabolic rate of its dominant life-form had to be correspondingly high.

The control of bleeding, both during a procedure and postoperatively, was difficult. And the internal decompression which was an unavoidable side effect of an operation could cause deformation and serious damage to major organs adjacent to the operative field. As a result the Hudlar information in his mind together with Conway's own experience of FROB surgery suggested caution, while the other mass of extraterrestrial experience advocated operating without delay. But a double amputation on a geriatric and dangerously weakened patient ... Angrily he shook his head and turned away.

The Kelgian nurse was watching him closely. It said, "Does that movement of the cranium indicate a yes or a no answer to my question, Doctor?"

"It means that I haven't yet made up my mind," Conway said as he turned and escaped thankfully into the infants' ward.

While it was true that for the greater proportion of their lifetimes the Hudlars were impervious to disease and all but the most severe injuries—which was the primary reason why medicine had been an unknown science on their world—this did not hold during the first and final few years of life. His recent harrowing experience had shown all too clearly the ills to which aged Hudlars were prone, and now he was seeing the other and much less distressing end of the clinical spectrum.

Infant FROBs seemed to catch every Hudlarian pathogen present in their atmospheric soup until, if they were able to survive the first few encounters with them, their bodies built up the natural resistance which lasted for the greater part of their very long lives. Fortunately, the majority of the diseases were spectacular in their symptomology but individually nonfatal. Federation medical science had been able to provide cures for several of them and was working on the others. Unfortunately, while no single disease could be considered fatal in itself, all were potentially lethal because the ailments which the infants contracted were cumulatively weakening, and it was the order in which they were contracted and the number of diseases present at a given time which determined the lethality. A complete solution was not possible until specifics against all of the diseases were produced.

As Conway entered and looked around the furiously busy ward, the Hudlar material in his mind suggested that mass immunization was not the proper solution. There was a strong feeling that protecting the FROB children in that way would ultimately lead to a weakening of the species as a whole. But the Hudlar who had donated his tape had not been a member of the medical profession, there being no such profession on Hudlar, and had instead been a strange combination of philosopher, psychiatrist, and teacher. Even so, the feeling bothered Conway until a six-legged, half-ton infant came charging down on him shouting that it wanted to play, and drove everything from his mind but the need to take urgent evasive action.

He set his gravity controls to one-quarter G and jumped straight upward to the rail of the observation catwalk, barely two seconds before the young Hudlar hit the wall with a crash which must have severely tested both the ward's soundproofing and its structure. From his elevated viewpoint Conway could see that there were fewer than twenty patients in the ward, and in spite of the four Gs at floor level, they were all moving so fast that there seemed to be at least three times that number. When they occasionally stopped to change direction, he could see that the majority of them were displaying a variety of horrifying skin conditions.

An adult Hudlar with nutrient tanks strapped to its back finished spraying an infant it had cornered and immobilized at the far end of the ward, then turned and moved ponderously toward him.

It bore the insignia of a nurse-in-training, and it was, on this duty at least, little more than a baby-minder. But Conway knew that it was one of three FROBs undergoing medical training at Sector General, and the first members of that species chosen to introduce to their world the concepts of preventive and curative medicine. It was in female mode a remarkably handsome specimen and, unlike the Kelgian nurse in the geriatrics section, very polite and respectful.

"May I help you, Doctor?" it said, looking up at him. A sudden rush of memories from his alter ego's life on Hudlar invaded his mind so that he could not speak.

"Patient Seven, young Metiglesh, the one who wanted to play with you," it went on, "is responding well to the new treatment devised by Diagnostician Thornnastor. I can quite easily immobilize it for you if you wish to make a scanner examination."

It would be easy, Conway thought wryly, for a Hudlar nurse. That was the reason why an FROB trainee was in charge there—it knew exactly how much force to use on the little terrors, while equally or higher-qualified nurses of other species would be afraid to use the amount of force required in case they might injure the patients.

Young Hudlars were incredibly tough, and some of the adults were unbelievably beautiful.

"I'm just passing through, Nurse," he managed to say finally.

"You seem to have everything under control here."

As Conway stared down at the being, his own knowledge of the FROB classification was being augmented by data on what it actually felt like to be a Hudlar in the male mode, as the donor had been at the time of making its tape, and he had memories only slightly less intense of being a female. He could remember the arrival of a recent offspring and how the birth process had drastically altered the hormone balance so that he became a male again. On Hudlar they were uniquely fortunate in that both life-mates were enabled to have their children in turn.

"Many life-forms carrying the Hudlar physiology tape visit here from the geriatric section," the nurse went on, unaware of the mental havoc it was causing him. His Hudlar alter ego was bringing up data, memories, experiences, wish-fulfillment fantasies of courtship, love-play, and of gargantuan couplings which made his Earth-human mind recoil in horror. But it was not Conway's mind that had control just then.

He tried desperately to regain possession, to fight against the overwhelming waves of raw instinct which were making it impossible for him to think. He tried to look only at his thinly gloved, non-Hudlar digits as they gripped the guardrail while the nurse went on. "It is distressing for a Hudlar, or for an entity bearing the Hudlar tape, to visit the geriatric section. I myself would not enter unless requested to do so, and I have the greatest respect and admiration for those of you who do so purely out of a sense of professional duty. Coming in here, it is said, frequently helps the overly distressed mind to think of something more pleasant.

"You are, of course, at liberty to remain as long as you deem necessary, Doctor. For whatever reason," it added sympathetically. "And if there is anything I can do to help you, you have only to ask."

His Hudlar component was doing its equivalent of baying at the moon. Conway croaked something which his translator was probably unable to handle and began moving along the catwalk toward the exit at a near run.

For Heaven's sake get control of yourself, he raged silently at himself. *It's six times bigger than you are!* ...

CHAPTER 12

The Menelden system was no stranger to catastrophe. It had been discovered some sixty years earlier by a Monitor Corps scoutship whose Captain had exercised the traditional right to name it because there were no indications that the system harbored indigenous intelligent life with its own name for the world. If such life had been present in the distant past, then all traces of it had been obliterated when a large, planet-size chunk of metal ore entered the system, colliding with the largest outer planet and causing havoc and ultimately further collision with the others, all in tight orbits around their primary.

When the system eventually restabilized itself, Menelde was an aging yellow sun tightly surrounded by a rapidly spinning cloud of asteroids, a large proportion of which were solid metal. Immediately following its discovery, life came to the Menelden system in the shape of mining and metal processing complexes and their operating crews from all over the Federation, and in that cosmic illustration of the Brownian movement of gases, accidents occurred.

The details of one did not become known until many weeks later, nor was the final responsibility for it ever determined.

An enormous multispecies accommodation module for housing mining and metal-processing workers was being moved by tugs from an exhausted area to a fresh one, and was ponderously following a path between the slowly moving or relatively motionless asteroids and the other mining traffic which was engaged in similar delicate exercises in three-dimensional navigation.

One of the vessels, whose course would take it safely but uncomfortably close to the accommodation module and its tugs, was a carrier fully loaded with finished metal girders and sheets. Between the thrusters aft and the tiny control module forward the structure of the carrier was completely open to facilitate the loading and unloading of its cargo. This meant that the clearly visible mass of metal held, apparently none too securely, to its lashing points was exerting undue psychological pressure on the senior tug Captain, who told the carrier Captain to sheer off.

The carrier Captain demurred, insisting that they would pass in perfect safety, while his ship and the vast accommodation module crept ponderously toward each other. The senior tug Captain, who was charged with the safety of a structure incapable of independent maneuver and containing more than one thousand people, as opposed to the carrier with its three-man crew, had the last word.

Very slowly, because of the tremendous weight and inertia of its cargo, the carrier began to swing broadside-on to the module, intending to use its main thrusters to drive it clear long before their paths could intersect. The two vessels were closing, but slowly. There was plenty of time.

It was at that point that the accommodation module's supervisor, although not really worried, decided that it would be a very good time to hold an emergency drill.

The urgent flashing of hazard lights and the braying of alarm sirens, heard in the background while he was in communication with the module, must have had an unsettling effect on the senior tug Captain. He decided that the carrier was turning too slowly and despatched two of his tugs to assist the process with their pressor beams. In spite of the caustic reassurances from the carrier Captain that there was ample time for the maneuver and that everything was under control, the carrier was quickly pushed broadside-on to the approaching module—the position from which a brief burn on its thrusters would take it clear within a few seconds.

The thrusters did not fire.

Whether the failure was due to the effect of the hastily focused pressor beams on the carrier's uncovered control linkages which ran between the crew pod and the thrusters astern—they may well have been warped into immobility—or Fate had decreed that the system

STAR HEALER · 505

would malfunction at precisely that moment would never be known. But there were still a few minutes remaining before the collision would occur.

Ignoring the orderly confusion on board the module, where the supervisor was trying desperately to make his people realize that the practice emergency drill had suddenly become a real one, the carrier used its attitude control jets at maximum overload in an attempt to return the vessel to its original and safe heading. But the tremendous weight of a ship fully laden with a cargo of dense metal was too much for them, and slowly, almost gently, the stern of the carrier made contact with the forward section of the accommodation module.

The carrier, whose structure had been designed to withstand loadings only in the vertical plane, broke up when subjected to the sudden, lateral shock. Gigantic lengths of metal tore free from their lashing points, the metal retaining bands snapping like so much thread, and the long, open racks which held the sheet metal disintegrated with the collapse of the ship's main structure, sending their contents spinning toward the accommodation module's side like a slow-moving flight of throwing-knives. And mixed with the spinning metal plates and beams and pieces of the carrier's structure was the radioactive material of its power pile.

Many of the plates struck the module edge-on, inflicting long, deep incisions several hundred meters long in the hull before bouncing away again. The metal beams smashed against the already weakened hull, opening dozens of compartments to space, or drove deep into the module's interior like enormous javelins. The collision abruptly checked the structure's forward motion and left it a slowly spinning half-wreck, which presented in turn a flank which was unmarked and another which showed a scene of utter devastation.

One of the tugs took off after the expanding cloud of metal which had been the carrier and its cargo, to chart its course for later retrieval and to search for possible survivors among its crew. The remaining tugs checked the spin on the accommodation module, then gave what help they could until the emergency teams from nearby mining installations, and ultimately *Rhabwar*, arrived.

Except for a few Hudlars who were not inconvenienced by vacuum conditions, and a number of Tralthans who could also survive

506 · JAMES WHITE

airlessness for short periods by going into hibernation mode and
sealing all their body orifices, nobody along the stricken side of the
module had survived. Even the immensely strong and tough-
skinned Hudlars and Tralthans could not live in zero pressure when
their bodies had been traumatically opened to space, and massive
explosive decompression was not a condition which could be cured,
even in Sector General.

The Hudlar and Tralthan quarters had suffered worst in the
collision. Elsewhere the structure had retained its air even though
the emergency drill condition meant that the occupants were in
spacesuits anyway, so a pressure drop would not have been a problem. But in these areas it was the sudden deceleration and spin
following the collision which had caused the casualties—hundreds
of them which, because of the protection given by the suits, were
serious rather than critical. When the module's artificial gravity was
restored, the majority of these were treated by the Menelden complex's same-species medics and held in makeshift wards to await
transfer to their home planets for further treatment or recuperation.

Only the really serious cases were sent to Sector General.

News of the Menelden accident had reached the hospital just in
time to allow Conway to avoid having to face another serious problem, although regarding a major accident as a handy excuse for
postponing a particularly worrying meeting was, he thought, neither
admirable nor unselfish.

His Educator tapes were becoming so well established that it
was difficult to tell when a set of feelings and reactions were his
own or those of one or all of the Others. So much so that the next
meeting with Murchison, when they would be together in their
quarters in circumstances which would inevitably lead to physical
intimacy, was something he had been dreading with increasing intensity as their next off-duty period drew closer. He just did not
know how he would react to her, how much if any control he would
have of the situation, and, most important of all, how she would
react to his reactions.

Then suddenly *Rhabwar* was despatched to the Menelden system to coordinate the rescue operation and bring back the more
serious casualties, and Murchison, a key member of its medical
team, was on board.

Conway was greatly relieved, at first. But as the ship's former medical team leader he was aware of the danger she was in, from the kind of accident which could so easily occur during a large-scale rescue mission, and he began to worry. Instead of being glad that he would not have to see her for a day or so, he found himself heading for the casualty reception lock just before the ambulance ship was due to dock after its first return trip.

He spotted Naydrad and Danalta standing by the transfer lock and keeping well clear of the casualty reception team, who needed no help at all in doing their job.

"Where is Pathologist Murchison?" Conway asked as a litter containing what looked like a Tralthan multiple traumatic amputation went past. The FGLI tape material in his mind was pushing to the fore, urgently suggesting methods of treatment for this patient. Conway shook his head in an instinctive attempt to clear it, and said more firmly, "I want to see Murchison."

Beside the uncharacteristically silent Naydrad, Danalta began to assume the bodily contours of an Earth-human female similar in shape and size to that of the pathologist. Then, sensing Conway's disapproval, it slumped back into shapelessness.

"Is she on board?" Conway asked sharply.

The nurse's fur was rippling and pulling itself into irregular patterns of tufting in a manner which, to his Kelgian alter ego, indicated an extreme reluctance to answer combined with the expectation of unpleasantness.

"I have a Kelgian tape," he said quietly, pointing at the other's telltale fur. "What's bothering you, Nurse?"

"Pathologist Murchison chose to remain at the disaster site," Naydrad replied finally, "to assist Doctor Prilicla with the triage."

"The *triage!*" Conway burst out. "Prilicla shouldn't be subjecting itself to . . . Dammit, I'd better go out there and help. There are more than enough doctors here to treat the casualties and if . . . You have an objection?"

Naydrad's fur was tufting and undulating in a new and more urgent sequence.

"Doctor Prilicla is the leader of the medical team," the Kelgian said. "Its proper place is at the disaster site, coordinating the rescue operation and disposition of casualties, regardless of the physical or mental trauma which might result. The presence of a former team leader could be considered as an implied criticism of its professional handling of the situation, which up until now has been exemplary."

Watching the movements of that expressive Kelgian fur, Conway was not really surprised at the strength of feeling that was being shown toward a superior who had been in the job for only a few days. By the nature of things, superiors were respected, sometimes feared, and usually obeyed with reluctance by their subordinates. But Prilicla had proved that it was possible to lead and instill absolute loyalty by making subordinates obey through another kind of fear, that of hurting the boss's feelings.

When Conway did not reply, Naydrad went on. "Your offer of assistance was foreseen, which is the reason why Pathologist Murchison remained to help Prilicla. The Cinrusskin's empathic faculty does not, as you well know, require that it work in close proximity to the injured, so it can remain in comparative safety while Murchison moves among the casualties as you would have done if you'd gone out there."

"Doctor," Danalta said, breaking its long silence, "Pathologist Murchison is in turn being assisted by several large, heavily muscled entities of its own and other species who are trained in heavy rescue techniques. These entities are charged with the responsibility for removing casualties from the wreckage at the Pathologist's direction, and for seeing that the same wreckage does not endanger Murchison.

"I mention this, Doctor," Danalta added, "so as to reassure you regarding the safety of your life-mate."

The polite and respectful tone of Danalta sounded almost obsequious after that of the more blunt-spoken Naydrad. But the TOBS, too, had developed a measure of empathy as a necessary adjunct to their species' faculty for defensive and offensive protective mimicry, and respectfulness made a nice change whether it was real or simulated.

"Thank you, Danalta. That is considerate of you," Conway said, but then turned to Naydrad. "But Prilicla, on triage! . . ."

The thought of it was enough to make Conway, and anyone else who knew the little empath, cringe.

The range and sensitivity of the Cinrusskin's empathic faculty had been invaluable when the empath had been a member of *Rhab-war*'s medical team, and now that Prilicla was heading that team the same circumstances would apply. The empath could feel among the casualties of a wrecked ship, especially those who were physically motionless, grievously injured and apparently lifeless, and state with absolute accuracy which protective suits held cadavers and which still-living survivors. It did so by attuning itself to the residual emotional radiation of the casualty's often deeply unconscious brain, and by feeling what the survivor's unconscious mind felt and analyzing the results, it could decide whether there was any hope of reviving the spark of life which remained. Space accidents had to be dealt with quickly if there was to be anyone left alive to rescue, and on countless occasions Prilicla's empathic faculty had saved vital time and a great many lives.

A high price had to be paid for this ability, because Prilicla had in many cases to suffer with each of the casualties, for a short or a lengthy period, before such diagnoses or assessments could be made. But triaging the Menelden accident would mean encountering emotional distress of a whole new order of magnitude, so far as Prilicla was concerned. Fortunately, Murchison's feelings toward the little empath could only be described as fanatically maternal, and she would ensure that the storm of emotional radiation—the pain and panic and grief of the injured and their bereaved friends—which raged within that devastated accommodation module was experienced by the empath at the longest possible range, and for the shortest possible duration.

Triage called for the presence of a Senior Surgeon at the disaster site. Prilicla was one of the hospital's finest surgeons, and it was being assisted by a pathologist who was second only to those of Diagnostician rank. Together they should be able to do that particularly harrowing job of casualty assessment without delay or indecision.

They would be following procedures laid down in the distant past to cover large-scale medical emergencies, from the time when air attacks, bombardments, terrorist bombings, and similar effects of the interracial mass psychosis called war had added unnecessarily to the death tolls of purely natural disasters. At times like these, medical resources could not be wasted, or time and effort devoted to hopeless cases. That had been the thinking behind triage.

Casualties were assessed and placed into three groups. The first contained the superficially or nonfatally injured, those suffering from psychological trauma, the people who would not die should treatment be delayed and who could wait until transportation was available to their home-planet hospitals. The second group comprised those beings who were so seriously injured that their condition would prove fatal no matter what was done for them, and who could only be made as comfortable as possible until they terminated. The third and most important of the groups contained those whose injuries were grievous, but who stood a fair chance of survival if the indicated treatment could be given without delay.

It was the Group Three injuries which were being sent to Sector General, Conway thought as he watched another litter go by with its pressure envelope inflated and its organic contents so hidden by life-support equipment that it was difficult even to be sure of its physiological classification. His own opinion was that this was a borderline case between Groups Two and Three.

"That is the last casualty on this trip, Doctor," said Naydrad quickly. "We must leave at once to bring back another batch."

The Kelgian turned and began undulating towards *Rhabwar*'s boarding tube. Danalta's shape became that of a dark green ball again, featureless except for an eye and a mouth which regarded him and spoke.

"You will already have noticed, Doctor," it said, "that Senior Physician Prilicla has a very high regard for the surgical ability of its colleagues and it is, moreover, extremely averse to placing any of the casualties in the hopeless category."

The mouth smoothed out and the eye withdrew as the TOBS rolled quickly away in Naydrad's wake.

CHAPTER 13

He learned of the return of *Rhabwar* with its last batch of Menelden casualties as he was about to attend his first Meeting of Diagnosticians. As he was the most recent probationary member, his sudden withdrawal for the purpose of exchanging a few words with Murchison would most certainly be considered impolite and downright insubordinate, and so their next meeting would again be delayed. His feelings about that were mostly of relief, and of shame at feeling relieved. He took his place, not expecting to make any important contribution to such august proceedings.

Nervously he looked across at O'Mara, the only other non-Diagnostician present, who sat dwarfed by the massive Thornnastor on one side and the coldly radiating spherical pressure envelope of Semlic, the SNLU methane-breathing Diagnostician from the cold levels. The Chief Psychologist stared back at him without expression. The features of the other Diagnosticians ranged around the room, sitting, crouching, hanging from or otherwise occupying the furniture designed for their bodily comfort, were likewise unreadable even though several of them were watching him.

Ergandhir, one of the Melfan ELNTs present, spoke first. "Before we discuss the Menelden casualties to be assigned to us, work which of necessity has the greatest priority, are there any less urgent matters requiring general discussion and guidance? Conway, as the most recent recruit to the ranks of the voluntary insane, you must be encountering a few problems."

"A few," Conway agreed. Hesitantly, he added, "At present they are mechanical, temporarily beyond my scope, or completely insoluble."

"Please specify," an unidentified entity said at the other side of the room. It could have been one of the Kelgians, whose speaking orifices barely moved during a conversation. "It is to be hoped that all of these problems are temporarily insoluble."

For a moment Conway felt like a junior intern again, being criticized by a senior tutor for loose and emotional thinking, and the criticism was well deserved. He had to get a grip on himself and start thinking straight, with all five of his minds.

He said clearly, "The mechanical problems arise from the necessity of providing a suitable environment and treatment facilities for the Protector of the Unborn, before it gives birth and—"

"Pardon the interruption, Conway," Semlic broke in, "but it is unlikely that we can help directly with this problem. You were instrumental in rescuing the being from its wrecked ship, you had brief telepathic communication with the intelligent embryo, and you are therefore the only entity with sufficient firsthand knowledge to solve it. May I say, with sympathy, that you are welcome to this problem."

"While I cannot help you directly," Ergandhir joined in, "I can make available physiological and behavioral data on a similar Melfan life-form which, like the young Protector, is born fully formed and capable of defending itself. Birth takes place only once in the parent's lifetime, and there are invariably four young as a result. They attack and endeavor to eat the parent, who usually manages to defend itself sufficiently well if not to survive, then at least to kill one or two of its offspring, who sometimes try to kill one another. Were this not so they would long since have overrun my planet. The species is not sentient . . ."

"Thank heaven for that," O'Mara murmured.

". . . Or ever likely to become so," Ergandhir went on. "I have studied your reports on the Protector with great interest, Conway, and shall be pleased to discuss this material with you if you think it might be helpful. But you mentioned other problems."

Conway nodded as the Melfan material in his mind surfaced with pictures of the tiny, lizardlike creatures which infested the food-growing areas of Melf, and which had survived in spite of the most large-scale and sophisticated efforts at extermination. He could see the parallels between them and the Protectors, and would certainly talk to the Melfan Diagnostician as soon as the opportunity arose.

He went on. "The apparently insoluble problem is Goglesk. This is not an urgent problem, except to me, because there is personal involvement. For this reason I should not waste your time by—"

"I was not aware," one of the two Illensan PVSJs present said, twitching restively inside its chlorine envelope, "that a Gogleskan tape was available."

Conway had forgotten for a moment that "personal involvement" was one of the phrases used by Diagnosticians and tape-bearing Senior Physicians to inform each other that their minds were carrying the memory-record of a member of the species under discussion. Before he could reply, O'Mara spoke quickly.

"There is no tape available," he said. "The memory transfer was accidental and involuntary, and occurred when Conway was visiting the planet. He may wish to discuss the details with you at some future date, but I agree with him that such a discussion now would be time-consuming and inconclusive."

They were all staring at him, but it was Semlic, who had changed lenses on its external vision pickup so as to see him more closely, who asked the question first.

"Am I to understand that you possess a memory record which cannot be erased, Conway?" it said. "This is a most disquieting thought for me. I myself am gravely troubled by my overcrowded mind and have seriously considered returning to Senior Physician status by drastically reducing the number of my tapes. But my alter egos are guests who can always be forced to leave should their presence become unbearable. But one memory record in permanent residence, without the possibility of erasure, is more than enough. None of your colleagues would think any less highly of you if you were to do as I am about to do and have the other tapes erased ..."

"Semlic has been about to do that," O'Mara said quietly, with his translator switched off so that only Conway could hear him, "every few days for the past sixteen years. But it is right. If there are serious problems as a result of the Gogleskan presence reacting against the others, erase them. There would be no discredit attached, no inadequacy of personality implied, and it would, in fact, be the sensible course. But then, nobody could describe you as being sensible."

"...And among my mind-guests," Semlic was saying when Conway returned his attention to the SNLU, "are a number of entities who have had, well, very interesting and unorthodox lives. With all this nonmedical experience available I may be able to advise you should you encounter personal problems with Pathologist Murchison—"

"With *Murchison!*..." Conway said, incredulously.

"It is possible," Semlic replied, missing or ignoring the overtones. "All here have the greatest respect for its professional competence and its personal disposition, and I, personally, would not like to think that it would suffer any emotional trauma because I had omitted to advise you, Conway. You are fortunate indeed to have such an entity as your life-mate. Naturally, I have no personal physical interest in this being..."

"I'm relieved to hear that," Conway said, looking frantically to O'Mara for help. It was beginning to sound as if the SNLU Diagnostician was going out of its super-cooled, crystalline mind. But the Chief Psychologist ignored him.

"...My enthusiasm stems from the DBDG Earth-human tape which has been occupying an undue portion of my mind since I began talking to you," the SNLU went on, "and which belonged to a very fine surgeon who was inordinately fond of activities associated with reproduction. For this reason I find your DBDG female most disturbing. It possesses the ability to communicate nonverbally, and perhaps unconsciously, during ambulation, and the mammary area is particularly—"

"With me," Conway broke in hastily, "it is that Hudlar trainee in the FROB infants' ward."

It turned out that several of the Diagnosticians present were carrying Hudlar physiology tapes and were not averse to discussing the nurse's professional competence and physical attributes at length, but the SNLU cut them short.

"This discussion must be giving Conway the wrong impression about us," Semlic said, its external vision pickups swiveling to include everyone in the room. "It might conceivably lower the high opinion Conway has of Diagnosticians, whose deliberations it would expect to be on a more rarefied professional level. Let me reassure it on your behalf that we are simply showing our latest potential member that the majority of its problems are not new and have been solved, in one way or another, and usually with the help of colleagues who are more than willing to assist it at any time."

"Thank you," Conway said.

"Judging by the continued silence of the Chief Psychologist," Semlic went on, "you must be coping fairly well up to now. But there is some small assistance I may be able to render you, and it is environmental rather than personal. You may visit my levels at any time, the only proviso being that you remain in the observation gallery.

"Few, indeed, are the warm-blooded, oxygen-breathers who take a professional interest in my patients," the SNLU added, "but if you should be the exception, then special arrangements will have to be made."

"No, thank you," Conway said. "I could not make any useful contribution to subzero crystalline medicine just now, if ever."

"Nevertheless," the methane-breather went on, "should you visit us, be sure to increase your audio sensitivity and switch off your translator, then listen. A number of your warm-blooded colleagues have derived a certain amount of comfort from the result."

"Cold comfort," O'Mara said dryly, and added, "We are devoting an unfair proportion of our time to Conway's personal problems rather than to those of his patients."

Conway looked around at the others, wondering how many of them were carrying FROB physiology tapes. He said, "There is the Hudlar geriatric problem. Specifically, the decision whether to involve the patient in a dangerous multiple amputation procedure which, if successful, will prolong life for a comparatively short time, or to allow nature to take its course. In the former event the quality of the prolonged life leaves much to be desired."

Ergandhir's beautifully marked exoskeletal body moved forward in its frame, and the lower mandible moved in time with its translated words. "That is a situation I have run against many times, as have we all, and with species other than the Hudlars. The result in my own case has been, to use a Melfan metaphor, a badly chipped carapace. Essentially it is an ethical decision, Conway."

"Of course it is!" one of the Kelgians said before Conway could reply. "The decision will be a close and personal one. However, from my knowledge of the Doctor concerned the probability is that Conway will opt for surgical intervention rather than a clinical observation of the patient to the terminal phase."

"I am inclined to agree," Thornnastor said, speaking for the first time. "If a situation is inherently hopeless, it is better to do something rather than nothing. And with an operating environment making it difficult for other species to work effectively, an experienced Earth-human surgeon might expect good results."

"Earth-human DBDGs are not the best surgeons in the Galaxy," the Kelgian joined in again, its rippling fur indicating to those carrying DBLF tapes the feelings which were concealed by its unsubtle mode of speech. "The Tralthans, Melfans, Cinrusskins, we Kelgians are more surgically adept in certain circumstances. But there are situations where this dexterity cannot be brought to bear because of environmental conditions . . ."

"The operating theater must suit the patient," a voice broke in, "and not the Doctor."

". . . Or physiological factors in the surgeon," the Kelgian went on. "Protective garments or vehicles required to work in hostile environments inhibit the finer movements of manipulatory appendages and digits, and remotely controlled manipulators lack precision or are subject to malfunction at the most critical times. The DBDG hand, however, can be protected against a large number of hostile environments by a ridiculously thin glove which does not inhibit digital movements, and the supporting musculature is such that they can operate with minimal loss of efficiency in the presence of elevated pressure and gravity. The hands remain operational even when projecting a short distance beyond the field of the gravity nullifiers. Although crudely formed and comparatively restricted in their movements, the DBDG hands can go anywhere, surgically speaking, and—"

"Not everywhere, Conway," Semlic broke in. "I'll thank you to keep your superheated hands off *my* patients."

"Diagnostician Kursedth is being diplomatic, for a Kelgian," Ergandhir said. "It is complimenting you while explaining why you are likely to get more than your share of the nasty jobs."

"I guessed as much," Conway said, laughing.

"Very well," Thornnastor said. "We shall now consider the urgent matter of the Menelden casualties. If you will kindly regard your displays, we will discuss their present clinical condition, projected treatment and the assignments of surgical responsibility . . ."

The polite inquiries, sympathy, and advice which, Conway now realized, had cloaked a searching examination of his feelings and professional attitudes, were over for the time being. Thornnastor, the hospital's most experienced and senior Diagnostician, had taken charge of the meeting.

". . . You can see that the majority of the cases," the Tralthan went on, "have been assigned to Senior Physicians of various physiological classifications whose capabilities are more than equal to the tasks. Should unforeseen difficulties arise, one of ourselves will be called on to assist. A much smaller number of casualties, the really nasty cases, will be our direct responsibility. Some of you have been given only one of these patients, for reasons which will become obvious when you study the case notes, and others have been given more. Before you begin organizing your surgical teams and planning the procedures in detail, are there any comments?"

For the first few minutes they were all too busy studying the details of the cases assigned to them to have anything useful to say, and the initial comments were more in the nature of complaints.

"These two cases you've given me, Thornnastor," Ergandhir said, tapping one of its hard, sharply tapered pincers against its display screen. "They have so many compound and comminuted fractures between them that if they survive at all, they will be carrying so much wiring, pins, and plating that induction will elevate their body temperatures every time they approach a power generator. And what were two Orligian DBDGs doing there anyway?"

"Wreckage subsistence casualties," the pathologist replied. "They were members of the rescue team from the nearby Orligian processing plant. You are always complaining that you never get enough DBDG surgical experience."

"You've given me just one case," Diagnostician Vosan said. The Crepellian octopod turned to regard Thornnastor, then it made a noise which did not translate before adding, "Rarely have I seen such a discouraging clinical picture, and I shall certainly have my hands full, all eight of them, with this one."

"It was the number and dexterity of your manipulatory appendages," Thornnastor replied, "which impelled me to assign the case to you in the first place. But the time for discussion grows short. Are there any other comments before we move to procedures?"

Ergandhir said quickly, "During the intercranial work, on one of my patients in particular, emotional radiation monitoring would be distinctly advantageous."

"And I," Vosan said, "would find it useful during the preoperative phase to check on the level of unconsciousness and required anesthesia."

"And I! And I!" clamored several of the others, and for a moment there were too many voices talking at once for the translators to handle them. Thornnastor gestured for silence.

"It seems," the Tralthan said, "that the Chief Psychologist must remind you once again of the physiological and psychological capabilities of our one and only medically qualified empath. Major?"

O'Mara cleared his throat and said dryly, "I have no doubt that Doctor Prilicla would be willing and anxious to help all of you, but as a Senior Physician who is being considered for elevation to Diagnostician status, it is in the best position to judge where and when its empathy can be used to best effect. There is also the fact that while it is useful to have an empathic sensitive constantly monitoring the condition of a deeply unconscious patient during an operation, the patient does not really require it and the only benefit lies in the mental comfort and reassurance of the surgeon.

"There is also the fact," the Chief Psychologist went on, ignoring the untranslatable sounds of protest from around the table, "that our empath functions best when among people who like and fully understand it. This being so, it should be clear to you that Prilicla is allowed a wide degree of latitude in its choice, not only in the cases it takes but in the surgeons it agrees to assist. And so, if the person who has worked with Senior Physician Prilicla since it joined us as a junior intern, and who helped it during its early medical training, if this Doctor requested the assistance of Prilicla during an operation, it would not be refused. Isn't that so, Conway?"

"I, yes, I expect so," Conway stammered. He had not been listening closely for the past few minutes, because his mind had been on his cases, his close to hopeless cases, and on thoughts of open professional rebellion.

"Do you need Prilicla?" O'Mara asked quietly. "You have first refusal. If you do not need, as opposed to merely want, the assistance of your empathic friend, say so. A line of your colleagues who do need Prilicla will form rapidly on the left."

Conway thought for a moment, trying to coordinate and evaluate the input from his other mind components. Even the friendly and perpetually frightened Khone was radiating sympathy for his cases, and previously the mere sight of an uninjured Hudlar was sufficient to throw it into a panic reaction. Finally, he said, "I do not think that an empath would be of much help to these cases. Prilicla cannot work miracles, and at least three separate acts of supernatural intervention would be needed if these cases are to make it. And even then, well, I very much doubt that the patients or their close relatives will thank us."

"You can refuse the cases," O'Mara said quietly, "but you will have to give us a better reason than that they appear to be hopeless. As we have mentioned before, as a Diagnostician on probationary status you will be given what seems like an unfair share of such cases. This is to accustom you to the idea that the hospital must deal with partial successes and failures as well as nice, tidy, and complete cures. Up until now you have never had to concern yourself with problems of aftercare, have you, Conway?"

"I realize that," he replied angrily, because it sounded as though he was being criticized for past successes, or being accused of grandstanding in some obscure fashion. And then he began to wonder if his anger was due to there being a certain amount of truth in the accusation. More quietly, he went on, "Perhaps I've been lucky . . ."

"As well as surgically adept," Thornnastor interjected.

". . . In the past with cases which could only be complete successes or utter failures," he went on. "But these patients . . . Even with the life-support systems in continuous operation it seems to me that they are only technically alive, and I would need Prilicla's empathic faculty simply to verify that fact."

"Prilicla sent these casualties to us," one of the Kelgians said who had not previously spoken. "Clearly, it did not consider them hopeless. Are you in difficulties deciding on procedure, Conway?"

"Certainly not!" Conway said sharply. He went on. "I know Prilicla and Cinrusskins tend to be incurable optimists. Unpleasant ideas like the thought of failure with a patient, or a case that is hopeless from the start, are utterly foreign to it. There have been times when it shamed me into feeling the same way. But now I am being realistic. It appears to me that two, perhaps three of these four cases are little more than not quite dead specimens for investigation by Pathology."

"At last you are showing signs of accepting your situation, Conway," Thornnastor said in its slow, ponderous voice. "You may never again be able to concentrate your entire mind and capabilities on a single patient, and you must learn to accept failure and make your failures contribute to your future successes. It is possible that you will lose all four of your patients, or you may save all of them. But no matter what procedure and treatment you decide upon, and the good or bad results which ensue, you will use your multiply augmented mind to learn whether or not that same mind is stable enough to endure and maintain control over your procedures, whether personally performed or delegated.

"You will also bear constantly in mind," the senior Diagnostician went on, "the fact that while treating your four cases from the Menelden emergency list, you have other concerns. The FROB geriatric problem, our presently unsatisfactory organ replacement postoperative difficulties, the approaching parturition of your Protector, and even, if its presence suggests a new viewpoint or procedure on any of these problems, the data provided by the nonerasable mind of your Gogleskan friend. And if you are bearing all these things in mind, and my own Earth-human mind partner is unhappy with that phrase because it is what your DBDGs call a pun, you have already realized that FROB replacement surgery will play a vital part in the treatment of your four cases, and any failure could provide ready access to the organs needed to ensure the success of a not quite so hopeless case.

"We all find it difficult to accept failure, Conway," Thornnastor continued, "and your past record will make it less easy for you. But these cases are not being assigned to you for psychological reasons. Your level of competence as a surgeon warrants—"

"What our overtalkative colleague is saying, once again," one of the Kelgians broke in, its fur tufting with impatience, "is that good Doctors are given the worst patients. And now, may I discuss my two cases before they both terminate, from old age?"

CHAPTER 14

The first three hours were spent on preparatory work, tidying up the traumatic amputations performed by flying metal at the accident site, charting the extent of the internal injuries, checking on the readiness of the operating teams, and, in spite of the cooling unit in his suit, sweating.

At this stage in the proceedings his work was chiefly supervisory, so his increased output of perspiration was unconnected with physical activity and was what O'Mara referred to as psychosomatic sweating, a condition which the Chief Psychologist would tolerate only on rare occasions.

When one of the patients died preoperatively, Conway's feelings lacked the intensity he had been expecting in that situation. The prognosis on that particular Hudlar had been very poor in any event, so when the sensors indicated termination it was not a surprise. The Melfan, Illensan, Kelgian, Tralthan, and Gogleskan components of his mind registered low-key professional regret at the loss; the Hudlar alter ego felt more strongly, but its sorrow was tinged with relief because it knew how drastically curtailed would have been the patient's quality of life had it survived, and because the other three cases were occupying so much of his attention, Conway's own reaction lay somewhere in between.

He maintained the cadaver's respiration and cardiac functions so that its undamaged organs and limbs, what few of them remained, would be in optimum condition for transplantation. A small part of his mind wondered if the Hudlar's parts were used for replacement surgery on its more fortunate colleagues, could it truly be considered to be dead? Which led, inevitably, to a minor conflict within his multiple mind between the Hudlar component and the others regarding the treatment of the physical remains after death.

For reasons which were not fully understood even by the members of the species themselves, the Hudlars, although in all other respects a race of highly intelligent, sensitive, and philosophically advanced beings, were unique in that they did not honor or show the slightest degree of respect for their recently deceased. The memory of the person while alive was treasured by its friends, and commemorated in various fashions, but these records invariably omitted any reference to the fact that the being concerned had died. The life and accomplishments of the entity were remembered; the death was studiously ignored, and the deceased disposed of quickly and without ceremony, as if it was a piece of unsightly litter.

In this case the Hudlar idiosyncrasy was a distinct advantage, because it removed the often time-consuming necessity for obtaining the consent of the next of kin for organ removal and transplant.

Realizing suddenly that he was mentally sidetracking himself and wasting time, Conway gave the signal to begin.

He joined the operating frame around FROB-Three, who was the patient with the fractionally better chance of making it, taking the observer's position beside Senior Physician Yarrence, the Kelgian surgeon who had charge of the team. His original intention had been to head the team on the recently deceased FROB-Eighteen's operation, but that patient's demise meant that he could now keep a close watch on the three operations, all of which were urgent and critical enough to require simultaneous rather than consecutive performance. The members of his original team had been divided up between Yarrence, Senior Physician Edanelt, the Melfan in charge of FROB-Ten, and the Tralthan Senior Hossantir who had taken FROB-Forty-three.

Even though the FROB life-form was capable of living and working in gravity-free and airless conditions, this was only possible when the immensely tough and flexible tegument remained intact. When the skin had been pierced and the underlying blood vessels and organs exposed, as had occurred in several areas with this patient, deep surgery was impossible unless the natural gravity and pressure environment was reproduced. To do otherwise was to invite massive hemorrhaging and organ displacement due to the high pressure of the internal fluids. For this reason the OR staff were forced to wear gravity repulsors set to four Gs and heavy-duty protective suits whose gauntlets had been replaced by tight-fitting operating membranes designed to minimize the effects of the high external pressure.

They clustered around the patient like a shoal of ungainly fish, Conway thought, about to begin their surgical nibbling.

"The rear limbs have escaped with superficial damage and will heal naturally," Yarrence said, more for the benefit of his recorders than for Conway. "The two midlimbs and left forelimb have been lost, and the stumps will require surgical trimming and capping in preparation for the fitting of prosthetics. The right forelimb is still attached but has been so badly crushed that in spite of efforts to reestablish circulation to the affected areas, necrosis has taken place. This limb will also require removal and capping..."

The FROB in his mind stirred restively and seemed to be raising objections, but Conway did not speak because he had no clear idea of what it was objecting to.

"... Of the stump," the Kelgian Senior went on. "There is a metal splinter which has been driven into the right thoracic area with associated damage to a major vein, the bleeding from which has been incompletely controlled by the application of external pressure. This situation must be rectified urgently. There is also cranial damage, a large depressed fracture which is compressing the main nerve trunk and affecting mobility in the rear limbs. Subject to approval"... Yarrence glanced briefly in Conway's direction... "we shall remove the damaged forelimb, which will allow easier access for the team-members working in the cranial area, and prepare the stumps for—"

"No," Conway said firmly. He could not see anything but the Kelgian's conical head inside the heavy protective garment, but he could imagine the silvery fur tufting in anger as he went on. "Do not cap the forelimb stumps, but prepare them instead for a transfer and transplant of the rear limbs. Otherwise your procedure as outlined is approved."

"The risk to the patient is increased," Yarrence said sharply, "and the operational time will be extended by at least twenty percent. Is this desirable?"

Conway was silent for a moment, thinking about the quality of life of the patient following the success of the simple as opposed to the more complex operation. Compared with the immensely strong and precisely controlled forelimbs possessed by a normal FROB, the telescoping, hinged, and swiveling prosthetic was ridiculously weak and inefficient. As well, Hudlar amputees found them aesthetically displeasing and distressing when the forelimbs—which were the members most conveniently placed to the eyes and used for the more delicate physical manipulations, including the long and involved preliminaries to mating—were artificial. Transplanting the rear limbs forward, although risky considering the weakened state of the patient, was infinitely preferable, because if the operation were successful, it would provide the FROB with forelimbs which would be only fractionally less sensitive and precise than the originals. Since the limbs would be coming from the same entity, there would be no immune system involvement or tissue rejection problems.

The Hudlar material in Conway's mind was insisting that he disregard the risks, while his own mind was trying desperately to find ways of reducing them.

He said, "Leave the forelimb transplant until the cranial and abdominal work is successfully completed; otherwise the transplant would be wasted effort. Don't forget to clean the tegument frequently and respray with anesthetic. In cases like this the absorption mechanism is affected by the general condition of—"

"I know that," Yarrence said.

"Of course you do," Conway went on. "You have the Hudlar tape, too, probably the same one as I have. The operation carries a strong element of risk, but it is well within your capabilities, and if the patient were conscious I have no doubt that—"

"It would want to take the risk, too," Yarrence broke in again. "But if the Hudlar in my mind feels that way, I, as the surgeon, feel obliged to express caution on its behalf. But I agree, Conway, the operation is desirable."

Conway detached himself from the operating frame, paying Yarrence the compliment of not watching the opening stages of the operation. In any case, incising an FROB's ultratough tegument required the tools of an engineering workshop rather than an operating theater, because the cauterization effects of using fine laser cutters, which were so necessary during internal surgery, seriously inhibited healing along the faces of tegument incisions. The blades which had to be used were two-handed Kelgian Six scalpels, and they required a lot of physical effort as well as a high degree of mental concentration in use, and frequently the medic was in greater danger from the blade than the patient. It was a good time to remove all unnecessary distractions from Yarrence, which included the presence of a would-be Diagnostician, and move to FROB-Ten.

It was obvious from the first look that this patient would never again see its home planet. Five of the six limbs had either been traumatically severed during the accident or damaged beyond the possibility of surgical reconstruction. In addition there was a deep incised wound in the left flank which had penetrated to and destroyed the function of the absorption organ on that side. Decompression, brief as it had been before the victim's self-sealing safety bubble had deployed inside its room, had damaged the organ's twin on the right side because of the sudden rush of body fluid toward the area which had been opened to zero pressure. As a result FROB-Ten was able to receive barely enough sustenance to continue living, providing that it did not exert itself in any way.

An FROB perpetually at rest was difficult to imagine. If such a thing were possible, it would certainly be a very unhappy Hudlar.

"A multiple replacement job," Senior Physician Edanelt said, curling an eye to regard Conway as he approached. "If we have to replace a major internal organ, there is no point in fitting prosthetic limbs rather than real ones. But it bothers me, Conway. My Hudlar alter ego suggests that we don't try too hard with this one, while my own purely selfish Melfan mind is concerned chiefly with gaining more other-species surgical experience."

"You are being too harsh with yourself," Conway said, then added thoughtfully, "At the same time, I'm very glad that the hospital discourages visits from patients' relatives. The postoperative talk with the patient, especially in a case like this one, is bad enough."

"If the prospect causes you serious mental distress," Edanelt said quickly, "I would willingly relieve you of it."

"Thank you, no," Conway said, feeling tempted. "It is supposed to be my job." He was, after all, the acting Diagnostician-in-Charge.

"Of course," said Edanelt. "Presumably the replacements are immediately available?"

"Patient Eighteen terminated a few minutes ago," Conway said. "The absorption and food-processing organs are intact, and there are three usable limbs. Thornnastor will let you have more as and when you need them. This was one accident which left us with no shortage of spare parts."

As he finished speaking, Conway attached himself to the operating frame beside Edanelt and began discussing the special problems which would be encountered with this case, and in particular the necessity for performing three major operations concurrently.

Because of the nature of FROB-Ten's injuries there was less than fifty percent of the patient's absorption system functioning, and that situation was being maintained with difficulty and with no certainty that there would not be further deterioration within the next few hours. The absorption mechanism could be used to assimilate the anesthetic or food, but not both, so it was essential that the patient's period under anesthesia be as short as possible. And while the limb replacements were relatively simple microsurgical procedures, removing the damaged organ from Ten and the healthy one from the deceased Eighteen was going to be tricky and only fractionally less difficult than resiting the donor organ in the receiving patient.

The organs of absorption of the physiological classification FROB were unique among the warm-blooded oxygen-breathing lifeforms known to the Galactic Federation—even though, properly speaking, the Hudlars did not breathe. Situated under the skin of each flank, the organs were large semicircular and extraordinarily complex structures covering more than one-sixth of the body area and separated along their upper edges by the spinal column. The organs were integral with the skin, which was pitted in those areas by several thousands of tiny slits whose opening and closure was controlled by a network of voluntary muscles, and extended deeply into the body to a depth which varied between nine and sixteen inches.

Serving as it did the functions of both stomach and lungs, the combination of nutrition and air which was the dense, souplike atmosphere of Hudlar was taken in by the two large organs, and in a remarkably short period of time, the usable content of the gaseous liquid and solid mixture was abstracted and the residue passed into a single smaller and biologically less complex organ sited on the underside where the wastes were evacuated as a milky liquid.

The two hearts, situated in tandem between the organs of absorption and protected by the central vertebrae, circulated the blood at a rate and pressure which had made the early attempts at Hudlar surgery extremely hazardous for the patients. Now, however, much FROB surgical experience had been amassed since the planet's inception into the Federation, and what was more important, a Hudlar was very hard to kill.

Unless, as in this case, it was more than half-dead already.

The team's one big advantage was that all of the procedures, the multiple replacements of limbs and organs of absorption, would be open surgery. There would be no delving and cutting and suturing in tiny, restricted interorgan spaces. More than one surgeon could enter the operative field when required, and Conway knew with certainty that the operating frame around FROB-Ten would shortly be the busiest place in the hospital.

Edanelt was giving final directions regarding the presentation of the patient to its nurses when Conway left to visit FROB-Forty-three. He was beginning to feel that he was in the way again, a feeling to which he had become increasingly accustomed as his growing seniority in recent years had necessitated greater delegation of authority and responsibility. But he knew that Edanelt, as one of the hospital's foremost Senior Physicians, was itself too responsible a Doctor to hesitate about calling for Conway's assistance should it get into trouble.

A superficial examination of FROB-Forty-three would have suggested that there was not very much wrong with the patient. All six of the limbs were present and clearly in an undamaged condition, the porous tegument covering its organs of absorption was intact, and it was apparent that the cranial casing and spine had retained their structural integrity in spite of this particular Hudlar having been in a section of the wrecked accommodation module which had sustained the heaviest casualties. The case notes made brief mention of the fact that it had been shielded by the body of another FROB who had little chance of survival.

But the sacrifice on the part of Forty-three's companion—in all probability its life-mate—could have been wasted. Just inside the midlimb on the right underside there was a pressure cap and temporary dressing which concealed the opening of a deep, punctured wound made by a length of bar metal which had penetrated the tegument like a blunt spear. It had torn the side of the womb—the patient had been in Hudlar female mode at the time of the accident—and while it had missed the major blood vessels in the area, it had stopped within a fraction of an inch of the rearmost heart.

The fetus seemed to be in good condition in spite of the metal bar having passed within a few inches of its spine. While the heart itself had not been damaged, the blunt end of the metal bar had pinched off the circulation to the heart muscles on that side to the point where irreversible deterioration had taken place. Cardiac activity was being maintained by the life-support system, but even with that assistance the heart was in imminent danger of arrest, and replacement was strongly indicated. Conway sighed, foreseeing yet another emotionally painful postoperative experience for himself.

"A replacement is available from Eighteen," he said to Hossantir, the Tralthan Senior in charge of Forty-three's surgery. "We are already taking its absorption organ and all of its undamaged limbs, so donating a heart as well should not worry it."

Hossantir turned one of its four eyes to regard Conway and said, "Since Eighteen and Forty-three were life-mates, you are almost certainly correct."

"I didn't know that," Conway said uncomfortably, sensing an implied criticism of his flippancy by the Tralthan whose species, unlike the Hudlars, held their recently deceased in high reverence. He went on. "How will you proceed?"

Hossantir's intention was to leave the section of metal bar still present in the wound in place. It had been cut where it passed beneath the skin by the rescuers to facilitate movement of the casualty, but they had wisely not removed the entire bar in case they might complicate the injuries. Since the inner end of the bar was performing a useful function in controlling some of the deeper hemorrhaging, the prior suturing of the tear in the womb would mean that the instruments necessary for the later heart replacement procedure would be able to pass it without risk of endangering the fetus.

The external wound was not in the position Hossantir would have chosen for a heart replacement operation, but it was close enough for the purpose following surgical enlargement—a course which would avoid subjecting the patient to the additional trauma of another deep incision.

When the Tralthan had finished speaking, Conway looked around the operating frame and at the surgical team drifting weightlessly nearby. There was a Melfan, two Orligians, and another Tralthan who were all junior surgeons, and five Kelgian and two Ian nurses, all of whom were watching him silently. He knew that Senior Physicians could be very touchy about seeming infringements of their authority, and especially when they were ordered to do something as a result of a simple omission on their own part. His Kelgian alter ego wanted him to come straight to the point, while the Tralthan component of his mind advised a more diplomatic approach.

"Even with surgical enlargement of the wound," he said carefully, "access to the operative field will be restricted."

"Naturally," Hossantir replied. Conway tried a more direct approach.

"No more than two surgeons will be able to operate at any given time," he went on, "so there will be a high degree of team redundancy."

"Of course," Hossantir said.

"Senior Physician Edanelt," Conway said firmly, "needs help."

Two of Hossantir's eyes curled around to regard the preparations going on around Edanelt's frame, then it quickly detailed his two Orligian and the Tralthan medics to help the other Senior with instructions to call on whatever nursing support as and when needed.

"That was unforgivably selfish and thoughtless of me," Hossantir went on to Conway. "I thank you for the tactful way in which you reminded me of the transgression in the presence of my subordinates. But please be more direct in future. I carry permanently a Kelgian Educator tape and will not take offense over any seeming infringement of my authority. Frankly, I am greatly reassured by your presence, Conway, since my experience of deep Hudlar surgery is not extensive."

If I were to detail my own experience of Hudlar surgery, Conway thought wryly, *you might not feel reassured at all.*

Then he smiled suddenly, remembered how O'Mara had sardonically described the function of a Diagnostician in an operating theater as being largely psychological—the being was there principally to worry and accept the responsibilities its subordinates might not be able to carry.

As he moved between the three patients, Conway recalled his first few years after promotion to Senior Physician and of how he had accepted, and at times jealously guarded, his responsibilities. While working under supervision he had attempted to show that the Diagnostician concerned was redundant. In time he had been successful, because the supervision had become minimal and at times nonexistent. But there had also been a few times when Thornnastor or one of the other Diagnosticians who had been breathing down his neck and causing an irritating distraction during surgery had stepped in and saved a patient's life as well as the professional career of a very new Senior Physician whose enthusiasm verged on the irresponsible.

How those Diagnosticians had been able to watch without intervening, or suggesting alternative procedures, or giving step-by-step instructions at every stage, Conway did not know, because he himself was finding it just barely possible to do so.

He managed to continue doing the near-impossible while the hours slid past, dividing his attention between the operating stations of Yarrence, Edanelt, and Hossantir as well as the activity around the deceased Eighteen, where the surgery required to withdraw the donor organs and limbs was as painstaking and precise as that being performed on the recipients. There were several aspects of the work he could have commented upon, although not in overly critical terms, so he remained silent and gave advice only when it was requested. But while the three Seniors were doing very well and he was careful to divide his time equally among them, the one he watched most carefully was Hossantir. If any of the patients were going to cause problems, it would be FROB-Forty-three.

It happened in the fifth hour of the operations. The depressed cranial fracture and arterial repair on Three had gone well, and the less critical work of limb replacement was proceeding in satisfactory fashion. On FROB-Ten the absorption organ replacement work was completed and the decompression damage had been repaired so that it, too, had only the time-consuming microsurgical work on the limbs to undergo. It was natural, therefore, for Conway to hook himself to Forty-three's frame to watch Hossantir performing the highly delicate initial stages of reconnecting the replacement heart.

There was a sudden, silent explosion of Hudlar blood.

CHAPTER 15

Hossantir made a sound which did not translate, and its manipulators holding the long-handled instruments moved with
incredible slowness as they felt about in the totally obscured operative field. Its assistant, also moving with a lack of urgency which
could only have been subjective to Conway's racing mind, introduced a clamp but could not find the vessel which was hemorrhaging. Trained as he was to react quickly and positively to such
emergencies, Conway did not move slowly.

He could not move at all.

His hands, his stupid five-fingered, Earth-human, and utterly
alien hands, trembled uncontrollably while his multiple mind tried
desperately to decide what to do with them.

He knew that this kind of thing could happen to medics who
were carrying too many tapes, but that it should not happen too
often if the Doctor concerned hoped to make it as a Diagnostician.
Frantically, he tried to impose order on the warring factions within
his mind by calling up the memory of O'Mara, who was totally
unsympathetic where disorderly thinkers were concerned—in particular, the memory of the Chief Psychologist telling him what the
Educator tapes were and, more importantly, what they were not.

No matter how he felt subjectively, his mind was *not* being taken
over by the alien personalities who were apparently sharing it—his
Earth-human mind had simply been given a large quantity of extraterrestrial knowledge on which it could draw. But it was very
difficult to convince himself of that when the other-species material

in his mind belonged to medical people with their own individual ideas on how he should react to this emergency.

The ideas were very good, particularly those of the Melfan and Tralthan components. But they required the use of ELNT pincers or FGLI primary manipulators, not Earth-human fingers, and he was being urged to do too many things at once with the wrong organic equipment.

Hossantir's Melfan assistant whose ID, like everything else in the immediate area, was obscured by the bloody spray, said urgently, "I can't see. My visor is—"

One of the nurses quickly cleaned the helmet in front of the eyes, not wasting time on the rest of the transparent bubble. But the fine red spray was re-covering it as Conway watched. And that was not the only problem, because, deep inside the operative field, the light sources on the instruments were likewise obscured.

The Tralthan Senior had been closest so that only the front of its bubble helmet had been affected. One of its eyes curled back to regard Conway through the still transparent rear section.

"We require assistance, Conway. Can you suggest a . . ." Hossantir began; then it noticed the trembling hands and added, "Are you indisposed?"

Conway clenched his fists slowly—everything seemed to be happening in the slowest of slow motion—and said, "It is temporary."

Silently he added, *I hope.*

But the alien personalities who were not really there were still clamoring for attention. He tried to ignore all but one of them at a time, thinking vaguely of the principle of divide and rule, but that did not work either. All of them were offering medical or surgical advice, all of it had potential value in the present situation, and all of it called for an immediate response. The only available material which did not force itself forward was the Gogleskan data accidentally provided by Khone, and that was of little value anyway. But for some reason his mind kept returning to it, holding on to that frightened but strong-willed alien personality as if it were some kind of psychological life-raft.

Khone's presence was not at all like the sharp, intense, and artificially enhanced impressions produced by the Educator tapes. He found himself concentrating on the little being's mental imprint, even though the strange and visually terrifying creatures around the operating frame threatened to throw it into a panic reaction. But the Gogleskan data also included material on Conway's work at the hospital, transferred to its mind during the mishap on Goglesk, and this to a certain extent had prepared Khone for just this kind of experience. It was also a member of a race of individualists whose mental processes were adept at avoiding contact with, or of negating the influence of, other beings around them.

More than any other entity in Conway's experience, Khone knew how to ignore people.

All at once his hands were no longer shaking and the alien babel within his mind had quieted to an insistent murmur which he could choose to ignore. He tapped the Melfan assisting Hossantir sharply on its carapace.

"Please withdraw and leave your instruments in position," he said. To the Tralthan Senior he added, "The bleeding is obscuring everything in the operative field, including the magnifiers and light sources of the instruments and, if we approach closely, our visors. We must . . ."

"Suction isn't working, Conway," Hossantir broke in, "and won't until the flow has been checked at source. But we can't see the source!"

". . . Use the scanners," Conway continued quietly, enclosing the tiny, hollow-coned handles of the Melfan clamp with his Earth-human fingers, "in conjunction with my hands and your eyes."

Since normal vision was useless because of his helmet's close proximity to the spray from the wound, Conway's idea was that Hossantir use two scanners angled so as to bear on the operative field from two viewpoints as far apart as possible. This would give an accurate stereoscopic picture of what was happening which the Senior could describe for him and guide the movements of his clamp. He would be operating blind, but only long enough to find and seal off the bleeder, after which the operation would proceed in the normal way. It would be a very uncomfortable few minutes for Hossantir, two of whose four eyes would be extended laterally to the limits of its flattened, ovoid helmet. It would also have to withdraw temporarily from the operation, Conway told it apologetically, so that its scanners and helmet would not be affected by the spray.

"This could give me a permanent squint," Hossantir said, "but no matter."

None of his alter egos saw anything funny in the idea of a great, elephantine Tralthan with a squint in two of its widely extensible eyes. Fortunately, a smothered Earth-human laugh was not translatable.

His hands and the instruments felt heavy and awkward, and not just because he was using Melfan clamps. The gravity nullification field surrounding him did not, of necessity, extend to the patient, so that everything at the operating site weighed four times heavier than normal. But the Tralthan used its scanners to guide him verbally to the blood vessel which had to be origin of the massive hemorrhaging, and considering the elevated blood pressure of the Hudlar life-form, he expected to feel resistance as he clamped it off.

There was none, and the bleeding continued with undiminished force.

One of his alter egos had encountered something like this situation during a transplant on an entirely different life-form, a diminutive Nidian whose blood pressure had been only a fraction of that of this Hudlar. On that occasion the blood flow had also been a fine spray rather than the pulsing stream characteristic of arterial bleeding, and the trouble had been due to a mechanical failure rather than to faulty surgical technique.

Conway was not sure if that was the problem here, but a part of his multiple mind felt sure, and he decided to trust that part.

"Stop the artificial heart," he said firmly. "Cut off the blood supply to the area."

"We can easily make good the blood loss," Hossantir objected, "but cutting off circulation for more than a few minutes could kill the patient."

"Do it now," Conway said.

Within a few seconds the bright red spray had subsided and died. A nurse cleaned Conway's visor while Hossantir used suction to clear the operative field. They did not need the scanners to see what had happened.

"Technician, quickly," Conway said.

Before he had finished speaking there was a furry little Nidian, looking like a gift-wrapped teddy bear in its transparent OR suit, hovering beside his elbow.

"The nonreturn valve of the connector is jammed in the closed position," the Nidian said in its staccato, barking speech. "This was caused, I would say, by the valve setting being altered accidentally when it was struck by one of the surgical instruments. The flow from the artificial heart has been blocked and was forcing its way out via the recess of the valve setting control, hence the fine, high-pressure spray. The valve itself isn't damaged, and if you will raise the organ so that I will have space to reset the valve . . ."

"I'd rather not move the heart," Conway said. "We are very short of time."

"I am not a doctor," the Nidian said crossly. "This repair should properly be performed on a workbench, or at least in an area with room for my admittedly small elbows. Working in close contact with living tissue is . . . is repugnant to me. However, my tools are sterile in readiness for such emergencies."

"Do you feel nauseous?" Conway asked worriedly. He had visions of the little being choking inside its helmet.

"No," the Nidian said, "just irritated."

Conway withdrew his Melfan instruments to give the technician more room to work. A nurse had clipped a tray of Earth-human DBDG instruments to the frame beside him, and by the time he had selected the ones he would need the Nidian had freed the jammed valve. Conway was thanking the little being for the speed of the repair when Hossantir broke in.

"I'm restarting the artificial heart," it said.

"No, wait," Conway said sharply. He was looking at the monitor and getting a feeling—a very vague feeling that was not strong enough even to be called a hunch—that any delay at all would be dangerous. "I don't like the vital signs. There is nothing there which should not be there, considering that the flow from the artificial heart was interrupted, initially by the jammed connector valve and later when the system was shut down during the repair. I realize that if the artificial heart is not restarted within the next few minutes, irreversible changes leading to termination will take place in the brain. Even so, I have the feeling that we should not restart but go instead for an immediate resection of the replacement organ . . ."

He knew that Hossantir would want to object and take the safer course, that of restarting the artificial heart and waiting until they were sure that the patient's circulation had returned to optimum, and then proceed as originally planned. Normally Conway would not have argued against this, because he, too, preferred not to take unnecessary risks. But there was something niggling at the back of his mind, or one of his minds, something about the effect of long-term trauma on certain gravid, heavy-gravity life-forms, and the feeling was so persistent that he had to act on it. And while he had been speaking, Conway had unclipped his instruments to show Hossantir, nonverbally so that the Senior's feelings would not be hurt too much, that he was not about to argue the point.

" . . . Will you work on the connection to the absorption organ, please," he ended, "and keep an eye on the monitor."

Sharing the operative field with the Tralthan, Conway worked quickly and carefully in the restricted space, clamping off the artery beyond the artificial heart connection, detaching it, and reconnecting it to the arterial stub projecting from the replacement organ. Unlike the first, shocking seconds of the earlier hemorrhaging, time seemed to have speeded up. His hands and instruments were well outside the field of the nullifiers, being acted on by four Earth-Gs, so they felt incredibly slow and awkward. Several times his instruments clinked loudly against those of Hossantir. He could sympathize with the surgeon, whoever it had been, who had accidentally knocked that connector valve off its setting. He had to concentrate hard to keep his instruments from leading a life of their own.

He did not watch Hossantir's work, because the Tralthan knew its stuff and there was no time for surgical sightseeing.

He inserted retaining sutures to hold the artery in position on each end of the connector, which was designed both to hold the ends firmly in position when circulation was restored and to keep the sections of original and replacement tissue apart so as to reduce postoperative rejection problems. There were times when, immunologically speaking, he wondered why a highly evolved and complex organism should be its own worst enemy. Next he began the linkup of the vessel which supplied nutrient from the absorption organ to one of the major heart muscles.

Hossantir had completed its connection and had turned its attention to the minor vessel which supplied one half of the womb when the Hudlar was in female mode—the second, undamaged heart had been performing double duty since the start of the operation. They were short of time, but as yet not dangerously so, when the Tralthan indicated the Monitor with a free appendage.

"Ectopics," Hossantir said. "One in five, no, one in four. Pressure is reducing. The indications are that the heart will go into fibrillation and arrest very quickly. The defibrillator is ready."

Conway took a quick look at the visual display where the irregular, ectopic heartbeat broke into the normal rhythm once in every four beats. From experience he knew how soon it could degenerate into a rapid, uncontrollable flutter and, with the subsequent loss of the pumping function, failure. The defibrillator would almost certainly shock it into action again, but that device could not be used while the operation on the replacement heart was in progress. He resumed his work with desperate, careful speed.

So deep was his concentration that all of his minds were becoming involved again, contributing their expertise and at the same time their irritation that it was a set of Earth-human hands which were doing the work and not the assorted manipulators, pincers, and digits of his alter egos. He looked up finally to find that Hossantir and he had finished their connections at the same time. But a few seconds later the other heart went into fibrillation, then arrest. Their time was really short now.

They eased the clamps on the main artery and secondary vessels and watched the flaccid replacement organ swell slowly as it was filled with Forty-three's blood, checking with their scanners for the formation of air embolisms. There were none, so Conway placed the four tiny electrodes in position preparatory to restarting the replacement heart. Unlike the defibrillator charge needed for the other heart, which would have to penetrate more than ten inches of hard, Hudlar tegument and underlying tissue, these electrodes would be acting directly on the surface muscles of the replacement organ and would be carrying a relatively mild charge.

The defibrillator brought negative results. Both hearts fluttered unsteadily for a few moments and then subsided.

"Again," Conway said.

"The embryo has arrested," Hossantir said suddenly.

"I was expecting that," Conway said, not wanting to sound omniscient, but neither did he have the time for explanations.

Now he knew why he had wanted to complete the replacement connections so fast after the emergency with the valve. It had been not a hunch but a memory from the past when he had been a very junior intern, and the memory was one of his own.

It had happened during his first lecture on the FROB life-form, which had been given by the Diagnostician-in-Charge of Pathology, Thornnastor. Conway had made a remark to the effect that the species was fortunate in having a standby heart if one should fail. Conway had meant it as a joke, but Thornnastor had jumped on him, figuratively speaking, with all six of its feet for making such a remark without first studying the Hudlar physiology in detail. It had gone on to describe the disadvantages of possessing two hearts, especially when the possessor was a gravid female-mode Hudlar nearing parturition, and the nerve network which controlled the involuntary muscle system was maintaining a delicate balance between the impulses to four hearts, two parental and two embryonic. At that particular stage the failure of one heart could quickly lead to the arrest of the other three.

"And again," Conway said worriedly. The incident had not been worth remembering then, because major surgery on FROBs was considered to be impossible in those days. He was wondering if survival for this particular Hudlar was impossible now when both of its hearts twitched, hesitated, then settled into a strong, steady beat.

"The fetal hearts are picking up," Hossantir said. A few seconds later it added, "Pulse-rate optimal."

On the sensor screen the cerebral traces were showing normal for a deeply unconscious Hudlar, indicating that there had been no brain damage as a result of the few minutes cessation of circulation, and Conway began to relax. But oddly, now that the emergency was over the other occupants of his mind were becoming uncomfortably obtrusive. It was as if they, too, were relieved and were reacting with too much enthusiasm to the situation. He shook his head irritably, telling himself once again that they were only recordings, simply stored masses of information and experience which were available to his, Conway's, mind to use or ignore as he saw fit. But then the uncomfortable thought came to him that his own mind was simply a collection of knowledge, impressions, and experience collected over his lifetime, and what made his mind data so much more important and significant than that of the others?

He tried to ignore that suddenly frightening thought by reminding himself that he was still alive and capable of receiving new impressions and continuously modifying his total experience as a result of them, while the taped material had been frozen at the time it had been donated. In any case, the donors were long since deceased or far removed from Sector General. But Conway's mind felt as though it was beginning to doubt its own authority, and he was suddenly afraid for his sanity.

O'Mara would be furious if he knew Conway was indulging in this kind of thinking. So far as the Chief Psychologist was concerned, a Doctor was responsible for his work and for the tools, both physical and psychological, which enabled him to do that work. If the Doctor could not perform satisfactorily, then the person concerned should seek a less demanding job.

There were few jobs more demanding than that of a Diagnostician.

His hands were beginning to feel wrong again, and the fat, pink, and strangely awkward fingers were trembling. Conway stowed away his DBDG instruments and turned to Hossantir's Melfan assistant, whose ID was still smeared with blood and only partly readable, and said, "Would you like to resume, Doctor?"

"Thank you, sir," the ELNT said. Obviously it had been worrying in case Conway, as a result of his intervention, had thought the Melfan incapable of doing the work. *Right now,* he thought grimly, *the opposite is true.*

"It is not expected," Hossantir said gravely, "that you should do everything yourself, Conway."

Plainly the Tralthan knew that something was wrong with him— Hossantir's eyes missed nothing, even when all four of them seemed to be looking in other directions. Conway watched for a few minutes until the team had closed up, then he left Forty-three to check on the progress of the other two patients. Psychologically he felt unwell.

The organ of absorption had been successfully transplanted into Ten, and Edanelt and his team were busy with the microsurgery required on the replacement limbs. The patient was out of danger, however, because the new organ had been tested with an application of nutrient paint and the sensors showed that it was performing satisfactorily. While he was complimenting the team on its work, Conway stared at the heavy staples which held the edges of the wound together—so closely sutured were they that the wound looked like an enormous zip-fastener. But nothing less would serve to hold an FROB's hard, thick, and incredibly tough hide together, and the material of the staples was molecularly unstable so that they could be rendered flexible for withdrawal when the healing process was complete.

But an almost invisible scar, the Hudlar component of Conway's mind insisted, would be the least of this patient's problems.

All at once Conway wanted to run away from all this major surgery and its attendant postoperative problems, instead of having to make yet another examination of a third Hudlar patient.

Yarrence had concentrated its efforts on the cranial injury, leaving FROB-Three's abdominal wound to the medics freed by the demise of FROB-Eighteen, while the remaining members of both teams were deployed on the limb amputation and replacement work. It was obvious after the first few minutes that they were engaged in performing a very complex but smooth-running operation.

From the talk around the frame he gathered that it was also an operation without precedent. To Conway it had seemed to be an obvious solution to FROB-Three's problem, replacing the missing forelimbs with two from the rear. While not as precise as the originals they would be much more satisfactory in every way than the prosthetics, and there would be no rejection problems. He had read in the old medical texts of Earth-human arm amputees learning to draw, write, and even eat with their feet, and the Hudlar feet were much more adaptable than those of an Earth-human DBDG. But the admiration that simple solution had aroused among the team was making Conway feel embarrassed, because, given the present circumstances, anyone could have thought of it.

It was the circumstances which were without precedent—the Menelden disaster with its aftermath of massively injured Hudlars requiring transplant surgery together with the ready availability of spare parts. The possibility of one of the transplant cases being able to return to its home planet with the bonus of a pair of forelimbs which were almost as good as the originals was an idea which would have occurred to any moral coward like himself, who dreaded those postop conversations with patients whose transplants were from normal donors rather than from themselves.

Conway made a mental note to separate FROB-Three from Ten and Forty-three before they returned to consciousness and could begin talking together. The atmosphere between Three and its two less fortunate colleagues would be strained to say the least, and their convalescence would be difficult enough without two of the three being eaten up with envy.

Consideration of the FROB's problems had brought his Hudlar component into prominence again, and it was difficult not to sympathize and suffer at the thought of his patient's postoperative lifestyle. He tried to bring forward the material on the Tralthan, Melfan, and Kelgian components who, as other-species medics, should have been more clinical regarding the situation. But they, too, were overly sympathetic and their responses painful. In desperation he called up the material of Khone, the Gogleskan, who retained its sanity and intelligence by isolating itself from all close contacts with its fellows.

The Gogleskan material was not at all like that of an ordinary Educator tape. It had more texture, more immediacy, as if another person were truly sharing his mind, however reluctantly. With this degree of understanding between them, he wondered how it would feel to meet and talk to Khone again.

It was unlikely to happen in the hospital, Conway was sure, because the experience of staying in Sector General would probably drive Khone insane, and O'Mara would never allow it anyway. One of the Chief Psychologist's strictest rules was that tape donors and carriers must never be allowed to meet because of the psychological trauma, incalculable in its intensity, which would result if two entities of widely different species, but possessing identical personalities, tried to communicate.

In the light of what had happened to Conway on Goglesk, O'Mara might have to modify that rule.

And now even the problems of the Gogleskans were clamoring for Conway's attention, as were the Tralthan, Kelgian, Melfan, and Illensan occupants of his mind. Conway moved back to a position where he could watch the activity around all three operating frames without the team-members being able to see his distress. But the alien babel in his mind was so bad that he could scarcely speak, and it was only with a great effort that he could comment on some aspect of the work or give a word of praise to one of the medics. All at once he wanted out, and to escape from his too-demanding selves.

With a tremendous effort he guided his alien fingers to the transmit key for his general communication and said carefully, "You people are too good and there is nothing here for me to do. If a problem should arise, call me on the Red Three frequency. There is a matter which I must attend to at once on the methane level."

As he was leaving, Hossantir bent an eye-stalk in his direction and said gravely, "Stay cool, Conway."

CHAPTER 16

The ward was cold and dark. Heavy shielding and insulation protected it against the radiation and heat given off by the ship traffic in the vicinity of the hospital, and there were no windows, because even the light which filtered in from the distant stars could not be allowed to penetrate to this level. For this reason the images appearing on his vehicle's screen had been converted from the nonvisible spectrum which gave the pictures the unreal quality of fantasy, and the scales covering Diagnostician Semlic's eight-limbed, starfish-shaped body shone coldly through the methane mist like multihued diamonds, making it resemble some wondrous, heraldic beast.

Conway had often studied pictures and scanner records of the SNLU life-form, but this was the first time he had seen Semlic outside its refrigerated life-support vehicle. In spite of the proven efficiency of Conway's own insulated vehicle, the Diagnostician was keeping its distance.

"I come in response to your recent invitation," Conway said hesitantly, "and to escape from that madhouse up there for a while. I have no intention of examining any of your patients."

"Oh, Conway, it's you inside that thing!" Semlic moved fractionally closer. "My patients will be greatly relieved by your lack of attention. That furnace you insist on occupying makes them nervous. But if you would park to the right of the observation gallery, just there, you will be able to see and hear everything that goes on. Have you been here before?"

"Twice," Conway replied. "Purely to satisfy my curiosity on both occasions, as well as to enjoy the peace and quiet."

Semlic made a sound which did not translate, then said, "Peace and quiet are relative, Conway. You have to turn the sensitivity of your outside microphone right up to hear me with sufficient volume for your translator to be able to handle my input, and I am speaking loudly for an SNLU. To a being like you, who are nearly deaf, it is quiet. I hope that the environment, busy and noisy as it is to me, will help bring the peace and calm which your mind requires so badly.

"And don't forget," it said as it moved away, "turn your sound sensitivity up and your translator off."

"Thank you," Conway said. For a moment the jeweled starfish shape of the Diagnostician aroused in him an almost childlike sense of wonder, so that a sudden wave of emotion misted his eyes and added to the blurring effect of the methane fog filling the ward as he added, "You are a kind, understanding, and warmhearted being."

Semlic made another untranslatable sound and said, "There is no need to be insulting . . ."

For a long time he watched the activity in the busy ward and noticed that a few of the low-temperature nursing staff attending the patients wore lightweight protective suits, indicating that their atmosphere requirements were somewhat different from the ward in general. He saw them doing things to and for their charges which made no sense at all, unless he was to take an SNLU tape, and they worked in the almost total silence of beings with a hypersensitivity to audible vibrations, and at first there was nothing to hear. But the more deeply he concentrated the more aware he became of delicate patterns of sound emerging, of a kind of alien music which was cold and pure and resembled nothing he had ever heard before, and eventually he could distinguish single voices and conversations which were like the cool, passionless, delicate, and ineffably sweet chiming of colliding snowflakes. Gradually the peace and beauty and utter strangeness of it all reached him and the other components of his mind, and gently dissolved away all the stress and conflict and mental confusion.

Even Khone, in whom xenophobia was an evolutionary imperative, could find nothing threatening in these surroundings, and it, too, found the peace and calm which enables the mind either to float without thinking or to think clearly and coolly and without worrying.

Except, that was, for a small, niggling worry over the fact that he had been here for several hours while there was important work awaiting his attention, and besides which, it had been nearly ten hours since he had eaten.

The cold level had served its purpose very well by leaving him in all respects cool. Conway looked around for Semlic, but the SNLU had disappeared into a side ward. He turned on his translator, meaning to ask two nearby patients to pass on his message of thanks to the Diagnostician, but hastily changed his mind.

The delicate chiming and tinkling speech of the two SNLU patients translated as "... Nothing but a whining, hypochondriac cow! If it wasn't such a kindly being, it would tell you so and probably kick you out of the hospital. And the shameless way you try to get its sympathy is not far short of seduction..." and, in reply, "You have nothing to be seductive with, you jealous old bitch! You're falling apart. But it still knows which one of us is really ill, even when I try to hide it..."

As he left Conway made a mental note to ask O'Mara what the ultrafrigid SNLUs did about cooling a situation which had become emotionally overheated. And what, for that matter, could he do to calm down the perpetually pregnant Protector of the Unborn he would be calling on as soon as he had something to eat. But he had the feeling that the answer would be the same in both cases, nothing at all.

When he had returned to the normal warmth and light of the interlevel corridors, he stopped to think.

The distance between his present position and the level occupied by the Protector was roughly the same as that to the main dining hall which lay in the opposite direction, which meant that he would have a double journey no matter which area he visited first. But his own quarters were between him and the Protector, and Murchison always liked to have food available—a habit dating back to her nursing days—in case a sudden emergency or sheer fatigue kept her from visiting the dining hall. The menu was not varied, but then all he wanted to do was refuel.

There was another reason for avoiding the dining hall. In spite of the fact that his limbs no longer seemed quite so foreign to him, and the people passing him in the corridor were not nearly so un-settling as they had been before his visit to Semlic's wards, and he felt in control of his alter egos, he was not sure that he could remain so if he were to be exposed to the proximity of masses of food which his taped entities might find nauseating.

It would not look good if he had to pay another visit to Semlic so soon. He did not think that the type of cold comfort he had received was habit-forming, but the law of diminishing returns would most certainly apply.

When he arrived Murchison was dressed, technically awake, but in a powered-down condition, and about to go on duty. They both knew, and they were careful not to mention to each other that they knew, that O'Mara had arranged their free periods to coincide as seldom as possible—the assumption being that it was sometimes better to put off a problem rather than cause unnecessary grief by trying to solve it too soon. Murchison yawned at him and wanted to know what he had been doing and what, apart from sleeping, he intended doing next.

"Food, first," Conway said, yawning in sympathy. "Then I have to check on the condition of the FSOJ. You remember that Protec-tor? You were in at its birth."

She remembered it, all right, and said so in terms which were less than ladylike.

"How long is it since you've had any sleep?" she went on, trying to hide her concern by pretending to be cross. "You look worse than some of the patients in intensive care. Your taped entities will not feel fatigue, because they weren't tired when they donated their brain recordings, but don't let that fool you into thinking that you are tireless."

Conway fought back another yawn, then reached forward sud-denly to grab her around the waist. He was pretty sure that his arms were not trembling as he held her, even though his arousal was being matched by equivalent feelings in his alter egos, but the kiss was much less lingering than was usual. Murchison pushed him away gently.

"Do you have to go right away?" he asked, fighting another mammoth yawn.

Murchison laughed. "I'm not going to fool about with you in

that condition. You'd probably arrest. Go to bed before you go to sleep. I'll fix you something before I leave, something hidden inside a sandwich so that your mind-friends won't object to what you're eating."

As she busied herself at their food dispenser, she went on, "Thorny is very interested in the birth process in the Protector, and it has asked me to check the patient at frequent intervals. I'll call you if anything unusual develops there, and I'm sure the Seniors in Hudlar OR will do the same."

"I really ought to check them myself," Conway said.

"What's the use of having assistants," she said impatiently, "if you insist on doing all the work yourself?"

Conway, with the remains of his first sandwich in one hand and an unspecified but no doubt nutritious cup of something in the other, sat down on their bed. He said, "Your argument is not without merit."

She gave him an almost sisterly peck on the cheek, a kiss designed to cause minimal arousal in his alter egos as well as his own, and left without another word. O'Mara must have lectured her pretty thoroughly regarding her behavior toward a life-mate who had recently become an acting Diagnostician and who still had to adjust to the attendant emotional confusion.

If he did not adjust soon, he could not look forward to having much fun. The trouble was, Murchison was not giving him much of an opportunity to try.

He awoke suddenly with her hand on his shoulder and the remains of a nightmare, or it might have been an alien wish-fulfillment dream, dissolving into the comfortable reality of their living quarters.

"You were snoring," she said. "You've probably been snoring for the past six hours. The Hudlar OR and Protector teams left recorded messages for you. They obviously didn't think them urgent or important enough to awaken you, and the rest of the hospital continues to go about its business much as usual. Do you want to go back to sleep?"

"No," Conway said, and reached up to grab her around the waist. Her resistance was a token one.

"I don't think O'Mara would approve of this," she said doubtfully. "He warned me that there would be emotional conflicts, serious enough to permanently affect our relationship, if the process of adaptation is not slow and carefully controlled, and—"

"And O'Mara isn't married to the most pulchritudinous female DBDG in the hospital," Conway broke in, and added, "And since when have I been fast and uncontrolled?"

"O'Mara isn't married to anything but his job," she said, laughing, "and I expect his job would divorce him if it could. But our Chief Psychologist knows his stuff, and I would not want to risk prematurely overstimulating your—"

"Shut up," Conway said softly.

It was possible that the Chief Psychologist was right, Conway thought as he gently rolled her onto the bed beside him; O'Mara usually was right. His alter egos were becoming increasingly aroused, and were looking with other-species disfavor on the features occupying the forward skull and the softly curving mammaries of the Earth-human DBDG in such close proximity to them. And when tactile sensations were added to the visual sensory input, their disfavor became extreme.

They reacted with mental images of what should have been going on in the Hudlar, Tralthan, Kelgian, Melfan, Illensan, and Gogleskan equivalent situation, and they insisted that this was utterly and quite revoltingly *wrong*. What was worse, they tried to make Conway feel that it was wrong, too, and that the life-mate beside him should have been of an entirely different physiological classification, the exact species being dependent on the emotional intensity of the entity who was protesting the most.

Even the Gogleskan was insisting that this activity was all wrong, but it was disassociating itself from the proceedings. Khone was a rugged individualist, a perfect example of a loner among a species which had evolved to the point where solitude was a prime survival characteristic. And suddenly Conway realized that he was using Khone's Gogleskan presence and ability, that he had already used it on several previous occasions to ignore those thoughts and feelings which had to be ignored and to focus his Earth-human mind on those which required the utmost concentration.

The alien protests were still strong, but the protestors were being put in their places and given a low order of priority. Even the Gogleskan objections were being noted but otherwise ignored. He was using the FOKTs unique ability against itself as well as the others, and Khone's race certainly knew how to concentrate on a subject.

"We shouldn't ... be doing ... this," Murchison said breathlessly.

Conway ignored her words but concentrated on everything else. There were times when other-species responses to equivalent situations obtruded, insisting that his partner was too large, too tiny, too fragile, the wrong shape, or in the wrong position. But his visual and tactile sensors were those of a male Earth-human, and the stimuli they were receiving overwhelmed the purely mental interference of the others. Sometimes his alter egos suggested certain actions and movements. These he ignored as well, except in a few instances when he was able to modify them to his own purpose. But toward the end all of the alien interference was swamped out, and the hospital's primary reactor could have blown and he would scarcely have noticed it.

When their elevated pulse and respiration rates had returned to something approaching normal, she continued to hold him tightly, not speaking and even more reluctant to let go. Suddenly she laughed softly.

"I was given precise instruction," she said in a tone which contained both puzzlement and relief, "regarding my behavior toward you for the next few weeks or months. The Chief Psychologist said that I should avoid intimate physical contact, maintain a professional and clinical manner during all conversations, and generally consider myself a widow until you had either come to terms with the tapes riding you, or you had been forced to resume your former Senior Physician status. It was an extremely serious matter, I was told, and great amounts of patience and sympathy would be required to see you through this difficult time. I was to consider you a multiple schizophrenic, with the majority of the personalities concerned feeling no emotional bond with me, and in many cases reacting toward me with physical revulsion. But I was to ignore all this because to do otherwise would be to subject you to the risk of permanent psychological damage."

She kissed the tip of his nose and gave a long, gentle sigh. She went on. "Instead I find no evidence of physical revulsion and ...

550 · JAMES WHITE

Well, you don't seem to be entirely your old self. I can't say exactly what the difference is, and I'm not complaining, but you don't appear to be having any psychological difficulties at all and . . . and O'Mara *will* be pleased!"

Conway grinned. "I wasn't trying to please O'Mara . . ." he began, when the communicator beeped urgently at them.

Murchison had set it to record any nonurgent messages so that he could sleep undisturbed, and obviously someone thought his problem urgent enough to wake him. He escaped from her clutches by tickling her under the arms, then directed the communicator's vision pickup away from the devastated bed before answering. It was possible that there was an Earth-human male DBDG at the other end.

Edanelt's angular, chitinous features filled the screen as the Melfan Senior said, "I hope I did not disturb you, Conway, but Hudlar's Forty-three and Ten have regained consciousness and are pain-free. They are feeling very lucky to be alive and have not yet had time to think about the disadvantages. This would be the best time to talk to them, if you still wish to do so."

"I do," Conway said. He could not think of anything he wanted to do less just then, and the watching Edanelt and Murchison both knew it. He added, "What about Three?"

"Still unconscious but stable," the Senior replied. "I checked its condition a few minutes before calling you. Hossantir and Yarrence left some hours ago to indulge in these periods of physical and mental collapse which you people seem to need at such ridiculously short intervals. I shall speak to Three when it comes to. The problems of adjustment there are not so serious."

Conway nodded. "I'm on my way."

The prospect of what lay ahead of him had brought the Hudlar material rushing in to fill virtually all of his mind, so that his goodbye to Murchison was nonphysical and lacked even verbal warmth. Fortunately, she had come to accept this kind of behavior from him and would ignore it until he was his old self again. As he turned to go, Conway wondered what there was so special about this pink, flabby, ridiculously weak and unbeautiful entity with whom he had spent most of his adult life.

CHAPTER 17

"Y ou have been very fortunate," Conway said, "very fortunate indeed that neither the baby nor you have suffered permanent damage."

Medically that was quite true, Conway told himself. But the Hudlar in his mind thought otherwise, as did the members of the recovery ward staff who had withdrawn to a discreet distance to enable the patient and its physician to talk privately.

"Having said that," Conway went on, "I regret to tell you that you, personally, have not escaped the long-term and perhaps emotionally distressing effects of your injuries."

He knew that he was not being very subtle in his approach, but in many ways the FROB life-form was as direct and forthright as the Kelgians, although much more polite.

"The reason for this is that organ replacement surgery was necessary to keep both of you alive," he continued, appealing to the patient's maternal instincts in the hope that the good news about the young Hudlar would in some measure diminish the misfortune which would shortly befall the older one. "Your offspring will be born without complications, will be healthy, and will be fully capable of leading a normal life on or off its home planet. You, regrettably, will not."

The Hudlar's speaking membrane vibrated with the expected question.

Conway thought for a moment before replying, not wanting to pitch the explanation at too elementary a level. This Hudlar was a mining specialist and highly intelligent; otherwise it and its life-mate would not have been working the Menelden asteroids. So he told Forty-three that while infant Hudlars sometimes fell seriously ill and a few might even die, adults were never sick, nor were they anything but physically perfect until the advent of senility. The reason for this was that they developed an immunity to their home planet's pathogens which was as complete and perfect as any purely biochemical system could be, and no other species known to Federation medical science could match it. The FROB immune system was such that it would not allow foreign biological material of any kind to attach itself to their bodies without instantly initiating the process of rejection. Fortunately, their superefficient immune system could be neutralized when necessary, and one of these occasions was when vital organs or limbs from a donor were used as surgical replacements.

He had been trying to make the explanation as simple and accurate as possible, but it was apparent that Forty-three's mind was going its own way.

"What about my life-mate?" it said, as if Conway had not been speaking.

Momentarily a mind picture of Eighteen's devastated body took form between the patient and himself, his own medical knowledge combining with that of his Hudlar component to suddenly involve his emotions. He cleared his throat and said, "I am deeply sorry, but your life-mate was so seriously injured that we were unable to maintain life, much less undertake curative surgery."

"It tried to shield us with its body. Did you know that?" the Hudlar said.

Conway nodded sympathetically, then realized that the small movement of an Earth-human head meant nothing to an FROB. His next words were chosen carefully, because he was sure that Forty-three—weakened by the recent major surgery, gravid, close to delivering its offspring, and in its ultimate female mode—would be susceptible to an emotional approach. His Hudlar alter ego was of the opinion that, at worst, some temporary psychological distress might result, while his own experience with other life-forms in similar situations suggested that he might do some good. But the situation was unique so far as this patient was concerned, and he could not be sure of anything.

Of one thing he was very sure. Somehow he had to keep the patient from becoming too deeply introspective regarding its own situation, so that it would be thinking of its unborn rather than itself when the really bad news had to be faced. But the idea of deliberately manipulating the other's emotions in this fashion was making him feel like a very low form of life indeed, somewhere on the level of an Earthly louse.

He wondered why he had not thought of discussing the case with O'Mara before proceeding further—it was potentially serious enough for the Chief Psychologist to be consulted. He might still need to if he made a mess of things now.

"We are all aware," Conway said finally, "of the action of your life-mate in trying to protect you. This type of behavior is common among the members of the more highly intelligent species, especially when the entity concerned is sacrificing itself to save the life of a loved one or a child. In this instance it was able to do both, and what is more, it was instrumental in giving life and unimpaired mobility to two very seriously injured survivors, one of whom is you, who would otherwise have died in spite of its earlier sacrifice."

This time, he thought, *the patient is paying attention.*

"Your life-mate donated its undamaged limbs and one lobe of its nutrient absorption organ to the patient you can see at the other side of the ward," Conway went on. "That patient, like you, will continue to live in a state of perfect physical health, except for some irksome restrictions regarding environment and own-species group activities. And in addition to its protecting you and your unborn child during the accident, you are both continuing to live because one of your hearts was also donated by your life-mate."

"While its presence is gone from you except as a memory," Conway added quietly, "it would not be completely true to say that it had died."

He watched closely to see how Forty-three was taking this blatantly emotional onslaught, but the tegument of the body was too hard and featureless to give any indication of its feelings.

"It tried very hard to keep you alive," he went on, "and so I think you owe it to your life-mate's memory to continue trying very hard to stay alive, although there will be times when this will not be easy."

And now for the bad news, Conway thought.

Gently, he went on to describe the effects of knocking out the FROB immune system—the aseptic environment which the patient would require, the specially prepared and treated food, and the barrier nursing and isolation ward procedures needed to guard against the possibility of any FROB infection invading the body which had been rendered utterly defenseless. Even the infant would have to be removed from the parent immediately after birth. Only visual contact with it would be possible, because the child would be normal in all respects and would therefore be a health hazard to the defenseless parent.

Conway knew that the child would be raised and well cared for on Hudlar—the FROB family and social structures were both highly complex and flexible, and the concept of "orphan" was completely unknown to them. The infant would be deprived of nothing.

"If you yourself were to return to your home world," Conway said in a firmer tone, "the same protective measures would be necessary to keep you alive, and at home your friends would not have the facilities and experience possessed by this hospital. You would be confined to your own quarters, you would have no physical contact with another Hudlar, and the normal range of exercise and work activities would be forbidden. There would also be the constant worry that your protective envelope would be breached or your nutrient infected and, with no natural defense against disease, you would die."

The native Hudlars were not yet medically advanced enough to maintain such a sophisticated facility, so its death would be certain.

The patient had been watching him steadily while he was speaking. Suddenly its membrane began to vibrate in reply.

"In the situation you describe," it said, "I might not worry too much about dying."

Conway's first inclination was to remind Forty-three of all the work that had gone into keeping it alive, the implication being that it was displaying a lack of gratitude. But the Hudlar component of his mind was making comparisons with the normal FROB life-style and that which Conway was offering it. From the patient's viewpoint he might not have done it a favor, other than by saving the life of its child-to-be. Conway sighed.

"There is an alternative," he said, trying to put some enthusiasm into his tone. "There is a way in which you could lead an active working life, without physical constraints on your movements. In fact, you could travel all over the Federation, return to asteroid mining if you like, or do anything else you have a mind to do so far as your working life is concerned, provided that you do not return to Hudlar."

The patient's membrane vibrated briefly, but the translator was silent. Probably it was a sound of surprise.

Conway had to spend the next few minutes explaining the basic tenets of multispecies medicine to the patient, and how disease and infection was transmissible only among the members of a species with a common evolutionary history and environment. An Ian or a Melfan or a member of any other species would be quite safe with an Earth-human with the most contagious and virulent Earthly diseases, because the victim's pathogens were ineffective against—in fact they would completely ignore and be ignored by—the tissues of any other off-planet species. An ailment could, therefore, only be contracted from a being's own world or people.

"You can see what this means," Conway went on quickly. "After your wounds are healed and the child is born, you will be discharged from the hospital. But instead of confining you to an aseptic prison on your home world and severely restricting your activities, you could elect to go to another planet, where your lack of resistance to Hudlar diseases would be unimportant, because the pathogens on that world would have no interest in you.

"Your nutrient would be synthesized locally and would not be a source of infection," he continued. "However, immunity suppressant medication will be required periodically to ensure that your immune system does not restart and begin to reject your artificial organs. This will be administered by a medic from the nearest Monitor Corps office, which will be given full instructions regarding your case. The Corps medic will also warn you of impending visits by members of your own species. When this happens you must not go anywhere near them. Do not occupy the same building as they do or, if possible, even the same town."

Unlike the transplant patients of many other species, who could accept donor organs with no rejection problems after a short time on suppressants, the Hudlar immune system had to be permanently neutralized. But this was not the time, Conway thought, to add another misfortune to the list.

"Exchanges of news between you and your friends at home should be by communicator only," Conway went on. "I must stress this point. A visitor of your own species, or even a package sent from home, would harbor the only kind of pathogens capable of infecting and killing you, and they would do so very quickly."

Conway paused to allow the full meaning of his words to sink in. The patient continued to regard him for a long time, its membrane showing no indication of it wanting to speak. This was a Hudlar in full female mode, and its present major concern would be for the safe delivery and future health and happiness of its off-spring.

When the birth was successfully accomplished, as it would be, the deceased male-mode life-mate should have been present to take care of the child and to slip gradually into female mode. Because of the death of its partner, that function would be taken over by close relatives. Immediately following the birth, however, this patient would begin the inevitable changeover to full male mode, and in that condition the absence of its life-mate would be particularly distressing.

People of many intelligent species had lost life-mates before now. They had learned to live with it or they had gone out and found another who would accept them. The trouble here was that FROB-Forty-three would not be able to make physical contact with any other member of its species, and would therefore remain in full male mode for the remainder of its life. That, for a young adult Hudlar, would be an intensely frustrating and unhappy condition to be in.

Through the torrent of sex-related Hudlar material which was flooding his mind, a purely Earth-human thought rose to the surface. What would it be like to be forever separated from Murchison and every other member of his species? If he could have Murchison he would not mind having only a bunch of extraterrestrials to talk to and work with—that was the everyday situation at Sector General. But to be cut off from the one form of warm, human, intimate, and mentally as well as physically stimulating contact which he had been taking for granted for so many years—he did not know what he would be able to do about that. The question was unanswerable because the situation was unthinkable.

"I understand," the patient said suddenly, "and thank you, Doctor."

His first thought was to refuse its thanks and instead apologize to it. He had the taped insight which made him in effect another Hudlar, and he wanted to tell how truly sorry he was for subjecting it to the trauma of this highly complex and professionally demanding operation which would give it so many more years of mental suffering. But he knew that his mind was oversensitized to the Hudlar material right now, and a Doctor should not speak to his patient in such a maudlin and unprofessional fashion.

Instead he said reassuringly, "Your species is very adaptable regarding working environments, and much in demand throughout the Federation on planetary and space projects, and your recovery will be complete. With certain personal restrictions, which will require a high order of mental discipline to negate, you can look forward to leading a very active and useful life."

He did not say a happy life, because he was not that big a liar.

"Thank you, Doctor," the patient said again.

"Please excuse me," Conway said, and escaped.

But not for long. The rapid, irregular tapping of six hard-tipped Melfan legs signaled the approach of Senior Physician Edanelt.

"That was well done, Conway," the Senior said. "A nice blend of clinical fact, sympathy, and encouragement, although you did spend a lot more time with the patient than is usual for a Diagnostician. However, there was a message for you from Thornnastor requesting a meeting as soon and wherever is convenient for you. It did not specify other than saying that it concerned your Protector and that it was urgent."

"If the time and place are of my choice," Conway said slowly, his mind still on the future troubles of FROB-Forty-three, "it can't be too urgent. What about Three and Ten?"

"They, too, are urgently in need of reassurance," Edanelt replied. "Three was the responsibility of Yarrence, who did some delicate and quite brilliant work relieving its depressed cranial fracture and underlying repairs, but no replacement surgery was necessary. Visually, Three will not be an aesthetically pleasing entity to its fellows, but unlike Ten and Forty-three, neither will it be a permanent exile from its home world and people.

"Ten will have the same long-term problems as Forty-three," the Melfan went on. "The procedures for the multiple limb and absorption organ replacements went well, and the prognosis is for a full recovery under the usual strict regimen of suppressants. Since you are short of time, perhaps I should talk to one of them while you speak to the other?

"I am a Senior Physician, Conway," it added, "and not a fledgling Diagnostician like you. But I would not want to keep Thornnastor waiting too long."

"Thank you," Conway said, "and I'll talk to Ten."

Unlike Forty-three, Ten was in male mode and would not be susceptible to emotional manipulation and arguments as the previous patient. He hoped that Thornnastor was being its usual impatient self and not really in a hurry to see him ...

When it was over he felt in much worse mental shape than the patient, who seemed to have taken the first steps toward the acceptance of its lot without too much emotional distress, probably because it did not have a life-mate. Conway desperately wanted to clear his mind of all things pertaining to the Hudlar life-form, but it was proving extremely difficult to do so.

"Surely it is theoretically possible for two suppressees, living away from their home planet, to meet without endangering each other?" he asked Edanelt when they were out of earshot of the Hudlar patients. "If both had their immune systems suppressed, they should be free of own-species pathogens which would otherwise infect each other. It might be possible to arrange periodic meetings of such exiles which would benefit—"

"A nice, softhearted, and, may I say, softheaded idea," Edanelt broke in. "But if one of these suppressees had an inherited immunity to a pathogen not directly involved with the rejection process, to which the other members of this group had no immunity, they would be in serious danger. But try the idea on Thornnastor, who is the recognized authority on—"

"Thornnastor!" Conway burst out. "I'd forgotten. Has it been? . . ."

"No," Edanelt said. "But O'Mara came in to see if you needed help talking to the replacement patients. It advised me regarding my approach to Three's problems, but said that you did not need help and seemed to be enjoying yourselves too much to be disturbed. Was that a remark denoting approval, or not? From my experience of working among Earth-human DBDGs I assume this was one of those occasions when incorrect verbal data is passed on in the belief that the listener will assume the opposite meaning to be true, but I do not understand this concept you call sarcasm."

"One never knows whether O'Mara is approving or otherwise," Conway said dryly, "because he is invariably uncomplimentary and sarcastic."

Nevertheless it gave him a warm feeling to think that the Chief Psychologist had thought enough of his handling of the postoperative interview with Ten not to interfere. Or maybe he had thought Conway was making such an unholy mess of things that O'Mara was unable, for reasons of discipline, to tell a probationary Diagnostician how abysmally wrong he was in front of junior members of the staff.

But the doubt Conway felt was being swamped by a feeling which was even stronger, a physical need which was being reinforced by the sudden realization that he had had nothing but a sandwich to eat during the past ten hours. He turned quickly to the ward terminal and called up the on- and off-duty rosters of the warm-blooded, oxygen-breathing members of the Senior Staff. He was in luck, their duty rosters coincided.

"Would you contact Thornnastor, please," Conway said as he turned to leave the ward, "and tell it that I will meet it in thirty minutes in the dining hall."

CHAPTER 18

Conway knew the Diagnostician-in-Charge of Pathology well enough to tell it apart from all the other Tralthans using the dining hall, and he was pleasantly surprised to see Murchison at the same table. Thornnastor, as was its wont, was purveying some interspecies gossip to its assistant, and so engrossed in it were they that they did not notice his approach.

". . . One would not think it likely or even possible," the Tralthan was rumbling pedantically through its translator, "for the urge toward indiscriminate procreative activity to be strong in a life-form which is only a few degrees above absolute zero. But believe me, a fractional elevation in body temperature, even when it is accidentally produced by the treatment, can cause acute embarrassment among the other SNLU genders present. Four genders in one species tends to be confusing anyway, even when one is carrying the SNLU tape, and a certain Melfan Senior, you know who I mean, was sufficiently disturbed emotionally to use its external manipulators to signal its readiness to—"

"Frankly, sir, my trouble is somewhat different . . ." Murchison began.

"I realize that," Thornnastor replied. "But really, there does not appear to be any great emotional, physical, or psychological problem. Naturally, the mechanics of this particular mating process are distasteful to me personally, but I am willing to consider the matter clinically and give what advice I can."

"My difficulty," Murchison said, "is the distinct feeling I experienced while it was happening that I was being unfaithful five times over."

They're talking about us! Conway thought, feeling his face beginning to redden. But they were still too deeply engrossed to notice either him or his embarrassment.

"I will gladly discuss this matter with my fellow Diagnosticians," Thornnastor resumed ponderously. "Some of them may have encountered similar difficulties. Not myself, of course, because the FGLI species indulges in this activity during a very small proportion of the Tralthan year, and during that period the activity is, well, frenetic and not subject to subtle self-analysis." All of its eyes took on faraway looks for a moment, then it went on. "However, a brief reference to my Earth-human component suggests that you do not concern yourself with minor and unnecessary emotional hairsplitting, and just relax and enjoy the process. In spite of the subtle differences which you mentioned earlier, the process *is* enjoyable? . . . Oh, hello, Conway."

Thornnastor had raised the eye which had been regarding its food to look at him. It said, "We were just talking about you. You seem to be adapting very well to your multiple tape problems, and now Murchison tells me that—"

"Yes," Conway said quickly. He looked appealingly into the Tralthan's one and Murchison's two eyes and went on. "Please, I would greatly appreciate it if you would not discuss this very personal matter with anyone else."

"I don't see why not," Thornnastor said, bringing another eye to bear on him. "Surely the matter is of intrinsic interest, and would no doubt prove enlightening to colleagues who have faced or are about to face similar problems. Sometimes your reactions are difficult to understand, Conway."

He glared at Murchison, who, he felt, had been far too free in talking about her intrinsically interesting problems with her Chief. But she smiled sweetly back at him, then said to Thornnastor, "You'll have to excuse him, sir. I think he is hungry, and hunger affects his sensorium as well as his blood sugar levels and sometimes makes him behave with a degree of irrationality."

"Ah, yes," the Tralthan said, returning the eye to its plate. "It has the same effect on me."

Murchison was already tapping instructions into the food console for one of his visually noncontroversial sandwiches. He said, "Make it three, please."

He was attacking the first one as Thornnastor, who had the advantage of being able to speak with all four of its mouths, went on. "It seems I must compliment you on the way you are adapting to operative procedures requiring other-species surgical data. Not only were you calling up this data with little or no delay; the indications are that you were initiating new procedures derived from a combination of different entities' experiences. The OR Seniors were most impressed, I have been told."

Chewing furiously, Conway swallowed and said, "It was the Seniors who did all the real work."

"That isn't the way Hossantir and Edanelt tell it," Thornnastor said. "But I suppose it is in the nature of things that Seniors do most of the work and the Diagnostician-in-Charge gets most of the credit, or all of the discredit if things go wrong. And speaking of cases which might not go well, I would like to discuss your plans for the birth of your Unborn. The endocrinology of its parent and Protector is quite complex, and I am most interested in this one. However, I can foresee a few purely physical problems which . . ."

Conway nearly choked at the understatement, and it was a moment before he was able to speak.

"Must all verbal communication cease while it is eating?" said Thornnastor impatiently, using the mouth closest to Murchison. "Why wasn't your species foresighted enough to evolve at least one additional orifice for the ingestion of food?"

"Pardon me," Conway said, smiling. "I would be delighted to have any assistance and advice you can give me. The Protectors of the Unborn are the most untreatable life-form we've encountered, and I don't think we have discovered all the problems yet, much less found solutions to them. In fact, I would be most grateful if your commitments would allow you to be present during the birth."

"I thought you'd never ask, Conway," Thornnastor rumbled.

"There are several problems," Conway said, rubbing his middle gently and wondering if one of them was going to be an attack of indigestion through eating his food too quickly. Apologetically, he went on. "But right now my mind is still sensitized to the Hudlar material and the questions which have arisen as a result of my recent experiences in the Hudlar OR and Geriatric wards. The questions are psychological as well as physiological, and so insistent that I find it very difficult to clear my mind for consideration of the Protector case. This is ridiculous!"

"But understandable, considering your recent total involvement with FROB life-forms," Thornnastor said. "But if you have unresolved problems regarding these Hudlars, the simplest way of clearing your mind of this troublesome material is to ask the questions at once and obtain as many answers as possible, even though they may be unsatisfactory or incomplete answers, so that you will have taken the matter as far as it is possible to go with it at the present time. Your mind will accept this and allow you to think of other things, including your perpetually pregnant Protector.

"Your particular mental quirk is far from rare, Conway," the Tralthan went on, slipping into its lecturing voice. "There must be a very good reason why your mind doesn't want to leave the subject. Perhaps it is close to drawing significant conclusions, and if the question is shelved now the pertinent data might fade and be lost. I realize that I am beginning to sound like a psychologist, but one cannot practice medicine without acquiring some knowledge in that field. I can, of course, help you with the physiological questions on the Hudlar life-form, but I suspect that it is the psychological aspect which is crucial. In which case you should consult the Chief Psychologist without delay."

"You mean," Conway said faintly, "call O'Mara right now?"

"Theoretically," the Tralthan replied, "a Diagnostician may request the assistance of any member of the hospital staff at any time, and vice versa."

Conway looked at Murchison, who smiled sympathetically and said, "Call him. On the intercom he can only indulge in verbal violence."

"That," Conway said as he reached for the communicator, "doesn't reassure me at all."

A few seconds later the scowling features of the Chief Psychologist filled the tiny screen, making it impossible to tell how or if he was fully dressed. O'Mara said coldly, "I can tell from the background noise and the fact that you are still masticating that you are calling from the main dining hall. I would point out that I am in the middle of my rest period. I do rest occasionally, you know, just to fool you people into thinking that I'm only human. Presumably there is a good reason for your making this call, or are you complaining about the food?"

Conway opened his mouth, but the combination of facing an angry O'Mara and a mind which was still too busily engaged in formulating his questions kept any words from coming out.

"Conway," O'Mara said with exaggerated patience, "what the blazes do you want?"

"Information," he replied angrily. Then he softened his tone and went on. "I need information which might help in the Hudlar geriatric work. Diagnostician Thornnastor, Pathologist Murchison, and I are presently in consultation regarding..."

"Which means," O'Mara said sourly, "that you've dreamed up some harebrained scheme over lunch."

"...A proposed method of treating their condition," Conway went on. "Regrettably, little can be done for the present occupants of the ward, since the degenerative condition is too far advanced in them. But early preventive treatment might be possible provided my idea has physiological and psychological support. Thornnastor and Murchison can give me detailed information on the former, but the key to their treatment, and any hope of its ultimate success, depends on the behavior under stress, adaptive ability, and potential for re-education in aged but pregeriatric FROBs. I have not yet discussed the clinical problems which would be encountered, because to do so would be a waste of time if the answers you give me preclude further investigation."

"Go on," O'Mara said, no longer sounding half-asleep.

Conway hesitated, thinking that his period of intensive Hudlar surgery, the visits to the FROB geriatric and infant wards, some old memories from his early childhood, and possibly material from his other-species mind partners had all contributed to an idea which was very likely unworkable, ethically questionable, and so ridiculous that O'Mara might well have second thoughts regarding his suitability as a future Diagnostician. But it was too late now to hold back.

"From my FROB tape and lectures at various times on Hudlar

pathology," he went on, nodding in acknowledgment toward Thornnastor, "it is clear that the various painful and incurable conditions
to which the aged of that species are prey are traceable to a common
cause. The loss of function in the limbs and the abnormal degree
of calcification and fissuring at the extremities can be ascribed to
the simple deterioration in circulation which is common to the aged
of any species.

"This is not a new idea," Conway said, glancing quickly toward
Thornnastor and Murchison. "However, as a result of working on
a large number of Hudlar limb and organ replacement operations
from the Menelden accident, it occurred to me that the deterioration
I observed in the organs of absorption and evacuation among the
aged FROBs was very similar to the temporary condition which
occurred during the replacement of a heart, although at the time I
was too busy to note the signs consciously. In short, the problems
of the FROB geriatrics are due to circulatory impairment or inadequacy."

"If the idea isn't new," O'Mara said with a flash of his characteristic sarcasm, "why am I listening to it?"

Murchison was watching him in silence. Thornnastor continued
to watch its food, Murchison, O'Mara, and Conway, also without
speaking.

"The Hudlars are a very energy-hungry species," Conway went
on. "They have an extremely high metabolic rate which requires a
virtually continuous supply of nutrient via their organs of absorption. The food thus metabolized serves the major organs, such as
the two hearts, the absorption organs themselves, the womb when
the entity is in gravid female mode, and, of course, the limbs.

"I had learned from the pathology lectures," he continued, "that
these six immensely strong limbs are the most energy-hungry system
of the body, and demand close to eighty percent of the nutrient
metabolized. But it was not until the recent Hudlar experience that
my mind was drawn forcibly to this data, and to the fact which is
also widely recognized, that it is the ultrahigh metabolic rate and
excessive food requirement which enables the adult Hudlar to be so
fantastically resistant to injury and disease."

O'Mara was getting ready to interrupt again, and Conway went
on quickly. "With the onset of old age their troubles invariably begin

in the limbs, which demand an even greater proportion of the body's available resources to fight it. This places increasing stress on the twin hearts, absorption, and evacuation organs, all of which require their share of and are interdependent on the circulatory system's nutrient content. As a result these systems go into partial failure, which further reduces the blood supply to the limbs, and the body as a whole slides into a degenerative spiral."

"Conway," O'Mara said firmly, "I assume this lengthy but no doubt oversimplified clinical picture is for the benefit of the poor, ignorant psychologist so that he will understand the psychological questions when they come, if they ever come."

Continuing with its meal, Thornnastor said, "The clinical picture is oversimplified, I agree, but essentially correct, although your method of describing it suggests a new approach to the problem. I, too, am impatient to know what it is that you intend."

Conway took a deep breath and said, "Very well. It seems to me that the drain on the age-reduced resources of these Hudlars, represented by the irreversible limb conditions, can be alleviated before onset. With reduced stress and a greater share of the available nutrient supply, the hearts and organs of absorption and elimination could maintain their functions for an additional several years while keeping up optimum levels of circulation to the remaining limb or limbs."

All at once it seemed that O'Mara's face in the screen had become a still picture; Murchison was staring at him with a shocked expression, and all four of Thornnastor's eyes had turned to regard him.

"Naturally the procedure would be one of elective surgery," Conway went on, "and would not take place except at the request and the expressed permission of the entity concerned. The surgical problems involved in the removal of four or five limbs are relatively simple. It is the psychological preparation and aftereffects which are paramount and which would determine whether or not the procedure should be tried."

O'Mara exhaled loudly through his nose, then said, "So you want me to tell you if it is possible to sell the pregeriatric Hudlars on the idea of voluntary multiple limb amputations?"

"The procedure," Thornnastor said, "does seem, well, radical."

"I realize that," Conway said. "But from the Hudlar material available to me it is obvious that there is a general and abject fear of growing old among that species, caused by the quite appalling clinical picture of the average geriatric FROB. The fear is increased by the knowledge that the minds of the aging Hudlars remain clear and active, although there is the tendency common to all aging entities to want to live in the past. But it is the situation of a normal mind being trapped inside a rapidly degenerating and often pain-racked body which causes the greatest distress. It is possible that the Hudlars may not have a lot of sales resistance to the idea, and may even welcome it.

"But my information is purely subjective," he went on, "and comes from recent personal experience and from the feelings of the Hudlar who donated my tape, so my thinking may not be com-pletely trustworthy. It requires the objective viewpoint of a psy-chologist with extraterrestrial experience, including that of the FROB life-form, to decide whether or not my idea has merit."

O'Mara was silent for a long time; then he nodded and said, "What can you offer these close-to-limbless Hudlars, Conway? What could they do which would make their extended, less painful lives worth living?"

"I have had time to consider only a few of the possibilities," he replied. "Their situation would be similar to that of the Hudlar amputees we will be sending home in a few weeks' time. They will have limited mobility on prosthetics, one or two of their forelimbs will remain fully functioning, and they should remain mentally and physically effective until shortly before termination. I shall have to discuss the physiological details with Thornnastor before I can be certain of this, but—"

"It is a fair assumption, Conway," the Tralthan broke in. "I have no doubt that you are right."

"Thank you, sir," Conway said, feeling his face growing warm at the compliment. To O'Mara he went on, "On Hudlar medical science is in the early stages and for some time it will be primarily concerned with the treatment of diseases in the very young, since the adult members of the species do not take sick. These pediatric cases, although ill, remain very active and require only minimal restraint and supervision while the administered medication is doing its work. Our aged amputees will still be physically capable of with-standing without injury the enthusiasm and playfulness of the half-ton Hudlar toddlers, and we are already training the first of a line of FROB pediatric nurses who will be able to instruct them . . ."

Mention of that very personable female-mode nurse had excited his Hudlar mind-partner, so Conway had to spend a few seconds telling it to behave itself. But when he tried to return his mind to what he had been about to say, memories of his extremely aged but alert great-grandmother and, at the time, only friend welled up in his mind. That touched off a sudden, intensely strong feeling of sorrow from Khone over the loss of parental physical contact, which was so necessary for the maintenance of mental coherency in Gog-leskan society, and which occurred at a very early age. He felt with Khone the past loss of that love and warmth and the expectation of future loss when its offspring would be born and remain close all too briefly before it departed. And strangely, although Khone's pres-ence had been reacting against nearly all of the material being thrown up by Conway and his other mind-partners, the little Gog-leskan was able to consider the sight and sounds and memories of Conway's incredibly old and fragile first friend without the slightest hint of distress.

This was important, he knew, because there were indications that the Gogleskan's mind was not entirely repelled by the thought of the geriatric FROBs, either. A bridge was being built between Khone and the other species, and Conway began blinking rapidly because his tear ducts seemed suddenly to have developed a leak.

He felt Murchison's hand squeezing his arm as she said urgently, "What's wrong?"

"Conway," O'Mara said, sounding concerned, "are you still with us?"

"Sorry, my mind went off at a tangent," he said, clearing his throat. "I'm all right. In fact, I feel very well indeed."

"I see," O'Mara said. "But I would like to discuss the reasons for and the content of your tangential thinking at a more convenient time. Continue."

"In common with elderly members of the majority of the in-telligent species," Conway resumed, "the very old Hudlars have a close affinity with the very young, and a great deal of benefit can

STAR HEALER · 569

be derived from this relationship by both parties if they are placed together. The aged entities are at the stage loosely described as second childhood, when the memories and feelings of their own younger days are thrown into prominence, and they have nothing much to do with their remaining time. The children would have an adult playmate who understands them, who enjoys their company, and who is not, like the younger adults and parents, perhaps too deeply concerned with the day-to-day business of life to have enough time to spend with them.

"Provided the geriatric amputee idea is acceptable to them," he continued, "I think they would be prime candidates for pediatric nursing training. The less elderly, whose mental age would be significantly greater, could be trained as teachers of older children and preadolescents. They might also be usefully engaged in supervising automated production processes, or on watch-keeping duty on the weather control stations, or as—"

"Enough!" O'Mara said, holding up one hand. He went on caustically. "Leave me something to do, Conway, to justify my existence. At least, your uncharacteristic behavior of a few minutes ago is no longer a mystery. The childhood material in your psych file and your suggestion regarding the geriatric Hudlars fully explain your temporary loss of control.

"Regarding your original question," O'Mara went on, "I cannot give you a quick answer, but I shall call up my Hudlar material at once and start work on it. You've given me too much to think about for me to be able to go back to sleep now."

"I'm sorry," Conway said, but the Chief Psychologist's face had already gone from the screen.

"And I'm sorry for the delay as well," he said to Thornnastor. "But now at last we can talk about the Protector . . ."

He broke off as the blue "Vacate" light began flashing on their table, indicating that they had remained for longer than was necessary to consume the food which had been ordered, and that they should move away so as to release the table for other would-be diners, of which there was a large number waiting.

"Your office or mine?" Thornnastor said.

CHAPTER 19

First contact with the species known as the Protectors of the Unborn had been made by *Rhabwar* when the ambulance ship had answered a distress signal from a vessel which had been transporting two members of that species under restraint. It discovered that the Protectors had broken free, and while they had been killing the ship's crew, one of them had died as well.

The surviving Protector had delivered itself of its Unborn shortly before it, too, died. That newly born Protector was the patient who, after more than a year's sojourn in Sector General, was about to give birth in its turn. The body of its parent had been thoroughly investigated by Pathology and had furnished information which might enable them to deliver the Unborn without it suffering complete obliteration of the higher functions of its mind.

". . . The primary purpose of the forthcoming operation is to save the mind of the Unborn," he repeated, looking around the crowded observation gallery before he returned his attention to the ward below, where the furiously battling Protector was engaging its life-support system and two Hudlar attendants in total war. "The problems are physical, surgical, and endocrinological, and Diagnostician Thornnastor and I have discussed little else for the past two days. And now, for the benefit of the support and after-care team members who have just joined us, as well as for the observers and the others who will be studying the recordings later, I shall briefly summarize the available information on this case.

"The adult, nonintelligent Protector is physiological classification FSOJ," Conway went on. "As you can see, it is a large, immensely strong being with a heavy, slitted carapace from which protrude four thick tentacles, a heavy, serrated tail, and a head. The tentacles terminate in a cluster of sharp, bony projections so that they resemble spiked clubs. The main features of the head are the well-protected, recessed eyes, the upper and lower mandibles, and teeth which are capable of deforming all but the strongest metal alloys.

"Flip it over, please," Conway said to the two Hudlars working on the patient with thin steel bars. "And hit it harder! You won't hurt it and will, in fact, maintain it in optimum condition prior to the birth." To the observers he went on. "The four stubby legs also have osseous projections which enable these limbs to be used as weapons as well. While the underside is not armored, as is the carapace, this area is rarely open to attack, and is covered by a thick tegument which apparently gives sufficient protection. In the center of the area you can see a thin, longitudinal fissure which opens into the birth canal. It will not open, however, until a few minutes before the event.

"But first, the evolutionary and environmental background . . ."

The Protectors had evolved on a world of shallow, steaming sea and swampy jungles where the line of demarcation between animal and vegetable life, so far as physical mobility and aggression were concerned, was difficult to define. To survive there at all, a life-form had to fight hard and move fast, and the dominant species on that hellish world had earned its place by fighting and moving and reproducing their kind with a greater potential for survival than any of the others.

At an early stage in their evolution the utter savagery of their environment had forced them into a physiological configuration which gave maximum protection to the vital organs. The brain, heart, lungs, and womb were all sited deep within that fantastically well-muscled and protected body, and compressed into a relatively small volume. During gestation the organ displacement was considerable, because the fetus had to grow virtually to maturity before birth. It was rarely that they were able to survive the reproduction

of more than three of their kind, because an aging parent was usually too weak to defend itself against the attack of a hungry last-
born.

But the principal reason why the Protectors of the Unborn had
risen to dominance on their world was that their young were already
educated in the techniques of survival *before they were born.*

The process had begun simply as the transmission of a complex
set of survival instincts at the genetic level, but the close juxtaposition of the brains of the parent and the developing embryo led to
an effect analogous to induction of the electrochemical activity associated with thought.

The fetuses became short-range telepaths receiving everything
the parents saw or felt or in any other way experienced.

And even before the growth of the fetus was complete, there
was another embryo beginning to take form inside the first one, and
the new one was also increasingly aware of the world outside its
self-fertilizing grandparent. Gradually the telepathic range had increased so that communication became possible between embryos
whose parents were close enough to see each other.

To minimize damage to the parent's internal organs, the growing
fetus was paralyzed while in the womb, with no degradation of later
muscle function. But the prebirth deparalyzing process, or possibly
the birth itself, also caused a complete loss of sentience and telepathic ability. A newborn Protector, it seemed, would not last very
long in its incredibly savage environment if the purity of its survival
instincts was clouded by the ability to think.

". . . With nothing to do but receive information from their outside world," Conway went on, "and exchange thoughts with other
Unborn, and try to widen their telepathic range by tuning to non-
sentient life-forms around them, the embryos developed minds of
great power and intelligence. But they cannot build anything, or
engage in any cooperative physical activity, or keep written records,
or, indeed, do anything at all to influence their parents and Protectors who have to fight and kill and eat continuously to maintain
their unsleeping bodies and the Unborn within them."

There was a moment's silence which was broken only by the
muffled clanking and thumping sounds made by the mechanical
life-support system and the Hudlars, who together were laboring

hard to make the FSOJ parent-to-be feel right at home. Then the Lieutenant in charge of the technical support team spoke up.

"I have asked this question already," he said quietly, "but I have trouble accepting the answer. Is it really true that we must continue beating the patient even while the birth is taking place?"

"Correct, Lieutenant," Conway said. "Before, during, and after. The only advance warning we will have of the event will be a marked increase in the Protector's activity level approximately half an hour before the birth. On its home world this activity would be aimed at clearing the immediate area of predators so as to give the young one an increased chance of survival.

"It will come out fighting," Conway added, "and its life-support must be the same as that needed by its parent except that the violence we administer will be scaled down, very slightly, because of its smaller size."

There were several beings in the gallery making untranslatable sounds of incredulity. Thornnastor gave a peremptory rumble and added its considerable weight, both physical and intellectual, to Conway's previous remarks.

"You must all realize and accept without question," the Diagnostician said ponderously, "that continual violence is normal for this creature. The FSOJ must remain in a condition of stress in order that its quite complex endocrine system will function properly. It requires, and has evolved the ability to accept, the continuous release of a hormone into its system which is the equivalent of Kelgian thullis or Earth-human adrenaline.

"Should the release of this hormone be inhibited," the Tralthan went on, "by the withdrawal of the ever-present threat of imminent injury or death, the Protector's movements become sluggish and erratic, and if the attack is not quickly resumed, unconsciousness follows. If the period of unconsciousness is prolonged, irreversible changes take place in the endocrine systems of both Protector and Unborn leading to termination."

This time the words were followed by an attentive silence. Conway indicated the ward below and said, "We shall now take you as close to the patient as it is possible to go in safety. You observers will be shown the details of the Protector's life-support mechanisms, and of the smaller version in the side-ward which will accommodate the young one when it arrives, both of which resemble nothing so much as the instruments of interrogation used during a very unsavory period in Earth's history. You new team-members will familiarize yourselves with these mechanisms and with the work expected of you, and ask as many questions as necessary to ensure that you fully understand your duties. But above all, do not be kind or gentle with this patient. That will not help it at all."

The various feet, tentacles, and pincers were beginning to shuffle, slither, and scrape along the floor as they turned toward the gallery exit. Conway held up his hand.

"Let me remind you once again," he said very seriously. "The purpose of this operation is not simply to assist at the FSOJ's birth, which will take place with or without our assistance, believe me. It is to ensure that the Unborn and soon-to-be new Protector retains the same level of intelligence and the telepathic ability it now possesses within the womb."

Thornnastor made a quiet sound which to the Tralthan component of Conway's mind signified pessimism and anxiety. Following two days of consultations with the Diagnostician, the precise details of the forthcoming operative procedure had still to be finalized. Radiating a confidence which he did not feel, he discussed the functioning of the combination operating frame and gimbal-mounted cage which accommodated the Protector before taking them through to the side-ward designed to receive its offspring.

Nicknamed the Rumpus Room by the maintenance engineers responsible for its construction, the ward was more than half-filled by a hollow, cylindrical structure, wide enough to allow unrestricted passage of the FSOJ infant, which curved and twisted back on itself so that the occupant would be able to use all of the available floor area of the ward in which to exercise. The entry point into this continuous cylinder was a heavily reinforced door in the side-wall, which was otherwise composed of an immensely strong open latticework of metal. The cylinder floor was shaped to reproduce the uneven ground and natural obstacles, such as the mobile and voracious trip-roots found on the Protector's home planet, and the open sections gave the occupant a continuous view of the screens positioned around the outer surface of the cylinder. Onto these screens were projected moving tri-di pictures of indigenous plant and animal life which the occupant would normally encounter.

The open structure also enabled the medical team to bring to bear on their patient the more positive aspects of life-support system—the fearsome-looking mechanisms positioned between the projection screens which were designed to beat, tear, and jab at the occupant with any desired degree of frequency or force.

Everything possible had been done to make the new arrival feel at home.

"As you are already aware," Conway went on, "the Unborn, by virtue of its telepathic faculty, is constantly aware of the events taking place outside its parent. We are not telepaths and may not be capable of receiving its thoughts, even during the period of intense mental stress which occurs just prior to birth, when it is transmitting at maximum power because it knows that its mind and personality are about to be obliterated.

"There are several telepathic races known to the Federation," he continued, his mind returning to its one and only contact with a telepathic Unborn. "These are usually species who have evolved this faculty so that their common organic receiver/transmitters are automatically in tune. For this reason telepathic contact between the members of different telepathic races is not always possible. When mental contact occurs between one of these entities and a non-telepath, it usually means that the faculty in the nontelepath is either dormant or atrophied. When such contact occurs the experience can be highly uncomfortable, but there are no physical changes in the brain affected, nor is there any lasting psychological damage."

As he switched on the Rumpus Room's screens and began projecting the visual record of that first, incredibly violent birth, his mind was adding the extra-sensory dimension of his own, minutes-long telepathic contact with the Unborn so soon to be born.

Conway was aware that his fists were clenched, and that beside him Murchison's face was pale as she watched the screen. Once again the rampaging Protector tried to get at them by battering at the partly open inner seal of the air lock. The opening was five or six inches wide, just enough for the pathologist, *Rhabwar*'s injured Captain, and Conway to see and hear and record everything which was happening. But their position was not a secure one. The Protector's hard-tipped tentacles had already wreaked havoc in the lock antechamber, tearing out sections of metal plating and deforming the underlying structure, and the lock's inner seal was not all that thick.

Their only safety lay in the fact that the lock antechamber was weightless, and the flailing tentacles of the Protector sent it spinning helplessly away from every wall or obstruction they encountered, which simply increased its anger and the savagery of its attack. It also made it more difficult to observe the birth which was taking place. But the violence of the Protector's attack was beginning to diminish. Weightlessness combined with physical damage sustained during encounters with the ship's now-dead crew and the subsequent malfunctioning of the on-board life-support system had left it with barely enough strength to complete the birth process, which was already well advanced as the parent spun slowly to give a good if intermittent view of the emergence of the Unborn.

Conway's mind was on an aspect of the birth which the recording could not reproduce—the last few moments of telepathic contact with the fetus before it left its parent and became just another vicious, insensate, completely nonsentient young Protector— and for a moment he could not speak.

Thornnastor must have sensed his difficulty because it reached past him and froze the picture. In its ponderous, lecturing manner it said, "You can see that the head and most of the carapace have appeared, and that the limbs which project from it are limp and unmoving. The reason for this is that the secretions which are released to reverse the prebirth paralysis of the Unborn, and at the same time obliterate all cerebral activity not associated with survival, have not yet taken effect. Up to this point the expulsion of the Unborn is solely the responsibility of the parent Protector."

In the characteristically forthright manner of a Kelgian, one of the nurses asked, "Is the nonsentient parent to be considered expendable?"

Thornnastor curled an eye to regard Conway, whose mind was still fixed immovably on the circumstances of that earlier birth.

"That is not our intention," the Tralthan said when he did not respond. "The parent Protector was once a sentient Unborn, and is capable of producing anything up to three more sentient Unborn.

Should the circumstances arise where a decision is needed whether to assist the birth of the sentient infant at the expense of the life of the presently nonsentient parent, or to allow the birth to proceed normally so that we end with two nonsentient Protectors, that must be the decision of the Surgeon-in-Charge.

"If the latter decision was to be considered," it went on, with one eye still fixed on Conway, "it could be argued in support that with two Protectors, a young and an old one who will both produce telepathic embryos in time, we will have another chance or chances to solve the problem. But this would mean subjecting the two FSOJs to lengthy gestation periods in a highly artificial life-support system, which might have long-term ill effects on the new embryos, and would simply mean deferring the decision. The whole procedure would have to be repeated with, in all likelihood, the same decision having to be taken by a different Surgeon-in-Charge."

Murchison's eyes were on him as well, and she was looking worried. Those last few words had been something more than a not particularly direct answer to the nurse's question; they were in the nature of a professional warning. Conway was being reminded that he was still very much on probation, and that the Diagnostician-in-Charge of Pathology did not, in spite of its seniority, bear the ultimate responsibility for this case. But still he could not speak.

"You will observe that the Unborn's tentacles are beginning to move, but slowly," Thornnastor continued. "And now it is beginning to pull itself out of the birth canal . . ."

It had been at that moment that the soundless telepathic voice in Conway's mind had lost its clarity. There had been a feeling of pain and confusion and deep anxiety muddying up the clear stream of communication, but the final message from the Unborn had been a simple one.

To be born is to die, friends, the silent voice had said. *My mind and my telepathic faculty are being destroyed, and I am becoming a Protector with my own Unborn to protect while it grows and thinks and tries to make contact with you.*

Please cherish it.

The trouble with telepathic communication, Conway thought bitterly, was that it lacked the ambiguity and verbal misdirection and diplomatic lying which was possible with the spoken word. A telepathic promise had no loopholes. It was impossible to break one without a serious loss of self-respect.

And now the Unborn with whom he had experienced mind-to-mind contact was his patient, a Protector with the Unborn he had promised to cherish about to enter the highly complex and alien world of Sector General. He was still not sure how best to proceed— or, more accurately, which of several unsatisfactory options to adopt.

To nobody in particular he said suddenly, "We don't even know that the fetus has grown normally in hospital conditions. Our reproduction of the environment may not have been accurate enough. The Unborn may not have developed sentience, much less the telepathic faculty. There have been no indications of . . ."

He broke off as a series of musical trills and clicks came from the ceiling above their heads, and from their translators came the words, "You may not be entirely correct in your assumption, friend Conway."

"Prilicla!" Murchison said, and added unnecessarily, "You're back!"

"Are you . . . well?" Conway asked. He was thinking of the Menelden casualties and the hell it must have been for an empath to be placed in charge of classifying them.

"I am well, friend Conway," Prilicla replied, the legs holding it to the ceiling twitching slowly as it bathed in the emotional radiation of friendship and concern emanating from those below. "I was careful to direct operations from as great a distance as possible, just as I am remaining well clear of your patient in the outer ward. The Protector's emotional radiation is unpleasant to me, but not so the radiation from the Unborn.

"Mentation of a high order is present," the Cinrusskin went on. "Regrettably, I am an empath rather than a true telepath, but the feelings I detect are of frustration which is caused, I would guess, by its inability to communicate with those outside, together with feelings of confusion and awe which are predominating."

"Awe?" Conway said, then added, "If it has been trying to communicate, we've felt nothing, not even the faintest tickle."

Prilicla dropped from the ceiling, executed a neat loop, and fluttered to the top of a nearby instrument cabinet so that the DBLFs and DBDGs present would not have to strain their cervical vertebrae watching it. "I cannot be completely sure, friend Conway, because feelings are less trustworthy for the conveyance of intelligence than coherent thoughts, but it seems to me that the trouble may simply be one of mental overcrowding. During your original contact with the then Unborn and present Protector, the being had only three minds to consider, those of friends Murchison, Fletcher, and yourself. The other crew and medical team members were aboard *Rhabwar* and at extreme telepathic range.

"Here there may be too many minds," the empath went on, "minds of a bewildering variety and degree of complexity, including two"—its eyes turned to regard Thornnastor and Conway—"which seem to contain a multiplicity of entities, and which might be truly confusing, and awe-inspiring."

"You're right, of course," Conway said. He thought for a moment, then went on. "I was hoping for telepathic contact with the Unborn before and during the birth. In this case the assistance of a conscious and cooperating patient would be of great help indeed. But you can see the size of the operating room staff and technical support people. There are dozens of them. I can't simply send them all away."

Prilicla began to tremble again, this time in agitation over the additional worry it was causing Conway, when its intention had been only to reassure him regarding the mental health of the Unborn. It made another attempt to improve the quality of its friend's emotional radiation.

"I called in at the Hudlar ward as soon as I got back," the Cinrusskin said, "and I must say that your people did very well. Those were bad cases I sent in, as nearly hopeless as it is possible to be, friend Conway, but you lost only one of them. It was very fine work, even though friend O'Mara says that you have handed him another freshly boiled vegetable."

"I think," Murchison said, laughing as she translated the translated words, "it means another hot potato."

"O'Mara?" Conway asked.

"The Chief Psychologist was talking to one of your patients," Prilicla replied, "and assessing its nonmedical condition after visiting one of the Hudlars in the geriatric section. Friend O'Mara knew that I was coming to see you, and it said to tell you that a signal from Goglesk has arrived to the effect that your friend Khone wants to come to the hospital as soon as—"

"Khone is sick, badly injured?" Conway broke in, the persona of his Gogleskan mind-partner and his feelings for the little being pushing everything and everybody else out of his mind. He knew, because Khone had known, of the many diseases and accidents to which the FOKTs were prey, and for which very little could be done because to approach each other for help was to invite disaster. Whatever had happened to Khone, it must have been pretty bad for it to want to come to Sector General, where the worst nightmares of its mind were a physical actuality.

"No, no, friend Conway," Prilicla said, trembling again with the violence of his emotional radiation. "Khone's condition is neither serious nor urgent. But it has asked that you, personally, collect it and convey it to the hospital lest fear of your physically monstrous friends causes it to change its mind. Friend O'Mara's precise words were that you seem to be attracting some odd maternity cases these days."

"But it can't be volunteering to come *here!*" Conway protested. He knew that Khone was mature and capable of producing offspring. There was nothing in the Gogleskan's mind regarding recent sexual encounters, which meant that it must have happened since Conway had left Goglesk. He began doing calculations based on the FOKT gestation period.

"That was my reaction as well, friend Conway," Prilicla said. "But friend O'Mara pointed out that you had lived with and adapted to the presence of your Gogleskan friend and that it, Heaven help it, had been similarly influenced by your Earth-human mind. That was the second boiled vegetable; the other was the geriatric Hudlar business.

"Sorting out the psychoses of a FOKT parent-to-be and offspring scared of their prehistoric shadows was not going to be easy," the empath went on, "and the geriatric Hudlar problem had grown to the stage where it was taking up practically all of his time. It sounded very irritated and at times angry, did friend O'Mara, but its emotional radiation was at variance with the spoken words. There

were strong feelings of anticipation and excitement, as if it was looking forward to the challenge . . ."

It broke off and began trembling again. Beside the instrument
cabinet it was clinging to, Thornnastor was lifting and lowering its
six elephantine feet one at a time and in no particular sequence.
Murchison looked at the Diagnostician, and even though she was
not an empath, she knew her chief well enough to be able to recognize a very impatient Tralthan.

"This is all very interesting, Prilicla," she said gently, "but unlike
that of Khone, the condition of the patient awaiting our attention
in the outer ward is both serious and urgent."

CHAPTER 20

I n spite of everyone else's sense of urgency the Protector seemed to be in no particular hurry to deliver its Unborn. Conway was secretly relieved. It gave him more time to think, to consider alternative procedures and, if he was honest with himself, more time to dither.

The normally phlegmatic Thornnastor, with three eyes on the patient and one on the scanner projection, was slowly stamping one foot as it watched the lack of activity in the area of the Protector's womb. Murchison was dividing her attention between the screen and the Kelgian nurse who was in charge of the patient's restraints, and Prilicla was a distant, fuzzy blob clinging to the ceiling at the other end of the ward, where the emotional radiation from the Protector was bearable if not comfortable, and linked to the OR Team by communicator.

It was there purely out of clinical curiosity, the little empath had insisted. But the true reason was probably that it sensed Conway's anxiety regarding the coming operation and it wanted to help.

"Of the alternative procedures you have mentioned," Thornnastor said suddenly, "the first is slightly more desirable. But prematurely enlarging the birth opening and withdrawing the Unborn while at the same time clamping off those gland ducts . . . It's tricky, Conway. You could be faced with an awakened and fully active young Protector tearing and eating its way out of the parent. Or have you now decided that the parent is expendable?"

Conway's mind was filled again with the memory of his telepathic contact with an Unborn, an Unborn who had been born as
a mindless Protector, *this* Protector. He knew that he was not being
logical, but he did not want to discard a being whose mind he had
known so intimately simply because, for evolutionary reasons, it had
suffered a form of brain death.

"No," Conway said firmly.

"The other alternatives are even worse," the Tralthan said.

"I was hoping you'd feel that way," Conway said.

"I understand," Thornnastor said. "But neither am I greatly in
favor of your primary suggestion. The procedure is radical, to say
the least, and unheard-of when the species concerned possesses a
carapace. Such delicate work on a fully conscious and mobile patient
is—"

"The patient," Conway broke in, "will be conscious, and immobilized."

"It seems, Conway," it said, speaking quietly for a Tralthan, "that
there is some confusion in your mind due, perhaps, to the multiplicity of tapes occupying it. Let me remind you that the patient
cannot be immobilized for any lengthy period of time, either by
physical restraint or anesthetics, without irreversible metabolic
changes taking place which lead quickly to unconsciousness and
termination. The FSOJ is constantly moving and constantly under
attack, and the response of its endocrine system is such that . . . But
you know this as well as I do, Conway! Are you well? Is there psychological, perhaps temporary, distress? Would you like me to assume charge for a time?"

Murchison had been listening to her communicator and had
missed Thornnastor's earlier words. She looked worriedly at Conway, obviously wondering what was wrong with him, or what her
Chief thought was wrong with him; then she said, "Prilicla called
me. It didn't want to interrupt you during what might have been
an important clinical discussion between its superiors, but it reports
a steady increase and change in the quality of emotional radiation
emanating from both the Protector and its Unborn. The indications
are that the Protector is preparing itself for a major effort, and this
in turn has caused an increase in the level of mentation in the

Unborn. Prilicla wants to know if you have detected any signs of an attempt at telepathic contact. It says the Unborn is trying very hard."

Conway shook his head. To Thornnastor he said, "With respect, this information was contained in my original report on the FSOJ life-form to you, and my memory is unimpaired. I thank you for the offer to take charge, and I welcome your advice and assistance, but I am not psychologically distressed, and my mental confusion is at a similar level to that at which I normally operate."

"Your remarks about immobilizing the patient suggested otherwise," Thornnastor said after a short pause. "I'm glad that you feel well, but I am not completely reassured regarding your surgical intentions."

"And I'm not completely sure that I'm right," Conway replied. "But my indecision has gone, and my intended procedure is based on the assumption that we have been too heavily influenced by the FSOJ's life-support machinery and the insistence on physical mobility . . ."

Out of the corner of his eye he saw the figure of Prilicla grow more blurred as it began to tremble violently. He broke off and said into his communicator, "Withdraw, little friend. Keep in contact but move out into the corridor. The emotional radiation around here is going to be pretty savage stuff, so move back quickly."

"I was about to do so, friend Conway," it replied. "But the quality of your own emotional radiation is not pleasant for either of us. There is determination, anxiety, and the feeling that you are forcing yourself to do something which normally you would not do. My apologies. In my concern for a friend I am discussing material which should properly be considered privileged. I am leaving now. Good luck, friend Conway."

Before he could reply one of the Kelgians, its fur rippling with urgency, reported that the birth opening was beginning to enlarge.

"Relax," he said, studying the scanner picture. "Nothing is happening internally as yet. Please position the patient on its left side with a right upper dorsal presentation. The operative field will be centered fifteen inches to the right of the carapacial median line in the position marked. Continue with the present life-support arrangements, but with a bit more enthusiasm if you can manage it, until I tell you to stop. On my signal the restraints team will im-mobilize the patient's limbs, being particularly careful to stretch the tentacles to full lateral extension and to anchor them with clamps and pressor beams. I have just decided that this job will be difficult enough without the patient jerking and wriggling all over the table while we are operating. While the operation is in progress, I want the minimum number of OR and support staff present, and those who are present must discipline their thinking as I will direct. Do you understand your instructions?"

"Yes, Doctor," the Kelgian replied, but its fur was showing doubt and disapproval. A series of shocks transmitted through his shoes from the floor told him that Thornnastor was stamping its feet again.

"Sorry about the interruptions," he said to the Tralthan. "I had been about to suggest that complete immobilization might be pos-sible during the period necessary to complete the operation without serious damage to the patient. To follow my reasoning in this we must first consider what happens before, during, and after a major operation on any of the life-forms who, unlike the FSOJ, become periodically and frequently unconscious in the condition we know as sleep. In such cases—"

"They are tranquilized to minimize preoperative worry," Thorn-nastor broke in, its feet still displaying its impatience, "anesthetized during the procedure, and monitored postoperatively until the metabolism and vital signs have stabilized. This is elementary, Con-way."

"I realize that," he replied, "and I'm hoping that the solution to the problem is also elementary."

He paused for a moment to marshal his thoughts, then went on. "You will agree that a normal patient, even though it is deeply anesthetized, reacts against the surgical intervention which is taking place. If it was conscious it would want to do what the Protector is trying to do to our operating staff, that is, trying to kill them and/or escape from the threat they represent. Even when anesthetized the normal patient is reacting unconsciously to a condition of severe stress, its system has been flooded with its equivalent of adrenaline, the available supplies of blood, sugars, and oxygen have been stepped up, and it is ready to fight or flee. This is a condition which our Protector enjoys, if that is the correct word, permanently. It is constantly fighting and fleeing because it is constantly under attack."

Thornnastor and Murchison were watching him intently, but neither spoke.

"Because we are showing it pictures in three dimensions and in quite terrifying detail of its natural environment," Conway went on, "and we will be attacking it, surgically, with an intensity that it has certainly not experienced before, I am hoping to fool it and its endocrine system into believing that its limbs are still engaged in fighting off the attack or trying to flee from it. The limbs are, after all, fighting against the restraints, and the muscular effort needed is comparable.

"We will be attacking it," he concluded, "with a major cesarean procedure through the carapace rather than in the abdominal area, without benefit of anesthesia, and I expect that there will be enough pain and confusion in its mind to make it forget that its body is not in motion, at least for the relatively short time it will take to complete the operation."

Murchison was staring at him, her face expressionless but as pale as her white uniform. The full meaning of what he had just been saying dawned on Conway, and he felt sick and ashamed. The words were in direct contradiction to everything he had been taught as a healer and a bringer of comfort. *You must be cruel to be kind,* someone had told him once, but surely they had not meant this cruel.

"The Earth-human DBDG component of my mind," Thornnastor said slowly, "is feeling shock and disgust at such unheard-of behavior."

"This DBDG," Conway said, tapping himself angrily on the chest, "feels the same way. But your taped DBDG never had to deliver a Protector."

"Neither," Thornnastor said, "has anyone else."

Murchison was about to speak when there was a double interruption.

"The birth opening is beginning to widen," the Kelgian charge nurse reported, "and there is a small change in the position of the fetus."

"The emotional radiation from both entities is reaching a peak,"

Prilicla said on the communicator. "You will not have long to wait, friend Conway. Please do not distress yourself. Your clinical thinking is usually trustworthy."

The Cinrusskin invariably said the right thing, Conway thought gratefully as Thornnastor followed him to the operating frame.

They checked the underside first, moving as close as they could while still avoiding the Protector's wildly thrashing legs and the Hudlar who was jabbing at them with a metal bar to reproduce the attacks of the small, sharp-toothed predators of its home world. The musculature associated with the limbs was in constant, writhing motion, and in the medial area the birth opening was slowly lengthening and widening.

For the recorders, Conway said, "Junior will not be coming out this way. Normally, a cesarean procedure calls for a long, abdominal incision through which the fetus is removed. That course is contraindicated in this case for two reasons. It would involve cutting through several of the leg muscles, and because this being is incapable of resting a damaged limb while healing takes place, the clinical injury would never heal and the limbs concerned would be permanently affected. Secondly, we would be going in very close to the two glands which, we are virtually certain, contain the secretions which reverse the prebirth paralysis and obliterate the mind. Both, as you can see in the scanner, are connected to the umbilical and are compressed, and their contents discharged into the fetus, during the later stages of the birth process. In this physiological classification, a traditional cesarean entry would almost certainly compress these glands prematurely, and the purpose of the operation, the delivery of an intelligent Unborn, would be defeated. So we'll have to do it the hard way, by going through the carapace at an angle which will cause minimum disturbance to the underlying vital organs."

While the charge nurse had been positioning the Protector for the operation, the movements of the Unborn had been imperceptible, but now the scanner showed a slow, steady motion toward the birth canal. He forced himself to walk around to the other side of the operating frame, when his instinct was to break into an undignified gallop; then he checked that Thornnastor and Murchison were in position and said quietly, "Immobilize the patient."

The four dorsal tentacles were at full extension, motionless except for the barest tremor caused by their efforts to overcome the restraints. He tried not to think of the devastation even one of those limbs would cause among the OR staff if it succeeded in pulling free, or that he was closest and would be the first casualty.

"It is desirable—in fact it may be vitally necessary—that we establish telepathic contact with the Unborn before the operation is completed," Conway said above the buzzing of his surgical saw. "The first time such contact took place, there was only one physiological classification present, the Earth-human DBDGs Pathologist Murchison, Captain Fletcher of *Rhabwar*, and I. A multiplicity of physiological types and thought patterns may be making it difficult to make contact, or it may be that DBDGs are fractionally easier to communicate with telepathically. For this reason . . ."

"Do you wish me to leave?" Thornnastor asked.

"No," Conway said very firmly. "I need your assistance, as both a surgeon and an endocrinologist. But it would be helpful if you tried to bring forward the DBDG component of your mind and concentrated on its thought processes."

"I understand," the Tralthan said.

Working quickly, Thornnastor and Conway excised a large, triangular section of carapace, then paused to control some minor bleeding from the underlying vessels. Murchison was not assisting directly, but was concentrating all of her attention on the scanner so that she could warn them if the trauma of the operation was giving indications of triggering premature delivery. They went deeper, cutting through the thick, almost transparent membrane which enclosed the lungs, clamping it back.

"Prilicla?" Conway asked.

"The patient is feeling anger, fear, and pain in steadily increasing intensity. It does not seem to be aware of anything other than that it is being savagely attacked and is defending itself. Apparently it has not realized that it isn't moving, and there are no emotional indications of endocrine misfunction . . .

"The effect of this attack on the Unborn," the empath went on, "is of markedly heightened sensation and mentation levels. There is greater awareness and intense effort. It is trying very hard to contact you, friend Conway."

"It's mutual," he replied. But he knew that too much of his mind was being devoted to the surgical aspect just then and not enough to communication for there to be any hope of success.

In the FSOJ the heart was not situated between the lungs, but there were several major blood vessels traversing the area, and these with their associated digestive organs had to be moved out of the way without cutting—surgery had to be kept to the irreducible minimum when the patient would be mobile minutes after the operation was completed. As he pressed them carefully apart and locked the dilators in position, he knew that the circulation in several of those vessels was being seriously impaired, and that he was constricting one of the lungs and rendering it little more than sixty percent effective.

"It will be for a short time only," he said defensively in answer to Thornnastor's unspoken comment, "and the patient is on pure oxygen, which should make up the deficiency..."

He broke off as his exploring fingers moved deeper and encountered a long, flat bone which had no business being there. He looked quickly at the position of his hand in the scanner and saw that he was, in fact, touching not a bone but one of the muscles of a dorsal tentacle. The muscle had locked in spasm as the patient tried to pull the limb free of the restraints. Or perhaps it was simply reacting—as did the members of other species who locked mandibles or clenched fists—to unbearable pain.

Suddenly his hands were trembling as all of his medically trained and caring alter egos reacted to that thought.

"Friend Conway," Prilicla said, its voice distorted by more than the translator, "you are distressing me. Concentrate on what you are doing and not on what you are feeling!"

"Don't bully me, Prilicla!" he snapped. Then he laughed as he realized the ridiculous thing he had just said, and went back to work. A few minutes later he was feeling out the contours of the Unborn's upper carapace and its limp dorsal tentacles. He grasped one of them and began to pull gently.

"That entity," Thornnastor rumbled at him, "is supposed to come out of the womb fighting and able to inflict serious damage with those particular limbs. I don't think the tentacle would come off if you were to pull a little harder, Conway."

He pulled harder and the Unborn moved, but only a few inches. The young FSOJ was no lightweight, and Conway was already sweating with the effort. He slipped his other hand down into the opening and found another dorsal tentacle; then he began a two-handed pull with one knee braced against the operating frame.

He had performed more delicate feats of surgery and manipulation in his time, Conway thought sourly, but even with this unsubtle procedure the little beastie was refusing to budge.

"The passage is too tight," he said, gasping. "So tight I think suction is holding it in. Can you slide a long probe between the inner face of the dilator and the inner surface of the carapace, just there, so that we can release . . ."

"The Protector is beginning to weaken, friend Conway," Prilicla said, the mere fact that it had been impolite enough to interrupt its Seniors stressing the urgency of its report.

But Thornnastor was moving in before the empath had finished speaking, using the slim, tapering extremity of a manipulatory tentacle instead of the probe. There was a brief hissing sound as suction was released. The Tralthan's tentacle moved deeper, curled around the Unborn's rear legs, and began helping Conway to lift and slide it out. Within a few seconds it was clear, but still connected to its parent by the umbilical.

"Well," Conway said, placing the newly born Unborn on the tray Murchison had already placed to receive it, "that was the easy part. And if ever we needed a conscious and cooperative patient, now is the time."

"The Unborn's feelings are of intense frustration verging on despair, friend Conway," Prilicla reported. "It must still be trying to contact you. The Protector's emotional radiation is weakening, and there is a change in the texture which suggests that it is becoming aware of its lack of motion."

To Thornnastor, Conway said quickly, "If we reduce the dilation, which is unnecessary now that the Unborn is out, that will enable the constricted lung to operate more effectively. How much room do we need to work in there?"

Thornnastor made a noise which did not translate, then went on. "I require a fairly small opening through which to work, and I am the endocrinologist. Those ridiculous DBDG knuckles and wrists are physiologically unsuited to this particular job. With respect, I suggest that you concentrate on the Unborn."

"Right," Conway said. He appreciated the Tralthan's recognition of the fact that he was in charge even though he was, at best, only a temporary Diagnostician whose recent operative behavior would almost certainly ensure the temporary nature of his rank. Without looking up he went on. "All non-DBDG members of the OR and support teams move back to the ward entrance. Do not talk, and try to keep your minds as blank as possible by looking at and thinking about a clear area of wall or ceiling, so as to make it easier for the telepath to tune in to the three of us here. Move quickly, please."

The scanner was already showing two of the Tralthan's slim tentacles sliding down into the womb on each side of the umbilical. They came to rest above two ovoid swellings which, over the past few days, had grown to the size and coloration of large, red plums. There was adequate space inside the now-empty womb for a number of different surgical procedures to be carried out, but Thornnastor, of necessity, was doing nothing.

"The two glands are identical, Conway," the Tralthan said, "and there is no rapid method of telling which secretes the deparalyzing agent and which the mind destroyer. There is one chance in two of being right. Shall I apply gentle pressure, and to which one?"

"No, wait," Conway said urgently. "I've had second thoughts about that. If the birth had been normal, both glands would have been compressed while the Unborn was exiting and the secretions discharged through ducts directly into the umbilical. Considering the degree of swelling present and the tightly stretched appearance of the containing membranes, it is possible that even the most gentle pressure would cause a sudden rather than a gradual discharge of the secretions. My original idea of metering the discharge by applying gentle pressure and observing the effect on the patient was not a good one. As well, there is the possibility that both glands secrete the same agency and that it performs both functions."

"Highly unlikely," Thornnastor said, "the effects are so markedly different. Regrettably, the material has a complex and unstable biochemical structure which breaks down very quickly; otherwise the cadaver of your first Protector would have contained sufficient residual material for us to have synthesized it. This is the first occasion that samples have been available from a living Protector, but the analysis would be a lengthy process and the patients might not survive for long in their present condition."

"I completely agree," Prilicla said, sounding unusually vehement for a Cinrusskin. "The Protector is going into a panic reaction, it is becoming aware of its abnormal condition of immobility, and the indications are of general and rapid deterioration. You must withdraw and close up, friend Conway, and quickly."

"I know," Conway replied, then went on fiercely.

"*Think!* Think *at* the Unborn, of the situation it is in, of our problems, of what we are trying to do for it. I need telepathic contact before I can risk—"

"I feel irregular, spasmodic contractions increasing in severity," Thornnastor broke in. "The movements are probably abnormal and associated with the panic reaction, but there is the danger of them compressing the glands prematurely. And I don't think that establishing telepathic contact with the Unborn will help identify the correct gland. A newly born infant, however intelligent, does not usually possess detailed anatomical knowledge of its parent."

"The Protector," Murchison said from the other side of the operating frame, "is no longer fighting against its restraints."

"Friend Conway," Prilicla said, "the patient is losing consciousness."

"All *right*!" Conway snapped. He was trying desperately to think at the Unborn and for himself, but all his alter egos were trying desperately to think as well and were confusing him. Some of the answers they were throwing up did not apply, some were ridiculous, and one—he had no idea who originated it—was so ridiculously simple that it had to be tried.

"Clamp the umbilical as close as possible to those glands so as to guard against accidental discharge," Conway said quickly, "then sever the cord on the other side of the clamp to separate the parent and infant. I'll draw out the remainder of the umbilical, and you go into the glands with two needles. Evacuate the contents of each by suction and store the secretions in separate containers for later use. You might have to speed up the process by compressing the glands as well. I'd help you, but there isn't much room down there."

Thornnastor did not reply. It was already lifting one of the suction needles from its instrument tray while Murchison was switching on the pump to test it and attaching two small, sterile containers. Within a few minutes the suction needles had been introduced and both of the bulging glands were visibly growing smaller.

When the scanner showed them as flattened, red patches on opposite sides of the birth canal, Conway said, "That's enough. Withdraw. I'll help you close up. And if there's an unoccupied corner of your mind, please use it to think at the Unborn."

"All the corners of my mind are occupied by other people," Thornnastor said, "but I shall try."

Withdrawing was much easier than the entry had been because the Protector was unconscious, its muscles were relaxed, and there were no internal tensions trying to pull the sutures apart while they were being inserted. Thornnastor repaired the incision they had made in the womb; then together they eased the temporarily displaced organs back into position and sutured the thick membrane enclosing the lungs. All that remained was the replacement of the triangular section of carapace with the inert metal staples used on the hard and flexible hide of the FROB Hudlars.

The Hudlar operations felt as if they had happened years ago, Conway was thinking, when Thornnastor began stamping its feet in agitation.

"I am suffering intense discomfort in the cranial area," the Diagnostician said. While it was speaking, Murchison put a finger in her ear and began to waggle it frantically, as if trying to relieve a deep itch. Then Conway felt it, too, and gritted his teeth, because his hands were otherwise engaged.

The sensations were exactly the same as those he had experienced when the Protector, then an Unborn, had made telepathic contact during that earlier ship rescue. It was a combination of pain and intense irritation and a kind of discordant, unheard noise which mounted steadily in intensity. He had theorized about it after that first experience, and decided that a faculty which was either dormant or atrophied was being forced to perform. As in the case of a muscle long unused, there was soreness and stiffness and protest against the change in the old, comfortable order of things.

On that first occasion the discomfort had built up to a climax, and then ...

I have been aware of the thoughts of the entities Thornnastor, Murchison, and Conway since a few moments before I was removed from my Protector, a clear, silent, and urgent voice said in their minds, from which the maddening mental itch was suddenly gone. *I am aware of your purpose, that of birthing a telepathic Unborn to become a young Protector without loss of faculties, and I am most grateful for your efforts no matter what the eventual outcome may be. I am also aware of the entity Conway's present intentions, and I urge you to act quickly. This will be my only chance. My mental faculties are dimming.*

"Leave the parent for the time being," he said firmly, "and set up to infuse Junior."

He did not tell them to make it fast, because both Murchison and Thornnastor had received that same telepathic message. With luck there might not be any permanent impairment of the Unborn's faculties, he thought, because the effect could be due to the newly born FSOJ being immobile like its parent. While the other two were working, he removed the surplus length of the umbilical and moved the infant's transporter cage to a more convenient position in readiness, should the procedure he planned be successful, to receive a suddenly active and dangerous young Protector. By the time he had done that, Thornnastor and Murchison had the infusion needle sited in the stub of the Unborn's umbilical and a length of fine tubing connecting it to one of the sterile containers of withdrawn gland secretion.

It might be the wrong one, Conway thought grimly as he eased open the delivery valve and watched the oily, yellowish secretion ooze slowly along the tube, but now the chances were much better than fifty-fifty.

"Prilicla," he said into the communicator, "I am in telepathic contact with the Unborn, who will, I hope, be able to tell me of any physical or psychological changes caused by this infusion which, because of its irreversible effects, will be delivered in minute doses until I know that I have the right one. But I need you, little friend, to serve as backup by reporting changes in its emotional radiation, changes of which it itself may not be aware. If the Unborn should break off contact, or lose consciousness, you could be its only hope."

"I understand, friend Conway," Prilicla said, moving along the ceiling toward them so as to decrease the range. "From here I can detect quite subtle changes in the Unborn's radiation, now that it is no longer being swamped by the Protector's emotional output."

Thornnastor had returned to suturing the parent's carapace, but with one eye on the scanner and another on Conway as he bent over the infusion equipment. He delivered the first minute dose.

I am not aware of any changes in my thinking other than an increasing difficulty . . . difficulty in maintaining contact with you, the silent voice sounded in his mind. *Neither am I conscious of any muscular activity.*

Conway tried another minute dose, then another followed, in desperation, by one which was not so minute.

No change, thought the Unborn.

There was no depth to the thinking, and the meaning was barely perceptible through a rush of telepathic noise. The precontact itching somewhere between his ears was returning.

"There is fear . . ." Prilicla began.

"I know there is fear," Conway broke in. "We're in telepathic contact, dammit!"

". . . On the unconscious as well as the conscious level, friend Conway," the Cinrusskin went on. "It is consciously afraid because of its physical weakening and loss of sensation due to its continued immobility. But at a lower level there is . . . Friend Conway, it may not be possible for a mind to regard itself other than subjectively, and perhaps a failing or occluded mind cannot subjectively perceive that failure."

"Little friend," Conway said, disconnecting the container he had been using and replacing it with the other one, "you're a genius!"

This time it was no minute dose because they were fast running out of time, for both patients. Conway straightened up to better observe the effect on the Unborn, then ducked frantically to avoid one of its tentacles which was swinging at his head.

"Grab it before it falls off the tray!" Conway shouted. "Forget the transporter. It's still partially paralyzed, so hold it by the tentacles and carry it to the Rumpus Room. I'd help you, but I want to protect this container . . ."

I am aware of an increasing feeling of physical well-being, the Unborn thought.

With Murchison gripping one of its tentacles and Thornnastor the other three, the Unborn was flopping up and down between them in its efforts to break free as Conway followed them to the door of the smaller scale FSOJ life-support complex. Using Tralthan tentacles, female Earth-human hands, and one of Conway's large feet, they were able to hold it still while he administered the remainder of the deparalyzing secretion, after which they pushed the patient inside and sealed the door.

The young Protector and recently Unborn began moving rapidly along the hollow cylinder, lashing out at the bars, clubs, and spikes which were beating and jabbing at it.

"How do you feel?" Conway asked and thought anxiously.

Fine. Very well indeed. This is exhilarating, came the reply. *But I am concerned about my parent.*

"So are we," Conway said, and led the way back to the operating frame where Prilicla was clinging to the ceiling directly above the Protector. The fact that the empath was at minimum range indicated both its concern for the patient's condition and the weakness of the FSOJ's emotional radiation.

"Life-support team!" Conway called to the beings who were waiting at the other end of the ward. "Get back here! Loosen the restraints on all limbs. Let it move, but not enough to endanger the operating team."

The suturing of the carapace had still to be completed, and with Thornnastor and him both working on it, that took about ten minutes. During that time there was no movement from the Protector other than the tiny quiverings caused by the blows and jabs being delivered by the life-support machinery. In deference to the patient's gravely weakened postoperative state, Conway had ordered the equipment to be operated at half-power and that positive pressure ventilation be used to force the FSOJ to breathe pure oxygen. But by the time the remaining sutures were in place and they had conducted a detailed scanner examination of their earlier internal work, there was still no physical response.

Somehow he had to awaken it, get through to its deeply unconscious brain, and there was only one channel of communication open. Pain.

"Step up life-support to full power," he said, concealing his desperation behind an air of confidence. "Is there any change, Prilicla?"

"No change," the empath said, trembling in the emotional gale which could only have been coming from Conway.

Suddenly he lost his temper.

"*Move,* dammit!" he shouted, bringing the edge of his hand down on the inside of the root of the nearest tentacle, which was still lying flaccidly at full extension. The area he struck was pink and relatively soft, because few of the Protector's natural enemies would have been able to make such a close approach and the tegument there was thin. Even so, it hurt his hand.

"Again, friend Conway," Prilicla said. "Hit it again, and harder!"

"Wh . . . What?" Conway asked.

Prilicla was quivering with excitement now. It said, "I think— no, I'm sure I caught a flicker of awareness just then. Hit it! Hit it again!"

Conway was about to do so when one of Thornnastor's tentacles curled tightly around his wrist. Ponderously, the Tralthan said, "Repeated misuse of that hand will not enhance the surgical dexterity of those ridiculous DBDG digits, Conway. Allow me."

The Diagnostician produced one of the dilators and brought it down heavily and accurately on the indicated area. It repeated the blows, varying the frequency and gradually increasing the power as Prilicla called, "Harder! *Harder!*"

Conway fought back the urge to break into hysterical laughter.

"Little friend," he said incredulously, "are you trying to be the Federation's first cruel and sadistic Cinrusskin? You certainly sound as if . . . Why are you running away?"

The empath was ducking and weaving its way between the lighting fixtures as it raced across the ceiling toward the ward entrance. Through the communicator it said, "The Protector is rapidly regaining consciousness and is feeling very angry. Its emotional radiation . . . Well, it is not a nice entity to be near when it is angry, or at any other time."

The relatively weak structure of the operating frame was demolished as the Protector came fully awake and began striking out in all directions with its tentacles, tail, and armored head. But the life-support machinery enclosing the frame had been designed to take such punishment, as well as hitting back. For a few minutes they stood watching the FSOJ in awed silence until Murchison laughed with evident relief.

"I suppose we can safely say," she said, "that parent and off-spring are doing fine."

Thornnastor, who had one of his eyes directed at the Rumpus Room, said, "I wouldn't be too sure. The young one has almost stopped moving."

They ran and lumbered back to the scaled-down life-support system of the young Protector. A few minutes earlier they had left it charging around the system, happily battering at everything mechanical that moved. Now, Conway saw with a sudden shock of despair, it was stationary inside its cudgel-lined tunnel, and only two of its tentacles were wrapped around a thick, projecting club trying to tear it free of its mounting while the other two hung perfectly still. Before Conway could speak, there was a cool, clear, and undistressed thought floating silently in his mind.

Thank you, my friends. You have saved my parent, and you have succeeded in achieving the birth of the first intelligent and telepathic Protector. I have, with great difficulty, tuned in to the thoughts of several different life-forms in this great hospital, none of whom, with the exceptions of the entities Conway, Thornnastor, and Murchison, have been able to receive me. But there are two additional entities with whom I shall be able to communicate fully and without difficulty, because of your efforts. They are the next Unborn, who is already taking form in my parent, and the other, which I myself am carrying. I can foresee a future when a growing number of Unborn will continue their mental growth as telepathic Protectors, with the technical, cultural, and philosophical development which that will make possible . . .

The clear, calm, and quietly joyous stream of thought was suddenly clouded by anxiety.

. . . I am assuming that this delicate and difficult operation can be repeated?

"Delicate!" Thornnastor said, and made an untranslatable sound. "It was the crudest procedure I have ever encountered. Difficult, yes, but not delicate. On future occasions we will not have to play guessing games with the gland secretions. We will have the correct one synthesized and ready, and the element of risk will be greatly reduced.

"You will have your telepathic companions," the Tralthan ended. "That I promise you."

Telepathic promises were very hard to keep and even more difficult to break. Conway wanted to warn the Tralthan against making such promises too lightly, but somehow he knew that Thornnastor understood.

Thank you, and everyone else who was and will be concerned. But now I must break off contact, because the mental effort required to stay in tune with your minds is becoming too much for me. Thank you again.

"Wait," Conway said urgently. "Why have you stopped moving?"

I am experimenting. I had assumed that I would have no voluntary control over my bodily movements, but apparently this is not so. For the past few minutes, and with much mental effort, I have been able to direct all of the energy necessary to my well-being into trying to destroy this one piece of metal rather than striking out at everything. But it is extremely difficult, and I must soon relax and allow my involuntary system to resume control. That is why I am so optimistic regarding future progress for our species. With constant practice I may be able to avoid attacking, for perhaps a whole hour at a time, those around me. The fear of attack is more difficult to reproduce, and I may need advice . . .

"This is great! . . ." Conway began enthusiastically, but for a moment the thinking resumed.

. . . But I do not wish to be released from this mechanism, and risk running amok among your patients and staff. My physical self-control is far from perfect, and I realize that I am not yet ready to mix with you socially.

There was an instant of itching between his ears, then a great, mental silence, which was slowly filled by Conway's own and strangely lonely thoughts.

CHAPTER 21

His second meeting of Diagnosticians was different in that Conway thought he knew what to expect—a searching and mercilessly professional interrogation regarding his recent surgical behavior. But this time there were two non-Diagnosticians present, the Chief Psychologist and Colonel Skempton, the Monitor Corps officer in charge of the hospital's supply and maintenance. It was these two who seemed to be the center of attention, interrogation, and criticism, to such an extent that Conway felt sorry for them as well as grateful for the extra time they were giving him to prepare his defense.

Diagnostician Semlic required reassurance regarding the power source for a new synthesizer which was being set up two levels above its dark and incredibly cold domain, particularly about the adequacy of the existing shielding against the increased risk of heat and radiation contamination of its wards. Diagnosticians Suggrod and Kursedth both wanted to know what, if any, progress had been made about providing additional accommodation for the Kelgian medical staff. Some of them were occupying the former Illensan accommodation, which, in spite of everything that had been done, still stank of chlorine.

While Colonel Skempton was trying to convince the two Kelgians that the smell was purely psychosomatic, because it did not register on his department's most sensitive detectors, Ergandhir, the Melfan Diagnostician, was already beginning to list a number of admittedly minor faults in ELNT ward equipment which were causing growing annoyance to both patients and staff. The Colonel replied that the replacement parts had been ordered, but because of their highly specialized nature, delays were to be expected. While they were still talking, Vosan, the water-breathing AMSL, began to question O'Mara regarding the desirability of assigning the diminutive and birdlike Nallajim to a ward designed for the thirty meters long, armored and tentacled Chalders, who were likely to inadvertently ingest them.

Before the Chief Psychologist could reply, the polite, sibilant voice of the PVSJ, Diagnostician Lachlichi, said that it, too, had similar reservations about the Melfans and Tralthans who were appearing in increasing numbers in the chlorine-breathing levels. It said that in the interests of saving time, O'Mara's answer might be modified to answer both questioners.

"A correct assumption, Lachlichi," O'Mara said. "Both questions have the same general answer." He waited until there was silence before going on. "Many years ago my department initiated a plan which called for the widest possible other-species experience being made available to those staff members with what I judged to be the required degree of psychological adaptability and professional aptitude. Rather than specializing in the treatment of patients belonging to their own or a similar physiological classification, these people were assigned an often-bewildering variety of cases and given responsibility for them which was not always commensurate with their rank at the time. The success of the plan can be measured by the fact that two of the original selectees are at this meeting"—he glanced at Conway and at someone else who was concealed by the intervening bulk of Semlic's life-support system—"and the others are coming along nicely. The degree of success achieved warranted the enlargement of the original project without, however, lowering the original high requirements."

"I had no knowledge of this," Lachlichi said, its spiny, membranous body stirring restively inside its envelope of yellow fog. Ergandhir clicked its lower mandible and added, "Nor I, although I suspected that something like this might be going on."

Both Diagnosticians were staring toward the head of the table, at Thornnastor.

"It is difficult to keep secrets in this place," the Senior Diagnostician said, "and particularly for me. The requirements are a much greater than average ability to understand, generally get along with, actually like, and instinctively do the right thing where a large number of different intelligent species are concerned. But it was decided that neither the entities selected nor their colleagues and immediate superiors should be made aware of the plan lest candidates displaying many of the required qualities fall short of reaching the top and end up as respected and professionally gifted Senior Physicians. In many cases, these entities are capable of better work than their, at times, multiply absentminded superiors; they have no reason to feel ashamed or dissatisfied . . ."

I've flunked it, Conway thought bitterly, *and Thorny is trying to tell me as gently as possible.*

"... And in any case," Thornnastor went on, "there is a fair chance that they will make it in time. For this reason the existence of the Chief Psychologist's plan and selection procedure must not, for obvious reasons, be discussed with anyone other than those here present."

Maybe there was still a chance for him, Conway thought, especially as he was being told of O'Mara's plan. But another part of his mind was still trying to accept the strange idea of a close-mouthed and secretive Thornnastor instead of the being who was reputed to be the worst gossip in the hospital, when O'Mara resumed speaking.

"It is not the intention," the Chief Psychologist said, "to promote people beyond the level of their professional competence. But the demands on this hospital make it necessary for us to put the medical and"—he glanced at Colonel Skempton—"maintenance resources to the fullest possible use. Regarding the Nallajim invasion of the Chalder wards, I have found that if a Doctor or nurse is in more danger from the patient than the patient is from the disease or, as will be the case in the chlorine wards, the patient is in greater danger from the sheer physical mass of its medical attendants than its disease, a great deal of extra care is exercised all around and there is a beneficial effect on the Doctor-patient relationship.

"And while we are on the subject of the plan," O'Mara went on, "I have a short list of names which, in my opinion, and subject to your judgment on their professional competence, merit a rise in status to Senior Physician. They are Doctors Seldal, Westimorral, Shu, and Tregmar. A Senior Physician who should be considered for elevation to Diagnostician is, of course, Prilicla . . . Your mouth is open, Conway. Do you have a comment?"

Conway shook his head, then stammered, "I . . . I was surprised that a Cinrusskin would be seriously considered. It is fragile, overly timid, and the mental confusion caused by the multiple personalities would endanger it further. But as a friend I would be biased in its favor and would not want to—"

"There is no entity on the hospital staff," Thornnastor said ponderously, "who would not be biased in favor of Prilicla."

O'Mara was staring at him with eyes, Conway knew, which opened into a mind so keenly analytical that together they gave the Chief Psychologist what amounted to a telepathic faculty. Conway was glad that his empath friend was not present, because his thoughts and feelings were nothing to be proud of—a mixture of hurt pride and jealousy. It was not that he was envious of Prilicla or that he wished to belittle the empath in any way. He was honestly delighted that its future prospects were so good. But to think of it being groomed for a position among the hospital's elite while he might well remain just an able and respected Senior Physician! . . .

"Conway," O'Mara said quietly, "suppose you tell me why Prilicla is being considered for Diagnostician status. Be as biased or unbiased as you like."

For a few seconds Conway was silent as he strove for objectivity in the minds of his alter egos as well as his own—when he was thinking petty thoughts his mind partners kept bringing forward their equivalents. Finally, he said, "The added danger of physical injury might not be as great, since Prilicla has spent its whole lifetime in avoiding physical and psychological damage, and this situation would continue even if it was confused initially by a number of mind-partners. The confusion might not be as bad as I had first assumed, because, as an empath, it is already familiar with the feelings of a very wide range of physiological types, and it is the presence of these alien thoughts and feelings which causes most of the mental confusion in us nonempaths.

"During many years' close professional association with this entity," Conway went on, "I have observed its special talents in use and have noted that it has assumed increased responsibilities which have, on many occasions, involved it in severe emotional discomfort. The most recent incidents were its organizing and direction of the Menelden rescue and its invaluable assistance during the delivery of the Unborn. When the Gogleskan Khone arrives I can think of nobody better able to reassure and . . ."

He broke off, aware that he was beginning to wander off the subject, and ended simply, "I think Prilicla will make a fine Diagnostician."

Silently, he added, *I wish someone were here saying nice things about me.*

The Chief Psychologist gave him a long, searching look, then said dryly, "I'm glad we agree, Conway. That little empath can obtain maximum effort from both its subordinates and superiors, and without being the slightest bit obnoxious about it the way some of us are forced to be." He smiled sourly and went on. "However, Prilicla will need more time, another year at least in charge of the medical team on *Rhabwar,* and additional responsibilities on the wards between ambulance calls."

Conway was silent, and O'Mara went on. "When your FOKT friend is admitted to the hospital and I have it available for the full spectrum of psych tests, I'm pretty sure that I will be able to eradicate its mind impression, and the one you left in its mind. I won't go into the details now, but you won't be burdened with that troublesome Gogleskan material for much longer."

O'Mara stared at him, obviously expecting a word of thanks, or some kind of response, but Conway could not speak. He was thinking about the lonely, long-suffering, nightmare-ridden, and yet not entirely unhappy individual who shared his thoughts and influenced his actions, so subtly on occasions that he was scarcely aware of it, and of how uncomplicated life would be if his mind were completely his own again—except, that was, for the taped entities, who could be erased at any time. He thought of the presence of Khone, who got the twitches every time a non-Gogleskan life-form went past, which was very often at Sector General, and of the implication its visit had toward the finding of a solution to its species-wide psychosis. But mostly he thought of its unique ability to withdraw and compartmentalize its thinking and its perpetually curious and careful viewpoint which made Conway want to double-check everything he thought and did and which would no longer be there to slow him down. He sighed.

"No," he said firmly, "I want to keep it."

There were a number of untranslatable sounds from around the table while O'Mara continued to watch him unblinkingly. It was Colonel Skempton who broke the silence.

"About this Gogleskan," he said briskly. "What particular problems will it give my department? After the Protector and Junior's Rumpus Room and the sudden demand for Hudlar prosthetic limbs—"

"There are no special requirements, Colonel," Conway broke in, smiling, "other than a small isolation compartment with a restricted visitors list and normal environment for a warm-blooded oxygen-breather."

"Thank Heaven for that," Skempton said with feeling.

"Regarding the Hudlar prosthetics," Thornnastor said, turning an eye toward the Colonel. "There will be an additional requirement there due to the pregeriatric amputation procedure suggested by Conway, which has since received the approval of the Chief Psychologist and, apparently, every aging FROB that O'Mara has approached. There are going to be far too many voluntary amputees for the hospital to accommodate, so your department will not be involved in the large-scale manufacture of Hudlar prosthetics, but . . ."

"I'm even more relieved," the Colonel said.

". . . We will have our designs mass-produced on Hudlar itself," Thornnastor went on. "The operations will be performed there as well, by Hudlar medics who will be trained at this hospital in the necessary surgical techniques. This will take time to organize, Conway, but I am making it your responsibility, and I would like you to give it a high degree of priority."

Conway was thinking of their one and only Hudlar medic under training, and the large numbers of same-species trainees who would be joining it, and wondering if their personalities and dispositions would be as attractive and friendly. But then he thought of the living hell the patients in Hudlar Geriatric were going through, with the fully functioning brains trapped inside their disease-ridden, degenerating, and pain-racked bodies, and he decided that the training program would be given a high degree of priority indeed.

"Yes, of course," he said to Thornnastor. To O'Mara he added, "Thank you."

Thornnastor's eyes curled disconcertingly to regard everyone at the same time, and it said, "Let us conclude this meeting as soon as possible so that we can get back to running the hospital instead of talking interminably about it. O'Mara, you have something to say?"

"Only the completion of my suggested list of promotions and appointments," the Chief Psychologist said. "I'll be brief. One name, Conway, subject to satisfactory completion of the verbal examination by those present, to be confirmed in his present status and appointed to the position of Diagnostician-in-Charge of Surgery."

Thornnastor's eyes waved briefly along the table before returning to O'Mara. It said, "Not necessary. No dissent. Confirmed."

When the congratulations were over, Conway sat staring at the Chief Psychologist while their more massive colleagues cleared the exit, thinking that he would feel very pleased with himself when the shock wore off. O'Mara was staring back at him, his expression as grim and sour-faced as ever, but with a look in his eyes which was very much like paternal pride.

"The way you've been hacking through patients these past few weeks," O'Mara said gruffly, "what else did you expect?"